# Amalina and the End of it All

Episode 5 in
The Count at Play
& Slaughter series

## C.L. Holmes

Bad Hound Press

Dedicated to T.H.W., J. S.A.C., and J.K.R.,
modern masters whose prose energized, and
inspired


Other books in the series:

Amalina and the Secrets of the Wailing Castle

Amalina and the Palace of Pleasure

Amalina and the Midnight Gift

Amalina and the Brocade Army


Amalina and the End of it All
Episode 5 in The Count at Play & Slaughter series
© 2023 C.L. Holmes


Bad Hound Press
A Division of Giant Dog Books
www.giantdogbooks.com
All rights reserved.

ISBN-13: 978-1-949043-37-2





Cover design and layout by Dominic Wilde

Preface

# What Came Before …
## (A Note for New Readers)

Death had existed in the Ardeel mountains ages before humanity arrived with its weak memories and fragile history—a past recorded on paper that can burn or turn to dust. However, death had a sudden insufferable uptick nearly five centuries ago, which they remembered well enough; because it arrived in the form of one man—who was capricious and wanton in his bloodthirstiness, and who as a terrifying, remorseless tyrant, had robbed them of night and the freedom of movement. They could point at the man, this creature, and sometimes knew where he lived. He even had a name by which they could call him and curse him: The Knight of Ardeel. Less formally, and to a certain knowing few, he was Count Miscael Ivanov Tepsji.

By way of example: he now stood with a young woman's arm bent at a painful angle in his powerful grip, and he glanced around the scene, noting the other young lady embedded in the trunk of a large oak, her impact when he'd thrown her into it cracking it more than her. He knew just by looking she would survive, so that wasn't a concern. Instead he centered his attention on the mortal standing near the burning building. The tremendous blaze lit the clearing more than the moon above did, and in its light the quaking body was white and naked and so very delicate. So was the one sitting on the ground, huddled nearby.

They hadn't seen him yet.

He knew by long practice, and with a pinch of delight at the memory, that he could snag a piece of dermis at that upright mortal's hairline, right between his forefinger and thumb, and then send the body spinning like a top, tearing away an endless strip of skin, spiral after spiral, like peeling an apple. And if the pain and horror of it did not cause the one to shriek an answer to his question, the other on the ground who watched it happen, getting showered with blood, would tell. He could already feel the shape of the question in his mouth: "Where are they? Where did they go?"

Nearly five centuries of training and practice and simple vicious inclination pushed at his back, and he almost leapt to it. But nearly five centuries living in that same mode of existence had begun to feel a little repetitive. A little stale. He understood the two poor wretches he performed the act on would not really be enjoying it as much as he. Which, of course, would be a let down.

He knew, too, there were other, superior pleasures to be had now …
After all, he'd met Amalina.

### Episode 1: Amalina and the Secrets of the Wailing Castle
On a quiet night in old Ardeel, Amalina is kidnapped from her childhood home, taken to a lonely mountain castle, and forced to work for the mysterious Count, a polished gentleman who is also a monster.

### Episode 2: Amalina and the Palace of Pleasures
Amalina struggles to remain above suspicion as she works against the Count, serving as an agent for the commander of a growing counterforce intent on bringing him down. All while trying to keep her friend, a guileless princess from the West, entertained unaware of her peril, and out of harm's way.

### Episode 3: Amalina and the Midnight Gift
Once an unwilling servant to a monster, Amalina finds reasons to stay in his service: to protect the lives of seven innocent young princesses while they visit the castle; to discover the identity of a malicious murderer and put him out of action before he can strike again; but even more compelling, to hide from a terrifying entity, much more powerful than her master, who seems to be hunting her down.

### Episode 4: Amalina and the Brocade Army
As much as Amalina enjoys her new noble life, the old one pulls her back. Weaving through a gauntlet of family, friends, and guests (common and royal), barely a step ahead of the law, revolutionaries, and a deadly conspiracy against her, Amalina begins the difficult steps to free herself from the creature she works for.

And now—and at last—the forces of human justice have gathered to battle an internal enemy, before they can move to strike at the Count, and so conclude his reign within the mountains …

Episode 5
Act One
Act Two
Act Three

# AMALINA AND THE END OF IT ALL

# ACT ONE

## LOST PHANTOMS

*OR,*

## IT'S ALL JUST TALK ...
## UNTIL THERE'S A MISUNDERSTANDING

Prologue

# A Friendly Chat

## I

Count Tepsji watched the dark figure trudge through the graveyard. Something in its slow, wary strides, as it approached the side gate, its frame a hunched shadow against the bright, moonlit snow, struck him oddly. Was it impatience at the thing's pace? or annoyance? or an obsessive need to fill the time? When the shape had started out, it appeared to him as if one of the many low tombstones, half-buried in the drifts, had suddenly come alive and slipped out of place. Only now, to his enlivened, energized, and transforming thoughts, it seemed something better: *a blackened tooth has freed itself from a fallen, sun-bleached skull, yesss, and it is carefully, quietly, almost fearfully, winding away from a broken socket, past all the other stone teeth, trying not to wake them in the night; to then cross down the field of immaculate white jaw; to make its escape.*

*Yes,* the Count smiled at his lively creation. *Yes, yes, yesss …*

Only, that thing—the man—wasn't coming to escape. The Count shut away his smile before the Cardinal reached the fence. Now wasn't the time for it.

. . .

"You wanted to speak with me?" said the Cardinal, bundled, shivering, and annoyed upon arrival. His eyes picked out the fence's high bars to confirm they were solidly between them both. However, in a chilling counter-point, the clouds of his breath passed through the barrier, whispering into pearly fragments on the Count's coal-black cloak: they were still within easy reach of each other. The Cardinal's expression neutralized, or rather became a natural mask of agony against the bitter cold. He was determined to show no fear.

"No doubt Rosczy has told you what's happening at the castle," said the Count, as if from mid-conversation. "My efforts there."

The Cardinal didn't answer, but when it appeared they would be standing there for the rest of the night unless he did, he gave a curt nod beneath his hood. "Rosczy's told me everything; I believe I understand well enough."

"And you've had word of *the incident*?"

The Cardinal raised his head, curious. The Count looked tired somehow. Or weary was a better word. But he reminded himself that looks could be misleading with this one. Misleading in the absolute.

"You'll hear of it soon enough," said the Count in an off-hand way. "An orphanage or workhouse or something like that, you see … "

It took only a moment for the Cardinal to put the words and their meaning together: orphanage, workhouse; *incident*. Even when the realization struck it did not move him to react, other than to acknowledge what had been said by crossing himself and muttering a prayer for the dead. Because if *he* was here, there were dead. After the requisite moment of silence: "Someone at this workhouse offended your … rules?"

"If only it were that simple. No."

"Then," said the Cardinal, his voice grave, his thin eyebrows pressing together in worry, "…then you've broken the agreement? The contract? Is that what you're saying?"

"I've broken nothing," said the Count, irritable. "It would be impossible for me to violate a contract—one of many, by the way, and I remind you— created by men and for men in order to adhere them to my will. That I've chosen to humor those scribbles all these years, all these years, if nothing more than to keep the peace so I could get on with my life, has little meaning here."

"I—I see," said the Cardinal. "I didn't realize. That wasn't how it was explained—"

"When I strike deals it is with an individual," explained the Count. "Anything more than that and things get messy. I prefer relationships where I can look someone in the eye and hold them accountable to their word." The Count stared at the Cardinal meaningfully.

The Cardinal bowed his head to acknowledge the point and to interrupt for a few seconds the unbearable attention, then said: "And so you've lost your humor with our contract, am I to understand, by this unfortunate occurrence at our orphanage?"

"*This* was not my doing," said the Count, sounding bothered in an abstract way. "I thought I'd cleaned it up well enough as I could, but a couple of the little ones escaped my Ladies' notice. And now those pitiful children have gotten word spreading."

"*Your* ladies … ?" said the Cardinal as if coming to terms with what was just revealed.

"I thought you said you understood what's been happening at the castle," grumbled the Count impatiently. "Didn't you just tell me so?"

"Yes." The Cardinal's lips twitched. But he was only just grasping the enormity of it, and yet had to act aware and impassive for his audience. "*Your ladies*. I'm only surprised you could not … um … control them."

"I suppose I can't expect a priest to appreciate the difficulty in 'controlling' a woman when she feels her own freedom, particularly when she's yet to realize the limits of her power; but now imagine her in a *group*," sniffed the Count, incensed at having some failing on his part suggested. He was that kind of brittle person, and if he didn't have such supreme control over his own body he would have suddenly erupted in a spasm of hand movements and shifting on his feet. Not realizing he was in effect doing so with his words, he continued on: "I'd left them to their own exercise, and a couple got it in their heads to give this wretched orphanage a try. You understand. I wasn't told what naughtiness they'd gotten up to until it was too late. My ladies were trusted to an unsupervised night out. I loathe children, but these ladies have little experience in the matter, so they had their way. And this was the unsurprising result. You understand how that goes. Forbidden fruit, etc. …"

• • •

The Cardinal cleared his throat. "What is it you wish from me?"

"Yes," said the Count, his lips slanting off, returning to business. "You will tamp down what's to come. What's already coming."

"Tamp it down?"

"I don't need this distraction. Nor do I want it to lead to any upset with the sweet atmosphere I have going in my home. It's been a pleasant winter so far, and I've much still planned for everyone. So you'll stem the tide of outrage."

"I see. And will you be—em, *tasking*—the mayor on this, too?"

"After what happened to his daughter? I don't think he'd be as convincing to the people of Netz, on my behalf, as you."

"Yes … what happened to his daughter, Ygardina …"

"That was not my fault, either," said the Count, defensively. "Not directly. And I shouldn't have to explain it to you. That's history."

"No," agreed the Cardinal, sensing a growing anger, which could be dangerous even with the security of the fence between them. The Cardinal reached out with a gloved hand and pretended to steady himself on the bars; to touch them again. They felt comfortably sturdy and protective. Or was he trying to subtly remind the Count that they were there, in case he got some new ideas? "But if you might suggest what I could possibly say to 'tamp down' the outrage?"

"You're the man of words and the conductor of hearts and souls, Cardinal. I can only imagine what you'll come up with." The Count made a face. "But I suggest you keep it simple. The workhouse was completely razed so there should be no lingering evidence. Say there was a *tragic occurrence*, as you've already put it to me, and the lucky ones who escaped are mere children with fanciful imaginations." The Count grinned suddenly, sharply. "Suggest *they* might have been the ones who started the fire in the first place and are now trying to shift blame. But you'll think of something clever, and even better, I'm sure. Along those lines, though."

"You think of everything," said the Cardinal, not so much as a compliment. The Cardinal would follow the Count's suggestion to the letter. He didn't know if it would work, but at least he could say that he'd done as instructed. Still, there was already the hint that if he did not resolve matters to the Count's liking, even if he worded it as laid out precisely, he could be blamed for not improving on the plan as the Count had also suggested. Either way, the Count would have his justification to punish the Cardinal for what came of it. The Cardinal nodded quick and sneered inwardly at the petty injustice which he saw but could do nothing about. Not here. Not now.

"You said word is spreading," said the Cardinal. "How far has it gotten that I should not have heard it yet?"

"You will. By morning if not tonight. Is everything understood, Cardinal?"

"If it hasn't spread too far … would it not be wiser to trim the rest of the contagion off before it spreads further?"

"Don't try to snake your way out of this," warned the Count.

"No. Never. I was just thinking while we are still under cover of night it might be easier for you to—"

"I know what I want," answered the Count, snippily. Then, after a thought, and with an intrigued lift of his eyebrow: "*Easier*, Cardinal? And here I expected to have to haggle with you, with you carping and carrying on about the laws of your book and of mercy, and warning I should rather stay my red hand."

"I wouldn't think to."

"The others would have."

"Others?"

"The ones before you, who've come down to me through the years."

"Oh, I see. Perhaps I am more pragmatic."

"Another strange word from you tonight, Cardinal," said the Count, appraisingly. "I thought you, in your realm, dealt in absolutes. If nothing else, I'd have thought you'd *appreciate* my staying this hand—staying it myself, of all people—and not lifting it high, and so preserve the lives of your blameless sheep; that you would compliment me for my making your life easier. If I did not care, or I wanted to make things easier *on myself*, I could do so much more than—"

"Yes, yes, I wasn't questioning," the Cardinal hurried in, before the man before him grew too excited. Already it seemed his eyes were lighting up and his shoulders expanding. Or was it that having been pulled out of a warm room, the cold and ice and full moon were playing tricks with his own eyes?

"See that you don't," said the Count. "Just do as I ask of you and we remain friends."

"Of course. Anything. It will be done."

"You know what happened in Kyrgil … ?"

"An earthquake, or a small volcanic eruption." But the Count stared levelly at him through the bars. It seemed there was a contemptuous smirk. There was a reason he'd asked the question, he wanted a reaction. "Or … that was … What happened in Kyrgil? That was *you*?"

"The same thing could happen here," said the Count in a low growl, "which would be unfortunate. To see your lovely church destroyed, not to mention the whole of Netz? It would only be a little more difficult for me than a rickety, flammable workhouse." He paused to allow the Cardinal to blink at the threat. "You know, I watched this church as it was built, stone by stone. How this fence went right up. I've watched this city grow and thrive, as it might never have if *I* hadn't chosen to settle here. I very much like these mountains and these valleys. I love my high castle. Grown to love it beyond reason, perhaps. But I've put in so much effort in this rock, I'd hate to have to wipe it all out—these innocent mountains and valleys—and start again."

"No. Heaven forbid."

"Heaven's got nothing to do with it," said the Count. "It's only decided by what happens here, between two friends, talking. We *are* friends, aren't we?"

"There's no need to worry, Count Tepsji. I do it gladly, think of it not as a favor. It will be taken care of."

"I'm not the one worrying."

It seemed that was as good a send-off as the Count could give him. The Cardinal bowed, ready to leave and rush back inside his church. But the man on the opposite side of the fence did not move. He was as still as the moonlit mountains behind him. The eyes seemed to glow brighter.

"Was there something else?" asked the Cardinal.

"I noticed … you didn't call me 'friend.'"

"Oh?"

"I don't think I'll leave here until I hear that warm, reassuring word, 'friend', come out of your mouth." His eyes flicked to the sky, then back down. "Remember, though, Cardinal, I haven't all night."


## II


A number of days later, Rosczy noted the Cardinal sprinkle the clear-liquid poison down his rings in an absent, nonchalant way. The Cardinal even paused to admire the gleam on one of the outset gems.

"You want me to prepare the antidote, your eminence?" said Rosczy, already heading for the vials of antidotes and the serving trays with the pitchers of water and wine—the refreshments. When the Cardinal did not answer he prompted: "Your eminence?"

"Do whatever you feel like," muttered the Cardinal in a heavy tone.

"Your eminence?"

"Apologies, of course," replied the Cardinal with a quick smirk, or was it a smile at himself in the mirror? He stared at his neatly trimmed beard, finding something to admire in it. "Much to think about. I'm glad I have you here though, Rosczy. As always, my loyal one; come down from the castle for me, at my call."

"Yes, your eminence. Of course. Always. I'm glad to be here to assist in any way I can."

"We've quite a mess to clean this morning. You and I."

"It must be done."

"Things have gotten out of hand. Are the city fathers ready?" The Cardinal was straightening his gloves now, making sure to remove the wrinkles around the poisoned rings.

"Yes, your eminence. Is *he* making you do this?"

"And those damnable children from the orphanage?" asked the Cardinal, not answering.

"Kind little Sergi, and Jarl, and Timothy—"

"I didn't ask their names!"

"They are outside as well," said Rosczy calmly. "And a good number of the villagers; witnesses, as you requested." He had no clue what the Cardinal intended for this moment, it was going to be tricky with so many watching. Rosczy would have to be deft and on his game, too. "Everyone is waiting for you."

"Let them wait."

"Your eminence?"

The Cardinal shot a smile at himself in the mirror again, but it didn't look like he liked himself all that much. "Still figuring what to do, the best course. What justice will be meted out today, by these hands."

He tested his fingers, flexing them, spinning them, flashing signals which Rosczy was only too keenly aware of and recognized immediately.

"Your decision will be, as always, sound, your eminence."

"Shut up."

"Your eminence?"

"I need to think, I just told you."

"Of course, your eminence. Forgive me. I forgot."

Cardinal moved his fingers in a way that told him to be quiet. Rosczy bowed his head.

"Would you say we are friends, Rosczy?"

"Impossible. You're above my station. You are my master."

"You're glad to be down here, back at St. Grigori, helping me, you said?"

"With anything."

The Cardinal glanced at him through the mirror's reflection. "But you *are* missing those women up in that castle. Aren't you?"

"What, sir? No, sir."

"By your negligent reports, you seem to be *missing* a lot, Rosczy."

"Sir?"

"The ladies. *His* ladies!" The Cardinal eyed Rosczy with such a look of accusation, as if not sure what his apprentice was ignorant of even now, or knowingly omitting. "Before I make up my mind what to do in this coming trial, and to whom, you will explain to me what is happening up in that castle. Some lives," he pointed to the outer rooms where the orphans, city fathers, and witnesses were waiting for him, his guidance, and his ultimate delivery of justice, "are depending on it."


III


Maybe what began the end of Amalina's dark adventure with the Count was when he'd summoned to the St. Grigori Cathedral's gates a powerful man whom he regarded as a simple pawn, and in turn this man, the Cardinal of the Netz church, viewed the other as a gamepiece as well; like his many underlings, such as Rosczy, to be moved and manipulated. Neither understanding the game, nor the value of the other. Nor how little either of them—much less all the rest—meant in the greater scheme.

Maybe that was, indeed, how the end began.

# PART ONE
# ONE SLAM-BANG MORNING (WITH TEA)

1

# Twilight's Last Hour:
# The Dream

It began with a blue sky.

. . .

The dreamer woke with a bolt from her bed, heart pounding, gasping for breath, sweat covering her whole body. But that was usual, wasn't it? A routine so well worked out by now it would take only a matter of seconds to recover.

But the vision, still fresh in her mind and so vivid, of a bright blue sky cut at the horizon by an endless sea of wheat—or was it barley? she can never quite tell—and the merry sound of chirping birds and buzzing bees zagging through the scene swept aside intermittently by a young girl's treacly-sweet song, it was as if this time around half her head had gotten stuck in the dream, though clearly she was awake and in her bedroom, and that she needed to throw the remaining bits away, like shucking a tight dress which stubbornly clings to the body.

However, with her mind not quite out of the trap, she was there: in the height of summer, the air a long hot breath, the crops in full. And as the song carries on, far off in the distance the dreadful, dead-faced, grey-white head pops up above the rows, its large, level eyes staring accusation at her. It's an angry head, then, despite its expressionless lips, which bobs up and down through the surface of swaying grain as it moves, a knitting needle poking a pattern as it scores a direct line toward her.

And over the cheery sounds of chirping birds and buzzing bees and that sickly sweet little tune, there comes, as ever, the grating words: "Kill him, Amalina! What's taking you so long? So *very* long! I'm counting on you for my revenge—but you must do it! You must! Kill him!"

With a smirk, a shrug of her head and shoulders, and then a slight laugh, Amalina shook off the remnants of the nightmare. She told the fading apparition—it crowing on, just short of reaching her, *"Kill, Amalina, Kill!"*: "Yes, yes, yes, Lucinda. I know. I know what you want. But what can I do about it? I *am* trying. You know I am."

She meant it, but felt foolish when she realized she was trying to push a lie—out loud at that—to a lost phantom of air.

"The dream again?" whispered Aklan cautiously from the middle of the room, dressed in his uniform, looking like he'd slept in it and had just stormed through the door with candle in hand as if brandishing a sword.

By breaking the stillness, Aklan's voice had frightened Amalina more than the dream, but by how soaked her bedclothes were he wouldn't believe it. Still, she caught a yelp in her mouth and began to shiver.

"What are you doing in here, boy?" scolded Amalina, not liking the feel of her vibrating nerves brought on by his sudden entrance—which she immediately resented; she'd rather be right back into her routine, the reassurance of it. Next she would be getting dressed and press on with her happy, comfortable day and forget all about Lucinda's deathly demand; what it meant.

"Thought I heard you scream, Pretty Princess. And you did!"

"You're getting a little too big to be barging in, don't you think? I'll call for you when I'm ready."

"Yes, Pretty Princess. But you said 'Lucinda'. It *was* the dream again, wasn't it?" he asked, not yet heading back out the door.

Amalina nodded. With a 'knew it' smile, Aklan left her alone to her thoughts, with the ragged edges of the nightmare thrown to the room's corner along with its last haunting cries: *"Kill him!"*

In the darkness, Amalina sensed the chill of winter reaching in through her boarded window and down the flue of her fireplace. Reality taking hold. She was no longer off in the heat of the blue-skied summer field, she was here in her castle; a spot quite different. Good. She reached out and lit a nearby three-stick candlestand and began planning out her day—because she did have plans for the day; important plans—her mind flying further and further from the dream.

There was a gentle knock at the door.

"Yes?"

Aklan spoke from the other side: "Hey, Pretty Princess, did you know Pia came to your room last night?"

"Did she?"

"A bunch of times," said Aklan, enthusiastically, like it was red-hot gossip. "All night long!"

"Really?" said Amalina, only a little interested. At the moment she had other things on her mind: not only plans, but joyful things; as always, little golden bits built up like a wall to counteract Lucinda's call for revenge. Amalina shivered and smirked as she searched her dresser for a new, dry shift. Well, she'd woke from a nightmare, but at least she'd been warm and dry in there.

"Princess?"

"Get in," called Amalina, having quickly changed out of her bedclothes.

As the boy scrambled back in and straight to her, he said, "I was right, wasn't—?"

"Hush," commanded Amalina. "I just need help with getting this dress on."

"Oh, you want me to fetch Anka?" he asked shyly, retreating a step. "She's better at—"

"Let's let the poor old woman rest, eh? She ran the party in the great hall last night. She needs time to recover, and you'll do fine. Just keep your mouth shut now. I'm composing myself."

"What's that, Pretty Princess?"

"Composing myself."

"What's that mean?"

"I'm trying to think."

"What about?"

"Never you mind."

"A secret, then?" he grinned hopefully.

This was the day she'd set aside to consider the revolutionary and the coming revolution, to make a final decision about it. But she wasn't about to tell the boy. The revolution *was* a secret, and would remain so until she'd made up her mind.

As Amalina dug out the layers of clothes, on went the undergarments, the stays, and the wire understructure, in preparation for her dress and overlayers, with the final skirt of fancy brocade silk cloth. It was the promise of a good day she was struggling into. Aklan helped her with the fitting and tightening, starting with the stays.

"So, yer meeting Lady Lampeda, then?" asked Aklan, as the stays went on.

"Not sure. Why?"

"She's been asking all night, like I said. She says you and she are seeing each other in the morning. I kept telling her it was the middle of the night and you were still sleeping, but—"

*That's something new,* thought Amalina: *up all night? What could that mean?* Was Pia experiencing a bout of insomnia? or was she finally changing hours? She'd always been an early sleeper, early riser. But now? *Well, why push* me *to change?* frowned Amalina. *Wanting* me *up, too? at all hours? I need my rest, that's for sure,* she thought. But at least Pia had been polite enough to ask Aklan, instead of simply barging in, as the man whom the Lady was taking after—the *thing* she was becoming—would have done.

"What time is it now?"

"Almost dawn, I think. Anytime now. So *are* you expecting to see her, Princess? This is a real fancy dress."

"I wasn't intending to, no. My only firm plan was to feed the pigeons before they starve. I'm sure Genadie's forgotten all about them again. This dress ... well, I just wanted to be ready for when the others start waking. But I can visit her, if she likes."

"This *is* a real fancy dress," said Aklan again, eyeing it with a down-turned lip and nervous hands, unsure with its unwieldy construction. Amalina noticed Aklan in detail now, as he danced around her working at the laces. *He's a faithful little guy*, she thought affectionately; he'd stood by her through many dangers and, during a crazy revenge attempt for her honor, almost had his neck snapped at the end of a rope. At his serious, cross-eyed look of concentration, she patted him tenderly on the head. With his unruly hair it was like patting a thick stack of blond cotton. "Why'd you do that, Princess?"

"Just being nice," answered Amalina.

"Uh-oh," he said, with a grin.

She looked curious at him. "What?"

"You get nice when you're up to something, Pretty Princess. So tell me."

"Do I really?"

"Well, *are* you up to something?"

"Not that I know of," said Amalina innocently—though still thinking of the secret decision she'd planned to make today—just as a knock sounded at the outer door. "Go see who it is. If it's Pia, let her know I'll join her in the Grand Gallery. She likes that place the best, and it should calm her down while she waits."

"I just say the part about the Grand Gallery, right?" he said, already moving for the other room. "Not that other stuff about calming her down?"

Amalina nodded, and smoothed the undercoats of the dress. *Give me another hour*, she thought sourly, growing annoyed at the fussiness of this dress, too. She wasn't even half-way done. Then there would be the make up and hair. But it wasn't Pia Lampeda at the door. After a terse exchange in the outer room, Lady Aria Ecci slouched into the bedroom, followed by a shamed Aklan.

"Katty," said Aria, immediately joining in Amalina's dressing. "I thought I might speak with you while we have the moment to ourselves."

"You're still in your dress ... from last night," observed Amalina. "You haven't been to bed?"

"Just on my way," said Aria matter-of-factly. "Figured I might catch you on your way up as I was on my way down, figuratively speaking."

"You've caught me," said Amalina, thinking her friend was looking drawn and needing a rest. How many other Ladies were still up? Or had Aria outlasted them all—again? She pictured the great hall strewn with passed out Ladies, their arms and feet twisted and sprawled in unladylike positions.

"Have you seen 'Maria' di Oscina?" began Aria. "I feel I might have been too hard on her the other day, as you said, and I should apologize."

Something awful appeared for an instant before Amalina's eyes—not Lucinda, and not 'Maria' di Oscina's off-putting face; something else—and she felt a strange lurch in her gut. But it was fleeting and gone in an instant. Wind?

"You don't have to apologize on my account," said Amalina, curtly, feeling that Lady Aria should have apologized long ago to poor homely 'Maria' di Oscina; done so on the spot when she'd offered the offensive remark. Or might never have said it in the first place.

"Your account's got nothing to do with it," laughed Aria ruefully, after reading Amalina's expression.

"As I recall, you weren't too friendly to me in that incident, either. You were a little insulting, in fact."

"Was I?" Aria sounded amused, confident Amalina had already forgiven her. "Well anyway, as I was saying, you've nothing to do with my apologizing to *her*, Kit-Kat, nor why I'd make the attempt. As if *you* could change my mind! My opinion about that hideous, cross-clutching, rubber-faced imposter, 'Maria', has not altered one inch since she arrived. But I *have* been thinking, and I just wouldn't want a petty offense against her—whatever it was I said—to end up standing against me." Aria's tugs on the stay's laces took on a sensual nature. This young woman knew her way around the fittings of a dress, and her touch was gentle and caressing, plying and almost apologetic. But she kept on, in a different tone: "Your uncle doesn't like her, does he? *'Maria'*? Well, it's hard to grasp what might happen next around here, you never know. And what happens if he favors her with his little gifts? Or worse, what happens if her friend, that tenacious barnacle, Margeta, should suddenly get some power? Get it before *I* do, that is. I wouldn't like to consider."

Another awful flash shot through Amalina's mind. This of torchlight and blood—*torchlit blood*—Amalina swallowed it.

"And all because of a little teasing on my part?"

"So you're saying you're really afraid of Margeta then?" Amalina asked Aria, who seemed to be not looking her in the eye but keeping her dark-haired head down, all about the work.

"I *am* afraid of the barnacle; if she gets accepted by your uncle before me, and takes his gift," acknowledged Aria, unabashed, "as I explained. I can't imagine what your uncle would want with a wife who'd find every one of his farts in bed as a cosmic tragedy, instead of something to laugh at. What a dreary thought how this castle would wilt, absolutely wilt, if Margeta la

Brichese were to be lofted over it … So *that* outcome I was worried about, Kat-Kat. But then, after Noka's little drama—" another flash, this time with Noka's eyes staring at Amalina, her bland smile, the blood, all the blood "—If somehow Noka—" Noka is back, bulging and distended but her expression sated, she is about to talk, flecks of flesh still on her lips, caught in her teeth— "If she got wind of it," Aria made a fearful face, "who knows what might come of it if she hears what I said to 'Maria'. I mean, *imagine.*"

Amalina tried to shake her head without Aria noticing, wanting to dispel the frightful sight of Noka—*Not* Noka!—drenched in her servant's blood, their bodies dismembered and strewn through the hallway, which Amalina had to wade through to confront her friend. Her friend smiling innocently at her, despite the rolling pool of gore around her; and on her … marking her as their murderer.

"You didn't tell Nok-Nok did you?" said Aria, a worried look on her face to match Amalina's. "About what I said to 'Maria'?"

"No." Amalina shook her head perhaps a little too hard.

"Well, Katty, I suppose I should apologize to you while I'm at it, eh? Not that that's why I came, but I can't have you thinking I meant anything by what I say, to you or anyone else, other than to pass the time and make things interesting. You know you can insult me all you like, every minute of the day, I'd laugh."

"I think everyone knows not to take you too seriously, Aria."

"My, my, Katty, am I all that bad?" But Aria wore a short smile that ended at her lips. She didn't care what anyone really thought. As long as it did not affect her relationship with their host, and what she hoped to gain from him.

*To gain from him.*

The vision of Noka, so many nights ago, slammed hard again into Amalina's memory; as if it were lurking at every turn, waiting for an opening to spring out and shock her. Noka, the sweetest woman Amalina had ever known, all bloated and no more human than any foul beast, sitting atop a display of her absolute savagery. The proof, the monstrous, undeniable proof that there was no such thing as sweet Noka anymore; that the skin, the act of being a kind, admirable princess between kills, had all just been a flimsy shell covering … And she whispers her dismissive little words to Amalina, *"C'est finis."* "The end." And why? To ease Amalina? To promise that it would never happen again? To pretend this proof to the contrary, which Amalina saw before her eyes, which soaked her dress and spattered her skin, wasn't true?


• • •

The carnage had been explained away, to the Ladies of Title and their entourages, as an internal fight between Noka's servants. One that claimed the lives of all, right up to her highest man, Oroco. And while Amalina's innocent guests might have bought the flimsy explanation, those in the know, like Aria, who hoped to enjoy the very power Noka had gained from their host, the Count—and the few that had already received his 'gift'—they could guess what had *really* happened, and Noka's reason for doing it.

After that night's horrifying events, the high castle had been haunted, its mood entirely changed, even as the servants struggled to scrub the stains from the hallways, and Noka withdrew below the Castle into its lowest cellar rooms to join the others like her. It had taken a week or so for the castle to regain its air of sorority and celebration, with the concerted will and effort on everyone's part to put things back the way it had once been. And Amalina had even managed to push it down so far in her mind that the only ugliness she had to contend with anymore was Lucinda's nightly visits and demands for revenge. *That* had been a relief.

*So why did Aria have to bring up Noka?* wondered Amalina, presently. *Dredge up the awful visions of her and that night ... so much more dreadful, and real, than the Lucinda nightmare?*

Amalina sneered at the obvious answer: Because Aria so wanted Count Tepsji's 'gift', and wanted reassurance it was still within reach, that her actions and her careless words hadn't hurt her chances to get it—and to snatch it before her rivals. The most boisterous and cocksure of any of the Ladies of Title in the castle, Aria Ecci, the longtime favorite of the Count, had been reduced to a conniving schemer, sneaking about at all hours and trying to gain advice and intimacy from 'Katarina', the Count's niece? Amalina felt embarrassed for her. And that embarrassment was another good way for Amalina to divert her irritating thoughts of Noka; to look on Aria with pity and tell herself, as the dress went on: *I would never be like her. I'd never want to be like her. Like Aria Ecci.*

• • •

"Go to bed," suggested Amalina. "You're tired. I know you'll do whatever you think is right."

"That's just it," snorted Aria, softly, "Even fully rested, I doubt I'm capable of knowing what's right. That's why I came to *you*. Will 'Maria' forgive me, do you think, if I can apologize somehow? Or would she even believe me? Oh, it's almost too tiring to consider. Maybe I should give up before I bother. I should just be me and let everyone live with it, come what may. Isn't that really *me*, after all?

"I'll say one thing," she said, finishing up as she slid back to the doorway, "all of this feels like so much work just to keep ahead. I can't imagine what *you're* waiting for, Katty. After all, he's a man and could've taken you—or done even worse—any time he liked. Instead, he hasn't. And that makes him more of a gentleman than I've ever met in my life; or heard of."

After Aria had gone, and with the insistent visions of Noka now biting her nerves, before Amalina went down to the Gallery to visit Pia, she snuck to different room on another floor. This room had become part of her morning routine, just as all the other parts that followed after waking from a Lucinda nightmare.

Amalina hesitated at the door. It was still very early, perhaps the sun not up. Would Cristine be awake by now? Amalina wanted to visit her old best friend and have a chat. That would be nice. Or no … at first, she'd thought so. But then Amalina realized she'd really come to have a look. That would be the safest thing to do, wouldn't it? No arguments or tough conversations if she only had a peek at her friend. But that wouldn't be fair, either, just eyeing her through a keyhole. They hadn't spoken in a number of days. And still not since that night of slaughter: *The Night of Noka*. She should really have a serious talk with Cristine, see if she'd changed her mind, or if Amalina could convince her to change it, about what was happening in this weird court and should rather like to leave after all; not take any further steps in the Count's—

With her mind made up, Amalina stepped confidently to the door, and readied her hand to knock. Just as she had for so many mornings, she sent her hand forward, once, twice, three times, but still it didn't make contact with the wood, only the air. Could she really *still* be too nervous to—?

"E-e-e-excuse, Princess?" said Bardina, Margeta's maid, appearing out of the hallway's darkness.

"Bardina, hello," said Amalina, trying to sound warm and collected, though the flashes of Noka's massacre, the irritation of Aria, and now the question of Cristine's wellness were sitting heavily on her.

"M-m-my Lady wishes to speak to you, Princess Tepsji. Princess la Brichese, eh? Y-y-y-you speak to her, m-m-most please?"

"Oh?" Amalina was curious how, and why, Bardina had found her out so early. And Margeta was also awake at this time? and wanting an audience? The castle seemed livelier than Amalina would have assumed. What was happening this morning?

"Y-y-you will come, Princess?"

"Do you know what it's about? It's rather early."

"Sh-she s-s-said if I saw L-L-Lady Ecci go to your room, Princess Katarina, I should bring you to her."

"You've been following Aria?" said Amalina, unsettled. What *was* going on this morning? "Or were you watching me?"

"W-w-will you c-c-come?"

"You know your lady has risen, and that she would want to see me now—right now, at this instant?" questioned Amalina, wishing she could be away from whatever business this was. Not that it was hard to guess with the constant feuding between the two Italian ladies, Aria and Margeta; and now that they were in an undeclared race with each other for a special *gift*, it could only be some bit of backbiting and maneuvering.

"Sh-sh-she w-w-will be awake," said Bardina, her eyes closed. "B-b-believe me. B-b-but you *w-w-will* c-come?"

"I think not," said Amalina. "I just wanted to visit my good friend, Cristine. See how she's feeling this morning. You can tell your Lady Margeta just so, Bardina. And now that I've seen to Miss Berzweck, and that she's resting comfortably, I will be returning to bed. Do tell her that also, Bardina, will you?"

Bardina did not answer, but bowed and handed Amalina a note.

"What's this?"

"I-i-if y-you won't c-come, I-I-I a-am t-t-to give you thi-thi-this."

Amalina unfolded the letter.

> Princess Katarina Tepsji,
> Do you think you can evade me so willfully when I have become a member of your family, the lawful spouse to your uncle, and a permanent feature to this very castle where you live? Think on the rightful actions you take now, and the wrongful. If you cannot do so, if it is too much trouble for you, let mine own actions be your righteous guide—and Aria Ecci's your example to the opposite.

Amalina could hear Margeta's scolding voice in the stilted, vicious script.

"Y-y-you've read it, Princess?" said Bardina.

"I have. And?"

Bardina bowed once more, deeper now, and turned round to scuttle back into the darkness.

Amalina imagined she saw Noka within the deeper shadows, smiling from them.

. . .

"Help me take this off," grumped Amalina, returning to her own apartment almost at a run. "I'll wear my old clothes. That's good enough for a trip out of the castle. I don't wish to see anyone anymore, and I don't want anybody recognizing me."

"Take it *all* off?" Aklan sounded exasperated. "But you just put—"

"Yes." As he started to work the laces at her back, she turned her chin to her shoulder and said softly, "I'm sorry Aklan. I woke a little out of sorts."

"No bother, Pretty Princess. Whatever you wish."

"And I've already had enough with those twin rocks, Aria and Margeta. While I get my other clothes on, I want you to go down and have Pils make sure Margeta isn't lurking anywhere. Heaven forbid she see me without a proper dress on."

"Doubt she'd be up at this hour."

"Why doubt that?" asked Amalina, innocently. "Does she ever leave that little chapel of hers to rest?"

"Ms. Dalll-ca," said the Count, suddenly in the room.

Aklan toppled backward to the floor as if blown over, holding in a shout, his eyes wide.

Amalina gasped, "Oh!"

There he stood in full, Count Tepsji. Amalina couldn't see the Count's face as it was hidden in the shadowed scoop of his shoulders, but he brought with him what he always dragged in with him: his enormous presence. And while he fit within a human frame—a large, imposing black shape, as tall and broad as he wished to be—he emanated the subtle but menacing vibrations of a door strained to its limit, creaking even as the monotonous knocks sound, at the rhythm of a slow heartbeat, of a dark, malevolent force pressing on the other side. One could almost hear the screams of the thousands of his previous victims; of that force that wanted in. Which was why Aklan, on the ground, continued to use the heel of his foot to scoot, inch-by-inch, away. There also came, on the swirling breeze that followed, the vague scent of rodent fur and some exotic herbs.

By the way the Count was stooped over and by his slow, grating words, he was in a mood. Was it *his* face she'd seen in the shadows of the hall just now, and not Noka's?

"Sir?"

"It's good to see you up so early. Your rising could have not been more perfectly timed."

"Oh? Really?"

He seemed to also be in one of his sluggish moods. Which meant it took prompting to get him to not just stand there and stare, as if he were trying to relay his words with his mind.

"Um ... Sir?"

"Ms. Dalca, you and I ... we need to talk. About *Princess Noka*."

# The Rising Tide

Amalina entered the Count's private study—as he'd instructed before becoming a black blur, a whir of air, and was gone. He wasn't in the study, but she could hear him through its passage to his secret countinghouse. Normally hidden by a massive portrait—where he stood in glorious triumph over the world—the painting was swung open and she could see him on the other side, free of his black cloak, counting out pieces of gold into a bag.

"Right here," said the Count needlessly. "Do hurry. I want you and Genadie to be out of my castle before any of the ladies are up."

Amalina looked around. Once upon a time the countinghouse's floor-to-ceiling shelves had been packed and stacked with bags of gold ingots. The last time she'd snuck through it, she'd noticed that the shelves had been substantially reduced, suggesting the Count had made a huge outlay of his wealth … on something. Presently, the shelves were depleted even more, but the reason was obvious: his workstation where he melted ingots and pressed his own coins was still puffing out acrid white clouds, and she could feel its heat. And all around on the several standing desks there were dozens upon dozens of towers of gold coins with his face stamped in relief on them.

For all the hot smelly smoke fouling the room, Amalina was glad she had changed out of her more formal gown and was now dressed down in a thin, plain, rougher blouse and skirt.

"I was going out," she told him, cautiously, pulling up a side of her coarse utility dress, unsure of the Count's meaning about leaving the castle, particularly when he'd said earlier they were to talk about Noka "Thought I'd see if I could find some berries to pick for our lunch."

He dismissed the idea with a wave of his white hand. His fingers and palms were dusted with gold, as if he'd been working the molten metal with his bare hands. "You can do that tomorrow, Ms. Dalca. I suppose you should be back by tonight."

"I'm going somewhere, sir?"

"You know that I love you," he said. "I just adore you."

"Sir?"

"That you'll soon, in no time at all, be mine. Hand-in-hand."

Besides uncomfortable, this seemed to be getting far afield. But if she didn't do anything about it, it could get worse. "Yes, sir. You've told me so, sir. It's something you've left me to think about, remember?"

"But there's no question of how I feel about you?"

"I would never question, sir."

"Good. It's good you know that I can't—we can't—wait for you to join us, and understand. You *do* understand?"

"As I've just … um, yes, sir."

"Very good." He finished tossing coins into the bag. "Now, as soon as I give you these monies, you and Genadie will run straight off to Netz."

"In the middle of winter?"

"That's why you must be quick about it, I don't want you two getting lost in any storms. I don't have time to be hunting you down and pulling you out of snowbanks."

"But why? And why Netz, sir? And … and why all this money?"

"We need to discuss our darling Princess Noka Kunuru Sowa Iwebo …"

"That *is* what you said. Originally, sir."

He put down the bag of coins and began fussing with his instruments again.

"… What *she* has done," he muttered darkly, distracted, not looking at Amalina anymore.

"What about her?" said Amalina, with a worried tone. "I thought she was over her little … whatever it was. She went through all her servants, there's no one left. She said she was done."

"*C'est finis …*" Noka's voice whispered to Amalina, the memory sharp.

"That she did," he agreed. "And she's behaving herself now, of course. She *is* a delight and a sweet one, yes." The Count said this nicely, but he sounded somewhat exhausted. He paused what he was doing to look at her. "But what I mean, Ms. Dalca, is what that sweet Lady has unleashed here in my castle."

*Unleashed?*

Immediately at the word, Amalina thought of the woman locked in a dungeon cell below, lashed to a turning wheel: the one who'd been there for ages and whose enduring urge must be to escape this endless torture and have her vengeance; and which, without meaning to, Amalina had once prevented. Had Noka learned of this poor wretch? Found her out? And now set her loose as a small bit of revenge? What would that mean for any of them?

"Unleashed, sir?" said Amalina, a little nervous.

The Count sighed, he dumped out the latest batch of coins from a steaming wood box. He began sorting and plunking select ones into the already full bag.

"I'm not certain how much you'll need, but I'm making sure you have enough," he said, sounding like he was more talking to himself. But then he turned to Amalina again: "Now, what you're to do, little mouse—both you and Genadie—is to visit our pleasant little village and spend some money there. Have a lunch. Make a day of it. Order up supplies for our guests. But be sure you're seen by as many of the people as you can. Now this is gold, so don't spend too much, of course, and be sensible; and make sure they see my coins—what face it bears—before you break them down for payment."

"Um, yes, sir."

He tried to hand the bag to Amalina but she wasn't ready for the weight and it smashed to the ground, spilling the coins to all corners. Some rolled under the shelves. He tried to catch them with his hands, in a blinding whirl.

"Clumsy, clumsy, my little mouse," he said, with a patient, forgiving, but tired voice.

"I couldn't possibly carry a bag that heavy, sir."

"Fetch your leather bag then, the one with the long handles. That should be big enough to work."

"Okay, but—"

"You'll watch them," he told her, one gold finger in the air. "Watch closely now, my clever Amalina. See how they react both to you and Genadie, and also how they react to my gold."

"How they react, sir?"

"You'll recall your reception in Netz, some years ago, when it was discovered that the mayor's daughter, Ygardina, had been killed and they thought you were responsible—"

"They thought *you* were responsible, sir, but that Genadie and I were your servants; and we were the only ones they could lay their hands on, because you were back in the castle—"

"However the case," interrupted the Count, seeming in a hurry now.

"They nearly killed us," said Amalina with some emphasis, trying to remind him what had happened. "They would have killed us if we'd been any slower and they'd caught us, sir."

"Very good, you remember," he smiled, oblivious and already running on his own track. "Well, for our own peace, I need to make sure that we aren't back to that same unfortunate situation. You remember how much it took to bring them back into order." The Count sounded testy at the memory.

"What? What's happened?"

"I can't bore you with the details, Ms. Dalca, as *I* feel you really now must be off. But *I* am forced to admit that *I*'ve been perhaps overly positive about the progress of *my* Special Ladies." Amalina noted, with a smirk, that though the Count was in a hurry, he couldn't help to curlicue his sentences with as many unnecessary I's, me's, and my's as he could. *Always referring to himself,* she thought in agitation, *his favorite subject.* But he was still talking: "But perhaps I've made a mistake by my doing so. Especially after our Princess Noka made such a fine point for me the other night. *Noka's night.* Strengthening herself by—um, let's say consuming—consuming as many of her people as she could in order to rival the number I have done in my days, and so equal *me* ... ho, ho! Well, it was not lost on those clever Ladies I've singled out for my favor. And Noka's *In-Yang* has spread its *In*. For you see, being in a charitable mood, I let my Ladies have a longer leash than I should have. Inspired by our Noka's actions then—her aggressive act presenting an out-sized impact and an undue influence upon them, leading to their clumsy imitation and abuse—during the last outing a number of days ago some of these Ladies took it on themselves to have their first ... shall I call it ... *atrocity*?"

"My god."

"No need for that," he frowned.

"I mean, what kind of ...?"

"It's all in the past," said the Count. "Or it should be. The Cardinal, my dear friend, has promised to smooth the waves for me. But the only way for me to prove it is if we have ourselves a little test. Which is why I am sending you down there. If he's telling me the truth, those citizens of Netz will meet you—or, that is, they will meet my niece, Katarina—as kindly as ever, and accept my money without hesitation."

"But if he's wrong," said Amalina, appalled, "They'll tear us to pieces. You really want *me* to go down there? alone in a hostile city ... and in danger?"

"You made it safely through last time," said the Count without concern. "But I insist that you do, yes, I think it should be done. It *has* to be."

Amalina made a small unhappy noise.

"This isn't just about me anymore, I can't have my Ladies, the valued daughters of important western families, learn they are under threat by the local population."

"So you'd sacrifice Genadie ... and *me*?"

"No need to be dramatic, my little mouse. How many times have I told you not to give in to your fears?"

*My* fears? she thought. But she said: "You have?"

"Is there something wrong, Ms. Dalca?" He'd noticed her, and turned to her a little more fully.

"Um, no, sir."

"You seem you have something to say."

"Um, no, sir."

"Nothing troubling you?"

"Um—"

"But I know what it is," he grinned.

"You do, sir?"

"Ms. Dalca," he hummed with a pedant tone, "you always seem to have an ample supply of catastrophes in the seasons—which you do an admirable job of cleaning up for me, I will give you that. But sometimes I need your attention … and for you to concentrate. Concentrate *here!*"

"Alright, sir, I'm sorry."

"I'm trying to remove one situation before it rises poorly and interferes with the grand work I am trying to do here, and it bothers us to no end. You should see the value in that."

"Yes, sir. I apologize. Really. Do go on."

But he was still talking. " … only it's this fear. This constant fear in you. Like the tides, it must be borne and accepted by me. And I try, I do try. And I don't know what else I can do to ease your mind and to still the unending *tides* you have. You know how much I adore you—as I've just told. I would never see you come to harm. Even in this little favor I ask of you. You know I'd do it myself, but I would be valueless to the experiment. You, however … You I count on the most, don't I? As ever. So just pop on down and have a look around—"

"Why can't you do it, sir?" she asked, as if unclear.

"Even if we were to discount what time of day it is, the burning hours, if I showed in their midst, what could they do but drop kindly to their knees? They couldn't help themselves. But you two, who they think are easy catches, will attest to how they'll treat my guests. It's the only way to prove it to my satisfaction, you see."

"I suppose," said Amalina, remembering back to when the streets of Netz were clogged with villagers chasing after her speeding cart, swearing at the top of their lungs that they will kill her and Genadie, and throwing bricks, sticks, and anything they could get their hands on. "We can't have Mr. Balbo come? He might provide better protection."

"Balbo?" he asked curiously. "Mr. Balbo has important duties here, which means I require his presence at my high castle. And he'd only muddle the process, as I've explained. It is to be Katarina and her footman, two innocents alone, for the good people to welcome; while I remain behind, deciding what's to be done about the rest of our troubles." He nodded, well convinced of his plan. "But I believe it has been made very clear to you now, by me, to your satisfaction. And if it helps turn your tide, know that, as I've said many time before, I have lived for a very long time, and I have allies everywhere. Hidden ones. They are already in place and watching, so that you will be protected, always, and suffer no harm. All righty? " He began ushering Amalina to the door with a gentle push at her back. " Go now, Ms.

Dalca, bring down your handle bag. And while you're up there, change out of this berry-picking costume and throw on one of your finer dresses. You should look the perfect part."

"Sir, you don't just throw on a—"

. . .

Amalina growled at Aklan: "Get up! Get me a dress!"

"Pretty Princess!" Aklan shot off the couch he'd been sleeping on. "What are you doing here?"

"Never mind that, help me get a new dress out. I'm putting one on."

"Again?" he gasped at the coming struggle.

Oh yes, thought Amalina with a miserable face, this morning she'd woke from one horror, the predictable Lucinda nightmare, which she'd felt she could easily forget, only to be quickly and harshly reminded of just where she really was: locked in a castle with a score or so Ladies of Title who were roiling with jealousies and ambition to marry the Count, and a hatred for each other which could lead to blood if you just scratched the surface. And, of course, there was plenty of blood to consider with the Ladies who the Count had already turned into monstrous creatures like himself—with Cristine still hanging in the balance between the two states of mortal kindredship and supernatural depravity—who've now, apparently, taken up Noka Kunuru Sowa Iwebo's unfortunate example to kill relentlessly to gain more power; Noka's example a ghastly, blood-gorged, unforgettable sight whose memory destroyed Amalina's calm to even contemplate. And so—

Oh, here it came, *the tide* … and it was rising past the mark. From the very start the morning had been pushing Amalina from her half-solid perch of denial, her painful attempts for peace, tranquility, and stability in her surroundings, so she could at least have a moment to think. But now, her thoughts were cascading one-over-the-other about her oh so lamentable life.

*No, never mind about the Ladies of Title. Never mind about Noka; or the Count's Changed Ladies, now acting like her. Never mind about Cristine—*

It went on, the flood-tide, because there were so many perils rolling in from years past, she could barely sense them as they swept over, to be replaced, dizzyingly, by another, she could not keep up. The first were the ones the Count knew about and related directly to him. But she had so many more that related directly to *her*, either alone or he'd forgotten; so many that she could scream. She admirably did not scream, but instead, did that thing Anne Brignol had once observed and titled 'Katarina's Survivor Energy': she tucked her head down to meet them:

*—and never mind AXP is still out there and is presumably still plotting my death …!*

*And never mind that poor, tortured woman is still turning on a wheel below the castle, in need of rescue, who I vowed to rescue, didn't I …?*

And never mind that Amalina was still the active spy for Sadra's revolutionary; and that this happened to be the day, the very morning, she'd set for herself to decide, finally, what to do about him and his pending attack on the castle—

It was all too much to think about, and as each problem submerged to be forgotten as another rose to take its place, she felt almost as if she actually was drowning.

*No, never mind all that*, thought Amalina finally, as she tried to put a stop to her thoughts before she fainted. No, never mind all that—to cap the morning off, the Count was now sending her down to Netz to test the waters after another outrage against its citizens, to see if she would *survive?*

*If she would survive!!!*

Amalina wished she had stayed asleep and was safely back in the dream with Lucinda.

"Right now, boy: the yellow one with the flowers, birds, and bees embroidered on it," decided Amalina presently, with a serious tone, pointing to the dress she wanted. "If I'm going to risk my life today, I'll be wearing my favorite. And maybe, even if Mr. Balbo can't go I should find him, borrow one of his fancy new pistols."

Amalina snapped her fingers and ran to her bed. She began rummaging under the mattress.

"Pistols? Risk your life?" chirped Aklan, excited now. "I'm going out with you, right?"

"Just ready my dress," said Amalina, as she pulled the magic item from its hiding place. "If I'm going to get myself killed this morning, I should at least say good bye to Cristine."

## 3

## "All is good."

With a couple grisly, battered heads of AXP henchmen skewered on spikes above the front gate to see Amalina and Genadie off, setting a certain mood, leaving the castle hadn't improved her spirit much.

And despite the fluffy white hillocks and frosted tree limbs scrolling in the distance—soft scenery so similar to the hypnotically rotating platters of iced pastries and delicate, foot-high cakes that had charmed Amalina in the Parisian royal court—even with their seeming desperation to cheer her up, a deep foreboding filled the trip down to Netz; its wraithlike gloom shriveled any pretty sight at a glance, and seemed to infuse everything with a sense of sinister menace. All while Genadie tried to calm Amalina so that she would stop fidgeting and glancing round with a sour, nervous look; which was now carrying over into him. *But how could it be helped?* she wondered, because *right there* she'd been attacked and nearly killed by the great black wolf. Only escaping by a sliver of luck. And *over there* just inside the mountain forest— behind and above the burnt-out wreckage of the farmhouse, where Commander Kralov had housed his ill-fated army before they'd launched themselves at the castle and to their deaths—that was where one of AXP's assassins, the scary tall man with the lame leg, had almost done Amalina in. And he would have if not for the appearance of the black haired, monstrous wolf and his pack once more; which had, just by luck again, taken him first. And somewhere, here or there, Katrina Flauna and Odetta had been torn apart by the Count, their bodies not found until the spring thaw. She'd been up and down these mountains, on foot and horseback, and everywhere was a bloody memory. And so what promise could Netz, waiting for them at the far end of the valley, hold?

Fear was drawing itself into a fine point just ahead.

Even the sleigh they rode in over this lovely, pristine landscape, had bullet holes in the bench where AXP's hired gun had tried his weapon on her and Genadie.

"Who fixed the roof?" wondered Amalina, now glancing up at the riding compartment's black leather cover, which once had a handful of holes shot into it to match the ones in the bench, when the sleigh had turned over and the assassin closed in for the kill. She still felt the press of that moment, the fear like a fist clenching her gut.

"Princess Margeta's people," answered Genadie, cheerfully. "Very nice of her. Lent the supplies reserved for repairs to her furniture and her chapel. Very kind, yes." His lips wriggled at a thought. "Though I could have done the work, no need for them to bother with it—the castle's sleigh, after all."

"Exactly," agreed Amalina, hotly. "I mean, just why *are* we here? There doesn't seem to be any sense in it with so many others up in the castle who can take this little trip of his instead of us ... people who'd love to do it. Margeta's servants, for one."

"He needed a *Lady*," Genadie reminded her.

"A lady he could *spare*," huffed Amalina. "I guess *we're* the ones who can be spared. Or *lost*—"

"Oh, now," said Genadie, trying to quiet her.

"He didn't even send Captain Durok or one of the other castle guards. Why no protection at all? At all!"

"Always trust his plans," he soothed. "You know how he thinks of everything. And so, well, he must have told you, with a guard in our company, it might scare those Netz people off if they see—"

"Right: if they see we're protected! Exactly! I can't believe we're just going to do this without protection. That we're actually doing it, Genadie!"

"*Someone* has to go," said Genadie, sunnily, lifting one edge of his smudged, wide-brimmed hat so he could wink and grin at her "Might as well be us."

Amalina let silence fall as yelling would begin if the conversation continued.

At least, thought Amalina, before she left the castle she'd been able to sneak into Cristine's room and had seen her—still asleep, and still alive it seemed, though greyer than ever. At one point in her visit, her friend had appeared to sense movement in the room, stirred and called out in her sleep, spun and clutched at the air, throwing her hand against an unseen attacker. In her dreams, Cristine was warding off a bad girl of Korr, one of the worst of them, who'd often left her sprawled in the street or stuffed in an alley beaten and covered in cuts and bruises. "No, Bessa! No! Leave me alone! Please, Bess! Amalina! Amalina, where are you? Amalina, help! Help me, Amalina!"

While Amalina would not dare wake Cristine and reveal herself, she had calmed her friend by gripping her pale flailing hands and soothing her with reassuring strokes and lullaby hums until she'd settled back down and looked at some peace. In this state, relaxed and snoring lightly, Cristine was just as before, the vulnerable girl from Korr ... if a part of her was waiting for the creature to come.

*Wouldn't want to be like that, either,* Amalina had thought.

But Amalina had done her old best friend a favor, had saved her one last time from Bessa, and done so before putting herself on this mission and directly in harm's way and might never see her ever again. That little visit—done with the help of her magic item—was comforting at least, in its own way.

After a few breezy minutes, the road, an invisible path in the snow Genadie could apparently see, or he knew from decades of practice, took a wide, meandering turn. The sloshing of the sleigh's runners, as Genadie expertly, and rather serenely, kept the sleigh on course, and the sound of the chirping birds through crystal clear winter air had an easing effect. Amalina clasped her hands together in the furry hand-warmer and tried to shrug off her nerves. She felt the magic item within the warmer beside her glasses and held onto it like a talisman, her invincible shield.

. . .

"I wish there was something I could do to make you feel better about it," mumbled Genadie a little later, testing the waters between them.

"We can can just *not* go, you know," suggested Amalina. "Turn around and tell him we went. How would he know if we didn't? Tell'm 'all is good in Netz'."

"Please don't be scared, Ms. Dalca. But, all *is* good."

"And how would you know that?" she began to seethe again. "Even *he* doesn't know. That's *why* he's sending us."

"Now, Ms. Dalca, I don't think he'd deliberately send us into something dangerous."

"That's exactly what he's doing! That's the point! He's *using* us to test Netz. Using *us!*"

This caused Genadie to shift uncomfortably on the bench. He wasn't ready for the renewed anger. Or he saw her point and believed it.

"Or he's testing us, eh?" she sneered. "To see if we're stupid enough to do it."

"Now, Ms. Dalca—"

"I mean is this how you treat the woman you claim you want to make your wife? I can't imagine!"

"Did he?" gaped Ganadie in surprise and delight.

"Enough times you wouldn't expect him to do this to me. But don't pretend you didn't know, Genadie, I know he tells you everything."

"Not much anymore," he said, somewhat lost. "Did you ... *accept?*"

"No!" cried Amalina. "Are you kidding? And this, the way he's treating me, just shows you what a liar he is."

Genadie frowned and made a small noise. "Liar ... well ..."

"Didn't he swear he'd gotten rid of AXP? He even put one of those heads up on that wall for me as guaranteed proof he'd done it—"

"I never heard him say—"

"—But then came another AXP letter, and then came another another assassin!"

"Another!"

"Oh, yes,"hissed Amalina, "There's no end to his lies, are there?" She turned to him with a deeper sneer: "But I'm sure you'd accept the deal he's offering me in a heartbeat. Wouldn't you? Look at you, all happy he's showing you a little attention by sending you off to get killed! Even if you know he's lying to you, you'd do it."

The miracle that her words began to work on Genadie was quite remarkable. His lips turned down and head shook side to side disagreeably in the effect. As if the Count being accused as a flagrant liar could be worse than actually being a monstrous, blood-thirsty beast who'd killed untold numbers. After a moment, though, he seemed to shake the objection off.

"Oooh, Ms. Dalca, you needn't take your nerves out on me like that," said Genadie, as if he'd discovered a hidden purpose in her rage. "We really should be fine."

"Heading into Netz?" she grumbled, continuing to push. "Right when they're upset at us, or him, or whatever? And you remember exactly what happened last time! Of course you do!"

His right eye began to blink very quickly, and the side of his face twitched. He played it off by taking both reins in one hand and using the other to dig in his jacket pockets.

"Trust in him!" said Amalina, acidly echoing Genadie's now visibly deflating confidence, "Well, at this point, if I knew it was going to come to this, I probably should have accepted his offer. Then someone else would be sitting here ... not me. Not me sitting here with *you*."

"I know what you meant."

. . .

Amalina leaned close and, with a sly look, nudged his bony shoulder and whispered. "Better yet, let's go back to Paris. Now we've got our golden opportunity, eh? a bag full of it!" She tried to prod her leather bag with her elbow but it was too heavy, it just made the wood handles clack against each other. "Let's just keep going then. Eh? Race him to the border, and then off again ... to *Par-ee*."

"You're dreaming, aren't you, Ms. Dalca?' he said with a forlorn smile."You know how poorly it turned out for us last time."

"Oh, come on." Amalina's tone flattened: "We should have stayed there. Eh? You know it."

"A little late now." Genadie adjusted his hat with a disgruntled look and continued to search his greasy jacket's pockets.

"If we hadn't come back here," said Amalina, in a calm but somehow accusatory voice, "we'd still *be* in France. Eh? Or somewhere out in the west. *Safe* out there, and not about to meet death—"

"Meet death," scoffed Genadie. His hand had found what it was looking for and it dropped in his lap the small millet bag he kept for such occasions as increasing nerves. "It was your idea to come back, not only mine."

"Well, I was out of my head, wasn't I? We both were mad to do something like that. Come back here? We were *free*!"

"As I said, nothing can be done about it now," said Genadie, also a little testily. As if he might agree with the thought. He opened the bag and began feeding himself the millet. Little grains started bouncing off his lower lip and out the front of the sleigh to join the snow. "This is our life now—as it is— isn't it?"

"But it's *still* my same life! Nothing's changed between France and now, you know? Only that we are, by our stupid mistake, here and not *there*. But everything I felt and said there I still feel and mean now. Do you understand what I'm saying, Genadie?"

"Only some things *must* have changed for you, Ms. Dalca. A lot has happened since then. Proposals for marriage by … our … what have you … "

"You're right," she allowed, "A lot's happened. But not enough to change my mind. To my core, I'm still the same person. And I don't see how anything that's happened from then to now, some of it quite horrible, mind you, could have changed *you* all that much, either. It should only have convinced you more you were right back then. You wanted to stay, Genadie. You *would* prefer to be there in France, of course. Only that monster—"

"Master," corrected Genadie, to which Amalina laughed caustically.

"Exactly. Dead on: your *Master*. Haven't heard that pathetic word from you in a while. After what he did to your family—"

"I asked that you never to bring that up again, Ms. Dalca. Don't be cruel—"

"There's absolutely no reason we shouldn't still be the good partners we found ourselves to be in Paris. You and I, Genadie, the same as before."

He munched on the millet in guilty silence, until he mumbled, "We are. But …"

"But … ?"

"But this is the life that I've known for so very long, silly girl … You can't know how hard it is to change one's ways. Try it yourself sometime. I mean … we did try, didn't we? And it didn't work, did it?"

"What's to change? You're on my side, I'm on your side, and we're both against *him*, because he's awful and what he did to your fam—um, well ..."

He looked a little choked up about that statement, but nodded.

"And you know we both wanted to stay on in the west," she continued. "So what's stopping us? I mean it ... I mean it!" As she enthused, she pushed the bag again, with her hip this time, until it gave off a feeble *clink*. "We could do it. Think about it, eh? *Think* about it."

"Oh, I know what *you're* thinking."

"I don't want to get killed before lunch, is what I'm thinking."

"You're thinking to get back in touch with that Lieutenant friend of yours, is what you're thinking." He mocked: "Back in *Par-ee*."

Though Amalina blushed, she denied it with a visible gust of air from her nose and mouth.

"That's what I thought," he said, wearing a proud smirk. "To get away from Master, you said we had to to run as far away as we can; you said we had to go to a *land beyond the sea*. And Paris, last I checked, is still attached to the continent. There's nothing there in that city but your lieu—"

"You have asked me to stop bringing up what your 'Master' did to your family," growled Amalina, "and I've asked you—asked more than once— never to mention that lieutenant again."

"And why not? He was just a friend to you, wasn't he? Not like he was family." Genadie stared at her as if he understood a deeper truth between her and the lieutenant, a more meaningful relationship. But he looked silly with the millet caught in the whiskers around his trembling lips. "Don't think I didn't hear you two in the general's tent."

"I can't imagine what you thought you heard!"

"What you two said to each other. There's nothing to guess about it: he dropped you pretty hard." Genadie smiled apologetically. "Oh, I suppose we're even now, eh? I say we cease fire against each other's broken hearts, Ms. Dalca. And we stop dreaming of Paris, there's nothing to get ourselves back to there; and you don't really mean it, anyway."

"Of course I mean it!"

"No, you don't," he said confidently. "You're just scared. Trust me, girl: there's nothing to get back to there, there is everything to do here ... and all there's to do now is to focus ourselves on our duties ahead."

"So just to be clear, even though we're riding on a fast sleigh with a full day still ahead of us, and we have enough gold to buy a whole city, we aren't going back to France or to try to escape at all?"

"No," he said, with a definitive nod that used his whole head.

Amalina cleared her throat, with a worried look. "You aren't afraid at all, Genadie? Of what's going to happen in Netz?"

"It isn't a matter of fear. You can't be afraid when you are focused."

"Is that true?"

Genadie chewed on his millet, his eyes and face twitching. Not looking as confident as a second before.

. . .

"Genadie, how did you know they were going to come after us?" asked Amalina quickly, her anxiety growing as the town neared. *How much time left? another hour, maybe?* "That time in Netz, you could see it coming?"

"Easy enough when they started throwing things at me. Then someone brought out a noose—"

"A noose!"

"It began with their looks, though."

"I remember," said Amalina, recalling clearly the cold looks, the way the people of Netz stayed at a distance and would change to the other side of the street, or duck into side alleys or doorways if too close. It had been such a peculiar morning, she'd known something didn't feel right. And it had gone down from there. Then came the bloody parade of Ygardina's body.

"They began to whisper to each other," recalled Genadie, his little rat-like eyes ticking side-to-side, as if he could see the awful scene conjuring before him. "They made little groups that would follow. Those groups started getting together, and then they were coming for me." Genadie swallowed hard and then grabbed another handful of millet. "Not even a word of warning before the first piece of brick struck me in the head. Then they grabbed me. Then came the noose around my neck."

"They had it around your neck!" gasped Amalina.

"Glad you didn't have to go through that, Ms. Dalca. Very scary. But I got away and rode straight to you, and got you out before they had a chance to really catch us."

"You would've rode right past me if I hadn't grabbed onto the wagon in time."

"Oh, Ms. Dalca, how could you say—?"

"I'm sorry, Genadie, it *is* just my nerves now. Really. We have to stick together. We have to have a plan. But how did you get away with a rope around your neck?"

Genadie's trembling hands opened his coat, revealing two knives tucked into his belt, and then two rusty looking pistols in the coat's large inside pocket. "Had my knives. They're sharp."

"You brought weapons!" cried Amalina, though not feeling too relieved.

"You can have the pistols if you want."

"Where would I put them? Maybe a knife, and you keep the guns. But these arms are much better than nothing ..." she looked at his crooked, misshapen, shaking fingers. "Well, maybe not much better."

But then:

"Wait!" Amalina pointed to a grey mass of skyward stones just past a hill. "Is that the spire of St. Grigori church? Already? It can't be."

"I believe it is," said Genadie with a gulp, and then a shrug of his shoulder. "We'd better get ready then, eh?"

They both tensed.

Amalina squeezed the magic item in her hand warmer, not sure if she would use it if trouble broke. She could only use it to save herself. Leaving Genadie to the mob. Could she really do *that*?

"I really don't think we have anything to worry about," he tried to comfort her again, unconvincingly, as he chewed the millet faster. "You're making this much direr than it needs to be."

"You know it's not just *them* we have to watch for, either. Mr. Balbo scared off another one of those assassins."

"Where?" gulped Genadie. "In the castle, you mean?"

"But he didn't catch him and he got away. The man could be waiting for us in town. Any number of them."

"Hadn't thought of that," said Genadie with a grimace. "Did you happen to bring your good luck charm?"

Amalina took the magic item out of her hand warmer and showed it. It looked like an old broken duck bone that had been strung back together using some strands of Amalina's hair and glue—which it had been when Genadie had repaired it, he unclear on just what magic it contained. He thought it had something to do with luck and good fortune.

"That should be all we need, then, some of your solid-gold luck." He smiled shakily, his eyes on the St. Grigori spire as if it might strike them if they got too close. But they *were* getting closer to it, and soon its shadow would cross them, and the walls and gates would slide into view. "Just some good old fashioned luck."

"Still, let's have a plan, Genadie."

"Of course, Ms. Dalca," he said. He took hold of her hand, maybe to steady hers, or perhaps to steady them both. Their clasped hands tightened into a nervous ball as they rode closer and closer to their final destination. "All is good," he muttered fearfully. "All is good, Ms. Dalca."

4

# Dawn:
## My Dear Lieutenant

Sadra paused for a moment over Attila Bronk, watching him sleep before she reached out to gently shake his shoulder. "Loverboy's here, Attila … It's time."

Attila nodded and sat up as if he'd been awake the whole time.

"I have some hot tea for you," she offered.

He shook his head.

• • •

Early dawn came with a thick, shrouding fog that Attila Bronk welcomed. It made stalking the streets unobserved much easier, and was especially helpful in a village like Korr, where the populace, whether out of extreme superstition or excessive boredom, seemed hyperattuned to movement on the grey cobblestones outside their homes and apartments. The people seemed to have an almost supernatural knack to sense strangers.

Along with the grey-white mist providing cover, Attila had a companion at his side who could dispel any ill-feelings should the night watch or other random Korrite notice him. Attila's regular companion for the past months had been Sadra Smidt who, as the wife of the popular minister of Korr, could easily quell too much curiosity about him in any encounter. But this morning his companion was much larger, and more broad-shouldered than Sadra; whose smaller frame, but purposeful strides Attila had grown used to. This new escort's gait was sturdy, yet it was also somewhat unsure. He followed Attila more than accompanied him. Though handsome and dressed in a martial cloak from a great western army, he reminded Attila of an old dog he'd known in Tsobl that would follow him on his patrol, scratching along at his heels, or even darting a little ahead sometimes. Always there was a momentary pause, here and there, and there'd be a slight turn of the head, and a sidelong glance from his bulbous eyes, as if making sure he was still with Attila, still attached to the constable and hadn't been lost. For the past half hour Attila could feel the young man's eyes glancing in his direction, in the same way that nervous pooch would, and it began to have a tempo. This grated lightly on Attila's nerves; though the companion wouldn't be able to tell because of Attila's set, slack face. But again the glance came, and the slight turn of the head. If it had been the dog, there might have been added to it a worried yap. That was enough for Attila. Sometimes it was important to speak. So he knew, and so he did.

"My dear Lieutenant," said Attila in a low voice and without expression, as he turned to have his say.

Lieutenant Ivanti Ion Vokent drew up close to Attila and halted with what seemed to be a click of his heels. "Yes, sir?"

"I'm not much older than you, Lieutenant, and I never entered into the military ranks, so there's no need to call me that."

"Oh, yes," said Lt. Vokent. "I guess not. What should I call you then?"

"We've known each other for only a short time and Dragomir has been more of our go-between. You don't really know who I am, I'll presume?"

"Well," said Lt. Vokent with a vague, handsome smile. "You're in charge is what I've gathered."

"Nobody's told you."

"Not much," nodded Vokent. "Just what I've been privy to in our meetings."

"For good reason. Absolute security is required around this whole operation."

"Oh, I understand *that*, sir." Vokent seemed unsure of what he'd just said, or what he should have called Attila. "Um … Sir."

"To succeed against this enemy, we can't be too careful."

"I really do understand," said Vokent, with a smile again.

"During your time in the west, you served under a highly esteemed general."

"General Volante. I was his adjutant."

"Yes, I've been told everything," assured Attila, cutting the young lieutenant off. "Now, so you understand, I will hold all the pieces of this revolution securely in my head. Your background is well known to me. That is: you've returned to this country to rescue a girl: Dragomir Dalca's daughter, Amalina. A young woman you met in Paris."

"We knew each other here first, sir."

"You're a son of Korr, yes. And she a daughter. But you reestablished your relationship with this baker's daughter, or strengthened it, in Paris, France; where she was there disguised as our enemy's niece, Katarina Tepsji … from what I've been told."

"That is very much true. What you said, sir." He gave a little embarrassed laugh. "I think I'd be comfortable just calling you 'sir', since you're in charge. If that's all right, sir. Feels easier."

"Your martial training," assumed Attila.

Vokent nodded once with his strong jaw.

"I've been negligent," said Attila, "in that we haven't yet discussed your role in *the Cause's* organization. But I want you to know there is one for you. I don't want you to just float along like a leaf upon the current of a river. I want you fully immersed in it." Recalling what had happened to the man previously in the role Attila intended for the lieutenant, it was a poor choice of words. For his own satisfaction, he added positively, if inartfully, "To *own* that body of water, like a king trout."

"If you don't mind, sir, I'd rather be a bear in the river and not a trout."

"So would we all," rejoined Attila, "but it must be understood that in this scenario the Count is, and will always be, the wading bear. With sharp teeth, ready claws, and an insatiable appetite. We are necessarily the multitude of fish attempting to knock him over."

"And the river, sir?" Vokent arched his perfect, rakish eyebrow with a spirited look.

"Time, certainly," said Attila. "But we're moving far from my intended point."

"Yes, of course, sir."

"You, Lieutenant," nodded Attila, "because of your military background and training, are going to be placed in charge of our forces. When it comes to it. Their training and then implementing and executing their battlefield tactics. Sounds fair to you?"

Lt. Vokent straightened, then relaxed, his body spreading his weight evenly on his legs. He nodded with a serious look.

"For my own part, so you understand, I was a low constable for the Tsobl government. Which makes me more familiar with the enforcement of laws than fielding armies."

"Yes, so I understand."

"But also understand, Lieutanant, that I do have some learning and experience in the operation of military force."

"Oh?"

Squinting through the mist it was difficult to determine how Vokent meant the little word. Was it disbelief? or mocking? Though it might have been innocent, Attila couldn't have it otherwise.

"I co-commanded Hak Vogoneyevic's retribution force for nearly two years. You've heard of Sir Hak Vogoneyevic?"

The lieutenant thought about it and shook his head. "Vogoneyevic's an old family name. Haven't heard of Hak. But that might've been before my time."

"Hak's army folded after his death. The men were more attached to his family name—even his father's reputation—than the mission." Attila shrugged. "How about General Zsolt Marosh?"

"Zsolt? Everyone's heard of him!" The lieutenant burst into a goofy smile that Attila could read clearly through the mist. The young man was impressed and waiting for the payoff to this story.

"Zsolt and his southern forces had an idea to stop me and my mission. As far as I know, all of his men are dead, to the last. But I can say for certain that Zsolt is no longer alive. And yet I'm still here."

"Oh," said Vokent. "I see."

"Let me help you see even clearer, Lieutenant," said Attila through straight lips and a seemingly bored expression, which helped Vokent realize he wasn't reprimanding the young man but continuing a point, "I am a man of the law. First it was for Tsobl, for Ardeel and its people. Then, after I learned of the forces of evil at play in this land, I understood it was for the supreme law of heaven and all that is good in this world that I work."

"I see."

"As a serious man of the law and military experience, however limited, there shouldn't be a question of my being in charge."

"There isn't a question of it," said Vokent with a sharp grin and nod. "The way you put old Boss Berzweck in his place, I've never seen such a thing. Even General Volante, who holds the respect of three emperors, would never work up the courage to question a sovereign, or snap the backside of an important financier. There isn't a question of your leadership from me at all, sir. Be assured."

"Good. I'm glad to hear it."

"Not sure how you're going to get the Boss back on your side," he said, still grinning, as if Attila might tell him how he would get *the Cause*'s top investor—and so, the proposed revolutionary army—back under his control.

"However … returning to my point," said Attila. "As a man of the law I've developed my own abilities to reason out what I need to know, and to place people where they need to be in order to work for good. Mr. Berzweck will rejoin us. His daughter is wrapped up in this affair as much as Dragomir's. He's only letting his anger and impatience get the better of him. He'll come 'round when he understands I have a better sense for these kind of matters. Not everything can be handled like a business."

"I think General Volante said as much to me. He always disliked having to kiss the boots of the moneymen."

"Pardon the digression," said Attila. "I was outlining my professional skills. Along with logical reasoning, I have developed, as well, a honed eye of observation."

"I should think so, sir."

"And so, my honed eye tells me: you're wondering why you are with me on this very early morning."

"Was I? Well, maybe it's ... but I trust Dragomir," said the lieutenant, with a shrug. "And if Dragomir trusts you, so do I. But I *did* wonder ..."

"We are hunting someone in this village, Lieutenant. I have kept this piece of information from you, but now I find it necessary you know."

"Please, sir, do tell." Vokent did not shift his feet. He was used to receiving important information, whatever it might be, in the tents of high command without reaction. "You can trust me."

"And that's why you are here. You see, there is a man in Korr who is secretly a close associate to our enemy. He has regularly corresponded with the high castle in Netz, and seems to have some working relationship, if not some strange hold over that creature there."

"Really?" Now Vokent rocked back on his heels, and sounded like a schoolboy who'd been impressed by some nonsense.

"Though he is known by an acronym, it is a code that has not yet been broken. I don't know who it is. But before we can even think to continue our plans against the creature we must root this evil agent out, so that he cannot warn our adversary and ruin any chances we have against him, including our most crucial advantage: surprise."

"I see."

"And before we resort to the crudest methods of sorting through our potential suspects, by asking questions and stirring suspicions in return, I thought it best to at least try to discover this traitor in our midst as quietly as possible. Doing as little damage to our more important effort."

"I see," the lieutenant repeated with a brief nod. "A traitor to us all. You said there's an acronym? What's the acronym?"

*A.X.P.? ... Or is it A.Z.B.? Or is it ...?* Attila's mind began to wander. He could still picture the water-smeared, blurry and perhaps ink-doubled letters in his mind. Attila held up his finger. "Not absolutely certain, and not your concern. But it won't be necessary to puzzle out if our actions are successful today.

The lieutenant nodded with a hopeful look. "Okay. I see, I see."

"So then, we get to the reasons—which are twofold—why you are with me today, Lieutenant," said Attila, looking like he might fall asleep on his feet. "I need someone I can trust in this effort to root out the Count's agent. And they must have my absolute confidence that they are not the one, or an associate of that one. And since I am not from this village, I cannot be 100% sure of anyone's loyalty. Not even—and this is a shame to say—Dragomir Dalca."

"Oh, he's all right."

"I'm sure he is," said Attila. "But there is only one person in our operation—as it stands—who never knew of the creature and remained ignorant of him until recent events. Who did not sign their name into the contract with that beast—"

"Sadra?" guessed the lieutenant.

"That wasn't the name I was going to say, Lieutenant. Let me finish, please."

"Oh, yes, do go on, sir."

"I understand that signing that ancient contract with the Knight of Ardeel, Count Tepsji, is meaningless, just a common rite of passage among Ardeel's *men* to do so, but to never have signed it makes one a standout; an innocent beyond innocent. And let us consider he's been away from Ardeel for more than several years, so it is impossible for him to have kept a personal correspondence with the creature or his agent in Korr during that time without leaving a trail. And so there is only one person who I can fully trust. And that is you."

Ivanti Vokent nodded and put his hand inside his coat to warm it. He waited on the next bit of information he sensed in the offing.

"This agent of the creature had other associates I encountered here. They tried to kill me," here Attila tapped the bandage at his throat, "and though they came close, they did not succeed in their orders. When I visited the high castle outside of Netz recently, I saw their heads on spikes over the gate. For what reason I cannot fathom and your friend, Amalina, could not furnish, either."

At the mention of Amalina's name, Vokent's thighs clenched like a bolt of electricity had shot through him. But he kept the ripples across his expression admirably to a minimum.

"Now," continued Attila, after allowing Vokent a moment to compose himself, "those associates are dead. But I know they were residents of this village. That means they have lodgings somewhere. And if we can locate them, we may be able to discover, through letters and notes and other pieces of incriminating what-may-be, who they allied with and perhaps took their orders from, and thereby identify who this higher Korr agent of Count Tepsji's is; the identity of this *agent-of-the-acronym*."

Vokent nodded sternly.

"So it is clear what we are doing this morning, and why you are with me?"

"Clear enough. We're tracking down where these two men lived."

"At least one of them. I believe I have the solution for that. But I could be wrong. We will see." Attila turned with a sweep of his cloak. "Now let's return to it."

"May I ask you a question, sir?" said Vokent, after clearing his throat.

"Yes?" Attila stopped to face the lieutenant again.

"You said there was a twofold reason I'm with you this morning."

"More than that, actually," allowed Attila. "But I am prepared to admit to two."

"You trust me."

"Yes."

"That was the first reason," said Vokent. "The second?"

"Simple enough," answered Attila. "You've been a soldier. You know how to fight."

"Ah," Vokent chuckled with macabre understanding.

. . .

After this exchange, the two continued on, with Lieutenant Vokent's strides a little easier beside Attila, giving him a short lead, though they would appear to anyone else as if moving shoulder-to-shoulder.

They wound their way through the hushed, pre-bell streets of Korr, avoiding patrols, as Attila quietly made notes in his head, and took notice of secret signs he was looking for. After half an hour, and nearly a mile of mist-shrouded cobblestones covered, he was ready with a conclusion, and he paused on the northern side of the village, where the incline of the mountains would be seen past the last row of buildings if the fog wasn't hiding the view.

"It's as I thought," whispered Attila, and drew Vokent close with a slight gesture. "I'm most certain, but see if you can follow my logic, Lieutenant. I am looking for a man who nobody claims to know, yet is a resident of this village, and is most distinctive in his features. If he is indeed no longer among us, how do we find where he lived? Since nobody knows him, it would seem almost impossible."

Lieutenant Vokent nodded, signaling Attila to continue.

"Cutting out what is sensational but irrelevant—that he was a casual murderer—because he had an off-putting look, and yet somehow remained unknown, that would suggest he lived secretively, and so his place of rest would be in an area of the village that has little traffic, allowing him anonymous comings and goings, and access to less frequented privies. Since he kept to himself mostly—though he had that brute of a friend, whose head is mounted on the castle wall right beside his—it would suggest he'd want an apartment, perhaps one to share with the brute, with large rooms so they would not grow to feel confined. Now, less traveled could mean a back room or basement apartment, perhaps in a hidden alley. Larger rooms coupled to the above, if my guess is right, would place him in an area for industrial work, or something such as a warehouse. But let's take this in steps. He was a man. Which means he needs to eat and fetch water. Which means he buys produce and goes to the well. Or sends his brute to do it. Someone would have to have seen one or both during those moments of purchases, dining, or dunking the bucket in the town square. But if we don't want to draw suspicion by our search, we don't have the luxury of asking around more than I have already. So that route is unworkable. But what else does a man need to survive, and must be compelled to use, and will give him out?"

Vokent shook his head and shrugged. "Besides privies? Sexual desire, you mean?"

Attila made note of the lieutenant's answer without reacting. Then he answered the question himself. "It is winter. A man—all men—need heat. And considering his furtive nature and that of his brute friend, they might not collect what's needed by themselves, but steal it from whatever buildings are nearby, which would leave us without resource to follow. Or, if we are favored … he has a service to deliver wood or coal to his home. And that service would be paid in advance, and might not be aware he is dead."

Vokent nodded appreciatively.

"When I first arrived in Korr," said Attila, "I made a tour of it, and since then have made regular strolls through all parts. I am keenly certain where the best spots for our subject to hide. And now that you have followed me on my route, and I have gathered more insight, I can say with almost certainty that the rooms we are looking for lay right down that alley."

Attila pointed with his left hand, which had a little shake to it. He dropped his hand and nodded to the alley's end.

"The fog is thick, the light not at its best, but if you look deep inside, you'll notice the stack of logs outside that low doorway. And further, you will notice how many layers of snow there are to the stack, and how much more snow is on each descending layer; the top ones, with just a dusting, might have been delivered yesterday. But here we are in the middle of winter. Who would not be using their hearth? And more, observe how the windows are not boarded over for the night, yet the morning bell hasn't rung. There isn't a man so poor in this village who can't comply with the night laws. So: he hasn't come home to put them up, and died before he knew he wasn't coming back. This must be it."

"That's a bit of genius," said Vokent, his eyes flashing with admiration. "You really know your stuff."

"It is simple, my dear Lieutenant. One must always look for the signs, the proper signs—determine them without prejudice, and withold placing unwanted weight upon one or the other—and then follow them. You know you are headed in the right direction when those signs align. I could still be wrong. But there is only one way to know."

Both men shook at the sound of the morning bell.

Attila blew out a breath. "The city is waking up. We don't have much time. Men will be coming to these warehouses before long. We should be gone by then. Come."

5

## Morning:
## The Smiling Ally

When Amalina and Genadie rode into Netz through its northern gate they'd already settled on a strategy. Their initial thought to circle the major streets, smiling at the people as if on parade to get a reading of the general atmosphere, was tossed when they decided it would be risky and reckless to enter too deep, or remain within the city long enough so a trap could be erected, or they might be forced down a cul-de-sac where their arrival would be cut violently short. Instead, cleverly, Genadie would find the first convenient place to stop, turn the sleigh to face outward, and then tie the horses there, not bothering to loose them from their harnesses; they would not be staying long. Then, as Amalina and Genadie moved inward on foot, both would keep sleigh and horses in sight as best they could, in case the Netzians had some surprises of their own—which might begin with an attack on their transport. She would work her way up the main thoroughfare while he took the large street angling one block over, so they would be within shouting distance. And they would move quickly but cautiously block by block into Netz, noting the looks on faces and alert for danger. Any bad sign—a piece of brick or a looped rope in hand—and one would send up the alarm and they'd dash for the sleigh.

It is with this agreeable plan they proceeded on their suicide mission.

• • •

With a face like a misshapen gourd, mouth cutting across its lower third at an uneven, downward slant, he never looked happy. Neither of the two—he or his comrade—ever did seem happy. But it was the first one, the one with the gloomy gourd, who talked first to the man sitting at the table: "Master."

"What is it?"

"The lookout reports a sleigh has arrived."

"Oh? Do tell. Is something wrong?"

"Came in from the northern route."

"The northern route!"

"Yes!" grumbled the gourd, his brow heavy. "Two've 'em, sir. The dog and a girl."

"A girl?"

"Young lady."

"Could it be … ? Did we know about this little morning excursion?"

"No, master. You want us to go get them, eh?"

"Make no moves. Either of you. We'll just wait and see. See where they are headed before taking any action. See if they separate. Wouldn't that be better?"

"They have separated."

"Have they? Well that's promising. Promising, all right. Still, we hold. Yes. We should be patient. Always patient, haven't I told you? But get things prepared for a quick move."

"While you wait, shall I prepare your tea?" asked the second one, who swept a mop of black hair out of his unhappy eyes.

"Oh! Tea! Yes!" exclaimed their master with a smile. "How thoughtful of you! Hm, hee!"

• • •

So early on a winter morning, Netz presented a clean, scenic tableau where anything could happen to two wanderers. The buildings, mostly still boarded over, were decorated with deep tufts of snow on the roofs, on shutters, on awnings, with sunlit ice stuck into the crevices and thickly lining spouts and gutters, lending them a gem-like quality. Chimneys puffed smoke, speaking of peaceful inside activities, and the undisturbed air in the streets and alleys was quiet enough to suggest a sedate, half-sleeping city—or portended murderous mobs holding their breaths just around any corner, listening to feet crunching down on the ice and snow, the sound of which echoed loudly through the frost-bitten silence, and waved off the brick buildings, giving even the mice away. Audible, too, past Amalina and Genadie's gulping, heavy breaths, was their shivering anticipation.

Very soon into her dreadful journey, Amalina realized she must be making an odd sight. As she walked nervously, stiffly, bent in a defensive posture, almost hunched, and keeping close to the buildings and walls, she attracted the attention of a Netzian who stared at her as if worried she didn't know how to tread slushy, ice-covered cobbles and needed his help. Amalina straightened her posture and gave him a reassuring smile as he approached; to warn him off. The man did not return the smile. But neither did he frown, as the people had, years ago, when they were geared to lynch a couple outsiders. He then nodded politely to her and turned back to his business, skating along a cross street.

Amalina hesitated to enter a store just yet. The last time Netz was angry and against them, she'd almost been trapped inside a small restaurant, caught between two large, brutal men. And who knows what would have happened if her capture hadn't been interrupted by the sorry sight of Ygardina's ravaged body hauled past the windows? Better to further test the people's friendliness before braving a doorway and giving a store a try. On the thought of entering a shop, she felt dumb for not having come up with a good shopping list. The Ladies back at the castle would chide her when she returned empty-handed for forgetting or ignoring what they'd been asking her and the Count for for weeks now. Chide her, that is: *if she returned!* Amalina tried to remember some of the goods they needed. But those memories were unhelpful, they clouded her probing for danger.

Perhaps expecting the trouble would begin immediately, Amalina and Genadie hadn't planned how far into Netz they'd dare. She waited at a crossing until she saw Genadie enter the intersection one block east, he bent over more than usual and awkwardly, with the heavy bag of gold coins on his shoulder. They nodded to each other as vaguely as she'd done with the Netzian. Should they go on? Genadie moved on. So they would keep going. Short of a welcoming committee appearing with drums and pipes ablaze, there was no telling what would be a satisfactory stopping point, where their safety, general acceptance and approval by Netz was understood and they could go home. And, unfortunately, since it was early on a cold winter day, the streets were near empty. Nothing like before, when it had been a pleasant spring afternoon, and it was only the mild weather of the populace that had darkened and turned on them.

With few people about presently, most huddled together, rushing from one place to another, their thoughts bent to a warm room at the end and not out hunting for strangers, Amalina was ignored.

Until a man stepped from a doorway. He moved as if to stop her. As if he'd been just inside the building watching her through the front windows and thought to come out.

"Hello, there," said the man. He was large and round, with sloping shoulders that would have looked broad if it wasn't for his much wider belly below. His head was round, too, and fringed with a light brown hair that ringed from top to chin. But the beard, sparse as it was, did not obscure his face, and gave only a suggestion of color. His eyes, squinted narrow by heavy lids, tilted upward and outward; they looked like sparkling, happy eyes. And his mouth was open with a generous, toothy grin. It was a boyish head, whatever his age, and it was a very happy one at that. He wasn't fat, but was rather like an enormous, delighted child. His smile seemed to glow from his red cheeks and it felt infectious. Amalina tried hard not to return the smile but look wary and warning. He said, smiling of course, undeterred, "I think I recognize you."

Amalina spotted some Netzian faces in the large window behind him. They stared at her non-committally, as if bored and just looking for something interesting to gawp at. One brushed his moppy hair off his brow, but did not change expression. She couldn't tell if they were with this man. She returned her eyes to him, but said nothing.

"You're the Countess Katarina Tepsji?" asked the man, his gorgeous smile positively beaming.

"Uh, yes," said Amalina, with a short nod. She had stopped because he'd stepped in her way. She wondered if it would be rude to push on around him. Now she allowed a polite smile. She felt for Genadie's knife within the hand warmer—pushed aside her glasses and the magic item, the bone, which would be useless here—and seized its handle.

"Yes, you're the Countess Tepsji," he said, "so young and beautiful. You will come inside and have something to eat with me?"

Amalina suddenly wondered if this man was a restauranteur out to snare some local royalty to burnish his credentials. But he wasn't dressed like a Netzian. And he didn't look like he'd just been working in the kitchen. He had the air, and wore the clothes, of a traveling merchant. A happy one, of course.

"I'm not very hungry at the moment," said Amalina, taking a step to make it clear she would prefer to move on.

"But you *have* to eat with me," insisted the man, his cheerful face not losing any of its warmth. "My name is Janusch. You *must* come."

"But if I'm not hungry, sir—"

"They have the most excellent food inside. And tea, very strong, good for a cold day. And *Janusch* would like to speak with you."

"Speak with … ? Do we know each other?" Again she tried another quick step forward. He stayed in place, would only have welcomed her to step into his outstretched arms. As it was, he was using those arms to guide her toward the open door. She gripped the handle of the knife tighter, wondering if she would really need to use it. Or if she could bring herself to use it.

"We don't know each other, Lady Tepsji. But you will speak to me, Janusch, anyway. And why not?" He bent forward confidentially, but didn't lower his voice. "You are Amalina Dalca, are you not? Yes, yes you are. The crazy revolutionary's spy, who lives up in the castle." He clapped his hands and pointed into the building. "You will tell me, now, about him, that crazy revolutionary. Tell me everything. Come, come. This way. Right here. Let's eat. I know you're hungry. But come, let's talk."

. . .

"My name is Janusch," the joyful man introduced himself again after they sat at a corner table far from the windows; where Amalina hoped she could still be seen from the street should Genadie come looking. Amalina hadn't removed her coat, but it didn't seem as if the man, who was happily adjusting himself, his chair, and the table to fit his size, would care if she ever took it off. With his great, warm grin, and his direct, undiverted eye-contact, he accepted her in full, as-is. As if she were a sudden treat to be eaten immediately or would be lost. "Janusch Timorak, hee hee. But my good friends call me 'Janushti'."

As soon as they'd entered the restaurant, the two Netzians who'd been staring through the window had wandered off to a back room. Amalina looked around and it seemed she and Janusch were alone, but no telling if they were nearby and listening.

"Hello, Janusch," said Amalina, timidly but politely.

"Please," he smiled brightly as he scolded her, almost reaching out to tweak her forearm, "*Janushti*. No Janusch, we are friends, you and I."

"So we *do* know each other, sir?"

"Not precisely, but we're both friends of that crazy revolutionary. Well, not friends, precisely, either, but we both worked for him. We should know each other. Eh?"

"You *worked* for him?"

"How do you think he got all his supplies? Janushti! Who else!" This he declared loudly and proudly, then he sighed: "So, I know it's been so long, Amalina, but tell me about our crazy revolutionary, what happened to him? Is he still alive, even now? Please tell me he is …"

Amalina didn't know what to say to the smiling man, who watched her with such eager openness it was like a dear friend reunited after years gone by. Janushti? A supplier to the revolutionary? *Or,* thought Amalina quickly as her mind turned … *is this AXP, come for me at last?* Or perhaps this was one of his many asssassins at work … just trying to get as much information out of her before he goes in for the kill? Or maybe a Count's minion, here to interrogate her, to test her loyalty? He didn't seem dangerous, though. Not yet anyway, besides the secrets he was willing to shout for anyone to hear. But was he telling the truth here? She didn't feel like answering directly until the situation was made clearer. "You said something about tea?"

"Ye-es, the be-est," sang Janushti. He called to the side, "Hey, there! He-ey! Tea please! Tea here!"

One of the men who'd disappeared through a door reappeared with a pretty, painted ceramic pot—dozens of pretty iris plants, with blue petals and swirling, entangled green vines, covered its body with an eastern overelaborateness. He set the pot at Janushti's elbow when done filling the cups on the table, then disappeared again. Janusch wagged his eyebrows and leaned over to snatch his own cup. It was like a bear taking up a thimble. A jovial, thirsty bear. He winked, and his head waggled from side to side like it was dancing atop his shoulders, then he drank down the whole cup with a long pleased sound. He let out a satisfied sigh at the end of it and looked at her expectantly, as if she were missing out.

"The best!" he said, encouraging.

Amalina picked up the cup, blew on the steam, then took a couple sips while he nodded, beaming at her. The tea tasted of an extremely fragrant jasmine.

"The best, no?" said Janusch, his eyes gleaming.

Amalina nodded politely. His eyebrows went up, begging her to go on. She said: "It's very good, yes."

Janusch clapped his hands, the satisfied bear, then relaxed into his chair. He almost knocked over the teapot in the process. His eyes went to it and he pushed it to the side. Then his eyes went to it again, and his smile faltered a little. His cheeks burned redder. But then his eyes were on Amalina and nothing else.

"Oh, it's so good to see you, Amalina Dalca."

"You know my real name," said Amalina.

"Of course, I know," said Janusch, waving a dismissive hand. "I know everyone."

Now where had Amalina heard *that* before? The Count was always saying something like it. *I know everyone.* But this Janusch … was a bit different. So merry, so confident, somehow. It didn't sound like an idle brag or threat.

"So do tell me what I'd like to know, Amalina: our revolutionary. I don't want my delicate ears injured with bad news, though I can only expect … But … if, perhaps, he *is* still alive? maybe being held up at the castle?" Janushti wagged his eyebrows at her as he had before. *Good news, please.*

Amalina felt a warm pulse within her. Maybe it was the heat in the room, or the excellent tea working its way into her system, but it was like what she felt on occasion with the Count, he staring at her, and the world—and she— melting slightly, relaxing, becoming almost malleable.

Though she had been drugged before, she had watched Janusch drink enthusiastically from the same pot, and the circumstances were so strange, and the effects were so much subtler, she didn't suspect it now.

. . .

"Held up at the castle?" said Amalina, still feeling cautious and forcing herself to keep her words vague, resisting the comfort. "I don't know of anyone being *held* at the castle." She thought quickly: *Forget the lady on the wheel in the cellar, forget the lady on the wheel!* "No revolutionary ... "

"No? But you know who I'm talking about, of course you do. When was the last time you saw him, eh? Our revolutionary?"

She shook her head as if she just didn't understand.

"Years gone, but still playing the cagey little spy for him, eh? This bodes well. My sister, Amalina, I'm talking about our dear commander, Commander Kralov!"

"Kralov!" she cried in surprise.

"Yes, the Commander, so crazy!"

"But that *was* years ago," said Amalina, almost tripping over her words, as a strange feeling of relief took hold. She sat up. "I thought you were talking about—"

Amalina caught herself. What was she saying? What was she *going* to say just now? *Why* would she volunteer any information not needed to be known? Wasn't that Sadra's revolutionary's greatest rule: secrecy? Amalina didn't even know his true name, he was that tight-lipped. He'd have been appalled at her lack of discipline.

"Kralov, Kralov," said Janusch, winking at her as if she were being silly. "Of course. Our friend, our commander. Now: is he still alive? All I know is that I got him the equipment he needed—because that is what I do, I help!— then I had to leave. But he was such a good man, and really believed in what he was doing. What happened to him, Amalina? Tell Janushti!"

"Well, uh ..." The way Janusch was looking at her, Amalina felt it was harmless; so very long ago. Amalina nodded slowly, then told him of Kralov's ill-fated storming of the castle, of how close they had gotten to killing the Count—*"And did my supplies help?" asked Janusch, proudly*—and the fatal error of Kralov's captain, the handsome and brave Piotr, whose need for vengeance overshadowed the Commander's careful planning and led to everyone's death, including Commander Kralov. With some effort, Amalina left her own part in it, and her guilt in his death, out of the recounting.

Janusch sighed, and for the first time his face fell and looked tremendously sad, as if the Commander had been a close friend. "Ah, that *is* too bad. I tried to help, but ... it's as I feared. And it's as I warned him, the poor crazy man. But he believed in what he was doing."

He crossed himself while Amalina took a few more sips of tea.

He smiled at her, then nodded with his chin thrust forward, looking sly, "And so, Amalina Dalca, why *are* you still there? Eh? You seemed to think I was talking about someone else than our crazy Commander. Is there *another* revolutionary? I can't imagine it, but is there?"

Amalina didn't know what to say, but her head nodded, shyly, before she could stop herself. She looked to see his reaction.

"Oh, a new one," said Janusch, his lips pursed. "And you're the spy again, eh? And still up at the castle; how some things never change. It's a strange life here in this world, it must be. And I wonder if I've heard of him, this new revolutionary. Can you tell me who it is, Amalina Dalca?"

She shook her head. But she did so without necessarily wanting to. It was as if body and mind were so relaxed next to this sympathetic, boyish man, it was a relief to just let go. To decompress a tight spring hidden inside her. She didn't think much about it after that, it was an irresistable urge, but tried to guide herself safely through this generous feeling.

"I've never known his name. But he's building an army, just like the Commander did, only this time he has some new ideas. I don't want to say where he is, but—"

Janusch steadied her with a gentle wave of his hand. "That's all right, Amalina. I was just curious. Janushti always likes to help where he can. But I never want to know too much if it might hurt someone. I, above anyone else, know these things. Now tell me ... is he as crazy as old Commander Kralov?"

Amalina shook her head. "The opposite. Younger, smaller, quieter. Always thinking. And I think he might be one of the Germans, from Germania—"

"Oh my—"

"—and he worked for the government—"

"Oh my! Oh my Hea-av-vens!" Janushti took his hand away from his mouth and shook his head, smiling, but looking somewhat dismayed. "You mean that old low constable from Tsobl? Attila Bronk?"

"I-I don't know," said Amalina, amazed to suddenly have this information. "Is it?"

"Looks like he might fall asleep on his feet? with these large, hooded eyes, eh? That one?" he didn't wait for Amalina to answer, he was already certain. "I'd wondered where he'd gotten off to! Oh, but don't tell me, I don't want to know!"

"You know him?"

"He's made an impression in certain circles—*many* circles. Too many."

"Well, that's who it is: the revolutionary, sir—"

"Janushti!" he chided. "Never 'sir'. I am your Janushti!"

"Yes, well, if you help people, and you helped the Commander with his supplies, do you think you might ...?"

Janusch slapped the table and laughed, but he still had that disconsolate look in his glittering, happy eyes. "I wouldn't touch that one with a hundred foot pole, Amalina. Never. I always work at a distance, three layers deep.

Listen: one does not go out in winter without three layers on. That's why winter is the safest time for me to work. Hm-hee. Well, that Bronk, he doesn't know what he's doing. He's as dangerous as they come. Right up front and pushing. Self-righteous, egotistical, nobody else is as correct, morally or otherwise, as he, so all must suffer. I'm surprised *he's* still alive, after the Commander. Anyone playing around with him will be dead soon enough. I've even heard the King has sent a force to root him out—"

"What?"

## 6

## The King's Army

Janusch Timorak was right, and that very subject was being discussed at almost the exact same moment less than three hundred yards from the restaurant.

Inside the St. Grigori cathedral, the Governor of Ardeel had dropped in, unannounced, to visit the Cardinal. They held their secret audience in a private chamber, where the Governor darted his eyes into every corner, while the Cardinal stared from his tall chair with the air of a large but thin spider observing a bug that had wandered into its web. This keen watchfulness did not relieve the Governor's nerves, who knew Governor Schluckgeld, his predecessor, had died not long after making a similar secret trip to the St. Grigori cathedral and meeting with this famous—this dangerous—Cardinal of Netz.

. . .

"Have something to eat, Governor? Or drink?" The Cardinal pointed to a sideboard where bread and a round of cheese sat, along with goblets, a couple of corroded-looking bottles of wine, and a wispy servant in priest robes waiting to serve. "No? You look hungry."

"No, thank you; the ride didn't agree with me," lied the Governor—he'd enjoyed the ride quite a bit, and in various ways. He adjusted his large body uncomfortably in the small chair provided. "Back to your old ways, Cardinal?"

"Old ways?" asked the Cardinal with a thin, arched eyebrow, and stroked his immaculately trimmed beard guiltily, no doubt suspecting he was hinting at ill-fated visits.

"The last time we met, you came to me in Sobelburg," explained the Governor, still adjusting himself.

"Tsobl," corrected the Cardinal.

"*Sobelburg*," smirked the Governor, "the council has voted it in. It's official now. But the point is, you actually left your church to come."

"Well, it was a desperate circumstance," admitted the Cardinal. "A one-time occurrence not likely to be repeated."

"Desperate? Done to save your friend. Your friend, the former low constable Bronk."

"'Friend' is greatly overstating our relationship."

"It brought you out of St. Grigori, and to the Capitol. Unheard of."

The Cardinal nodded, his eyes unyielding. "It wasn't the relationship at work, you see, but *the Cause*."

"Which returns us to the matter," said the Governor, clearing his throat. "Do you wish to spare Attila Bronk? or, anyway, this *'Cause'* you two are involved in?"

"You ask me because of the military force that has just arrived in Ardeel— some extra-territorial apportionment of the king's own army, I understand," surmised the Cardinal. When the Governor nodded: "And are you saying you can *divert* the King's Army?"

"It's the Crown 1ˢᵗ Dragoons, a whole regiment," said the Governor, elaborating with a provocative lilt, "the king's personal reserve guard."

The Cardinal made a face as if such a thing were meaningless. "Yes, as I said, a vaguely legal, *extra-territorial* force. However, you can divert them?"

"But haven't I already? by convincing them to come straight to Sobelburg, which means avoiding Netz … and *you-know-who*?" the Governor pointed in the direction of the high castle, of course meaning the Count, and smirked again to emphasize. "The impetus of this 'reinforcement action' by the king was the discovery of the Germanian delegation's wreckage— slaughtered to a man, mutilated in the most grotesque possible way—just across the border; the delegation who'd been sent to visit *you-know-who*. And yet, even in their fury for retribution, at my word they've already bypassed Netz. I *can* divert."

"Hm. I'd thought the Army's aim here is to stabilize and suppress any unrest after Kyrgil's collapse and destruction."

"All of that, yes, and the other. But, as I said, *you-know-who*'s presumed disposal of the delegation was the impetus. And I was convincing enough for them to come to me instead. Directly to me. For instruction. I repeat, *for instruction*."

. . .

The Cardinal nodded, running his fingers over his sculpted beard. The Governor's face, so swollen by fat, was clean-shaven, or would not grow hair, and was entirely round, almost featureless but for the required ornaments stuck into it; the eyes, nose, and mouth. It was an uncomfortable thing for the Cardinal to look at without sensing his own body beginning to bulge and swell, or to not think condescendingly about the Governor's abject corpulence. There were ripples in his chins! But the Governor appeared oblivious and, at the moment, seemed to be experiencing a moment of power, and enjoyment of it; despite the inadequate chair he'd been given.

"So I'm being handed a weapon," said the Governor. "What should be done with it? Because something must be done. The Army won't just sit still."

"No?"

"The King's son's at its head, or so I'm told. Unless we're lucky, that he's a drunk or a ne'er-do-well, he'll not sit idly but seek to punish. Someone. I have to give him something to entertain him before he starts casting his bored or ambitious eyes around and finds me interesting enough to play with. My first thought was Bronk."

The Cardinal made a face.

"Well, he would be the easiest," explained the Governor.

"And your first choice," said the Cardinal. "Because you don't like him."

"Why shouldn't he be *your* first choice?" asked the Governor, rubbing his upper chin. "But I see it: your *Cause*; again. And this *Cause* is necessary?"

The 'Cause' they were referring to was the common people's effort to destroy the Knight of Ardeel: The revolution!

"I thought we'd finally convinced you the merits of it, Governor."

"I see it from both sides. Killing *that one*—" meaning the Count "—might only be the end of one problem, but the beginning of a real one for the Sobelburg council."

"And for you," expounded the Cardinal.

"Maybe even you," said the Governor with a grin that moved his large cheeks. "All authority will come into question, even yours, once *the-greatest-authority-of-all* to these people falls."

"I am one of 'these people'," cautioned the Cardinal.

"Heaven forbid," chortled the Governor, to which the Cardinal couldn't help but also smile. They both knew he wasn't *that*; one of the common people. "Our interests are aligned, until they're not. Now, how do we handle this?"

*How do we handle this, indeed*, agreed the Cardinal. Could he admit to the Governor just how much had changed in Ardeel? After what the Count had revealed of his 'Ladies', and the evidence that proved itself out with the orphanage and the children: the creature was producing more of his own kind. Was it prudent to keep Bronk on his path, to exterminate this growing threat? But …the monster could give others his power! And wouldn't that be something to get hold of? How would one persuade the creature to share? Doing favors could be a start. Perhaps crushing a rebellion—or revealing it to him—would be just the thing to buy a piece of super-mortality. *Yet, still,* went the Cardinal's thoughts, *would I really want to become such an unnatural thing, no matter how powerful?*

. . .

After a time, the decision was made to spare Attila. Left unsaid, but the Cardinal knew, the King's Army could always be used to tame the revolutionary if need be, if Bronk were to get out of line.

And for the Governor, who'd grown cozy with his station and its attendant power; and with the world quieting and feeling the humane warmth of his wise governorship (after the Kyrgil tragedy had the Ardeelian people appealing to *him* for help and answers—being genuinely comforted *by him*—something he'd never experienced in his life: it was addictive) he knew he could always use the King's Army as a mighty hammer against the Cardinal, and against *the Cause* (which threatened to upend all his institutional and personal progress) and especially use it against Bronk.

But the Governor needed the Cardinal on his side for now, to pretend at stability and to get some answers.

"What would you say would be the best way to control the King's pup?" asked the Governor, presently.

The Cardinal looked surprised: "They're reformists, unrepentant Protestants—as are you—and so how could I hope to have any influence?"

"Not asking for your influence, Cardinal. You take confession in your church, though. You know private matters and thoughts. You understand the humanity that lays behind raw power. How could I best work our prince the way I want, and send him in the right direction, even if it's only sending him back home to papa? Your opinion. That's all."

"If he's anything like his father, it will be pride," declared the Cardinal, confidently. "Pride is a miracle worker with the mighty. You could have him risk his life, have him crush an infant under his horse's hoof, if you make him believe his power is at stake; that any upstart might challenge his god-given birthright and will capture his natural, divine superiority before the masses."

They both laughed cynically, but they knew he could have been speaking for either of them, as well.

"Glad to see you were able to calm the storm over that orphan-workhouse, by the way," said the Governor, making to leave. "All went well?"

"Without you mentioning that terrible tragedy just now, I doubt I will ever hear of it again." The Cardinal smiled complacently.

"Very good."

"You sure you don't want anything to eat, Governor? I can't tempt you?"

· · ·

The Governor headed for his carriage knowing inside was a quarter of lamb, which he could reheat using a specially vented coal device within the central compartment. He looked forward to this: a hot, tasty reward for having resisted the bait and survived his sit down with the Cardinal. He'd successfully avoided Schluckgeld's fate.

The Governor also looked forward to the return trip to Sobelburg *(once Tsobl)* now made quicker by a new pass miraculously opened up after the collapse of Kyrgil mountain *(soon to be a forgotten formation of rock … and city)* shaving off days of travel between Sobelburg and Netz *(Nettenburg, eventually, in time)*. So much faster a route was this new passage, he would announce, after returning from his expeditionary trip through the ruins—which had been his excuse to travel in the first place—he would begin construction on a highway between the two cities; a modern road that might surpass the methods of the Romans and would last for centuries, and would even carry the stamp of his name. The applause of future generations tickled his eardrums.

"It was good of you to show me this," the Governor had thanked the odd businessman who had alerted him to the potential of the Kyrgil collapse, what could be exploited from it.

Though the destruction of the mountain and its valley was enormous, with the rock pulverized to near gravel, trees flattened and scorched to haunted coal sticks, and the cross-breezes in the new, titanic gulley, hinting at fires still burning, the businessman had already explored and patted down a single-lane path that was serviceable by cart and carriage, even in winter. It flouted the surrounding devastation's demand to be in awe, and offered the mountain's collapse up as merely a constructive happenstance.

Not that one could ignore the terror contained in the event without feeling disrespectful to the Kyrgil people or the reason for it. One unsettling rumor was this calamity had been the work of the creature!—or two of them!—but that seemed as inconceivable as the rumors of dragons. So the Governor shoved the thought of the creature's incredible power deep away; this was god-like wrathful stuff, on an entirely inhuman scale; which ordinarily shrieked of other-worldy horror and a need to escape it, avoid it … unless you were someone charged with unblinking foresight, daring, and a uniquely entrepreneurial spirit.

The Governor had said as much to the helpful merchant: "You impress me with your vision of a most pleasing future. And you say you have the workforce to complete the highway?"

"The materials will be the trickier part," admitted the businessman, looking not put off by the prospect. "There are always men to work. They love to work, and this will give them something to do. They've been begging for it for years, something meaningful to do. And you giving it to them, they will be thankful and everyone will be happy, happy, happy!"

"The materials?" the Governor had then inquired with an economy of words.

"Trickier, as I said, but I will have it all, never you worry, Governor," the man smiled brightly. "Just think of how you will be remembered down the years when it's done. Have some more tea."

"Oh, yes, quite tasty. Jasmine, is it? Don't mind if I do, Mr. Grandiere, was it? How have I never heard of you, and we've never met?"

"But you were speaking of the King's Army? And meeting with the Cardinal? Do tell," the businessman had smiled, or continued to smile. He hadn't ever seemed to stop smiling.

"Oh … yes … that …" muttered the Governor, cautiously. "The King's Army."

"Do tell, do tell, do tell, hee hee, hm-hee."

The tea was delicious, and the businessman so accommodating … and the Governor really had come to love being the governor of Ardeel. What he could do with the position and power and how he could affect the lives of so many. And knowing Ardeel had once been a country of its own, he felt and fancied—dare he? *he did*—that with his new title, the territory he now governed, and the people he controlled, he was as powerful as any king! What could stop him from wresting control of this land and make it his own? Take power and become a king in his own right!

And so, in a manner of thinking, this Germanian army *was* a force of interlopers, led by *another* King's son, a foreigner; who would now be his hostage and a violent playtoy of his own. He couldn't wait to begin playing with it.

*Attila Bronk*, smirked the Governor presently, in a dark turn of thought, whatever the Cardinal wished for him, whatever Bronk's use to the Ardeelian people (who were now, in all law, *the Governor's* people) *that upstart low constable, he might not have that much longer to live.*

• • •

A sentiment which dovetailed finely with the matter that was discussed a short while ago, not more than three hundred yards away, in a restaurant, between Janusch Timorak and Amalina:

"…No," Janusthi had wrapped up his short diatribe against the revolutionary or anyone who might be thinking to join him, "I'd wish them all luck, I really would. But the deck is stacked against him. At this point, all

Bronk needs to do is poke his head up high enough, then his head—and everyone else's—will come off."

"Really?" said Amalina, feeling a sick rumbling in her stomach.

7

# The Lair

Attila Bronk and Lt. Vokent strode with purpose to the low doorway in the rear wall of some kind of immense warehouse. Five worn stone stairs led down to it. They paused outside the chipped, black-painted door.

"You're sure this is it?" asked Vokent turning an ear toward the door. "How do we know he doesn't have a wife, or that someone else isn't inside?"

"We don't," answered Attila, before he knocked loudly. "Hello? Hello!"

Half a minute passed before he tried again. After a full minute he nodded and pulled from his cloak a small leather roll of metal picks; another gift from studying and learning from the criminals he had jailed. In seconds, shoving picks through the wide mouth of the door's simple lock, it clacked loudly, announcing it was open.

"Let's be prepared," said Attila. He pointed at Vokent's sword. The lieutenant nodded and drew it out of its scabbard in a smooth pull. He held the pointed tip at the edge of the door.

Attila swung open the door and planted himself with his feet wide apart, as if to defy the darkness that met them.

"Cold as stone," said Attila. "Nobody's been here for days."

"I can't see anything," said Vokent.

Attila was already digging out the tinderbox from his cloak. "Haven't much time," he muttered, looking unconcerned with a half-lidded stare. "Best get to it. If we take too long, I'm afraid we'll be trapped here until night."

Attila got a light and stuck a small makeshift torch into the air.

Lieutenant Vokent nodded at the hallway, asking, *me first?* Attila stared down the hall and squinted. He shook his head. He said in a low voice, "Nobody's home. We should be okay." Attila entered. "But stay close, just in case."

Attila didn't know what he'd find here but threw any preconceptions out as they came. He was looking with an open mind. But it didn't take long to spot a doorless wardrobe with squat black leather cloaks on pegs at the back, and a few wide-brimmed hats that matched the ones Attila could still see in his mind, floating in front of his face as the green-skinned man wearing it laughed, and the brute slashed Attila's neck. Attila swallowed heavily.

"This it?" asked the lieutenant, his sword still hoisted with caution. His head was turning on his muscled neck, eyes dancing to the corners. From the lieutenant's practiced movement, Attila decided Vokent must have seen combat inside buildings, not just on the battlefield.

Attila didn't answer the question, instead he searched the wardrobe, and then switched to a desk along the wall. His eyes alert for documents, weapons, anything that could be used as a sign.

Vokent made a noise of appreciation from the back of his throat. When Attila looked up, he saw the sword jab at a line of small framed pictures along the wall. They were hand-drawn portraits of pretty young girls, or, leaving Attila with a disturbed jangle to his nerves, squared off studies of well-formed hands or legs, giving the impression that the limbs were all there was to see, as if detached from the principal subject entirely. Other frames contained parts of bodies which at first Attila could not identify, and then with a creeping acid sickness, understood they were even more minute studies of something quite obscene. He returned to the desk and his search for the incriminating documents he was sure must be there. A letter. A handwritten note. A small strip of paper that could attach to a pigeon leg.

A quarter hour passed in the heat of the search, Attila mindful of their limited time, and knowing they were quickly coming to the end of it, if not already out.

In a ceramic cup on the desk he found a handful of small silverish marbles—*silver? Curious, must determine.* Without the lieutenant noticing, Attila dumped them into his side pocket. He set the cup quickly back into place with a few left in it, in case any unknown associates might return and notice the marbles missing. This way, they might think the green man had simply taken a few with him before whatever happened to him had happened. But maybe *that* was overthinking it, Attila considered. His hands froze for a moment on the desk in a fit of indecision.

"Sir," said Vokent. Now he pointed his sword at a curious section of wall around the corner from the desk.

There was a small enclosure. Almost like a jail cell, it was made of strips of thin, rough metal, which ran crosswise from wall to cornerbend to wall, or descended from ceiling to floor, the bars embedding in cones of cement-like material at either end, securing them to the room's superstructure. It looked roughly built by an untrained hand, but solid anyway. A short rectangular stool sat inside this seemingly improvised cage, with a suggestive pair of open and discarded iron cuffs beside it. A strong box was also inside, shoved up against the wall. And there was a door to the cell, shut and locked.

"Will your keys work on this?" asked Vokent.

"Hold," said Attila. He pointed at the wall outside the cell and pushed the small torch toward it. Hanging off numerous nails, placed in a deranged sort of disorder, were rusty pieces of iron. Some resembled saws, some jointed whips, some lengthy needles. One semi-circular bit of iron had a handle just behind the curve, with two small corkscrewed skewers, set an inch or two apart from each other, extending outward.

"What is all this?" murmured the lieutenant needlessly, his uneasy tone revealing he already knew.

"Unfortunately it is very obvious. Instruments of his—or their—trade. For business or entertainment. By the stains running down on the wall beneath them, they haven't rusted, but it shows their use; dripped and dried blood. One can imagine, if one wishes to consider the twisted mind at work, the tools were placed here for convenience, so that his partner, whichever had grown exhausted by their exertions on the victim, or whoever hadn't won the toss of the coin to go first, could take down whichever implement was desired by the deviant still inside the cell, and hand it to them." Attila nodded, as if picturing it clearly. "And also this arrangement was well-placed outside the cell, for the poor subject to contemplate in rising fear, as they awaited their session. Imagine the chill driven into their heart, before the work began."

*Thank Heaven they didn't bring me here that night*, thought Attila. But then his eyebrow twitched at an errant suspicion: *Why didn't they?*

Attila gestured towards the crescent of iron with the skewers. "I suppose this was meant to punch with, leaving marks much like that of the creature. To cast blame his way when the body was found with incriminating tears and punctures, or perhaps to emulate his crimes, to try to capture the feeling of it. What fiends."

The lieutenant grimaced at the crusted black pieces on the wall. "Shadows of the torturer."

"But you are right, Lieutenant, we're not here for these. Eyes forward. What secrets might our dark agents be protecting within this cage while they are away?"

Still holding the torch, Attila tried to locate his roll of metal picks with his free hand. He gave the torch to Lieutenant Vokent then went to work on the lock. It was simple enough design, and after some fiddling and a gentle click the door swung out with a tug. Attila put away his picks and took back the torch, allowing Vokent to go in.

"Looks like old blood all right," said Vokent from inside the small cell, his lips tight, scraping the tip of his sword on the streaked, red-stained floor. "Murderers and then some, eh?"

"Let's not get distracted by the meaningless," reprimanded Attila, though his tone was level and his eyelids at half mast. "Check the box."

"No lock," agreed Vokent. He used the sword to pry up the lid. Inside were stacks of letters and pieces of paper; folded, some rough-edged.

Attila leaned forward and made his decision. "Good enough. We leave now. Let's grab everything. If it doesn't have what we need, we can always come back and search again. This is most definitely the place."

"You've a bag or some extra pockets on you?" asked the lieutenant, riffling his fingers on the papers inside but not grabbing yet."

"Just take the box."

"The whole thing?"

"It's got handles, easier than wasting time trying to pocket it all."

"But this was meant to be locked away," he said, pointing to the box. "If we take it, then they'll know we have his—"

"*Who* will know?" said Attila, bemused in his deadpan way. "He's in no position to miss it."

"Right, you're thinking," said the lieutenant, pointing to his head with a wink. "I'll shut up now."

"Let's hurry."

The way Vokent put up his sword in its scabbard, it was so smooth and practiced that it was like he'd swung and placed the blade on his hip. Then he shoved open the sides of his cloak, hiked up his pants and knelt for the box. With just as easy and graceful a swooping motion, without even testing its weight, the lieutenant grabbed hold of the brass handles and lifted.

As the strongbox came off the floor, a series of pointed metal rods shot out of the wall through holes that might have always been there or were hidden behind the plaster.

"No!" cried Attila. He threw himself into the cell, but it was too late.

Lieutenant Vokent, with the speed of a true soldier, and reflexes that seemed to border on the clairvoyant, spun to avoid the rods. But one suddenly stuck out the side of his heavy brown cloak along where his ribs would be. He shouted. One of the rods also slammed into the strongbox. Its papers spilled out as the box tumbled to the floor like a giant's gambling die.

Then, appearing in the center of the cell as if by magic, five small metal balls with hissing fuses rolled around, clanking into each other, seeking a place to stop.

"Bomb!" shouted the lieutenant, as he scrambled stiffly with the length of iron sticking through him.

"Bombs," corrected Attila, staring at them, then looked to Vokent, impaled but still writhing on the end of the spear, trying to understand the situation and solve it.

8

# Mid-Morning:
# Janushti Lessons

"**O**h, Amalina ... you don't want to follow that Attila Bronk fellow," said Janusch, regarding her fondly. "Let me tell you one of Janushti's little secrets, eh? Let me give you some lessons. Then maybe you'll take my example instead of his. You'll change your life by it and make yourself happy—happier than you've ever been! For he and I are nothing the same!"

"I'm happy," said Amalina, defensively.

"Happy, Amalina? How can you say that to your good friend, Janushti?"

"Happier than I've *ever* been, you said?" she asked to push past the attempted lie.

"Well, I look *soo-oo* happy, do I not?" At Amalina's slight nod, Janushti then declared with arms in the air: "Very happy, is our Janushti!

"And why?" he continued his lesson. "Well, it's simple: I'm the only one around here who's figured out this strange world we're in, and the game being played. Eh? You see? As soon as I learned about the Knight of Ardeel, and how oppressed the land is, it all became clear to happy little Janusch. Look at these moping faces, the bent backs, the miserable lives lived out under the crush, crush, crushing superstitions and the hate and defeat by the invaders. I mean, why? Why do they do this? Why does *anyone* want to allow one bit of unhappiness into their lives? Well, this Knight—your Count Tepsji—has made everyone's lives so unhappy. So I decided not to play *his* game. Let him hide where he likes, and pop out when he likes to give everyone a hard time. But he can only do it to you once! And how long would it take for him to get you, eh? Why spend your life worried about that one time; a little moment? Live instead! That's what I shall do, and Janushti will help *everyone* do! Instead of making everyone unhappy as he does, if the Knight should be the darkness, I will be the light." At this Janusch slapped the table again and beamed prouder than he had yet. He seemed to glow angelically. "And so I *am* the light. Where he cuts off, I make things happen. Where he recedes, I fill in. I see to the happiness of the people.

"But how do I do this?" he asked Amalina. Then he seemed to levitate himself above his chair, his arms and hands above the table setting. "I keep myself as light as can be, so I float above these mountains like a cloud. Many people may see me, but they don't notice me, and only a chosen few know my name. I am a secret, a happy secret. And I can only be that way if I keep myself to those who seek to better their lives—*and don't care about overturning others*! Rock the boat, and you might call the waves to you and then you drown. I never work with agitators; radicals like that Bronk."

"You gave Commander Kralov his weapons," countered Amalina.

"Those so many dozen mirrors and the wonderful crystal balls—and the cart and drayhorse which I threw in for good measure—were not weapons at all. The Astounding Kralov was a circus performer and so were his men. I supplied them only what could be wanted in their profession—and of the highest quality, Janushti does not skimp!—but I gave them nothing more, and where he got his explosives and weapons of war I haven't a clue, and don't want to know. Now what the commander and those big boys chose to do with what *I* gave them—"

"But you knew what he was going to do with them," said Amalina, the truth coming up like a bubble, or what felt almost like a real bubble pushing it up her throat.

"That crazy man," said Janushti, sadly. "I *did* know, though I warned him not to. And I have to admit, I knew what I was doing. He told me everything, right down to his spy up in the Knight's hideout in the castle. I thought it might work. I even told him where he might source the guns and ammunition, it's true. I lied there, even to myself. He wouldn't have had those guns and powder but for me pointing him in the right direction. I thought to myself: why not? If I give Commander Kralov what he wants, and he does with it what he will, and if he succeeds, we're all happy. But he did not succeed, and people are sad; as Janushti predicted. I will never make that mistake again."

Amalina nodded, only half-understanding, and sipped the teacup empty, feeling more thirsty than worried.

"But I can tell by looking in your eye: you and I are the same, Amalina. We want to make people happy. Don't you, Amalina?"

"I think so."

"Of course you do!" smiled Janusch, his eyes glimmering with pride at her as if she were his firstborn. "But this is why I would never work with that Attila Bronk—in fact, I will never say his name again—" at this, he spit (though without losing his smile) "—as he means to bring only sadness to everyone." At Amalina's look he tilted his head: "Well, maybe he doesn't mean to, really, but he *has* a hardened heart." He grinned knowingly and looked like he wanted to nudge her elbow, which was a miniature to his. "You know what I mean! In that way I am as opposite him as he is the same as the Knight. Bronk's *exactly* like the Knight of Ardeel: everyone must follow him and sacrifice and suffer in order to make the world the way he wants it. That is not my way, and that is why I loathe government and defy all laws, as they are not *human*, and why I shall never join him or anything like him. But for you …"

Janusch stirred in his chair and it creaked and sighed under his weight, but he was too invested in what he had to tell Amalina to care. For this next part he leaned forward quickly over the table, almost upsetting the tea service, his wide face the most extreme expression of joy: "But for you, Amalina Dalca, here is what I will do! Now that we are reacquainted, my sister, my comrade—Kralov's faithful and brave spy—as sad as the circumstances are, let me make them light. I will work for your happiness!"

"Oh," said Amalina, startled. "Oh, really …?"

She couldn't imagine what he meant, but she began to picture vague, blurry futures full of bright sunlight.

"Of course! Janushti will take you away from here! Right now! We will leave here, and you'll be rid of this sad life forever!"

"What!" now she was *beyond* startled. That strange energy boiling inside her hiccupped and fizzed. Sweat sheened her forehead, back, and trembling limbs.

Janusch grinned proudly, his great strawberry red cheeks glowed. "It will make me so happy. I'm willing to take the risk—any risk—to show you to a life that will be a paradise. I saw that you came here today with one of his servants … ?"

"Genadie."

"My people here will distract him while I sneak you away to your new life."

"You mean you won't take him?"

"This Genadie? No."

"But he's my friend."

"No Genadie."

"Why not?"

"I don't know him."

"But you don't really know me, do you?"

"I know what you've *done*. Him? what do I know? I've seen him and the way he moves; by the looks of it he's not to be trusted. Maybe you know him better than I, but what can I do about that? No. Too dangerous, Amalina. I know he's not like me, anyway … as you are."

"But, really, he's not so bad," she mumbled unsurely now, though feeling fond for the little rat-like man. "You could ask him questions; to satisfy yourself."

"Why would I do that?"

"But he's had such a hard life," and here came another bubble, much larger now, a wave of pressure within her that spilled her thoughts out in a torrent. But it felt right somehow as she released it: how the Count had wiped out Genadie's whole family. Then, afterward, Genadie'd been enslaved and tortured at the castle for years. Decades maybe.

"Sounds like a dark fairy tale."

"But it's true."

"He doesn't look so *un*happy."

"He's miserable, I'm telling you."

"This offer is for you, Amalina Dalca," smiled Janusch, patiently. "I'm your guardian angel alone. Now, here is how it will be, you'll be out of Netz by the hour; and out of the country in less than two days. Then this will all be behind you. You can only imagine how happy you'll be once you are outside these mountains, with the future yours, and you can breathe free." To provide an example for Amalina he took a big breath in through his nostrils that expanded his wide chest. Then he grinned, also as an example. His smile was a man tasting freedom for the first time. "You will thank Janushti for the rest of your life."

"Well," began Amalina, her expression fluttering between happiness and something else, but not wanting to disappoint this self-happy man, "that's very nice of you. Very kind. But I can't. Can't do it, that is. I mean, it's impossible."

His expression didn't change, but he did look at her curiously. "Why? You will be so happy, I can't tell you."

"No, I'm sure you're right, that's true. I've had a little taste of it before. But you see … Janushti—" his eyelids fluttered and he smiled broadly at his name "—I just *can't*."

"Why not?"

"Well …" she said, feeling her raucous unhappy 'tide' rising within, loosened by and lifting on this strange bubbling action inside her, her mind clearer than ever before and dumping its secrets into the surge; coming up in a rush. She *had* been thinking to escape just this morning on her way into Netz, hadn't she? She'd been pushing for it. But: " … but I suppose Genadie *was* right after all, really—"

"Genadie!" erupted Janusch. "Didn't I say! He has brought you into his confidence, to his side, by a spell of clever words he has gotten you to question yourself and what is good for you!"

"Genadie?" said Amalina, taken aback. "No, sir. But he was right: I only wanted to get away from here because I was afraid. And—"

"And why *shouldn't* you be?"

"Because I have responsibilities here."

"Have you?"

"Oh, yes! There's the revolutionary, Attila."

"Bronk'll be the death of you. Of everyone, I'm telling you."

"But it isn't that simple …"

"That's what everyone tells me—every sad person. But it *is* that simple."

"Only, we had a deal," said Amalina, riding the upward tide, "the revolutionar—that is, Mr. Bronk and I: Five birds I am supposed to send him; five birds' worth of information, then I can leave. But I've only sent one so far. That means there's still—"

"That's one too many!"

"And … well … there's not only he and I and the revolution. Then there are the Ladies up in the castle," she went on. "They came because of me, and so I couldn't just leave them."

"Why can't you?" he asked, as if mystified.

"They're my friends! And my best friend—from when we were young— Cristine Berzweck, she's there, too! I'm responsible for her, I have to be. Really, I'm responsible for them all."

"You're responsible for yourself, first of all. Second of all. Third of all." he counted this off on his thick, soft fingers. "Nothing more. Once we get you away, we can see what we can do about the rest. I'm not sure *how*, but—"

"Well, there's still more, though," said Amalina, her 'tide' continuing to rise up her throat and out of her mouth atop the inner force of bubbles. "My family, you see. If I disobey Count Tepsji, he promised he will kill them."

"Ah!" cried Janusch brightly, as if he'd just discovered treasure. "That's what I was waiting to hear! Your motivation; there it is! I wondered how that abominable Count could keep you in his grip, such a nice young girl, for so long, and trusting you all this time. And even after Kralov. But it isn't by clever, intoxicating words—it's with *incentive*! The very thing Janushti uses, how I can trust my people: incentive. But nothing as unpleasant as threats and ugly treatment, like *that* one. I'd never be like *him*. Instead I give them things, and get them the things they most want or need—the best things! I say it's better to use incentive that is positive, or people's hearts will still be set against you." Janusch pointed at Amalina knowingly, "As you are set against *him*."

Amalina dipped her head, feeling caught out and shamed.

"So," said Janusch, returning to the original thought, "just like your friends, after you're away, I can see what I can do about your family."

"But it's not that simple, either. I don't know how much time we'd have—how quickly—before the Count might carry through with his awful promise."

"There's always a danger," agreed Janusch, sympathetically but with a smile.

"And I've already been over this with my father. He refuses to leave the country. Even for his own safety."

"Your father knows where you are, Amalina? what's happening to you?"

Amalina nodded, and his lips slanted, appalled, "And that is why Papa's going to join the revolution. And not just him, many, many people I know. They're planning to attack the castle, very soon." She gave a brief, simple, but strangely accurate description of Sadra's revolutionary's plan—*Attila Bronk*'s plan. Amalina couldn't believe how easily it fell out of her mouth, she didn't know why she was bursting forth with all these secrets but she felt relieved when it was done. Janushti rocked back in his chair and gasped, again.

"So I can't leave now, Mr. Janushti. Leave *them*, when they are caught up in it all. You understand?"

"But that is their decision to follow him, then, no?"

"My family," she tried to explain.

"But we're all individuals here."

"I don't think I can see it that way."

"You must try. We *are* all individuals in this world. And we must see to our own happiness. We can't save everyone, sister Amalina, or we should never live our own lives. Forget about them for the moment and act for yourself, while you have the chance!"

"You make it sound so easy."

"Well … I suppose I do," he said with a bashful smile, almost embarrassed. "But anyone can do it. Everyone, they like Janushti because he enjoys himself, yes? He knows how to, and how it's done. And what's his secret?"

"Enjoying yourself."

"As an individual, Amalina Dalca!" he declared merrily. "This is my last lesson to you, sister Amalina, though perhaps you're still too young to understand: But see, what profit's in raging at the world, I ask you? Nothing! The world enjoys those who enjoy themselves." He wasn't ashamed to say it, but explained to Amalina's perplexed look with a winning smile: "Well, Marcus Aurelius said as much! And his are words to live by! He was a great Caesar! Not many people can pull it off, of course. That's why I wanted to meet you. It can get lonely for poor Janushti, and I thought, seeing as how you've been up there on that mountain for so long, and got through many an event, and you have so many friends, and you can still smile, that you might really be just like me … just a little bit? No? That's what I hoped for. Oh, well." He shrugged, then, happily: "Why should you care about them, those other people, whoever they are, past your own happiness? your own life? Do you see what I mean?"

However, Janusch's words were a startling, alien concept. Despite how it contradicted his apparent profession, his idea of freedom struck Amalina as an extremely selfish one, one that ignored responsibility to others, so unlike the life lessons which her father Dragomir, Minister Smidt, or his wife

Sadra would instruct her when she was growing up. Now Janusch's babyishness was more obvious to her. *He's never been hurt*, she thought. He'd never been too close to anyone.

He was as simple as a child!

*I could never be like you! Never at all! And nor would I ever want to be!* she thought with the same reproachful heat with which he had declared he was not like the Count; but not letting her smile slip, though it began to strain at how emphatic she'd thought it.

And then, at his look, when his smile fell, she realized she had said it out loud.

9

## Boom, Boom, Boom, Boom, Boom

"**B**ombs!" repeated the lieutenant. "Here, get me off this damned spike!"

The fuses continued to hiss, but Attila could not estimate how many seconds before they entered the metal housings and the bombs exploded. Was there time to kick them out of the cell, out of the apartment? How powerful were they? A host of questions and observations flooded his mind. And as he noticed how similar to a large shot from a cannon the bombs were, and noted the high pitch of the sparking fuses, and detected a faint scent of lubricating oil, presumably on the spikes, perceived over the mold of the apartment and the strong taste of fire and spent gunpowder of the fast shortening wicks—a taste like sulphur, or eggs that had gone off—looking as half-lidded as ever, though his eyebrows had definitely risen half a notch, Attila wrestled the lieutenant in the small confines of the cell; as the lieutenant, by himself, slid his body off the pointed metal rod. The torch had been dropped, and light came in wild flashes, with a steady flicker of red and orange from the bombs. With a sickening tearing sound, as soon as Lieutenant Vokent was free, he had Attila around the waist and was charging down the black hall, out the door, up the small stairs.

And still Attila's mind was working: Vokent wore some kind of cologne. That meant he had taken up the habits of a western gallant, and whether by forced training or desire, was shedding his more colloquial eastern habits. The large brown cloak he had was rough cloth, but his military jacket underneath was a smooth and expensive weave of wool. You could tell when he had come off the cement floor and onto the cobblestones just by the sound of his bootfalls on the different surfaces. The brightness of the morning traveled further into the apartment because of the mist pushing in through the door, but outside the apartment the mist made the light all-encompassing, directionless.

When Attila's feet met the ground outside, the observations stopped, he grabbed the lieutenant and kept them both running. "Move, move, move," he said quicker than he'd ever said anything before. "We can't be found here when—"

Five blasts sounded behind them, staggered just enough to know that there was more than one bomb. The two men were flattened to the ground as debris shot past them. The mist was joined by smoke and it sounded as if the three-story wall of bricks was beginning to crash down.

"Can't stop," insisted Attila. "Not the streets! The alleys!"

It wasn't until they'd gotten to a whole new district that Attila allowed them to stop. Or was it that he'd tripped? They both tumbled to the grey stones and gasped for breath, their limbs thrashing and whirling as if to draw the air closer.

"Was it meant to be that way?" muttered Attila through his heavy inhalations. "I don't know if he had extra wick on those explosives, and so meant for any thief to be trapped on those spears so they can see their doom coming as they are stuck there dying; he was a murderer and a torturer after all, and it might have been intentional. Or was it the cold from the apartment that hindered the bombs' action? Some chemical starter delayed? I could only know if I could get a better look at those bombs. Only they are gone. And so is the apartment. And so is everything I could ever have found useful. And, as no doubt was their secondary purpose, their blasts have let this higher agent know his underlings' lair has been found and compromised. Fell right into his—"

Attila came off his feet and slammed into the alley's brick wall. The lieutenant pressed him up there with one strong fist. The other had a knife out under Attila's bandaged jaw.

"I'm going to kill you," snarled Vokent, his nose up close to Attila's, his dreamy hazel eyes, no doubt seductive to the women, staring violently, hatefully into Attila's. And it looked like he meant what he was screaming. "Going to kill you! Kill you!"

"What's this—?"

"You goddamn idiot! With all those brains of yours you couldn't figure there would be a trap?"

"I didn't—"

"No, you didn't! Did you!" Vokent's panting was only getting stronger, his eyes clouding over into a blind rage. He took the knife away from Attila's throat only for a second to flip the front of his own cloak and see where the rod had rammed through. It must have been a split second difference that kept him from being gored, and only having the cold metal rod's point scrape through the material. Then the knife was back at Attila's throat. "You could have gotten me killed! ... for *nothing! Nothing!*"

Ivanti panted directly into Attila's face, which looked utterly at ease. He seethed resentfully at the dead, though twitchingly analytical eyes staring back at him.

"I suppose this is how you do it," said the lieutenant. "Send the ox in to get gored for you. Eh?"

Attila tried to lift his finger to point at the bandage on his neck being pressed by the knife. "I do plenty on my own. And I've seen death up close, more than once. I wouldn't ask anyone to do something I wouldn't do. As a matter of fact, if you cut any deeper, it will match the wound I already have."

"Made by someone like me? who you used, and who almost came to ruin?"

"Let me down," said Attila, calmly.

The lieutenant had to wait a number of seconds to consider his options. Then he lowered Attila so that the former low constable was standing again.

"She doesn't know you're here," said Attila, with an unimpressed tone but analyzing Ivanti up and down and delivering his assessment. "Does she?"

Lieutenant Vokent swallowed hard.

"No, she doesn't," said Attila, sorely. "That's why you said if you'd died just now, you would have died for 'nothing'. Because Amalina Dalca won't have known you were here fighting for her. And you will have come all this way without taking her into your arms again." The way Attila said it made the lieutenant feel stupid, he lowered his head, but kept his eyes up and steady on him. Attila flapped the sides of his jacket as if he were idly waiting for a carriage to arrive. "My dear Lieutenant," said Attila, finally, "what you are doing here isn't for a girl. And it's not for 'nothing', as you'd have it. You must see that. What you are doing here is fighting in the righteous struggle for law, and for justice, and to free your—*our*—people from an evil that has persisted here beyond all bounds of reason. Any move you make, should you live or die from it, from here on out and until this creature is vanquished, is for the greatest good you could ever do. You were willing to spill your blood, toss your life out like a common mercenary in foreign lands, and for a foreign cause. For what? *That* would have been for nothing. You have a higher cause here. *The* Cause. *This* is something."

Lieutenant Vokent, clamping his fists, still looked overcome with anger, but he nodded in shame.

"Never mind Ms. Dalca, my dear Lieutenant. Never mind her, and never mind love. Remove any thought of it from your mind until we are done. It is only a distraction. Love can only—and will—get you killed."

The lieutenant barked out a derisive laugh. "That's a fancy thing to say, sir. And so what about you?"

Attila stared uncomprehending at Vokent.

"What about me?"

10

## Late-Morning:
## The Impossible

Janusch didn't appear to be too put out by Amalina's insult. He hulked over the table in front of him like an oversized, gurgling baby who'd caught sight of the interesting, mischievous housecat.

"Did you *mean* to say that, sister Amalina?" said Janusch with a bashful smile and a wink, recovering nicely from any upset. "That you would never want to be like me? like Janusch Timorak? *Little, harmless Janushti?*"

"Oh, no," insisted Amalina, embarrassed.

"Don't worry if it's true," assured Janusch. "But just because you think you *aren't* someone, sister Amalina, doesn't make it so."

"What I meant is, maybe you're mistaken," said Amalina in a diplomatic tone. "I'm afraid I'm a little different."

"Oh," he said with an accepting smile at the blow. "So you're really going to stay on here? You won't take Janushti's helping hand to leave?"

"I would if I could. But Mr. Janushti, you must understand, though I wish I didn't feel compelled to … " another bubble was coming, another release of tension: Amalina had not told him yet of Noka's slaughter of her people. It was still too awful to consider, much less relate to a stranger, but she felt it brewing upward in her system involuntarily. With so many things left unsaid percolating and jostling in her chest, by only thinking of Noka's face briefly she'd just given this one an opening, and it was on its way. On its way! "I feel I must tell you: recently I witnessed what can only be described as a living nightmare …"

"I can only imagine," he said, sympathetically, spotting what was coming and looking like he'd prefer to avoid the gruesome details.

"It's embarrassing to say," she went on, trying to hold it back, or sideline it, "but I've managed to push it down, to ignore it, to forget it ever happened."

"There's nothing wrong with—"

At the last second, she shoved and diverted it to another track: "The revolutionary—um, Attila Bronk—warned me once that I had fallen asleep. That at the castle I was enjoying myself too much—"

"Only *he* would say something like that," interjected Janusch, as if insulted.

"But I think he's right. Part of me was enjoying so very much that life I had, I wanted it to go on forever—"

"Naturally. And why not!"

"So I was ignoring what needed to be done," *and then horrible things happened—The Night of Noka.*

"What needs to be done, eh?" said Janusch, with his sweet, innocent smile. "What ever really *needs* to be done?" he gave it a thought. "Other than kindness to others, and, above all, to enjoy oneself? I tell you: *nothing.*"

"But, because what happened … I feel worse for having done nothing for this long already," said Amalina, quietly, not wanting to offend this happy man. "Let me tell you, ever since I woke up this morning, I've been slapped in the face with what I'm responsible for, what innocence I've harmed and endangered by my own inaction and what I really need to do before I can just walk away. I can only walk away if I have a clean conscience."

"But what can you possibly do for them up there, for anyone … especially against him?"

"If nothing else, I have to do something, *something*, before they—my father and my friends—come to the castle. You see?"

"Yes, I see. And?" he stared at her like she was telling a story, and he couldn't imagine what miracle she would come up with.

"The math is simple: I have to stop one side or the other—the Count or the revolutionary—or my people will die. And while I've tried to delay the revolutionary, I sent him off to find AXP—" Amalina looked as if she'd stunned herself, *Oh, AXP!*, and a new bubble rose quickly to replace the first "… sorry, do you know who AXP is?"

"AXP?" he said, looking puzzled. "Um, no?"

Amalina rattled off AXP's crimes, as if that would help him figure it out, while he continued to shake his head. But, following this new feeling of release, she had to get it all out.

"You're full of so many secrets and surprises, little Amalina," gasped Janusch when she was done, as if being tickled. "Not the simple girl you appear to be at first sight! Not at all!"

"… So I'd hoped this Mr. Bronk," said Amalina, in conclusion, "who is very smart, whatever you might think of him, would spend his time finding out who AXP is, and so delay the attack. But he's very smart, and I'm sure he must have figured out who it is by now, or soon will. And then the attack will be back on. Which means I need to find another distraction, or a permanent solution."

"I've never heard of an AXP," said Janushti, a little thrown and lost in thought, though still smiling. "Em … In all my years."

"You're sure?"

He nodded, and a shadow of unease crossed his face. "But this concerns me, Amalina. Not this bad man, this AXP, as there are so many bad men in life. But first you asked me to help Attila Bronk, or seemed to want me to. Yet now ..." He angled his head, as if to come at her from a different direction. "So you're saying in essence you're not working *with* him, you're actually in a race *against* him. Either you do what you can to stop him, or it will be Bronk and your village that tries to remove the Count, and they all die there. It's a *race!*"

"I suppose you're right," she admitted.

"But in that, you see, Amalina, you're running in the same direction as Attila! and taking his direction!" He tsked at her, with a reproving smile. "You haven't been listening to *me*. But listen now: You aren't in a contest with anyone but yourself, you've only set your own trap—*against yourself*—with ideas that were given to you by strangers who had no interest in your happiness. Don't you see?"

*Sheer sophistry*, the revolutionary would say. But of course from Mr. Timorak it would only be easy and selfish, self-serving answers, thought Amalina. She said: "But—"

"But I'm telling you—Janushti is telling you!—you aren't in a race at all; you're being given a choice: continue what you are doing, or do something else!"

Amalina nodded, trying to understand, feeling his beliefs weighing on her head like his big bottom was crushing down and she was a soft couch. He seemed to blur in front of her. She was thinking: *Is there something else? Some alternative besides this race? Anything?* Of course there was. But that could include accepting the Count's own plan, which would be the easiest thing; to take his hand and allow him to transform her ...

"And of course *I'm* offering you a choice right now which should be the easiest of all!" said Janusch, in a strange echo of her thoughts, cutting her off before she started blabbing the worst secret of all: her option to take the Count's hand and change forever. Ending all argument. "Mine is the easiest and the cleanest of paths, and you remain you!"

*You remain you!* How eerily accurate Janusch's sentiments were. But he couldn't know what alternative she was trying to resist. And as much as she wanted to tell him of the Count's proposal, she forced the words to stay in her chest. It was so difficult to hold back with the closeness of the room, the ease of his charm, and the loosening of the spring inside her. The caressing bubbles encouraging a release. She shook her head again.

"What is it, comrade Amalina?" said Janushti. "You wish to tell me something. But I've declared the truth and have an escape for you! Is there really anything left to be said? Look here, for your own good, I'm going to have to insist you—"

"You're going to kidnap me?"

"What? No. No no no. But if you'd only tell me what is it you feel you must reveal—I see it in your eyes, comrade—because if you don't, then I would have to … well …"

Amalina had to talk: to admit the Count could alter her, give her his power; or, that is, put his power into her through a vile exchange of blood. He was doing it already to others! She must tell Janusch, and tell him right now. To warn him. To get it over with, all she had to do was open her mouth and give voice …

*No, no no!* As the energy welled up, she quickly redirected her thoughts: what had she been talking about before? AXP?

"Well, anyway," she mumbled awkwardly, "what I meant to say … what I *was* saying, what I mean—and thank you very much for all of that escape stuff—but if I haven't stopped the timing of the revolution, which is all I had control of—you understand, the *timing* of it—then, as you say, I *am* in a race. And so: in order to prevent Count Tepsji from killing everyone, just as he did our Commander Kralov and all the brave men who've tried to bring him to justice, if I can do nothing else, it will have to be the Count who I—"

"You're going to stop Tepsji?" he howled. "The Knight of Ardeel?"

She nodded shallowly, feeling stupid.

"I'm afraid he *must* be stopped," she said. "Or delayed, or distracted. Worst come to worst, if I can't find a way to bend him before the revolutionary arrives, he must come down."

. . .

Janusch nodded back, gravely, and then bent forward, hands clasped seriously in front of him, a look of realization and acceptance. It was the most sober he'd looked yet, his smile was at its smallest. "*'Come down'*. Okay," he said. He raised his eyebrow. "But how are you going to do this?"

"I've had thoughts."

"Thoughts, Amalina? You should need more than that. This is a serious decision, and if you're going to do it you need a plan."

"I know," said Amalina, her cheeks reddened. "It kind of sounds silly out loud, but there *are* plans … "

"*A* plan. One plan. A good, solid plan."

" … I have ideas … Ideas for one."

"The Knight is impossible to stop, to trap, or to kill. As you say, everyone has tried. Even our Commander."

"There are the bees," mumbled Amalina.

"Bees?" Janusch sounded incredulous.

She told him of a little anecdote Genadie had of the Count versus a swarm of bees, and how disturbed and helpless the monster had been.

"Bees," said Janusch again, looking dismayed. "But they did not *kill* him."

"I also once had an idea to use the chandelier in the great hall," said Amalina, feeling dumb for admitting this, even as she said it. And as much as she tried to explain it the details came down to dropping it on him.

"The chandelier ... in the great hall ..." he kept repeating the most ridiculous parts of what Amalina proposed. She felt her half-baked ideas coming apart in the air, she almost wanted to cry. But still there was that strange pressure behind her words, as if she wanted to confess, or else had to convince this pleasant doubter.

"You'd have to see it, Janushti, the chandelier, it is huge. I thought I'd—"

"Yes, drop it on him."

"I know it sounds silly, and it probably is, but I've thought about it some, and it might still be a way to ... but that's just one thing among ..." She swallowed on a drying throat. "I know his weaknesses and he has many, and I'm sure I'll be able to ..."

"Stop him" he said, seriously. "Hold him. Bind him. Prevent him. Or bring him down. Somehow."

Amalina nodded, and then mumbled on with more ideas, almost in a trance; by the end of it, she didn't know everything she'd said.

"None of what you're saying is making you reconsider my offer, Amalina Dalca?"

"I wish I could ... but ..."

Janusch nodded with a smile that said he pitied her. Her decision.

"If you're going to do this," he began, "you also need to have people on your side. Do you have people who can help you up there? *Someone* you can count on, anyway?"

"Oh, yes," said Amalina, her happiness suddenly inflating, and she immediately—beyond her control—rattled off their names to the skeptical Janusch.

"A handful," he murmured, assessing their numbers on his fingers as she went along. "And do you have *incentive* for these people you've named, to make sure they help you?"

"I don't think they'd need ..." she said unsurely and trailed off.

"It's the only way to be sure ... and even then ... but really ... " he said, starting and stopping. He ended with: "I hope you can find *some* incentive for them, just to be sure. Or *that one* up there in the castle, your adversary Amalina, might have incentive of his own on them, to work them against you."

Amalina made a face.

"And *still* you won't take Janushti's offer, Amalina Dalca?" said Janusch, with a hopeful smile.

Amalina moved quickly to wrap this up: "I do appreciate this talk and your tea, Mr. Janusch. I feel it has really stirred my mind. I mean it. And while I wish I had never left *Ivanti*—"

Janushti's eyebrows raised.

"I mean, I hadn't left *Ivanti Ion Vokent*—"

Janushti's eyebrows raised higher.

"I mean," said Amalina, speaking slowly, deliberately, trying to get hold of the reins on this continuing fizz of confession, "what I mean to say is—not Lieutenant Vokent, never mind him—what I meant to say is: while I wish I had never left *Paris*—Paris, France, that is to say—that I had stayed there, and … or that I really would have liked to be able to take you up on your kind, generous offer … it is all the same … Here-there, Him-you … um, *it*-you … um …" Amalina shook her head, polite apology in her eyes. "I can't."

He nodded. She nodded back.

"So bees, or chandeliers, or a colonel's pistols, or something," said Janusch, cheerily recalling her words, shifting uncomfortably on his chair. "You've been there long enough, survived even where our Commander did not, I'm sure you will stop him, trap him, bring him down, whatever. Even if it is all by yourself. I have confidence in you, Amalina Dalca."

"Thank you."

Still, he stared at her like she was an unfolding tragedy. She didn't like that look. Smiling, he lifted his cup of tea only to find it empty, he motioned with it self-consciously.

"All gone," he said.

Amalina was immediately visited by Noka's image, blood-laden and sated, *"C'est finis."*

*No, I could never be like her*, she thought, *and I can never be like him.*

At least she didn't say it this time.

"I *want* to help you, Amalina Dalca," said Janusch, looking at her with a smile as if he'd just noticed how beautiful she was. "I so very much want to help. If only you'd let me be your guardian angel. That is what Janushti does, and can do. But I am only here this morning by chance. This will be the only time I can extend to you my offer. As your guardian angel I can plant you somewhere safe where you can do your good work," he winked a wet eye at her, "Paris even, if you like, and without *this infernal villain* to bother you. And still you won't accept me but choose to go your own way? This is your last chance, Amalina, to get out of the race. Will you take it?"

11

# High Noon:
## Journey into night

Amalina felt the blade tucked in her handwarmer and noted how dull it was. What could she have done with it, really? Or with the little magic bone? At the thought of how ridiculous it was, she might have burst out a big laugh there in the street, but she was still too unsettled by her meeting with the jovial giant Janusch, and anyway it was too cold. She stamped her feet, trying to generate some extra heat as she walked through the near empty avenues, smiling at the Netzians who passed with polite return smiles of their own.

"Good morning," she burbled at them, for some reason barely able to control the link between her thoughts and her mouth.

She'd cut over to Genadie's street. Feeling somehow defeated she just wanted to get back in the sleigh and go home, but she didn't see him. Even when she peered deeper into the city. Even when she fumbled her glasses onto her face, there was no sign of the little, raggedy man. Panic passed through Amalina for a moment—he might have been grabbed by a mob. But the streets were quiet and the people unconcerned with anyone else. They hadn't been roused into a violent lynch. This wasn't what the Count had worried them over. Maybe Genadie had gone back to the sleigh, or was out searching for where she'd disappeared to for so long. Because she'd never find him if she started chasing him up and down the streets, she headed back to the sleigh to wait, if he wasn't there already.

Amalina almost missed Genadie when, from behind, she came upon him bent over and cooing at a small boy who was sitting atop a barrel set against a building. The boy stared up in wonder at the rat-faced man with delight. Genadie had hold of one of the child's tiny hands between his finger and thumb and he was swaying the arm back and forth, up and down. Amalina realized he wasn't cooing exactly but lightly warbling a fanciful tune.

"Come now," chimed Genadie. "Doo—dee—doo—dee—dah! Fa—la—la—la—lah! There my boy, I think you've got it." The child imitated the song and swung Genadie's hand, with Genadie nodding along and helping him with the rhythm. "Doo—dee—dah—dee—dee! Tummity—tah—tee—tee! Yes, oh, yes, you've got it! Oh, my, now isn't this fun? And what a splendid musician you will beee—"

"Genadie, who's this?"

Genadie spun like a frightened cat, head down below his shoulders, and threw away the child's hand. The boy, startled, glanced at his rat-faced conductor, and then was about to cry.

"Oh, Ms. Dalca!" said Genadie, putting himself in front of the barrel and the boy on it. "Done already?"

"Who do you have there? What were you doing?"

"Oh, nothing, Ms. Dalca. Just waiting for you. Now that you've returned, we can go."

"But you were having some fun," said Amalina, smiling because she'd never seen him so happy and the feeling had caught on. "You were singing with him. Don't let me stop you. Do continue."

"Oh, it's nothing," said Genadie with a swipe of his hand. "Nothing at all. Fun? No, no, no."

The boy leaned to tap Genadie's back. Genadie turned to him.

"Ah, yes, there you are. Shuh-shuh-shuh, don't you cry now. Go inside and find your parents, I should think they'd be worried about you. Run along. Now, don't forget the song! But run along, run along, it's too cold to be hanging about outside." Genadie had taken the boy off the frosty barrel and waved him away with the same swingy up-and-down gesture as before. He said to the boy's back "Doo—dee—doo—dee—dah! Fa—la—la—la—laaah!"

"But that wasn't … *your* boy … ?" said Amalina. But of course it couldn't be. His son would have been so much older by now. She couldn't help asking, though. The thought pushed up her throat and out her mouth before she knew it.

"What a fool thing to say," said Genadie, looking a little pained as he heaved the handle bag with the gold from the ground. "Just an innocent little child who's gotten lost in the snow and I was trying to calm him. Now, let's get on, Ms. Dalca. I would swear to anyone it *was* 'good in Netz', wouldn't you?"

"But it was so nice of you, Genadie," said Amalina, feeling warmed by the sight. "You were so good to him. And that cute song!"

"I like to think I'm good with everyone," said Genadie. "I've been good to you, too. Haven't I?"

"I've never seen you so happy," repeated Amalina, noticing that Genadie's eyes were wetted with tears. So much so he had to wipe them with the back of his dirty sleeve. "He reminds you of your boy, then? He must."

"Please now," growled Genadie, pushing past her and crunching through the snow to the sleigh. Pointing to it and their horses further up the block. "I've told you to leave off that! Haven't I! Why are you so cruel sometimes?"

"But I'm not done yet," she said as she hurried away. "Almost, though. Just give me a second, I'll be right back!"

Amalina ran to the restaurant she'd left just minutes ago. Inside the dining room there was the lonely feeling of a private party being cleared out. Janusch was shrugging a great coat onto his shoulders as he stared blankly at the table they'd been sitting, its tea service still in place. He swung his head at her in surprise as she entered.

"Glad I caught you!"

"You have," said Janushti with a polite smile, his eyes darting to either side to make sure nobody was watching. "And wearing opticals, quite the disguise. And so now what will you do with me, eh?"

She removed the glasses, self-consciously and because they'd begun to fog over. Into the handwarmer they went, adding to the clutter there. "I'll ask you a favor."

"Oh!"

"But not that. Something else. One I can pay you for. Whatever the cost."

"I *do* like money, hee-hee, hm hee," he giggled. "How can I resist? While I'm here. As long as it isn't too dangerous."

"Listen," said Amalina in a confidential whisper. "You've a good knowledge of the gypsies in these mountains?"

His eyebrow lifted, she was moving into an intriguing area. "I work with all types, of course. I do trade and operate with them quite often."

"Years ago, I don't know when, but a long time ago, there was a King of the gypsies whose daughter married a talented musician."

"*King* of the gypsies? " he scoffed. "No such thing. If there's one such king then there's a hundred of them. But that will narrow the search nonetheless. Someone who would dare to claim such a grandiose, presumptuous title. Yes, do go on."

"The king and his men went after *you-know-who* and were all killed. Then *you-know-who* went after the rest of the tribe, their families. He killed the whole caravan except this one musician—who was not a gypsy—and also spared the musician's son. He separated the two, and promised the musician he would allow the boy to live, as long as the musician would serve him and obey his every command."

"Mm. Sounds like a storybook again. But didn't you tell me it earlier?"

"But it happened," assured Amalina. "I know it did."

"And why not? And such a bargain, there you go—incentive. Dark incentive, but incentive. Didn't I tell you? This is about Genadie, eh?"

"And now I'd like you to find that boy," concluded Amalina. "I can't imagine where he might have gone, or how old he'd be. He might even be older than you."

"That's pretty old," chuckled Janusch. "If he's made it this long, he's got some of that gypsy good fortune."

"Well, I need you to find him," said Amalina. "Or at least find out what happened to him. Please, if you can. As soon as you can. I need to know." She handed him three gold coins from her hand warmer. "Please."

"I can't perform miracles," said Janusch. "But gold sure can."

Then glancing down, looking at the coins in his hand, his smile changed. "Yuck. What an ugly face. I hate that Knight of yours."

"Don't look at them. But it should be enough. Or do you think you'll need more?" She squeezed the small bag of coins on her belt, wondering how many she could give away without the Count asking for receipts.

Janushti shook his head and handed the coins back with a pleasant smile. "Ah, incentive! I smell incentive for *me*. Eh? That is what you are looking for. Never mind. For your thoughtfulness, Amalina Dalca, here is what I will do, I will do it for free!"

"No," said Amalina, "You should take something …"

"You may ask why, and the answer is simple enough: Because you're doing this not for yourself, but for others. Risking yourself to give happiness to an unhappy world. In that way, you *are* like Janushti, no? You can't deny it. Even if you don't want to admit it. If you'd taken my first offer, you'd have been ordinary, like anyone else, but you're not. You're a pleaser, *just* like Janushti, eh!" He took her hand before she could object. "And because I see you're learning from me already, no? Incentive for Genadie?"

"No, its just a favor—"

"No need to be downcast, it is sweet. Perhaps in time, you will see the value in *all* my lessons. But for now, I will do this for you, *gratis*. It'll make me happy to do so, and happiness is all there is or we can ever want." He bounced her hand in his, "I'll have one of my many, many happy people reach out to you in the castle when this boy is found. May it be done in time, eh!"

"You know, there is one more thing," said Amalina, retrieving her hand and pulling out the magic bone from the hand warmer. She did not know why she felt compelled to share this, but it had been nagging her, as if it were a piece left out that she should have shared earlier, that would—or might—clear up his doubts. A residual bubble lifting. "Besides the bees and whatever, I also have this."

"And what is this?" he said, giving the old repaired bone a charitable smile, as if hoping it wasn't as ridiculous as it looked.

"I was told this came from some old gypsy magic. At least it was fixed by it."

"Yes? And?"

Amalina set it between her teeth and bit gently down, tasting the lint that had been building on it since its last use. She vanished. Or, that is, her body disappeared, leaving only her hat, dress, winter coat, bag of coins on her belt, and hand warmer floating in the air in front of Janusch.

His eyes goggled wide, and it looked like he might scream.

"But what is this!" he could barely comprehend. "Do tell! Do tell Janushti!"

Amalina spit the bone back in her hand, returned to view, still not sure why she felt so confident and obliged to show him. "Gypsy magic."

"Gypsy *magic*?"

"My secret weapon, maybe? Even *you-know-who* doesn't know about—"

His hand reached for the bone but she put it back in the handwarmer, next to her glasses and the blade, which she grabbed hold of again, in case he got greedy. As it was, he was starting to lean over her.

"Can Janushti have it?" he asked.

"I really don't know how much power it has left. I can't waste any. But I *had* to show you. So you'd understand."

"Yes, that's good. But I think I would take it as payment, yes? To find the son?"

"You just said you'd do it for free."

"Yes, but …"

"This one I need," said Amalina, with a strong look, shaking the hand warmer. "But if you go to the gypsies, when you look for the missing son for me, you can also ask if they can make one for you. No?"

"Ah!" he said almost proudly, but still regarding her as if mesmerized. "You *are* being clever, giving *incentive* to old Janushti, eh? For Janushti to go brave the gypsies! To seek after the son. Yes. The incentive of *the magic*."

"It's not like that."

"No? But I think so."

"If you can get a dozen or so more for me, that would help free the Ladies, you see; more than you could imagine," explained Amalina. "If you do that, I'll give you all the gold you could ever want. A full bag for each."

"Yes," said Janusch, with a nod. His eyes were focused on Amalina's hand warmer and what was hidden inside. "Yes, I see. *More* bones, yes …"

There was a quiet knock at one of the inside doors, and a voice whispered, "Symolsza, sir, it is time …"

Janusch looked stunned—more so than just a moment ago—as he froze, gaping at the side door, then burst out in an uproarious laugh. Then he smiled down at Amalina with red-cheeked embarrassment. "Well, you've heard my code name. And so what? What can be done about *that*? But, um, listen, Amalina Dalca, you should be careful for the rest of the day. My friends informed me, after you left, that they introduced an additive to the tea, so that you'd be more comfortable with me ... and talk easier, maybe share your secrets ..." He glanced guiltily at the hand warmer, imagining the magic item within it. "They thought I had wanted to ask you an important question: if you're acting as *his* agent now."

"I'm not—" blurted Amalina on top of another surprise bubble, her fingers coming up to her lips at the wonder of the additive's effect.

"No, of course you aren't," smiled Janusch, abashed. "I wasn't going to ask, I wouldn't even suspect. But they also thought I'd try to find from you what he's up to these days."

"He's—" she hiccupped.

"No, no, no," hurried Janusch, before she began reeling out the Count's scheme to transform his many foreign women—and for them to descend on the world!—which she would have done. Or might have, with the unsuspected return of the warm fizzing. Amalina had her hand firmly over her mouth now. "I don't want to know these things. Even if I knew, what could I do about it? He has his sphere and I have mine. And we should never meet. But sometimes my people get ahead of themselves." He pointed to the teapot to make it the example, but then, when she stared at it, Janusch took the teapot off the table and held it between them.

"But you drank from the same pot," said Amalina. "You had a whole cup! Swallowed it right down!"

"I did, I did, but well ..."

"So how did you not—?"

"Therein lies their trick," he said in an off-hand voice, as if to distract from what had happened, though his eyes transmitted his mortification. "I am really very sorry, please forgive them, they were just trying to—well, they did this for Janushti, to help him, what can I say? You understand. I hope you can excuse them, anyway. And think nothing bad of it, as I *am* on your side. As no one else. But do be careful, for Janushti's sake, eh? Don't mention to anyone me—Janushti—or my *other* name."

"No, I promise. Thank you."

"And take this humiliation as a helpful reminder, my sister Amalina: your agents may be your best people, and want to help you any way they can. But that doesn't mean they'll do what you want, or be good at it. Take it to heart, Amalina. This is the drawback of using other people." He grinned widely, with a wink: "But then, if you don't have any people by your side, well, then you're in it all by yourself, eh?"

"Thank you for your help, Janushti."

"Good luck to you and with your life, Amalina Dalca," he smiled brightly, "and, in this most dangerous race—which, mind you, is a path you're freely choosing for yourself—to stop the Count in time. I do hope to see you again. Hee hee."

. . .

Earlier that morning, Amalina hadn't been able to go hunting for breakfast berries. She hadn't gotten alone to think about how to handle the revolutionary—*Attila Bronk*, she reminded herself—and how to further delay his disastrous plans. Amalina's day then, from her thwarted berrywalk onward, felt ruined. And so when she arrived at the castle in the evening she reported her positive findings in Netz to the Count—*"Yessss, most excellent, you've come through for me again, my little mouse, as always, and without harm, as I promised you. And the people of Netz have been properly pacified. My plans will continue! Haven't I told you how much I adore you …?"*—rolled her eyes at him, and went straight to her room and tried to forget it all. But the day ran back through her mind, beginning with her meeting with Janusch, where he'd insisted she was like him or he was like her. And putting that memory aside, she decided she would only count on the large smiling man for nothing but that he might succeed in finding Genadie's son—*"Incentive!"* came his voice. But now …

Under Janusch Timorak's lesson, Amalina understood that all her fanciful flights of taking the Count's offer and staying on at the high castle indefinitely, without consequence, or escaping these mountains and abandoning everyone else to their fates, would be selfish and, for her, impossible; she had to end her endless delays and finally put her own plan into motion—if not to kill, if she refused to kill at all, then—to thwart, trap, entirely bring down and make powerless the Count. Do so immediately. And she had to act fast, even if alone. But how?

How could she *ever* stop the almost-infinitely powerful being on earth? There must be something!

For another restless night, between tender squeezes by a restless Pia, visits by Lucinda Skeldar's soul demanding revenge against her murderer, and now fretful thoughts of hidden men throwing tainted tea cups at her head and whispering "Szymolza, sir", Amalina's mind worked on.

# ENTR'ACTE: MIDNIGHT CODA

## 12

## Affair's End

### I

At the last chime of midnight, a tall man with a pitiable face finished his report to a more important man who sat behind a large oak desk.

"Well, that settles that, another end to things." The man who'd received the report glanced up from his desk with a melancholic look and grumbled softly. "You say their heads are stuck on spikes above the castle walls?"

"Frozen like two blocks of bad ice—real ugly ice—clear as day." Across the room, the tall man shifted awkwardly, his cracked lips scraped against each other in an unsure way. "Very sorry to tell you."

Yes, thought the man behind the desk, looking appraisingly at his midnight informant, this one isn't too differently ugly than that one whose head was now stuck on a spike. About as tall, too. And as well, that one, whose head was now fully detached, hanging out over the Count's high castle's walls as a display—or *a warning*—had once stood across this same room and upon the same oriental carpet; looking dreadful, but useful. And already, here was his possible replacement? *There were always replacements.* That this one was a near doppelganger was somewhat disturbing, and yet comforting. Or was it the other way around?

He glanced across his desk again at the tall, ugly man, who looked expectantly, almost worshipful at him.

*Perhaps*, thought the man behind the desk, feeling encouraged. *Perhaps ...* But in this unsure time there needed to be tests.

"You weren't observed?"

"I was seen, but nobody knew what I was up to. They've no idea."

"You can never be too careful." He eyed his new underling. "You understand that, right?"

"Oh. Yes, yes."

Behind his desk, the important man shifted, rubbed his cheek thoughtfully. "You were very helpful. I appreciate your service. Expect more, but know you'll be well rewarded for it."

The tall man thanked him and left the room. As he did, he mumbled, as if uncontrollably, "I'll do anything for you, you know, sir. Anything for you … Anything for you … Anything for you …"

Watching him, the other chuckled to himself.

*Definitely useful*, thought he. *I'll have to look into the man's family, delve into his true ancestry. Blood will tell his character, his significance, his destiny. Blood—one's bloodline—is the most important thing in the world.*

But still, his own blood was boiling; this was the end of something, wasn't it? He'd do all he could, but it seemed everything was conspiring against his deal with the Count. His two loyal lieutenants had been cut down by the creature? And for what? It was one thing to ignore their terms of agreement, but to send such a brutal signal … Was it defiance? After all these happy years? And on top of it, this morning's blowing of the holding-house? What there? *His* work, too? What was happening up in that castle? Had all those foreign girls bedeviled him, corrupted him with their western ways, so that he no longer knew how to honor an ally?

*Not a false ally, either*, thought he, *like any old commoner who's signed that contract with the Knight of Ardeel.*

He'd done that, too, of course; signed the old contract. But that was a passive thing. A capitulation by the local population to an immortal destructive force. A bending of the knee to it. An abject prostration. For centuries the Knight had terrified with his inhuman abilities and power and unquenchable thirst. Malevolence that could threaten the entire populace to extinction. And yet, on one sunny day, the Knight had allowed himself to be penned in, reduced to savaging just one young lady or two a month. This man behind the desk had seen the victims: the white corpses, their throats ripped and torn, the blood drained of every drop, sometimes their sweat-slicked breasts exposed through torn bodices. And yet *he* hadn't been afraid! He'd signed the contract like anyone else, in order to fit in, but he knew how the world worked, and he was stronger than the others—he had good, strong blood—and he had positioned himself deliberately *closer* to the ancient monster. After centuries alone to itself, the man had figured out how to be an equal, of sorts, to the creature. He had something of value to offer, to trade, to prove himself worthy. So that he could not just bend the knee, but offer himself up as a true ally.

*Not just a true ally, either*, cackled the man further, with a thrill: *a life-long friend now.* A friend who'd eased his immortal life immensely and would continue to do so—gladly—even in spite of a few wrinkles. Didn't the Count know how important he was to him? Did the Count truly not ken how he had him surrounded at every side? what a formidable enemy he could become if he so chose? With such a long-lived life, had the monster not gleaned the most important lesson: how dangerous a dear close friend can be?

*But is it really too late to save our friendship?*

There didn't seem to be a way to resolve the current matter positively, thought the man with a shake of his head, other than to fully make the break. Make it first. He would send more notes to the castle, but knew already they'd be met with silence. And so what? It was all just a formality in what was to come. And whatever he did, he had to control the situation. Now, when everything was on his side.

But that meant clearing the field for battle. No diversions. The concentration of his wits. The shutting away of meaningless, inconsequential affairs.

With a sad throb to his heart, he opened the secret compartment in his desk and withdrew the papers. He looked tenderly and longingly at the warm words written on them, already feeling the ache at their loss, and breathed in the rich floral scent of the paper, remembering erotic scenes he did not wish to forget, only to renew. But he knew what must be done. One can never be too careful, and this was nothing but a distraction. One that perhaps could be picked up at a later time, when all was said and done. But for now ... He stood and crossed the room with a resolute step, papers in hand, the hint of flowers wafting from them.

"Are you coming to bed?" asked his wife tentatively. She was at the edge of the room looking in.

"I told you never to bother me in my office when I'm working," he said gruffly at the surprise.

"I'm sorry, I thought you were done. Your visitor left just now. Who was he? Or ..." She glanced down at his hands. "What are you holding there?"

"Are you going to insist on talking to me while I'm conducting business?" he hissed. "Or do I have to teach you once more how *to listen*?"

"They look like letters. Is that smell ... perfume?" His wife's large eyes grew watery, and her lips trembled. "But tell me you haven't—"

"Mind your own business," he hissed again, her sad face making his blood boil even hotter.

"Those *are* what I think they are," she said timorously, hands folding together in front of her mouth as if in prayer, "aren't they?"

"I said to mind your own business, didn't I? And yet you *persist*!"

She realized he was using the voice, that low, ugly, whispering voice, the one he used when he was up to something wrong. So husky and unnatural. A secretive half. Conspiratorial. Creepy. It wasn't really him, she thought. Or ... *or was it?* She had a sudden fiery notion: that this was the voice he used when trying to seduce those poor—

"Don't I please you *enough*, my dear husband?" she cried out suddenly, to drive away the image of he and them; all of *them*. And here it was before her eyes, as if she'd just caught him with a girl in his arms; in his hands: those sweet smelling papers—another one of *them*. And for her to see! She couldn't simply ignore it now … "Don't I do everything for you? Just tell me what I can do that would please you and I'll do it. You know that. Anything for you. Anything for you. Anything for you …"

"There's nothing you can do to please me," he grunted cruelly, "but to *endure* me."

"Please," she said, stepping toward him, reaching for the letters, or maybe to embrace him.

"Mind your business, old crow!"

He lunged at her, shoved her, and kicked her out of the room. His blood was at top boil, turning to flames.

"Where does all this anger come from?" she cried as she retreated.

. . .

He spun around and looked one last time upon the papers in his hand. He shuffled them to regard the page with the drawing. Such a pretty face there, lovingly inked.

*Why does he,* my old friend, *defy me?* he grumbled to himself. *Is he protecting that girl, though I warned him? I've unmasked her threat, so it shouldn't bother him to do away with her just as he's done the countless beauties before. Is it because he really cannot believe she could bring him to harm? Well, he's disregarded my own potential against him, hasn't he? And so that's his constant mistake: Hubris; the folly of every great man.* Then, at a turn in thought: *Or …? could it be … ? does he honestly have feelings for her? What* is *happening up there in that castle?* The man chortled suddenly, and stared at the portrait of his own young lady. *I suppose I can't blame him if he's been seduced. Why not? Though it reveals another weakness if he doesn't recognize the value between that Amalina Dalca and I.*

With a final sniff of the sweet bottom pages, the letters he threw into the fire. Then, with a sigh, he threw in the drawing, too. But he couldn't bear to watch it crackle apart. Better to keep the image complete in his head.

*Just the latest,* he told himself sanguinely, cooling his blood. Calming himself. *Just the latest, she was. And there will always be more …*

He left the room debating whether he should work more often with the tall man who had visited tonight, who was loyal and did not shrink from a bit of hard, bloody, risky business. Useful, indeed. And he was perhaps more reliable to work with than that ridiculous menace he'd been dealing with for so long now, who held everything over his head. The one who could destroy him in a flash—and now looked like he just might do so.

Just look at the destruction of the holding house ... that was close. Much too close.

While there was a question of whether the monster might do him harm, this man—who only a select few in the world knew as AXP—wasn't safe. Nobody in his family was.

*Yes,* he grinned a sharp grin at the challenge. *Maybe it* is *a good time for a change. Time to bring things to an end. Time to take him down.*

## II

He didn't notice his wife hiding in the hall's shadows. Or hear her enter the abandoned room as he climbed the stairs. She went straight for the fireplace. The letters were blackened and curled and crumbled. Useless. The drawing was still in there, it had fluttered to the side and only its corner had caught the heat of the fire. Before it burned she swatted it out with an iron. She picked the crisped paper up and stared at it; scowled at the face of the smiling girl there.

Then, later, she added this portrait to her secret collection.

# PART TWO
# PARTNERS IN REVOLUTION

## 13

# A Plan into Place, Pt. 1 (of 3)
# The Examples

Amalina woke with a sense of relief, clarity, and focus she hadn't experienced in a long while. She barely remembered Pia growing bored and restless and slipping from the bed, or her latest nightmare of the haunting and hectoring Lucinda Skeldar, or even the worry of tainted tea cups. At the front of her mind was something more important.

To her amazement, Amalina found lying next to her on the goose down mattress, a couple long pieces of paper scrawled with ink. Somewhere in the night, no doubt inspired by and in response to Janusch, and driven by her tidal worries—and powered also by an odd somnambulance brought on, apparently, by Lucinda Skeldar—Amalina had written out a kind of manifesto: a summation of her current predicament and a plan of action to overcome it all.

It began, in her tiny, precise—though clearly hurried—hand:

Lucinda won't let me rest tonight and neither will my thoughts. So let me set some down here on this secret page and get them organized. Then I can proceed tomorrow clear in what I must do. Because—I know, I know—the time has come for me to act …

Included in its body, much lower down, was a list of those Ladies of Title, her guests in the high castle, whom she must save at any cost:

<u>Friends, yet well</u>
1. Aria Ecci
2. Giordina 'Maria' di Oscina
3. Halma Inovala
4. Genevieve de Roye
5. Maibrigg Smeehaute
6. Elle VandeGarde
7. Claire Montraine
8. Elisavet Pattipo
9. Greta La Nevers

10.  Terza 'Fandine' Fleccevocarre
11.  Marie Daume
12.  Ivareta Bolso
13.  Berrille de Jeane-Miesse
14.  Cece Mineau
15.  Stasia Auster
16.  Charlotte Jottes Chemirouge-Guillat
17.  Eustine Keller
18.  Candace Multiford
19.  Dora Patin

Following that came a brief catalogue of the four who'd already changed and now resided below the castle and might be beyond saving, but she still needed to try:

<u>Friends, below</u>
1.  Pia Lampeda
2.  Noka Kunuru Sowa Iwebo
3.  Erin Epris
4.  Anne Brignol

With one soul mentioned, finally, still teetering between the two states, perhaps the most important on whom to concentrate her efforts:

<u>My longest, dearest friend of all</u>
Cristine Berzweck, sister in blood!

Left unsaid were the countless anonymous servants, also innocent and also worth saving. But naturally they came along with their charges, the Ladies of Title. She also noted with a short hum that she'd somehow left off Margeta la Brichese from the first grouping of names, and felt guilty enough to want to quickly add it. She didn't, but returned to the beginning to read the whole thing over several times more.

Part passionate screed, part meticulous call to action, which boldly incriminated her and Sadra's revolutionary should it be found by the wrong party, she would normally burn, tear to pieces, or otherwise destroy such a paper—so it could never come back to haunt her. But because she agreed with its every sentiment, even its omissions, and since she didn't remember writing a word of it—and tossing aside the errant thought it had been composed by someone else, who'd forged her handwriting, and left it there to baffle her, or send her off on the wrong path—she believed it was a direct communication from a deeper region within herself, perhaps her own soul, admonishing her for her earlier hesitations. And because the letter's origin was significant in that heavier way—from her unknown depths—she believed it might possess some of the good-luck energy she was feeling right now and so she could never dare destroy it, but would fold it away into the hidden pockets in her dresses. And she did just that, immediately after studying it, tucking it in beside her glasses and that other private talisman she possessed, the magic bone. But still, she was amazed she'd created it at all, and could not comprehend when she'd had time to in the restless night. But she could only thank herself for writing it. It was, she saw in the end, her solution.

A solution to the impossible!

. . .

Even before she was asleep Amalina had been wracked with despair at her position, the direness of it made oh-so real in her chat with Janusch. The simple fact was that the stakes could not get any more dangerous. Pia Lampeda was kind enough to Amalina, in her way, and it was comforting to have one of the Count's transformed Ladies as a friend, but she was only one in the rising quartet. And the others might not be as willing as Pia to side with her, or agree to remain 'civilized', considering what had happened with the orphanage workhouse. Or could she trust any of them at all, whatever they said or did? No matter. In time, if nothing were done to stop this progress of transforming his uncorrupted women, and the Count's dreams reached full fruition, his eyes would turn to Amalina, and she would be incorporated into their fold. Folded-in almost as easily as the others had been. She didn't see a way out of that dark future.

Also Sadra's revolutionary, Attila Bronk, *was* still out in the wild, preparing his assault. If he launched his attack—*when* he launched it—they would—all those men—be killed. And some of those ill-aimed men included her father. That tragic future seemed unavoidable, as well.

So there was no question, as her thoughts went in the night, that she must renew her efforts to neutralize the Count. Never mind the revolutionary's—and then Janusch's—dismissal of her plan, she had to firm it up, get it into place, and spring it before any of the more unthinkable scenarios above played out. She had to change those futures.

But what, the monotonous refrain crowed again, could be done?

As she'd wondered and wondered restlessly to find some way to counteract what was coming, turning from Pia and tugging the blankets over her shoulder—

*"You fool, you could have left!" yelled Amalina in her sleep. "You had your chance and didn't take it. You could have left. You should have left!"*

*Pia, hearing this, came round and said, "Are you talking to me?"*

*"There's no reason to stay, you idiot, but go, go!"*

*"How could you say that?"*

*Pia, not sure what to make of it, but feeling a pout coming on, slipped out, while trying not to take it personally.*

—the task seemed too impossible while still tucked in her bed. But when at some point Amalina's mind softened and fitted into her dreams, the impossible seemed less so. In her dreams she could swim against the fastest river and fly high enough to touch clouds. So what *couldn't* she do if she set her mind to it? Control something as powerful, as seemingly indestructible as the Count? Amalina, having witnessed personally the many failed attempts to destroy the Count—not to forget her own foolhardy stabs at it— could at least take pointers from the various, and often fatal mistakes revealed within those sad examples. There was that.

And knowing the Strange Man, a creature like the Count, *had* been killed, and that the Count, who'd arranged said killing, had not only explained to Amalina his own method on how to do it, but had been so confident enough in her ability to accomplish the feat that he'd asked her to give it a try, she was lifted by a wave of positivity about her prospects. It could be done. Oh, yes.

In fact, there were several pat principals she would need to follow.

. . .

The fantastic display of raw power in the Count's battle with the Strange Man; the destruction of Kyrgil Castle, the collapse of Kyrgil Mountain, and the flattening of the town of Kyrgil itself, had been terrifying. But the Count's strategy to destroy a creature like himself had been relatively simple, and it went like this. He'd known he could not beat the Strange Man outright, as the two were an even match. But the Strange Man, a warped buffoon, was overconfident and had believed to the core he could win a fight against any other creature on earth. So the Count had led the Strange Man to think he had done just that, that he had killed the Count (with poor loyal Vezel Umalasju taking the fall in Kyrgil; sacrificing himself for the ruse to succeed), thereby lulling his enemy into a smug, and false, sense of security. Relaxed and supine in victory, with nothing left to fear of the world, or so he thought, the Strange Man was then quietly smoked into passivity while he slept, where the real blow was struck. He fell to a stake and knife, two simple weapons, completely unawares.

*One must be clever like that*, thought Amalina, a smile in her sleep. Attack these creatures unexpectedly. Though they may be vulnerable to sunlight, and certain elements such as silver and fire, they have heightened awareness of these things if one were cheap enough to try. No, no. One must lower their guard first, before the attempt even begins. And how to do that?

With another turn, and a brighter, clever grin, Amalina's face dug into the cool pillow, her thoughts flowed as naturally wild as a stream, all impossibilities clearing out of the way, and she remembered instances in her career here in the castle, and recalled what she knew of the Count and creatures like him.

These things—for that is what these creatures were, *things*—were easily distracted. Perhaps it is the hyperactivity in their sped-up brains, but if there is enough of a fog set around them, it will sap their ability to move like lightning as they try to process all the threats against them. She'd seen that in Commander Kralov's invasion of the castle, where his many men had continuously blasted daylight through the building, focusing it like beams, and fencing in the Count wherever they could with a hail of bullets. Too much to handle at once. As well, and on a smaller scale, Genadie had elaborated on the Count's hatred of bees, describing the incident where his master had been immobilized inside the angry swarm's frenzied center, unable to deal with their—to the creature's mind—overwhelming chaos.

While the bees were never a mortal threat to the Count, in the end, Kralov's much deadlier attack failed only because of his second-in-command. They could have buried the Count in the rubble of his castle with their strategy and their explosives. But Piotr had needed to personally punish the Count for killing his brother, Roti, and that instant of hesitation cost everyone their lives. *There can be no hesitation!* The attack must be uniform, cold, and unrelenting.

And to match the Count *a plan had to be flexible*: Brave Erik Kosche had taken the Count head-on after a brilliant deception, holding Amalina out a window, pretending Amalina was the lovely and talented Katrina Flauna, threatening to drop her to the courtyard below, while the real Katrina escaped. Erik Kosche's strategy had worked for only so long, holding his rival at bay with fire and daylight, before night came; when his options extinguished.

So, as Amalina spun again on the goose feather mattress and readied herself for Lucinda to make her expected appearance, it was quite clear now: For the plot against the Count to succeed it had to have an element of surprise, it had to be somewhat confusing and unrelenting, and it had to be merciless in its delivery, but it also had to be supple enough to account for any unexpected turns by the Count, or mistakes or slip ups in the delivery.

The last part, the flexibility, was the most important because she had to rely on others for its success.

As she came awake, Amalina had read on the paper six names; six who were on her side in the castle, who she could count on in any plan:

Allies
1. Genadie
2. Aklan
3. Pia
4. Anka
5. Pils
6. Mr. Balbo (and his new pistols)

Despite the six names, Anka and Pils—the Count's main servants—were a little too rubbery with their courage. Conscripted into their positions, they still had thoughts of making it out of this service in one piece. And being from Ardeel, they weren't too canny, either. Nor to be honest were they physically up to most tasks. Perhaps that left four. She couldn't help but amend the list immediately.

Allies, amended
1. Genadie
2. Aklan
3. Pia
4. Mr. Balbo (and his pistols)

But maybe that wasn't so, she'd have to think about it. It felt mean to trim off Pils and Anka.

Regarding these soon-to-be enlisted partners, while Attila and Janusch— and even Ion Vokent's General Volante—had, in their turns, cautioned Amalina on the need for good, loyal soldiers, or she would face the enemy alone—a unanimous opinion she'd not ignore—with it she would take another shrewd bit of the revolutionary's advice: no element within the plan must know of the other until absolutely necessary. To make it frictionless, each agent had to believe they were vital elements to the cause, working alone for their own particular purposes.

Tossing on her plain dress now with renewed vigor, after hiding away her twin talismans—the manifesto/plan and the magic bone—Amalina realized the conversation with Sadra's revolutionary might have helped her in another way. It had forced her to hone her ideas. Where she'd seen the weaknesses in his plan and critiqued them to his face, he had located the failures in her own and broken it to pieces before her. But now, in her sleep, she'd taken those pieces and formed them into something more solid. And, to tweak both Attila's and Janusch's noses, it would include, among other mocked items, as listed in her own confident hand:

Items
1. the great hall chandelier
2. a dose of bees
3. the emergency bell
4. Genadie's weapons – stakes and knives
5. Mr. Balbo's pistols
6. the magic bone.

See if that wouldn't be so.

• • •

"Berry picking," Amalina sang at Aklan (Ally #2, she noted) when he came through the door holding his candle high. He must have heard her poking around the room.

"You sure this time?" he said, looking somewhat relieved she wasn't asking for a ball gown.

"Definitely. I have no use for the fluffy stuff today."

"I say! And up real early too, Pretty Princess. You had the dream again?"

Amalina nodded. She must have, she supposed. But she was already on to her plotting and planning, refining the details, and couldn't bother with his excitable distractions.

"Did you hear me writing last night?" she asked.

"Were you writing, Pretty Princess?"

"Seems I wrote a whole book almost, yet I don't remember any of it."

"I didn't see a light under the door until shortly ago," he said, immediately concerned. "And I didn't notice any in the night. And I would have. So you wrote in the dark, you think?"

"I hardly think that's possible," said Amalina, still not feeling touched by his worry. "I imagine I did it when you were asleep."

"But I'm on my guard at all hours for you, Pretty Princess! It would be impossible."

"You must have slept. Everyone sleeps." At his troubled look: "There's no fault in it."

"Or ... does it mean *she* took possession of you?"

"Who?"

"Your ghost, Lucinda Skeldar."

Amalina experienced a chill. "Who says she's a ghost?"

"Well then what is she, Princess?"

"A spirit. She's calling for revenge. But she isn't a *ghost*."

"How do you know?"

"Because she's in my dreams, not flying around my room."

"What exactly is it like, your dream?"

"I've told you before."

"Say again for me."

She did so, blue sky and all. She had no idea where this was headed, but doing so nipped her burst of enthusiasm and confidence. She had to get out on her own to put the finishing touches on how to approach her people before she tried her first real stab at the ally list. Not that Aklan would take much convincing, from the look of it.

"… but I wake up before Lucinda's head shoots up again," concluded Amalina.

"Oh, right," he said with a snap of his fingers.

There came a low, dull, resonating clang from behind the boarded window.

"Visitors?" said Amalina in surprise. "At this hour? In this season? Whoever could it—?"

"But that's the *service* bell," Aklan reminded her. "Not a proper visitor—"

"Still, at this hour? And now that might have woken up our guests. I really don't want to be seen, not yet. I just want to get out by myself so I can think."

"I thought you were picking some berries for us."

"Well, both."

"You'll be thinking about what, exactly, Pretty Princess?" he persisted.

"In time."

"You sure been thinkin' a lot," he seemed to complain with a playful frown but inquiring eyes. "You still won't tell me what happened down in Netz yesterday?"

"Nothing happened down in Netz yesterday."

"You never tell me nothin'," groused Aklan.

"In time. In time. And didn't I just tell you my dream? Now go make sure my route's clear."

"Yes, Princess!" smiled Aklan, bouncing back cheerily, as if he were in on a fun scheme.

*He'll be happy to have a bigger role soon*, she thought.

"You know, about that nightmare of yours," he said, before leaving, popping back into the room. "I keep telling you, you need to grab her! While she's still in the field and when she gets close enough, just rush the girl, throw your arms hard around her waist and pull her out of your dream as you wake up. If she flies out into the room, then she's a ghost."

"And if she's real. A real ghost?"

"Then ..." Aklan pretended to slam some weapon down on her head. "Wham! I'll get her."

He looked like a little boy again, wrapped up in a childish fantasy. It was a wonder he'd survived this long, she thought. Or maybe it was his sense of wonder that had allowed him to pass through all the unthinkable horrors like a gleeful child thrilling to a story told 'round a campfire; as if it were all as simple as one.

But Aklan had been in that corridor with Amalina when they came upon Noka in all her ghastly glory. Funny how he didn't seem to have been affected by it. Not at all. So now she wasn't sure how to regard him. As a potential agent? Or a whimsical innocent to be left alone? This was one of the things she would have to consider on her walk: *Cut Aklan in on the plot, or no?* Maybe the list would go down to three, she thought, the fact not really bothering her at all; now that she had a plan!

When Amalina finally left her suite—wrapped up in private thoughts, positive energy, and set on making it a good day; full of fun, a basketful of wild berries, and a solid strategy for how to approach her three or four allies on return—by having troubled herself with describing the dream to Aklan, she was oddly possessed with a notion that what waited outside was a pleasant, blue-skied summer day.

## 14

## A Plan into Place Pt. 2
## Mr. Balbo and the Special Delivery

On her way to the the courtyard, passing through *l'entrée grande*, Amalina met Mr. Balbo, of the Wanger, Regio, and Balbo group. Besides a couple sleepy servants Balbo seemed to be the only one within the large entry hall, and he appeared well-rested and wide awake for the time of morning it must be. When Balbo spotted Amalina, he squinted at her, to make sure he knew who it was, then smiled and proceded to slick down his white hair with a tongue-wetted palm. He often did this, unselfconsciously, at the sudden appearance of a pretty, titled young woman. Balbo bowed to her in a creaky, martial way.

"Good morning, Mr. Balbo," said Amalina, for some reason wishing he wasn't there, like he was a block put there to stop her. Since she needed him for her own greater purposes (Ally #4, she recalled), at first contact—the reality of it—she nervously clasped her hands together, making it look like she might drive right past him, or around him, or over him, or through him. She would not be stopping. This was too soon to meet; she had yet to work out the delicate proposition needed to ply him. "Should be a great day today."

"Should it?" he said with a look of surprise, sidestepping to allow her to pass. His eyes were opened wide at the thought.

"Of course!"

"Well, I ... um ..." he regarded her as if she might be acting strange, or considering whether *he* was in the wrong.

She stopped to shrug her light coat over her shoulders and pull on her hood.

"I see you're still wearing your new pistols in your belt," Amalina noted off-hand. She was glad to see those guns, weapons not under the purview of Captain Durok or the Count. Not in any castle inventory, and better cared for than Genadie's rusty ones. As she thought this, her mouth carried on: "Not sure they're needed at this point, though, Mr. Balbo. What could they be good for anymore? The sight of them might alarm or frighten some of our guests."

"Well," he mumbled, looking somewhat embarrassed that she'd noticed. "Some of our Ladies, yes I think so; frightened, alarmed. You might very well be right. But, I suppose, you never know when you'll need them, eh, Countess?"

Fortunately, Balbo left his comments there and didn't apologize, as he'd done on every occasion since that awful night—Noka's night—though the sparkle of an apology was there in his eyes—*"So very sorry I let that dangerous rogue give me the slip, Countess ... and to take my old pistols, no less!"*. She supposed she had a counter-sparkle too, telling him the apology was no longer sought for, nor welcome—*"You did fine, Mr. Balbo. At least you drove him away and he didn't kill me. I'd rather just forget it happened. Forget everything that happened."* She was more interested in acquiring him and his pistols at this point, than reminiscing.

"I can put those fancy pistols up, and keep them for you, if you'd like, Mr. Balbo," she offered with an innocent look.

He clutched at their handles protectively.

Amalina suddenly felt she'd missed her opportunity here with #4, muddled it with her usual worn dialogue and her stumbling offer. While she hadn't fully worked out her proper approach, if she didn't leave him soon, she might keep talking and make it worse. At the cost of her first recruit.

There was another look in Balbo's eyes now, as he glanced away from her and to the courtyard door.

"What *did* bring you down here so early, Mr. Balbo?" she asked to move things along, with a cheery lilt, and absently guessed the logical reason he was there. "The bell, was it? You *do* know there won't be a princess this morning." She chided him playfully, to dispel his awkwardness, "I don't think we should be expecting another Lady—a *new* Lady—again for some time, if at all."

"Milady, I *did* recognize the *service* bell and that it was not indeed an *arrival* bell," said Balbo, defensive, his back straightening and his whole body stiffening, as a thief who'd been accused unfairly when he hadn't yet begun to steal. "Wanger, Regio, and I are concerned at our dwindling cheese stock. I've ascended like a scouting rat to do an inventory of the delivery, you see," here he winked, and tried to wiggle his nose, "to assure them we are in the clear for at least another month."

"Very thoughtful of you," said Amalina, aware she'd dented his dignity with her little jibe, despite his wink and return joke to say otherwise. Balbo was a good man, she knew, despite himself, and she didn't mean to be cruel. She'd bungled it for certain, now. *Better get away!* She'd have a chance some other time, she thought, maybe in a more suitable location and under favorable circumstance. Just to paper things over, she thought quickly: "I knew there was a sensible explanation, of course, sir, than common ... um ... I would never think ill of you. Have a good day, *Colonel.*"

The honorific of 'Colonel' made him blush red throughout his whole head, so that he resembled an inflamed pustule. He couldn't help but smile that she'd remembered he'd once been an officer in some army somewhere, and so he closed his eyes and bent low at the waist. "*Countess*. But, wait—!"

When Amalina opened the large door to the courtyard she was blasted backward by a cold wind and stinging particles of snow and ice. He helped her battle the door to shut it.

"Thank you, Mr. Balbo! You're always a good help!"

"Always, Countess."

"You *will* always help me, won't you?" Amalina held her eyes on his. "Whatever the trouble."

"Always."

"*Whatever* the trouble?"

"I should think so."

"I might hold you to that one day, Colonel."

"Do so! But this weather is a bit of a bear at the moment, wouldn't you rather—?"

"I suppose I'll need my heavy coat," smiled Amalina, waving her hand to a servant.

"Or as I was going to say, perhaps I can save you again, Countess. I could keep you company right here beside the fireplace, and we'll see what they bring in."

"Oh, no, Mr. Balbo. I should be fine once I'm in the forest. I'm off to pick wild berries."

"Ah, wild berries! Splendid! Pairs so well with our cheese and wine!" He adjusted his hair with a licked palm. "No other ladies will be joining you on the hunt, though, did you say?"

Eventually, Amalina made her way out the door.

. . .

The priest Rosczy had returned to the high castle to renew the chapel services. Riding an unsaddled mule, he was followed into the courtyard by two massive four-horse sleighs. The sleighs had identical, tall, blocky back ends almost too tall to fit through the gate, and were enclosed by tied-down leather tarps, making them a curiosity, and garnering more attention from the handful of palace guards along the walls than the more prosaic, mum-faced priest.

On Amalina's way out of the main building, still taken by the pelting wind and the blanket of snow everywhere in the courtyard, she greeted Rosczy with a quick wave. He met her with a half-hearted one of his own— low and odd, seeming forlorn, almost as if he were waving goodbye—his lips angled off in a grim line. More grim than she'd ever seen him. Had he heard about what happened with Noka? The 'civil war' and slaughter of all her people? Or was he simply spent by a long trek through a pre-dawn blizzard? It *was* quite intensely cold. In the moment, she didn't consider that she might never see him again. And so Amalina didn't stop to talk, thinking: *for another time then, inside.* Could *he* be an ally? she wondered now, noting his potential along the same lines as Mr. Balbo. But she walked straight past him for the oversized sleighs, to pat the hot flanks of the horses.

Always enamored with draft-horses, these large, powerful beasts, Amalina couldn't keep her hands off them, whatever the weather. But with the steam coming off their brawny sides they looked wonderfully warm. And, she thought as she neared the first set, they could use some pampering after a trip up from Netz.

"*Lady Tepsji*," called a voice from atop the closest outer walls, almost sarcastically.

"*Captain* Durok," returned Amalina, also sarcastically.

"Early morning, enh? Come to check out the delivery, enh? Big stuff!"

Amalina nodded, and would ignore the captain further, as he would no doubt ignore her, and she went for the pretty horses. Touched their steaming, shifting bodies.

The driver of the first sleigh was a giant farmer stuffed in furs, who busily drank from a flask, white puffs of breath spouted out his nose on either side of the bottle. At first she thought he might be Janusch Timorak in disguise, she wasn't wearing her glasses, he was a bit of a blur, but it wasn't him. She moved on from the horses, circuited the driver's bench, then petted the tarp that covered the sleigh's massive cargo area. This produced an uproar of squeals and grunts.

Lifting, with a sharp crackling sound, the side of the frozen leather tarp, Amalina saw twenty or so pigs scramble around on the icy wood of the sleigh-bed. The grunting white-pink animals strived for the new opening, as if they thought food, which they were clearly starved for, was about to be dumped there. Behind them, in the middle of the enclosure, two cows lay serene and incurious to the scramble. Amalina fell back a step at the lunging mouths, but then giggled at the pink snouts shooting puffs of steam and snuffling at her hands between the wood bars. She touched a couple of the driest noses just to know what they felt like; something like animated mushrooms.

It was strange to see so many healthy looking pigs this deep into the winter when they would have been slaughtered and processed into jerky months ago. Where had the Count found so many of these prime animals so late? From someone's private stock? Were they a gift from the Cardinal?

"Yes, give them some love," said the driver, looking round the side from his riding bench. "So kind of you, little girl, to show your heart to those that are condemned. Bound for the slaughter, these are."

He drew his thumb across his neck and laughed, before taking another healthy swig from his flask.

She moved on to the next set of horses. She patted them as they nickered agreeably, studied their thick, damp hair under her fingers, and contented herself.

The two drivers on this sleigh did not look as cheerful as the one on the last. They wore helmets and had weapons loose beside them. They smiled down at her but not in a welcoming way as she continued to pet the heavy-shouldered carthorses. Under their drivers' stares, she didn't stay long, but moved on to the sleigh itself.

Touching the tarp, there were no sounds from within. She lifted a corner, wondering if it would be more pigs. Or perhaps pigs that had already been rendered, stacks of frozen pork. Something valuable that would have needed an armed guard. Amalina was confronted instead by the slack and sorrowful face of a man who turned to peer at her through iron bars.

She had seen such a face before, with the hollowed cheeks and empty, staring eyes; hopeless, and resigned to his coming fate. It was the face of the traitor on his way to the town square for execution.

The stink from this cage was worse than the pigs, it carried with it the sickening tart odor of human fear sweat. The early dawn light penetrated enough for Amalina to count at least fifteen men packed and shackled inside.

"Oh, hello Ms. Dalca," said Genadie, who had lifted the tarp from the other side. He counted off the lumps of half-frozen men.

"What is this?" she asked, coming around the back of the sleigh to meet him.

"Master has given me a task that can be trusted to nobody else," he boasted with a proud, grizzle-jawed grin. "He has decided to act as a better partner to the people of this land, to relieve them the burden and maintenance of the criminal population that crowd its jails."

"Where did they come from?"

"The *jails*, Ms. Dalca."

"But why would he want … ? *What* is he going to do with a bunch of criminals when there are Ladies of Privilege staying in this very castle?" Then Amalina added, with a note of hopefulness which she prayed Genadie didn't detect, because she was now filled with the intent to immediately begin circulating such unhappy information among those Ladies—*prisoners held inside the castle!*—as soon as this conversation was over; because that should get at least some of them running: "It will drive them right out of here!"

"Maybe a few will object," admitted Genadie. "But aren't you more than half the reason these men are here, Ms. Dalca?"

"What! Never!"

"Well, it was your idea … wasn't it?"

Amalina began to feel dizzy. The pigs and the convicts had arrived together. Did that mean—?

Genadie threw down the tarp with a disgusted flick of his wrist. "Not that they will do for us. All wrong. I suspect near death already."

"What do you mean it was my idea?"

"Not all of it, of course," said Genadie. "But you were the inspirational spark for our Master. You remember? Your bit of advice, along with the lesson we learned from Princess Noka?"

"And what's the inspiration, Genadie? What was my advice? Don't tell me …"

As he hobbled the long route back to his shed at the rear of the main building his whole body trembled with a jaunt of purpose.

"The Ladies—Master's *Special Ones*—don't have their full strength yet and they lack the range to hunt. Only Princess Noka will consume any old thing she meets in the forest. Oh, without question, she's game for it. But they *all* need to eat, don't they, Ms. Dalca? And we can't become a pestilence on Netz, nor to the unfortunate farmers in the valley … nor random workhouses. It would be too much. Our master and his guests at the high castle will be blamed if we aren't careful. But you know that. As it is now, word *is* spreading …"

"They—these poor men," she said with a sour look, "they're to feed our Ladies? Just like the pigs?"

"Need to be fattened first," said Genadie critically, with a shake of his head. "The men, that is. Their blood must be very thin. A low quality lot."

Amalina felt her stomach turn. Meanwhile Genadie was humming a tune.

"You were right, Ms. Dalca," he said with a remnant of his slight idiotic smile turned up to her. "You said you did not want the innocent to suffer. You suggested our Master help the common people rid these lands of the condemned."

"When did he tell you I said that?"

"Didn't you?" He scratched his chin and cocked his head. "These are *not* innocent men, Ms. Dalca."

When they entered Genadie's shack, Amalina's stomach dropped further. The Count was sitting in a chair wrapped all around in an oversized and heavy, hooded cloak.

"Master!" Genadie dropped flat onto the grey floorboards.

"How are they?" said the Count, keeping himself out of the light. "Inferior? But what can one expect."

"Yes, Master." He turned his head to sound the words clearly. "They'll need fattening before they can be of any use. Not a good constitution among them."

"The additional livestock will do the work. It shouldn't take too long … and we have time."

"You think of everything, Master," groveled Genadie at the Count's boot.

The Count's head moved at his servant's dramatic prostration and he must have spotted Amalina's feet beside the body. "Ah, my mouse. My favorite little mouse. Up early, are you?"

"I can't believe you're doing this, sir," said Amalina, feeling sick. She wasn't sure if the thought of these doomed men nauseated her, or it was that Genadie had so quickly returned to his nauseating servility by being given a real job again, not just serving as his master as fodder. "I *never* told you to do this."

"Of course you did," said the Count. "And what would you want instead? a countryside ravaged by your friends? Don't be squeamish, my little mouse, when facing the reality of your own perfectly reasonable and respectable plan."

"*My* plan?"

"A plan based on your constant harping and arguments, Ms. Dalca. But I've listened. Isn't this all for you? Now these pieces of meat are rapists and murderers, tramps and foreigners. The worst of this country and marked for death, anyway. I—or, that is, your friends—will now provide a great benefit to this country. They will deserve medals for their service."

"I don't think so," she said, her nostrils flaring. "One look at them and they wouldn't touch such … revolting creatures."

"Don't underestimate your friends," he laughed confidently. "And I'll have this shipment washed and readied so they make a fine presentation. But your sisters will not hesitate once they learn of the crimes these men have committed. They'll gladly give them their just reward," he made a tasty noise, "and reap from them a profit of their own."

"Where will you put them in the meantime, sir?" questioned Amalina. "All the other Ladies—the ones still innocent of your gift—will know what's being raised here within their company."

"Let me handle that. They'll know nothing of it so long as you keep our confidence. Which I rely on your better judgement to do; if only for the happiness of your friends who *do* have my gift. And I guarantee, to appeal to your softer side, little mouse, these degenerates—these vile wretches, who deserve nothing—will be treated comfortably and liberally and will enjoy, to the very utmost, their final hours, believing they are here as a reprieve and to be reformed—not consumed. They will think *they* are taking advantage of *us*. Of course."

"The governor knows what's to happen to them? Their real purpose here? He's gone along with it?" said Amalina, incredulous.

"What do you know of governments, little mouse?" sneered the Count. "Who said the governor knows anything about it? How do you know where I got them? Let's just say that those who have remanded these lowlifes to my custody and care, care little for their fate. But to keep their consciences clean there will be rumors that these men, at some point, tried to escape the castle and were killed in pursuit."

"You think of everything, Master," said Genadie from the floor.

"I know." The Count rose from the grey bench, tightening the thick black cloak around himself. He eyed Amalina. "This is *my* plan for how to deal with our current, troublesome situation, Ms. Dalca. Who knows what flies through anyone's head at any moment, but by recent events, these Special Ladies—who *you* brought to me—are either overly-enthusiastic and incautious, impulsive and indiscriminate, or they are *willful*, and therefore problematic for us. For they are *ours*. Do you have some other way out of our situation, one that you wish to propose, my little mouse? Do *you* have some *other* plan?"

"I can't think of anything, sir," she said, disgusted and mollified, resentfully so, staring down at Genadie's groveling body.

"Then what more could you want, Ms. Dalca?" begged the Count, his palms up in the air almost helplessly, but with a strange, enigmatic smile.

15

# A Sudden Detour:
# Count Tepsji's Plan

## I

*"What more could you want, Ms. Dalca?"* the Count's words circled dizzyingly in Amalina's head; their meaning shifting in terrible ways, from regrettable to worse. Her world seemed to have turned over.

He had a plan of his own.

Of course he did, he thinks of everything.

•  •  •

"He's gone," said Amalina, after the Count had vanished through a hidden exit in the wall. She switched to an obscure French mountain dialect which she and Genadie had found intriguing enough to study to fluency, and she was certain the Count knew nothing about; to him it should sound like gibberish, she thought, before continuing. "We need to talk about this."

"About what?" said Genadie dumbly, coming off the floor and brushing the dust from his patchy pants. At least he'd followed her choice of language; to him it seemed a playful decision.

But then she snapped: "You know exactly what! You're not bothered by any of this … this … this … *vile*—?"

"Now, Ms. Dalca—"

"Oh-hh-hh!" growled Amalina before he could say another word. "Tell me you aren't back to your old pathetic ways, Genadie; your groveling and simpering!"

"I don't know what you mean, 'groveling' and 'simpering'," he protested; surprised by her outrage after a pleasant and elucidating conversation with the Count.

The trouble was, Amalina had just seen one of Janusch Timorak's lessons! Played out before her eyes and enacted skillfully by her opponent. Amalina resented how Janusch's words of caution seemed to have infected her world view, skewed her perception so much that she saw it through his lens and sensed life as a balance of competing transactions; she could almost smell the enticing sweet jasmine vapors in the back of her nose.

"Oh, I get it," said Amalina, hotly. "You've been moping around forever about 'being worthless' at the castle, haven't you? Eh? And I suppose you've been out of sorts so long now, just because he gave you a little job to do he's brought you right back to heel."

"Ms. Dalca!"

"He's bought you!"

"Bought me?"

"You're calling him 'Master' again," she accused. "And I guess you've gone back to thinking he's Zeus, too? Is that it? Even if he defiles your precious Olympus by hauling into it criminals of the basest order, like these dreadful prisoners?"

"Sacrifices—"

"Even after he tried to have us killed yesterday?"

"Now that isn't true, Ms. Dalca."

"Of course it is true," she whispered in a staccato rage. "Stop lying. At least for my sake, stop lying to yourself. It should not require *incentive* for you to do what's right."

"Incentive?" he wondered, confused. "What's right?"

"I thought we had an agreement. You swore to me!"

"I can't imagine what you think I swore to you, Ms. Dalca."

"That we're on each other's side! That we'll protect each other! That you'll protect me!"

"Oooh, Ms. Dalca," soothed Genadie. "Of course I'll protect you. Never doubt that!"

"But you know what he wants to do to me! You know exactly *what*."

"Marry, didn't you say …?"

"He just about said it right there: he's going to kill me! And you aren't going to do anything to stop—?"

"Oh, now," said Genadie, his lower lip outthrust, though with eyes rounding in a joyful way, relieved, hopeful, almost in a laugh, as if she'd just told him a joke. "I wouldn't say *that*. Kill you? Oh, no. Master cares deeply for you, Ms. Dalca."

"*'Master'*," echoed Amalina in an aggrieved tone, "cares for me just like he did the other Ladies. Like he did Noka. And he does plan to do *that*, to me, eh? And he will do it. One night he'll come around and—"

"No, no," said Genadie, in a positive tone, "but you'll still be *alive*, you understand."

"Not alive, I'll be like him. And he'll have me eating criminals for breakfast!"

"But you *will* still be alive, see, Ms. Dalca." He was grinning as if he hoped she'd join him in the good news. "You will. And you and I can still talk and have our language lessons and—"

"That wasn't our agreement, Genadie," she snarled. "That's not protecting me! I'm telling you, I won't let him do it. Do you understand? If he tries to make me one of them, I will kill myself before he can. I swear it. And then I *will* be dead."

"I wish you wouldn't be so angry," said Genadie. "He doesn't see it as wrong, you know."

"I see: *he* doesn't see it as wrong," she sneered.

"Well, why do you?"

"If you're so forgiving about it. Would you let him do it to *you*?"

This gave Genadie pause, where his eyes gleamed and then dried, and then gleamed again, his lips wriggled and twitched like unearthed worms, part smiling part frowning. Maybe he *would* accept the rite, she thought, appalled.

"What about your wife, eh, Genadie?" said Amalina, before he could think too much more. "If he'd proposed to do it to Mala, would you have gone along with it?"

Now he frowned. His eyes blinked and squinted as if she'd just striped him with a whip.

"Well ... Mala ..." he mumbled. "That's not who *you* are ... are you, Ms. Dalca ... my Mala ... ?"

"That's not the point. You know what your answer would be, and you'd never let him do it to her. To *change* her."

• • •

Turning away from earlier events and to clear her mind, Amalina escaped to the aviary to take care of her messenger pigeons.

Among the many birds on the counter were four in a cage that were set to Sadra's revolutionary in Korr; what remained of the handful of pigeons Amalina was required to send as Attila's castle-spy. The ones she *must* send to him, loaded with notes of useful information, before he'd consider her free of her obligations to *the Cause*.

She wondered if this arrival of criminal stock would make for a piece of worthy information for the revolutionary. She didn't see how. Not without revealing their purpose, which might send him into a panic.

Seeing the pigeons' blank eyed, hungry looks in their cage, she recalled the men in the prison sleigh, stuck helplessly behind bars, unaware of their future. Against her will, Amalina contemplated what the prisoners' fate in this castle would be. And try as she might to shut it out, she pictured their grisly doom anyway: torn to pieces, strewn about the woods, stringy chunks of their meat caught in her friends' teeth. *And was this bloody hunting-scheme meant for her to join, too?* If the Count's plan was to continue and he gave her his gift, was this how Amalina was to survive forever onward?

Amalina couldn't want to leave the castle now more than in any other episode with this monstrous creature. And the thought of not having taken Janusch's offer seemed almost as senseless a blunder as returning from Paris. So stupid. She felt sick to her stomach, and could barely feed the pigeons out of antipathy toward the prisoners' sordid guilt, which she unfairly transferred onto the birds because they looked so similar in their cages with the same empty eyes.

Amalina abruptly opened the cage door and then the window, letting the fresh, cold and crisp wind swirl in. She'd just granted the birds their freedom. If they left now, they will have made the decision for her. With no pigeons left to send, her duties as a spy would more-or-less be met, and she would leave immediately. Even if she had to toss the bone in her mouth and run naked to the forest to make her escape, she'd do it.

She watched the pigeons with nervous expectation. But the freezing wind, now howling through the window, did not encourage them. They huddled together at the back of the cage. Going nowhere. She slammed the cage door and felt trapped again.

To punish them for their cruel decision she would leave the window open, letting them shiver until she returned for their next feeding. *May they be frozen to death!*

Before Amalina got too far, she hurried back and, with a guilty conscience and short apology to them, sealed the window.

Thinking her restless thoughts were a remaining product of Janusch's lackey's exotic tea 'additive', she had Aklan get her some hot water to drink to flush the pollutants from her body, then shut herself away in her room, blankets over her head.

After stewing with her anger for an hour, Amalina now realized that besides her race with the revolutionary she was also running one against the Count. A secondary race. And if she lost, if the Count beat her to the mark before anyone else reached their own, she would be eating prisoner—

*I could never do that, I could never do* that!

How could anyone?

*But what more could you want?* the Count's voice mocked.

## II

Amalina's upset was not undone when she spoke to Pia later in the afternoon, when the redhead crawled into bed and tried to comfort the pouting mound underneath the covers.

"I can't even consider killing someone … anyone," said Amalina, agonizing about the prisoners, their intended use, and what the Count expected of her. "… Not even people like *that*."

"Who would you consider?" asked Pia, idly curious. "Say, if you had to."

"Nobody! But it's even worse with *them*." Amalina felt near tears and a resentment toward Pia's cool indifference. "And don't you see how ridiculous it is: He once told me one of the most valuable things about me is I would never harm anyone, that I am a *blood innocent*. And yet if he changes me over, I'll have to kill. Kill, kill, k—"

"But you don't have to *kill* them. You said it yourself, you set the rules for our 'civilized behavior': only a little sample here and there. Nobody has to die if you don't like it, and nobody would *force* you to kill anyone."

"Just touching them, though," said Amalina, recoiling at the new prospect. "Imagine it. A rapist or a murderer's skin, putting your mouth to it, tasting him. Eating of his flesh. It's like you're accepting him, making his foul soul—and all his crimes—a part of you. Forever. Like an unholy, inverted sacrament."

"You're thinking too much about it," said Pia, petting Amalina. "And it's the blood we're after, not the skin or the soul."

"You'd do it?" Then, realizing her friend's tone: "You're *going* to do it?"

"I don't know. But you don't understand the hunger. What you just said, about their nature and how objectionable they are, wouldn't even occur to you once you've felt the need. Knowing how bad these men are might even make it more *acceptable*, you see, because it would feel like you're serving them some justice. Think what I did to the Germanian delegation when I learned they meant you harm. Doing the same to these criminals would be more justified. Wouldn't it?"

Amalina's stomach turned again, this time at Pia's blasé acceptance and embrace of animal slaughter, the easy justification delivered in her friend's pleasing voice. But there was more here. Never mind her sudden disgust with Pia—someone she had considered only that morning could make a great ally against her own 'Master'—it was obvious Pia Lampeda was a monster in her own right now; perhaps to the core. If there really was a race between Amalina and the Count, between Amalina putting him down or he converting her into him, Pia was on his side, rooting for the seduction to work. And if it worked …

... Amalina tasted blood in her mouth, from when she'd drank it from Noka's ritual cup, with everyone staring at her, seeing how she reacted. The Count thrilling at her first try.

How awful it was.

*That would be the rest of my life!*

. . .

*If one could call it 'life'.* Amalina considered this aspect, drifting off from the conversation as Pia gently stroked her. *Could one call it life?* That depended.

With Amalina's prolonged contact with Count Tepsji, the innumerable interactions when he was in his mode of human normalcy, and having experienced his wide range of oddball quirks and foibles, she could not think of him as anything other than an eccentric royal—or, under Genadie's influence, a landed, mercurial god—among whose many idiosyncracies included two pronounced ones: the immeasurable power of a minor diety, and a monstrous appetite for blood which occupied, surprisingly, only a fraction of his soul, if one could call it that, but gained control of him and burst out when he felt weak. That was the Count.

No matter how she tried, Amalina could not think the same of her changed friends, but suspected them instead as senseless—though canny— beasts using their old skins and previous regular behaviors and personalities as a screen to hide from detection; the outer shell thinning as time went on, with the bestial nature growing into line with the one that had created it. Their masks slipping as time progressed. Not themselves in the least bit.

This dual conception of Count as a living being and others as enslaved, mindless monsters, worked because from the very beginning, when Amalina had learned of the Count, he had always been this way, starting from the horror of it, and learning of his more human bits along the way. But for the Ladies, they'd begun normal as anyone else, only now his personality was dissolving them from the inside out; until they would be only him.

Not knowing if this was true, but because the potential was real, it was nothing to ignore, only to suspect, and to seek for signs of its truth. To never lower her guard once, or give up her suspicions of the enemy, or her probing of them for those signs. As this was a matter of preserving her own private being.

*Her own private being.* This above all else, Amalina wished to retain. Personal freedom and will to action. She could think of nothing more horrible than if, by taking the rite and converting, one lost absolute command of oneself. Her experience in life as a child had begun much this powerless way, facing tragedy beyond her control, and being put to work in the family business as soon as she could lift her arms and walk, and push a broom or brush, or carry a bucket of water, or knead some dough. But at least that had been a happy, contented passivity compared to what came next. She felt her life had been completely stripped away once she'd met the Count. All was in service to him. And to have that become her life for an eternal length? If not his will, but to be subservient to an all-consuming *need* and *instinct* was unthinkable. She imagined it like when Genadie—when he was still an abject lackey to the Count—had dragged Amalina to the western kingdoms against her will, she locked in chains in the middle of the carriage floor, helplessly watching the world pass outside the windows, unable to guide the course or to call out for help. If what she feared of the altered life were true, that is what it would be like forever! No, no. Amalina already resented how her actions and movements were hampered by an ever-watchful Count, and how she could not develop true friendships, and every real stride she attempted had to be—was forced to be—indirect, cautious, and clever. If her fear was true of this change, she could not want to *ever* take that final, fateful step.

So then, for the Ladies who'd joined him: constant vigilance for their untruth, and always suspicion and doubt!

Which was difficult. An inhuman deception would be hard to believe with Pia Lampeda; the Roman Lady almost always affectionately at her side in the most familiar way.

## III

"That first time with the delegation … um …" Amalina paused, her voice remarkably calm, returning to the moment, picturing Pia—who was still petting her—with vicious animal eyes, tearing away the bearded neck of the delegation's sheriff with her elongated teeth, "when it happened, you didn't know how to control yourself. You were starving. With this need. This hunger. But you wouldn't do it again, right? You've felt sorry since … and apologized for it."

"I understand what you're saying," said Pia delicately. "But it really is different. Haven't you ever had a favorite pet during a long and hungry winter? Of course you'd *never* eat them. But there *is* the thought … from time to time … And when the spring comes you thank heaven you did not." She rubbed Amalina's shoulder, and looked reflective. "But anyway, what's to bother anymore about what I do, and what's it all to do with heaven? My entry there is no longer a consideration, now is it? And it's only an offense in the beyond, not here where I'm staying. So what's the crime? Not saying I would, Katty. But it really *is* different."

Amalina scowled and cursed, hugging herself tight and rolling away from Pia.

"Oh, don't be mad," soothed Pia, with a gentle laugh. "Curious how much you've tried to correct our behavior, to modify us, and we've come a long way to meet you—"

"We?"

"Well, it's being tried, isn't it? And only a week or so ago, didn't I say you could civilize me? I welcomed it and you seemed to be satisfied. But now that the method, which you yourself advised for the Master of this house, has been taken up, by him, it's a medicine you'd refuse? Kind of silly if you think about it. But maybe it's just cold feet; now that you're looking straight at it."

"Looking at it realistically you mean, the reality of it."

"Realistically, though? You're acting as if there *is* a higher moral choice to be had here, Kat. But what if there isn't a choice at all? Realistically. What if when we die, that's all there was? We're just beings of solid flesh and it all comes to an end when we cease? No final judgement and no heaven. Then this route of escape that I've taken—and which you're being kindly offered, nobody is forcing it on you—just becomes a way to prolong that which is enjoyable. And so then what would be the point of denying it; and yourself? What more could you want?"

*What more could you want?* The Count had said that very thing, with a strange smile, little more than an hour ago.

"A bit of neat logic you picked up from *him*?" accused Amalina.

"No, no," said Pia. "This puzzle I've been working on since the very beginning; when I was bored at church and my mind wandered and my parents would pinch me to stay awake: *What if there's nothing else?* Then these religious, dogmatic rules of morality become arbitrary and pointless. Hm? It *is* a question. And a different answer would change the whole equation. You must admit that."

Amalina tried to see it Pia's way, to envision life from a higher—if earthly—perspective. But she'd been taught the reality of her religion and its permanence by the minister, and Sadra, and her father while growing up; presented its comforting explanation on the death of her mother, and how that piece of her personal tragedy fit into the grand scheme of the universe. To have the universe suddenly change shape, coldly so, where the tragic piece, large as it was, would now be robbed of meaning because it did not exist in a greater spiritual structure—a structure which also did not exist— was an impossibility. She knew Pia's argument wasn't improbable and could be studied and weighed at some other time. But it could not happen here and now, when everything felt like it *did* hold meaning: there should be, must be, and *is* a heaven above, to keep a good order below.

Anyway, Amalina felt sore about the whole subject of introducing these prisoners as acceptable victims, and couldn't help but think the Count was cruel and purposefully using her own words against her; which was unfair besides.

But it *had* been her idea, hadn't it?

And while Pia's arguing in this sophisticated way made it impossible to think of her as a 'mindless monster', again she couldn't help but wonder if it wasn't somehow *He* speaking through her, a program he'd left in her shell.

"Blast him," muttered Amalina.

"D'j'you say something?" said Pia into Amalina's ear; they entwined, she half asleep. They must have been drifting off.

"Just one more question," said Amalina. "Don't take this the wrong way, but … I'm just curious about what it's like. This change. The 'need' you talk about."

"Yes?"

"You didn't have it before."

"Maybe I did. Who can say? It's just so much more."

"But you would say Noka's changed, wouldn't you? And into something she never really was? I don't know, something completely different, it seems, than the person we ever really knew?"

"Not really. What are you asking? Are you saying *I've* changed?"

"Not exactly."

"Then what?"

"You're changing your hours. Don't sleep at night anymore."

"Maybe a little."

"And you used to wrap your hair around me. Remember? Like a blanket. You haven't done that … since …"

Pia immediately did so, spreading a scarlet curtain of hair across Amalina's shoulder and arm. "Oh, I didn't know that you liked when I did it. I never really thought."

"I did. I do." Amalina threaded her fingers between Pia's red tresses, not sure they weren't now a calculated net more than a genuine show of affection.

"What's that look, Kat?"

"Do you *think* you're the same, really? After all this?"

"Of course."

"Do you still *feel?* Like you did before? Emotions, that is?"

"What a thing to say."

"Well … do you?"

"This is more than one question," said Pia. Then she nodded her head forward with a light smile. "Would I be in this bed if I didn't feel?"

"I don't know," said Amalina, sincerely. "Would you?"

"This is starting to get offensive," said Pia, with a mock pout. "What you must think of me! I'm beginning to think *you* don't have emotions for *me* and you're just trying to cover."

"But that isn't true. It's just that I'm trying to understand, and how could I know what you're really thinking and feeling?"

"How can anyone ever know such a thing of anyone else?" answered Pia. "How can *I* believe *you*? You just have to take their word for it. Or do I have to prove it or something now? Is that what you're asking? Too bad there aren't any dragons anymore that I can go and slay for you to prove my love." Pia made a face: "So what should I do to prove it, pitch myself off the nearest mountain? You first."

"Sorry, I—"

Suddenly Pia grabbed Amalina with both her arms, reeling her in, a naughty grin on her face, tickling her with cool fingers. "Come here, I'll show you my feelings."

. . .

Oh, what a conniving beast the Count was! Where Amalina aimed to build out her plan against him, he'd already been constructing his around her: corralling Amalina with his treacherous schemes the way a storm, closing in too suddenly on an unwary hiker, might force them in one direction and then another, until their only escape is a dry narrow canyon—which appears the best and safest route—but where they'll find themselves boxed in, trapped, and overrun by the storm floodwaters.

*Oh, Pia, Pia!* If Amalina left now, and Pia was still herself—or at least a good portion of her remained so—she'd break Pia Lampeda's spotless heart. And Pia had come to the castle and then had taken the rite only because of her; it would be unfair and coldhearted to do so. And in the same act, she'd also be abandoning Cristine. Unthinkable. And all the same, to abandon her other, still innocent guests, no matter how unworthy they might be, without first alerting them to the dangers, would be cowardly. But say she could see her way around those snares, by claiming self-preservation above all, by doing so, and thereby, at her betrayal, unleashing the wrath of the Count on her father, it would be the most selfish act of all! No! Impossible! She could not do it. None of those things she'd ever wish to be, or have it thought about her.

The Count had known this all along, of course. And he'd driven her further and further into his trap, blindly, until now, upon realization, she saw the waters rising. But nothing more could be done about it! There was no escape!

Unless she could just ... do as he wanted? ... accept his offer?

*Accept it?* she wondered.

Was that *really* a way? To give in?

Never mind *him*, it felt a bit like freedom there. No stress. Open air. Where all the dark clouds suddenly parted.

And there was a clear, bright blue sky.

IV

Amalina leaned over the town of Netz with legs that went on for hundreds of yards—as tall as the Count and the Strange Man had been when they'd battled over Kyrgil. She stood astride the tallest of Netz's mountains, sure this is what it felt like to have *the power*. And how exciting would it be then to change into a bird or a different creature, as Pia now could. But she needed to refresh herself, she felt her body weakening as the moments passed, her power draining. And suddenly below her Genadie waved from the highway and called out, hand cupped at the side of his mouth, as he marched the ugly and awful prisoners down from the castle. "Eat! You must eat, Ms. Dalca!" he cried. And she knew she must eat, no matter how vile they were. She *needed* the power.

*"No! This isn't me!"*

"Of course it is!" crowed Lucinda Skeldar. "This is the deal. You must eat like Noka! This *is* who you are! What they want to turn you into. What you *will* turn into."

Before Amalina could have another thought, her arms, longer than the highest of trees, had swept down and she caught the prisoners by the handful. *She* was the one to eat them. Not Noka. Not Pia. Not anyone else. She shoved them into her mouth, any feeling of guilt flung away. They were so tiny, it was like eating bugs. Not as unpleasant a meal than if they were larger—larger than she was—and she could see them whole, and know exactly where she was biting in. She just ground her teeth against their slick, crunching bodies.

But the taste! Like wet, dusty linen with a touch of mildew to them.

Amalina woke with a corner of a pillow in her mouth.

*What a way to wake up*, she smirked, feeling the day was already trouble, and now this nightmarish afternoon daydream? Or was it premonition?

"I don't want to be like them," muttered Amalina. "I don't want to be like that."

"If you don't stop him soon, that's exactly what you'll be!" shouted Lucinda. "Or else you'll end up like me! Those are your only two options. Your only *real* choices. And one of them would make you just like my assassin. Think on that … and get my revenge, already!"

Amalina looked about the dark room. "Did I just … ? Did I just pull you out of my dream, Lucinda?"

"What's that?"

Amalina looked to her side. Pia wasn't in the bed.

"Where are you?" she asked Lucinda.

"Right here, watching you."

"Are you a ghost? Or a specter? Or …?"

"I'm me."

"But *what* are you?"

"Do you suspect me of something? If nothing else, think of me as your conscience. You must get my vengeance, not *join* them. Why do you persist in talking to them? Why are you listening to them, Amalina, at all?"

"But if I was holding onto you and woke up," said Amalina, "and I pulled you out of my dream, would you be alive again?"

"These aren't the questions you should be asking, Amalina. You should be killing who murdered me."

"So you *are* dead … But I am trying, you know. And he isn't the one responsible. Did you know that? Do you know who AXP is?"

"Who?" cried Lucinda in frustration. "I don't see you working on anything at all. You're still here. You place your head on a pillow in this bed every night. What does it take, Amalina? You shouldn't need *incentive* to do what is right!"

Amalina blushed at those words—her own words—rebounding on her and grew angry. "How dare you say that to me? You've no idea what I've been doing for you!"

"No I don't. If you're not all talk, get to work. I want to see real action. You are mine, and you must do this now."

*You are mine?*

"Is that really you?" huffed Amalina.

"What?"

"Come out so I can see you," she challenged. "So I know it's really you."

There was a hush, a menacing pause, as the air seemed to chill and contract within the room. And Amalina realized suddenly maybe she didn't want to see what was to come. What if Lucinda did appear? Would it be Lucinda's sad, pale face, or would it be the headless body, with a meaty red stump of a neck between the shivering shoulders, blood running from the round of its open veins?

"No, never mind," said Amalina, quickly. "You don't have to. But you have to understand, you aren't my only priority. But it is coming soon, I promise."

"How am I not your only priority? You stood there watching me die, watching him kill me, and said nothing. You might have saved me. You *owe* me. You owe me like no one else! Enough. Already. Get. My. Revenge."

A bee zigged by, and she could smell the field of grain—or was that jasmine?—hear it swaying in the warm wind, and the image of it flickered over the room.

*Oh, I'm still in the dream*, thought Amalina. In the moment, a realization appeared along with the changing scenery: *And this is still* another *race I'm in, I suppose*. A third race, for Lucinda's revenge. Then she said into the air: "You aren't helping."

"Enact your plan!" screamed Lucinda, as if *that* would help. *Do it before he does*, was left unsaid.

At least Lucinda's last scream woke Amalina.

## 16

## A Plan into Place, Pt. 3
## The Recruits

"What do you think?" asked Amalina.

"It's huge," said Aklan, as they both stared up at the enormous chandelier. "And real high."

"Well, that's because you're short."

"I'm not that short," he said, sounding wounded. He stretched upward in his tight servant's outfit. "I'm almost as tall as you now."

"Well, even for me it's high, I suppose," admitted Amalina. "But that's part of the point."

They looked at it hovering over the great hall with open mouths and a bit of awe—the immense piece of wood, created in a remote time, shaped like the wheel of some mythical giant's chariot. Having avoided replacement by the more fashionable and lighter, narrow-metal constructs found in the western courts and palaces, the chandelier was suspended over the stone floor by a web-work of heavy iron chain; which met higher above at something like a pulley, where the webbing connected to a longer, stouter single chain used to raise and lower the piece for cleaning, maintenance, and to light its hundreds of candles. Amalina *had* once thought of using the great hall's chandelier to crush the Count (method #1 on her list). Having known of men being crushed by ceiling beams, Amalina imagined by just throwing the chain's release at the wall, the chandelier would drop on a pre-positioned, unaware Count; right on his head. To her great delight, she'd imagined him squashed like a stewed tomato.

The greater mystery at the time was how she could lure the Count to the rarely used hall and position him directly underneath it. Amalina had pictured herself marrying him in a private ceremony, a marriage contrived with some unimaginable, completely implausible reason. And when he joined her under the chandelier to take her hand, in full witness of the greatest religious leader in the land ... Crash! But even at the time she knew it would have to be some other ploy than their preposterous wedding. She didn't want to mash herself to bits alongside him. But, as her thinking went on, how he got there didn't matter. All that mattered was to get him there without him noticing the quivering hammer of Thor right above his head and what was about to happen. Then make it happen.

That was before. Since that time she'd seen the Count in action too many times to believe it would work. His hearing was so sensitive, he would hear the snap of the catch at the wall, and the whir of the chains zipping through the various pulleys. His speed and reflexes were so superior, nimbler than a fly, he could almost dematerialize and then rematerialize at the bottom of the mountain before the chandelier smashed into the stone floor. But having also seen him lobbing boulders and bringing down mountains with his incredible strength, she knew that he could also simply stay put and toss the wheel aside as easily as waving off a falling leaf.

Still, the idea persisted in Amalina's head. Almost as relentless as Lucinda and her demands for justice. She kept picturing the chandelier in her head, and her brain scrambled to solve the many faults of using it as a weapon. Troubled by the way it tickled and burrowed into her thoughts, she puzzled over why it did so. And eventually she settled on the explanation that the great hall's chandelier, with all its chains, reminded her of the wheel in the cellar with the wailing woman fastened to it. The Count and Genadie had somehow trapped that woman, who was a creature like him, on that spinning wheel and bound her there with silver chain. Something inside Amalina saw the chance to achieve a kind of symmetry, or thematic justice if she could end the Count's reign with a wheel and some silver links; it became a minor obsession to get it to work.

In time, after hours spent in deep thought when she should have been sleeping, Amalina had created an elaborate fantasy which appeared plausible in weaker moments. The wheel itself would just be the delivery system. The chains would be his undoing. The iron chains of the chandelier would be replaced by silver ones. When the chandelier dropped it would capture the Count in its supporting web, and then he'd be buried by more silver uncoiling from above, which he could not easily escape. The silver would shrivel him and strip him of his energy as it did the woman. And then Amalina could bind him to that wheel, and lift it to the ceiling again, and send it spinning, spinning, spinning; he crying out in pain, as the wailing woman had for far too long.

So now, Amalina knew no dreams, no afternoons spent sulking in bed, could put off Sadra's revolutionary from throwing himself—and her hometown—against this constant death machine. Even with a warmer third route of escape opening for her—easy, tempting, and unthinkable as it was to join his side—Amalina's only real option was action. Stick to the plan. Get her allies on board. Prepare and put everything in place; at the ready for when.

She would thank herself later.


• • •

Aklan was an easy sell for a thrilling adventure. He was more concerned with its logistics.

"It *is* pretty high," he squinted warily at the distant circle of oak, then measuring the gap, then imagined riding the thing. "Um, uh, just so you know, after what happened down the privy … nearly killing myself falling out the castle, I'm not as keen on heights anymore, Pretty Princess."

"But you don't need to climb the thing," she explained "I just need you at the release, and to make sure you aren't seen at it." Amalina held out the magic bone to Aklan. *Incentive*, she heard Janusch declare proudly. She shook it off; this had been her idea. "A reward for helping me with the chandelier issue."

"You're giving it to me?" he said, his eyes wide, transfixed on what she was holding. "I am helping you really, aren't I …?"

"You've become a keen expert on hiding. Which is kind of what I'm counting on."

"But I can't believe you're going to give it—"

"For when the time comes," said Amalina, poised to place the bone in his open hand, which was shaking eagerly to receive. "You understand? If it comes time, it's just you and me. And I'll need all your help. If you fail, nothing'll work. Don't make me regret it."

"You can count on me, always," he said, licking his lips as he stared at the bone he'd once broke but was now repaired and ready to go again, coming back to him. Then he looked up, with a weird gleam in his eye: "But didn't you say Genadie flooded the Count's bed chamber with smoke to kill that other one?"

"Yes?"

"Why can't I just do *that*? I'd chop off a head, no problem. And with this thing I could go sneak in and—"

"Because," said Amalina with a sigh, "if we try something like that, the Count would be right onto it. That was *his* plan. We have ours—"

"*Yours*—"

"—and if we do this right, he'll never see it coming." She began emphasizing her points with downsweeps of the bone, so that it nearly touched his waiting palm. "Now, when I've made sure everything's in place, and when the time comes and he's standing directly under the chandelier, you're just going to let it all drop. Never see it coming. And I'm thinking I'll add some bottles of Netz lake water around its rim, and some extra chain too, so when the chandelier hits, the extra chain will be thrown onto him, more and more and more, and the silver water will soak him, even through his clothes. Really agonize him, eh? so he can't move at all."

She could see the glorious scene play in Aklan's eyes. All her musing painted it clearer in his head. He wore a huge, bloodthirsty smile. She placed the bone into his hand and he gaped at it, not closing his fingers, still amazed he was being trusted with it after what happened before.

"Are you sure, Pretty Princess?" he asked, looking to her.

She nodded. "Just do what you're supposed to. No telling how much power is left. I can't have you running off, like in—"

"Never," he said. "I learned my lesson. Oh, I promise you. I'll do it all bang right, just like you say." He had another thought: "But, Pretty Princess, where are we gonna get silver chain?"

"I know," said Amalina, thinking breezily of the wailing woman on the wheel. "Hmmm, yes, maybe we could get some off the woman. That should be easy enough."

"And how can we string it on the chandelier without it getting noticed?" asked Aklan, skeptically, still looking for faults. "Pils and Anka clean the thing, remember. They're the ones who light the candles. They'll see everything."

"That's not a problem at all."

"No?"

• • •

"The Count leaves the castle for extended periods of time," Amalina told Anka and Pils, after she'd tracked them down in the dusty cellar. By their surprised faces, it looked as if she'd caught them doing something wrong instead of sweeping, which was what they were doing. "And if you've noticed, he's been disappearing more and more lately."

"Too bad he comes back," said Anka, only to flinch and duck and hold her broom in defense as if the man in question might sweep down from the ceiling at her. He didn't. He wasn't in the castle. Amalina had made sure he was gone on one of his mysterious jaunts again before she renewed her recruiting drive.

"No need for that," said Amalina with a charitable smile.

"No, milady," they both answered, eyes rounded.

"Has he told you where he disappears to?"

"No, milady," both in unison again.

"No?"

"No, milady." Sidelong glances traded between them.

"Very well," said Amalina. "From now on you'll inform me whenever Count Tepsji leaves the castle. At some point, during one of his absences, when I deem opportune, you will help me lower the chandelier in the great hall and leave Aklan and I to work on it."

"Yes, milady," they chorused without expression, though they glanced at each other once again.

"If you ever wish to bring it down after it is back in place, you'll have Aklan help."

"Yes, milady."

Amalina stared at them, judged their nervousness, or curiosity, and did some calculations in her head.

"You might notice that some things have changed about that chandelier, after Aklan and I have been at it. The chains different, wine bottles placed around the rim, and other such things we may add. You'll take no notice of it. And never … *never* … mention it to your master. This is my wish, and this is your command."

"Oh, yes, milady," said Anka. They both nodded. It seemed that what Amalina said was important to them and not to be questioned. But would they really not report it to the Count?

"Do you want to know why?" asked Amalina, eyeing them both.

"If you wish to tell us, milady," said Anka, politely, subserviently. "There's no need."

"I'm going to share with you a secret."

The two said nothing but waited.

"As you know, silver is outlawed in this country. But in my travels in the western kingdoms, I've come to love it. It's my weakness. As well as silk. And certain drink. I don't want the Count to know about such things or to concern himself with them. I feel the chandelier will be the perfect hiding place. He hardly goes to that room and I doubt he'd ever notice the chandelier was there, not being in his direct line of sight. It's not like he needs its light. The candles on it will more probably irritate him when they're lit and he'd ignore them, and so overlook what's up there with them, you understand? Like my silver."

"Yes, milady."

"So that is my secret," concluded Amalina. "You two will keep it for me?"

"Oh, of course. Yes, milady. Quite safe with us. Didn't have to tell us, certainly, but it's locked tight. We'd never tell *him*. You secret's our own, milady."

Speaking of secrets, Amalina remembered weeks ago finding Anka and Pils talking quietly between themselves about something they felt they should reveal but were afraid to do so. What kind of secrets would they keep from her—*were* keeping from her?

"And in the spirit of openness, do either of you have secrets *you*'d like to share with me?"

Anka fidgeted first.

"Anka? You've something?"

"Well," said Anka in a shy voice. She worried her lower lip with her teeth. Pils stared at her, horrified, but hung on her next words. "Well, to be honest … milady …"

"Go on."

"And this is the last of it, I swear to you. There's nothin' else."

"I haven't all day, for pity's sake, Anka."

"I suppose … well, I suppose I do have a fair helping of silver of my own," said Anka, sheepishly. "Some nice necklaces that have been passed down through my family. Always worried he might sniff it out. Might I store it up there, too, along with yours, milady?"

. . .

Her confidence rallied, Amalina now turned to the more difficult, but crucial players in her scheme. Sticking to the revolutionary's admonition of secrecy, and that each individual agent must be ignorant of any other, and have their own private reasoning to join in while seeing within their leader a unique motive as well, Amalina cornered Genadie in his grey shed and took up their old argument; her heart beating faster at the thought she might actually pluck away the Count's most fervent defender, almost in direct retaliation for how he was collecting her friends just to control her.

Amalina whispered quickly as Genadie stared at her from his table, spoon clutched in his hand, bowl of soup growing cold: "Listen, this isn't a game anymore. Do you still have those special weapons? You know the ones. The ones I found in our old traveling carriage?" She meant the specialty knives and the stakes, some of which he'd used on the Strange Man. Genadie looked around nervously. "You didn't throw them away, did you?"

"Uh …" he hesitated. "Why do you want to know *that*?"

"We're going to need them. Now more than ever."

"Em, what for, Ms. Dalca?" his voice quavered.

"Against one of these women here, eh? If they decide to come after you or me. Think of Noka Iwebo, and what could have happened to us if she hadn't stopped."

"Noka?" said Genadie, wide eyed with shock. " … One of the Ladies? Us? Why? The Master would certainly protect us—"

"Like he did when he left us all on our own, to fend for ourselves against Noka? Protect us like that, you mean? Or like when he sent us down to Netz?"

"Now, Ms. Dalca—"

"And what if they run out of prisoners to eat? Think about it! Who'll he feed them next if their supply suddenly runs out?"

"Ms. Dalca, no …"

"Yes! He's losing control here, Genadie, if he hasn't lost it already. Don't you see that? How many has he made so far? Pia, Noka, Erin Epris, Anne Brignol? He is outnumbered, and he'll soon be overwhelmed."

"Ludicrous," argued Genadie, looking worried but hopeful. "Master's much more powerful—"

"Ha!" she interrupted this thought. "Now, do you still have the weapons or not, Genadie?" Then, at his look. "*Where* are they?"

"In safe keeping, of course. But what is so important about *those* weapons, anyway? Why can't we use just any old one that looks like them, and with a sharp blade?

Amalina nodded. "What about my magic bone, eh? Looks like any old bone, doesn't it? But you and I know it does a whole lot more than a piece of kitchen scrap. Eh? The Strange Man gave it to me. And didn't the Count give you those weapons that did him in? Who's to say there isn't something in them, some enchantment that we can't see with our eyes. Better to use the things that have accomplished the deed."

When he didn't look entirely convinced, or was trying to push his doubt on her with a lowered brow, she added: "You could be right, but why take the chance? I know you know what I'm saying. There *is* a reason he gave them to you to use, there *is* a reason he told you to get rid of them when you were done. And there is a reason you haven't done that part yet, but have been holding onto them. Saving them."

"Oh … umm …"

The argument was decided.

"And what about your emergency bell?" Amalina went on. "We'll need that too, so we can let each other know if we're attacked. Did you get it back from Captain Durok yet?"

"Ms. Dalca, please, really though … our Master's Special Ladies—?"

"We don't have enough wheels in the cellar to strap them on, do we? What then, if they should run amok and he's gone from the castle, as he's been so often lately? As he is right now! What then, Genadie, if it's just us two alone against *them*?"

Genadie's eyes fluttered, his stubbled chin moved from side-to-side as if he didn't understand what she was talking about, but also agreeing: they didn't have enough spinning wheels on which to chain all the Special Ones.

"But I'm also talking about *him*, too, of course," said Amalina, with a heavier, more forceful whisper. *Now was the time*. Channeling Sadra or Sadra's revolutionary, she leaned in, touching his arm: "Genadie, I'm not asking you to do anything I wouldn't do. I've stood up to him for you before, just as you have for me. We *are* in this together, you and I. And I know you *will* do the right thing if it comes to it. *When* it comes to it."

"What are you saying, Ms. Dalca?" grumbled Genadie in his hoarse voice, spooning up some colorless, odorless soup to distract himself. "I wish you wouldn't press me. You know how it pains me so."

"I'd kill anyone for you if you were in danger," said Amalina, grabbing his spoon hand for effect, "even if it's *him*. I'm only asking for you to do the same now. And it doesn't even have to be killing, eh? especially not for him. But if *we're* in trouble, why *not* trap him, like you did with that poor woman on the wheel? And only use the weapons if we have to. It only makes sense. To save ourselves."

"I suppose …" He then said, in a low scratch, "Master put her there, though, y'know."

"But you helped him. Won't you help *me*?"

Again his eyes batted and twitched. It looked like he might agree, or he might not. Or he might break. She wished she could have had Janusch's special tea right about now to get the truth out of him. That would have settled things. But for right now she wouldn't push him any further.

• • •

Pia Lampeda knew of the brewing revolution in Korr and had yet to say anything of it to the Count. Which meant she was keeping Amalina's secrets. Maybe there was something hopeful in it. Was there? With Pia's more direct bond to Count Tepsji, this recruitment would be trickier than Balbo, or maybe even Genadie. But it was necessary. So Amalina arranged for a quiet, private, intimately domestic moment in which to make her moves. They were in Amalina's bedroom, Amalina sitting on a chair, with Pia standing behind her, brushing her hair, eyes half-closed, relaxed and unsuspecting, when she'd begun her approach.

"You do understand I can't have my father die," said Amalina to Pia, cautiously, carefully. "I told you the people are unhappy, and that there's at least one revolutionary out there."

"Yes," said Pia.

"My father will be caught up in it and come to rescue me. Just as your father would, if he knew what was happening here, and with you being … *taken*. I'm sure he'd come from Rome with a whole army for you."

Pia's breath hitched at the mention of her father—or was it that Amalina had said she was 'taken'?

Amalina didn't turn just yet, it was easier to talk to Pia this way, with Pia behind her and out of sight. Staring at the candle on the nightstand, then out into the room's darkness, Amalina could have been talking to anyone. Or just practicing. With nothing to risk.

If Lucinda were somehow watching this scene, Amalina was sure she'd be appalled at the soft intimacy, not knowing what was coming.

"And if—and when—the revolution comes here to challenge Count Tepsji, or to rescue me, they'll all die. All of them. And it won't just be my father who comes, it will be every single man in my village I grew up with. I just can't allow it ..."

"I understand," said Pia Lampeda, sympathetically. "I'm sorry."

"I can't be on his side—the Count's side—for that. You understand, don't you?"

"Of course."

"If I can't find it in me now to do what he asks of me ... to become ... you know ... *different*—" Pia chuckled sadly at the word "—yes, like you ... that's what I meant ... If I can't do that for my own elevation, how could I ever allow him to hurt my people?"

"It's sweet how hard you're trying to save your old life. But I hope you aren't forsaking your part in the new one, which you created."

"You mean the new one with you."

"Of course I mean me," she said, with an innocent voice. "I don't know if you think the old one you grew up with is just a dream that you want to preserve or recapture somehow, though you've moved on physically, or if you feel this new one is the illusion, Katty. But we *are* all real here."

"As my village is. I'm just trying to keep them alive."

"You don't think you will ever accept ... *become*, as you say ... one of us? ... you don't think so?"

"Maybe not before they arrive, anyway. I don't know when that'll be; for them or me. But I will never do it—ever—should *he* hurt them."

"I see," said Pia, sounding worried.

"If they come, I'd need to stop him," said Amalina, in a low breath, but firmly. "And I couldn't do it alone. I'd need help. Don't you think?"

Amalina now turned to look Pia in the eye. She pushed back her friend's red locks from her face, keeping her hands cupped to the skin, to make it clear what she was asking. The importance of it. "I'd need a friend, a good friend."

"I don't know what I could do," said Pia, softly. Concerned. "His blood flows through my veins now, Katty. I don't think I could ever do anything to actually *hurt* him."

"I'm not asking you to hurt him," assured Amalina, still firmly but now hurrying. She heard the howl of the wolves outside, the Count was coming back from wherever he'd been. Or he *might* be. No reason to risk it. "It's not like I'm trying to kill him. I just need to *stop* him from hurting the ones I love, if it should come to it. I don't really have anyone else I can turn to for help. You may not be as strong as he is yet, but you are stronger and faster than anyone else."

Pia nodded slowly.

"I'm begging you. I need your help. Won't you help me, Pia?"

After a long thought, stroking Amalina's arm affectionately, an apologetic look on her face, a giant ornate gold brush caught in her hand, Pia said, "As best that I can, yes. Any way I can, I promise … *If* I can."

"I'd just need you to lead him through the castle. Lead him to where I want him to go."

"So you've thought of something already?" she sounded a little disappointed, but there was a small admiring glint in those green eyes—a light through emeralds. "But of course you have, little mouse. Always thinking."

Amalina felt she'd given some of the game away, fumbled this. And: *Little mouse?* She held her gaze steady, "It's just an idea." whispered Amalina, to remind her to do the same. "It's more just putting him out of the way, you see. It's to keep him from doing something to my people I could never forgive him for."

"But not kill him, though."

"Only distract him, at least long enough so I can get out of the castle and talk to Papa, and the villagers too, and get them safely away before an attack, I don't care about the rest. Only that. I can't have them die for me. Never. Not them. You understand."

"But you *aren't* going to kill him, either," reasserted Pia, with a tightening grip on the back of Amalina's hand, pressing it to her cool cheek. "Right?"

"How could I ever? Who in the world *could*? I wouldn't even know how, Pia."

"But you would kill him," she persisted, "if you could?"

"Not if I can help it."

"But …" said Pia, looking worried and not relieved.

"If it came to it," whispered Amalina, confirming something Pia must've see in her eye, at the back of her thoughts. Better to get it out. Be honest. "I mean, *only* if it comes to it. Only *if* it does. Who knows what will happen. But whatever happens, you wouldn't want him to kill *me*, would you?"

"Never."

No hesitation. At least not in that moment. Amalina supposed it was as good of an answer as she could have hoped for. She turned back around to be brushed, straightening her hair over her back. Staring into the candle's light again.

"Lead him … where you want him to go …" murmured Pia. "Where? A trap, Katty? Is it a trap?"

"I didn't say. But maybe it won't even happen …"

"But … is it a trap?"

• • •

"You said silver chains," said Aklan, when he returned to her room, long after Pia left, Amalina's scalp well massaged, and she feeling a little sleepy. But he was too excited to let her rest, he'd discovered another problem: "They won't look a thing like the old ones, will they? All shiny. You think he won't see the damned things above his head, Pretty Princess—like a coiled snake in a tree?"

"Who sees snakes in trees?" smiled Amalina confidently. "Until it's too late?"

"Well, I don't know about that—"

"We'll just cover them up."

"With what?"

"Just something dark. We'll figure it out. It won't really matter if he hasn't noticed by the time we're pulling it off. We just need a good trick to get him there, which I've already taken care of, and—"

"You have?" grinned Aklan. "What is it?"

"Oh, it isn't much," said Amalina, her cheeks flushed at almost giving something away again. "I'm handling that, don't worry. But what I meant was: If we can lure him there, which we can, and then *distract*—" here she really emphasized the word to get him onto that "—give him some kind of shock that'll throw him off for a second … something he thinks is an even bigger threat, even if its for just for a moment, then we can drop the chandelier on him before he can react."

"Well, if you hugged him and gave him a big kiss," said Aklan, with a boyish delight. "He wouldn't hear or see anything, he'd be too excited!"

"No, not me," continued Amalina, before he carried on. "I'm not the bait or the *distraction*, or else I'd be pulverized—"

"Oh, that's right," said Aklan, his momentary brainwave snuffed. She noticed he was still holding the magic bone tight in one fist, one grey knobby end sticking out. "But maybe not if you were in just the right place."

"Never mind all that. The *distraction* is simple as a bunch of bees—"

"Bees!"

"Quiet," said Amalina. "He hates them and a swarm would throw him off. Yes, that'll give him one hell of a distraction. An angry swarm or two of bees will keep him so turned around, you could probably just walk up to him and throw the chains right on. You'll never have seen him so distracted, they scare him that much."

"Now wait … wait … what are *you* going to be doing, again?" he asked, sounding suspicious.

"Setting off the bees."

"And so the bees are going to be *where?*"

"The first floor."

"In the great hall?"

"Yes."

"With us?" To which she nodded. "*We* aren't going to get stung?"

"*I* might," admitted Amalina. "But you should be fine if they can't see you."

Aklan looked unsure of this.

For Amalina it was simple enough, Genadie sets some cover smoke in the cellars (initial distraction), and brings up the weapons (if they should be needed). Pia leads the Count to the great hall—or if she fails to, Amalina rings the emergency bell—and then Amalina sets off the swarm. When the Count appears under the target he'll be overloaded by the bees and the lighting fixture will fall. *Fait accompli.*

"It'll be a sight to see," she assured the boy. "Just be in your spot and ready. I'll be counting on you." At his nervous look: "What is it? You're afraid of heights *and* harmless little b—?"

"No, no, it's okay," he said. "But for this swarm of yours …where are you even going to *get* the bees?"

"That's easy enough."

•  •  •

So, counting on her fingers:

1. Aklan – absolutely

2 & 3. Pils and Anka – clueless, but on board

4. Genadie – a maybe, the sheep, but probably

5. Pia – probably more so than Genadie, though only to a limited degree

6. Mr. Balbo – undetermined, but he'd *have* to be there for her since he'd been her absolute savior on the Night of Noka, when AXP's assassin made his move.

After only the first round of recruiting, that was her six to a good probability. Four or five would work out when it came to it, as she'd first supposed. Maybe they all would.

Following Attila Bronk's policy of information containment, each recruit had their own task, and believed it was a personal obligation to Amalina and with their own tailored reason; well separated from each other. Though Aklan knew of Pils and Anka's part, and they knew he was involved with their mistress in some harmless sport, those two elements needed to be aware of each other since they were going to be laying down her plot's physical preparations in close proximity.

Amalina was satisfied then, and assumed Sadra's revolutionary would have been satisfied too, if not entirely impressed.

But Mr. Bronk would never have assumed, expected, nor approved of her final agent. She waited for the right moment anyway, and then proceeded.

## 17

## The Most Secret Agent of All

The last person Amalina needed to fold into her plot against the Count was going to be the thorniest, so she waited until she felt confident enough to approach him. With her original six roughly signed on, there was no reason to delay, so she went to talk to Count Tepsji, who had returned from wherever he'd been for the past couple days.

"*Bees?*" said the Count, looking like he'd tasted something bitter, not sweet.

" … along with a cask of light wine, as I said, and some saffron," said Amalina quickly, to keep her list rolling along, "and the wheat and the jasmine to add to the next order before spring. Oh, and a good weight of seed oil and daffodil root—"

"For what, is this?" asked the Count, shifting on his divan as if coming awake.

"For the hair salon. Seed oil and the root help thicken hair."

"And the bees?"

"For Elisavet, Elisavet Pattipo. To make her hair dye we need light wine, saffron, and some bees."

"Bees."

"For honey."

"Just how much honey does Lady Pattipo expect she needs?"

"Well, her hair—"

"And what's the matter with her hair, anyway?" sneered the Count. "I like the color the way it is."

"Yes, sir, but she keeps this color, which you like, by maintaining it with the proper mixture of—"

"Will she insist on doing this forever?" said the Count, irritably. "Will I be able to tolerate these things, or will she learn the superior way? Maybe I should elevate her now just so she can have what she wants without all this fuss. Saffron! Bees! No, I don't see it. We can leave off with the bees entirely."

"You're *changing* Elisavet, then?"

"I didn't say that." He frowned at the ceiling. "Though if it will influence her away from stuffing her hair … I might."

"But … well … *I* would still like the bees, sir."

"Why?"

"The honey. Bees *make* honey and—"

"We can purchase honey by the barrel; bee pollen, bee's wax: without resorting to creating it and dirtying our hands."

"But you know I've always been interested in raising them myself, sir. It's a fascinating study. And on top of that, it would be better to have bees of our own so we won't have to rely on someone else. If we buy honey, it will cut into the profits. If we raise them ourselves, it will be all profit."

"Profit?"

"Oh, yes," said Amalina eagerly, widening her eyes, really trying to sell this new bit as hard as she could. *Just keep coming at him from different angles until he crumples.* "I'll be making those candies with the honey. You remember, the candies you used to make? You heard Aria, she loved them. Everyone who's tried them does. They will be very, very popular on the market."

"*Popular?*" The Count seemed surprised to hear that his underhanded ruse to medicate his lady guests, which he'd employed early-on in the castle, would have some legitimate application and interest, or just what the import of it would be. Though his eyes looked rather tired and his posture somewhat sunken, he tickled his lips with yellow-stained fingers, which left marks there.

"Never mind how good they taste, sir," Amalina went on. "Their effects! Many ladies, and young families, and maybe parents, too, will appreciate a say over the inconvenience and unruly humors—as well as balance the risk of an untimely baby. No pregnancy, and delicious besides! It'll be *very* profitable. What a business. It might be more popular than bread!"

"Bread," snorted the Count.

"Yes, sir. Very, very profitable, sir."

"Profit is not flattering for a lady to discuss or to need contemplate," said the Count, beginning to stroke his sudden mustache with enervated flicks.

"Why not? What does commerce have to do with sex? I helped my father run a bakery."

"Nothing to do with it," said the Count. "However, crass money generation concerns are not the realm of a Lady—or even a Gentleman—*of Title*. Mercantilism runs beneath the nobility as a sewer does the majesty of a city. It is a necessity, but to be avoided."

"But trade *is* the future of nobility, sir!" she chirped excitedly; though it wasn't her true passion yet, but she couldn't lose him here.

He looked as if she were speaking some blasphemy.

She explained, in a calm voice, hoping she hadn't lost him and he'd follow: "Sir, the aristocracy, as important as they are, *spend* the money; they run through it. That's what they do. It's the merchant class who innovate and *make* the money. They also buy up the land with it. The nobility, when they begin to run short, need to tax the merchants and marry into their finances. So you see they, the merchants, before long, will *be* the nobility."

"That kind of thinking tried to take root here, and I drove those Boyars out of this land before I ever did the Ottomans," he muttered hotly. "They nearly rotted the country. But how do you explain why these Ladies of Title, guests by the permission of their parents, are here with me and not out corraling a scion of caravans, trade, and transportation?"

"Because you are too good to be true," she said, adding quickly, "Sir. You're the dream of the western aristocracy. A Man of Title *with* money? How could they resist?"

"Though I'm impressed, as always, at your fertile imagination, Ms. Dalca," he sniffed, "this line of thought is unbecoming of your station. Don't offend our guests with these wild thoughts. After all, once they're free of this mortal need for commerce, the oils and the seeds and the saffron ... when immortality comes the merchant class will hold no more importance than a tangle of rats."

"If nothing else, sir, these women will still need clothes, which wear out and change in fashion. And who will make those? Tradesmen will."

"They will only need *hand-tailored* clothes if they want it. If you recall, Ms. Dalca, clothes are the unfortunate necessity of mortals. We here in my Palace of Pleasures will enter a new Garden of Eden."

This thought made Amalina suddenly very uncomfortable and she studied his shirt to see if it was real.

He didn't notice, but was lost in his own reverie, to which, by Amalina's lively looks, he naturally assumed she was rapt: "And to speak of the temporary nature of things, and profitability ... *think naturally*, my little mouse: Imagine what happens when the body changes against you, and against your will, but it pleases you. Oh! And imagine when it changes and causes displeasure. And then imagine if you always had control; one way or the other. Which is what you can have, you understand. So much better than honey and medicines ... and those all important *profits*."

"But I don't understand," said Erin Epris, yawning and uncoiling out of the darkness. It took Amalina all of her self-control not to jump several feet backward. Her heart hammered.

Even the Count looked surprised, as if he'd forgotten she was in the room, lumped up in a chair. "What are you doing there, my lovely Lady Epris?"

"Those candies," said Epris. "What have they to do with preventing babies?"

"They have the side-effect of inhibiting menstruation," said Amalina, cutting a look at the Count. "Or so we've noticed."

"But you were talking about preventing a pregnancy. What does one have to do with the other?"

"It has to do with fertility," said Amalina, but suddenly sounded unsure. "When one bleeds, that's the beginning of our ability to have children. When it stops, that is the end. So if you can turn it on and off …"

"Like the flow of a river?" laughed Lady Epris, lazily. "Stop the rivers and you stop the fish from existing in lakes and oceans? One of these does *not* have to do with the other."

"But it does," said the Count matter-of-factly with a sniff, as if ignorance was another offense to him, "in that blood is life. Blood is life, you see. One can almost *sense* it."

"You mean it's true?" said Lady Epris, whirling up and waking. "Without our *natural stir* a woman cannot have a child?"

"No."

"But I haven't had one since …" she muttered unhappily, her eyes ticking back and forth at the thoughts running through her head. She hadn't had any 'natural stir' since he'd performed the ritual on her, to transform her "Will I, dearest husband? Now that I'm like you, won't I be able to have children?"

"I don't know," he said rather indifferently, unaware of the seething within the woman beside him. He was still wrapped up in the distasteful thought of Amalina as a honey mogul. "I don't think so."

"But I *want* one!" gasped Lady Epris. "I want five, six, a whole dozen! I wanted a large family, just like my own, and I told you as much! What have you done to me, Count Tepsji? You lied to me! You betrayed me!"

Lady Epris departed the room screaming.

"Now look what you've done," said the Count to Amalina as he rose wearily to go after his woman.

"May I have the bees?" she called after him.

"Not in sight of this castle."

Elation!

He hadn't said no. The plan was now in place.

# Part Three
# Ladies, Ladies, Ladies
## *or,*
## AXP, Exposed

18

## The Sadra Smidt Problem

### I

From the high castle of Netz, via pigeon post, the Dalca girl had warned of a Count's minion in Korr. Reported it dutifully. And while she was prudent not to have written the man's name out in full—in case the letter was intercepted—if she'd only taken care to compose it in an optimum environment, or salted some sand over the paper and ink so that it hadn't suffered in transit and the letters she'd written blurred to confusion, Attila might have already figured out who it was. Though he didn't need to look at it again, with the image perfectly captured in his mind, Attila now pulled out the little slip of paper and studied it. But it was still the same. Nothing had changed. He folded it back into his pocket.

Attila turned the puzzling, waterstained and smeared hand-written message every direction in his mind, but the AXP (or *XB* or *ZP* or *ZB*; the last two letters were entirely undefined, and could still be, arguably, any of the above options) persisted in looking like initials. Amalina had said it was a person, and there were three letters to it; making it easy to fall into lazy thought that, indeed, they were the parts of an Ardeelian middle-to-upper-middle class name. He reprimanded himself. It could be a contraction of some kind, or an acronym of anything. Perhaps there was a code to it, then. Maybe instead it hinted at a profession or location. Why hadn't the girl been clearer? Without clarity, her letter only sowed discord and suspicion of anyone and everyone. And it brought Attila to mind-numbing torment.

But there was still another way to work through this knotted puzzle. Assuming there was no new pigeon arriving soon, he considered another instrument close to hand. So *very* close to hand:

"If I could just get my hands on that *damned book*—" he meant the Secret History of the Sheriff of Korr, locked away in a drawer somewhere within the town "—it might give us the answer immediately! The signed contract contained inside it is a virtual—no, a *literal*—inventory of our suspects." Attila held his shaking left hand. "Why is it so difficult for me to get at?"

"We're back to *the book* again?" asked Sadra Smidt, at his side and whispering concernedly to him. "The *Secret History* seems to be becoming an obsession."

"That book is why I came to Korr. I wanted information on my adversary. But since my arrival here I've been provided with distraction after endless distraction." He looked at her as if realizing she were one such distraction, then darted his eyes away. He said in vague frustration, "I've had to survive cutthroats, heal from my wounds, and then puzzle out mysterious agents, before I can begin to do anything I wanted. What stands in the way? I want it ... that book ... now."

"As I've explained countless times already, Attila, it isn't easy."

"But I could use it more than ever. You must see that. The names, *the names!*"

"Desperate," she said, her lips tensed. "I'm not sure you know how to handle everything that's going on here."

"What's going on?"

"Never mind."

"I just want that book."

"The deputy sheriff has it," said Sadra with a resigned sigh, seeing he would not leave the subject. "I assume only he knows where it is, and he won't part with it without a reasonable explanation."

"Aren't Dragomir and Boss Berzweck on some unofficial club of city fathers? They can't persuade the deputy sheriff or the mayor to let them have it? If only for an hour or two?"

Sadra raised a sharp, angular, challenging eyebrow. "Are you going to trust either of those two to speak freely with Mayor Daniel or the deputy about what you're up to here? That's what they must do, you know, if you want that book, Attila. Or do you continue to insist—?"

"And I *will* insist until the time is right," he interrupted. "Powerful men don't take kindly to rivals to their influence. Only when we have collected the majority of this town into our camp can we present ourselves and the plan *openly* to either the mayor or the deputy sheriff. Especially after the destruction of one of Korr's buildings. What would they possibly think? The timing of it? We must be careful. Otherwise these men of high station might easily overturn the will of our fledgling army. Or talk sense into them. And then we'll have lost the fight before it started. I've seen it happen many times in this endless crusade against our foe. Many times."

"Sensible reasoning, Attila," said Sadra, her lips tightening even more, until they couldn't hold the smirk. "But it won't get you your book. Maybe we should tell Dragomir what we're looking for; if he knows anyone with those initials."

"Let's have another roundup," said Attila. "Like when we presented Berzweck's silver to the men. Only, let's see what they might have to offer us of their own, any information for *the Cause,* and we'll make note of what they have to say, and, of course, pay attention to their names. AXP—or whatever it is—might very well be among them."

II

At Sadra's insistence, she went first to clear things with Dragomir and have him set appointments. While she and the baker busied themselves with lists and messages, Attila used his sudden freedom to trace his old route through town, noting differences here and there, swallowing down the sick feeling when he passed the alley where the two killers had slit his neck. But soon he was at the scene of his own crime.

The building which Attila and the lieutenant had destroyed had once been a warehouse storing flammable products—*a neat design by the green-faced killer?* wondered Attila. And so while its wild conflagration and collapse was a sensation, sending Korr's masses into the streets to mingle and puzzle out what might have been the real cause, there was no deeper, official inquiry. It all seemed matter-of-fact to the men of reason and law. Attila was relieved. Still, he took care not to remain too long at the site of the smoking ruin lest anyone come to gape at it and then notice him, the hooded stranger sifting the scattered rubble with his boots as if searching for something particular, and become suspicious.

Standing across the street, the warehouse's fallen timbers resembled blackened femurs knotted together inside a blown kiln wall. Attila longed to dig through the greater debris within, see if he couldn't fish out the strongbox and its secrets. But he knew the wood box and its papers would have been the first turned to ash. He had nothing to expect if he tried poking around—except for a vicious looking bloody piece of iron or two. And still he caught himself returning to the scene for a third time. *Maybe*, thought Attila, analyzing his motives as closely he would any hardened criminal's, *I secretly hope to be caught here by AXP, if only to end the suspense, whatever may come of the encounter.*

Suddenly Attila wished Lieutenant Vokent was there with him, in case of trouble. And considering the deeper perspective, with the lieutenant still hanging around, Vokent's youth, martial abilities, and being a native son, he'd be the best candidate to lead the revolutionary army; and so would be a splendid bulwark against Boss Berzweck's possible—inevitable— interference with said army. Who could Attila possibly use to counter the Boss now, with Vokent gone, if Berzweck suddenly made a power play? Sadra? Despite her sway as the minister's wife, and her natural born abilities, the men would never go for a woman.

"And where is your shadow?" said a surly but trumpeting voice. A voice of authority.

Attila turned his head with a sleepy expression and saw it was Boss Berzweck, dressed in an expensive, full-length fox fur coat. Attila then glanced down to look for his own shadow that the Boss had mentioned and which was clearly there, in the morning light, cutting a sharp, blue-grey figure on the snow.

"Sadra Smidt," said the Boss, explaining his meaning. "She's always attached to your side. You haven't had a falling out, have you?"

"A falling out?" said Attila, his gaze at Boss Berzweck half-lidded.

"Losing your allies, Bronk?" it was a gloating, mocking voice now. "Word is that Lieutenant Vokent has disappeared, too."

"Who said this?" said Attila, as if uninterested.

"Wasn't he staying at the Rock Cup? His room's been paid, but they haven't seen him for days."

"You've been talking to the innkeeper?"

"And why not? He's a friend. More than can be said for you. But I see that look. Don't you worry, former low constable, I haven't said anything out of turn. I keep my promises."

"Lieutenant Vokent is conducting a mission, if you must know," said Attila blandly. "He hasn't deserted our cause, if that's what you mean to imply."

"Vokent's a good boy, of course, I'd never think he'd desert us. But rather he might've lost confidence in you," Berzweck grunted a laugh and lowered one eyebrow to stab his look at Attila. "Only a matter of time."

"Why do you say that?"

"I will remind you, former low constable, that two weeks ago I proved my ability to provision this force with silver against our ... Well, you know the *who* we're talking about here. And I set a timetable for you to do the same. For you to prove your worth, shall we say?"

"I'm fully aware."

"Time's up. I'm not pressing you yet because I want to make it clear to everyone my case: I am a reasonable man, and you, even given extra time, can't prove yourself. And so, with the hour to present your goods lapsed, I think it isn't too unreasonable to assume there might be those, no matter how close to you, who'll begin to lose faith."

"As I said," murmured Attila, his face a blank, "Lieutenant Vokent is running an errand. And my shadow, as you'd have her, is running one of her own. She has important duties within Korr that have to do with the church and her husband's ministry."

"Well, good for you," said Boss Berzweck. "With friends still faithful. But I'm glad we've met. I wanted to remind you of the challenge. I can't guarantee how much longer I'll hold back. That's *my* daughter up in that castle. I can't imagine what's happening there and I shall have Cristine back. You can't expect a father to keep himself in check forever."

*And this is the problem*, thought Attila. With the Boss' immense wealth, and proof he can supply the necessary ton of silver that would make a military force untouchable, and that he can produce weapons using this illegal substance that'd do the Count in, at any time he could buy off Attila's nascent army. And with his local power and deep roots within the community, he could persuade them to his command. But even worse, if Berzweck were to let them know his daughter was now tucked up in the high castle as a hostage of their enemy, he'd have a handle on their sympathy too. He would have them to a man, absolutely. It was only Berzweck's pride, and sensible need for discretion on the matter, that prevented him from whispering a word of it outside their inner circle. But his daughter was a trump card, if he wanted. And if he ever reached the end of his patience …

"I would counsel you to follow Dragomir Dalca's example, Mr. Berzweck. His daughter Amalina has been there for years."

"I can't explain Drag," said Boss Berzweck. "You find his exceptional forbearance admirable … and not suspicious?"

That actually got a reaction from Attila, his eyebrows rose at the suggestion.

"All that yeast has softened his head," shrugged Berzweck. "I'm sure he thinks he's doing right. But I keep my own counsel. In my business I deal in timetables, and you're lucky we've a strong winter that allows you extra room, and my tolerance to pretend you've the resources which I command at a whim."

"You must be patient," muttered Attila, his body slumping slightly.

"And then part of me just likes to watch you wriggle, you cold-blooded gargoyle," said Boss Berzweck. "If you had a daughter up there, you wouldn't be so smug about it."

"Perhaps not. But consider, that just means I have a clearer head. And I just need a little more time. As you say, the winter has been strong, my resources aren't as readily at hand."

"So have your added time," said Boss Berzweck, shifting his boots in the snow. "My season's gift to you. But when I decide it is up, you'd better be sensible and willing to turn over your factions, and give me your full-throated endorsement, eh? We can't have a divided force."

"On that I agree," said Attila.

"There's been some activity around Dragomir's bakery this morning," said the Boss, as he leaned his head close to Attila's, eyeing him suspiciously. "I'd better not find out you're trying to pass off my silver ingot as your own. Melt it down, recast it, whatever you might do to it, you'll be found out. I can have chemists prove its alloy and its provenance from my own mines. And then where will you be? A fraud on top of your other disgraces, former low constable Bronk."

*Focus*, thought Attila, stalking away. There was still time to put off a Berzweck coup, he was sure of it. Never mind the original plan to take down the Knight of Ardeel was his in the first place, Attila was also the one who'd cautiously grown its ranks, the only one who knew all the names. It was rightfully his, not Berzweck's. And it always would be. What mattered right now was locating and eliminating the Count's enemy agent—

*Allowing there's only one*, he thought suddenly ... *and not more.*

*Be moderate always*, he calmed himself, before he noted that, in this circumstance, with potential enemies everywhere, it was wise to be overly cautious and suspicious. Amalina's warning, no matter how obscure, no matter how wide its scope, no matter how it put his nerves on edge, was better than complete ignorance of the threat itself. If only his research into the ugly green killer hadn't turned out as it had. *Boom-Boom-Boom-Boom-Boom.* What a disaster. Away went the evidence, which might have ...

Thinking again, sadly, on that last encounter with the lieutenant, he wondered if there was something he could have done that would have made things turn out differently. So that he didn't have to lose Vokent from his side so soon. But that morning had changed the dynamic entirely, and forced a new shape to his plans.

Attila shook his head. *Focus. Focus.* Forget Vokent. No army could be claimed, trained, or fielded, by either Boss Berzweck or Attila, even with the lieutenant's help, if a nearby enemy gave the game away to their greater adversary.

*So*, thought Attila: *Focus, focus, focus!*

But that was impossible when his agitated mind was already at work: What had Berzweck grumbled, almost mirthfully, at their parting, "Give your shadow my regards"? And why did that remark feel so similar in tone— and somehow share meaning—to what Vokent had said at his recent departure, after Attila had reminded him again, a second time, forcefully, and adamantly about *focus* ... and to put aside love? Vokent had said with a straight face, "I hope you're good at taking your own advice."

*And what did he mean with* that *crack?* wondered Attila presently as he moved on, alone, back toward the bakery. *What was he talking about? Was he hinting at a personal distraction of my own? Accusing me of something untoward, though in a chiding, friendly way? What* could *he be talking about?* Attila's agile mind honed in: *Did he mean ... 'love', as well? To* me*? As if my motives are compromised by it? By whom? What would even make him think such a ... such a thing of me?* This meshed inside Attila's mind with Berzweck's mocking 'shadow' comment: *Did he mean Sadra Smidt?*

Sadra?

*No*, thought Attila, *Focus, focus*.

But something in this day would not let him, it seemed: Attila saw Sadra waiting for him outside the bakery, and supposed, without evidence, that she must be the point of the lieutenant's jest. But Vokent hadn't actually seen anything untoward between them, Attila and Sadra. Had he?

III

As he watched Sadra at the entrance to the bakery, and she looked about expectantly for him, Attila recognized a warmth there he hadn't seen in her before. Attila felt her hand slide into his, as it had weeks ago. His hand reflexively closed on the memory, hoping to experience, once again, that extraordinary passion he'd enjoyed for the first time in his life.

"Again with *her*?" said a scornful voice.

Bishop Perdu, behind Attila, stood as solid and still as a cloth draped pyramid, his stare from under the deep hood of his cowl, like shooting lightning, was concentrated past him, up the street, on Sadra Smidt. The Bishop was the head of the Roman Catholic Church in Korr, a loyal soldier for the Cardinal, and a jealous competitor to the Protestant Minister, Minister Smidt, for the souls of these people. His envy naturally extended to the minister's wife, who was at least ten times more popular and influential than he. Attila had made a point of ignoring the inconvenient religious enmity, pretending it was a matter of logistics and scheduling that caused him to keep them separated, and kept Perdu out of *the Cause*'s inner circle.

"Bishop," said Attila with a nod, his eyes low and inexpressive. "I can't make proper introductions between the two of you just yet. But I've already explained to the Cardinal how best to handle the delicate situation here in Korr, with our various factions, and how best to time it. You will be brought in. In due course."

"Introductions?" scoffed the bishop. "I shouldn't wish for any. I've already known the Smidts for some time, and they me. But I can't see how an outsider like yourself can credibly instruct the Cardinal, much less *me*, on how to conduct business here in Korr. As if you can understand, truly understand, the *delicacies* that exist." He nodded his head to the thin black figure outside the bakery with a contemptuous smirk. "And who you choose, day-in and day-out, to share the path."

Attila followed the man's look and felt sorry for Sadra's lonely figure.

"You mean Sadra?" said Attila. "Specifically her? You've something you wish to tell me, Bishop?"

"Only a caution. A warning."

"What have you to warn me about her? She's been most helpful." Attila couldn't help but touch the bandage at his throat, where she'd sewn him up against a fatal slash. "But don't let me stop you."

"This operation of yours," began Bishop Perdu. He stopped, still staring venomously down the street. Was his grudge against the Smidts' rival religion—its success in Korr, compared to his own native church—so bitter and so troubling to him?

"No," said Perdu, finally, with a shake of his head.

"'No', what? If you've something to tell me, there's nothing to gain from withholding information. And I should wish to hear it if it helps our great cause. Please."

"Because you're searching for the truth," said Bishop Perdu, and eyed Attila doubtfully. "Are you? Really? The *full* truth?"

"Always. Especially when a particular truth springs words of caution and warning from a trusted ally; such as yourself, Bishop."

Perdu nodded gravely, then shrugged. He closed and opened his eyes slowly, and seemed to comport himself and his stance, centering on Attila, all seriousness between them. "How much do you know of her, this Sadra Smidt?"

"Very little, but fate seems to have placed us together."

Perdu grunted and shook his head. "*Very little*, yes. Fate? I thought you were a godly man."

"Tell me what you know," said Attila, willing him to do so.

"This Sadra Smidt, for certain reasons, and until very recently, she assumed her role in life was to be the pinnacle of all that is *righteous* in the town of Korr." The bishop raised his hand to indicate Attila: "Until the arrival of the stranger; whose mind is sharper than hers, as well as his moral center superior, and holds a compulsion to drive out the town's—and the land's—wrongs and moral ills. In that, she stands in awe of *him*, and would gladly defer to *him*. Now, for the first time, you see, there is someone in her world who stirs her admiration, and up to whom even *she* can look. More so than her husband." Perdu paused. "*Does* the minister know who she's been spending her daily hours with, as he pens his homilies for his flock?"

Attila did not answer, but waited, feeling the winter chill biting in.

"Along with our stranger has come the revolutionary winds of change," Perdu carried on, "for the good of the world. Eh? This man is the beginning of a new age for Ardeel and its people—so long as he should succeed in his mission. Eh? Well, she'll be there to assist him in any way she can, and no doubt has sworn to use her accumulated power within the community to deliver his success. And while she is ignorant of many aspects of what's taking place—*as am I, eh?*—if she were privy to that which will be revealed in the end, Sadra would no doubt assign the proper blame—a certain blame—for everything that's happened, is happening, will happen, and how it will fall out. Taking center stage *back* for herself. Do you understand what I'm saying?"

"Are you talking about taking credit?" said Attila. "Are you exercising my jealousy? Be assured, I've none. But that the job gets done, anyone, Sadra Smidt, even you, can have all its glory."

"Jealousy, though?" said Bishop Perdu, surprised. "A quality I don't possess, either. No."

"No?" challenged Attila.

"Sadra is a woman," he said dismissively. "If we're to talk of jealousy, then I can only wonder again whether the minister, her husband, knows completely who occupies the greater part of her day, and perhaps her heart?" He let the statement hang heavily, portentously, between them. Then: "But that is not my point at all, former low constable. I can only emphasize that you're standing in this community on a spot that she's used to owning. In what you hope to do here, you will now usurp her, eh?"

"I haven't much time, Bishop," said Attila, staring dully at the heated, protuberant eyes within the cowl, sensing the man was confidently arriving at a point that would soon put him on an uncomfortable edge. "I don't think she's prey to jealousy, either."

"I'll arrive at my point, momentarily."

"If jealousy is not it, please do, Bishop Perdu. Your warning."

"It's rather, blame. The blame I mentioned before."

"Blame?"

"To fix blame on someone or something is rather easy, isn't it, Attila Bronk?" said Perdu, as if beginning a sermon, a lesson of some kind. Attila assumed it was the easiest, most practiced way for this strange holy man to express himself, and settled in for the Bishop's truth to finally spill out; somewhere. "Take Sadra Smidt, the minister's wife, eh?" Perdu smirked and nodded resentfully at her, "who when, occasionally, it comes time to do so— to place blame, eh?—everyone in this village relies on for guidance as to who or what to blame; because the people of Korr *revere* her as an artist in the practice of blame, you see. Sadra is so preternaturally quick about it she rightly arouses our admiration." Though he grinned lightly, and his voice sing-songed, his tone was spiteful. "The way she goes about her business, when it's time to nail guilt somewhere, and with everyone—*everyone*— drawing close to take note on how it's done, eh? first off, she discounts herself, eh? as she is *naturally* faultless; then, if there's someone she does not like, or she knows they don't like her, or some object has troubled her in some way—whichever thing at the moment has her in a bad mood most— her long, bony finger rises ..." he lifted his finger as an example. "And then it's all over, the guilt is set, eh? The best possible reason for *why* so-and-so or such-and-such is responsible can always be worked out later." His teeth ground together in a now choleric grin. "But to her awed watchers, the whole operation seems to have been well-considered."

Attila stared untroubled at Bishop Perdu, and wondered where the point was.

"Sadra's husband," continued Perdu, with a further note of insinuation that bugged Attila, "*the* Minister Smidt, however, is so woefully slow at it; placing blame. He hums absently as he sloshes the merits of a case from side to side in his head—the timidest appraiser of any kind of trouble, eh?— wrestling each fact to a draw in his painful, methodic way, as if it were the most important thing he will ever do in his life on this earth. Whether innocent or guilty, rest assured, if there's only one person to stand between you and the hangman, you will pray on your knees, with hands raised to the sky, eh? the minister caught the case, and that you've not attracted the interest of his wife. Eh? Eh??? But for everyone else, Sadra *is* the crowd favorite; for dramatic flair, for precise aim, and for lightning certitude. Sadra, she is most satisfying, and *instructive.* And while she, that shrewd woman, knows there's a difference between her and her husband, a disparity in likeability, she doesn't see the trouble in being the people's lightning rod of moral and religious fear. I'm sure it feels like a comfortable place to be at any time for her, lofted high on a pedestal. Terrifying.

"But if Sadra is taken down from her mount after the people following her lead for so long, won't there be many around the village who, having derived a certain training from her, know well how to work the same levers their *grand example* set for them? And might they not use those levers against you, the righteous stranger—but a *stranger,* after all? Eh? If she falls in her lofted position by your actions here, then by dismounting her, you might fall, too. Eh? Anyone could do it, even that ineffectual husband of hers, the minister, if he got the sudden cravings you have."

There was something ugly in the words, and the way he was using them, suggestive. *Dismount her? Sudden cravings?*

"I have better faith in the people of this town," said Attila, almost sneering as he lied.

"You're not that much of a fool."

"Every single one of them. When the time comes."

"When the time comes, there's only one being in this universe, under heaven, in which to properly place your faith." He pointed upwards, but it almost seemed as if he were pointing at his own head.

"I'll introduce you soon," said Attila, nodding to indicate Sadra, coldly concluding business with Bishop Perdu and turning. "I promise. Not to worry."

"Everyone in Korr has eyes and ears," he called after Attila. "Everything under the sun is seen or known. Or it will be, eventually. Bear that in mind, former low constable."

Attila stewed: *Sadra, again?* First Vokent, then Perdu, and, now that he reflected on it further, that dark something hinted in Boss Berzweck's 'your shadow' comments? They seemed to be of one mind. What were they warning him? What did they know?

Attila resented the way everyone seemed to be plucking at him, and as if they could see his imperfections like they were erected and framed in the middle of the village square. As he walked toward the lonely, boney, black clad figure outside the bakery, he once more felt her hand join his, as it had weeks ago. And as his hand closed in reflex upon the memory again, he thought: *Danger there!*

Or was this disagreeable result the bishop's whole intent? Had he accomplished what he'd set out to do? to sew doubt and discord? To throw Attila off his game by striking a soft spot, an obvious hole in his armor? That might have been it. Perdu could just as easily be the Count's Korr agent, the man-of-the-acronym, besides being the Cardinal's lackey. Or he could have come after Attila on the Cardinal's orders, to break apart Attila's union with the rival church. Anything was possible, and so it should be disregarded until further data could be gained, and signs pointed in the right direction. Until then, everyone was to be suspected.

Only, that didn't explain what Vokent and Boss Berzweck had said. Was he simply discounting the Bishop's more direct declarations in order to forget the other two? Clearing Sadra Smidt of any suspicion out of fondness or pity for her? But there *were* three separate voices here. Three signs. All in accord. By Attila's own rules he must pay attention to signs. And three of them presented in close order and aligned in a single direction was something significant. But the problem here was that these weren't *objective* signs; physical and concrete objects, to be observed. They were opinions, and suppositions, and surmisings, and insinuations, possibly errant or corrupted by malicious intent. So were they really signs at all?

*Focus, Attila!*

"What did *he* want?" asked Sadra, with acid contempt toward the robed pyramid-shape waddling away.

*Focus, focus, focus, focus, focus: AXP!*

"Nothing, Sadra. Let's go in and resume the work."

## 19

# Sadra's Controlling Hand
## Or,
## All Suspects Suspected

**D**ragomir Dalca spoke with members of the revolution at an arranged time in his store while Attila listened and watched from the kitchen. Sadra, breathing heavily at Attila's elbow, pressed close.

As the men came, their names were checked off a list, watching for signs of the acronym: Gorga the Street Sweeper. Lygo the Painter. Harszu the Clockmaker. Jenz Timer. Elto Pop the Miller. Simyon the Tailor. Ronal Niszu the Physician. Homer Tolchok the Occulist. Miden the Trapper. Paulu the Woodsman. Gulgas the Hunter. Reiku the Shop Keeper. Jeno the Inn Keeper. Bardoz the Inn Keeper. Hector the Restaurant Owner. Gyemes the Candler. Ilyanos the Painter. Midas the Perfumier. Kodyu the Blacksmith. Tosjk the Peasant. Etrensil the Other Peasant. 'Dog' the Serf. Luto the Idiot. Askan Zugan Borga the Forager. Ngaszy the Farmer. James the Farmer. Orson the Town Clerk. Szocs the Artist. Lexio the Apothecary. Ivanszony Spillyonskyu the Astrologer. Efraim the Barber. Matteus the Butcher. Konstantin Krumb the Carpenter. Dan the Shoemaker. Jon the Architect. Taszu the Herbalist. Lemn the Messenger. Pacinto the Money Lender. Laszerball the Porter. Anzi the Porter. Zakreba the Farrier. Orgo the Veterinarian. Yat the Cooper. Kastar the Woodworker. Docra the Sign Maker. Vladimy the Fine Cabinetmaker. Nashyu the Fine-Metal Smith. Borszova the Hatter. Han the Watchmaker. Horvak the Printer. Juda the Leatherer. Desclu the Tanner. Besel the Bookbinder. Szimy the Ropemaker. Grayol the Saddler. Moshecai the Weaver. Lenn the Wheelwright. Castor the Whitesmith. Balaszi Naeblin the Jeweler. Ilya the Glass Maker. John the Boat Maker. Hans Klepp the Undertaker. Eigru the Sharpener and Wirepuller. Gralya the Fisherman. Steegkan the brewer, and his Apprentice. Opps the Compass Maker. Karl the Waremonger. Boris the Pig Farmer. Hadriani the Carter. Gavril Denk the Muler. Kedrik Strock the Hayer. Decebal the Coalmaker...

As Dragomir pushed for any helpful information they might have about any strange men in the city or goings on that were suspicious, they more than eagerly helped with a laundry list of rumors:

"Have you heard about the school of witches who've taken over the eastern mountains?" one said …

"Young daughters of royal blood are being lured by an evil old king into the mountains so he can dine on their bones and make clothes of their skin," said another …

"The great general of Ardeel, Vezel Umalasju, fought a battle against the Sobelburg council and he won, but has agreed to go into hiding as long as the new government doesn't exceed its bounds … he hides in a great, old castle in the east …"

"Kyrgil was destroyed when a couple dragons fought above its mountains …"

"Kyrgil was eaten whole by one *single* dragon, sent there by a vengeful sorcerer who controlled it …"

"The sorcerer who sent the dragon must belong to the school of witches in the mountains, and is very powerful …"

"A strange sorcerer has been travelling all over Ardeel, appearing as a young man with wild blond hair, who claims to be a prince but wears pauper's clothes …"

"A young man with blond locks like a haystack begs for money, but is seen elsewhere handing out gold coins …"

"If someone doesn't give charity to this poor boy, the sorcerer, who is related to the little urchin, is gravely offended and sends a dragon to destroy the unkind city …"

"Kyrgil wasn't destroyed, it never really existed. It was just a story, a legend … Did *you* ever see it?"

"Neku Jonker was the great great great great grandson of St. Grigori, and the rightful King of Ardeel, but chose to humble himself to its people, and by heaven's will did battle against the greatest forces of evil …"

With so many able-bodied men passing through the bakery or congregating there, it was a surprise to the women of Korr who came simply to purchase a loaf or cake. They thought to themselves that it resembled days when some newsworthy event, such as a plague or a war or a crumbling mountain or a scandalous piece of gossip had hit the town. So they made reasons to linger within the shop, trying to pick up what was happening, convinced it had something to do with the blown warehouse, and grew frustrated when the men stood awkwardly mute while they loitered with their ears outside their caps. This slowed the inquiry.

. . .

"This is taking longer than I'd hoped. You aren't needed elsewhere?" an irritated Attila whispered to Sadra. "Your husband isn't missing you?"

"He's used to my circulating and having business with the women in their homes. As long as I make our walks, and the meals are ready on time, he won't know the difference."

"At this rate we'll be here until the bell rings."

"I can stay." Sadra patted Attila's back to reassure him, and then left her hand on his shoulder. "But I'm not sure how much good this'll do. There hasn't been anything useful yet. Not anyone matches the letters, 'A'-whatever."

For Attila, too many did. His mind worked on finding signs and communicating lines of logic that proved themselves true. And this caused him to search for paths that connected, and through-lines that stood out, and tested it all by looking from a hundred different angles. And by not coming out of the back room and asking them directly what he wanted to know, this caused a fog, with dark shapes within it that he took to be promising. It was like the child's game of looking at clouds and seeing what one wanted to see within them. He had nearly ten suspects so far, because of the way they answered questions, and how the imprecise initials the Dalca girl had sent could be interpreted beyond a simple name. Askan Zukan Borga (if AZB)? Anzi the Porter (if AZP)? The Painter, whose shop sits at the cross section of the Main Street (the first street in the town grid next to Amalina's, which would be A) and the sixteenth perpendicular street in from the beginning of town (which in the alphabet would be P). And so on.

Though the word paranoia did not exist at the time, Attila Bronk became subject to it, and began to feel that everyone was AXP (or whatever those letters really were). That they were all in a conspiracy against him, with their ludicrous fairy tales, to frustrate and degrade him.

In this state, Attila felt Sadra's hand on his back might even be the controlling hand of a puppeteer. He hadn't seen the pigeon with Amalina's message arrive. Had she, Sadra, written the note to throw him off? Could this woman, constantly at his side, guiding him, testing him, be none other than the essence of AXP? What else could explain why, since he'd met her, had it only become more difficult to get the Secret History of Korr into his hands? Had the killers who'd slit his throat really, out of duty, held off taking him to their chamber of torture and death, and instead delivered his unconscious body to her, so she could heal him, gain his confidence, and plumb him for information? Could *she* be the Count's thrall?

What was it that Vokent had said? His counter warning about love? Did he think that Sadra, the minister's wife was really …?

Attila blinked thoughtfully.

Hadn't there been something in the air since this morning, incessantly pointing signs in Sadra's direction? Was it divinely inspired, then? Who was Attila to question, but to interpret? But *was* there something to it? For Attila's mind there was always something, and his mind locked onto Sadra now. Hadn't he, by his—what else could it be called?—*fumbling transgressions* with Sadra Smidt given Heaven a just reason to twist the world and those he cared for against him? Was this all a personal punishment? And so everyone must suffer for his guilt?

*While the crimes of the monster go unpunished?*

Sadra's hand remained on his back.

Attila shook his head, knowing he had to clear his thoughts. It was a rare movement for him. Sadra's full arm came down on his shoulders, tightened around him into a comforting hug. He felt like he wanted to throw her off and run out of the stifling heat of the kitchen.

• • •

"Maybe you should rest, Attila," said Sadra. "It's been a long day."

"It's not much into afternoon," mumbled Attila. "My resolve only strengthens. You can go home if you need a rest. I'll be fine here."

Her arms withdrew from him stiffly.

"You're sure you aren't tired?" she asked with concern. "Many children fuss when they tire, refusing to go to sleep when they should."

"Comparing me to a child?" said Attila, turning his bored eyes on her. "Have you had any children to know this?"

"I've raised scores," she said, slightly affronted. "Parenting for hundreds, some from cradle to the grave. But you knew that before you asked, so why did you? I'm saying *you* are a man of great will, Attila. Those types, those great men, unfortunately, sometimes resemble a willful child."

"I know my limits. And what's limiting me here is the lack of good information. This town is a fountain of fantastic rumors and worthless gossip."

"If you won't tell Dragomir to ask them *specifically* what you need to know—"

"I need you to leave me alone!" said Attila, cutting her off, his teeth clamped together. "Leave me alone ... to think!"

"Very well," she said, stepping sideways, looking down at him. "I'll come round before the bell to fetch you."

Attila cleared his throat before looking up at her.

"It seems Dragomir has two bedrooms available," he said, matter-of-factly. "Continuing forward, I'll stay here."

Sadra's eyes flared, the corners of her mouth tensed. "Very well ... Very well ... As you please." She moved as if to leave, but only made it a few feet away when she stopped. "Is there some reason for this change?"

"For this next phase of our mission it makes more sense to remain close to the front line of communication. Dragging me back and forth and stuffing me in your church's cellar only opens us to detection and cuts me off from potentially vital news. As it is, we're waiting for Lt. Vokent to return, and his instructions are to rendezvous here at the bakery. I want to receive him."

"That sounded rehearsed," remarked Sadra. "You've been thinking about this. Is it rather that you want to stay here to be rid of me? Our brief association has already made you uncomfortable? What are you afraid of?"

"To this very day you haven't told your husband of my presence within his church."

"First it's *my* church, now it is *his?*" observed Sadra, coolly.

"It feels illicit. Not something that should happen in a holy place. Much less one the minister presides over."

"It's not only a church. Its private quarters are my home ... as well as my husband's. And if it matters at all to you, Attila Bronk, I *want* you there with me." She sighed once, heavily, then concluded as if speaking to a clueless child: "I want it."

## 20

# The Lady Princess and the First Book

## I

The Count was in the castle.

So went the word after a strange tremble within the building—or from the ground on which it stood—and Ladies of Title looked worryingly to each other—but not *too* worryingly—as if mildly concerned something like a roof or a wall might fall on them, or hoping it might just do so on the other. There was no way to tell if Tepsji really was there without asking for him, which might bring him around, chanting 'all is good' and raising an eye at any doubt, and then you had his full attention. So let others do it, thought Amalina, she would rather not. But if he *was* up and wandering, that meant she could not continue the physical preparations for her trap. Which meant she had to do something else, then. Fresh from her victories on the planning front, and humming with that peculiar energy which sometimes visited Amalina—the type of positive spark she must do everything with while it lasts; when *anything* is possible if she only tries—Attila Bronk's revolution came to mind, and then AXP's looming threat, and she figured she'd give one of those two concerns a crack. *Why not?* What else could she do while she waited for the Count to leave?

"Where's the AXP book?" Amalina asked Aklan, preparing some sheets of paper, several quills, and a bottle of ink at her desk. "Bring it here so I can decipher more pages, see if we can't finally figure out who he is."

"Um," said Aklan, with uncharacteristic hesitation and discomfort. "Aren't you supposed to have his permission for me to get the book out?"

"I can look at the book whenever I like, that's the deal."

Aklan shook his head slowly, eyes wide, "The deal was that you can have it whenever you wish, but you have to get *his* permission first. Remember?"

Amalina gave the boy a sour look. "Whose side are you on? You know where it is and I want it. Just go and get it for me."

"Oh, of course I'm on your side, Pretty Princess," cried Aklan. "Of course. Always!"

"But you aren't going to get it for me?"

"Welllll," he grimaced.

"So tell me where it is and I'll get it."

"Wellll ..."

"You're going to make me go find him, and talk to him, and ask him?"

"If you really want it, Pretty Princess."

"What a stupid deal that is," frowned Amalina. "How can I have the thing 'when I wish', if I have to ask him for it first—though he cannot refuse me—so he can then tell you that I can have it, and so you can then get it out of hiding, when you could just get it out of hiding for me in the first place when I ask?"

"That's the deal, though."

"I know, I'm just remarking how stupid it is."

"But you agreed to it."

Amalina scowled.

"I think it's so he can know *when* you're looking at it." He cleared his throat as her mood darkened, her color deepening. "I mean, do you really want it?"

"No," said Amalina, blowing out a breath to relieve the internal pressure. "That's fine. I don't have time to waste on nonsense."

"I mean I would get it out if he said it was okay," he assured her. "It's just ... *the deal*, you know ...? Please don't be disappointed."

"That's okay, I understand." But Amalina worried at this ding to her good energy—which she sensed as if the vessel holding it had suddenly sprung a leak. She couldn't let any free moment go to waste. "I've got plenty of other things ... "

• • •

*So what else?* A second objective, as laid out in Amalina's midnight manifesto, when the primary cannot be pursued: ease the Ladies out of the castle. *Time to begin that.*

Amalina put the movements of the revolution, and counter maneuvers against AXP, far from her mind to focus her energy. It's not like she'd been looking forward to pouring over AXP's messages anyway; teasing out his crimes from them, looking at all the tiny drawings of pretty young women who she knew had suffered and died at his command. No, in fact, she was glad to be rid of that odious task. Better that she used her energy on the living. And tangling with any of the Ladies of Title on the touchiest of subjects, of their returning home, especially when their competitors lacked the interest in doing so, was a little daunting. It would occupy all her concentration.

Helpfully, Amalina's unconscious self—her dreamself—had laid out some good ideas how it could be done. Just as the Count had wound the Ladies' hearts, over the preceding months, by playing on their distinct personalities, shifting himself to meet and engage their individual interests, and exploiting their unique appetites and weaknesses as he strutted about the castle, on display like a peacock with a thousand distinct, pretty plumes to awe them, so could she, while he was distracted, unravel them. Amalina would pluck as many loose feathers on that old bird as she found; some easier than others, but there would be ones to come fully out in her hand. She just had to keep yanking to find which might cause a Lady to turn their confidence from him, to lose interest, and to question her dedication to this contest.

Wasn't Erin Epris, disillusioned because he'd robbed her of her bushel of children, a prime example? *And she was an already changed Lady!*

Most targets would be obvious after awhile, and she would begin her campaign with the simpler Ladies until she'd gained enough experience. But until the end, when her skill was well honed, Amalina would make it a point to avoid the most challenging of the lot, like *the Barnacle*, Margeta la Brichese, whose mind was firmly fixed on taking a place beside the Count.

Only, to Amalina's great surprise, it was Margeta la Brichese she faced first.

• • •

As a bit of easy practice, Amalina headed to Cristine's room, intent on talking sense into her old friend, wean her away from the Count's empty seductions—with Cristine, *that* angle might be difficult—and then get her to leave.

Cristine's entrance to the castle—her introduction to the Ladies of Title as 'Miss Berzweck'—had been a significant distraction for Amalina. And in the tumult and chaos of the Count's romancings that naturally followed, and the upheaval of the *Night of Noka*, their childhood bond had seemed to fade and fade, until it was almost forgotten. They were growing apart as many friends moving into adulthood do; painful, but nothing important in the grand scheme of things; even when Cristine became laid out in bed, with her life nearly drained away.

But Amalina felt lively now, and so she paced the route to Cristine's rooms in what felt like three long strides, thinking: *get her out of the castle, get this duty out of the way; deal with Cristine now and clear my head before all the trouble really begins.* Amalina sensed the greatest freedom waiting for her if she did this one good deed, she didn't even pause before opening the door.

She opened the door.

Amalina stood on the threshold with a candle, and with that and what little light there was added from the petering fireplace, she surveyed the room. It was difficult to see Cristine's face from that angle, but the way she lay there on the bed, flat on her back, with the covers pulled up to her chin, arms straight down on either side, reminded Amalina of a dead body. Her pale skin did not help matters. Amalina tried to spot the covers' rise and fall, a sign she was still alive. Instead, and to her relief, she heard a light snore. Not wanting to disturb her friend while resting so peacefully, an innocent (if an unhealthy one), for fear she would raise the other half of the young woman, the half who was cold, defiant, and eager for the Count's attention, she hesitated in the doorway.

Before she stepped in, she made a promise to herself. If Cristine did not wake up she was worse than before; insensible. If she were completely without consciousness, Amalina supposed there was nothing her friend could to do stop her from writing ol' Boss Berzweck. Calling him to fetch his daughter home. It might be something to try. And that's what she'd do. With that decision made, Amalina entered.

Cristine did not stir as Amalina tip-toed her way to the bed, nor when she came to a stop beside it, nor when she bent over her.

Amalina inched the cover down from Cristine's chin. The bloody gouges were still on her throat, of course. Cristine had created some of the marks to obscure the obvious, incriminating gashes the Count had left; to pretend (to the other Ladies) the damage was of her own making. The top of the covers were still damp and stained from where they touched her neck, and painted sticky dark patches where it met Amalina's fingers and sleeve.

But Amalina was staring at Cristine's face. The peaceful look was like all the times before, when she'd come running from a brutal encounter, to cry herself out and then fall asleep in Amalina's arms. Not the cocksure beauty who'd come strutting through the gates some weeks ago. It took Amalina back. So sad and innocent and vulnerable she appeared in the candlelight. But now, those horrible black and crimson holes below her jawline …

Fascinated, Amalina found her hand reaching to the ruin of Cristine's neck. But what a ruin! Those wounds were entirely Amalina's fault. Or so she felt, with a throb of guilt.

"I'm sorry," muttered Amalina, troubled that she couldn't protect Cristine from the Count the way she had from Bessa. "It's all my fault. I'm so, so sorry … so sorry …"

"If you want to confess something, Lady Tepsji," said Margeta, beside the bed, "I *will* be available in the chapel, later."

• • •

"Margeta, what are you doing here?" hissed Amalina, trying to quiet her.

"Is it your guilty conscience that keeps you up at all hours, Lady Tepsji?" the thin, severe, almost prematurely aged young woman carried on, her harsh voice growing louder.

By mentioning a guilty conscience keeping her up, Amalina at first thought Margeta was talking about Lucinda Skeldar, then, looking at Cristine, realized they were actually reasoning along the same line: Amalina's responsibility was with the one lying in the room, nearly bloodless.

"Wh-whaat?" murmured Cristine from the bed. Strangely, her voice sounded younger. More like from years ago: slightly breathy, cautious, vulnerable. Her lids fluttered as if they might open, revealing slivers of her crystal blue eyes. Her body shifted, her arm rose along the covers, sliding toward her mottled neck. Then she seemed to fall back into deep sleep, her hand stopping where it was, with a long, drawn out: "Whooo?"

Amalina ushered Margeta out before Cristine woke. Then, shutting the door, Amalina rephrased the question.

"Princess la Brichese, what *are* you doing here? Are you following me?"

"Since Bardina hasn't worked, I knew it was time I applied myself," said Margeta. "Though there's no need to follow you. Finding you isn't hard at all, knowing how constant your pilgrimages are to Ms. Cristine Berzwecken's door." Margeta's eyes flashed. "When you aren't losing your hours in Lady Lampeda's company."

"I'm not sure what you're talking about," said Amalina, now confused by Margeta's knowing look and what she seemed to be trying to imply with it. "What do either of them have to do with my conscience?"

"*Guilty* conscience," reminded Margeta.

"What are you talking about?"

"Well, isn't it obvious, Lady Tepsji? Your best friend's condition aside—which, despite your uncle's effort, has not changed but for the worse—you *are* letting go that once-valuable friendship, aren't you?" She pointed her grey thumb at Cristine's room. "Letting that one go for another which you know—or you *suppose*, anyway—is superior. Superior in rank, superior in quality, and now superior in pure *power*."

Margeta meant her friendship with Pia, of course: the new, changed friend. Or did she somehow mean her relationship with the Count?

"I hadn't thought of it that way," said Amalina, truthfully, though feeling appalled that Margeta might have hit on something. *I just want Cristine out and safe, don't I? Not to lose our friendship in order to free myself for Pia—?*

But it wasn't as if Margeta's assessment was entirely wrong. There had been a shifting of ground. By their altering interests in Amalina alone, Pia was occupying most of her time while Cristine was breaking away. It couldn't be denied. But those were changes caused not by Amalina's direct choice. So why did Margeta's cynical accusation raise such a tremendous feeling of guilt? Amalina wondered against her better judgment if there wasn't some disappointing truth to it after all.

"If there's some guilt inside you," simmered Margeta, with a grim smile at what she saw in Amalina's expression. "I can relieve you; I will be hearing confession today."

"You want me to confess, Princess?"

"Only if it would *relieve* you, Lady Tepsji. I don't know when you've last had it. It is like missing a regular bleeding, the blood becomes stagnant without outlet and renewal." Margeta's smile angled down, her tone changed to something worse. "But … but I'm afraid it will be up to me, as Father Rosczy has left us again, this time without notice." Again, Margeta's dark, wizened eyes flashed. "I don't suppose *you* knew of that, Lady Tepsji?"

"No."

"Or had a hand in it?"

"I don't know what you mean."

Margeta's teeth clenched, and her voice rose in accusation: "You wouldn't admit it, but you've been trying to convey everyone out of this castle ever since I got here. And more so ever since you've returned. Now Rosczy is gone again. And I haven't seen those architects, Misters Wanger, Regio, and Balbo, in the chapel for services in too long a time. It's not like them."

"That isn't my doing."

"But you did speak to Mr. Balbo last, I know this for a fact." Margeta's left lip curled upward slightly, like a tortured, contracted snail. "I don't suppose you could prevail on the Cardinal to send that other priest who visited us previously? He was so much better than Rosczy. Remember the one, Lady Tepsji? The one you *also* scared away?"

"I didn't scare him away."

"He met with you, good lady, after I told you I preferred him to Father Rosczy, and then he was out the door without excusing himself," she said, full of rebuke. "Well, I'd like that one back if we can't have Rosczy anymore. But I don't have time to manage everything. And so I ask you."

Amalina didn't know how to tell Margeta that the priest she'd enjoyed so much had been no religious man at all. He was Attila Bronk, who, in disguise, had come to meet with his spy, Amalina, to introduce her to Lucinda Skeldar's father, Lazru, who was tasked to manufacture the revolutionary army's armor; a brief meeting of *the Cause*'s inner forces right under the Count's nose. If ever Attila Bronk were to appear in the castle again, it would all be over, for everyone.

"And what does *that* look mean, Lady Tepsji?" said Margeta at Amalina's clever smile. "Will you send a note to the Cardinal? Can I have my priest and my services again, Lady Tepsji, or, I ask you plainly, is this your way to *push me out*?"

Amalina hesitated instead of answering, unsure how to play the question. With Margeta so worked up, Amalina realized she might have an opportunity here. Cristine was a bust now, but ... should she try to work on Margeta, instead?

"Why do you always seek to turn me away, girl?" Margeta cried out, as if reading Amalina's thoughts. "Why! Is it because of your friendship with Lady Lampeda? I can only assume it is your advice and counsel to your uncle that has prevented him from taking the final step and accepting me into this family. I know he wants to. He has assured me of my elevation again and again. And so there could be no other reason but you!"

"Is this why you really wanted to talk to me, Lady Margeta?" said Amalina, trying to remain cool in her delivery, trying to find the route she needed. "To accuse me of working against you ... even though there are plenty of others besides me who'd do it? and even though it might be your own obvious faults that do it nicely for my uncle on their own? Or can't you understand he might be lying to you?"

"Lying to me?"

"If you'd just stop to think for one moment, I couldn't care less about whether you—"

"When he *does* finally elevate me," snapped Margeta, cutting off whatever else Amalina was about to say, her cheeks puffing, her head shaking atop her neck, "he will realize his mistake for waiting so long. And perhaps you and Lampeda will also regret your mistake in standing against me. Don't you understand, Katarina, I can give you anything Pia gives you— and better than she can—if you'd only let me? If only you'd recognize me for who I am!"

*Ah!* thought Amalina with an inward smile, *that's right! Who she is! Margeta la Brichese is a stuffy, snooty snob; an unarrested aristocratic elitist of the highest order, and obsessed with rankings and titles. So there!* Amalina remembered her intention to pluck the peacock: she saw Tepsji's assumed claim to royalty was the perfect place to strike for one like Margeta la Brichese.

"Unless ..." said Amalina, carefully, as if not wanting to say more, placing the lure, "unless everything he's promised you just isn't true. All his assurances to you. How do you know you can believe anything you're being told here?"

"You've something to say about your uncle, Countess?" said Margeta, squaring her shoulders, bracing for a blow. "These supposed lies? As if you two aren't the ones pushing him into it!"

*No, the Count is the liar,* Amalina thought, to spread the heat in her mind. *He promised he stopped AXP, even stuck a head up on the wall as 'proof' he'd ended that menace, only to be proven wrong within a week!* This roused Amalina more, like a bellows into a fire, and she would use this kindled flame to push

Margeta in the right direction: the Count is not to be trusted, much less pursued with such obstinacy. He is an imposter, a charlatan.

Amalina shook her head, and, thinking quickly, said in a low, confident voice: "He told you he was once, once long ago, a prince, didn't he? and then he was a king? from a royal family? But then, why say he's just a count now, eh? And didn't you hear the man who came to Kyrgil Castle? The one who wasn't really a man at all and who tried to kill him? He said uncle was nothing but a slave to a royal family, who slew them and took their title just for show; that Uncle Tepsji was nothing, from nothing."

"And so what does that make you?" challenged Margeta. "Wouldn't what you've just said demote you? Or are you saying your family accepted him into your lineage, this interloper you now claim him to be? Really, you should put more thought into your fictions before you begin trying to weave them to me."

"It doesn't matter what it makes me," argued Amalina. "If it's all based on a lie, Margeta, then—"

"What lie!" Margeta's face had gone greyer than usual, her lips a sour pucker. But there was the look of a deep upset in her eyes. "Who is telling lies here? Shouldn't I simply understand that you're lying to me as yet another way to push me out, by making me question everything? I think that's more the case—"

"But I'm *not* the one lying, Princess la Brichese—"

Margeta had a different line of thought, then: "And again what is the difference if any of it is true, when he *is* Count Tepsji now, and I see the very truth of his amazing gift written on four Ladies who've stolen it before me? What shall I believe then, Lady Tepsji, you or *my own eyes*? I *know* what I'm getting—"

A shake of the hall, as if the whole castle had shifted.

The Count appeared between Amalina and Margeta. Amalina fell away with a stifled gasp. Margeta simply stepped back with a light bow to allow him space, as if he'd been expected all along.

"Ah! Glad I caught you, Ms. Dalca," said the Count in a pleasant mellow voice, sweeping his large brown eyes across them both, to hold them in place. He glanced down at his hand, where he held a green glass bottle. He gave them a toothy, distracting smile as he slipped the bottle into a cape pocket. "So good to see everyone getting along, no matter the hour. But let's not disturb Miss Berzweck, she has said she needs rest. Now, my little mouse, you were on your way back to your room at the conclusion of this pleasant conversation, I assume?"

"I—" Amalina looked at Margeta. "Yes, sir."

"Ah, good, then one more thing, my little mouse, come this way," said the Count, motioning for her to follow. "If you don't mind me borrowing my niece from you, Princess la Brichese?"

"By all means, Lord Tepsji," said Margeta, in an undeniable show of exquisite poise. She did not shudder under his stare, she did not bend, she did not fear him; somehow. And her face had turned into something of a slightly pleased, though dour, grand dame. "I think we were done for now. Wouldn't you say so, Lady Tepsji? *For now?*"


## II


"What are you up to, Ms. Dalca?" asked the Count, as he led her down the dark stone staircase to wherever they were going. "Was something happening between you and Margeta that I should know about? You know I'm counting on you as our resident peacemaker."

"Are you, sir?" she asked in surprise.

"I believe your skills in diplomacy are beyond compare," he answered. "And I go back a-ways, understand."

"Yes, sir."

"You do seem to have an excess of energy lately," he commented. "You know how much I've praised you for that energy, seemingly inexhaustible. But these last few months ... such vitality and bustling around at all hours, and with your dark 'tides'. Are you having trouble sleeping? You know, in the end, I am convinced sleep is essential for one's good health."

She wondered if he was regurgitating some bit of random information he'd picked up from one of the Ladies of Title to impress her.

"What about you? You're looking tired, sir."

"Essential for *mortal* health," he amended. "You see the advantage in the other path, hm? But do not concern yourself with me, I'm perfectly fine, as long as there's happiness and accord within my castle." The Count petted his mustache. "Our Princess Margeta la Brichese is unhappy, then? Or ... discontent?"

"She is herself," said Amalina.

"Which means?" he said suddenly testy, not liking her tart answer.

"Both, sir. More discontent I'd say."

"Ah! I wonder why this time," he said without enthusiasm, as if he really wouldn't care to be enlightened.

"She blames me for you not ... um ... not 'accepting her into the family', as she puts it."

"The 'family', eh?" he giggled, his mood brightened again. "Does she know *your* little secret yet?"

"Hard to tell," said Amalina. "You haven't told her who I really am, sir?"

"Only if it comes to it," said the Count, almost cheekily, lifting an eyebrow, intrigued and attentive. "No doubt *you* will be joining us soon enough. *Whenever* you like. And then you will no longer be of that unfortunate class."

Amalina didn't answer, though she saw he was watching for her reaction. She looked away, "No saying if any of the others might not have told her about my past, either."

"But not Lady Lampeda I would assume," he said with a suggestive intonation. "Your good friend."

"I wouldn't think so," she grumbled at him.

"Nor Lady Berzweck."

This didn't improve Amalina's mood, she grumbled harder: "I don't think *she* can talk to anyone anymore, really. The way she is, sir."

He nodded lightly with an unconcerned expression.

"If you wish to visit your friend Cristine again, I suggest you give her another hour or two after we're done here. She should be back to herself by then, I should think."

"You mean?"

"Her former self, that is," tutted the Count. "I too, am not overjoyed by her persistent languor. But as per your restrictions, I am not hurrying her along. Perhaps we can share the best of both worlds, hm? But that is for another time, and another conversation, my little mouse."

*What are* you *up to, Tepsji?* wondered Amalina as they arrived at his salon.

• • •

"Is there something wrong, sir?"

The Count led Amalina through to the countinghouse—now entirely dark, the firechambers cold, the unbagged towers of coins spilled off the counters with uncharacteristic disorder in the high castle—and then out and down the long set of stairs that fed into the vast chamber that was his message center.

As sizeable as the room that stored his gold was, the message center was ten times greater, or even more. The shelves were deep and filled with various correspondence from his minions throughout Ardeel, carried on through the centuries. Each town had its own set of shelves, or just one, depending on the level of communication, with their name etched into it. The room smelled of old vellum and paper, and still held a slight sour tinge from the amount of Kralov's gunpowder that had almost—*almost!*—been used to blow the whole castle to pieces.

The high-ceilinged room was so deep, Amalina could not see the far end. But there was a lit torch at the bottom of the stairs next to the Count's standing desk, where he worked on his private exchanges. Amalina stopped at the desk, but the Count moved further in, and she thought he might be taking her to some other secret chamber attached to this one, one of his many hidden quarters, where his Special Ladies stayed, and where Noka might be. She pictured Noka's smiling face waiting for her around the corner, and bit her lip.

But the Count went to the single shelf that was named 'Korr', Amalina's village, to pull something out, and she blew a breath of relief. When he returned to her, he held the item behind his back as if preparing a pleasant surprise.

"Since you're going back to your room, before you naturally put on a better dress—one without those provocative drops of Miss Berzweck's blood on the sleeve—to then play my ambassador of calm and happiness in my home (which is your sworn duty to me while you remain my servant, you understand, little baker's daughter) and ease our guests' worries over these minor tremors within the mountains—as if what happened in Kyrgil could happen here—or to forgive my occasional absences—"

"The tremors *are* coming more often," interrupted Amalina, rushing in with concern. "And some Ladies *are* asking questions, sir, many questions, yes. May I tell them they can go home if they don't feel safe—?"

"No—"

"Or that you're gone so often because you're supervising the construction of another castle, somewhere else, where we'll soon be moving—?"

"Move from my favorite place in the world, my lovely Palace of Pleasures—?"

"—which will reassure them, or if they don't want to wait for the new place, they can leave—"

"Absolutely not, Ms. Dalca," his eyebrows angled down in annoyance. "While my other castles might have suffered at the hand of that midget, I still have plenty more that survived—not to mention my *hidden castle* in the north, which will never fall—so there's no need to build elsewhere. And this castle here, on this sturdy mountain, I refuse to abandon. But you must stop interrupting me, Ms. Dalca."

"Yes, sir."

"What I was saying was that, before you go off to do your work to play my ambassador," his voice dripped like syrup now, his eyes widened and softened over a generous smile, "I thought *you* might like to return *this* to your boy."

. . .

Amalina's heart skipped a beat as she recognized the book he brought forward and held in his bloodless hands. On its cover, reflecting the bright flickers of the torch, were three large metal letters: AXP. He held the book before her, tapping it with a slight flourish.

Amalina felt her face flush. "But ... what are you doing with that! Um, I mean... sir. You gave it to *me*."

"With the promise that I might borrow it if ever I felt like doing so," he reminded her. "What can I tell you, but that I felt a burst of wistfulness and I took it from your boy. He offered no objection to my request, whatever that look on your face. But never mind, I'm keeping my word to you, and I am delivering it up when done with it. You see?"

He now placed the book in her hands.

"Um, yes, sir."

"You see that nothing has changed with it, I didn't harm it in any way." The way he said it made Amalina think otherwise, but then he explained: "You know how I dote on my things."

"Um, yes, sir."

"A weakness of mine. But I can forgive myself. However, now, before you do your rounds of our guests you will get that boy to hide it again. As was our agreement. For I am not a liar. No matter how much that distasteful word seems to be floating about on the air in my castle these days; *Liar*." He paused. "*You* would never think of me as a *liar*, would you, my fair little mouse?"

But Amalina couldn't answer, she was holding a dangerous book she'd thought she'd left safely in Aklan's possession.

"Very good. Sometimes I wonder if there are those in this castle—both above and below—who question me."

"Question you ..." still she was transfixed by the book, only barely listening.

"Yes, question *me*. Haven't you heard? If I were once a king in Ardeel, why am I now just a count? How could that be? It must be questioned. It must be a *lie*, and I must be a *liar*." He petted his mustache with a haughty look. "That hedgehog I was forced to kill the other year said as much. Well, for your information—" he said this, but seemed to be talking into the air, or himself "—after I withdrew myself from my throne-*regnant*—you know, to purchase some anonymity and peace—I had tried to forward myself as some minor prince, much below my true station. But still, such a title brought too much notice, unfortunate scrutiny, and a constant need to prove myself. Easier then to disappear into the obscure nobility of a count; much more difficult for the rabble to challenge my name and rank.

"*Liar*," he carried on, his mood sinking, his eyelids lowering along with the corners of his lips; as if this was the actual purpose of taking her aside for a talk. So had he heard what she'd said to Margeta? Was he warning her that he's listening, always? That she shouldn't speak carelessly, or against him? "Liar? Call me so, eh? And who are *they*? Are they all actual princesses? *Really?* 'Lady Princess', indeed! Noka's the only one who would survive such a test. She is the true daughter of a true king! Yet it shouldn't bother me if they all weren't. As you very well know, I haven't shaken their tree for their true pedigrees, and it would seem more realistic if most of them were common high borns, with no ounce of legitimate royal blood. Did you not make mistakes somewhere when verifying their credentials, Ms. Dalca? An oversight here or there? Did you give in to *their* lies, or wishful thinking, or did you boast them above their level to me? But see how easy, and comforting, and acceptable it is for a beautiful young woman to lift her rank a step or two. A young *man*, no matter how handsome, I doubt could get away with it. Anyway, what do I care of it? Let them *lie* to me. Let them all be *true* princesses if they like, even if it is only so in their minds, for they shall all be queens; those who prove themselves equal to the task, those whom I choose, and those who accept me—and those who don't disobey. I will see to their promotion myself, eh, little mouse?"

"Uh, yes, sir."

"As my goodwill ambassador," he said, falling out of his tangent, "how do you think you might best smooth these many wrinkles within my Palace of Pleasures?"

"I-I'm sure I will think of something … sir"

"Wouldn't it be best practice to dispel any rumors and lies, and not encourage their spread?"

"Uh … yes, sir."

He saw she was still staring at the book, preoccupied with it. He turned his attention directly to her and pushed a finger down on the gleaming letters.

"As you see, from what I've done here, by restoring this book to you, that I am not a liar, as some might claim, and *I* keep *my* word," said the Count. "Now, Ms. Dalca, my dearest, deepest friend, *you* keep *yours* to *me*."

## 21

# Katarina Tepsji and the Second Book

Amalina couldn't believe she was holding the AXP book again, she kept glancing down at the metal letters as she wound her way up the backstairs. Here was the abhorrent thing she'd been asking for less than an hour ago: a compendium of coded messages from AXP to the Count, which the Count had methodically assembled for an uncertain purpose; sentimentality? a device to aid in his recall of history? a catalogue of damning letters to hold over his treacherous friend? So thorough was this bound collection, spanning decades, she had used it in attempts to discover AXP's identity. And while the true answer to who the criminal was might still lay within its unexplored pages, when she first thought she'd solved the mystery it had only resulted in the death of men who weren't him at all, whose heads now stood on spikes above the entrance to the castle; and though unintentional, remained as unsettling reminders of her guilt in their end. *So caution there.*

When she got to her room, Amalina threw the heavy book down on her mattress and growled at Aklan, who immediately fell startled against his tall cabinet: "All right, get me a dress!"

"Pretty princess! What are you doing here?" Aklan saw the shining letters on her bed. "What's that?"

"What do you think? The book!" she rounded on him. "Why didn't you tell me he took it?"

"He told me not to tell you."

"Whose side are you on?"

"*He* told me not to. What was I supposed to do? You aren't even supposed to know where I hide it, so what does it matter if he has it or not? It's not like you'd know."

"Where *do* you hide it? You can at least tell me that."

"You trying to get me killed, Princess?"

"What a stupid deal," huffed Amalina as she began to remove her dress. That positive spark she'd started the day with now felt like it had ricocheted, she hadn't even spoken to Cristine and now she was fizzling. She stared at the book suspiciously, as if it had betrayed her somehow. "Who knows what he did with it—or to it? For sure he did *something*. He doesn't want me to know who AXP is. For whatever reason, he doesn't; I just *know* it. But ..."

she thought of how little the book's mysteries meant to her anymore considering Attila Bronk and his coming revolution, and just how disturbing it would be to start reading it again; talking herself out of its value. "Well, it'll have to wait until later. Now hold on ..."

Amalina had stretched out on the bed, and while she enjoyed the moment free from her dress, she'd opened the book just to have a glance. There *were* a few more notes pasted into it, or so it appeared. But, more interesting and drawing her eyes, she also saw writing in gold ink filling the margins and the spaces between the notes, especially surrounding one considerable wide gap where Amalina had once removed a slip. Amalina threw on her glasses. Spidery gold-ink arrows pointed at the empty spot from all directions, and starting from the tail end of one of them began a message, in the Count's hand:

> *What is this? Something's gone missing! Has someone tampered with my book? Remember to search the shelf when you are done with the project, this book must remain whole. Or death to the saboteur!— was it Mouse's boy, perhaps?*

"What's that?" said Aklan, when Amalina took in a quick breath. "You see something? Wait, should you be reading it?"

"Whenever I want," said Amalina, shutting the book quickly.

"*After* you've got his permission," he reminded her.

"Doesn't he handing it over to me mean I've gotten it?"

"I don't know."

"If I tell you he gave me permission, would you believe?"

Aklan stared at her, unsure how to answer.

"I haven't the time, just put it away." Amalina slapped it across the mattress. "Somewhere he can't find it, either."

"He doesn't need to find it, he just needs to ask for it."

"And *I* approve he takes it. That he has *my* permission. Remember that."

"Well, that isn't how the deal works, as far as I understand. I mean, how can I really question *him* when he asks for it? I can only take his word he's asked you. And even if he hasn't, what can I say if he asks me nicely?"

True enough, the deal was unbalanced as long as he could push Aklan around. And he could push anyone around. Even now, Amalina knew she'd have to be more careful. It seemed definite now, by what the Count had said, that he *had* heard what she'd said to Margeta, said about him, his past, and his lies. He'd overheard it in the hallway then, as he was on his way to Cristine's room? Or had he heard it from somewhere else in the castle, through all of the thick stone blocks between them, just idly minding his own business on another task and noticing her voice? Could anything she said be overheard from anywhere? If nothing else, from now on she would only speak to Genadie in the French mountain dialect; and, with everyone else … ?

"Fine," said Amalina with a frustrated tone. Then she wiggled a finger for Aklan to get closer and she whispered: "Forget it. Next time, if *he* ever takes the book from you again, just place one of your shoes on my desk. You won't have said a thing to me, and you and I can swear to it also, but I'll know what it means, and I won't be taken by surprise."

"That's clever," said Aklan.

"Never mind that," she said, returning to her regular voice, "help me get a new dress. I'm putting another one on."

"Again?" he gasped at the coming struggle once more. "What I do for you, Pretty Princess!"

"Come on, expert. One that doesn't have Cristine's blood on it."

. . .

There *had* been grumblings among the Ladies of Title and their circles over the recent shakes in the castle, spurred on by tales of Kyrgil Mountain's utter collapse and the destruction it had wreaked throughout that valley—the castle and town pulverized and removed from the earth, the Ladies and their people who'd survived the catastrophe having done so by a complete miracle. These haunting and harrowing tales of near-miss escapes through an immense devastation were spread at every turn and emphasized quite aggressively, to perhaps make some of the weaker souls bolt from the high castle for their own safety. Katarina Tepsji emerged from her room that day to make her rounds as a counter-balance to the uneasiness, to assure everyone that her uncle had assured *her* that the engineers, Wanger, Regio, and Balbo, had assured *him* that all was good: the activity within the rock was a natural occurrence, a sympathetic vibration from the events at Kyrgil, but that it would not be repeated in full. Or at least not happen to them in the high castle, Tepsji's vaunted Palace of Pleasures.

Amalina delivered the reassurances as Lady Katarina with much eye rolling and sarcasm to make sure it was no actual reassurance at all—though if the Count was listening in, he would be unclear.

But everyone was fastened to these rocks, nobody bolted.

. . .

And it should be noted here: while a problem regarding the condemned prisoners did present itself on Katarina's tour, their fate within the castle would take care of itself, bares little measure on the main events of this story, and could use a whole departing piece to recount; but it resolved itself eventually, and separately from this narrative. The most to be said within these pages was that Amalina didn't find the unchanged Ladies too bothered by the introduction of a private prison to the Palace of Pleasures, but that it more became a curious attraction, like a zoo; which many wished to visit to relieve their boredom, and the Count soon forbid.

As for the Ladies below the castle, whom the prisoners were there to feed, Amalina, when she spoke to Erin Epris or Anne Brignol in their private apartments—bare, gloomy, low-ceilinged chambers within the cellars, tucked alongside the Count's—always came away with the same thought. She would never want to be like them: hidden away from the sun, from their vulnerabilities, and from common life; cramped together in a sorority of fears and stale air; and addicted to blood no matter the source. She would not wish herself to be that, not at all. Even if Anne Brignol, in her challenging, keen, and proud fashion, presented their situation as superior, and managed to drag down everyone else into that of beggars jealously waiting outside a senate for entry, or grubs or larvae hoping to reach the final stage of their evolution—including the Barnacle, who she accused of being an utter faithless fraud, as nobody wishing to ascend to the Special Ladies' station could truly believe in an outdated religion.

Also, while some small mystery emerged regarding the prisoners, the transformed Princess Noka Iwebo was avoided during this time; successfully dodged on Amalina's part; or the princess had otherwise ducked Amalina, which was just as well.

But the prisoners will be mentioned no more.

. . .

The most surprising—and surprisingly important—moment in her tour that day was when 'Katarina' was steered by servants into the Grand Library and found Mr. Balbo inside with his new pistols on his hip and a book in his hand. Amalina felt a burst of excitement when she saw him, knowing they were alone and she was free to test his loyalty and solidify his interest—to guage his appetite in her plan.

But then she felt another sudden rush from something else, when Balbo tried to slick down his hair and she saw the book he was holding.

"Mr. Balbo, what is that book you have there?"

"What, this?" he said, sounding flummoxed. "Oh, well, nothing that would be of interest to you, I suppose. Just a bit of odd science, unusual and obscure, but quite technical. I was just returning it."

She told him she wished to have the room for a half hour of private reflection and settled down in a chair, head tucked down. When Balbo politely left she went straight for the book.

So many years ago, Amalina had snuck this very volume up to her room, from the inventory she'd been conducting, and tried to puzzle out what to make of it. The work was a scientific one, written in Latin and, at the time, beyond Amalina's understanding. Its intrigue was in the back. Numbers and tabulations had been written in by hand in the Count's handwriting. And then he'd left a message there. And adjoining his message was a reply by none other than AXP.

*Wasn't that so?* Or was she just remembering it that way? No, it seemed so clear. It had to be true!

Amalina had tried to find this book again, from time to time, when she would remember it and thought it would be a help in her quest to identify him. As she recalled, the words were written in regular roman letters and plain text. That meant it must predate their strange coded exchanges. And since it was before AXP had felt the need to be discreet, it just might give away some important clues. Was there some detail there she could exploit?

But after the discovery of the wailing woman below the castle, the book had immediately become unimportant; being returned to the inventory at some point long ago, and then placed in the library by Georg, and then promptly forgotten.

Until now.

With a shiver of excitement, she pulled from the low shelf the old, heavily bound tome with the title *In Unum De Re Metallica et De La Pirotechnia*; 'On The Use Of Metals and Fire', she could read it better now, as she couldn't before. She was going to have to find some way to reward Genadie for his brilliant language instruction. Opening the book, and flipping eagerly through the pages, she studied again the numbers the Count had written into the margins and flipped her way to the back.

*In here you will find all that you require*, the Count wrote in his spidery script.

Following that, in the oddly distinct solid print which Amalina had grown familiar with from the pigeon-posted slips: *Most helpful indeed. Thank you, estimable Count. I am indebted to all your help, as you are to mine.* (Signed, of course:) *AXP*

'*I am indebted to all your help, as you are to mine* ...?' wondered Amalina.

'*All your help*'? ... a reference to the Count's murder service, perhaps? But it seemed here that the Count was providing AXP science books and calculations. Was that done in addition to killing people for him? And what about '*indebted* ... *as you are to mine?*' How was AXP helping the Count so that he, too, would feel indebted? How could the Count be given anything he didn't already own or could possess? What was the exchange here? Or ... was this just another of the Count's strange one-way deals: providing a profane service to a mortal just to keep himself tantalized by the infinite dark doings of humans?

Far from hearing a cry of delight from Linda Skeldar's spirit at this rediscovery of the long forgotten book, Amalina felt a plunge of disappointment as she stared at the writing and knew that the strange hope she had once placed in finding it was misguided. There were no answers, only more questions.

But as she held the book, and saw the weird exchanges inside it, she was left wondering if there wasn't some greater meaning, and what that meaning could be; that her morning had been pushed constantly in one direction, as if by a higher force, filling her moments with memories of the mysterious criminal who lurked behind the deaths of innocent women, and twice now, within a few short hours, she'd been handed a book touching on that very abominable AXP.

22

# The Widow and the Minister's Wife

After Korr's bell had rung, the boards went up over the bakery windows and doors, and the bolts were secured; leaving the two men alone in the store. Dragomir breathed heavily after dropping the last bar. He was bent at the shoulders from a long day of odd, aimless conversations with his fellow townsmen.

"Well, that's that," said Dragomir.

Attila, appearing bored, nodded more to himself than Dragomir.

"The Vokent lad didn't come inside for a private meeting this afternoon," said Dragomir, curious.

Attila stared at the wall and didn't answer, his fingers mindlessly playing with crumbs on the side board.

It's not that Attila was talkative, he was rather the most reserved of men, yet even so it seemed to Dragomir that ever since Sadra had left, he had gone completely silent and had deflated in some indiscernable way. Just a sunken mound of lightly breathing, occasionally sighing, cloak, with wide eyes that roamed at random; like a sleepy newborn seeking shapes before its face, but not really focusing. His mind had wandered off into the woods, and Dragomir couldn't fathom how to call him out.

"No need to bother with that," chortled the baker, pointing to the crumbs Attila was playing with, "I sweep before bed. Gives the mice time enough to get some bold ideas after I've gone for supper, and to sneak out their holes for a quick snack … then I catch them! Eh! Ha, ha!"

Even though Dragomir laughed heartily, encouragingly, and swatted him on the back playfully, Attila still did not react. It seemed he was lost in his thoughts, which Dragomir assumed to be as labyrinthine and inescapable as a mythological maze. Dragomir shrugged to himself and with a gesture guided the docile fellow out of the front area of the store and into the kitchen.

"Our lieutenant has left town," explained Attila with a mutter, stepping slowly after the baker, the movement seeming to have prompted an internal mechanism that produced his voice. "Left on an important assignment: to fetch our metal, you see. Not to worry though, I spoke with him privately. Gave him guidance."

"I see," said Dragomir, not exactly understanding but continuing on, shutting the door to the outer area—against the mice—and beginning to cover bins. "I don't know what you were after today, Mr. Bronk. Did you learn anything?"

. . .

The kitchen, with its floor-to-ceiling cabinets and wide counters on one side, a bulky rolling/kneading/cutting table dominating the floor's center, and several imposing brick ovens and still more cabinets on the opposite, eastern wall, was not as confining as it might have been, Attila noted. Because—Attila also couldn't help but note—its space had been designed for Dragomir Dalca's hefty body; his comfort and movement. And yet despite the ample room, for Attila, who was smaller than the baker and who'd been hunched over with his ear pressed to the doorway to the outer sales area for most of the day, it had felt oppressive. The ovens' residual heat, the ever-present smells of yeast, and almost perceptible haze of flour in the air, had crammed in at his back, on top, around his body, and down his mouth and nostrils.

The only relief during his vigil had been when Dragomir's wife, the Widow Lidsz, opened the door from the living quarters to procure one thing or another—before being startled at Attila's crouched figure and thrown into hand-waving retreat—and then the air would cool and the smells of common cooking, fragrances of a naïve life; one detached from the troubles brewing in the rest of the bakery and the outer world, would blossom and bloom, and for a few seconds enliven Attila's senses. He'd begun to look forward to the disturbances, and would remark to himself how enviable it must be to live as free from this land's darkness as the old Widow Lidsz, a plain woman from a small rustic town who'd lived her life simply with simple rules; so different from Sadra Smidt, whose life it was, and had always been, to know the darkness intimately, and to provide relief to her people; just the way Attila had done in his position as low constable of Tsobl. And Sadra—

*Sadra …*

The name echoed.

Attila shook his head to free it.

Sadra Smidt's leaving the bakery had not had the lifting effect Attila had hoped for. While he'd aimed to rid himself of an impediment to his considerable concentration, the many questions surrounding the minister's wife, and Attila's relationship with her, and the several warnings he'd received about the very woman—from surprising quarters, with almost astrological import—had instead weighed down his mind. But even thinking about this meant he was distracted again.

*Focus, Attila.*

" ... Mr. Bronk?"

"I was 'looking for' clues," said Attila, somewhat dully, belatedly answering Dragomir's question. "Looking for the signs I need. But I believe I've explained my process."

"Yes," agreed Dragomir his wide face turning red as he closed up the ovens. "So you did. And did you find any, eh? These signs?"

Again, Attila seemed to freeze, his eyes distant, half asleep.

"Well, supper's waiting for us. A good stew is known to help a man think, eh? Let's not let the wife wait."

*... Sadra ...*

"*Who* did you say?" said Attila, too quickly, almost blurting it before recovering himself.

"My wife," said Dragomir, wondering at the odd little statue of a man. He waved him on through the doorway to the living quarters. "You remember her now, eh? Right through here?"

"Forgive me, um ..." said Attila, following the baker. "Yes, of course. Forgive me."

"I'd say this man needs some of your stew," declared Dragomir to Widow Lidsz, as they entered the common room. He pointed a meaty finger at his head. "He's quite a lot on the mind."

"Oh," said the Widow Lidsz, only half-turning from her work at the fire. Then she sang, "Very soon, very soon, my boys. Sit yourselves down and have something to drink. Did everything turn out okay for you, Mr. Bronk?"

Attila did not answer, and Dragomir shrugged helplessly at her.

"Right away," said the Widow Lidsz excitedly, as if her stew were a needed elixir and she had just been presented a desperate case. "I promise, dumpling! Right away!"

Attila's eyes roamed to the Widow and then settled there, his features slack.

From the table, he observed her busy movements at the hearth, the sure but still clumsy way the old woman banged around the pots, wooden plates, and bowls. Her lips were lifted into a smile of happy absorption, so much different than the hard scowl of Sadra ... *Sadra* ... when she puttered around with his meals, before delivering it, setting a sparely loaded pewter disk on a cold crate in the church's supply room.

*... Sadra ...*

. . .

Maybe it was because he was missing her, Attila supposed, but he couldn't keep from continuing to compare the two women: Dragomir's woman and his own; *well, that is, with* Minister Smidt's *woman*, he corrected himself guiltily, *his wife, Sadra Smidt, anyway.* Attila tried to be neutral about it, but where Sadra was thin and angular, her features pulled tight, without an age, and with eyes that flamed and cut and examined as deep as a person's soul, the Widow Lidsz was loose and baggy with little rolls and deposits of fat that hung on in ungainly places, even dripping in wrinkly pockets off her whithered cheeks and jawline, her skin all-over decorated with bumps and moles and wiry hairs, with eyes that were soft and accepting, and which only played over the surface of a subject, as if, and with all her might, she couldn't penetrate a person nor, with a kindly smile, would she ever wish to; it would be *impolite.* But though matched to this old, inadequate woman, Dragomir Dalca appeared a contented man! His daughter was held captive in the monster's castle some great distance from his home, and he was satisfied! Satisfied with his life, satisfied with his wife, and … perhaps that satisfaction was because of *her?*

*Observe*, thought Attila presently, as if dissecting the moment with a scalpel and forceps: The old woman dotes and prances around him, almost in a spring festival dance, constantly calling him 'dumpling', and it appears to bring her genuine joy to give him a smile. In that way, reflected Attila, with her earnest devotion, her warmth and caring, there was a similarity to the woman who'd raised Attila from infancy, and who he loved even to this day. If Attila wanted to push the comparison, he could even claim that same quality was shared by Gug Vogoneyevic, who had rescued him from the river and nursed his broken, bullet shattered body back to health before delivering him to her husband, the great hope of Ardeel, Sir Hak. And so it was with Sadra Smidt, too, who had found him left for dead, had tucked him safely away in a hiding place in the woods and mended him, and then had nourished his grander designs and gave him lodgings in her church. But even if all their warmth and caring matched Dragomir's wife, when compared to those shining examples from Attila's past, the Widow Lidsz was too horribly sweet, and somehow untouched, and willfully—almost shamefully—withdrawn from the real world, and existed only in a bizarre state of second childhood, where, to her, Dragomir was father, son, king, and God. This strange zealotry caused Attila to shiver when he experienced its effects.

Attila also noted Dragomir watching him now, giving curious glances to the Widow Lidsz to follow his guest's dull stare, as if wondering what Attila's looks were about—and then, seeing his wife going about her business, suddenly being stricken with a bland smile of his own, to match the Widow's. These two were both simple people, so Attila's thoughts went, with simple lives. So simple and so unlike Sa—

. . .

"... Sadra, eh?"

"What's that?" said Attila, realizing the Widow had been talking to him.

"I said: 'Staying here with us tonight?'" repeated the Widow, mocking her own warbling voice. "'Poor you. You must be missing your Sadra, eh?'"

Attila was stunned by the statement, and would have inferred a cheap insinuation if it weren't for her empty cheerfulness.

*... Sadra ... My Sadra ...*

*My God, have I been bewitched?* thundered Attila inside at the continuing echo of her name, though with a passive outward face.

"Missing her *already*, I'd imagine," said the old woman to herself, continuing on with unintended deadly accuracy. "Dearly so. Remarkable woman."

The arrows landed in a perfect grouping at the bulls-eye, 1-2-3.

"Admirable," said Attila, trying to steady the strange throbs inside himself. "As are all those of the fairer sex in this village."

The Widow laughed and giggled and fanned herself with the ladle. "'Fairer sex.' Did you hear that?"

"Yes, dumpling," answered her husband, still with a puzzled look at Attila, and had himself a long drink to break off the eye contact.

"Such a thing for a young boy to say these days. I'd thought all of them had lost their manners."

*Young boy?* wondered Attila. But then he supposed he *was* very young compared to—

"You love your new wife," mumbled Attila, sidelong to Dragomir, pointing to her back.

"What's that?" said Dragomir, setting down his mug. But he must have heard the question.

"When did you meet her?"

"I've known her my whole life!" Dragomir whispered his answer as if it was part of a secret.

"But when did *this* come about? Your attaching yourselves? After Amalina left or before?"

"After?" as if a question, but it was his answer.

"The deputy sheriff proposed the match," said Attila quickly. "I heard that right, didn't I?"

Dragomir looked at Attila in wonder at how this odd subject had woken up the man who'd been close to falling asleep. And now he was asking Dragomir questions about—?

"And how much do you share?" said Attila, probing. "How much does she know about your daughter's situation and ... and *you-know-who*? About what *we* are doing here, Mr. Dalca? How much have you told her?"

Dragomir's face turned red again, looking shamed. "She knows. But not *too* much."

"But knows enough. A dangerous thing, knowledge. Particularly when the recipient isn't ready for it."

"Or is too innocent to understand," said Dragomir, "but such is love, to trust. Love is about trust."

"But some information is too dangerous," insisted Attila.

"Yes, I suppose," said Dragomir, his face growing redder, unable to look Attila in the eye.

"It's all right," assured Attila, scratching idly at the table. In a most uncharitable thought, he supposed Dragomir had shared *everything* with her. *And why not?* Attila realized the baker was so taken by his wife, that she was so overwhelmingly innocent, he thought nothing of speaking on any matter in front of her, confident that, even if she were to begin to understand what was being spoken of, she would never share it with another person, nor think to. In all probability, because it did not touch on the immediate pleasures of home life, she would simply choose to forget the conversation or the subject. That's what it seemed might be the case ... but could this be true? He'd have to test the possibility.

And if it were true, maybe he could use that to his own purpose ... to gain that one simple item for which he'd come to Korr, and which he'd been wanting all along.

23

# Surprising Quarters:
# The Innocent Wife and the Silver Sign

Attila waited patiently for Widow Lidsz to serve their night's meal. As Dragomir ladled the soup into his mouth, taking care with a large napkin not to lose any in his beard, Attila appeared to wake again from his stony silence: "I was speaking to your husband earlier about today's enquiries with the men."

Dragomir looked up, surprised not only that Attila had said something, but something he was not sure was true. Lidsz nodded her head politely to Attila, "Oh?"

"Yes, I have a particular way I work, you see, and I need certain pieces of information before I can establish a line of thinking that will profit the labor."

"Oh, I see."

"But it's always difficult coming to any conclusions when the general population of Korr are such easy recipients of lies. Their lack of discernment troubles me. Schools of witches? Paupers that are princes who are sorcerors? *Dragons?*"

"I'm sure you did your best," Widow Lidsz comforted Dragomir with a kind tone, though she had no idea what Attila was talking about but simply had to chime in to his defense. She paid no attention to the nonsense the *boy* was saying.

"I just need the right information," said Attila, almost acting. "Just the *right* information."

"What information is that?" she asked, seemingly more interested in spooning the soup over her wide, stubby tongue. This fascinated Attila.

"About the ... " Attila then said, in a drawn out way: "Everyone ... knows ... do you suppose? ... *Count Tepsji* ...—" The Widow did not react to the name, but waited politely for Attila to finish; she didn't know the Knight of Ardeel by name "—... has spies here?"

"Does he?" said Dragomir, astounded. "Spies! Who?"

"He has informants in many places," said Attila. "It's logical they would be here, too. I thought I'd told you ..."

"But do you know any?" said Dragomir. "I've only ever seen that little rat he keeps with him. But someone here in Korr? One of *us*? I can't imagine!"

"Certainly," said Attila, sleepily, as he worked through his prepared conversation. "But I'd know better who it was if I could get access to …" here he took a breath " … *the contract* … inside *the Secret History of Korr*."

Dragomir sent a look of horror toward his wife. Attila's own heart hammered, though he did not show his anxiety. For her part, Widow Lidsz looked at them as if she understood, though of course she could not. *The Secret History* was a book known only to the men who had been initiated into it. From Dragomir's reaction, at least Attila knew the baker hadn't shared *that* much with her. He had some discretion, then. Too bad though, thought the former low constable, this might have been the route to what he'd coveted for so long now.

"Why should you want such a thing?" asked Dragomir, his eyes continuing to tick almost ruefully toward his wife.

"I've received some intelligence and if I should see the name listed on the contract I'd know for sure. Do you know who keeps it? The mayor? The *deputy sheriff*?"

"The deputy," said Dragomir, certainly but with a gulp. "I've no idea where."

"But would he allow you to see it? If you asked for it?"

"He'd want to know why."

"I think at this point we might have to let him in on our little project. You think we can trust him?"

"He's been a loyal friend. I'd trust him with my life."

"The deputy sheriff is the one who encouraged our marriage," said Dragomir's wife, happy to have something she could share with some knowledge.

"What a lucky coincidence," said Attila, casually. He turned to Dragomir, drawing his eyes from Widow Lidsz's smile to her husband. "So he'd let us have it, this book, if you asked him and he knew our purpose?"

"Maybe," he answered nervously. "I haven't seen it since I was a young man. Who knows if it still exists? And, the recent years, with Amalina gone, he might have different thoughts. Yes, Boss B might have better success with the deputy sheriff than I; to convince him, if that's what you want. He has greater standing and influence there. Especially if we're still cutting out Mayor Daniel on this, like you said …"

Attila nodded they were. "Your mayor will be the very last to know, when it comes to it. But—"

"You said you'd recognize somebody's name in this book?" said Dragomir's wife, curiously; but not too curious, she wouldn't dare ever pry. She lifted an eyebrow between some hairy moles.

"There are many things in *the Secret History* that can shed light on our Tepsji, who he is, how we might take advantage—"

"But you said it had to do with a spy," said the Widow. "A confederate of some kind … and a name."

Attila nodded and cursed inwardly for getting too excited in his enthusiasm for laying hands on the *History* and forgetting how to conduct himself. But it was a thrill to have escaped Sadra's control, and to now be free of limitations and to finally reach out for what he wanted—"Yes, of course, that would be the most important. But there are other—"

"But does that mean you *have* a name?" she carried on. "You don't want to trust it to *us* until you have verified it yourself, then? or … ?"

"I only know the first name," said Attila, reluctantly, after a short sigh, dreading to part with any bit of information. But this was the plan to procure that book, one way or another, and if it would help …: "That is, I have an initial, the first name begins with an A."

Dragomir's wife made a little gasp. Both men turned to her.

"Oh, I'm sorry. It's just. You said the name begins with A? Remember Alexei the doctor? But he was so *nice*. And he's gone away to the south because of his gout. More than a year ago. He was so good with everyone's health but his own. A pity. Begins with A, you say? What about …?"

Dragomir and his wife traded names back and forth. Of course there was Anzi the Porter, and the Boss, Alexandru Berzweck, along with some others.

"But all of those do not fit exactly, do they?" said Attila, feeling a strange inward shift. It was as if, though he was not directly holding *the Secret History* open in his hands, as he'd thought he might achieve this night, he were onto some profitable line with which they could help. It was a tingling sense he'd learned not to ignore even when it countered his cautious nature. But with their combined ages and experience, Dragomir and the Widow might make the book unnecessary. "Maybe we shouldn't consider names within our circle who are already established, such as Boss Berzwecken, but those who exist completely *outside* of it. Is there anyone with a first name 'A' in town who's of prominence but hasn't been considered for our operation?"

"Argus," said Dragomir, and explained who he was: a brother in the baker's guild who sold his cheap goods to the poorer sort on the other side of town.

"Yes," said Attila, feeling the vibrations build. "A man by trade who deals with those in poverty and distress. Those who might be willing to talk for a little relief of their hunger. Those who might know secrets of the wealthier families due to their laboring for them. What's his full name? Does he have a surname? Or is he just known as 'Argus the Baker'?"

"I can't say," said Dragomir, looking distracted by any unhappy suspicion about his brother in the guild. "I don't think I've ever known."

The Widow shook her head and shrugged.

"Anyone else?" prompted Attila. "Someone along those lines as this Argus fellow? Perhaps with a middle name or a last name that is unusual? Like an X or a Z?"

Dragomir shook his head too and then brooded silently.

It seemed the baker had lost his mind and was done talking for the night, until Widow Lidsz encouraged him with more suggestions. The names she brought up, innocuous as they were, led them down a pleasant path of remembrance, far away from the purpose of the conversation, and continued on until it was well beyond reclaiming. In a short time they were smiling and giggling, their heads down together, or leaning back, Dragomir's hand trapped in hers. The Widow had rescued her husband from unhappiness once again; and far from a malevolent cunning on her part, she'd undone their work, his and Attila's work. And the baker was satisfied with that, too. It was as if the old woman's innocence were a prevailing current. Or rather, it was a heavy lid that sat firmly down on top of the large man, sealing his brains with it.

. . .

*And wasn't this the same miracle Sadra had performed—in her own way—on me?* wondered Attila. Because Dragomir was a simple man, he only needed someone simple to distract him. With Attila, it would naturally require someone significantly more intelligent and shrewd to keep him in check. And so, Sadra. Yes, the baffling mists were parting now. The morning's warning signs had been for a purpose after all, it must be. Heaven had recognized Attila's need for *the Secret History*. And for his having deviated from the proper path, as Attila had, a just penalty, an equal obstruction, was sent his way; a ready tool to prevent him from reaching the book. Sadra Smidt.

Or, was this an uncharitable thought?

Widow Lidsz, noting Attila's cold, observant look, shot him one of her own, a quizzical one, one to weigh his appropriateness for her husband's company, as if their guest were on the verge of announcing he was a rodent. She excused herself and left the table, her head shaking slightly.

This allowed Dragomir to lift his eyebrows, strain his fingers through his thick beard, and grumble on helplessly, not sure what he could do for Attila, or on his behalf, to improve the situation. But while he did so, Attila watched the Widow wander shakily to the small pantry, and begin sweeping, then duck and dart out of the rooms attached to the living area, and he thought how remarkable it was. She exists like a bird! Finding needed pieces for her nest, willfully ignorant of the plots of the poachers seeking her eggs; unconcerned, their threat against her forgotten.

It wasn't an uncharitable thought about the Widow this time, by Attila, but one of near envy. Attila suddenly realized that the turmoil in his head was brought on not by Sadra the woman, but the lack of true objective *signs*—the all-important physical signs that point him, and have always guided him to his solutions; to deliver justice. But facing a faceless enemy now, and without guidance, he was left to flail. Absolutely flail. And part of that flailing was to grasp onto someone he felt he could trust: Sadra Smidt, of course. Then, in a lesser way, Lieutenant Vokent, Boss Berzweck, and Bishop Perdu. But they begged the greater point: didn't the act of grasping for a companion weaken him instead of strengthen him? In his desperation he'd farmed out his intellect, most of all to Sadra. Sadra was smart, but by just how much? Smart *enough*? And what happened if she were AXP? Wouldn't he be blinded and led by the nose? led by the very culprit he was after? like a fool? Anyone in Korr could be this agent—even the seeming innocent Widow Lidsz!—so how could he permit anyone but himself to occupy his central mental ground? If the Widow could exist as a preoccupied bird, ignoring the plots of the world while concentrating on her programmed tasks, why couldn't Attila find comfort in his own tasks and programming, and live as a lone wolf, concentrating on hunting his prey, even if the scent should be lost? Hadn't he always lived this way before? Before Sadra Smidt? There was a time he had, and there was power in that oneness. And freedom. There was no conflict, no reliance, no possibility of befuddlement, as witnessed in Dragomir's seeming drop in intelligence when his wife starts talking—

"I must apologize," said Attila, turning his half closed eyes at the baker, who came to visit the guest room, on the second floor, later in the evening, where Attila had gone to meditate on his displeasing circumstances, confident now that any association with love—or perhaps the Widow Lidsz, at least—was the beginning of idiocy and defeat. "I should never wish to insult your wife."

Dragomir's thick, black, brambly eyebrows went up. "Have you?"

Attila looked blank again as he rethought his words, then, explaining or excusing himself, he said with a vague wave of his hand, "Imprecise. My apologies again, but I've been distracted."

"You've never struck me as a fellow that lets himself be distracted," said Dragomir, with a tired, bouncy chuckle.

"And still ..."

"You must forgive my wife, she really does want to be helpful."

"She seems to know much more than the average woman about men's business."

"*Men's business,*" echoed Dragomir with a laugh, until he noted Attila wasn't laughing. He admitted: "I *do* share with her everything."

"She understands what's at stake here? What's happened with your daughter? And the danger her abductor poses to the world? The entire world, should he get loose?"

"I've explained to her as well as I can. I think so. She's a cheerful woman, anyway."

Attila nodded gravely.

"No one's perfect, Mr. Bronk," said Dragomir, sounding apologetic on his part. "Even *her*, I admit." He leaned in confidentially, "I swear to you, though I haven't found a single difference between their two recipes, my first wife's mamaliga, god rest her soul, is so much better. I don't know how. But don't go telling Lidsz I said that."

"I didn't mean to start anything," said Attila, feeling uncomfortable, though looking sedated. Dragomir nodded and turned his head to take in the small room.

"This was Amalina's bedroom once upon a time," said Dragomir, with a lost smile.

This made Attila awkward under the covers. With the flowery blanket, it *was* like something a young girl might own. He had assumed it was Dragomir's wife's taste in bedroom décor. Returning his attention to the baker: Dragomir was nervous, his eyes bound to the rough wood panel over the window—as if his daughter was hovering outside it—more than they lingered on him.

"Our mission is not to return your daughter to you," reminded Attila, flatly. "But you understand that, no? Our purpose is to right a centuries-long injustice."

"Yes," nodded Dragomir. "I can only hope that … Well, she's a smart girl and will do her part. If we all do our part, she'll be fine. I know that. She *is* very clever."

"But there's something else you wanted to say to me?" said Attila. "You came to my room, privately, without your wife?"

"I suppose there is," mumbled Dragomir softly. After a reluctant glance into Attila's inscrutable stare, he became serious, he lost his smile and his voice changed, went lower and conspiratorial: "However, at supper, you said the first letter in the name you were looking for was an 'A'?"

"That's so," answered Attila, sensing something in the air might have changed once again. "Has some other person occurred to you, Mr. Dalca? Someone you don't want your wife to know about?"

"And that's it?" said Dragomir, not acknowledging the last question. "You said something about an X or a Z in there, too. What about 'A.X.I.'?"

Attila's eyes lowered to slits, his body seemed to relax into the bed as if he were falling asleep. But he said: "You've a reason to ask me something like this, Mr. Dalca?"

"It was strange when you said it," whispered Dragomir hoarsely, as he began to fumble at his smudged apron. "And I got to thinking about these letters I found on this bar. I wasn't sure if it meant anything …"

Dragomir handed Attila the little silver ingot the Boss had given him, turning up the wider bottom-side as he did so. Crudely pressed into the metal, as if by thumbnail, were the letters A. X. and then what appeared to be an I. But, of course, the 'I' could have been the long mark of an unfinished P or a B.

*Here's the sign!* thought Attila, with a sense of incredible relief. By freeing himself from a wrongful entanglement—an unsavory relationship with a woman—it seemed as a reward he had now received a clue! Which was another boon, for it was a second sign on top of the first. It confirmed that the warmth of a woman, any woman, perhaps *all* women, is a deception, a lure into falsehoods—a reach into the same darkness Attila sought to defeat.

"Mr. Dalca," said Attila, his eyes heavy. "Tomorrow, if Mrs. Smidt comes, tell her she's no longer needed. From here on out."

"Oh?" this surprised Dragomir, confusing him, they'd been discussing something else; something he'd thought important to his odd guest. He held up the ingot closer to Attila's face, turning it to the light. But: "I will. That's sensible. Okay."

"Now," Attila pointed to the ingot and the initials etched into it, and pivoted back to the matter at hand, "this is Boss Berzweck's metal. But we already ruled him out. Did we not?"

"Yes, of course. And these are kind of scratched in, you see, so I didn't suspect … I *don't* suspect …"

"Well, who *do* you suspect put the marks there?" Attila paused to study Dragomir deeply. "Or *is* there a reason we should be questioning your friend Alexandru after all, Mr. Dalca?"

## 24

## Lady Berzweck and the Crucial Link

With the day's coincidental book revelations and its seeming insistence Amalina think about AXP, it occurred to her this might be a subtle but atmospheric warning that the criminal was after her again; perhaps he'd sent a stealthier and more dangerous assassin this time—as he'd warned he'd do in one of his later notes. She'd best beware the castle's darkened corners.

As for her trying to solve that mystery, on further reflection, to discover and root out AXP right now could light a fuse too early, set in motion an unstoppable process which might result in a confrontation—possibly deadly—which could, in turn, free Attila. Bronk from his own diversion down that road of hunting and eliminating the enemy agent, allowing him to return to *the Cause*'s mission. And then the revolutionary army would arrive at the gate far sooner than she would like. Better to hold off until a later time, keep on guard, and clear people out of the way who may get hurt.

*Proceed as normal, then.*

But what was normal? especially if the Count was awake and paying attention to her movements, like a bug with its antennae up?

. . .

Presently, Amalina decided to take the Count's advice. The day had passed, allowing whatever he intended to do with—or for—Cristine to be done. It was time to visit, see if she'd finally found some energy to rise. If not, if she was still caught up in her dreams, half-in half-out of the world, Amalina would write a letter to her father, Boss Berzweck, immediately, to demand he come and remove his daughter from the castle.

With a light sneer of contempt for Margeta which didn't hurt her pretty face, Claire Montraine informed Amalina she'd noticed *the Barnacle* heading off to take confession in her chapel. Hoping to thread the needle and avoid Margeta—or Bardina—Amalina ran to Cristine's room, and for the third time in so many days, knocked once and entered.

. . .

On the small bed, Cristine was now sprawled under the blankets; her head, the only part sticking out, lay heavy on the pillow. Though definitely alive, her face looked drawn as ever, even more so than earlier; Amalina had seen livelier corpses. Whatever the Count had done, nothing had changed. Amalina thought sadly that the blond haired girl with the sharp features and striking eyes had disappeared forever.

" ... Yeah, you really don't look well, do you ...?" muttered Amalina gently to her unconscious friend. "Don't worry, I'll write your father ... tell him you're here. He'll take you home, and away from this. To where it's safe and—"

"Eh?" said Cristine, turning her head on the pillow, her eyes slitted but open. "Amalina? Amalinaaa ...?"

"*Katarina*," whispered Amalina helpfully, as she stepped forward, joining Cristine at her side. "We're still pretending I'm Tepsji's niece, remember?"

"Yes, dear sister," smirked Cristine, sounding more awake than Amalina had thought. "You just surprised me, I'm not that out of it. But I'm up now and I remember well enough ... *Katarina*. Did you hear that, *Katarina*? You happy?"

Cristine groaned as she tried to sit. She lay back down. With the blankets pulled away by the movement, Amalina saw her neck was now wrapped with a dark scarlet scarf, stained even darker by dried motes of blood. Where had that scarf come from? Cristine's hand idly played with one end.

"I'd be happier if you were back to normal," said Amalina. "Or better, back home."

"What time is it?" moaned Cristine. She struggled to open her dark, puffy eyes as wide as they would normally go. Then fought to keep them open as her head lolled and drooped to the side. "Supper already?"

"Not for a couple hours, I think."

"So early! Amalina ... I mean ...uh ... *whatever* ..." Cristine rolled back under the covers, but only to slide herself along the mattress to get out of bed. "*Katya*, help me get my clothes on, will you?"

"Just stay in bed," ordered Amalina with genuine concern. "Really. You look so very, very tired."

"Greta's makeup will help with that ... A touch of it, if you could, for me. No servants for such small things anymore, please ... they're no longer *en vogue*." Cristine intoned sarcastically, "Thank you very much, *Noka*."

"I meant you need more sleep, not make up."

"Sleep later," said Cristine drowsily, then added with a grim smile, "When I don't need sleep anymore ..."

"What does *that* mean?" But Amalina knew, of course.

Cristine managed to get herself out of the bed but fell, smacking fleshily on the stone floor. She laughed with shallow snuffles at her own clumsiness.

Then she crawled toward the mirrored table, dribbling a little line of spit from her lips, and pointed weakly to indicate where she wanted Amalina to help her. Amalina tried to turn her around.

"No, let's just get you back to—"

"Get me into my dress!" demanded Cristine. "C'mon!"

"I can't believe you. You need rest. You know it. Look at you."

"I need *that*." Cristine now pointed to a small bottle on the desk. It was made of a uniquely colored green glass with a rough but very angular body, which made it look as if it had been chipped out of a larger block of dark emerald stone. Was that green bottle the one the Count had been holding earlier? It must've been. "Get it, Katarina. For me."

"What is it?" asked Amalina, rushing ahead to retrieve it.

"Another of your uncle's presents," said Cristine. But this gift was not much like the ruby necklace which she'd used to hide the first set of neck wounds—and she had become, over time, indifferent to. She sounded hungry for it, "Yes, bring it here. To me."

Cristine took the bottle from Amalina with both hands. She removed the stopper and held its open mouth to her nose. When she breathed in hard she fell back, her eyes wide. "Aaaah …" But then she surged up onto her knees. "Ah, yes!" And then she stood, as if she might launch herself to the ceiling. "*Yes!* That's all I needed! Who needs to sleep?"

"We all do," said Amalina, disturbed by the sudden transformation.

"Not with this stuff," Cristine smiled with smug satisfaction. She sat down before the mirrored desk and plunked the green bottle onto it, carelessly discarding the tonic now that it wasn't needed. She began searching through the other bottles and canisters in front of her. Tins of powder, chalk, cherise, crushed cochineal, rouge for the the cheeks and then the lips, a basin of tiny diamond shaped patches, and jarred, pleasant smelling syrups, jellies, and creams. The armaments of a young woman who wishes to present as a proper Lady. "Now help your best-friend-in-the-world get ready, won't you?" Cristine was bursting with energy, her hands jittery with overflowing power, her words a rapid staccato. "Now listen, now listen, I'm so glad you came. I really am, I can't tell you. It seems like you never want to be with me anymore these days. You know?" She leered, her pupils were like pinpricks: "But *was* there a reason you're here, *Katya*?"

"You don't really have to call me that if you don't want," said Amalina, not quite liking the tone in it.

"Of course I want to. Just for you. I'm only playing the part, *Katty-Katty*."

"Well, there's nobody around. I'd prefer you didn't. And I don't care for the way you say it, to be honest. I'd prefer if you didn't say it at all."

"Oh? Would you say I don't have to call you 'Katarina' if, instead, I kept calling you *Amali—*?"

"Never mind," Amalina cut her off. She frowned at the dress Cristine was looking for, and channeled her attention to that. "This dress again?"

"Is there something wrong with it?"

"There's blood around the neckline."

Cristine snickered. Now seemingly bounding with energy, her skin still hadn't lost its claylike appearance, but something inside her had been pulled tight; her features were honed once again, and her eyes were ice-blue. "You know, I heard you before. When you said you were going to report me to Papa."

"I didn't say I was going to report you. I said I was going to have him come get you."

"Same thing."

"Welll ..."

"Why can't you stop trying to butt in when you see I'm happy, eh?" She shot a look at Amalina in the mirror. "So very happy!"

"How can you say you're happy when you look like this?" asked Amalina, using the folded dress in her hands to gesture at her friend.

"Thank you, dear sister."

"You can't say you're looking your best. I mean, just look at yourself in that mirror. Look. I don't see what's so great about being here if it's near killing you."

Cristine proceeded to obscure her lifeless color with a coating of stiff white paint, applied by her fingers. She changed her mind and scraped it off.

"Easy for you to say. You've been all over the world, I've been planted in Ardeel. Well, now you have the whole world here, why shouldn't I want to be here, too? To at least have some kind of life."

"And what he's doing to you ..."

"*What he's doing to you*," she mocked.

"Changing you."

"He's helping me *become*, Katty. Isn't he?" said Cristine, sampling more make up from the desk, checking its color against her drained pallor, everything seeming to clash with skin like a week-old boiled potato.

"At best he's changing you into something you don't know," cautioned Amalina, "even I don't know. And that's if it works. How you're looking ... I've been so worried for you, Cristine, I'd told myself today, when I came to your room, if you were still asleep I'd have the Boss come get you. And—"

"Well, I wasn't sleeping, was I?"

She shrugged. "I thought you were, anyway."

"No, I never do. I'm always awake."

"You *have* been sleeping, though. You've been asleep for days now, actually. Did you know that?"

"Maybe that's what you *thought*. I can't sleep hardly at all with the excitement and activities. Problem is, I can't get up, either. I just lay there and listen, and can't move ..."

"Hmmm, but you were definitely asleep the other day I came," said Amalina. "You were having a bad dream; a nightmare about Bessa, from the sound of it."

"Bessa? Bossy Bessa?" scoffed Cristine. Her pale hand flicked down the edge of the scarf, for a second revealing the scabs that ringed her neck. She blew out an impatient breath: "Ama—*Katarina*, dearest, can you *please* help me get dressed here, or not?"

Amalina nodded, but then had a clever thought. The leverage to get Cristine moving in the right direction.

"I have trouble sleeping, too," said Amalina, trying to sound nonchalant as she smoothed out the dress and prepared to help Cristine into it. She eyed all the underlayers to the side that needed to be arranged and put in place first. "All kinds of bad dreams, too. All kinds. Not about Bossy, though. I keep having ones about Lucinda Skeldar."

"Lucind—who? What? *That* girl?" Cristine played with the scarf some more, sneering at its pitifulness, or because it wouldn't obey where she wanted it to stay. "Why would you *ever*?"

"Seems like it only happens here," murmured Amalina, suggestively. "When I'm in this castle. I—I don't know why. But she comes to me at night, very often."

"She's dead."

"Yes. That's why it is so strange. She's a spirit haunting me. And it seems she wasn't killed by wolves like everyone said. But that she was killed by *someone*. And she wants me to take revenge on him."

"Rea-l-ly?" said Cristine, not sounding interested. The drifting way someone would let you know they aren't paying attention anymore.

"So you haven't had nightmares like that? I thought, with the one you had of Bessa ... oh, never mind."

"And why would a dream like that bother me, anyway? It would almost be a fantasy; her crying for mercy?"

"For help."

"Lucinda was just a bunch of trouble and deserved anything that happened to her. Bessa, too."

Amalina held back the dress from Cristine's leg and gave her a look.

"What?" said Cristine. "I mean, it's sad for Limpy Skeldy. But those things happen. She *was* one of *those* girls, remember?"

"Well, I suppose I thought you might get the dream, too. Like it happens to girls from Korr who visit the castle. Or it comes with the castle. Like she's really here," she added weight to the next words: "an avenging ghost."

Cristine eyed her critically. "Katarina! Are you now going to try to scare me out of here with a ghost story? Is that what you're seriously trying to do?"

"Well, not scare …" Amalina didn't know how to finish the sentence so she just blushed.

"C'mon, hold the dress open like a good little princess," Cristine instructed, somehow she'd already wormed her way into the stays. When Amalina opened the waistband, Cristine shot her legs through it. "Now get me a necklace, I've got the rest. Should be some over there by the chest."

"Well, anyway," said Amalina, pattering on to cover her lame attempt to frighten Cristine, "Ghost or not, I feel that she's calling out to me for help. Poor Lucinda. And I feel I have to help her."

"Of course you do," snarled Cristine, impatiently. "When do you *not*?"

"What?"

"I guess because it was your 'uncle' who did it, eh?" said Cristine. "Or is *that* not something we're allowed to talk about, either?"

"Not really. But, well, he didn't."

"No?"

"Not exactly."

"Did *you* kill her, Katya?" grinned Cristine, in mock surprise.

"No!"

"Swear it, my sister."

"I swear."

Cristine turned on the small bench. "I mean *really* swear it."

Amalina gawped at Cristine, who watched her out of a grey face with those icy blue eyes. "I swear, Cristine. I did not kill Lucinda Skeldar."

"*Noooo*," said Cristine, holding her arms out as if she wanted a hug. "I mean *reeaally* swear it."

Amalina nodded. She came forward and bowed her head down. "I swear, I did *not* kill Lucinda Skeldar." Since it looked like Amalina was going to be shy about it, Cristine pressed her forehead against Amalina's and then rolled it so her left eye and Amalina's right eye met, and she blinked so that their lashes kissed; their old custom of swearing on their blood-sisterhood.

But this meeting-of-the-eyes, so meaningful and solemn to two girls once-upon-a-time, it felt like some nonsense out of a simple, long-past childhood. Something not real anymore. Left behind. Cristine, sitting back, looked as if she had the same thought: that she'd just lost something. She frowned. Then glanced at the green bottle, shrugged and smiled an 'oh, well' smile.

• • •

"I guess you're telling the truth," smirked Cristine. "Luckless Limpy L died a bit of mystery, eh? Now get me my jewelry. What are you waiting for, princess?"

Amalina went back to the trunk, opened it, and stared at the bounty of polished jewelry and stones inside. She didn't see the Count's old ruby necklace, so she started rooting around, feeling the rich, cool metals against her skin.

"Luckless Limpy Lucinda Skeldar," Cristine was saying. "I swear, it's like you have some kind of *constant* guilty conscience, Ama—ah—Katarina. I wonder why? Why do you always bother about everyone else, good sister? I mean, first, when I got here, you were going on and on about all your obligations here and in Korr, and what you need to do, and what you need to do for your father, how you need to set him right. Now it's some savaged hick girl from Korr you've got to help? A bad girl who was nobody to us, ever? I guess you're going to be adding *me* to your crusades next, if you haven't already. Well, don't bother. See to yourself, Amalina. See to yourself … As it is, I'm leaving everything behind. I am growing *away* from it."

Amalina stopped sifting through the nest of gold loops, interlocking links, and bands studded with gems of all cut and color. She shut her eyes against the dizzy array.

"I can't find your necklace."

"There are at least ten in there. Are you blind?"

"Oh, I thought you meant uncle's ruby one."

"Don't you see I'm wearing a *scarf?*" cried Cristine in disbelief. "I need his big, clunky thing like I need dungeon irons around my neck. Something else there. Long, with a pendant that hangs low so it'll draw the eye away. *Away.*"

"Since when did you have so many necklaces?" asked Amalina, sorting through them again.

"Always. But how could I ever get away with wearing one in a place like Korr? Would've been stolen or smashed in a minute. I hid them."

"And never showed them to *me?* What about our oath? No secrets, remember?"

"What would be the point of showing you? I wouldn't want to get you *jealous.*"

"I wouldn't be jealous."

"Of course you would, that's what you've been from the very beginning. You never wanted to share your toys, and you were always grabbing mine. Remember how many fights we had over them? I think you even pulled my hair."

"It was the other way around, and you pulled *my* hair. What would I have to be jealous about?"

"Always a jealous little girl," said Cristine, patly, as if in conclusion. "But never mind, it's not like these little trifles are my *best* jewelry. Papa wouldn't let me take *those*. And well, besides, I couldn't have ever shown you any of this stuff here, because I got most of these ones after you left. Papa saw how unhappy I was with you gone and was trying to cheer me up."

Amalina picked out a long gold chain with a swirly metal disk hung from it. The metal had a finely crafted but deliberately beaten look. There was something about the chain itself that struck Amalina as oddly familiar. The design of the chain's loops, a bit squared off at the corners. Rectangular. She looked at it. Then she studied the disk. On the back, in small block letters pressed into the gold, were the letters: AXP.

Amalina gasped.

"What?" said Cristine, annoyed.

The design of this gold chain, though much smaller and far more delicate, was just like the silver link she'd found hidden in the Count's cellar. And just like it, this jewelry had the AXP initials. So AXP ... was a tradesman in Korr! Someone who worked with metals and could create fine pieces of jewelry. Like the Blacksmith? or the Jeweler? or the Clockmaker?

Surnames beginning with P, which Amalina might have seen written in the accord with the Count, began furiously flooding her mind: Polau, Pfinzu, Pstorak, Paul, Pontifax? Yes, Pontifax: she'd seen that one in Korr's Secret History. But that name did not belong to the tradesmen she knew. It had to be an artist, certainly, or someone with artistic talent who she didn't yet know. But ...

"Cristine? Where did you get this necklace? Did the Count give it to you?"

"No not that one," said Cristine. "Find the one with the blue rock on it."

"But where did you get it?"

"I already told you. Papa got it for me as a present."

"Where did *he* get it?"

"How would I know? He travels all over the country, picking up surprises for me."

"But this one was made in Korr."

"How do you know?"

"I just ... Never mind." Amalina figured maybe, seeing the letters there, and how, for some reason, and for the third time that day, AXP had become the focus, maybe it *was* a good time to push for an answer: "I just noticed it was stamped with some initials. Say, do you know anyone in the village who has a last name that starts with P? Such an *unusual* letter for a last name, don't you think? I can only think of old Wolk Pontifax, because you could never forget a name like that. But I can't think of anyone else. Can you think of anyone?"

"P?" said Cristine.

"Yes."
"You mean besides me?"

## 25

## Cristine Przek

"Why?" said Cristine, not noticing Amalina's face had suddenly gone white.

"But … I thought your last name is Berzweck."

"Berzwecken's the company name. Grandpapa changed it after the invasion to make it more appealing to *those* people. Which it did. *Przek*, with a 'P', doesn't fit as well as a 'B' does into a Germanian mouth; or their prejudices. Therefore: Przek … Berzweck. Ol' Boss *Berzweck*, y'know?"

Amalina felt her world spinning and she blathered just to cover again. "How did I ever not know this?"

"Because you never needed to?" said Cristine, in her own far-off world. "I must've told you a hundred times. But you only listen when you want, Amalina *Dalca*. See, I know *your* name." Cristine gulped at her mistake, then waved it away. "Oh, I mean … well, you know what I mean: Katarina *Tepsji*. *That* 'your name'. And so on. Now forget all that and find me the necklace with the blue rock."

"You don't have any uncles, right?" said Amalina, trying to sound casual as she set the necklace with the AXP stamp off to the side and began sorting through the trunk for a blue rock on a chain.

"None like *your* uncle," said Cristine snarkily. "Wouldn't that have been something?"

"But you do have an uncle?"

"No."

"Anyone with your old family name who works with metal?"

"What do you mean 'works with metal'? My father owns mines all over the mountains. That's the Berzwecken business."

Amalina swallowed a lump in her throat. "I mean *works* with the metal. Directly. Like making jewelry and stuff."

"No."

*This is impossible*, thought Amalina, thinking of Cristine's father, old Boss Berzweck; always so pleasant and friendly and generous to them both. But she felt the truth, the ugly truth, pulling hard like a magnet toward the man. How could this be? It couldn't. But …

"What's your father's real name, then?"

"I told you: Przek."

"His Christian name."

"Um, Alexi …um, *Alexandru*, I mean. Why?"

"So his full name is Alexandru Przek? Or does he have any middle names?"

"My father's name is Alexandru Xerxes Przek."

"Xerxes?"

"It's a strange name. One you remember. Not sure where that comes from, but it sounds powerful."

"How do you spell it?"

"Xerxes? 'X'—"

*AXP!*

Amalina gasped again.

"Why?" growled Cristine, impatiently. "And haven't you found that necklace yet? What's going on over there?"

Amalina took the gold necklace with the initials and brought it to her friend.

"That thing? I *specifically* said—!" began Cristine.

"I know, I know! But look! Here on the necklace. AXP? You see it?"

"Hm! So what? I told you Papa gave it to me. So it must be him. What's the matter with you, Amalina? Are you … Are you crying?"

"No," said Amalina, trying to hold back the confusing waves of panic and sadness. "I just don't understand."

"You don't understand what?"

Amalina didn't know what to say. She pictured the big AXP book. But what could she gain by telling her friend—proving to her—that her father was, in some sense … no, *he was!* … a murderer?

. . .

What possible reason could Cristine's father have to want young women killed? Why Lucinda Skeldar? Was it in revenge for those brutish girls' kicks to his daughter? If so, then why hadn't Bossy Bessa been the first to go? She was their ring leader; for many years, anyway. But there had to be a reason for him to target the girls, and always one of the 'bad girl'-set had found their way into AXP's deal with the Count. For decades before Bessa. Before Cristine was born. And so …?

There didn't seem to be any other logical reason if it was him. And it *was* him, it must be.

"What?" said Cristine, frowning down at the three letters stamped into the gold, then looking to Amalina's teary eyes. "What, Amalina? … What's the matter with you? It's just a silly necklace."

Amalina drew close, pulled Cristine into a loose hug. Then she leaned forward to push her forehead against Cristine's and winked one eye against the other, one side then the other, as they'd done just minutes ago. So childlike. And she did this again and again, until Cristine began to pull away, disgusted. Amalina hugged her harder now.

"Cristine, I have to tell you something. I *must*. But you can't tell anyone else, ever. You understand? Not one of these ladies here. Not one of the servants. Not the Count. Not even your mother or father. *No one*. We are sworn in blood, remember? What I have to tell you, you cannot let slip or speak aloud for the rest of your life unless I release you."

Cristine's eyes, which had been animated by the Count's drug, opened fully, and she looked like a cat woke to a bird sitting on her own tail. She hugged Amalina back; firm and reassuring. "Yes, of course. I can see how *much* you're pained to keep this secret to yourself. Say it and release your heavy burden. But don't tell me you're just a silly little girl; that you're embarrassed by how your father could never afford to buy you such a nice necklace as this. You're just as worthy as any of us to be here in this castle, no matter how humble your beginnings."

This reaction of nearly-pure condescension almost made Amalina laugh. It was a hitch in her gentle sobs, though. Of course Cristine would be weighing everything against her own world. She had no idea how fragile that world was—or that it was about to shatter.

"Come," said Amalina. She dried her eyes on the back of her sleeve and led Cristine carefully through the halls, avoiding the other guests, until they reached her own room. There, she went to her desk. But she turned before opening its large lower right drawer.

"You must swear to me never to reveal what I am going to show you. You must keep this secret to your grave."

Again this produced a ravenous delight in her friend. She would swear anything just to find out what could move Amalina so severely. "I swear it, Amalina. We *are* sisters in blood. Always."

Amalina nodded, put on her glasses and opened the drawer. She rustled through various envelopes and boxes and along the way opened secret flaps and doors, until she had all the pieces of paper she needed. She laid them out on top of her desk.

"See these here?" whispered Amalina, rounding her eyes at the walls first, as if checking for ears poking through. "These are little notes that are sent to the Castle. To Count Tepsji."

"They're *very* little," said Cristine, trying to peer closer, wondering what could be so important about them.

"They're sent by pigeon."

"Pigeon?"

"Never mind that. Look at them. Can you see? They have all this strange lettering. It's a secret code."

"Who's sending them?" asked Cristine, maybe already seeing this was headed in a certain direction, though not at all where.

"On these pages here," said Amalina, switching to the larger sheets which she'd copied out, "are code solutions. Different ones, you see? And sometimes these secret little messages use a tricky pattern between the codes themselves, to make it all that much harder to understand what they say."

"Okay? But what—?"

"And sometimes there are drawings." Amalina lifted one such message, one strip of paper with a portrait inked on it, and brought it close to Cristine's face. She stared at it crosseyed. "Look. Who do you see here? Who does this look like?"

"You?"

"Yes."

"How can they draw your picture so small?"

"That's not the point," said Amalina. "Look at the writing here. And we use these cyphers to work out the message." Amalina took up a quill and pointed to each tiny character on the note, then, after referencing it to a code's letter, jotted that one down on a blank parchment. Cristine tried to follow along, not quite understanding how Amalina was arriving at one letter or another when comparing them to the code keys. But the final message quickly became clear: *Kill Amalina Dalca.*

Cristine emitted a little whimper and put both arms around Amalina; and by her weight it felt as if she were about to swoon and wanted Amalina to catch her. "Who, though? What could this mean? *Why?*"

"There are many of these orders. Maybe hundreds. All sent here to Count Tepsji, asking him—directing him—to kill people. I'm just the latest. The last of their number."

"Oh, Amalina!" She gripped Amalina now as if she wanted to shield her from an incoming arrow. But her hold was weak, fatigued. She was tiring. She'd need another dose from the green bottle soon.

"The Count provides him a deadly service. I mean, that is, Tepsji kills women for him. Whomever he asks."

"He hasn't killed you, though."

"And he won't. I'm the first he's refused. Because I work for him, I think. He even showed me this little message with my portrait on it to prove I had nothing to fear."

"Well, that's wonderful! I know he likes you, Amalina."

"But that's still not the point," whispered Amalina, trying to get Cristine to quiet down. Even as she said this her lips trembled and her body began to shake. What she was about to say, what she was about to reveal, was the hardest part. She took the strip and brought it closer to Cristine, pointing to the three little letters at the bottom of the note. "You see? Right here: … AXP."

Cristine's glimmering excitement shook. "What?"

"A.X.P. It's on every note. There are enough of these messages to fill a whole book. And every one has those initials on it."

Cristine pulled back from Amalina. "What—what are you …? What are you trying to say?"

"I'm not trying to say anything," said Amalina, feeling her tears welling up again, her eyes already stinging. "I don't want to say it. It's just a fact."

"That what?" Now Cristine's lips trembled. The rims of her icy eyes turned red and her grey cheeks were flushing a faded pink. "That my father … ?"

"I don't know … I can't believe it … But …"

"*Why* did you show me this, Amalina? Why would you show me such a thing?"

"We're sisters in blood—"

"And you'd show me something like that? No. You're lying. I don't know why, but …" she pointed at the strip quickly, desperately, "but you didn't translate *that*. You translated everything else but those last letters."

"That's because, whatever the code—and they're all different—the messages all end with these three letters, no matter what. And the book they're bound in—there *is* a book, Cristine—has these very same letters on the cover."

"That doesn't mean anything. It could be something else, not a name, or a different … Or why does AXP have to be my father, even? How many people in the world have those initials? But you think it has to be *him*, do you?"

"I'm telling you, I don't want to think it." Amalina held onto Cristine's hands to keep her from pulling away. "But who else knows me and Lucinda? Lucinda is in the book, too. And there was a message sent right before she died, ordering the Count to kill her. Eh? And did you ever complain to your father about Lucinda?"

Cristine gasped, her eyes twitched back and forth, and then she said, "Oh, you think *I'm* responsible now?"

"No, no! I just mean, this makes the most sense, doesn't it? Why would he ask the Count for such a terrible thing but to protect his beloved daughter? If they were picking on you, they had to be stopped. But *he* couldn't be seen doing it or he'd get in trouble. So he asks the Count—"

Cristine shouted, pulled her hands violently from Amalina's, and began to stagger around the room like a crazed animal.

"What are you saying? What are you saying, Amalina? It makes no sense at all! But you have the whole story perfectly ready, don't you? And why you? Why would he come for you?"

"Because he's afraid I'm taking you away from him. Leading you here to the Count. If I wasn't here, you wouldn't have come. You wouldn't be here now. And if I were gone, gone now, you would leave."

Cristine's face contorted: "You can think that awfulness about my father? The man who was so kind and generous to you and your family? And you would accuse him of *this*?"

Amalina pointed back to her desk. "But you see the—"

"I've seen nothing!" wailed Cristine, her eyes drying with a hot blink. But then they were raining again. "Nothing at all! I just saw you pull some little papers out of your desk, showed me a bunch of meaningless scribble and then wrote down whatever you liked, and then told me how this proves my father's some kind of assassin. That's all you've done. Well I'm not going to believe it! It's all a lie."

"No. Cristine—"

But Cristine's face flattened, tensed strangely, and her eyes narrowed and centered as if an unpleasant reality had come into hard focus two feet in front of her.

"You just don't want me here. It's you all over again, you just won't ever share your toys with me. You want to keep the Ladies to yourself. You're sick with jealousy that *your* Tepsji favors me more. Yes, that's it. So you come to me with some insane story of a ghost, and when that doesn't work you break out crying, to try to drive me away with this wild, ludicrous story that my father—my great father! who stands above all the men in Korr and is a thousand times a man than your father—is … is a … I won't say it anymore; to repeat your disgusting lies, Amalina. But know I see you now, and I can't believe it. But if you want to start a contest—a war!—to see who can win everyone's heart, well then this is where it starts, but remember: you're the one who started it."

Before Cristine left the room, with Amalina on the floor wailing in sorrow, she declared, "Of course *I* won't tell anyone this *secret*. And if I find *you* repeating it to anyone else, Amalina Dalca, I swear to you, as your sister in blood, I will kill you myself!"

. . .

With tears slowed but still damping's her cheeks, Amalina tore a scrap of paper to match those scattered on the desk. Glancing twice at her image on the one strip that marked her for death, she encouraged her hand to write, because she *must*:

*Thank AXP for me. That is <u>Alexandru Xerxes Przek</u>, owner of Berzwecken mines.*

Amalina ran to the pigeon coop, seized the second of her Korr pigeons and launched it with the message tied firmly to its leg. As she watched it fly, she realized she'd been too hasty. The revolutionary might have already cracked AXP's identity. Yes or no, she should have added a more critical instruction for him. She looked tentatively at the remaining birds. Bronk had given her five. She was down to three. Could she afford to lose a third?

But a new message had to go.

26

# The Lesson Learned and the Lady

I

With the revolution's fuse now definitely sparking down fast—AXP's identity winging its way to Mr. Bronk—Amalina needed the Count out of the high castle immediately and for a good long while, or at least more regularly, so she could prime the physical parts of her trap. His recent disappearances were erratic and their timing unpredictable, but if Attila Bronk were to employ the Count's emergency birds—fancy pigeons fitted with bells on their legs, stored at his other fortresses and hideouts in case of attack—to send up alarms of a distant seige and capture to bait him out, when she heard those peculiar chiming bells, and if the Count left to investigate a far off property, she'd know with confidence he'd be gone for at least a day. Giving her time to maneuver.

Amalina reviewed the message she'd crammed onto the tiny strip of paper:

> *C must be drawn from the castle. Remember the wonderful trick I told you worked so well last time? The bird distractions? Please, if you could manage to do it again. As soon as possible. Thank you.*

She shook her head. It was too obvious. There was no telling what spies might get hold of the note before it made its way into the revolutionary's hands. And where would they all be then if Attila was nabbed as a traitor to the country's established order and he crumbled under their questioning and began to name names? No, it had to be more finely worded.

Amalina threw the first draft into the fire, and penned on the next strip:

> *Any of his castles in the south, if you please. Thank you for your help.*

Still too opaque and yet suggestive; open to a negative interpretation by prying eyes. It went into the fire.

> *Birds with bells. Jing, Jing, Jing.*

Innocent enough and indecipherable to an outsider. But Sadra's revolutionary should be able to get the hint, shouldn't he? She'd told him of the Count's emergency birds, described them with their pretty little ringing bells—"Jing, jing, jing". He was clever, and if he had a good memory why not catch a critical piece of information which Amalina had told him, almost in passing, on their way to the castle gate?

Still, it felt too late to send; that it would take too long to have its effect. Her pigeon would have to get to Korr, the message to Bronk, and then the revolutionary to find and destroy one of the Count's other castles—if there were any left—which would launch a bell-bird. Then that particular jinging pigeon would have to make its way back to the high castle. How long would the whole process take? Two weeks? More? Over a month before she got the room she needed to move freely?

But this new diversion to find the Count's emergency birds was the only thing she could think to aid her efforts here at the castle while also occupying Attila Bronk; which might tie him down for a week or two longer. And, now more than ever, Amalina would need as much added time as she could get. If Cristine began causing problems, it might focus extra attention to Amalina; restricting her; locking her down. Spring wasn't too far off, but given a few hours of freedom there might still be enough time to ready her snare. Who knew where the revolutionary's own plan stood, or how quickly it was coming along, really? But again, some of Amalina's items had to be gotten; and there was always the secondary plot to convince some Ladies to leave. And if her movements were hampered too much …?

Amalina felt she'd bungled it. In her rash, emotional response to finding out AXP's identity, she'd overcomplicated everything. If she had just kept quiet at the moment of discovery, and not immediately poured her accusations all over Cristine—someone the worst to receive the news—this wouldn't have happened. If she had handled it right she might have even added Cristine Berzweck to her list of allies.

*But could I really pretend to Cristine's face that her father isn't a force of evil? one who wants me dead? Shouldn't she know the truth, no matter what?*

*Shouldn't Cristine side with me?*

With tension knotting her stomach—over the few days left and how much had yet to be done—Amalina went back to the aviary and sent out her new message. As she let go the bird, she understood whether Sadra's revolutionary had found AXP or not, with this note fancy birds with bells on their legs were in the offing.

As she waited on those few precious moments those pigeons would buy her to act, Amalina knew she should gather any pieces of her plan that were close to hand. Like the most crucial …? … the silver chains?

Her mind leapt: *from the wailing woman … below the castle!*

Amalina gulped. The thought of facing the wailer alone in that cellar room … it was terrifying. Even with the Count by her side last time, Amalina had almost died.

But wasn't she now committed to getting the silver there? It's not like any extra lengths were hanging about in a spare room or a hidden drawer. Anka's modest collection couldn't be enough to cover the chandelier. There was no time to track down an alternative source. Amalina would have to enter that dark, dreadful place all by herself and …

Her heart sank …

… Because it wasn't as simple as that small burst of fear-memory a second ago, a shard from a horrific event. Entering the wheel chamber on her own was beyond terrifying, and grew worse as the reality set in. She pictured the room now as she'd seen it the last time she was there. But in her vision it was lit eerily, so that all its darkness and shadows were as deep and as richly black as ink on oil, and what colors were there in it were ghastly and vivid; the woman's withered, dessicated skin greenish-yellow and almost hollow, like a locust shell, her moldy dress a saturated blood red. The silver chains around her, holding her down to the wheel while they sapped the life out of her, glowed in an unearthly way. And no matter how many yards of chain secured each part of her body, Amalina knew if she made one indelicate or imprecise touch it would all unravel in a stream of silver to the floor—and that loathsome body would be on the move! Alive again! If Amalina loosed the head or any of the upper limbs, the wailer might snake out to attack. It would transform itself, just as it had before, the head becoming a giant serpent's that can unhinge its jaw so wide it could suck down a full-grown moose, antlers and all; as it had almost devoured Amalina. It had scooped her up and squeezed her body as its throat gulped her in, head first, inch by inch. If the Count hadn't been there, she would have been …

…and this time, there'd be no Count to save her.

Amalina shuddered, knowing there was no possible way she could face the wailer alone to brave removing any of those chains. Though she'd bound herself to the task—it *had* to be done or her plan would fail—she would have to find a way to get that silver with some help. It couldn't be Tepsji, of course, nor Genadie. And always eager Aklan wouldn't do. As Amalina's mind raced, the options ran out, she couldn't picture anyone else in that scenario: the person would have to be willing and fearless, but also be a much stronger force, a masculine force, tough enough to handle the woman—which negated old Balbo—and someone who was, or could be, read in on her plan.

As she watched her pigeon gliding high above the valley on its way to Korr, now only a small dot on a field of blue, Amalina realized she hadn't sufficiently thought her plan through—an oversite as bad as having riled Cristine. By dreaming up this hopeful scheme and not questioning its finer— and impossible—points, she'd dazzled herself into a state of blinkered foolhardiness; or plain stupidity.

*Am I losing it? With everything going on here am I now unable to juggle it all as I could before? Is it just too much?* Amalina thought critically now: *And where else have I failed?*

Amalina's heart, though already sunken low at the thought of a lonely, fearful trip down to the cellar, sank again: there *was* something else.

Rising back into the moment, as Amalina's pigeon blinked out of sight, it dawned on her if someone other than Attila Bronk captured and read the note, its bizarre and outwardly frivolous wording sent at great cost by using a trained bird, it must *necessarily* be a coded message. And whomever it was sent to would be an agent of some kind.

Genadie had once warned Amalina not to be too clever, and it seemed she'd just done it all over the place, and she couldn't stop doing it.

Thinking on it now, she should have placed something innocuous on either side of her six silly words. Or maybe it should have read:

> *Jing, Jing, Jing. I wish I could hear those merry bells <u>now</u>. Send here when you find them.*

Now *that* would have been much better and clearer, while looking entirely innocent, thought Amalina, sourly. But there was no getting back the bird.

"Sent out another one?" sighed a voice behind her.

II

Amalina spun, shocked at the unexpected sighing voice, one hand on the bench to catch herself, the other over her pounding heart, and saw Lady Lampeda, who'd apparently been standing behind her for some time. Pia was getting to be as stealthy as the Count. From practice? ... Or was this the latent instincts of a predator emerging? As Amalina tried to still her anxious, rampaging mind as quietly as she could, with her disjointed worries and misgivings sparking in every direction, the vision of the wailing woman— the fearful sense of her—merged with Pia's surprise appearance, and superimposed its ugly face onto her. Unfairly so, but just for a moment.

"Who did you send that one to?" added Pia with a tentative smile, though sounded a bit disappointed; and seemed unaware of Amalina's fright. "*Another* invitation? Someone I know?"

Amalina shook her head and closed the window against the cold, her breath curling into clouds even with the window shut. "No invitations anymore; we've enough. Or ... *he* has enough, I mean." She was still breathing heavily and tried to tamp it down by looking indifferent, and wiped down the spotted counter with her bare hand. "Um-uh ...what brings you up here?"

"Katty," Pia stepped forward gently from the door, chin down, eyes up, with a sympathetic look, her tone changing, "you're upset ... I-I heard you shouting ... and crying. I don't mean to pry, really. It's just that I can *hear* things now and ..."

As Pia continued to talk, something mysterious tugged at Amalina's deeper conscious, moving like a shape behind a curtain. She pulled her coat tighter, and was surprised to find, in the moment, at the slightest mention of crying, that she was still close to fighting off tears over Cristine; Amalina's feelings from the argument were welling back up, or hadn't fully receded.

Amalina sighed as Pia had, to cover her sadness, but suddenly looked worried: "You heard us? Our little quarrel? How can I hope to have any secrets around here when half my friends can listen through walls, eh? But ... *you* heard ... or *who* all—?"

"Don't worry about *him*," said Pia. "Your uncle's been very tired lately and left word this morning that he was *'not to be disturbed'*." She imitated his deep, heavy voice. A good rendition, including the haughty downward angle of his lips. Pia shrugged at the end of it. "He's either sleeping or he's gone away again. Who knows? He's had posted in the entrance hall a schedule-of-availability for this week, and today's crossed off. As far as I know, I was the only one who noticed what happened upstairs. It's only me here, anyway ... here asking ... making sure you're okay."

Though Pia's expression was innocent, Amalina could only suspect her sudden appearance—and her warm, liquidy looks—was a rush to take advantage of a falling out with her rival after overhearing a good fight. Irritated, Amalina wanted to squeeze past Pia and her coming attempt to drive the wedge in further; to find some dark, quiet corner where, in blissful solitude, she might prize out a solution to her problem of the silver chain. She'd feel better if she could be left alone to think. *I need to think!*

"But I don't have to explain myself," said Amalina, preparing to leave, "or what happened, if I don't want."

"Of course not," assured Pia with a nod. Her emerald eyes seemed larger. Also kinder and comforting. Also somewhat infinite. She stepped within touching distance. "I just wanted to help if I can, Kat. Can I?"

Glancing at Pia once more, Amalina's thoughts shifted.

And she was thunderstruck.

· · ·

It seemed one of those odd moments in Amalina's life had come once again, where an answer she despaired ever finding presented itself whole, almost unbidden. Amalina had been at a dead end who could possibly help her get those silver chains off the wailing woman—and then came the miraculous bolt from the sky: Pia Lampeda!

Why she hadn't considered Pia before she couldn't guess. But Lady Lampeda satisfied all Amalina's needs. And now she suddenly stood before her!

The conversation had begun awkwardly enough, of course, as the realization began forming, and Amalina tried to interpret the lurking shadow in her thoughts. The earlier blending of Pia's face with the woman on the wheel had reasserted itself with a rude flicker. And as Pia carried on with the conversation, and Amalina followed superficially, an inner part of her had worked things out. Now came the revelation! The odd miracle solution had shown, again!

*Can I help?* Pia had asked. Yes, you can!

At this point, Amalina was barely aware of the course the dialogue had taken, but was visited by positive visions of Pia restraining the wailer while Amalina pulled the thick silver strands off that wheel. It was certain now, and Amalina only had to force the conversation in the right direction. The remaining question was how could the subject be subtly introduced, and the secret woman within the building explained away to Pia ... or better, used? This couldn't be a simple conversation, but it had to appear to be one, as it headed in a single direction.

Down into the cellars.

## 27

# Lady Lampeda, the Race …
# and the Secrets of the Wailing Castle

## I

*D*on't be too clever, Genadie warned.
*Get to work*, demanded Lucinda.

"Are you all right?" asked Pia, looking concerned.

"What?" said Amalina "Oh, mm-hmm. I'm all right, yes. Never mind. Go on."

But what Amalina was thinking was: *Okay, I need to be clear; consider this next move carefully and don't mess it up. What, exactly, am I doing here?*

*Getting Pia downstairs to help me remove those chains.*

The danger in it: Doing so would let Pia in on a number of secrets—the wailing woman on the wheel, the presence of silver within the castle and how hazardous it is to creatures like her (if she didn't know it already), and it would confirm that Amalina was indeed preparing a trap—while at the same time it would challenge Pia's full commitment to the conspiracy against the Count. Any of these untried pieces might break her friend. And some of the possible consequences of that might very well expose Amalina's entire plan. This would be a problem.

There was an upside, though: Succeed, and Amalina would have the silver chains.

Also: She would know where Pia finally stood.

Also: Whatever the results, it would get things over with.

There was some relief in that.

But this would be a much more treacherous conversation than the one earlier in which she'd stamped on Cristine's foot. It had been a rushed, ill-considered decision to reveal, and then insist to Cristine's offended face, her father's outrageous criminality. But at least Cristine herself was straightforward. Cristine Berzweck, though being drained of her blood—the syphoning conducted at a leisurely pace, one determined by the Count—was still a human.

Pia, however, was already transformed, and was suffering through taking on the aspects of a creature itself: an excruciatingly protracted period where the power grew within the flesh like an infection, while weaknesses set in as a kind of balance to it; and according to the Count, who was nearly half a millennium old, he was still discovering new alterations to his mind and body. So it was an enduring progression. And the prevailing question returned, and was pressing now: unclear was how much of a true character, a genuine soul, one kept, if at all. That the Count's converts weren't simply hollowed out beasts performing as a human would be expected to, cannily keeping up some kind of pretense to serve as camouflage, to allow them better movement among their prey.

Pia's killing of the delegation had been one thing; the Strange Man's incredible example of tearing apart a small army by mutating his body into a two-story bug, another; but Noka Iwebo's rampage had solidified the fear that the alteration was a very deep one, and that the original person no longer existed in any real way but as a shadow that could hold its initial, physical form, and emulate its old personality, when needed.

Amalina had been able to forget that chilling aspect to Pia when in her arms, or disbelieve it to save her sanity, or discount it to allow herself to entertain taking the Count's offer; that she *could* continue to be herself after changing. And it was easy to believe the transformation left the primary nature untouched, when someone like Pia continued to perform warmly and familiarly. And when it felt so real. And when, maddeningly, there just was no way to know for sure.

So now, who was Amalina facing?

. . .

After nodding blankly, Amalina dropped back into what seemed to be a heavier discussion than she'd realized. And she noticed something else at work here. Pia had grown serious, running her fingers through her thick, red hair, giving it a thoughtful twist at the end.

*What was she saying?*

At first, what Amalina heard confirmed her assumption that Pia was there to knock Cristine aside: "I mean, you said she was your best friend," said Pia with a bemused look and an even, soft, rational tone. "But *that* was a long time ago, wasn't it? Cristine knew you—and has only ever known you—when you were someone else; just a common little baker's daughter. She doesn't know you—who you *really* are—now. Not really. Not like *I* do, Katty. She couldn't know—or perhaps can't appreciate, or accept—who you've become: the niece to a powerful count; and my friend. She could *never* understand your new qualities to that finer level, not if she's from *here*. But *I* can."

Of course, Pia, who sounded a bit vain and arrogant there, had come to the aviary with her own agenda. Amalina understood this. And that was all right; she would have been overjoyed if Pia had come only to oust Cristine in order to supplant her. Doing so would have been a sign of jealousy and envy; a sign of genuine human emotions; which would have meant a continued attachment to the old Pia, and the mortal she'd once been; still of a quasi-human race.

But then Pia's words took on another aspect, as she went on in the same understanding tone: "And so it really doesn't matter if you're worried whether you can live together peacefully and happily with *her*, Katty. as your uncle envisions it, however long, even if she's the way she is, and sore at you now; no, what should it matter when I'm here too, and she might always come around? And I'm sure she *will* because—"

*What's this?* thought Amalina. *She's lightly banging away at Cristine and puffing herself up, but it's more an explanation of Cristine's frustration and anger, for me to understand and accept her perspective. Wasn't that it? She hadn't heard everything said in the fight; she doesn't know what's happened and assumes the blow-up has to do with some kind of status envy, or a breaking of long held roles. She's here to convince me the situation isn't all that bad. That's what she's doing; which means she isn't really making a play for my affection, is she? She's more trying to calm me down, trying to convince me to stay—for* her *sake, presumably; the way she's telling it.*

Amalina smirked, suddenly overcome with suspicion—because, she remembered, there must always be suspicion with these Special Ladies. And here it seemed obvious now: the thin veneer of jealousy and competition that Pia was using, shrewdly so, because she must know Amalina would be expecting it (as, that *is* what Pia used to be), was to screen her promotion of the Count's greater message of harmony. This performance was just that: pure artifice—for a deeper purpose. And this minor intuition rankled Amalina more than she would have expected. Pia had tried to be as subtle as she could at first, but it was still a game. The game! The one Amalina had suspected before: the great second race. Well, there'd been a fight between Cristine and Amalina, and now Pia had leapt into the breach to repair it, *to convince me to go through with the change, and to stay with her—which means: to stay with Count Tepsji—here—forever. Pia doesn't really care about me, so much as what* he *wants done! You see! For him to have me!*

Unless it wasn't, so Amalina's thoughts continued on. Pia Lampeda, lifting a hand thoughtfully to the strong line of her jaw, studying Amalina, remained an enigma: had Pia really come here to win her away from Cristine while she had the chance, as the real Pia might have? Or did she come as a diplomat to mend sore feelings for the Count—as a kind of automaton, a helpless slave to his desires, and at his request, perhaps?—to calm Amalina, after whatever had happened between the two old friends, so she would just relax and settle into her proper, intended role?

*And so what do I care, what difference does it make?* thought Amalina, recovering, thinking quickly, coolly, cynically, and snapping into that 'survivor energy', knowing she had her own purpose here, though feeling a little unhappy about it all as she waited for the right opportunity to pounce: *If Pia can use me, I can use her too, no need to feel bad about it. It's all well and good, maybe I can use this to knock two targets down at once.*

*Now be careful,* she heard Genadie's voice again, *don't be too clever.*

But she'd just sighted this field of battle from all angles. She felt forearmed and ready.

Let the contest begin.

II

Pia continued to press Amalina, sure she had an opening, hoping to strengthen her case: "So Lady Berzweck's grown out of your friendship. Or *you* have, Kat. But you know what I'm talking about or you'd protest; if just a little. But you haven't said anything. And you're looking away because you don't want to admit it.

"Here, come, let me put my arms around you," said Pia, now brightly, coming forward out of the shadows, but still keeping clear of the direct sunlight from the window, snaking her arms through Amalina's as she always did, pressing their bodies together, their cheeks. "I don't know what to do but if I could only take away your sadness, make you feel better."

"Here?" mumbled Amalina coolly, dismissive and detached. "And now? It's a little cold, isn't it?"

"Is it?" said Pia, glancing at Amalina's clearly visible breath. She gamely redoubled her effort to bundle Amalina into her arms. "Well, this should warm you, I should think."

"That's nice of you, really," said Amalina, shifting away from their embrace, tapping Pia's arm like a pet animal she'd had enough of. "But it *is* cold. A little *too* cold. But I suppose you don't feel it."

"If you're mad at her," said Pia in a relaxed attitude, reading Amalina's mood but gently resisting her withdrawal, "please don't be mad at *me*. If Miss Berzweck being here displeases you so much, never mind. I can speak to your uncle, make him see the disadvantages of keeping her on and convince him to leave her alone. Or get him to set her free. It can be just you and I, and nobody has to deal with her nonsense anymore. Whatever you want."

*And wouldn't you like that?* noted Amalina, at Pia's quietly voiced—if sham—jealousy. *You'd love to deliver that message to him, but only to improve your standing with the Count by playing me. And then once I have given in, what would it matter if Cristine returned? was added back to the nest? It'd be too late for me, as we'd all be mindlessly enslaved.*

Again, Amalina was overcome, seeing in those nearly incandescent eyes, within the shadows of the room, a different mind at work than she had met and known in Rome. Could it really be? *Oh, Pia, if there is anything real left of you in there, please ...*

"If you tell him," said Amalina, matter-of-factly, "he'll just think you're jealous."

"And *you* cannot persuade him to send her away, Kat? I think you could."

"To hear it from me, it'll only look like I'm trying to stop him from doing what he's doing to her. He thinks *I* think if Cristine changes I won't be able to resist him. I'll have to go along with her, too."

"Oh." This seemed to disappoint Pia. But then she shrugged. "And there's no way you can convince her to end this on her own?"

"Cristine isn't going to listen," said Amalina. "To me or anyone else anymore. She knows what she's getting here and it's too much to give up. I couldn't even drive her away if I tried. Easier if I went."

Pia sighed.

"It's so interesting, Katty," said Pia, on a different note, "how you aren't tempted by his offer. Even when I tell you how amazing it is. What you have to *gain* from it. Cristine wants it. Everyone does. But not you. You can just walk away without a second thought."

"What I have to *lose* is what bothers me," argued Amalina, surprised at this change in direction, an almost honest admission by Pia why she was really here; to evangelize and advocate for her master. "Lose the connection to my family? What I was before? The world that I love?"

"But that isn't true, Katty. That's only your fear. I'm telling you, the connection to the world becomes so much *stronger*."

"A stronger connection, but only to a *piece* of it," countered Amalina. "More will be cut off, won't it? To never experience the day again? I can't imagine it."

"You're very right, you can't imagine it, and I could never fully describe it. You just have to feel it."

"And you *can* feel it?"

"What do you mean? Haven't I told you? And shown you?"

"Maybe that isn't enough, though. For me to understand."

"We're back to this again? Honestly, you're making me feel like you feel I'm some kind of insect to be studied. You don't trust me. It's like you don't even care for me anymore."

"It's not that."

"Do you?"

"I do. Of course I do."

"Then what is it?"

"Pia, I don't want you to feel bad for the decision you've made," said Amalina. "I'm sure you made the right one; for you. I see how tempting it is. I feel it. It's just, I've had a different kind of life. You see? Working since I was young. Having little, lost much. But I *was* happy with what I had. Maybe you don't appreciate that part of it. I like my freedom. I don't see what he can offer stuck forever in this castle with him."

"He's not all bad, you know," said Pia, not looking too put out.

"Says the one who fell in love with him. Or he seduced … as he has with so many others. God knows how he does it."

"You've seen a different side of him, Katty."

"The real one, I think."

"Who's to say?" said Pia dreamily. "People have many, many sides, Katty. I'm sure you have your bad side, too. Maybe you don't think it compares to his, but that's for others to judge. And he exists on a different scale than most, so his faults might appear bigger than if you were his equal."

"Do you love him, Pia?"

"I doubt it," said Pia, with a grin. "But I *am* captivated."

"By what?" They were moving in the right direction. "What is he to you?"

Pia didn't answer at first, embarrassed. "I don't know how to describe it. I don't remember how it started. How I felt about him or what he was to me before the … well, you know." She shrugged and twisted a long lock of red hair again, pulling it across her white throat. "But now he speaks to me on my own plane. It is as if I fit into him. Like a piece of a chair, fashioned to be a part of him. Or we both are a piece of something much larger, I can't tell. But he's important, somehow, to me. And I'm one with him, even if I don't wish it to be the case. And I don't."

"And I would feel the same way if I took up his offer?" said Amalina. "That I'd fit with him? and even maybe fit with you, too? and Cristine? So that we are all one in the end?"

"I think so," she answered with a hopeful smile. "It should be. Why not?"

"And Cristine *would* suddenly fit with me? No matter how she hates me now?"

"Kat, the difference here—between her and I—is that I can accept you; the way you were, and the way you are now. And even what you will become. Any which way. She can only accept one part of you: what you *were*."

"Only that's not the way it works, I think," laughed Amalina lightly at the naïvete. "If what you said is true, she's got a problem with what I have become. For you though, if I went back to being *just* a baker's daughter, as you say—"

"I'd be okay with it."

"Would you? Or are you only saying *that* because you want me to become something *even more?* with you?"

"I swear, I love you," said Pia, suddenly stricken. The heartfelt earnestness in the statement and those radiant green eyes, and the twitch at the side of her mouth, was more than convincing, it was heartbreaking. Amalina felt a lump in her throat. Maybe she'd been wrong, and this conversation was so much more innocent.

Or was that what Amalina was supposed to think? Anyway, this wasn't the right direction for their conversation. A misstep.

"Never mind, I didn't want to be mean," said Amalina. "I just wanted to be honest here, since that's what it seems we're doing here right now."

"Yes."

"I'd very much like to know what you two are trying to get me into."

"And I could say the same thing of you."

"But are you *his*, or are you yourself? Do you belong to yourself entirely?"

"Come on, Katty." A pain was in her eyes. It looked real enough.

Maybe, thought Amalina suspiciously, Pia was resisting the change— unlike Anne, or Noka or the others—feeling and knowing what was coming, the deeper loss of self, but was trying while she still had time to drag Amalina down into the pit with her. So that she wouldn't be alone. And so that she would also satisfy the Count's claim on Amalina.

"And so you are trying," said Amalina, as if for confirmation, "*on your own*, to get me to make this decision because you feel you care for me?"

*Or, you just want to win the race. To get me to—*

"I love you, I *do* love you." She sniffled, and it wasn't against the cold. But it still felt unreal; if Amalina looked hard enough it was, perhaps, performed. This didn't stop Pia. "I can't stand how my changing has only driven you away from me, it seems, instead of bringing us closer. That is what I wanted. That is what I'd hoped. I'd wished you'd've come to me, because I couldn't love anyone more in my life."

"Any old way that I am," said Amalina, almost coldly, like it was a challenge and not quite sure what was happening here. "Are you sure? Even if you don't really know *all* of me?"

"But I want to, all of it."

"And *him* to?"

"What?"

"Him. The one I'd be joined with, along with you. If I stay on here. *He's* important, no? What I think of him. What you think of him. What he thinks of us?"

"Yes I suppose. But it's you and I that matters more ... most of all ... you understand ..."

*Perfect*, thought Amalina. *You've stepped right where I wanted.*

"And if he is ever done with us," she said, "done with this new important piece of ourselves that he's creating, where we all fit in together so nicely, as you say … then what?"

Pia looked at Amalina curiously. "Done with us?"

"He's not here in the castle, you said? Or he's deep asleep? He isn't listening?"

Pia shook her head.

"You swear?"

Pia nodded.

"I need you to come with me."


## III


"Do you hear anything?" asked Amalina.

"Mm. Lots of things of course," said Pia. "What do you mean?"

They were walking down the stone stairs from the kitchens to the cellars, their steps a light sandy-skritching, Amalina's torch a hissing-snuffling-snapping, all of it gently echoing around them.

The Count's false walls he usually had set up throughout this area to conceal parts he preferred hidden were gone. Was it to allow his turned Special Ladies easier passage out of the castle, to escape into the night unobserved? wondered Amalina. *Well, good, he's made it easier for me, too.*

Amalina counted out the steps downward, picking the fastest route.

"A wheel turning," said Amalina, keeping her voice low. "Like a great water wheel without the water. Wood against oiled wood."

"Yes," said Pia with her ear to the air, nodding shallowly. "Yes, I believe so. Though I think I hear water, too, a little. Rushing. Maybe somewhere else?"

"We're almost there."

When they arrived at the door, Amalina pointed her torch at it. The key was still in the lock; no doubt forgotten in the hurried, distracted departure the last time she and the Count had entered—and had battled what lay inside.

"Behind this door," she said. "Open it. See for yourself."

"But what …?" Pia didn't have the patience to finish her question, she turned the key, used the latch, and opened the door.


• • •

Amalina tried to keep Pia in front, to block her own view into the room. But she needed to hold the torch far forward to make sure her friend saw everything.

"Katty," muttered Pia. "What … what is this?"

This was Amalina's third time looking on the massive spinning wheel with the woman pinned to it. Secured at all points by a silver chain that wrapped around her body and ankles and wrists and neck and mouth: an old corpse in a decaying dress. Her jellied eyes were torn from their sockets, drooping onto her cheeks like withered prunes, and her mouth was a shriveled black hole brutally gagged. Where her skin touched the shining metal, the wrinkles and damage was the worst. If Pia looked closer, as Amalina now did, the links around the head were fastened to the wood by large, fanglike teeth that had been hammered in.

"She was the Count's first," said Amalina. "He didn't really know what he was doing, but he created her. And now she lives forever here. Bound to the wheel."

"She's alive?" said Pia, marveling.

"As much as the Count is and you are, I suppose."

Pia's nose wrinkled as she inched closer, trying to study the body as it rotated round and round. She reached out tentatively and touched the withered hand. She flinched with a yelp, yanking her arm away, holding her fingers as if bitten.

"It … It moved."

Amalina nodded, looking serious. "I told you."

"But why does she look so …?"

"It's the chains. They're made of silver. I suppose he told you how dangerous that kind of metal can be."

"Silver …" said Pia. She stared at the long, heavy, shiny strands now, ignoring the wasted body under them. "But I love silver …"

She reached out again.

"Don't touch—!"

Pia flew back and hit the far wall with a crunching sound, her forearm folded protectively against her stomach, as she let out a long, ugly squeal. She held her hand out and shook it and gaped at it. Amalina brought the torch close and saw that the ends of her fingers were flaky and a bit shriveled, and grey instead of pale white. "Oh …" moaned Pia, pitifully.

"I told you not to," said Amalina as she stroked Pia's back.

Pia turned to the wheel, or the woman on it, a dull frown on her face.

"To you," said Amalina, "silver is what salt is to snails. Never touch it."

"But I love silver so."

"Well, don't touch it, whatever you do."

After another moment, Pia stood fully and tossed her hair back behind her shoulders. "She's still alive though."

"It doesn't kill you completely. It withers you away enough so that ... well ..." Amalina gestured at the woman.

"How long has she been here?"

"Since you've been here."

"I mean, how long? When did he put her there?"

"I don't know. Long before I came. Maybe twenty years or more. It happened a long time ago."

"Why?"

"He didn't want her," answered Amalina. When Pia said nothing more, she went on: "That's why I'm asking: what does *he* have to offer us, Pia? really? *Forever?* But look at *her*. She has forever, too. She had that same bond with him you were talking about, and yet here she is. And he's so cruel he doesn't even kill her, just leaves her there for some reason. What if he grows tired of us like he did her? What happens when we don't please him anymore? Then where are we?"

From the hot spark in Pia's eye, Amalina could tell that this threat was much more personal than it ever could be for her. By the way Pia's nostrils flared and the corners of her mouth turned down, Amalina knew she had just won the race.

"So maybe helping me with my—"

"How long did you know about this, Katty?" asked Pia, interrupting.

"For a while now."

"When you visited me in my home, when you invited me here to stay with you and to meet your uncle, you knew about this?" Pia's face squirmed with anger and disgust. "When you allowed him to court me, to make love to me, you knew she was down here all along, and you said nothing to me? Until now?"

"I—I'm sorry, Pia. But—"

"You betrayed me!" Pia stepped away from Amalina, as if recoiling. "Don't touch me. Don't ever touch me again! You heartless ... You never cared about me! Never!" She wailed: "Never!!!"

*Oh my*, thought Amalina, entirely shocked as Pia broke down into tears, feeling stupid, *maybe she actually* does *care for me.*

*Is there anything I* can't *get wrong today?*

28

# The Woman on the Wheel

As Pia's sobs fell in the distance, having fled the room with hands over her face, her shoulders shaking between the swooped lengths of red hair, Amalina filled with a self pity of her own, and experienced the amazement at having lost—having *driven off*—two best friends in so many hours.

*That must be some kind of record, you idiot!* she swore.

*Stop acting clever, Ms. Dalca,* Genadie reminded her. *Haven't I warned you? Didn't I just?*

"Shut up. I was just trying …"

Amalina turned back to the woman on the wheel. She was now alone in the room with the hideous—the tragic—wailing woman, but for some reason didn't feel as afraid as she might have before. *Probably the upset of Pia storming off,* thought Amalina. Only, on a second thought, Amalina considered that Pia had the power to kill her, to do what Noka had done to Oroco, to all her people, and worse, but had, mercifully, turned her anger and sadness inward. Another sign of human caring and self-possession within a changed person?

Amalina wasn't sure what she'd just done; what she'd hoped to do by bringing Pia here. She'd thought it had been to have the powerful Lady Lampeda protect her from the wailer as she got some chain off the wheel. But was it really something else? To provoke some reaction in Pia and prove she was still the same loving friend—the one capable of genuine emotions— whom Amalina had known from the start? Or was it a deeper calculation in her unconscious mind to drive Pia away? to win the race against the Count by angering Pia, and so delay for a time, if not actually put off, Amalina's own transition? She began to suspect she didn't know herself any better than she understood the changed women. In any case, and if nothing else, she'd accomplished the last part: she'd upset Pia.

But was it really a win here? Amalina had not only lost a good friend— for understandable reasons—she'd also lost one of her most important allies. Pia was the only one strong enough to even come close to matching the Count, steering him, moving him where he needed to be. Into the great hall, and underneath his own waiting, welcoming wheel.

Who knew if Pia would now run crying to the Count and report everything? Tell him Amalina was devising a trap. What would Pia do in her anger—in her justifiable feeling of betrayal?

*There's no counting on her anymore, anyway*, thought Amalina. She was no longer the plan's crucial element: the Count's neutralizer.

Amalina stared at the turning wheel. The silver chains glowed in the torchlight. They seemed more than plain silver. Maybe they had a spell working over them, too. Or maybe it was in her head. She stared at them, turning and turning, transfixed.

She didn't know how long she stood there, but she began to feel dizzy. She felt drawn in. It wasn't until she'd moved forward, touched the chain, felt it spinning against her fingers, did she snap awake, alert.

*What am I doing?*

The woman's head rotated into view. Amalina glanced away. What *was* she doing? Had the woman controlled her mind? Caused her to try to unwrap the chains?

Amalina shook her head to wake herself.

She was here, in the room now, and alone with the silver!

She needed it—at least a good length of it—for her own purposes. *Get going.*

Amalina tried to follow one of the loops around the woman's foot. It was nailed and tied into place, but it was full length. She supposed the other chains at different points on her body were the same. If she took one away, would it be enough? Well, it would be a start.

Amalina remembered again the time she and the Count had tried to loosen the woman just a little, and her body began to shift and expand and elongate, to come after Amalina.

But she couldn't let this opportunity pass.

The blown conversation with Pia had accomplished this much too, getting her here.

Above and below the center of the wheel's hub, the woman's midsection was tightly wrapped to the rungs. There was a bit of a gap around her hips. Studying the chain closer, Amalina believed that there were no less than several sets, one for above the waist, one for the upper hips, before the legs parted in their own directions, and perhaps another all around. It was hard to tell with the interweaving and the overlapping, but it definitely *seemed* to be three very long lengths that circled the center of her mass. At the very least. If she could separate just one of *those* from the wheel right now ...

· · ·

*Up.*

*Then. Down.*

*Up.*

*Then down.*

"Hello?"

*Hm?*

"Hello, hello?"

*Is someone talking to me? Yes. One of the voices I heard arguing; arguing so long ago. Decades? Centuries? A minute?*

"Can you hear me?"

*That voice. I've heard it before. Yes. Yes, I can hear you.*

"I'm Amalina. Do you remember?"

*Yes. Yessss. Amalina. The brat who put me here.*

"I'm here with you now. Do you understand?"

*Lucky I'm tied down or you'd be in my belly, Amalina.*

"I want to free you. Do you understand me? I want to let you go. Forever."

*Moon above! I can hardly believe. You're torturing me still? Mocking me? As I stay locked here; up then down, up then down … ?*

"Do you understand what I am saying? I have a plan. I have a plan that will save you from the Count."

*The man from the moonlit falls! The Count! Yes, that monster who did this to me. Yes. Yessss.*

"I promise you, you won't have to suffer here anymore."

*Oh, yes, please. Release me. Take this muzzle from my face. Remove the weight. Let me stretch my limbs. Oh, I will be so happy!*

"I'll just need to borrow some of this chain."

*Do so. Take it all. Set me free!*

"A few minutes here, I think, it's very tricky …"

*No trick about it, it's simple enough, just get it off, stupid girl!*

"I don't really know your name, but at least I know that you're real, you know? And I can help *you*. I mean, I want to help Lucinda but … Oops, careful there, hope that didn't hurt … But what if I'm just imagining her? It's so hard to tell, you know? Or is she *actually, really* a spirit? I mean, if she's real, why won't she tell me how to get out of this, or why didn't she ever tell me who AXP was, instead of just yelling at me? It would've made things easier, you know? … Oh, I see, there's a knot there, just another second or so … And so I was thinking, if she's not real, and I'm only imagining her, I really shouldn't bother with her, should I? That'd be one less person I'm responsible for. I mean, I feel I'm working for her, and I *have* to work for Tepsji and also Mr. Bronk. But I refuse to be a girl eaten by circumstance!

I'm working for me now. And I'm working for you. And we can work together, you know? *We work together?*

*What the hell are you babbling about, girl?*

"Yes, there we go! Coming off now. It's very, very long. Oops! And it will do very nicely, I think."

*That's right, girl! That's right! Oh, the relief! Ahhhhh! So much better!*

"Now, listen, when I come back, I shall remove the rest."

*? … Remove it all now.*

"It might take a while, I'm sorry, but I promise I will."

*What's stopping you? Keep going!*

"And when I do, you'll never suffer this way again."

*Oh, but it still burns, it holds me fast! They weigh a thousand stone. Take them off!*

"Just remember that we can—and will—work together. And that it is I, Amalina, who let you go."

*But you haven't, girl! You're torturing me again! How long must I stay here?*

"And when I free you, I will ask one favor and I hope you'll grant it."

*Only if you free me now. Free me this instant, or I will never forgive you!*

"On that day I'll tell you what I need, but know, just as I'm helping you now, when the time comes you'll be helping me stop him. And I know that you want *him* to be stopped. You and I together. You and I. Right?"

*What are you saying? You're just as bad as he. You're even worse! You keep giving me hope and then returning me to this cursed wheel.*

"And so you *will* help me, won't you? You promise me, as much as I promise you?"

*If you don't free me right now, I promise I will kill you. I will tear you into pieces! Do you hear me?*

"Thank you. I'll be back as soon as I can."

*No, don't go! If you go now, I will kill you worse than you could believe. Take off these chains!*

"Don't forget our promise."

*I won't forget a thing! But—*

"All right. Good bye."

*No! Remove the chains! Take them! I've promised no favor to you! I swear, to my dying breath, if I ever get free, I am going to kill you, Amalina! Kill you!*

• • •

Amalina blew out a breath and leaned her back on the door, now locked, its little iron key in her pocket. A silver chain from the wheel, one end gripped in her left hand, was coiled around her feet. She didn't know yet how she was going to sneak it upstairs, but she knew she'd have to move soon before someone came to fetch something from the cellar.

Still, Amalina waited, catching her breath, and reflected for a moment on what had just happened in the wheel room.

The poor old wailing woman had seemed to move sympathetically when Amalina whispered to her, hadn't she? She must have been so relieved when Amalina had removed the first layer of those awful chains. *How grateful she will be*, considered Amalina, *when the rest come off!*

*And she will be an even better ally against the Count than Pia. A distraction to him and truly a deadly foe——intent on his absolute destruction. She must hate him beyond reason for putting her there. Oh, yes!*

Pia Lampeda hadn't been needed in the first place, Amalina decided coolly, and with some relief. It'd probably be better to move her far out of the way now. Who knows what will happen when the wailing woman is finally unleashed; what level of destruction. Amalina would try to find some way—despite their falling out—to send Pia safely from the castle; as far as she can. Maybe this fracture would make it easier. And she would do the same for Cristine too if it was possible anymore. Those two, along with the rest of the castle's upstairs guests. Get them all out.

And so when the time came, and the Count was to finally be confronted, Amalina would set the wailing woman free.

*And then*, grinned Amalina, with a certain sense of victory, *let her rip!*

# Act Two

## Deeds & Action

# Part Four
# The Fresh Prince

29

# Confessional

"Whoah, look at this! A fortune!" said Aklan, greedily dipping his hands into the barrel to then bring out the bright, shiny links of silver chain. "You did it, Princess!"

"Now we've only to get it all on that chandelier," muttered Amalina, feeling exhausted from her trip up from the cellar, which had been an oddly prolonged process, and not wanting to really think about what comes next.

"But look how flashy these are, Princess!" He eyed the chain unfavorably, and then turned his critical eye toward her; to his excitement and pleasure, one of his 'problems' had been vindicated: "I was right! He's *gonna* see 'em up there! There's no way he won't with them sparkling like that!"

Amalina shushed the boy with a look and said, "Not if they're covered—*like I already told you.*"

"But—"

"And I've already got the 'how' figured out."

"Have you? Covered?"

"I was thinking," she said, her voice confident. "These chains feel solid as iron, but I don't know how strong they really are. And I wouldn't even know how to begin swapping them. It's not like we're smiths."

"No."

"So I figure we'll just wind the silver ones around the iron ones. Tie them on. And then, because they're so shiny, we can wrap them in black cloth. Real loose, though, like a sleeve. And have the cloth fixed by a thread to the ceiling block. Then when it comes down, the wraps'll tear free and it'll be silver all over the place."

"That's brilliant, Pretty Princess!" cheered Aklan, his eyes gleaming in admiration. "How'd you think of that?"

Amalina shrugged, and caught herself chewing nervously on a fingernail. "I just saw the chains and knew we had to do something. Then for some reason I thought of how a lady slips off her stockings to reveal what they have hiding underneath."

From Aklan's expression, it looked like she'd opened a new door in his head.

"And these ladies we've got here have plenty of old stockings. That's my next get." Amalina smiled at him encouragingly. "Look, you just go on keep finding holes in my plan, I'll keep fixing 'em."

"I'll do anything for you, Princess!"

"We make a great team," she added with a wink.

"I'll say! We're going to get him good, aren't we?"

Amalina felt it would be bad luck to answer that. But then by not answering, it felt she was adding something negative by leaving something out, like withholding straws from brick. Instead, Amalina blew out a breath and told Aklan: "You know, this place is getting very strange."

"Oh? How so?"

Thinking about it, Amalina didn't really want to say too much, but reflected for a moment on her short adventure getting the chains up to her room, a bit of a twisty trail, and what it all had meant; and if there wasn't something there she should tell him.

• • •

"Are you all right, milady?" Anka had asked. She was the first to find Amalina on her trip from the wheel room, struggling and staggering through the corridor.

Gasping heavily, Amalina had then slouched against the wall, doubled over, holding her stomach. Her midsection was grossly distended. It also clinked.

"Ill, milady?"

"No," said Amalina. "Listen, I'm carrying some of that … um … *stuff.*" Amalina mouthed: 'Silver'.

"Oh!"

"Very heavy."

"Looks quite a lot. Under your dress, is it?"

"I think I can make it to a privy. Have Pils fetch a good sized barrel and get him to help me move it to my room."

"Yes, milady."

"But first to the stall. Would you take my arm, Anka?"

"Of course, milady."

Amalina whispered a prayer she wouldn't run into anyone else. A set of stairs stood ahead of them, and then no telling if someone might notice their ungainly progress to the end of the next long passage.

"Have you seen Lady Lampeda?" whispered Amalina, sounding a little worried. "Or, has Miss Berzweck been around?"

"I've only just risen," whispered Anka in return. "Last night went so very late, you know. These ladies …"

"Yes, that's all right …"

She must have noticed Amalina cautiously scanning the way ahead and leapt to a terrible conclusion.

"But Lady Lampeda and Miss Berzweck …?" gulped Anka. "Has something happened? … happened … *again*?"

Whatever the weight of terror is, *Night of Noka*'s load of it buckled Anka's shoulders suddenly, depressing her into a low and undignified posture, like a squashed ball, and her eyes darted around. If Amalina hadn't been as distressed as she was and Anka's dropping made her lose her balance she might have laughed at the comedic appearance.

"Steady, steady! Nothing like that," assured Amalina with another heavy breath, grasping at the loose chain underneath her dress before it shook loose. She thought: *I certainly hope I haven't started something like that. Pia would never rampage …*

Anka eyed Amalina fighting to keep on her feet. "Oh, dear, take it slow! That's more of the stuff than I could ever imagine! Very daring of you, milady. Quite a secret you've kept to yourself all this while. Where were you hiding it?"

"That's quite *another* secret," joked Amalina, trying to keep her energy up—and cover the passage's silence as the chains chinked on noisily.

"Yes, milady. Oh, secrets … secrets …" She mumbled on in a different tone: "Yes, secrets … *secrets* … secrets …"

Amalina glanced over. Anka's haunted look reminded Amalina again of when she'd run across the maid and Pils speaking in whispers of secrets they wanted to tell someone but couldn't. Hadn't the old maid confessed already? Amalina gripped Anka's hand as if to keep balance, but then wrung it to draw her attention.

"Anka, do you have something you want to tell me?" she whispered even lower now.

"What, milady?"

"It seems you've something you'd like to say. Some secret, eh? We're alone now, not even Pils is here, if you want to speak."

Anka was overcome. She tried to hide her face with part of the veil from her puffy hat. "But I already told you about—"

"Not jewelry. There's something more, isn't there? You can trust me, Anka. You know that. You always could. Tell me now while we have the time."

"Oh, well," mumbled Anka, her eyes jumping back and forth. "Well … when do you think you'll be taking … em, that is … You *will* be taking the Master's offer, will you be?"

Amalina stared at her maid. Had Anka seen a secret decision within her, or was somehow foretelling the future; had foreseen Amalina's changing?

The old woman took the look as a sign of anger and dropped to her knees and petted Amalina's leg.

"Oh, forgive me, milady. Don't think it bad of me. Of course we don't want you to! Of course we don't!"

"Get up, get up," urged Amalina, almost toppling, "we have to keep moving."

"Yes, of course, milady," said Anka, as she wiped her tears and scrambled up to support her mistress again.

"'We', Anka? Who else are you talking about that doesn't want me to—?"

"Pils and I, of course. We should never wish you to change into something other than what you've always been. Such a great mistress …"

"But?"

"Well …"

"There is a 'but'?"

Anka shrugged. And then she whispered, putting her head near Amalina's "There's a worry if you don't, we're not too sure we'll be needed around here anymore. And I can't think of anyone else who'd argue for us, milady. No one besides you." Anka squeezed her arm. "Would you still argue for us—to keep us on in the castle—if you do change? Do you think?"

"You two *want* to stay on?"

"Well, we don't rightly know what happens if we aren't kept. You saw what Noka Iwebo did to her people. I think she set an example for the other 'blessed' ladies. They've taken it as a good idea, oh, yes. And when all is said and done, and it's just them and us left, they might just turn on each other's people to whittle down the numbers. And Pils and I, what chance do we have if we aren't … um … wanted anymore?"

"And what happens if I deny the Count's offer? Or he changes his mind, as he so often does?"

"I suppose, milady, then we don't know what will happen to any of us. Including you."

"That's true."

Amalina wondered if she should tell Anka the deeper part of her plan, that it might be some relief to her and Pils to know they were included in an intrigue to overturn the entire order of things; and that she wouldn't be changing after all. Or was having their simple cooperation enough?

Anka, nervous and sweaty, had glanced up at Amalina, looking wavy-lipped and guilty somehow.

"Is that all, Anka?" asked Amalina, feeling suspicious. "Is there is something *else*? Come on, spit it out."

Anka stared into Amalina's eyes, then nodded, seriously.

"Still more?" panted Amalina, in surprise.

But suddenly Anka stopped them before a low door. "Only, we're here, milady." She sounded relieved. "Another time then, eh? No matter. In you go. I'll send Pils right away with a barrel."

"Thank you."

. . .

Once inside the stall, Amalina had heaved a sigh of relief as she sat down on the bench. The blood seemed to pulse into her legs, and she stretched them out to the door; wondering if this was what it was like to be pregnant. She then worried for a second that the chain might accidentally slip from her waist and somehow fall down the hole. A silly fear. Amalina began unloading the chain onto the floor in preparation for Pils. Even with the dim light seeping in under the door, the silver shone enough to light her feet and ankles.

*Now what am I going to do with all this shine?* she wondered.

A sound of wood against stone. Amalina thought Pils had arrived but gone to the wrong door, but then she heard movement in the compartment to her left. Someone had entered the adjacent stall.

"Katty?" said a voice. "That you?"

"Um," said Amalina.

"Saw Anka tottering away after shoving somebody in. It looked like you."

"Well, yes, it's me," said Amalina, supposing it was too late to pretend the stall was unoccupied. "Pia?"

"No!" growled the voice. "Do I sound like Pia Lampeda?"

Whoever it was, she *did* sound like Pia. But she also sounded like Cristine. Amalina could picture either of them next door. Maybe it was dread, or even hopefulness, putting those two in her head, but then it had to be someone else. It wouldn't help to guess wrong again. It wasn't Noka, anyway. Not Aria, not 'Maria', not …

"Never mind, it's me, Jenny!" sounded Lady Genevieve de Roye's positive voice from next door, much clearer now, she must have pressed her head closer to the thin partition. "You feeling all right, Katty?"

"Oh, yes. Yes." After a lengthy pause. "And you?"

"Great."

"Well, that's good." She didn't know where to carry the conversation and hoped Pils would not suddenly arrive with a barrel. How could she possibly explain? And no doubt Genevieve would spread wide and far the tale of Katarina's strange 'privy barrel delivery'. Better to hurry this along if she could. Get her away.

"While I have you here, though," said de Roye first, lowering her voice, sounding contrite, "I should apologize again about bringing Lady Camper here. Jane *was* a bit of a bumpy toad, wasn't she? With all her low breeding and colonial hogwash."

"Don't worry about it."

"Can't say she wasn't wrong about Noka, though."

Amalina regarded the chain she was still feeding out of her dress—as quietly as she could—into a tight coil between her legs. Her bare feet and calves were bathed in its soft, silvery shimmer, the pile seeming to glow with the power of three candles. Noticing the hem of her dress blocked its strange luminescence, she suddenly felt sly with an idea: "Say Jenny that reminds me. I'm looking for stockings, black stockings, if you might be getting rid of any, or have some you can spare. I'm going to donate them to those poor orphans from the workhouse outside of Netz, the one that burned down; and who could use them in all this cold, don't you think?"

"Orphans?" said de Roye confused. "Stockings?"

"I'm sorry, what's that about the princess, did you say?" said Amalina, making it sound as if she'd been distracted, while she fed out the endless glimmering chain.

"I was saying … Well, I was saying we weren't wrong about *her*, Camper and I," said de Roye, louder this time. "Noka and her people I mean. We all had them sized up just about right from the start, didn't we? I suppose Noka's still nice, though. It was really Oroco and her servants to blame, I know that … But all the same … all Jackals and Hyenas from the savannah they are … I think it's good she's keeping out of sight. Would be better if she just left entirely, don't you think? That's what Jane said."

"It's really up to Noka," said Amalina, diplomatically. "Uncle wants her to stay."

De Roye cleared her throat.

"So good to spend time with you again, Katarina," said de Roye, after a moment.

"Oh, yes, I suppose …"

Then, with a sudden flurry, Genevieve seemed to get to her greater reason for this visit: "You know, Katty, I've a confession to make."

"Oh?"

"To everyone—I'm not just speaking for me—you seem to devote most of your energies to running between Lady Lampeda and the merchant's daughter, Miss Berzweck."

"I do?"

"That's what it seems like, yes."

"Everyone feels that way?"

"Most everyone, yes. But to be fair, I should speak for myself alone."

"I had no idea where I pass my time was a topic of conversation."

"And why wouldn't it be? You're the reason we're here, so why wouldn't we all notice where you run off to? But for my part, while I allow it is true, I tell them it is very understandable: both Pia and Cristine have been here or have known you longer than the rest of us." She paused for a breath and to prepare her next approach, her words came slower and more cautious, as if on tip-toes, "But those two aren't really human, though, are they?"

"What do you mean?" said Amalina, cautious in return. Did de Roye *know*?

"Well, they're both like a couple of animals aren't they?" declared de Roye boldly from her cubicle. "Lampeda is a dog; dogs are loyal but profligate in their affection. So much so they would protect their master to their dying breath if they had to, or any old stranger they attached themselves to.

"Cristine, however, is a cat," she carried on. "Oh, that kind is loving, too. Very much so. But only when they want to be. They're very selfish otherwise and capable of withdrawing to the vantage of a ruthless observer, biding time and determining what's in their own interest. Cats, you see, have the slitted eyes of a snake. And for good reason. Its nature's warning."

"Interesting comparison," said Amalina, trying to sound diplomatic again. She felt awful having her friends reduced in such a taxonomic fashion: Cristine, cat; Pia, dog? And who knows how far this conversation was carrying down the corridor? But at least it sounded like de Roye didn't know what they were *really* turning into.

"And what would you compare yourself too, Jenny?" Amalina had asked, conversationally.

"I don't, because I can't," said Genevieve, in an assured way. "You know, if I were to confess—which is what I said I'm doing here, ha! This whole animal business …—you're part of the reason I wanted to get away from my home. I was tormented by thoughts that people—everyone else but me— are so natural, pious, and proper—appear to be and behave that way, anyway—but the instant they get behind closed doors they immediately strip off their clothes and become uncivilized howling beasts, with untamed natures."

"I … I … never knew …" said Amalina.

"No you didn't. I never told anybody. But it's all true, that's what I believed. And I'd hoped you might cure me."

"Of this fear?" assumed Amalina.

"Of my inability to *transform* myself," moaned de Roye behind the partition, though it sounded as if she were mocking herself. "'When will it happen?' I would ask me. When you were in France, Katty, I requested to meet you in my home, and had hoped your visits would perform the miracle.

Because I thought, being from a wild country, you'd be more ... well ... base and bestial, and show me the way ... Well, obviously that didn't happen. And I was so frustrated, I supposed I needed to get away from my own house and land in order to stimulate my wilder spirits." Genevieve made a noise, it sounded like frustration. But then she seemed to laugh: "When, oh, when*ever* will I overcome this unnatural lock on my body, so I can be like everyone else?"

*Why does she think I would or could help her with that?* Amalina wondered in shock.

"But, as I've learned, in the end, we're both—both you and I—very much *human beings,*" said de Roye cheerily, in conclusion. "As if we wouldn't know it as we sit here smelling each other's shit!"

De Roye laughed loud and hard at this.

"But, rather, I mean," said de Roye after clearing her throat again, "you and I hold the rainbow of emotions, interests, compassion, and empathy, don't we? That's why I miss your company when you're off frolicking with the wild animals. The dogs and the cats and the hyenas. We should stick together more, us humans, *don't you think*?"

"Oh ... yes."

"That's a good girl. Wasn't so hard was it?"

"Wasn't so hard?"

"Giving *other* people some of your valuable time, Katty. It invigorates the mind and the soul, doesn't it? I think so."

"Yes," answered Amalina. She smirked to herself and couldn't decide what was preferable, Anne Brignol's indifference and contempt, or de Roye's very human and needy latching.

"Yes it does invigorate ... But if you don't mind, Jenny, may I have privacy?"

"Ah!" said de Roye with a laugh. "One of those, eh? Well thanks for hearing my confession."


. . .


As Pils rolled the heavy barrel up the hall, Amalina had been tempted to run ahead. She couldn't believe how long it was taking to transfer this chain to her room, it had become some endless, meandering trail. But she'd also felt that she mustn't dare let the barrel out of her sight until it was safely stashed away.

Amalina then noticed Pils glancing at her between rolls. Had Anka told him—warned him—of their 'secrets' conversation?

"Is there something you wanted to tell me?" asked Amalina.

"Um, well," he pursed his lips. "You're looking very nice today, milady."

"Not some idle praise." Amalina gave him a serious look, a conspiratorial look; the same kind she and Anka had shared. "Something *of concern*."

"Oh, no, milady," he gulped. "I shouldn't think …you mean, hiding from you?"

"*Are* you hiding something from me?"

"No! Never! We'd never from you, I promise."

"*We?*"

"Well, Anka and I," sweated Pils.

"I already spoke to Anka about your worries … over my accepting that new position. I'll tell you what I told her: you two have nothing to worry about."

"Well, well, that is a bit of a relief, milady, yes …" Somehow Pils seemed more distraught than relieved.

"But there's something else?" said Amalina. "If you *are* hiding something from me, I won't like it."

"We hide nothing from you," he declared solemnly. Then, after a thought: "Nothing *voluntarily*, that is. Everything we do is on orders. Strict orders. We are the best and most loyal of servants and should never violate a trust."

"You've been ordered to keep something from me?" asked Amalina.

Pils did not answer, but his eyes saucered. This sent up a worried nerve.

"Who?" she whispered. "Who's wanting you to keep secrets from me?"

"I've said nothing like that," whispered Pils, still looking guilty.

"What is it? I order you to tell me."

"We can't say anything, milady. You know how it is. But I can say … Yes, I can say this: You know Wanger, Regio, and Balbo?"

"Yes. What about them?"

"I can say nothing more. Just that you are aware of them was my question. And now you've answered."

"What about them?"

"They're nice and learned gentlemen, those architects and engineers, Misters Wanger, Regio, and Balbo—though I don't understand half of what they're saying, and I think it's the same thing for them. But very nice. For the most part. And if they're here to keep the Castle or the mountain from falling apart, I pray for their lives they stay healthy and succeed. Well, here we are at your rooms. Where do you want it, milady?"

When Amalina tried to follow up this conversation, as Pils rolled the barrel around the room looking for an inconspicuous spot to settle it, he'd pretended not to hear. And then, when cornered, he'd sworn not to know anything else about the group, Misters Wanger, Regio, and Balbo.

Growing suspicious at Pils' mumphering, she had thought at the time: *suddenly Pils is interested in the architects? and has some secret about them he* must *keep from me? on orders of the Count?*

Far from being a slumbering heap anymore, to Amalina—who had been unaware of any danger while circulating in her own dramas—the castle seemed at once to be like an anthill that had been kicked; a chaos of disparate effort, activity, and movement, hastening below the surface.

• • •

"This place *is* getting very strange," repeated Amalina, done with reflecting. Her opinion hadn't changed "I'm glad I've got you to trust."

"Always, Pretty Princess," said Aklan.

"Well, I think I have another favor to ask."

"I'll always do anything for you, Pretty Princess," he said, dropping the chain and staring at her. He looked like a hound waiting to be sent to collect a downed bird. "Tell me."

"You *really* don't have to keep calling me that," said Amalina. "*Pretty princess?*"

"But I want to! I don't mind. Is that all you wanted, Pretty Princess?"

She smirked at him. Then she cleared her throat. "What do you know about Wanger, Regio, and Balbo? The architects?"

"Not much," said Aklan. "They don't talk to me, you know. But I think Balbo's headed for the Marosh treatment."

For effect, Aklan drew a finger across his neck and stuck out his tongue.

"He's sleeping with one of our Ladies?" said Amalina in disbelief. That's what had cost Zsolt Marosh his life. But Marosh had been a formidable man. Balbo was an old, red-faced, white-haired academic, not much a skirt draw.

"No one's interested," confirmed Aklan. "But he's definitely not gonna stop trying until he runs into trouble. I know it."

"Well, that's interesting. But I don't think that's it. Go hang around Anka and Pils, see if you can get them to tell you anything about those old fellows."

"Like what?"

"I don't know. But those two seem to know something the Count doesn't want us knowing. I can't imagine why, but maybe Anka and Pils won't think twice about talking in front of you."

"You got it, Princess. I might use the …" he made a gesture to signify the magic bone.

"Let's not use it if we don't have to."

"Would make it easier."

Amalina let out a long sigh and rolled back on her bed. Having secured the chain, and by attaching the wailing woman to her cause, it felt like she had accomplished a lot after the day's loss of Cristine and Pia. But there was still more to do. There always seemed to be more to do.

"Well, at least we don't have to rely on Pia anymore," said Amalina to herself, thinking of the greater promise of the woman on the wheel. "We don't need her at all."

"We were relying on Princess Lampeda?" Aklan raised his fuzzy blonde eyebrow at her. "For what?"

"Never mind. Shouldn't have said anything. But we've got a good replacement now. Someone a lot more committed than her, and who will really be able to help us when the time comes."

"Who is it?"

"I can't say yet. But you'll see."

"You know you can always count on me," said Aklan. He sealed the lid on the barrel, then hopped to sit on it. When he landed, he gave it a pat.

"I *am* counting on you," said Amalina. "But we need as much help as we can get, you know. And so ..."

"Who is it, I wonder?" he said from atop the barrel, leaning back, hand on knee, looking blankly into the distance of the room. His imagination spinning.

"Never mind, boy. It'll all come out later. Trust me."

## 30

# A Force at Work

Lieutenant Ivanti Ion Vokent paused in the ruins. The air smelled of smoke and charred wood. The old bones of the fortress were black and collapsed and hadn't been pulled out of the lower stone structure before the builders had begun reconstruction. The lieutenant didn't know if the builders had been in a rush or were simply incompetent. It would be hard to ask at this point. Their whole encampment, the architects, the engineers, the workers and their train of hangers on, had fled as soon as the flames in the woodwork were rekindled and the grounds overrun by his little force. None captured.

"We'll find one," promised Basz, who with a spyglass was studying the upper side of the mountain and forest, looking for trails in the patchy snow of quarry on the move. "Ran like white-tail hares, but my boys are half bloodhound. We'll get them. And not just the lame whores."

"It's all right," said the lieutenant, patting Basz on the back. "Let 'em run and spread the news. The only thing I'd like to know is how all this work was getting paid for, who was doing the paying, and who ordered it."

Behind it all would be the Count, of course. This was old Tepsji property. But better to hear it from the lips of the contractor or an engineer, or any of the others in charge, who must be maniacs to build in the height of winter, or the Count had frightened them into it. This was the sixth such castle: razed but being rebuilt at a hasty clip, with what little there was of the recovered paperwork pointing to a vast reward for a completion date by the end of Spring, at the latest the end of Summer. A lot of money was being spent across Ardeel, to its very corners, or debt was mounting. How the capital was flowing would be a good bit of information to have, so the fight against their adversary could be waged at every level.

In each wrecked castle's case, so Vokent had found, wood was the redevelopment's understructure, as stone was cut or sourced nearby, for the building's soon-to-be-real resurrection. Even if Count Tepsji's castles weren't laid out on any map, they were easy enough to find; they stood out along the mountainsides like great, broken, stony heads piercing through the snow, with trails and ruts of workmen leading to them. Easy enough.

The real genius of Attila Bronk had shown not in locating these castles, but in rooting out the Count's emergency pigeons, with their tinkling bells;

Tepsji's elaborate remote alarm-system. Always two or three were hidden within the nearby town, with a nervous minion on the lookout for mischief that needed reporting—and who would kill themselves upon discovery, stabbing daggers into their hearts, declaring loudly, forebodingly, "This is the best I can hope for, you don't know what he can do!" But despite the frustrating results, the pigeons and hideouts were pinned down with ease. Attila's pointers, as he and Vokent had searched around Korr for AXP's henchman's lair, had been, all along, rather subtle lessons to the lieutenant on how to observe minutely and detect acutely. Upon arrival in a new town, it took Ivanti little time to identify, isolate, and capture a bird and its keeper. The lieutenant's respect for Mr. Bronk grew.

. . .

Attila Bronk had also been right about the lieutenant returning home to his father.

Ivanti wasn't sure why he hadn't immediately sought his old home for lodging, but had tucked himself into the Rock Cup Inn. Vokent supposed he'd told himself it was for the immediacy of the moment: he was on a mission, after all; believing this even before tumbling into the growing revolution. He'd likely convinced himself as well, there was no reason *to* return there, he was no longer a Vokent from Korr, and so he had no real home here. Besides, his mind had knotted around the belief that to wander out to the family farm would only have weakened him, as his father would thoroughly diminish him there—just as he had driven Vokent away, to join the King's Army, in the first place.

But Attila Bronk had looked the lieutenant in the eye and pronounced that, with all these petty excuses, he was avoiding a reckoning with his father and himself. And it was an important step to free his soul and mind for the coming fight. The lieutenant had nodded and promised he would. He'd even once made it to the property's outer gate, stared in at the long house with the pens attached, frosted over, set in the lower roll of a hill at the mountain's foot, and imagined how the homecoming would play out if he entered.

When his father found him loitering at the broken down gate, he swore at the young man as if Vokent were still twelve years old and then ordered him inside. His father didn't ask much about his military life, though he did stare resentfully at the uniform from the corner of his eyes, but he led him on a tour of the house as if Ivanti might have forgotten where he'd come from, ending at the pens with the hogs left over from the slaughter, wintering for next season, and reminded Ivanti what he should be doing; his real work. His father was drunk, and continued to drink, as he heckled and berated his grown child. And more, through his rants, he explained in bits and pieces why he'd sent young Ivanti away with the king's recruiters; laughed how he'd wanted him gone from the Ardeel. Because with his son's good looks the boy would soon enough have some fool lass pregnant, but he could barely pay for Ivanti, much less a daughter-in-law and a drove of children. Better the boy find a girl on the other side of the continent. "Heard you were 'round here last year sniffing for the Dalca girl. She's a nice 'un— that tribe are, all of them—but she's also had some hard turns and that can only mean bad luck. You don't want to be touching that. No, get yourself far, and farther, and farther away. As far as you can go. Like you were meant to. As if you didn't *want* to go, anyway ... " Then the monologue descended, step-by-step, into blaming Ivanti for driving off his mother and sister, and maybe there came a hard blow to his ear.

And so, imagining this sour reunion, and feeling it as real as anything, Ivanti had turned on his heel resentfully, screwing his foot into the frozen mud, and returned to the Rock Cup, where he cleaned and polished his boots, having been unable to see it through. *Why bother?* He'd thought.

But when the revolutionary gave him his latest orders, the first was to finally go home.

With no right of refusal, Vokent did as ordered.

The old man hadn't come out as he'd imagined. Ivanti had had to climb over the broken gate, the latch had completely rusted into a solid piece, and then he'd searched the farmhouse until he found his father at the kitchen table, peaceably eating some cabbage soup. His father had only nodded, pointed to the old, iron, wide-bellied pot hung off a hook, if he might be hungry, and at the sideboard with the water or mead, should he want a drink. His father said nothing, expected nothing, only nodded now and again at some thoughts in his head. Ivanti thought he might have winked at him once. He could have stayed, taken up his old room. But the gloom and the promise of a more lively time at the Rock Cup Inn called him out. They, Ivanti and his father, never touched, never hugged. The only words said were, "Think you'll be coming back, then?" and later, as a side thought, and in a soft, sweet voice of concern, "When you're over there, d'ya ever remember your mother at all? do ya?" His father didn't say it, but the blame for her abandoning him, and her death by a broken heart, was in his rheumy eyes. Ivanti left without promising anything and spreading a handful of coins on the kitchen table, which should last his father a year or more, from the look of it.

The visit had been liberating after all. He'd emerged from this contest with himself as the true Lieutenant Ivanti Ion Vokent, future commander of the revolutionary army and a pig farmer's son no more.

Thanks again to Attila Bronk, he'd felt ascendant.

. . .

"Thinkin' 'bout that girl?" said Basz, breaking into Ivanti's thoughts. The burning structure around them was hot enough that Basz, like many of the men, had shed his jacket.

"What girl?"

"That nice girl whose heart ya broke?"

"Blast you!"

"You broke some pretty young lady's heart, ya cruel bastard, by picking too many peaches in the wrong orchard, eh?" grinned Basz, as if he'd just nailed a guilty secret which he could now poke Ivanti with in dull moments, "And now you're here to win her back. That's why you're in it."

"Where did you hear that?" growled Ivanti.

"Word gets around."

"But how? Who's saying this?" Ivanti gritted his teeth. "I thought I left all that nonsense in Korr. Will it follow me to the ends of the earth?"

"It's true ain't it?" said Basz, mystified by the emotional reaction from his commander and not knowing what to say.

Ivanti didn't answer at first. After a long while, almost after too long to say it was an answer, he muttered, "I'm on a mission here. What more do you want? How much more do I have to do to prove myself?"

"Nothin', sir, you're great," said Basz, wandering to the other wall with his spyglass and allowing his commander whatever time he needed. It wouldn't be long. "Was just trying to get your ass off the log."

"All right Basz," said the lieutenant, in a solid, confident voice less than a minute later, rising from the charred timber he'd been sitting, to become commander again. "Let's call the men back. You get the rest of this heap down. Have our cargo in the carriage and the horses readied, I've got a meeting I can't afford to miss."

"Sir, what's that?" said Basz. He was now directing the spyglass over the far wall, his body pressed to it, peering at an angle down the mountain's slope. Vokent heard the note of concern from his normally unflappable subcommander.

Ivanti took the spyglass and directed it where Basz stabbed his thick, dirty finger. Down below the mountain, after the last row of buildings in the small town, a force of a hundred men on horseback were riding slowly onto the castle road. They sat tall, were sharply dressed in leathers, with carbines slung behind them, polished swords at their hips, most with long spears or lances reaching into the air from their stirrups, and with fashionable beards, and severe faces as if something in their saddle was biting them. The upward brush of polearms from this force made it appear almost like a light hair over their body. But they were dressed in uniform, royal blue colors, with some having pendants of the same dominant color hanging from the tops of their spears. The horses had similarly colored blankets under their saddles, which were studded with bright, flashing pieces of metal. The square pendants were emblazoned with larger versions of those metal trinkets: Horns. Tethers. Nooses. Collars; symbols of the hunt. These hundred men moved as a tightly packed rectangle onto the road, a column of color and brilliant polish, flickering in the sunlight. And the lieutenant noticed, behind this column, two more columns of equal size were emerging from different streets within the town. And still more behind them.

Lt. Vokent swore as he watched the gloriously decked horde press onto the castle road, linked to each other to begin the climb. Well over a thousand.

"Bronk's done it again," muttered Vokent under his breath. "Going to get me killed."

"What's that, sir?" said Basz.

Vokent and Basz were now joined along the wall by twenty men, all cupping their hands over their eyes. They could see the mass of the force below, though not the detail.

"The King's Army," said Vokent. "What are they doing here? Where the hell did they come from?"

"What do we do, sir?"

"Get out," said Vokent with a hard smile. "Have your men follow those *rabbits* in the forest. But I need all the carriages and cargo out of here, fast. Let's disperse, we'll take the side trails, and we'll meet up in Tsobl at the signal, eh?"

"What about *them*?" his eyes daggered to the King's Army.

"Look nice, don't they?" said Vokent. "We should probably take some pointers."

"Yes, sir. But—"

"No buts, we're done here, we leave now. Everyone. Set off the barrels and bring this all down. Give *them* something impressive to look at." The lieutenant snapped his fingers and put the spyglass in the large leather bag slung over his shoulder. He rooted around in it until he pulled out a mallet and a sharp piece of shiny metal. "This spot won't burn, eh? Good enough."

The men at the wall watched as the lieutenant unhurriedly, almost casually, strolled to a fallen beam and then with one blow hammered the small bit into its upturned end. Anyone entering the hulk of the castle would first spot this rough cross of silver.

## 31

## Castle Mouse

### I

When Aklan came down from the castle wall, after attempting to question Captain Durok—and maybe locate the emergency bell (Item #3)—without him suspecting any motive behind it, Amalina couldn't help but admire the revolutionary's ability to secure and maintain immaculate secrecy within his organization; the way Attila Bronk could fit all the pieces together without them really touching. It seemed impossible for Amalina, and that by the way she'd handled things on her own that her secrets might erupt at any moment. Captain Durok's suspicious scowl from the wall when Aklan was done confirmed her feeling. She wished she could've had more time with Mr. Bronk; for him to guide or instruct her; or she had an open line of communication with him so she could at least voice to a knowing ear her frustrations. As it was now, she had to keep them to herself, didn't she? And bottling it up wasn't doing her nerves any good.

"No one's seen *him* for a couple days, nor Pia, nor Cristine," said Aklan, joining Amalina in the courtyard. "Durok says he doesn't know a thing about any of 'em. As for the Count, well, he wouldn't say otherwise anyway, would he?"

"Did he look worried?" asked Amalina, her expression neutral.

"I don't know. Not worried enough to have the emergency bell on him. Why?"

"If Captain Durok looked nervous, then he's telling the truth. Because if he really doesn't know where the Count's gone that'll worry him."

*And it'll worry me,* thought Amalina, *because maybe, after what Pia told him* …

If Pia had gone and told the Count everything she knew—and she knew very little about the specifics of Amalina's plan, but for *why* she had one in the first place—any extended absence could mean he'd sped off to Korr to rip the revolutionaries into red fragments. She could picture Attila Bronk suffering under the blows, wondering what had happened. If Amalina had failed somehow, or had turned on him. Amalina wouldn't know if that had happened until it was over, and the Count returned with some questions of his own.

Or his long, unexplained absences could simply be a tactical ploy to keep the Ladies' interest.

She had no choice but to keep moving forward. But with her eyes open.

"Can you ever tell with that big ox what he is?" asked Aklan philosophically of Captain Durok. "He doesn't have the bell, anyway."

She shook her head. "Let's just assume you-know-who could show up any moment."

"That good or bad, Pretty Princess?"

"Who knows?" said Amalina. "Anyway, he can't accuse me of not trying. His little 'ambassador of happiness'—"

"—*Ambassador of Happiness*—?"

Amalina hadn't told him yet what had happened with Cristine and Pia. She could do so right now, but thought better of it.

. . .

Standing in the chilly courtyard under a sheeted grey sky next to Aklan, Amalina sank into a melancholy loneliness, and a deep resentment at her circumstances. To be surrounded by people on every side but have nobody to confide in. The way Genevieve de Roye had relieved herself of her private, almost embarrassing worries in that stall, and so openly to Amalina, seemed like it could be refreshing. But life had kept Amalina cut off from the very beginning: where, after removing her mother at such a young age, her mother's substitute was Sadra: a severe woman with no qualms in meting out divine justice when she found Amalina had strayed too far, and might very well report whatever error she'd confessed to Dragomir; or circulate it in the village for public consumption, ridicule, and for Amalina's own edification. *Not exactly the same as a mother.*

Well, there had been Cristine, too. But Amalina had had to spend more time looking out for her, defending her, and healing the girl's sores, that they'd never felt like equals really, when you got down to it, but more like Cristine was a troubled younger sister; a daring girl who would spur her into adventures that, on her own, she'd never take out of fear. You don't get too honest with someone like that.

Or there was—after all things considered—prayer; opening one's thoughts to heaven. The eternal place which seemed could only listen impassively, and seldom articulated anything to Amalina which she didn't have to then interpret, later, by herself, from signs and circumstances.

*Well, what's to be done about that?* thought Amalina, shrugging her shoulders to throw off the mood and bracing herself, standing taller. So Attila Bronk had impressed her with his cautious organization. So what? How had he? The only surprise so far had been Lazru Skeldar—who he'd brought into the castle and had revealed to her, hadn't he? Where was the wall of mystery there? He'd told her his full plan. She supposed she could name off all his associates and soldiers, knowing the town better than he. His admonition for secrecy had been more of a boast then, hadn't it? Or, she now suspected, it had been a way to humble Amalina in order to intimidate her, or dissuade her from acting on her own. Rely on Attila; only *he* knew how to do it. Amalina rankled at how easily he'd convinced her of his superiority.

She could beat him.

• • •

Amalina handed Aklan one of the large bags. "I only wish I'd have known he'd be gone this long. But for all we know he's having himself a nice big sleep, but could wake up to have a look around. Then we have to be a little more careful, eh? But let's just carry on and keep an eye out for him … Oh, and for Cristine, and Pia … especially Lady Lampeda."

"Why her, especially?" said Aklan.

"Just let me know if you see her, okay? Any of them, but especially her."

"You never tell me nothin'."

"Look, the point of what we're about to do now is to find them—"

"I thought we're trying to get some—"

"That too," growled Amalina. "Would you quit interrupting me? *That*, and to find them before either of them can mess up our plan."

"Well, how can they do that, Pretty Princess?"

"Do you always have to ask questions?"

"I just want to know," he said, sounding nipped. "Only *we* know the plan. And Anka and Pils, right? Or is there something else going on? You know you can tell me anything, Pretty Princess."

"That's great, but it's annoying—"

"Aw, Pretty Princess—"

"—when I'm trying to get things going and you keep interrupting. You see? I swear, I'm going to buy you a little jester's outfit. Make you wear that, if you won't let me talk and finish a sentence once in awhile."

"Okay, go on," said Aklan, quelled. "We're looking for *him* and the two Ladies, Berzweck and Lampeda. What if we don't find any of them?"

"No bother, we just get done what we can for ourselves," said Amalina. She shook her body and prepared it for the coming run. "Well, those orphans' feet can't be getting any warmer, so—"

"What orphans?"

"Some orphans, I don't know."

"What happens if they ask me about them—the orphans?"

"Must you be so annoying, boy? Just say you don't know. I mean, *I* don't really know what's happened to them, do I? They're just some orphans down in Netz that need—"

"Okay, I got it. Let's do it."

"You know what to do?"

"Hands out, eyes up. I'll meet you back at the room when we're done," he said confidently with a wink and a grin.

"Good luck!" Amalina shoved him off. He ran away excitedly, his open bag billowed like a wind sock.


## II


"Care to give to the cause?" said Amalina, somberly, as she asked around the main building, taking an inventory of her guests; eyes alert for Cristine or Pia. "I'm looking for all scrap hose or socks, and any kind of spare cloth. Black preferred. It was a tragic affair, requiring sympathy."

She collected whatever donations in her large sack, which got heavier as she made her way up the floors.

Stopping in the eerie silence of one dark corridor, Amalina took a couple breaths to calm herself before she headed for the single door at the end.

"Eh-eh-eh-excuse me, Countess Katarina Tepji," said Bardina, bustling up behind Amalina and bowing at her side. "My Princess Margeta would like to … eh … su-su-speak to you. Eh?"

Bardina gestured back up the hall, in the opposite direction, with a polite, apologetic smile.

"Now?"

"I-i-i-if you please, Princess. I-i-it's not be long. My lady, P-P-Princess la Brichese w-w-waits."

It won't be long, but it will be obnoxious, thought Amalina, unhappily. "Certainly, Bardina; for you."

Amalina dragged the bag behind her as Bardina led the way.

But Margeta was already leaning out from her suite's doorway, not too far along, watching.

"Where are you going to in *that* direction, Princess Tepsji?" asked Margeta now, as they approached. The dour Lady of Rome stepped halfway out of her room to glare.

Amalina began: "Aria—"

"You heard what insult Aria Ecci did to Princess 'Maria' di Oscina, did you not? You know of that decadent Venetian's ever devolving depravity. Debauchery's new home is at that end of the hall."

"She just … knows how to entertain herself," said Amalina in a tone of tolerance she hoped would catch on.

"Is that so?" snipped Margeta. "Stay away from her. This I caution you. Princess Smeehaute, Princess di Oscina—the good ones here in this place— we have quit her company already. Quit her *completely*. Aria Ecci is an infernal influence upon even the strongest-willed heart, and reduces all levels of discourse to the chattering of imps—in the lowest depths of damnation itself. You can gain nothing from entering her chambers."

The last time Amalina had been to Aria's suite, it had been choked with incense. It was difficult enough to force herself to visit there without Margeta shaming her.

"I have to see to all my guests," said Amalina with a polite smile.

"Yet you haven't visited *my* room in a long time. Have you?"

She'd felt no need to attend to introverted stragglers like Margeta, 'Maria', Maibrigg, etc. But she didn't say it.

"Later," said Amalina.

"However, wait too long, Lady Tepsji, and you might find it is too late, and you'll be trapped in unending, consuming flames." Margeta's nostrils flared as she clicked through her rosary beads. "But there's something unnatural going on here already, isn't there, Lady Tepsji?"

"Bardina, leave us, please," said Amalina. When Bardina received a confirming nod from her mistress, she scuttled inside the apartment and shut the door.

"Well?" said Margeta, now that they were alone. "You've something more to say in your defense, Lady Katarina Tepsji? I can't imagine what. Or do you intend to insult me, or renew your lies?"

"I thought you had something to say to me. Or was it only to accuse me of something vaguely *unnatural* in front of your servant?"

"The reason for your attempts to drive me out of the high castle have been exposed," intoned Margeta, as if about to read out a declaration of crimes. "I never understood why Lord Tepsji hadn't shared his powers with his own family. But that was his choice. Now I hear that you are in line to become his wife? His own niece—!"

"Who said that?"

"That being *the truth*," continued Margeta, with ringing confidence, "of course you would do all you can to secure his power, even if it means seducing him to take advantage of him; to press your immoral flesh to his."

"Who told you—?"

"And then, it follows logically," she concluded, her grey nostrils flaring once more, "you would throw from this comfortable nest everyone you can—especially the only one here who would challenge such an abomination of corruption. And it doesn't matter where I heard it, if it's true."

"I'm still confused," said Amalina derisively at Margeta's condescending air, as she switched track. "I don't get it. Why do you pretend at piety, Princess, when your heart is so set on accepting Uncle and his offer? Which, I'll remind you, he's already given to others, like he's building a harem. And that *family* you want to join could easily include the lady down the hall who you hate so much."

Margeta choked back her indignation, and pressed it under a thick, hairy, lowered brow, and behind an agitated, prematurely wrinkled scowl: "As I have explained before, Lady Tepsji, who your uncle chooses, within reason, is his own business, and the *number* of wives he proposes to take does not contradict the founding members of our religion—"

Feeling the challenging spirit of Anne Brignol within her rising, Amalina interrupted in exasperation: "Oh, why *are* you still coming at me about this, Margeta? What does any of it matter to *you*: housing a priest here, your Catholic services, your chapel, and your confessions, all your play-acting piety, when you can't possibly believe in your religion anymore?"

"*Dio Santo!*"

"That's what Anne thinks."

"What do I care what Anne thinks!"

"She says if you want to join with them downstairs—anyone who does— who does accept his rite—doesn't *really* believe in—"

"Of course I believe! I will never doubt! Never!"

"But *why* would you ever, how could you believe in it, if you will become a killer and violate the very laws of heaven?"

When she answered, Margeta lifted her head and torso to its stiffest height and glared down her nose: "I don't *doubt*, and will never doubt those laws! But while your uncle has not yet accepted me into the family, I must look after my eternal soul; as I always have. I cannot know how many days have been allotted to me by Heaven, the exact hours written, and so I must take care, at every second that passes—" as she said this she brought up her hand again to show Amalina her fingers still clicking through the beads on her rosary, marking the seconds, doing so even now, displaying her unending devotion "—when I exist as a *pure* being. But once I take his vow, and I join with your uncle, I will have been liberated from such mortal concerns as purity, soul, sin, and what is required to sustain me—sustain me for eternity. Not when I forever place myself outside those white walls of the higher, divine realm." Her eyes flashed. "But, having escaped their grasp, moving in a parallel existence, it will be an equitable trade, never you worry, Lady Tepsji."

"Have you anything for the orphans?" Amalina asked Margeta sweetly, shaking her donation bag, when Bardina peeked out the door to check on her mistress.

## III

Aria Ecci's suite was no longer stuffed to intoxication with the heavy scent of burnt, exotic herbs, as it had been weeks before, but was now cut with the clean edge of winter. The windows were open in a communicating room to her inner lounge, and a cold draft whistled through. The fireplace was unlit. Only a few torches and some candles brightened the space but provided no heat.

Bundled under blankets, Aria and her closest allies were laughing quietly among themselves until Amalina showed with her donation bag. There seemed to be five Ladies of Title, whom Amalina couldn't immediately identify, scattered about the room. Their movement under the blankets continued, but the low murmuring of the Ladies was almost secretive now, conspiratorial, uninviting. The room had the air of a party that had gone on much too long, where a strange and darker element had entered the space, harder in its qualities, adding a meaner spirit; and the people within it need drive themselves to regain the fun so easily had just an hour before. Amalina had experienced this more than a handful of times already as the Ladies sought to outlast the others. From experience, one time would have been enough.

But Amalina had work to do.

"Countess," said Aria coldly. "How *nice* of you to visit us in the Antarctic."

"What's that?" asked Amalina, confused and feeling foolish lugging the heavy, half-filled sack into the center of the room.

"Careful where you step, icebergs all around. They'll sink you if you aren't careful."

"Is everyone all right here?" she asked, worried.

"It's a game, Katarina," said Greta La Nevers, helpfully. "We're on the hunt for penguins. Have you seen one?"

"What are penguins?" said Amalina, wrapping an arm around herself and hefting the bag over her shoulder. "What game is this?"

"How to keep ourselves sane," said Aria, with a slight grin. "If we can't go into the world, it will come to us. Some of us have been reading on expeditions to the south. What they've found at the southern continent."

"How intriguing."

"We do what we can to pass the hours. You'll be proud, I have been telling them all about the fun we had the last time I was here. The delights of Kyrgil? Even Margeta couldn't resist, eh, Katty? We had some real fun before the … well … before the going got rough, and the mountains came apart."

"I don't recall you liking Kyrgil all that much."

"Remember the day we came off the mountain to visit the town? And the excitement we had in the snow? Sliding and sliding. Or were you already gone by then?"

"I was there," said Amalina, remembering the day she had returned to Kyrgil, after an emergency trip to Korr, to find everyone flying down the mountain in sleighs, or riding on pieces of furniture, which the townfolk had hauled up past the treeline for them to use.

"Well, how am I supposed to remember?" said Aria irritably. "You were always disappearing, to here, to there, to who-knows-where. As you and your uncle do. As if avoiding us sometimes, I think."

"Oh, that's not true at all."

"What do I care?" snapped Aria. "Now Katty, that time at Kyrgil, you said you were off to visit your folks in the *countryside*, isn't that right?"

Amalina's stomach lurched, thinking she meant visiting her father in Korr, until she remembered that Katarina's cover story was that her parents, the royal blood relations to Count Tepsji, who did not care for him or his lifestyle, lived in an obscure rural mountain town. A town secreted *somewhere* in Ardeel. Always a good excuse for her to escape the castle for awhile. Amalina nodded after the pause.

"Busy making *bread* or something?" sneered Aria. "Is that right, Katty?"

There was a distant laugh from under one of the blankets.

Amalina shot Aria a look. *Or* was *there some hidden meaning behind what she'd said?* Aria had learned about her real life as a baker's daughter, then? How? Pillow talk with the Count? And was she now going to reveal it to everyone in the room; trot it out for some unkind amusement?

"Bread did you say? What are you talking about, Aria?"

"We've heard rumors, Kat-Kat, on our trip below the arctic circle. Word is you were taken in by Count Tepsji as a favor to some poor small-village baker. A baker who was afraid his neighbors would learn of your *illegitimacy*."

"What! I'm a bastard? Who told you this?"

"The natives around here are prone to gossip," said Aria. "Much of it very scandalous, and it is hard to tell what's true and what's not. But sometimes it's hard to resist a good story."

Suddenly the chill in the room grew ten degrees colder, and emanated from all the eyes staring at Amalina, waiting for her to react. Perhaps

Margeta had been right about these damned chattering imps. Amalina felt like turning around and walking out. She thrust her jaw out and said: "A scandalous lie about your good friend; you consider it worthy of your entertainment, Aria? Well, you must be at wits end, then. Don't keep the windows open too much longer or you'll all catch your deaths of cold."

"Oh, *Katty*, don't be like that," said Cristine, poking her head above the covers and smiling like a knife at Amalina. "It's not like we *believed* it, but it does pass the time in a harmless way. Of course, we wouldn't think any less of you if it were true."

"Cristine!" said Amalina. "I know you didn't tell them such a thing!"

"Never," cried Cristine with a laugh. Her eyes glimmered with that false energy from the green bottle. "Who can tell where it comes from? I was telling them it *wasn't* true, that you are *not* a common baker's daughter, and a bastard one at that. But I'm sure there are worse rumors about *me* and my family that people tell; out of spite, or boredom, or jealousy. It never pays to worry oneself over such things. Or spread them."

"You'll be happy to hear," said Aria in a commanding but conciliatory tone, as if to take the attention back from Cristine, "I've spoken to your uncle, Kat-Kat. Well, it was Pia, Margeta and I who spoke to him. We will have those winter games again this year. As we did in Kyrgil. But at Lady Berzweck's *informed* recommendation, it will be in a quaint little town named Korr. That should be great fun, don't you think? It should put all this nasty rumor-mongering out of our heads, and in the meantime air the castle for our return, letting our friends who are still suffering from whatever it is that is going around—in this beautiful, timeless castle—to recover their health."

"Margeta has accepted?" said Amalina. "Pia too? You've spoken to Pia?"

"Everyone loves the idea, Katty. *Everyone*. Don't you?"

"And if your parents aren't willing to open their home to so many of us," said Cristine, "Papa Szeful will be happy to host everyone for a week. I'm sure your parents will though. The both of them. Your mother, too? I mean, why not? And it will be so nice for us to visit them. Over there in Korr. Where they live. Where we grew up together as the closest of childhood friends. Don't you think, dearest Katarina? Your parents have a castle there, too, don't they? Something like that?"

Cristine waited for Amalina's answer, with an ugly, razorsharp smile and eyes that cut around to the other Ladies, making sure they were in this entertainment with her.

32

## "Yes, My Love. Never, My Love"

"**I** love the idea!" declared Amalina to Pia Lampeda, when she finally found the Lady drifting aimlessly inside the Grand Gallery.

Amalina had felt a warm throb at seeing Pia again; and then another hopeful pulse when her friend didn't plunge into a inhuman rage but looked to be herself, if a little sad. Still, Amalina knew she had no time to get caught up in sentimental relief. She set her donation bag inside the door to this arcade of gargantuan paintings and elaborate sculptures to join Pia's side and spread the happy news. "A trip should be great fun! no matter how dangerous! Some people got injured in the snow, if I recall … But it'll be good for everyone to get away from here!"

Amalina found it hard to sell her enthusiasm to someone ignoring her.

"Didn't there used to be a wonderful painting on that wall of a picnicking couple?" said Pia, pointing vaguely at an empty patch. "A woman on a swing, laughing, with a dog nipping at her heel. It was so beautifully done, it looked so real. And the dog reminded me of me and my puppy, little Ge Ge, at play."

"You *will* be coming with us on our trip, won't you?" asked Amalina. "Aria wants us to repeat the fun we had last time, for our newcomers, before winter runs out. And she said you asked *him* to go, too. So you will be … yes?"

"Who can say, who can say?" said Pia vacantly. "But, well, *didn't* there used to be a painting? I swear it was there. Or did I imagine it all? … Is this whole castle just a dismal illusion that forgets itself sometimes?"

"Pia, I'm trying to talk to you," said Amalina, gently touching her arm. "Look, I'm so very sorry. I never meant to … I don't want to lose you as a friend. I want to make things up for what's happened. Do you hear me?"

Pia stopped and smiled warmly, taking up Amalina's hand in hers. "That *is* nice of you to say. Do you really mean it, I wonder?"

"I'm trying my hardest to prove it to you."

"And I wonder if anyone can ever really recapture their innocence once it's demonstrated to be false," said Pia. "What do you think? I've never pretended to be anything I'm not. I've always spoken the truth. But from the very first we met, our relationship was balanced and sold on a lie." Pia's eyes drooped. "Wasn't it?"

"Let's not forget," said Amalina with a sterner delivery now, but a lower voice, "It wasn't *my* lie. *He* was the one sending me out under threat if I didn't do what he wanted. Do you understand that?"

Pia nodded. "It's just a shame it had to begin that way, our friendship. The doubt, however undeserved, eats at my love for you. Even now, Katty."

"So you really do love me," said Amalina.

"I don't know what I'm doing wrong that I can't convince you."

"You certainly did your part the other day," replied Amalina with a distant smile. "I didn't know you were such a fragile flower. All those tears, girl. And running off like that …"

"And here you keep insisting I'm no longer myself. Accusing me I can't possibly have feelings anymore."

"I'm catching on. So … besides your hunger and need, you *can* have emotions too …"

"Of course." But the look in Pia's eye: there was a suggestion—the hope—of a *belief* in human emotions, which held like the strain on the edge of a bubble, shivering, uncertain. Maybe Pia wasn't sure. For Amalina, even now, it was difficult to reconcile a normal Pia with the grotesque animal she'd watched tear through half a dozen men, and the distorted, savage monstrosity the once-sweet Noka became so many nights ago; so opposite to creatures of sympathy and compassion and *feelings*. But Pia's forlorn smile pushed against that, even as her eyes showed some hesitation. "And now I never wish to have a single emotion ever again. How do you like that?"

"And a sense of humor," said Amalina, with an encouraging grin.

"I'm working on that, too," said Pia, half-returning the smile. "Shutting it up a little, anyway, the best I can. If I could find a way to banish every stray palpitation, I would."

*Is it real*, wondered Amalina at Pia's seeming genuine vulnerability, fumbled with accepting it, *or is it just a part of an act?*

Not knowing the truth was so frustrating, Amalina began chewing her lower lip.

"Never mind," said Pia.

"Yeah, never mind."

"You know, Kat, I think everyone here is just trying to understand each other."

"Everyone?" said Amalina, doubtfully " … Even *him*?"

"I think so."

"Hardly seems like it to me."

"Well, he's in no rush, is he? He's the only one here who knows how much time we have to get around to doing things; like *knowing* each other."

"Never thought of it that way."

"That's because maybe you don't have the ability, yet, to understand." Pia's mood appeared to sink again, listing toward her aimless sulk. "Or you've never *wanted* to."

"Then let's not worry about it right now," said Amalina, shaking their held hands encouragingly, trying to boost her up. Or was there something else there? Some reason Pia was acting like this? "Say, though, you didn't tell him about …?"

"About what, Kat?" Pia's eyes lowered as she frowned, predicting in her sullen thoughts some disappointment, perhaps suspecting Amalina was only worried she had spoiled the revolution, or given away Amalina's own little plot, to the Count.

Amalina, recovering with another positive shake of their hands, said quickly: "Hey, hey. Look, you have to understand, Pia. However much you felt I lied to you, that I shut you out, that I betrayed you, this whole time I've been thinking of some way to save everyone. Especially you. It's just that, before, I didn't really know—I never knew before you came—what was in his power to do. And even once I'd learned it, I didn't know what he planned to do *to you* until it was too late. I never would have invited *any* of you if I had known what he could do. And now it is my sole concern to get you away."

"Your sole concern?" echoed Pia, doubtfully.

Amalina nodded. "Listen: you love your family, don't you? You can doubt me, but there's nothing false about *that* love. That love is pure."

"No … I mean, yes … I mean, what do you mean?"

"If you think, even now, this castle is just a dismal illusion and you were lied into it, maybe by me—" Pia's lips shifted into a cynical smile at this, as Amalina lowered her voice once more "—why not return to your family while you have the chance? You can still stand the sunlight, can't you?"

She tilted her head, regarded Amalina with surprise. But she thought about it. "I'm not sure I could survive so long a journey as that. And to what purpose? So I can disappoint them at what I've become? The godless choice I made? I'd rather they thought I'd died and remember me as I was."

"But it doesn't have to be that way," soothed Amalina. "Don't think like that. You're stronger than him. You're better moraled. You can control yourself. All that's needed is a little discipline and you're no better or worse than anyone else. You don't have to go around killing, eh? You can sustain yourself on the blood of animals."

Pia made a face. "You've no idea what you're talking about. There's no comparing the two, animal or human. And I couldn't imagine living with that awful, awful taste every day—"

"You don't have to kill, anyway. Cristine is the very proof."

"But even with her, your uncle still goes hunting. And look how drained he is … by holding back."

"That's another matter then," said Amalina, "for another time. The important thing is for you to get home to the people you belong, in the land you are familiar with and love, while you still can. Remember your little Ge Ge. And if you go home, *if you dare*, you will be out of *his* range. You can do whatever you want. Live whatever life you see for yourself … and *you can protect your family*." Amalina squeezed Pia's hand. "And now we have the means to make it happen. If we're in Korr, you see, as they propose—in order to discredit and shame me, I guess—the border is not far away. Even in winter you can make it through the pass and into the frontier before nightfall, as long as you start early enough. He won't go over, there's nowhere for him to hide. You'll be free. If you dare."

"You're trying to get rid of me," said Pia, unsurely.

"Who said I wasn't coming with you?" whispered Amalina breathily. "This is *our* escape."

. . .

Before Pia could smile, there was a rumble and the castle shook and rocked from side to side. Stone squealed briefly as grit and dust fell from the ceiling and the walls.

"My, what's happening here?" said Pia.

The air in the gallery hummed and filled with grey dust as the wall on the far end of the room appeared to dissolve and reshape itself, a black blur hovering just in front of it. Then the blur slowed and hardened into the Count; who stood in front of the now-solid wall, staring at it. The castle's stones were uniformly light grey and smooth, the joins almost imperceptible. But this wall had transformed in a matter of seconds, and there was a newer projecting part, a little rougher both in shape and color. It looked like a massive rustic, jutting fireplace made with the kind of boulders found along the mountain's river. And though it had a fireplace shape, it was without a defined central hearth. This pile of rocks extended into the room as if to form a foot with a couple overly-large, seperated toes on either side. The top of the leg braced the ceiling.

The Count, his back to Pia and Amalina, teeter-tottered his hands before the remade wall as if willing it to stay in place. When it didn't collapse, he put his hands on his hips and made a small noise of satisfaction, which was disturbed by Amalina's coughing on the dust. He turned.

"I think it should hold," said the Count, who looked older than usual; even more so with the layer of dust delineating a few extra wrinkles. "Yesssss, it will hold very well. This science of architecture is quite sound, I think, despite its questionable origins. Don't you agree with me?"

*I, me, I me;* Amalina would have rolled her eyes but she was squinting hard and blinking back tears against the rough, floating particles. The wall and air felt incredibly hot, it smelled of charred stone.

Pia knelt before him, her head bowed. "Is the castle in danger, my love?"

"In danger of what?" said the Count, patting his arms and chest.

"I hope it isn't going to collapse."

"So you disagree with me? The science of architecture is not sound, and this bracing column will not bear the load it carries for a thousand years or more? Regio assured me so."

"Oh, I wouldn't know," said Pia with a shake of her head. She looked at Amalina until Amalina felt the need to get down on a knee next to her. "But your desire to shore up the castle does make one question."

"Interesting," he said, mostly to himself, his habitual smile elongating into consternation. "I'm improving the integrity of this great building, and it gives the impression to everyone that it is on the verge of collapse?"

"The mountain has been shaking—"

"Natural occurrences. From time to time. And the improvements I'm making are meant to buttress it all so the occasional shocks will be less noticeable. I'm sure Katarina has said as much."

"This is why you brought in the architects? to prevent a collapse? What will we do if it falls to pieces like the castle in Kyrgil before you can finish?"

"Please, Pia, you aren't hearing what I'm telling you."

"Sir," said Amalina. "If you're shoring up the castle, I suppose then our trip to Korr is well timed?"

The Count looked surprised. "Trip to Korr?"

"Aria asked you to—"

"She hasn't," said the Count with distaste. But to that: "What should she have asked me, then? to where?"

"Or maybe it was Cristine? But before we run out of winter, we—that is all the Ladies and I—and Pia—and you—will be visiting Korr." Amalina explained the concept of recreating the fun they'd had so long ago in Kyrgil, just as Aria had put it.

"Ah! Yes. *Yessss.* But nobody asked me. It was *my* idea, Katarina. To recreate that great fun, a pleasure I was not able to share with you ladies then. And it seems, from what I hear, to have been the most splendid way to pass the hours. Oh, yes, it was my idea to join you on this delightful excursion, so we will have plenty of things to talk about and reminisce in the years to come."

"Oh."

"And your old friend Cristine *did* try to talk me into a certain out-of-the-way venue, but we aren't going to Korr, after all."

"No?"

"No. *Noooo*." The Count caressed one side of his mustache as he stepped forward to guide Pia to her feet. "Please stand, my lovely. One never has to kneel before one who shares your own heart."

"You're saying we aren't going to Korr?" said Amalina, pressing him.

"Why go all the way there when there is a perfectly suitable city at our feet? I believe Netz will be perfect, don't you agree? With so many more establishments suited to the refined tastes of our princesses, and hotels of comfort. Nothing like that backwards little town of yours, Ms. Dal—I mean, Katarina."

"She knows who I am," muttered Amalina, indicating Pia with her eyes. "Sir."

The Count looked at Pia almost as if he were suddenly afraid of her. Then he recovered with a smile and pulled on his mustache again. "But the rest are comfortably unaware, and Pia promises not to tell a soul about your secrets, little mouse. You promised me, didn't you, Pia Lampeda? You won't say a thing about Ms. Dalca's unfortunate past?"

"Yes, my love. Never, my love." Pia was looking at Amalina when she said this, and hit the *my love* hard as she did so.

"Come, Amalina, does your desire to see your father never flag?" asked the Count. "So that you lose all sense of danger? Are you so blinded by your love of your best friend, Cristine, that you cannot see she might be wanting to humiliate you in front of our other guests? To reveal your true history?"

"Um—"

The Count continued on with a delicious purr, always the admirer of politicking and intrigue, "Why would she not? She's jealous of your elevated station, even as I lift her up into a higher place. Well, let's not be angry. Such things are natural while she remains a mortal. Their kind is undyingly petty, no? Unless you should wish me to bring her over quicker, to end it?"

"No, sir," said Amalina. "I don't think you should 'bring her over' at all."

"I understand. But you have no reason to worry. If it pleases you, she can't mar the Dalca name, whatever her prejudices. You've seen how I have already begun to alter the flow of history, blotting out the memory of that undeserving General Marosh, whose name will never pass my lips from this day forward, and I am writing into stone for all time the valor and nobility of his replacement, my loyal General Umalasju, *Vezel* Umalasju. I have not forgotten. So will I do with your father's family name. I shall make him and his ancestors known to all as the very founders of this grand nation."

"You really don't have to do that," said Amalina, feeling her pride bitten a little. She had always thought her father and their bakery were noble in their own way and didn't require an artificial boost to be well regarded. "I am fine the way it is."

"Now, ladies, why don't you go run and play while I get back to work here. I haven't the time for these transient palpitations of the minor realm. You will understand my meaning in time. Especially you, Ms. Dal—ah, *Katarina*. Forgive me." He wiped his brow, looking tired again. "I keep forgetting. Well, we can all look forward to these coming days of play and rest down in Netz—"

"But, sir," said Amalina —

"—which I think is a much better place to have our fun. The mountains of Netz valley are more suited to adventure. And they are closer to home, my high castle, so I can keep everything comfortably within my sight. Oh, the Ladies will think it is all their idea, of course, to discount Korr and embrace Netz, instead. But they *will* come to that very conclusion I have set for them.Yes. *Yesssss.*"

"Will they?"

"They certainly will, my dear. I shape the will of all." He took Amalina's hand, and his herbal scent stirred the air. "And as for you, I've given instructions to Netz's master apiar: you may have whatever part of his trade you like. Those bees you were wanting, remember? Simply ask from him what you want and he will supply. Whatever you like."

Amalina was shocked by the sudden turn, but made the right sounding noises: "Oh, thank you, sir. I do get my bees, then?"

"You may raise those loathesome insects as you will," he said officiously. "That is my concession. You may make the special candies with their honey if you wish, or use it to broadcoat Ms. Pattipo's hair. The matter of whether you'll conduct yourself as a common candy monger and scrounge after profit, however, is yet to be settled, and I still have a mind against it."

"Well, thank you, sir."

"And so *you* will prefer for us to remain in Netz instead of pushing on to Korr?" he smiled indulgently, "knowing now what is waiting for you there, *yes?*"

She couldn't help but admit: "You think of everything, sir."

. . .

And as it seemed he *did* think of everything, from a hundred different directions—and had now, by tempting her with the bees, cut off Pia's route of escape by withholding her nearness to the border, as if he'd heard them talking and suddenly formulated the counter-plan—Amalina realized that if she intended to best him, she'd have to be thinking at least one degree better.

## 33

## More Tea

**"I** wanted to thank you," said Rosczy, formally, "for putting me in touch with the southern partisans, Vogoneyevic's people."

"More than easy enough," replied the large, babyish looking man, who, at his unusual size, crowded almost the entire back half of the comfortably furnished compartment of the closed vardo wagon. With the number of loudly colored cushions lining the space and surrounding him, from a different perspective he could be a tot standing within a crib. "I couldn't guarantee how they'd receive you. Hm, hee. Though I did my best to keep it friendly—so everyone would be happy. Do tell how it went. But the tea is ready, would you like some?"

"No, thank you," said Rosczy.

"It's quite delicious. The best!"

The large man continued to stand there with his stupid smile, holding a teapot aloft, his eyebrows halfway up his forehead, as if his visitor might suddenly change his mind. Rosczy scowled until he gave up and happily poured his own cup. The man operated under the name Mr. Simulzja.

• • •

Mr. Simulzja had first entered the wagon belatedly, after being called by his people from the rough winter landscape, stark naked. With his out-sized proportions he resembled an overgrown infant. As amiably as if he'd just been out for a stroll in the woods, he'd explained to Rosczy: "Practicing to be natural in all elements! as all creatures do! even in winter! Hee, hee, hm, hee!"

Why it was so important Simulzja gain this particular advantage was left unspoken. But after Rosczy reminded him coolly how man's intellect had furnished him not only with reason but the ability to make clothes, which elevated him above the beasts, Simulzja had simply shrugged his white, rubbery shoulders, and said with a great smile, clapping his rosy cheeks to get them warm, "Still ... quite invigorating. I'm going to put a pot on for some tea; sooo good! Would you like?"

And though he'd draped a red silk robe over his frame like a furniture cover, its size, material, and design displaying the opulence of a wealthy merchant, Rosczy hadn't been able to shake the sight of his massive bare body. Even when it came down to business. The man lacked the stern brow of the deep thinkers Rosczy had known, but had the open, over-joyed face of a startled and credulous baby. And Simulzja was to be his …? Rosczy still couldn't believe that this cherubic simpleton, with his rawness and oddness, could actually be his link to the future—his route to redemption; his divine conduit. He couldn't believe that he'd ever believed it at all, much less now. But to get what he wanted, he *needed* to believe it.

"It's amazing how far a man will stretch when he thinks something is in reach," muttered Rosczy, dolefully.

"Hm?"

"It's nothing. I find myself speaking my thoughts aloud sometimes, now that I have the freedom to talk."

This didn't change Simulzja's smile, but his eyes blinked reassurances. Maybe he thought the comment touched on his recent nudity, though he hadn't seemed self-conscious before. "Well, we're all friends here, my dear comrade. We can be open about *everything*. Feel free to speak your mind. Do tell, do tell. Hm, hee."

Both seated now, Simulzja mindlessly played his fingers on the table and around his cup; as if, on its own, the hand was searching for something. The movement reminded Rosczy of a signal the Cardinal would make—an order his body almost reflexively obeyed.

"Oh!" started Simulzja, as Rosczy half rose, before he caught himself, hesitated, and then sat back down. "Something wrong?"

Rosczy just shook his head. And he loathed himself—and those terrible fingers that had trained him too well. *How I'd love to still those fingers forever!*

Mr. Simulzja noticed the heated stare and he pulled back his paw, a look of curiosity now on his face, eyebrows lifted halfway up his head again, a wondrous smile beaming out below. "What is that look you're giving me, eh? No, it's the least I could do for someone like you."

"Tell me, is what you've said about Attila's man, the young lieutenant, true? All of it? I need to know everything to make this work."

"It must be," smiled Simulzja. "His life, his love, and his honor? I heard it all from a reliable source … and I've good contacts. Are you *sure* you don't want any tea?"

Rosczy made a face and fiddled a flask in his hand as an answer.

"Quite delicious though. You were saying you wanted to thank Simulzja?"

"I will reward you greatly for what you've done. And if everything comes off."

"Ye-es, comes off!" chorused Simulzja. Then he made a face of his own, the smile curved differently. "From what everyone's been saying—the way they've been talking, and you've been talking—it seems like these mountains are about to have a reckoning that will alter their history forever."

"If all goes to plan."

"We-ell," smiled Simulzja. "Whichever way it goes, it all goes to *someone's* plan. Hm, hee. Or somewhere in between. But if things change in *your* direction everything will be different. It'll be a glorious and happy day for these mountains! But, you see, from my way of thinking, it's not whether *your* plan succeeds or not, you know. It's about finding happiness, whatever happens, whatever the circumstance."

"Right." Rosczy didn't enjoy the unpredictability of this merchant, much less when he cheerfully reminded him of his shifty, cantilevered nature: the status quo could stay or go, he'd ride it. Rosczy wanted to return the favor.

Rosczy frowned: "You're always smiling."

"Nothing wrong with that."

"Must be nice."

"You could give it a try, comrade. Here, some tea, Comrade Rosczy. Please, please. It *is* the best, I pro-omise! Now, what were you saying …?"

At the offered cup, one edge of Rosczy's mouth came up scornfully before he fought it back down. "You once put it, Mr. Simulzja, that you are the light in Ardeel's darkness; set against that darkness." Simulzja smiled and nodded. "You've pitted yourself against that creature in Netz. Well … the way I see it, that creature is the force of power here in your equation. And I believe you want to be a part of things when he finally goes down?"

"Very much so!"

"Very good. But your potential here is limited, you work *against* his power. When he's gone, it'll be like when the candle is extinguished: the face in the mirror disappears. You'll no longer be seen. You'll be out of your old job, you see."

"How awful you put it that way," said Simulzja, his smile faltering in the revelation. He glanced in an aggrieved way at Rosczy, as if the blow had been deliberate. But then he rebounded suddenly. His smile grew as if by divine inspiration: "Oh, well! What can I do about that, eh? What comes will come. If nothing else: what of the lieutenant and his *amour*? …" he whispered excitedly, confidentially, "I think I know who his lost love is. Oh, yes! A good girl, a very good girl, who deserves some happiness; the both of them. Hee, hee. Whatever happens, I'd like to help those two come together!" Simulzja, cocked his head back, his eyes batting, a beatific grin on his face, sighed. "It would be sooo-oooo romantic. If I could work something like a cupid, and bind them together before I'm done—"

"Stay away from him," warned Rosczy.

"What? Well, it's just a thought. But shouldn't I help everyone I can? Why not? Now, he *is* Attila Bronk's man, and I refuse to get too close to that one—"

"Right."

"But then again, though he may be too close to Bronk, it might still be worth it. It could make *everyone* happy, all my friends, their lovers …"

Rosczy understood his little push-back had gotten the meddler worried, maybe a little desperate. Doing so might have been poor judgment. It could be dangerous.

"Stay out of it. I won't allow any distractions."

"But if you reject my good and kind effort to settle things happily for everyone," mumbled Simulzja, sounding stung, testing a counter-strike, "might you only be accepting Tepji's bitter world instead?"

"Leave Vokent to me." ordered Rosczy. "Leave everything to me. We'll worry about the taste of the world later. Just keep your smiling face out of it, Simulzja. You've done your part and that's good enough. Now it's time to keep out of the way for those who are truly *in* the fight."

A voice whispered through the door. "*Mr. Timorak.* Time to go."

A look of horror spread across Simulzja's face, before he changed course and giggled with embarrassment. "Never mind you heard that name, Comrade Rosczy. If you please. A mistake on my servant's part is all. Just a meaningless, *temporary* code name."

Rosczy shrugged. What did he care? "I've forgotten many names already. What's one more? It's easy enough."

The large, babyish man shifted in his chair, uncomfortable, wincing, he leaned forward to pick up the conversation. "Anyway … let's not be mean or unfair to each other, I've never questioned *why* you are doing what you're doing—"

"And you shouldn't. According to your own words, this is *our* history, not *yours.*"

"But you really think there's a chance it'll work? Your plans?" he asked, innocently. "Do you really?"

"The time is coming. Tepsji must take responsibility for all he's done and pay."

"Must he, though? At all costs? What greatness can we hope to achieve in this world without a little evil?"

Rosczy's body tensed and contracted dangerously as his eyes sparked, "I can't imagine what you mean."

Mr. Simulzja looked only a little abashed, tugging at the robe, as he explained: "If we tame a lion, and can control him and bring him to our side as a tool we can use, would it not be wiser to do so? Than to risk it all for nothing, by trying to kill the lion outright?"

"What kind of rubbish!"

"Well, Marcus Aurelius would have said—"

"The *Roman* Emperor?" growled Rosczy.

"I know you're a devout and pious man, and I'm not sure you'd have read Aurelius' treatise on life, but he explains his philosophy all very well: how a man should be willing to accept his fate, whatever his fate, and play his role as best he can; and leave the rest to—"

"If that is your understanding of an *Emperor's* take on the meaning of life—" he pronounced the word 'emperor' with as much disdain as he could fit it with "—I'd say you have a very limited grasp."

"Well," Mr. Simulzja's head teetered back and forth, "I suppose we can agree to disagree."

"For all the creature has done, there's no question he must die. And that is the role *he* is going to play, Simulzja."

"Oh, yes, I suppose …" the man-child smiled bleakly. "… and if you're right, if you win, I suppose then … I suppose … I'll just be *forgotten* … Hm, hee."

## 34

## A Rival in Netz

The trip from the Count's high castle down to Netz—the first leg in the voyage to Korr—was a chaotic caravan of sleighs, unsteady carriages with slippery wheels, and raucous Ladies' laughter; with the Ladies' ever-mindful servants attached. It took most of the day and the sun was sinking on the mountain's shoulder when they finally slid into the city's northern quarter.

In the hours along the way, bundled inside their own private sleigh with a silent Pia Lampeda as their only witness, Amalina rehearsed Aklan on his role in their coming adventure. Because Amalina had built into her grand plan against the Count a degree of flexibility, and if with this unexpected outing she could not work its primary objective—neutralizing the Count— then she could very well continue easing the Ladies out of his clutches—and then out of Ardeel. This long jaunt provided the perfect opportunity, or so she felt. And who better to send the Ladies packing than the boy who never goes home: "What will you say to them exactly?"

"I will announce myself ..." said Aklan, twiddling his snow cap in his hand, kicking his feet excitedly, "as *myself*. The Prince of—"

"But only through a servant," cautioned Amalina. "Some trusty footman we hire in Netz. You must let *him* do the talking ... and you try to stay out of sight as much as you can. Stick to the shadows."

"How do I know if I'm in a shadow or not?" smirked Aklan. "Really, I think your players' makeup and the false mustache will convince them I'm worthy, even if I'm a little short. I'll bundle up and wear some tall boots with padding at the bottoms. It's good enough. I *am* a prince."

"Keep to the shadows anyway," said Amalina, "However convincing you think you are, I'm telling you: *Shadows*. Let your money do the work. Maybe put some padding in your shoulders, too. How much gold did you bring?"

"Fifty, um, coins."

"Coins? Aklan, I told you to get some of the little bars and then we can—"

"Come on, Pretty Princess," cheered Aklan, "How was I going to make coins in the city? I got the bars just as you asked, but then since the master wasn't around I went ahead and turned them into coins myself."

Amalina fell back in the compartment and stared at the young boy. "Right in the counting house? You could have been caught!"

"I wasn't."

"Still, he might know someone's fooled around in his treasury."

"I think not," said Aklan, calmly. "You know, he seems to have been at work there pretty hard recently, most of the bags and gold bars have gone." Here Amalina nodded. "And the fire was still hot in the forge when I snuck in. Hot enough to melt metal."

"You mean he's making *more* money? *again*?"

"He's planning on spending a lot pretty soon, eh? Or he's just readying 'em now before he needs 'em. You're friends will be pretty expensive if they're staying out for awhile."

Amalina also thought of the Count's plan to purchase lands and build castles into Western Europe, so that he and his chosen women can skip safely from one fortress to the other, to rest in well-guarded shelters during the daylight hours, like leaping from one stone to the next while crossing a dangerous river—another of Amalina's dumb ideas she'd unwisely bothered to suggest to him and he'd seized upon as if it were his own stroke of genius.

Or ... *was* his newest round of coins really for their expensive little pleasure trip? Or might there be another, unknown expense?

"You're lucky you weren't caught anyway," said Amalina, stowing away the unpleasant, unsure feeling. "And using his forge just means you've created more of *his* money, which they've seen a hundred times—"

Aklan stopped Amalina midsentence by holding up a gold disk. On it was a rough likeness of Aklan—Prince Aklan Spaarvierlet—looking quite dashing with a playful eye and clenched jaw and sporting a manly mustache. His initials circled its edge, along with his title and a message in Flemish that read *"Prince Aklan Forever"*.

"Made 'em by myself, *of* myself, for myself. Good enough, Pretty Princess?"

"Maybe a little much, but how'd you do it?" she marveled. It looked properly minted. She tried to take it but he shoved it back in his pocket.

"The other side is blank," he admitted with a shrug. "But who cares? It's gold, anyone will honor it."

"But how *did* you ...?"

"You've seen me carving and whittling before. I've had art lessons and it isn't too hard to alter his stamping blocks. And don't look at me like that. I only changed one old block and got rid of it when I was done."

"I don't know whether to kiss you or smack you. But thank you, Aklan. Those should work. *A rival in Netz!* Let them see how you spend your little fortune and send them some notes in your handsome handwriting, with some flowery lines, and we'll catch someone's interest. Um, since you made the coins without being caught, I assume you still have my, um—?"

Again he cut her off, now holding up the magic bone. "You mean this?"

She snatched it from his fingers. He tried to grab it back but she already had it under the blanket.

"Give it!"

"You'll never get it again," said Amalina. "Not unless it's necessary."

"But that isn't very fair. Why not?"

"Need I remind you of how the last time we were out in the wild you ran away with it the first chance you got? And you broke it! And you probably wouldn't have come back if it *hadn't* broken."

"You'll never let me forget," he grumbled crossly. "I did good with it, this time."

"Do a great job now and get these Ladies to leave and you can have it *forever*." She felt heartened by saying it aloud. It made the possibility of the venture coming off feel more real. The trip out of the castle had seemed a bad idea all round, particularly if they did push on to Korr. The Ladies were still clamoring for it when they were leaving; how they couldn't wait to meet Katty's parents and spend time in their castle, spurred on by Cristine of course. The Count had assured Amalina they would be stopped in Netz, and she just had to assume he'd deliver on his word somehow. Well, to turn this excursion into something positive, no matter what, Amalina would milk every chance along the way however she could, by reminding the Ladies of Title there are better things in the world; and spin them home on that promise. Getting all, or some. But even if, in the end, it was only one, Amalina would count it as a success. Come what may down the line in Korr.

"I can't wait," giggled Aklan, rubbing his hands greedily together, not meaning the Ladies but picturing the fun he'd have with the magic bone again. All his own, forever.

Pia moaned.

"Are you all right?" said Amalina and Aklan together.

Pia pulled her hat over her face. Before they disappeared behind its brim, her eyes were closed and her lips were set in a grimace.

"I—I don't know if it's because I haven't fed for a while, or because I am further into the change. But the light is so very hot. More than before. Maybe if there were some clouds or something to shield me. My skin feels like it's burning."

"Oh, no," said Amalina, while Aklan privately made a face at her, showing how disturbed he was to be sitting beside a budding creature. "Should we go back? Or ...?"

"I'll be all right," said Pia. "Just, let's get to the city soon, and me out of the sun. My fair skin always burns easy and I look awful when I start peeling."

She suddenly screamed. A burst of icy snow had shot across their faces and into their laps, and Pia jerked up so hard the wood bench cracked. As the three tried to recover from the shock, they saw next to them the open-mouthed, whooping, laughing faces of Aria Ecci and Elle VandeGarde, inside their own sleigh, with more handfuls of snow ready to go just in case Amalina, Aklan, or Pia made a counterattack.

. . .

One of the expensive restaurants which had suddenly sprung up in Netz last year to cater to the foreign princesses—but then had foundered and sunk after those same Ladies had abandoned Netz for Kygil—was quickly revived and reopened, with magnanimous, Netzian smiles, upon their return. The Ladies all agreed to meet for a lavish five course dinner there, only after first seeing to their apartments and changing out of their damp travel clothes. But when they reconvened in the restaurant, and Amalina gave an excuse for Pia's absence—*"she wishes to rest, but sends her love"*—she noticed strange looks from some of the other Ladies of Title. It was explained that among themselves, while Amalina was tucking Pia into a darkened bedroom, they'd come to an agreement: instead of pressing on for Korr tomorrow, the party would stay in Netz for a few days or so, and then return; the tough business of traveling in an Ardeelian mountain winter had impressed them by just trying to slip down to the city.

Or had the Count worked some hidden magic on them, to influence them?

"Enough is enough. What difference does it make where we land in 'Garlic Place'?" said Aria with a caustic leer, referring to the garlic garlands and wreaths fastened to most Ardeelian buildings and over doorways. As if she were already tired of the trip. "Anywhere is as good as the next."

"*Garlic Place*," echoed VandeGarde. "That's a good one."

They all laughed about Ardeel and the change in plans. But Cristine's eyes were cold, her conversation terse, and her tone hostile. "I guess we won't be seeing your parents, poor Katty. For this *next* week, anyway. You must feel the most let down of us all, missing a family reunion."

She cornered Amalina alone the first chance she had, the skirt of her wide, expensive dress rustling loudly against Amalina's; crinkling like fire: "This is all your doing, I know it!"

"What is?"

"Your 'uncle' has them convinced, but I know you put him up to it," snarled Cristine. Her eyes were burning again with that unusual intensity: the effect of the Count's drug. It almost left a trace scent in the user, but it definitely produced an uncanny aura. Cristine's body seemed to be vibrating with its energy. "Are you *that* afraid of me, Amalina? Is that what it comes down to? You won't ever let me share any of your friends?"

"You need to calm down, I'm not trying to—"

"Of course you're 'trying to'. I come up with a perfectly simple and amusing idea to pass our time, but you can't have that because they'll get to know me and *my* family better since you have to keep yours hidden. And so you deliberately destroy everything. Just to thwart me."

"Have them all," said Amalina in frustration. "What do I care? What is the matter with you, Cristine? You're acting just like *them*!"

"Yes, I'm the bad one, aren't I?" hissed Cristine, playing with the scarf and necklace at her throat. "That's *your* story. I'm bad, so's the Boss. Spreading it like poison in their ears against me. Trying to sabotage me and my family name!"

"That's what *you're* doing! I haven't said a word about your fa—"

Cristine shot forward with both arms. Amalina found herself on the floor, legs in the air.

"You'll keep that ugly, fat mouth of yours shut," growled Cristine. "Or I'll shut it like I did Bessa's. I'd tell you to go ask *her* if I'm someone who can be pushed around, but where that cow is now *she can't talk*. You understand? I don't need my father to handle my bullies, and I never did. I can do it all by myself. See if I can't!"

"Please," said Amalina, holding up her arm to protect herself, feeling like she wanted to cry. "Have them all, Cristine. I mean it. I'm not trying to harm you in any way, and I never would. I don't know what's come over you. Just have your fun here and leave me alone."

"Don't look at me like that. It's you're fault you're on the floor. Here, let me pick you up, and we'll pretend you tripped and I'm being so very kind to you."

"Don't touch me. Do you hear me? Leave me alone!"

Cristine stood back with hands on hips, looking down on Amalina with a savage smile. "I believe you're tired, *Katarina*. You need to go back to your room now, don't you think?"

Cristine's command was fitting to someone so like Bossy Bessa of Korr. Forgetting the irony that it should come from one of Bessa's favorite victims, it was an ugly look for her friend. Amalina did not argue, though. She rolled over and stood up without looking back and walked stiffly out of the restaurant. Cristine laughing.

· · ·

Amalina found Aklan fussing in the mirror with his mustache and a small pot of glue when she entered her room. Dressed in the oversized princely costume, he looked too young. Like a little boy who'd found his way into his older brother's closet. The fake mustache wasn't going to help.

"You're back quick," said Aklan, holding up one end of the mustache.

"Remember to stay in the shadows," said Amalina as she stomped to her cases and began to throw clothes onto the bed, determinedly searching for something. She was seething, breathing heavily, tear-stained and red. But it was like she was trying to keep up the appearance of being good-mannered. "Have your footman do most of the exchanges. *Have* you found someone to be your footman yet?"

"I know just the man! Don't you worry, ol' Jakob's the best." Aklan groaned in frustration at the mustache: "How does this glue work? I'm making a complete mess of the whiskers. I think I'll just forget it." His eyes focused on her and the growing pile she was making. "Say, what are you doing?"

Amalina found her sodden traveling clothes and pulled the small bone from its pocket. "Turn around, boy. I'm about to solve my problems with Cristine."

## 35

# The Intoxicant

Without clothes, Amalina shivered against the cold, biting down harder onto the bone as she did so. Though the Strange Man had claimed the magic item was fashioned from a cat's leg, it tasted like a dusty old duck bone. After it had broke, and Genadie mended it with some gypsy magic of his own, it now tasted like a dusty duck bone plus glue, burnt hair, and pocket lint.

She patted her invisible hands together and warmed herself by staying in motion and thinking of how she would exact revenge on her former best friend. As cold as she was, she noted, at least she didn't have to go outside for what she was about to do.

Each of the Ladies had several rooms assigned to them within the large inn. Amalina had gone straight to her own room upon arrival, and then to Pia's. So she didn't know which one Cristine had taken. Amalina would have to search until she found it. She knew she only had so much time. The sun had been fully setting on her way back from the restaurant, and the Netzian doors would remain open for only so long to accommodate the foreign princesses, even with the blinding light of their money. The Ladies must all return shortly.

Amalina assumed that Cristine, as angry as she was, would have tried to bunk as far away from her as she could. Amalina moved in the opposite direction from her own quarters, quietly opening doors along the way, just in case she was assuming wrong—and peeked only briefly into each new room. Most were empty, or had a Lady's servant so preoccupied with readying their clothes and toiletries they didn't notice the mysteriously opening door.

Amalina blundered into an old man who was carrying a heavy case in the hallway. He dropped the case and it broke open with a slam, sending clothes in all directions.

"Husband!" shouted the old woman who'd been behind him. She zoomed forward to grab up the clothes. "What's the matter with you!"

"Something ran into me," he said, looking confused.

"*What* ran into you?" clamored his wife. "Nothing ran into you, you old goat. The trunk fell open. And of course it fell open, look how much you jammed in there. You'll worsen your piles carrying all that!"

"These are *your* clothes," he said, as she slapped at his hands so she could take up the clothes herself. Amalina had tumbled over and was sitting on a skirt. She tried to roll out of the way before she was grabbed. "All of them, yours."

"What does it matter *whose* clothes they are, old goat? Your piles! Your piles!"

"You don't have to yell, dear."

"But don't you know how to pack things properly, eh?"

"I suppose not, my dear, you haven't yelled at me yet how to pack things properly," he said drily. "Or only less than ten times."

"*Must* I always have to yell at you to get things done right?"

"Is there a choice?" he asked from the floor, still looking befuddled.

"It's bad enough we're being cleared out and shoved into some little pantry closet just to make room for a bunch of lazy, late-arriving, tarted-up slatterns," sneered the woman, as she tried to fold the items before tossing them in the case; while the man watched her from the floor, almost helplessly, frozen mid scramble to help, like a small animal awestruck before a thundering hurricane. "But it's a shame I don't know any better: that you didn't create this commotion so you can get a better look at them."

"What's that, dear?"

"We were here first! Weren't we, eh? You should have told them! My, god, you don't even know how to argue for us. Well, while you're down there, I hope you get your wish and some of these ladies come out, so your old eyes can have their fill of them. I hope so!"

Watching the two, Amalina was suddenly overcome by a shiver, and a presentiment she was seeing her and Ivanti in some future of their life, she brutishly standing over him, he cowed; this current darker time in their life with the Count—their past—near forgotten but instructing their roles. She couldn't tell if she felt more appalled at herself or sorry for Ion. But then, wasn't her lieutenant long, long gone? And she detached from him? It was such an odd thought at such an odd time.

Amalina dodged the woman's hands and ran up the hallway. She'd have to return to check the apartments on this floor later if she didn't succeed when searching upstairs.

. . .

Amalina knew she'd found the right room on the third floor when, inside, she spotted the cases and trunks she'd seen many times before in Cristine's home. Cristine's maid—one she'd borrowed from a generous Lady—had, in a precise manner, laid out all Cristine's jewelry on the nightstand; in almost geometric configurations. But the bottle Amalina had come for wasn't there.

Amalina's hopes sunk. Cristine might be carrying it with her, which meant Amalina would have to wait for her to return. Or go seek her friend out, wherever she was now, and try to pry it off her.

But Amalina decided to search the rest of the apartment. She felt a sudden thrill when she opened the large jewelry box, which should have been empty considering the hoard of necklaces, rings, and earrings arranged on the desk, and discovered the Count's vial of stimulant. She picked up the peculiar, angular green bottle. What was in it? Amalina opened the top and carefully sniffed at it. A sharp, harsh smell sent a shiver up her scalp and back. She almost opened her mouth and dropped the bone. Then came another wave and her legs flexed and sprung Amalina into the air. She landed, feeling chemical tickles all over her skin, and it was like a live, wriggling eel was looped around her spine. Her head hummed and her eyes seemed ready to push out of her skull; swirling colorful amoebas floated and swam within her intensified view.

That had been a small inhalation, a slight taste.

Whatever it was, this tonic was powering Cristine. Without it, she'd be laid out in a bed succumbing to anemic stupor. *And without it*, thought Amalina, *she can't stir any more trouble!*

Trying to shut away the extraordinary sensation animating her body, Amalina stoppered the bottle and headed for the door.

But what was she going to do with it? Just take it? How many people might report sighting a little green bottle floating down the hallway? And when Cristine discovered the theft, and heard the rumors of ghosts and green bottles, what would she think of it?

Amalina went to the window and opened it. If she threw it hard enough, it might land on a neighboring roof. Or get lost in a snowbank. Or maybe it might survive the fall and be found.

And in either case, once again, when Cristine found it missing, what would she think? Who would she suspect? Even if Amalina stole the entire box and all her jewelry with it, pretending a thief had ransacked her room, where could Amalina hide the bottle where it wouldn't be found if the authorities searched for it? And what could convince Cristine that Amalina hadn't been behind the burglary?

Amalina closed the window and went back to the jewelry box. She set the vial inside as she'd found it. But she pulled open the stopper and let the liquid pour out. With the bitter fumes rising in her face, Amalina turned her head, sucked in a breath and held it, tilted the bottle just to make sure, and placed the stopper weakly back into the neck. Cristine might still suspect Amalina had somehow gotten into her room and done this, but she also couldn't deny she might have just been too careless with it. The stopper had come loose. The loss her fault.

She wondered: How long before Cristine could get the intoxicant replenished?

*Any kind of breathing room*, thought Amalina, *however short, will help.*

Satisfied she'd evened things between them, looking forward to the Cristine-free days ahead, Amalina slipped out of the room and headed down the corridor, then the stairs. Her head was still buzzing from the essence. It was a strange ecstasy. Not like being drunk at all, it held a crystal clarity and an overabundance of energy. No doubt this was one of the Count's many discoveries during his constant, obsessive, tinkering in the lab. A marvel to set alongside the scientist's honey 'candies'. But for this tonic's powerful effect … was this what it was like to go through the change? Was it just a sampling *fraction* of it? If so, Amalina could see how it could be tempting. She felt so alive. As if she could simply wish herself invisible and it would happen—no magic items required—and she could brave the winter without a cloak or clothes and be fine.

*Add to its effects: overconfidence*, she thought.

But it would also be popular in the market. *Maybe get the recipe.*

Back on her floor, Amalina felt a cold breeze and then saw the open window at the end of the hall. By the hall's dim light, flakes of snow were visible outside. She would have turned away but noticed the wet footprints in the corridor leading from the window to a nearby door. The door to Pia's room. Her heart skipped. She adjusted the bone between her teeth and crept forward.

Even before reaching the room, she heard that low hum she was so familiar with, which penetrated her chest and vibrated her whole body. But he was talking in a soothing voice. The door was open enough to get her head in. She saw the Count's back, his large black cloak tapering toward his head with snow still on his shoulders. Pia, in bed before him, had her face lowered, her posture slumped but casual, as she started to speak.

"I can hear everything," said Pia. "It feels like they are all talking to me. And I … I understand them more and more. It's a little *too* much, I think. All these living things, with their hearts pumping blood through their systems. They feel like living flowers with a giant throbbing pod, around which everything else—the organs, the skeleton, the limbs—are centered: like almost meaningless, tissue-thin leaves." Pia angled her chin, ran a hand through her hair pensively. "They are to me now these incredible fountains of life. But they are asking for me to tear them open like an overripe fruit, willing me to. And that they can move around, and speak, and have thoughts, it is almost amazing. It seems unnatural, impossible. It is crazy sometimes that I am talking to them, like I'm talking to a speaking monkey."

As Pia said this, Amalina slipped sideways into the room to try to see her face better, to understand how much what her friend was saying was true and how much was to satisfy the man. The room was an interior one with no windows. A candle on a table by the bed, which Amalina had left there nearly an hour ago for Pia's comfort, lit the scene. It guttered dangerously as she crept alongside the unmoving figures, as if it wanted to put itself out.

"Yes, *yesss*, you see how you pull away from them," rumbled the Count, "as you come to understand they are nothing like *us*. That you are nothing like them anymore. We are separate; and they are nothing. As immaterial as air. What they say and what they want and what they fear mean nothing."

Pia's face twitched with torment as he spoke, then she settled down to say: "Only because I know I was once like them do I keep my head together. But, of course, I fear I will eventually forget." She smiled woefully. "Hopefully it won't happen until everyone I love is already dead, so I can't hurt them."

The Count's face twitched too, from impatient anger to understanding, then further to warm commiseration and indulgence. "Eventually, my lady, if you are to keep your sanity, to avoid loneliness, to divert yourself, you will pretend that they *are* important, and force yourself to enjoy their meaningless company. And you might come to convince yourself they *do* matter, as I have. It feels real. Some more than others. It might actually be true."

The wind was whipping through the window outside and winding through the room, circling Amalina, stripping the heat from her, cutting through the drug's effect. There was no way to warm herself other than crouch low and hug her body. Neither of the unnatural pair looked as if they noticed the temperature, the room's fireplace was unlit. As pale white as they were, they were talking marble statues.

Amalina decided she'd heard enough, that if she listened more she might feel worse for Pia's loss of her humanity and that she might begin crying; or she might abandon any notion of a human connection to her friend, and then cry. Before she began blubbering either way she slipped out.

Without thinking, she went to the hallway's window to close it, stepping in the Count's puddle-shoeprints to do so, but at the last second, she realized she shouldn't. She had to get back to her room as fast as she could. She paused though, for a moment, looking out at the evening village, with the white flakes in random gusts falling down to meet the mushy cobblestones. How lonely, yet serenely beautiful it was.

That's when she saw the figure walking below.

· · ·

Netz was not as cosmopolitan a city as Tsobl (or now *'Sobelburg'*). Here in Netz, the villagers sealed themselves up at sundown, as custom dictated in any proper Ardeelian town—unless pressured into staying open by outsiders. The streets should have been empty except for the foreign Ladies of Title and their servants. But here was a man walking confidently along in the darkness, a dashing figure even in a bulky winter overcoat with a lively bounce to his step.

Amalina's jaw dropped, and she had to quickly catch the bone and replace it in her mouth. She didn't know what to do, but her body decided for her. She ran down the several flights of stairs, pushed past the people in her way and shoved open doors; even opened the bolted front door with little care.

In the street she ignored the cold, and stamped crescent-moon-shaped prints into the snow, as she tore after the man she only thought she recognized—though it was impossible he could be there! But the impossible had already happened before; and how many times now? even thousands of miles from this spot? and with the exact same person? As she raced up to him, she tried to aim her unseen bare feet at the already packed snow, so he wouldn't notice her approach.

And with a heavily beating heart she saw it really was him. Lieutenant Ivanti Ion Vokent, trudging with a certain purpose and a serious look.

She didn't know what to do or how to react. It *was* impossible that he was here, wasn't it? And that she'd caught sight of him on a meaningless glance out a window! But here he was, and going who knows where. Just the sheer improbability of it wiped away any anger she might have still held. Instead, she could only feel that deep elation experienced when his handsome face entered the scene.

Or was it Cristine's intoxicant still working on her?

No.

With Cristine now a hostile enemy, and Pia was—who knows what was happening with her, but it felt like she was drifting away—finding Ion was like discovering a floating branch next to her in a wild river, Amalina wanted to grab on. She didn't want to lose him.

"Hey," she said around the small bone clamped in her mouth. "Hey!"

Ivanti froze. He turned around and looked in every direction.

"Hey, I-on." His name didn't come out right with the cat-bone impediment between her teeth.

He looked unsure, and blinked his eyes, searching the nearby sealed windows and doorways. He peered up at the sky, then he turned and hurried along.

Amalina knew she wouldn't be able to stay outside much longer, the wet cold was biting at her skin and going deeper. She sprinted past him when she saw an alcove, and spun to meet him there. She hunched down and spit out the bone.

"Ivanti! Here!"

Ivanti's foot slipped in the slick road as he spun in her direction. His face was pulled taught, with a flicker of anger, then delight, and then finally settled into confusion. "What? Amalina! What are you—*Where are your clothes?*"

"Get in here. Give me your coat!"

Ivanti was already pulling off his overcoat. He looked back to make sure nobody was watching. There was no guarantee the Count wouldn't suddenly appear, Amalina knew, considering he was right up the street and through an open window. This would have to be fast, whatever she was going to do with him.

"I can't believe it," whispered Ivanti, sounding angry. "What's going on?"

"What are *you* doing here?" she countered.

"I—" he hesitated. He looked around again.

"Never mind," she said. "Let's go somewhere we can talk. Where were you going?"

"You can't come."

"Do you have a little time?" she asked, trying to sound rational and not driven by the drug, or anything else. He probably saw a touch of wildness in her eyes. Her mind was racing, shoving, splintering into a thousand thoughts. "How long are you going to be in town? We need to talk."

"Can't say how long. I'm afraid I just can't!" He hugged her to him, to warm her up. "But of course, let's talk. Quick, let's get to my carriage before a patrol passes and we're put in stocks. My word, as naked as Eve in the streets of Netz on a winter's night." He laughed and looked at her affectionately. "By god, I can't believe you, girl. I can never, ever believe what you get up to!"

"Well then, just wait til you hear what I have to tell," she said confidently, though not knowing what she was going to say next, only feeling the welling charge of it.

36

## Lt. Ivanti Ion Vokent, Renewed

Inside a massive, block-wide storagehouse packed wheel-to-runner with sleighs, carts, and broken-down transports, hidden in its darkest, cobwebbed corner, sat Ion's closed carriage; a worn and unassuming coach built for hard, long distance travel.

"A gift from the Cardinal," he told Amalina.

When they entered the coach's central compartment, they were met with a protesting warble. Its interior was cramped, half the space filled with tarp-covered boxes.

"*Many* gifts from the Cardinal," he laughed.

Ion had his arms around Amalina and guided her onto the seat opposite this canvas wall, all the while he continued vigorously stroking her shoulders and back. He paused only to light a lamp.

"I doubt it'll provide much heat for you," he said.

But the warbles continued from behind the tarps. Sensing she knew just what was there, Amalina could not resist. She reached out and lifted a corner.

Staring from within a cage were a couple pigeons; confirming her suspicion. But when she threw up the canvas, the birds moved back and she heard the light jingle of bells on their legs. Amalina gasped and her eyes goggled. Ivanti pushed her hand down and bundled her again.

"You'll let the breeze in," he said.

"Those are the Count's birds!"

Ivanti nodded. "Well, they're *going* to him, anyway, with luck. To bother the hell out of him."

"But they're *his*."

"You don't say," he said a little too blandly, losing some of his initial excitement, his eyes narrowing.

But what he'd said: 'Going to him'—to the Count—'to bother the hell out of him.' Wasn't that *her* plan? *And*, she remembered, *hadn't it also become a part of Attila Bronk's plan—if he received my note? But so many birds, and so soon?*

"Where did you get them?" she asked. "The Cardinal, did you say?"

"A joke," he said, guardedly. "I was given them."

"By who? And where did *they* find them?"

"I've no idea. I was just given these birds and that's it; and by someone I'm afraid I'm not allowed to say. My job's to ruffle your gentleman up in the Netz castle with their messages."

*It's the plan!* thought Amalina, astonished. *That means my note got through to Sadra's revolutionary!*

"You're with the revolution, Ion?" she asked eagerly.

"Eh?" he watched her in surprise, his eyes wide.

"The revolutionary! Attila Bronk! You've spoken to him? You're working with him?"

"Now, Amalina," said Ion, trying to calm her.

"These birds are part of the plan," said Amalina, adamantly, tapping the tarp with her foot. "It's part of *my* plan. I told him to do it. I know he won't want you to say anything, of course, or to admit it, or admit to anything, that's his stupid high-secrecy technique: 'never let information out that isn't necessary'—" at this Ion grinned, before he caught himself and corrected "—but you can tell me, Ion!"

Breathlessly, her eyes went to the tarps again, thinking: *And they've already found the pigeons? Now what? They're sending the birds to distract the Count? Is his army already on the move?*

Ivanti Vokent saw the look on her face, and she saw the look on his.

"But *what* exactly are you—?" she started. "No … *Why* are you—?"

Ivanti shook his head. "No, no, no, dear Amalina. Now *you're* going to tell me why you are here … instead of up there, in the castle. And, if you like, you can add how I found you completely naked in a snow storm?"

"I found *you*," countered Amalina. Her hand came out from under the jacket and she held the bone for him to see. She would give him this much, a secret of her own, something to think about. "How? Here, watch this."

Amalina clamped the bone between her teeth. Ivanti shook violently and slammed backwards in the compartment. Then his arm tightened around her, and he sent his opposite hand rushing toward the emptiness in his jacket. His over-sized fingers dug into her neck and face.

"Ah-ow!" shouted Amalina, as the magic bone popped out of her mouth and she caught it. He was stunned again when she reappeared. "Take care. I'm still here. See, but it only works on me, not on clothes. So I have to be …"

"This … !" he gulped as he pointed to the bone. Then he got that look on his face, the one Amalina had seen too many times before; on Erik Kosche, Piotr, Crutio. It was a horrible lost expression, and had preceded their tragic deaths. Now Ion had it. It was the realization: "This is real. It's impossible … but it is *real*."

"Yes," said Amalina. "Everything I told you. Including how dangerous he is. Why didn't you believe me?"

"I believed you," he said defensively. "Of course. But why didn't you show me this trick before? It would have helped. It wouldn't have changed anything, but ... Here, let me see that."

"Don't bite too hard," cautioned Amalina, as Ivanti tested the bone himself. He blinked in and out of sight several times before she took it away.

"I'm spending some time in the village, a few days or so," said Amalina. "The princesses and I. That's why I'm here. Now what are *you* doing here? just collecting birds, or ...?"

"Trying to save you."

• • •

Amalina's heart gushed at Ion's words, delivered so earnestly. She bit her lip to stopper any flood of emotion as he spoke on. But, wrapped up in emotions of his own, or something else, his brows knitted and he began stumbling.

"I—I just couldn't let ... let you ... how could I ...? not when you ..." But then he looked angry all over again. "Amalina, this is all *true*! And you came back here? To him? I thought you were running away! I thought you were going to sail off to England or something. Why didn't you?"

"Huh! Why do *you* care?" snapped Amalina, her face flushing, her words striking in a surprising, and vastly different direction than where her heart was telling her to go. Instead directed by pride to meet the manly, almost possessive rage she saw in Ivanti. *How dare he question?* Or was it the drug that fed the rage? "It shouldn't have mattered where I went, should it? *You* couldn't care a thing about me!"

"You can't say that! I have, and always will, care about you, Amalina. Deeply!"

"*Huh!* You think I don't remember?"

"Oh, don't hold my words against me," he said, "what I told you in Paris: I didn't know what I was saying."

"It's not what you said that was the problem, it's what you *did*, wasn't it? What you were doing."

"When I told you you were standing in my way, I thought that was the most hurtful thing anyone could say to another person. Those women ... those other women ... they were meaningless."

"I get to decide what's meaningless."

"You're right," he nodded, chastened. He looked at her shyly and suddenly contrite. He was trying to speed them along to some reconciliation, or so it felt, as if they were pressed for time. "But it's all in the past now, eh? Never mind that. I'm here. Only ... why *did* you come back here ... ? If it's all true about him, and you said you were never going to return ..."

"It was my decision," she said firmly. "If it was a mistake, then it's mine."

"Well, a mistake …" He wiped his face with his big, strong hand. "When I heard that young Lady Tepsji had not gone to England after all but returned to Ardeel …" His jaw flexed admirably. "I couldn't believe it. I had to find out for myself; that it was true … I felt so responsible. I'd hurt you and made you angry, and so you'd made a decision out of pure spite without thinking. But then I figured, maybe things weren't as bad here in Ardeel and with this count as you'd let on. That had to be it."

"But it wasn't," she said.

"No."

"I told you before, Ion, I have to look out for Papa and Cousin Jenna. So really I had no other choice but to—"

"Of course you had a choice," he said, breathily. "And you chose to return to protect those you love the most." Ivanti's lips moved soundlessly for a moment, hesitating. His chest began to swell. "And now, you see, Amalina … so have I."

For her, the words felt too much again. She'd seen his beautiful eyes swear things to her before. It touched the wrong nerve, the haywire of the intoxicant sped it along. She could only respond coldly once more, "Huh!"

"You keep saying that, Amalina," he protested. "But I *am* here, aren't I? And I'm telling you, I came back to rescue you. To free you from *him*, once and for all."

"An easy thing to say," muttered Amalina, feeling that, with his serious look and his continued effort, it was unfair for her to say. But … but she couldn't help her pangs of doubt, even with him here in front of her; that he *was* here was the hardest, clearest proof of his sincerity. He'd traveled across the continent for her.

But when he'd betrayed her, had lied to her, she'd been wounded to the core. And though in that first moment of finding him all was forgotten, the old dark clouds closed in again with each and every of his ardent declarations. And those clouds weren't clearing fast enough in her heart. They caused her to search for the lies in him, which must be there. She couldn't control it. She accused: "Your army disbanded for winter and you came home. That's all."

"*My* army?" laughed Ivanti, softly. "That would be something. They *did* disband, but I mustered out early. Please, do believe, I'm here for you."

"Well … Well, Good. I—I …" She wanted to say something hurtful. But then, suddenly, her anger broke. Finally. "Oh, never mind. I'm sorry," she said, and scooted forward into his embrace. "I don't know why I—I was just confused. Thank you, Ivanti … *Ion*." She touched his arm. It was as solid and strong as she remembered it. It helped her melt a little more. "Well, you have me now, don't you?"

His eyes met hers and they shivered nervously together.

"Yes, I have you ..." said Ivanti. "But I didn't expect ... *This* wasn't the plan, Ama. I thought I'd have to get you out of that castle. It was going to be a larger operation."

"Oh, yes, with the birds."

"Yes," he said, glancing cleverly at the covered cages. "And then some. These're just a part. Your master'll be getting his first communique any hour. And that'll take him away from the castle. Hopefully for a day, or a few. We'll see. Then things can really start happening. We're a little late as it—"

"You *are* working with the revolutionary in Korr," said Amalina in a steady voice, but with a deep swallow. "Attila Bronk."

Ivanti nodded soberly.

"His plan isn't to rescue me, you know," she said.

"No. But it is *mine*. If *his* succeeds, all the better. You'll be rid of ... *Him*. We all will. Done."

"It won't work."

"You know Bronk's plan—?"

"I know it. And I know him. I know everything."

He blinked, surprised. "Maybe not all of it."

"Maybe," she allowed. "But most of it."

"It sounds good enough."

"But don't do it," said Amalina. "Listen to me—"

He held up his finger to his lips, gently silencing her. "All I'm here to do is a little part. We wait for this Count to get the birds and leave, and then I secure what we need in Netz, then ... Well I can't say. Just another week or so and—"

"What else do you need here?"

"If you don't already know, I can't say."

"Ion."

"Battle provisions," grinned Ion. "If you must."

"So he's going to go through with it? all of it?"

"I don't know how much you know, but if you know him ... well, all I can tell you is, it's going to happen."

"Really?" she said, disappointed, worried.

"Yes."

They stared into each other's eyes, his tender, hers questioning and desperate. Attila Bronk *was* on the move, and much faster than she'd ever thought. Too fast. The scheme with the warning birds was fine, but Amalina couldn't have her diligent, efficient, and helpful Ion working anything else for the revolution until the time was right. Until it was too late and Amalina had worked her own plot through to the end, which would make the revolution moot. So she had to delay him however she could. In their shared look, Amalina's mind scrambled for any possible way she could throw him off track.

Suddenly Ion was kissing her.

. . .

Amalina made a surprised noise and fell back. She pushed him away with a gasp.

"I … I thought you wanted me to kiss you," he said.

"No."

"No? But the way you were staring at me." He looked sorry and destroyed at once.

"I was just *thinking* … I mean, yes, of course. But not right now. Right now, something else."

He glanced off shyly and cleared his throat. "Well, you're right, though. I suppose." He turned to her. "I do have you with me now. We don't have to wait if you don't want. I will finish my part, because I must, and then we can go." He scratched his head unsurely, but with a soft smile, warming again. "We'll take anyone you want, your father, your new mother, your cousin, or whoever, and we'll hire the fastest sleigh and head to France. Right away. No stopping."

His words were similar to Janusch's, his offer to rescue her held the same promise, but with Ion's selflessness, fearlessness, and boldness to action, it felt entirely different. It made her want to gush over him and his shy smile; or afraid that he could actually convince her.

"But no," said Amalina, her frenetic thoughts locking onto a strange new track. "There's more, Ion. These princesses can't be here for what's coming. They're in danger as it is, and if a siege hits the castle … They don't deserve it. I need to get them out. Out of Ardeel, you see."

"Then we take them with us too?" he suggested, not seeing that she was winding up for something else.

"They're dug in, Ion," said Amalina. "Nothing I say will ever convince them to leave. And so … as I said before, I needed to tell you something—or ask of you …"

She pressed her index fingers underneath his handsome, straight nose, and then brushed them outwards on each side, describing a large, suave, invisible mustache.

"You *can* look like a prince."

"What?"

"And now that I know you're expecting to be here for a while," she cooed breathily, with an assured intonation, "this little favor for me should work brilliantly."

"Now, I'll be leaving tomorrow night," he said as if reminding her. "The next after, or the next after that, at the latest. However long it takes, but—"

"Or maybe a little longer, can't you? Didn't you say before it would be a week?"

"At the end of the week I'll be back," he corrected. "The supplies should be prepared. But there've been delays already. Too many. I was expected somewhere else long ago. I *do* need to leave … and very soon. I can't say too much, now …"

"But if there've been delays already, what's a little more, Ion?" she asked pulling on his sleeve. "It can't hurt that much. Nothing can really happen—*really* happen, according to Mr. Bronk—until spring anyway, right? Right?"

"Is that right?" Ion looked confused, he didn't know. "Did Mr. Bronk tell you that?"

"That's when all armies march, isn't it?"

He cleared his throat and frowned. "That all depends. Do you really know what's going on—?"

"But that was his plan, Ion," she insisted. "Now, if you truly *want* to help me …"

"I will if I can," he said, no longer frowning but with his brow furrowed, a worried look in his eyes. "But how long are you talking?"

"Not too long."

"What is it?"

After she'd done explaining, Amalina smiled and tugged at his collar and regarded him admiringly.

Ivanti's kissable lips hung open. "That's ridiculous."

"There's nothing ridiculous about it. You'll be helping me save the innocent lives of as many princesses as we can. Just say you'll do it."

## 37

# The Three Princes

Amalina hadn't actually been sure what she wanted to say to Ion when she'd grabbed him on the street. Maybe just tell him what had happened to her since they'd last seen each other. Maybe warn him the Count was bent on changing her into what *he* was; that he had the power to do so. Perhaps tell him the Count was already transforming Cristine. But, she considered now, maybe her mind had already had it all reckoned when she'd spotted him out the window, and just needed to put her into the right position. Then, when she was there, the words came for her.

Amalina couldn't help but admire how perfect her plan was now. With Ion as the seducing Prince, the Ladies of Title would be led so easily astray, and he would send them home with promises to reunite, and soon enough this Netz hotel, emptied of the Ladies, would be as bare as an after dinner chicken, stripped to the bone and gutted. What a surprise for the Count.

Coming awake, and Amalina spotting Aklan at the mirror, dressed in a horribly over-sized royal uniform, playing with the fake mustache on his face, only made it that much clearer how foolish her earlier plans had been.

"No," said Amalina, coming to take the mustache. "Off. Take it off."

"But I need it, Pretty Princess."

"Everything," she said. "Off. I've got someone else."

"Oh?" said a voice from the corner of the room.

Amalina yelped and turned around, to see an old, ragged man smiling at her from the corner loveseat.

"Who're you!"

"Milady."

"That's Jakob," said Aklan. "I told you about him. But what do you mean you've—?"

There was a knock at the door, with a prearranged pattern. Ion, right on time, just after the morning bell, and long before the Ladies might wake.

"That's him," said Amalina, shooing Aklan to the corner, his mustache now in her hand. "Get over there and stay quiet."

"Well," said Aklan, resentfully. "Who is it? And why?"

"He looks the part," said Amalina, rushing to the door to let Ion in. "Just stay quiet, you two."

When she opened the door, Ivanti Vokent entered. The hood of his great overcoat hid his head, but once inside the room and with the door closed, he shrugged his thick shoulders and the hood flipped back. He continued forward with a glum, wilted look, his back slightly bent, his eyes on the floor.

"Good morning," twittered Amalina, excitedly.

"Him!" growled Aklan.

Vokent's eyes shot up, and recognized the young man standing by the mirror, wearing an over-sized and silly looking uniform. Then he saw the decrepit man in the other corner and grew confused.

"You remember Aklan," said Amalina. "My house boy."

"You!" quaked Aklan now, his face turning red.

He was a small quivering figure trying to glare down a man who was three heads taller and double the breadth in the shoulders.

"Back from the dead," quipped Ion, with a gentle, muted laugh. "I guess. Good to see you, Aklan. No harm done."

"What are *you* doing here?" demanded Aklan, glancing at Amalina, too. Wanting answers. Good ones.

"I already told you," said Amalina, trying to usher Ion further into the room. "He's to be our prince."

"Our Prince!" howled Aklan.

"Quiet down," said Amalina. She pointed to the old man. "And this is Jakob. He'll be your servant."

"Well," said Jakob, his adam's apple bobbing under his whiskered jaw. "A military man. Pleasure. You're handsome enough."

Ion almost laughed, but his eyes were downcast, and he quickly returned his sad gaze to Amalina. "Didn't know there'd be an audience for this, Ama—"

"That's *Lady Katarina* to you."

Ion nodded briefly, eyes closed, looking unhappy, deflated.

"You slept in the carriage the whole night?" she asked with sudden motherly concern. And when he nodded again: "But it's so cold."

"Slept in worse," he said with a lost smile.

"You're feeling all right, Ion?"

"Look," he said. "I've been thinking since last night …"

"So have I," said Amalina, sensing his reluctance, trying to prod him in the right direction with a positive feeling. "And look at you. You're going to be perfect. Absolutely perfect. Just need to fix you up."

Smiling, she reached out and tried to put the mustache under his nose. It held askew, comically, at the corner.

Glancing at himself in the mirror, Ivanti made a noise of disgust. "Ama—"

"*Katty*, please."

"... I—I'm not a stage player."

"You aren't playing on a stage, Ion," she reminded him. "This is all real enough. The whiskers and the uniform, which I will supply—right here on Aklan—are just disguises. You simply have to play yourself, eh? A young and incredibly handsome man, which you are; who happens to have distinguished himself in military affairs, which you have; who is also very, very rich—" Amalina poured gold coins out of a bag onto the bed, driving Ion's eyebrows up, and Jakob to hoot, and Aklan to grind his teeth "—which you can't deny you suddenly are. And you are of noble lineage; because, considering we all descend from the first man and woman, Adam and Eve, the chosen of God, who lived and ruled in Eden, you can't say that it is an exact lie."

"Well said, milady," enthused Jakob from the corner.

"*Who* will I be, exactly?" said Ion, curiously, but his eyes pleaded for her not to go on.

"You speak French pretty well, so ..."

"I can carry it off," mumbled Ivanti in French, with only a slight accent.

"... You'll be *Prince Phillipe Castion of the Outer Meldines*."

"Who? Where?" he said as he stared at her, unbelieving. "I've campaigned all over this continent. Never heard of either."

"And neither have they. And luckily there are enough kingdoms scattered through all the empires, my friends won't look past the pretty letters you send and the gold coins you flash in front of them."

Ivanti seemed to lose a shade of color, while Aklan's fair skin gained a darker pink.

"It'll be easy," she soothed. "The letters, which will be written for you in the most exquisite hand, will be conceived by me and penned by Aklan here. You just make sure you're seated and seen in the best light—you are too handsome for your own good to be hidden in the shadows, not to be ogled— and wink at them, pass them notes through your servant—" she indicated Jakob "—and speak as little as possible, only the right words, so they won't notice the accent."

"I see," said Ion, noticing how agitated Aklan was now.

"Jakob's already been provided for. I will make further introductions later, so that you can get acquainted in your roles."

Ivanti stared at her. His expression hardened. His voice was low, soft, and ashamed, as if he didn't want to say it in front of their onlookers, but he had to have it out. "You've well ordered the whole thing, I'll give you that. But it's ... it's, um ..." he was having a hard time getting it out. "It's perverse."

"Perverse?"

It seemed too big a word for a hogger's son. He'd definitely matured out of Korr, thought Amalina.

"That is *not* what I came back for, Ama. I came for you and you alone, and not—"

"You came here to salve your guilty conscience," she grinned hopefully. "And *that* you will do. But for what you did to me, I get to set the price. And I say you must pay me back *with interest*."

"But you can't seriously—"

"Stop complaining. This mission will be so much easier than anything else you've ever done; and you can't deny it won't be fun, and that you have the necessary talent to pull it off."

"You cursed me for doing something like this before, Ama. You know that. And now you are asking me to do it … again?"

"Right," agreed Aklan.

"But I need you—"

"I don't think I can go through with this … this … this farce," he said as his face turned red, stumbling on his words again, trying not to hurt Amalina, but needing to speak his mind. His hands balled into fists at his side. "I've something *real* to do, do you understand, Amalina?"

"*Lady Katarina*," she reminded him. "But, this *is* real."

"However real, *Lady Katarina*, it feels like a waste of time." When she began to protest, he held up his hand, "And I won't … can't … waste my time trying to save a bunch of … a bunch of whores."

"Whores!"

"I'm sorry. But aren't they here for his money?" Amalina made a face at this, still uncertain if she shouldn't have told him what else the Count was offering now, his greater bargain. "Instead of having me toss around a bunch of money, acting a fool, seducing them, why don't you just set a trail of your gold over the border? They should be gone in no time."

"Ion," said Amalina, sternly. "I'm serious about this."

"The problem is, I can't be. I don't think so. Not for this."

"Where are you going?"

"I just need to think," he said, shuffling crimson-faced for the door. "I've waited so long for this moment," he gestured between he and her, "you have to understand. But now this …? There's so much to do, people are counting on me. And this … I really want to, really … for you … but I just … have to think."

"Where are you going?"

"Meet me at the carriage house in an hour. Let me alone to breathe, eh? Then you'll have your answer. I just need time to think."

After he'd flipped his hood over his head and left, Aklan cried out.

"Scared him off," he said. "There he goes. Again!"

"He just needs to think."

"But why!" cried Aklan. "You've got me here!"

"But Ion—"

"How is that fair?" wailed Aklan, his fair features now near purple even to his hairline. "I'm the one who found Jakob. He's *my* man. I can't believe you were just going to give *him* my job." He leaped onto the bed with the coins and glowered. "I can do it, I was going to do it, so why give it to *him*?"

"Because he was so perfect for it and he owes me."

"He doesn't owe you. He betrayed you. *I've* never done that. And how's *he* so perfect? He's just a backwoods hick in a French uniform."

"He fills out the clothes. With you we'd be lucky if they don't spot you right away. And they already know who *you* are. So if they recognize you, it would make things difficult."

"How do you mean, they know me?"

"You're my lad for errands and things."

"I'm a prince. A real prince!"

Astonished, Jakob touched his weathered head and stared at the boy.

"You're my servant," corrected Amalina.

"And a prince! All I need do is write home and my parents will clear everything up for these ladies. I'll have a real carriage and a real valet and real footmen and tons of money and proper letters of introduction, and it will all be *real*. Not like *him*."

"If only you could get those here so Ion can use them," she said thoughtlessly.

"Ion? *Ion!*" snarled Aklan. "No! He's gone!"

"Oh, right."

"And they're *mine*. Because *I* am real. He doesn't get to use my birthright, even for you."

"I wish you'd write your parents, anyway," said Amalina, starting to feel annoyed, wanting to get off the subject and figure out how to mend things. "They'd take you home and out of danger. I wish you had stayed home as it is …"

Aklan paused, considering her.

"You don't really want me gone," said Aklan, confidently. "You were glad to have me back. I've saved your life, you know. At least once."

"It's not that I'm not glad you're around—"

"Look how much I do for you."

"I just want you out of danger. I still feel responsible for you."

"Well, you're just changing the subject if you keep saying that. Better to have someone who can stand up to danger than run away, which is the only thing that louse is good at."

"He said he'll have his decision in an hour, and I believe he'll do the right thing."

"He'll do the right thing, all right," snarled Aklan. "The right thing for him!"

Amalina made a sour face.

• • •

They waited the uncomfortable hour, until Amalina could no longer stand the suspense and left for Ion's carriage. As a fetish for good luck, she took the mustache off the floor, intent on putting it right back on his face. She returned half an hour later with red eyes and a small note, with the mustache inadvertently hanging from it.

"He was gone," predicted Aklan in a snarling triumph.

"His carriage was there."

"But he was gone," said Aklan again, prompting her.

"His horse was gone."

"And so you scared him away. Just as I told you. Did I not?"

"I didn't scare him away," said Amalina, crestfallen. "He had his reasons."

"So now it comes back to me! *I* am your prince! Return my mustache!" Aklan held out his hand.

"Look, never mind this whole prince thing, it was another one of my stupid ideas." Amalina peeked over at Jakob then switched to French: "If you want to do something for me, Aklan, someone still needs to fill up the wine bottles at Netz Lake and stow them in the sleigh so Genadie and the guards don't find them. You can—"

"Yes, yes. I'll do it," He answered in the local language so Jakob could understand. "I can do that, too. You know I'll do anything for you, anything you want. But I'm perfect for this job and you know it."

"No, Aklan, you're young," she said. "You need to put on make up and mustaches and padding to pull it off."

"Is that really how you see me, *too young*?" He squinted his blueberry eyes at her, puffed out his chest and mussed his golden curls on his bushy head. "How can I be, eh? I've had plenty of women interested in me already these past years."

"Have you?"

"Yes," he said resentfully. "And I'm loyal, ain't I? I haven't wasted myself on them as he would've. And I'm more a man than him in many other ways, besides. I bet I've killed more men than that ox-head of an ex-fiancé of yours."

"He's been in the army," she reminded him. "And you haven't killed anyone."

"Haven't I?"

"You have?" she asked, shocked.

"I'm a handsome young prince alone in a savage land, you think I haven't had to defend myself?"

The thought of Aklan, this innocent looking boy, killing someone seemed impossible, disturbing, and depressing. Even more so than applying the same dark deeds to Ion, or even Genadie. "Really, though? Have you?"

"You don't believe me?" He sounded as if she'd pulled off an important piece of his body.

She didn't want to answer and fiddled with the little letter in her hand. "Still I think, maybe the plan wasn't right ... I just don't know ..."

"But it was a great plan, and when else are you going to be able to do it? We *have* to do it."

"I know you want to, Aklan, but ..." sighed Amalina. "Let me have a look at Jakob, maybe he'll do. As long as we can find a footman for him. Or you, Aklan, could be his—"

"Footman!" screamed Aklan.

"—and he can be an older baron or something," said Amalina, almost warming up to the idea. "How old can a prince be? How old is he, did you say?" Amalina turned to Jakob, who rocked on his feet at the surprise, and she said in their native tongue: "How old are you, sir?"

"Well ..." hesitated Jakob, patting the whiskers and wrinkles on his face.

"You couldn't stuff him far enough in the shadows to pass as a royal gentleman," said Aklan, even more offended now. "Sotted footman certainly, aristocracy, never."

"I'll be the judge of that."

"It'll be *me* or no one else," said Aklan. "Do you understand?"

"Well then, no one else, I suppose," decided Amalina, with a sigh.

"You're wounding me, Pretty Princess! And just when I was about to help you and you were happy for it. That isn't right!"

"I'm sorry, Aklan. I don't mean to hurt you, but after seeing Ion ..." Amalina realized with a trailing mutter that was precisely the wrong way to start her sentence, but also knew, by the way he was staring at her, she'd better finish it somehow. "Jakob *may* be too old—"

"But you're simply *too young*, little crab," finished Jakob for her, jovially, catching on to his potential improved employment.

"Traitor!" shouted Aklan.

"And I'm just as strong and handsome as that officer who just left," intoned Jakob, thrusting out his sunken chest, his ribs nearly visible through his shirt.

"Only in your drunken, ale-soaked brains," snarled Aklan.

"But Mr. Jakob's right," said Amalina. "Honestly though, *way* too young for the part. Aklan, please. You must see that."

"Must I? *Still* too young? *Way* too young?" Suddenly Aklan had tears welling in his eyes that he wiped away. "You're never going to give me a chance, are you?" He quickly said in French: "So there it is. But I'll show you. I'll show you!"

"You'll show me *what*?"

"You don't love me, but you'll see." Aklan's tears broke over his lids, as his pert little lips turned purple and trembled, and his shell-like nostrils flared, near crying. His face was a mass of unhappy bubbles. "You *will* see ..."

"What are you talking about?"

Sensing his emotions were about to run away with him, Aklan scrambled off the bed and darted out of the room, slamming the door behind him with a last, mortally wounded, "Never mind! Forget it! Have Jakob as your prince if that's what you want!"

"Aklan!"

"Little rascal," giggled Jakob. "I believe he's in love, eh? Pardon my sayin', milady."

. . .

Amalina opened the letter in her hand and, with a sigh, read it again.

> Amalina, I've already laid out my reasons, so I won't repeat them other than to say that I have more important things to do than play at games. And what would you have me do if this Count got wind of what I was up to, and he came for me as a jealous lover? Just me alone against him? It shouldn't be tried, you must be reasonable and understand. I will be back later this week for the carriage, if you wish to take up my first offer. I will always be there for you, Amalina. And to hell with Lady Katarina. Burn this note. Love, Ion.

Amalina sighed for what must have been the hundredth time this morning. Everyone seemed to be right in this affair but her. Ion wasn't wrong: it was perverse for Amalina to suggest he romance the Ladies, and that it would be a bit ludicrous, and potentially dangerous, to even try. And Aklan had been right too: would there ever be a better time?

"Milady?" said Jakob, shuffling in place, unsure of what he should be doing.

"Will you be my prince, Jakob?" asked Amalina, removing her glasses and staring at him levelly.

"Oh!" Jakob bowed deeply, and shakily, at the waist. "Don't know how to write, though," he said when he straightened up. "Understood that was the boy's job."

"So it was. I'll take care of the letters."

"Then I am your prince, milady."

"You aren't afraid of the Count?"

"Haven't met a man on this earth I cannot lick in a stand-up fight."

"He's Count Tepsji, the Count of Ardeel."

"An' I'll be a Prince. Won't I outrank him or something?"

"You'll need a shave and to wash your hair," said Amalina, worried for him already. "Leave the side whiskers. And you'll have to do without a footman."

"Always have, milady," he said confidently.

"And don't talk to any of them. Not a word. Let the money do the work. Maybe stick to the darker parts of the rooms."

"Aye," he said. "The shadows, was it?"

After a thought, "Did the boy *do* anything while I was gone?"

"Beat about the room a little. Went through your dress over there."

Amalina checked the dress. In the hidden pocket, the folded manifesto was there but the magic bone was gone.

"*Aklan*," she swore.

"The little rascal," said Jakob, tenderly. "And don't worry, milady, I can get another prince suit from the theater. He only bought the one."

"You know what, Jakob? Never mind. It was a bad idea all around. You can go."

"Oh, that's too bad," said Jakob, kind and stoic at his dismissal, and with the philosophical nod of a sensible sage, added: "Yet understandable, understandable … Yes … yes … But, milady, who then will rescue all your princesses?"

"Not you."

## 38

## Return of the Man of Action

Attila held up the small oblong silver block to Boss Berzweck and said, "Since we won't be needing this anymore, I'm sure you'd like it back." As he returned it, he spun it bottoms-up and asked blankly, "Oh by the way, do you know what these markings are?"

Dragomir, who'd been leaning casually against a counter to watch the two men at the central table, eagled his eyes on the Boss' reaction. And because Attila had told Dragomir that he would allow Sadra to attend the meeting after all, because he felt an additional witness to this event would be helpful—and perhaps to show his generosity of spirit, and that he could stand on his own even with her present—she was there, too, at the opposite counter. With Sadra unaware of Attila's private crisis, or his monumental decision to renew her *Cause* privileges, she was undistracted, and focused especially hard on Berzweck, her eyes narrowed. This was a moment of truth and revelation.

. . .

"Hm?" The Boss glanced at the ingot. Then he took it from Attila, tossed it into a jacket pocket and returned to looking irritable. "Shaving it, eh? Do I have to check its weight, Dragomir? My scales are precise and I'll know how much has been shaved. I left it for a purpose, not as charity to be poached from. But how could I not have suspected it would happen? Shaving! As if nobody's ever thought of doing that. Remember that it's an illegal metal to possess."

"However, if you will observe again the markings," said Attila. "It wasn't shaved, Mr. Berzweck."

Confused at first, the Boss smirked and retrieved the ingot from his pocket, and flipped it around in his hand adroitly, in a practiced way, like a magic act. He brought it closer to his eyes. He chortled. "What markings? these?"

"They look like ..." Attila made his voice soft and suggestive as he pointed, "...initials? An A; an X; an I."

"I wouldn't call them markings," he said dismissively. "Someone dug into my silver with a fingernail. They were testing its purity."

"They aren't letters?"

"A coincidence. Why, is it supposed to be some kind of message?"

"You didn't make it?"

"Why would I devalue my own bullion?"

"I thought maybe they were your initials."

"Alexandru Berzweck; of the Berzwecken Mines and Mining Concern," he reminded them as if introducing himself. "No 'X'. No 'I'. And we don't deface our material with our initials, much less scratch in inauthentic ones."

"So you didn't put those markings there?"

"It was as smooth as a placid winter lake when I gave it to you." He glanced around for back-up. "Dragomir?"

"I didn't notice," said Dragomir nervously, though trying to look offhand about it all.

"Did anyone else touch it?" asked the Boss.

"Well, of course I showed it to some of the men we're recruiting."

"Who!" demanded Berzweck, his face turning red, his pale eyes shining that much brighter, a large vein appearing along his temple. "I warned you not to pretend it was yours."

"We didn't," murmured Attila. "They know it was yours."

"And who were *they* that got their dirty fingers on it? I want names."

"Let's not get into the specific names at this time," said Attila. "To preserve secrecy."

"Well, how many then?" the Boss glared at the baker.

Dragomir shrugged.

"One? Five? Ten? One hundred? How many people were fondling my little bullion?"

"The number is unimportant," said Attila.

"What's the point of this?" bellowed the Boss. "I've had it with you, former low constable. I'll take my silver, thank you. And if I lost a tenth of an ounce, I'll be back for compensation." He shoved his finger into Attila's face. "But you still haven't shown us your own, eh? And I have given you your time. More than enough! You haven't produced so much as a sprinkling of dust. I warned you! Again and again I've warned you. But you always look at me with that same insipid face. Now see if I don't show you what action really means."

"Give us seven days. Just one more week. There was another storm, and Lt. Vokent might've had trouble getting through the highway."

"Same excuse as the purported letter of warrant from that governor of yours—which he was to send to you long ago, I expect? Where is that?"

Attila did not react.

"Right, take all the time you want," said the Boss as he slammed his way out of the back room and out of the store, their meeting at an end.

Attila's eyes remained on the door, as if he could follow the Boss' progress outside. But his index finger tapped the central table. Then he turned.

"How many people touched it?" Attila asked Dragomir.

"I don't know," answered the baker guiltily, wiping his hands on his apron like he needed to remove something. "Everyone, wasn't it? I showed them all. I wasn't paying attention. You both saw me do it, though. Of course they all held it. It's forbidden, how could they help themselves?"

"Were those markings on the piece at the very beginning, or was it smooth as he said?"

"I only noticed the letters at the end of the day, when I went to put it back in my pocket. I-I think I made a mistake about what happened. I'm sorry, Mr. Bronk, maybe I was wrong."

"You weren't," said Attila.

Dragomir and Sadra looked at him. He stared back dully.

"Is there some strong reason you suspect him, Attila?" said Sadra. "*Boss Berzweck?*"

"These very letters on his own block? It seems too much of a coincidence."

"Why would he scratch anything into a block he owns?" countered Sadra. "And the initials don't match entirely."

"It could have been anyone," admitted Dragomir. "A shame I noticed too late. I really didn't think ..."

"Attila," said Sadra. "You should go apologize. Give him as much as you can of our efforts without letting on too much. No names if you can, obviously. But if you don't stop him now, he's going to start on his own. He will, there's no doubt. *On his own.*"

"If Berzweck begins his own campaign," said Attila, calculating, "at least we know he isn't the Count's man in Korr. However, if he doesn't start, we will have another reason to suspect. This turn could be good for us, then."

"But if he does move," said Sadra, looking grave, "need I remind you he might not succeed. He's just a distraught father and a mineral monger. He doesn't know what he's doing. But he will let the Count know something's happening here; a threat that requires his attention. And *he* will come and root out any movement against him."

Attila stared blindly at the oven as he considered matters.

"It makes no sense," said Attila, "that a man of ambition and power like Berzweck would join with this creature. The government, the Cardinal's church, and the people acquiesce to him because they have no choice. They need him for their interests and self-preservation. But for one to actively seek enslavement to this monster's will, when one has means of freeing himself, on his own, with his own money and resources, does not logically follow."

"No, it doesn't," agreed Sadra. "So go to him. If you can't bring yourself to do it, Dragomir should. Or I will talk to his wife—or to him directly if I have to. But I won't see all this work, this good work, ended on a mistaken suspicion."

"There's no mistake," said Attila. "Not yet. And the Boss can't just snap his fingers and make things happen, even if that's what he wants. So let's give our good lieutenant at least a few more days to show. He's on a critical mission, but it shouldn't be long now. I'm positive."

"Why wait when an apology right now is for the best?"

"Because despite the logical view, which declares him innocent, the Boss is in league with the Count. It must be so."

Dragomir grumbled his simmering doubts.

"How can you be so sure?" asked Sadra.

"There's nothing sure. It's no more than a hunch, I admit it. That's all."

"And those signs you're always talking about are missing," she reminded him.

He shrugged. "True. But we'll see if the lieutenant has more useful information for us, one way or another, when he returns."

"Would you mind telling us what the lieutenant is doing, what he could possibly return with that would change matters as they are?"

Attila remained quiet. His lowered gaze was set vaguely on the table between them.

"If it's too much to explain, or if it's too much to reveal with Dragomir here," said Sadra, rather boldly, "perhaps you can come back with me to the church tonight, and help *me* understand."

"No. I'll be staying here." Attila's eyes lifted, then listed back and forth between Dragomir and Sadra. "Please, allow me this one thing: we wait."

## 39

## Three Men Walk into a Tavern

Three men walked into a tavern at its busiest hour, one man followed by another followed by another. Each settled at a different spot; the last two overlooking the first. The first man stared into his drink thoughtfully, the others accepted their cups but their eyes were watchful, amid the crowd, to the next one over. Everyone inside this dark, low-ceilinged space wore the same sort of bulky, leather, hooded overcoat, ornamented variously with blobs of melting snow; making them nearly identical, and so, anonymous—which was part of the point of the place.

The second man made a decision, and with an unseen nod of his head he found his way to the end of the long counter where the first one sat. The first eyed the second suspiciously, even as the second, with a benevolent look, made himself at home, facing him, while he placed at his back the wide wall of wine casks, allowing for, and keeping, a clear view toward the entrance.

"You're thinking about your men," said the second, his voice low but confident. He didn't lift his head too much or remove his hood. Neither did the first.

"My men?"

"Your name is Vokent."

This further surprised the first man—Lieutenant Ivanti Ion Vokent. His eyes narrowed, trying to place the newcomer. He'd been trying to think about his men, that was true, and considering the next moves needed to be made, but had ended up brooding about Amalina Dalca and her crazy plan for him to pose as a prince. He now realized in his distraction he'd lost awareness of his surroundings. He'd missed someone moving up on him. And this one knew something about him few should.

He tried to focus on the man's face, a wispy bearded face, with soulful, wounded eyes set inside deep, dark sockets. But he wasn't familiar.

"I am one of yours," said the second. "One of your men that is. You wouldn't remember me, I'm good at blending in."

"I haven't raised the signal," cautioned the lieutenant. "The king's men are still about, looking for any of us. You should have waited for the sign from Basz."

"You enjoy maybe a couple hundred strong," said the second man, undeterred. "Not much against the king's forces."

"No."

"I have in my possession near a thousand. Perhaps more so."

Vokent's eyebrow arched handsomely. "What are you saying, sir? *Who* are you?"

"I have pieced together Hak Vogoneyevic's southern partisans, and added a little to them myself. They can be at your disposal at any time, Ivanti Vokent. I've brought them north to Tsobl."

"Could be dangerous with so many native menfolk in one place with no authorization or excuse," said Vokent, and the second man nodded; while the third watched.

"But, as I said, they are yours," murmured the second man seductively, "to deal with the king's men and anything else."

"Thank you, sir." But the lieutenant didn't ask where this force camped at the moment, or why they'd been offered. He sensed there was something else coming.

"I have a question for you first," said the second man. "At every site you visit, you place a silver cross. Why?"

"You don't care for the church?" asked the lieutenant, reading the man's face.

"This cross: it bears the shape of the Cardinal's Roman Orthodoxy. Are you working with him, the Cardinal of Netz?"

"The blade tucked here in my belt could be chewing your guts before you ask one more question," muttered the lieutenant with a smile. "Spies are always so full of questions, aren't they? My old general's motto was to answer them with a bite of steel."

"Spies don't come offering you five times the men you have."

"They offer as much as their target wants to hear," countered Vokent.

"And they don't ask direct questions about seemingly meaningless aspects to your personal conduct. Or do they?"

"I'll tell you why I do it," said Vokent, still with a predatory grin, admiring the second man's calm, "this bit with the cross, if you really want to know. You see, when the people find it placed over the ruins they will know *we've* been there, and it'll help spread the word of the silver army. *The silver army.*"

"Yes, it works. I've heard of it. But, to answer my next question, then, you aren't with the Cardinal of Netz?"

"No."

Now the second man smiled. It was a small, tentative one. Like he wasn't used to it. "I see. But you use the Cardinal's favored cross anyway. You're with low constable Attila Bronk?"

"That's true," nodded Vokent. "And?"

"But only him, you do not serve directly the Cardinal of Netz?"

"Not that I know of. You've something against the Cardinal, then?"

"I do not wish to say."

"Why does this matter to you?"

"I've my personal reasons."

"Personal? And how do you know Mr. Bronk?"

"I've known him for a while. An interesting man."

"But you've nothing against him?"

"I think I understand," said the second man, as if he'd been considering something else the whole time. "You place the cross so people will remember the silver—which is highly illegal, and so you set yourselves directly against the council laws—and it *is* the Cardinal's Roman Cross. Not so the Cardinal can claim your work in his name, but so that the heat your work gathers will be pointed at him in Netz and away from Bronk, who I believe is in Korr. I see the constable's tricky mind in that."

"That could be the case," allowed Vokent with a sly grin. "You *have* met him then."

"The first time I met Attila I was unsure of him. He held some conversation I didn't really understand, seemed to be about beards or something. Only later did it become clear he was giving us a peek into his methods of thought. Very unusual. Made me feel stupid and I didn't care for that."

"What's your name?"

"It doesn't matter."

"So you'll allow me to have your men if I serve under *him*, Bronk?"

"No," said the second man.

"You're confusing. You can still enjoy a talk with my blade if it will help."

"Listen to me, Ivanti Vokent," said the second man, with serious eyes. "Don't work for anyone but yourself. Ever. For yourself and the good of the people. Never put your trust in one man, especially one at the top."

"Well, where does that leave me?"

"As far as I know, there are only two people in Ardeel who are straightforward and working for the good of the people: me and this man, the low constable of Tsobl, Attila Bronk. And even *he* I won't put my full trust in. Because you can only ever really trust yourself, and then, only so much."

"You have to start somewhere," said the lieutenant. "That's how armies work."

"So it is," said the second man, drinking from his flask, which he pulled from his robes. "I'm warming up to you. But I know Bronk has compromised himself with the Cardinal. I know this. He has dealings with him."

"I'm to meet with the Cardinal soon enough," admitted the lieutenant. "But as far as I know, it is only for a small trade. And Mr. Bronk is in charge. If you trust him …"

The second man nodded, but said: "As much as I can allow myself to rely on Bronk, it may look to you like he has the command position, but I know the Cardinal, and he might be trickier than the low constable after all. And so … But you said you'll be meeting the Cardinal soon?"

"Business," said Vokent.

"How can it be just business?" scoffed the second man. "It's never just business with *them*."

"The Cardinal, you mean? Or the whole Roman order?"

"Never get involved with a religious man or religion in general," warned the second man. "It only wants one thing, and it will take that only thing you have of value."

The man seemed to want him to ask the question, so he did: "Which is?"

"*Your soul.*"

"Is that all?" joked Ivanti. "Still haven't figured out if I have one."

But the second man went on, placing his hand on the lieutenant's arm, staring directly into his eyes, growling his dire warning: "The religious will lie to you, my friend, and cheat you for what you're worth and make you think whatever they put you up to is justified in the moment, believe me. Before you know it, *pfft*, your soul is theirs to play with, and you can only look on, knowing they've stolen it. But they can never take what you don't give away, so keep it yours. Always."

"A thousand men, you say?" said the lieutenant shifting uncomfortably.


· · ·


The second man would never forget the loss of his own soul—his most precious possession—though it happened in countless slices over the years. He knew when it had finally gone, felt it when the Cardinal had cut and taken the finishing piece. How could he ever tell anyone about that fateful instant when at the end of his confession they could only damn him?

But still he remembered it at nearly every waking moment since, his dark-socketed eyes drooping wide open and haunted, every cell in his body crying in lament for what he'd done for that infernal monster at the St. Grigori church: having already watched with disgust the toadying by all those supposedly superior women at the Count's high castle, those Ladies of Title from the west, taking their confession, a carnival of offenses, and then witnessing his own wretchedness when he was summoned away from them and down to St. Grigori, to take part in the worst crime of all.

The Cardinal had smiled as he secretly doused his rings with poison, and with the same smile he'd offered his rings to the orphans—the children who'd escaped the workhouse massacre—to kiss.

"Paulo was already in two ragged pieces," mumbled the littlest one, Sergi, with wide eyes, unaware he was delivering more narrative than was wanted; or delivering *exactly* the kind of carnal candy on which many ears there exhilarated.

"Speak up, boy!"

"Paulo was already chopped up in a couple, red-and-white chunks, sir," the little one spoke up again with an innocent voice. "Mostly red, sir. The skin left of him, sir, shivered inhuman-like, sir, like pieces of loose fat floatin' in a spicy sauce." This colorful detail, though excessive, met with an agreeable noise from the congregation, and the second man, standing at a side table, had marked the boy as a born raconteur. "I swear at the sight of it I never wanted to open my eyes again. I looked away quick and saw Jarl pointing to the wide hole in the wall. The one we use to escape chores— sorry for that sin, sir, but it's what we done when we didn't want to work. I wanted to dive through the hole, but others were ahead of me. And I had to wait."

"That's how you survived," crooned the Cardinal, "but how do you know that—?"

"Well, I heard them, sir. Didn't I, sir? Right behind us I heard them; their hoarse, screeching voices, almost in a chant, sir: 'Where are they...?' one says. 'Find them all ...' says another. "More, more, more, more, more ..." says the third, and them all."

It was a fine testimony.

"You've sworn to this audience," said the Cardinal, appearing unmoved, and withholding the rings from the eager children, indicating to them the assembled fathers of the village, and all the witnesses, "that it was one or several women with incredible power and the savage lusts of the strigoi who burnt down your building and killed all of your masters and friends?"

The three orphans nodded in religious fear of the holy man.

"You swear that it was not your own doing, that you did not by negligence nor thoughtless horsing around, or even worse, by malevolent intent, cause a fire within the workhouse, which then would consume it and all inside, and that you have not concocted a vibrant fairytale—summoned into my solemn and holy house the most gaudy of chimeras ever witnessed—to raise the fears of, and thereby beguile even the smartest and wisest men of Netz, in order to cover your crime?"

The orphans, mouths agape, nodded or shook their heads, unsure what answer he was looking for.

"You claim you are innocent?" he helped them.

"Yes, sir!" they said, little Sergi's meek voice trailing after his older brothers'.

"Then by all that is righteous and in heaven, you will press your lips to my holy signets. And if you are truly innocent, and with this fateful kiss as your seal, you will thrive. But if you are lying to me, you lie to heaven itself, and will suffer death. Do you understand? The truth will be known!"

They all nodded and gladly pressed their little lips to his rings, grabbing his lethal hand as if it were pulling them from a river. He nodded, and there came his smile of satisfaction. Even the fathers of Netz were relieved.

And when the second man saw this scene, with the orphans having sworn true, and knowing what should be done, he came forward with the goblet filled with wine mixed with the poison's antidote. The children had done right and they would live.

"What are you doing, Rosczy?" said the Cardinal.

"They should drink of the wine?"

"Put that away."

"Too young? Water, then?" There was a pitcher of water with the antidote as well, for when a potential victim abstains from alcohol. That is what the Cardinal must have meant.

"Not that one," groused the Cardinal, when he saw Rosczy going for the pitcher. "Here, the three boys may drink from *my* cup, if they must. Touched only by the mouth of an innocent. Or better, no drink at all, so our esteemed witnesses know I've not tampered with them in any way. It is their words, and their oaths to heaven, that will sustain them or, heaven forbid, condemn them."

Rosczy shook his head, questioning.

The Cardinal knew what would happen to the boys without the antidote, but he smiled back at Rosczy in a self-pleased way, and had one of the other servants show the boys out to the village; where the fathers of Netz, and the whole enervated population, would watch them for the first signs of a writhing, painful death, to see if they had been false in their testimony before the Cardinal. That it had all been a lie.

Rosczy could still hear the Cardinal's words when he'd worried to his master about withholding the antidote from the children:

"Don't you know that you owe me for everything I have given you?" the Cardinal had snapped in his reedy, whip-saw voice. "Are you really so selfish, Rosczy, that you don't feel you must repay me for this rich education I have provided freely through the years—done out of my own interest in bettering you—and you will instead persist in this … this … your perpetual *mediocrity?* Don't you feel ashamed by it?"

"Your eminence?"

"Well, get out of here if you can't stomach real work and you prefer instead those cushions up there in the castle. But if you're going to be any help to *me*, stop being a complete disappointment, pay more attention to what is happening there. *Those women.* I can't be left in the dark … and it isn't all soft cushions up there, let me tell you."

"Yes, your eminence."

And without Rosczy crying foul to the people of Netz about the underhanded poisoning of the orphans, away went the last slice of his soul. He didn't need to hear when they died, their tragic deaths conveniently placing the guilt of the workhouse fire on them alone, leaving the real monsters standing blameless; he knew it would happen. And he'd already felt the diaphanous tearing away from his body.

• • •

"I am the man it happened to, Ivanti Vokent," said the second man, Father Rosczy, presently. "So know I'm telling the truth, because I ask nothing from you, even though I'm now without what is most precious to any honest man on this earth, his soul. I've lost it, but I do not seek it from anyone. I don't want yours. I only wish to reclaim my own. Now, with what I have done so far, I'm taking mine back; or rebuilding it, piece by piece. You believe me."

"I feel I couldn't otherwise," said Vokent to the man quivering before him.

"Love is what brought you back here?"

Vokent seemed to recoil for a second.

"Could be," he said cautiously. "It's what I've been told. But wh—?"

"There's nothing wrong with that," he assured the lieutenant quickly, gripping his arm again and squeezing it. "Love is pure. It is *of the soul*. Your motives must be pure, Ivanti. So it is true?"

"We'll see. Right now there's only the mission. You understand?"

"If you must go to him, the Cardinal of Netz, don't drink anything he offers you. And never touch or kiss those rings he wears, even if he insists. Tell him you've converted away from the orthodoxy if you have to. It will anger him, but it will keep you safe."

"Sounds like you know something about him."

"Treat him as if his entire body is as poisonous as his soul."

"You can trust me on that," said Ivanti Vokent. "But then you *will* bring me to your men, and turn them over to *the Cause?*"

"If I know Bronk well enough," said Rosczy, not exactly answering, "and with the sudden appearance of the 1st Regiment Dragoons, the plan here for you and your men is to make a direct attack on the Sobelburg council, a raid of some sort, to destroy the physical structures but no intentional violence on the members themselves. To simply enrage them, and leave clues that send the King's Army against the Count. To thereby harass him in his lair, and have him whittle down their numbers if not wipe them out for you, while you continue to draw him off and harass him elsewhere, by chipping away at his castles. Wearing him down by keeping him occupied all over the map."

"Could be," grinned Vokent, impressed at the guess.

"It is *a* plan," said Rosczy, without enthusiasm. "And if it were the Cardinal's, your orders would have been to kill or kidnap the Governor instead, or in the mix of it. Since *that*'s not on your agenda, I see, you *are* working for Bronk alone."

"And is it a good enough plan for you to sign on to? And your people?"

Before Rosczy could answer, the third man stood before them both, with a handsome grin of his own.

"You are the owner of the revolutionists," said the third man to the first, confidently, but with a heavy accent.

"Who are you?" said Vokent.

After he removed his royal blue leather gloves, the third said in a cheerful, clipped voice, "I am the man here to kill you."

## 40

## Au Contraire

Rosczy fell back a foot, shoulders landing against the wine casks, and turned his head, wide eyes searching the room for other threats, mouth hung open like a breathless fish. Lieutenant Vokent did not react, but also did not drop his tight gaze from the third man.

The third man had taken off his gloves and parted his heavy coat, revealing a high ranking Germanian military uniform. But he was really showing them he had no sword or pistol. No doubt, just as the lieutenant did, the man had a deadly blade stashed in an easy place, but this was enough of a display, with a carefree smile that polluted his whole lean, attractive, rakish face, he was someone to get along with. Vokent ignored the pangs of alarm caused because he hadn't noticed this potential threat—*two of them now*—until it had arrived within striking distance.

"However," said the third man "How would you like to not have a fight?"

"Who are you, sir?"

"I am the prince."

"A real prince?" said Vokent, eyeing the military uniform.

"*Your* prince. I'm here to sue for peace, how does that sound?"

"Easy."

"You're an odd one," continued the Prince, in French now. "But I suppose nobody else can understand what we're talking about if we speak in a proper tongue, one I assume you know?"

Vokent cast a look around, saw Rosczy's bewildered expression, and then shook his head in agreement.

"I'm here now to see if we can come to some kind of arrangement. You look like a smart man, not too much older than I. You've an officer's rank, I've seen you in uniform. French, isn't it? I'd guess you've experienced about as much of the world as I, and crave a bit more of it."

"Not much of a guess," said Vokent. "Wouldn't anyone? But being a prince—someone who's had much more of the world under his feet, and definitely owns a rank, and means, which I haven't—what exactly would you want from me? What can I possibly offer?"

"As I said: not have a fight. I've seen your numbers, you've seen mine. We know each other's weaponry and supplies, and can guess the disparity in our training. Won't be much of a scrap. I'd say it could be an afternoon's work. It would be bloody. And none of you would be walking off the field. I won't ask you to confirm I'm right, because I am. And you know it."

"Suing for peace, did you say?" said Vokent with a carefree, jovial tone.

"In so many words. Whatever your aims are, I know, with your taste for vandalism against historical properties, your target here is that Black Castle above Sobelburg."

"Could be."

"We could have a bloody contest over it, in which you lose."

"Or."

"Push on," said the Prince. "Leave. Forget the castle, at least for now. We won't pursue. I command here, and my forces will stay put. Or rather, with you gone, ostensibly, we will leave. Why not?"

"That's all you're asking?" said Vokent, honestly surprised.

"Yes."

"What happens if we stay?"

"Events occur as I just described, and your untimely death," said the Prince. "But I don't want that."

"Why not?"

"Because I don't want a fight," said the Prince, cocking his head, with a look that said it should be obvious, he'd already been over this part. "I want to achieve my objective, but I do not wish to do battle here. Not with you, or your people."

Now it was Vokent's turn to tilt his handsome head, shoot him a curious look.

"Don't think me a coward," cautioned the Prince, with a smile angled sharply up toward the right cheek. "I can face combat. But … "

"Didn't you just say you'd make a fast meal of us?" It seemed somewhat offensive to Vokent, this hard battle being denied, turned down by an almost childish, pusillanimous foe, and for no real reason. The lieutenant himself would welcome the sound of the trumpet and drums, even with the odds appallingly against him.

"Notwithstanding an outcome as certain as this one," began the Prince, "there's no telling what might happen on the ground, yes? Anything can happen to anyone, the mightiest king laid low by an accidental swing by the most abject slave. The conqueror felled by a wayward arrow. An untouchable man in the rear maimed or worse by the chance spin of a tiny lead ball deflected at the front."

"Something any soldier knows and accepts when they accept the challenge," said Vokent.

"But that's just it, man," the prince's smile grew, but he looked somewhat abashed. "I *don't* accept this fight. I don't want to fight here. I don't want to bear the chance that I could be brought down *here*. In this country? In these mountains? This is no place to die. Do you know what I mean? I don't wish it. I've other much greater places to stake my glory. My father sent me along because he doesn't want me to risk myself, he wants me to have victory after victory, no matter how embarrassing the foe." This seemed to really pain him. "But I've lost my mother unfairly—"

"The Queen is dead?"

"Oh, yes, I suppose that is the case," he murmured to himself. "*Your* queen, *my* mother. Queen consort. Don't worry, she's been replaced … handily. No matter." He lifted his head, a smile on his lips again. "And I simply don't feel like playing the dice here. Even if they're loaded. They can always fail. Not here, my man. It won't be here. Not if I can help it. And not if we can find a better agreement for our sides—with drinks between us."

"What is he saying?" asked Rosczy, his eyes wide, lips still hung absurdly open. "I think this is the Prince of Germania. He leads the dragoons."

"Go wait outside," said the lieutenant. "I'll meet you shortly."

Rosczy did as ordered, his eyes never leaving the third man on his way to the door. Some of the patrons had noticed the strange movements of these three, and were looking up from their drinks. The Prince shrugged his cloak closed and, after pulling the chair back a couple steps, he lowered himself carefully to sit where Rosczy had been. In a few seconds, the rest of the room went back to sleep.

"Your uniform," said the Prince.

"I served in the King's Army; your father's army. But when we fought in the west I met General Volante. He bought me out into his service."

"Ah, Volante," said the Prince with a knowing smile. "Those are the colors. That means you have some real fight in you! And yet you somehow escaped him to return home and pick up a strange cause I see no sense in."

"It would take too long to explain."

"I doubt it. There can be only so many reasons, especially for a man as good looking as yourself. And to break from General Volante's clutches? It's family, or a woman." At Vokent's look. "A woman. Why not? And she likes you tearing down castles for her, as if it will lift her up somehow? Or it lifts you, anyway, in her eyes? Never mind, I do not ridicule, but show you how much we are the same. That's how things go with women, enh?"

The lieutenant shrugged at the Prince, and idly wondered what Amalina might be up to now without a prince of her own. He'd called her plan a farce, but somehow this felt much the same. Two leaders of opposing military forces meeting in a gutter-level tavern, bargaining a peace … or that is, arranging not to fight.

"Since you were under General Volante, I'm surprised I've seen no hint of cannon. That should have made me a little afraid. But that kind of firepower is hard to come by. And makes my job easier, now that I know you are without his beloved battlefield superiority."

"Were we going to have a drink, you said?"

"Yes, we will drink together as friends ... as old comrades of the King's Army. And if you're a good 'un, since you know the city better, you'll point me to a quality restaurant—I don't know if my spies have turned on me, but they can't seem to tell me where I can get a bit of currywurst, or even a *decent* peppered hare; Ach, my cook isn't worth a turd in piss, and you know what camp food is like. But where you take us we will stuff our bellies till they ache. And we will speak of modern battle tactics, and the women who follow along. Why, I even have some easy beauties where I'm staying right now, whom I'll gladly share like a good brother-in-arms, if you're inclined ... But only after I hear you swear that you'll stand down your men. Grant me this and I can say the rebellion is quelled, and I'll return home the hero. If you should start again, months later, or next year, what would it be to me? I will have already done my job and have no cause to return. I'll have moved on to greater challenges ...

"But to secure ugly castles, and break the hearts of pretty women in Ardeel ...? I've no wish to die for that. So tell me what I long to hear."

. . .

The Prince wound his way through Tsobl whistling a tune while shaking off the wrath of the low-quality but potent back-water ale. He felt triumphant and laughed to himself, recalling the faces of the rebel commander and his shocked lackey. But upon entering the boardinghouse's quarters he'd privately rented—had *anonymously* taken—he found himself just as shocked.

"What are you doing in here?" rumbled the Prince, trying to keep his face neutral.

Though the room was supposed to have been a secret, sitting on the stuffed chair inside was his military advisor, Rancik; and taking up almost a whole sofa with his enormous body was the local governor. On the other side of the room two soldiers stood at attention with their hands locked on the the hilts of their swords as if ready to draw them.

"The question is, Lord Prince," said his advisor, eyes glinting, not even bothering to rise—though everyone else bowed reverently, the governor causing the sofa's cheap wood to squawk, "What are *you* doing here? Away from camp? I can only pray you have overcome your resistance to the local bordellos."

"And why are you here, Governor?" said the Prince, switching targets.

"We were just discussing the situation with the Black Castle," said the governor, his upper chin jiggling above the lower one. "Our fear for it."

"I won't ask how you found out about this apartment," said the Prince, airily, "but I'm glad you're here, Rancik. My legs aren't fit to stand on for the rest of the night. While I sleep off my drunk, you can tell the captains that we are returning home. Have the men ready to go in the morning."

"*Merde alors!*" cried the advisor, his stony blue eyes staring in disbelief.

"I've completed my mission, and I have secured the peace." The Prince sat on the arm of a facing chair as he briefly explained how he'd gotten the commander of Ardeel's rebel 'silver army' to give in.

"They've surrendered?" gaped the Governor.

"You went to him unarmed?" gasped the advisor. "*Incroyable! Tu es Fou!*"

"*Tu es?* Call me a fool, Rancik? Treat me so? And are we all French now?" The Prince switched to French, with a wry smile: "Or are you trying to seduce this fatso with your sauce-licking tongue, enh?"

"*Fou! Fou! Fou!*" cried Rancik, indignantly. Then back to German: "Your father would say as much. What job I've been given to look after the child! *Enfante absolute!* To risk your life like that, Lord Prince!"

"What's to risk?" yawned the Prince. "Unarmed, as you say, I've beaten them. *I've won the war.*"

"They've surrendered?" asked the Governor again, his jowls atremble.

"Something like that," said the Prince, with a vague smile. "They shouldn't trouble you and the council any more; not so much that we should hear of it back at the king's castle anytime soon."

"You've taken them into custody?" persisted the Governor, his fat eyes thinning.

"Why bother?" said the Prince, unconcerned. "They can see themselves back to their garlic-topped shacks without wasting any more of my time."

"But that isn't the mission," said Rancik, growing cross. "That isn't your mission at all. We need to smash them down!"

"Then you do it," said the Prince. "I'm going home."

"But you can't!"

"Can't I?" challenged the Prince.

"But, your lordship," said the Governor, his voice fluttering up and down the scales, a smile and a frown competing for room on his face. "This outburst of nativism began just months after your own Germanian delegation was found dead at the border. The rumors of subornation and rebellion have proven out. They must be made an example."

"I have *made* them an example: Live in peace and you may live in peace." He opened his hands to them with a charming smile. "An example for us all."

"But, your lordship," the Governor began again. "A fire not extinguished will smolder and spread."

"Or not," said the Prince.

"But I cannot believe it," said Rancik, his tone chastising. "To let the enemy, who is sitting in your palm, waiting to be crushed, slip away? The queen will be displeased."

"Who?" snarled the Prince, coming awake, standing, his face flushing. "What queen?"

"Your mother," said the advisor.

"The *new* one, you mean," snapped the Prince. "The one who has wrapped my father around her finger and sent me off … here."

"To prove yourself," said the advisor.

"Or get me killed."

"The King, your father, loves her and agrees that if you are to command the same respect as he, to sit on the throne, to gain the love of the people, you must prove yourself just as he did in his youth."

"This makes sense," agreed the Governor.

"I've just gotten done what everyone wanted without one musket ball being fired, and I'm to learn that this doesn't qualify as something to be respected?"

"Falling back from an easily trounced enemy cannot be respected," declared Rancik the Advisor. "And it won't be respected by every other rebel standing in the wings, observing and taking note of your mettle."

"You have your orders, Rancik," said the Prince, his face red. "Ready the men for the return march in the morning. I command here. And I'll be back at father's castle before the sunflowers bloom."

"But, my Prince," said the Governor, his hands cupping the air before his chest in a supplicating motion. "You must reconsider."

"Must I?"

"Lord Prince," said Rancik. "You will now return to camp. You will ready the forces and throw them against these rebels, with yourself in the saddle, leading them to victory."

Though shaking with rage—and sobered, which was a pity—the Prince laughed. "What a picture! But *I* am the Prince, and you don't give orders here."

"*Au contraire—*"

"*Au contraire*, Rancik?"

"It is the will of your father and the queen. You *will* do as you were commanded."

"And if I refuse?"

Rancik nodded at the two soldiers to the Prince's right. They were older and looked rough, and like they didn't love any cowardice. As if for example, they snapped their heels to attention and drew their swords out in a ring of metal on metal. Their hard eyes announced they would enjoy a fight. On second glance, perhaps there was the hint of the egg sucking *Gallier* to them, as well, and a provincial animus ticking their lips.

"Is that how you all feel?" asked the Prince, addressing the soldiers. "But, *au contraire,* I *am* the Prince. I am *your* Prince."

"And as the prince," said Rancik with a condescending smile, "you will now return to camp, and you will ready the forces—"

"*Au contraire!*" declared the Prince, as he, with a smile, lifted his arm.

With a *shoof* sound, a thin stream of smoke shot out laterally from a pistol the Prince now held toward Rancik, and then a sudden deafening burst of flame and black clouds fired at the advisor. Rancik fell to the floor in agony, grasping his leg, as blood spurted from a tear in his thigh.

The Prince tossed his spent pistol at the nearest soldier, at the same time coming forward in a flash with his hands. Even as the sound of the shot still filled the air, along with the stinging smoke, the Prince batted the nearest soldier into the other, and then with a duck and a twist of his arms and torso, had their swords clattering to the floor, while he brandished a deadly sharp rapier of his own.

Whirling again he slapped the thin strip of metal across Rancik's head, yelling, "I am the Prince! I am the Prince! I am the Prince!"

He poked the tip of the blade into the Governor's chest, piercing the uppermost layer of his cloak. The Governor gasped and gabbled incoherently, his grossly inflated hands waving in some kind of surrender. Rancik's screams were earsplitting, and caused the fat man's eyes to blink and water on the beat.

"I am the Prince!"

"Yes," said the Governor. "Yes, my Lord Prince. Of course you are."

"I am not unreasonable."

"No, sir. No you are not. Of course you are not."

"Does everyone in *my* army feel this way, as Rancik has said? That I am a coward? So much so that they'd come at me with swords? With mutinous, treasonous swords?"

"I cannot say, your lordship, my Prince."

"But you agreed with Rancik, just a minute ago, didn't you?"

"I—I—I—"

"Listen to me, Governor."

"Yes, yes, yes, of course—"

"I am the Prince here."

"There's no doubt."

"And you are just a figurehead that has been placed by the crown—*my father*—to keep these people in order."

"A point I do not disagree with, my Lord Prince."

•  •  •

*This pup is as dangerous as Attila Bronk ever was*, thought the Governor as the tip of the blade nipped into his chest, reminding him to regret his once heated ambitions to this governor's post, while thinking as fast as he could to save his skin. *No, he's even worse than Bronk. A prideful thing.*

"So as the last voice of any reason in this room, Governor," intoned the Prince melodically, "I must ask you to come up with a good reason why I should ever change my mind, why I should take contrary advice, why I should even *listen* to someone who is not the son of the King!"

The Governor's mouth opened. *What had the Cardinal advised to manipulate this prince?* Oh, yes, it was so clear, so easy. But the words were still deep in his head, being unlocked as the blade pressed.

## 41

## The Black Castle

Basz stepped back as his efforts inside the mammoth fireplace produced a ball of flame that sped up the flue and licked the surrounding mantle, before it eased down into a decent blaze. He kicked the end of a log to settle the whole, and Ivanti felt its crackling heat from across the room. The lieutenant leaned in a chair and let his eyes roam, but the room was too dark to see much, even with Basz's fire and several torches, because its cavernous size matched that of the fireplace, and everything notable was in the vast, gloomy distance. The place seemed built for giants.

"I wonder what this room used to be," mumbled the lieutenant, grimly. "Whatever it was, it'll serve our purposes well enough. Basz, get a handful more rooms going. But before you do, let the surgeon know he can start using this one. Quickly, now."

Basz nodded, then trotted with purpose out a disconcertingly tall door.

"You're a good man, Basz."

"It's eerie," said Rosczy, his eyes glassy and rounded. "How quiet it is, eh? Don't you think?"

The lieutenant shrugged. "That happens."

"Restful … you'd never know …"

"It'll be a good warm place to rest, just as long as we do our jobs. But it is about to get noisier. Come, we should see how things are."

As they arrived at the tall door, they made way for two men hauling a third man between them, whose body was slack and bloody, with two deep lacerations on his chest and a wide chunk taken out of his shoulder. His skin was grey, lifeless, but he was blinking and he was moaning through grizzly lips. Rosczy, surprised, stared after the man and muttered a quick prayer.

Vokent noted this. Rosczy's prayer.

Ivanti and Rosczy might have gotten lost on the network of staircases, but for the trail of torches and nervous men staring their way down to the action, and the growing clamor and roar from below. When they arrived at their destination, Vokent swore under his breath. One of the men, noticing the arrival of the lieutenant, said needlessly, "They're almost through."

Looking out the thin aperture that overlooked the scene, it was obvious enough.

. . .

The day had begun with a light, celebratory mood at the announcement of the King's Army's retreat, only to be surprised by the appearance of that very army, the Crown's 1ˢᵗ Dragoon Regiment of it, advancing on them in the street, the Prince, surly-faced, sitting tall on his saddle in the front row of the first column.

At the time, Rosczy was with the lieutenant and his small band of the 'silver army', which had gathered at the town's end for their 'victory' announcement. While there was the immediate impulse to run, to abandon them to their fate, Rosczy had grabbed Ivanti's arm and told them to fall back to the Black Castle.

Ivanti knew well there was a choice to be made. They *could* simply scatter. But this went against training: General Volante routinely kept order in his ranks by having watchful sergeants shoot and stab anyone breaking, as breaking ranks meant the loss of cohesion, spelling a rout; which was just as good as defeat and capture—or death, once the victors swept up the various fragmented pieces, one-by-one. So Lieutenant Vokent organized the retreat, and the men of the outnumbered silver army, taking note of his confidence and courage, followed. They swore and fired arrows and took intermittent musket shots at the dense body of German cavaliers—doing little damage—as they fought off their enemy's occasional charge, with those high riders' long, sharp spears picking off their numbers like a cat nipping off tail feathers.

It had been a drawn-out, tiring, nerveshattering climb through the wild, snowy path to the Black Castle, and then matters got only worse when they found the gates locked. The men were pressed against the high walls, staring at the widening regimental column behind them, as muskets and harkebusses from within the King's Army opened up without order; using Vokent's men as target practice. Chests exploded with unexpected spouts of blood while heads burst and bodies collapsed. The kingsmen laughed and jeered, but the cornered 'silver' soon realized they could use each other and the thick vines growing on the castle wall to clamber to the top of it. Half of them were over before the Prince called for a new, cautious advance.

As the sun began to drop behind the mountains in the west, casting them in shadow, Ivanti organized what defense he could along the top of the battlements, observing the number of men he had, and then the sprawl of the King's Army below; all mounted on horses and relatively fresh, fanning further down the descent back through the valley. He didn't want to say it, but it was growing more hopeless by the second.

At Rosczy's insistence, he left the defense along the parapet—cutting back the ivy they'd climbed—to see what might be done inside the main building, once the outer wall was inevitably breached. Entering through the Black Castle's front doors, his jaw dropped. The main building was gigantic and an imposing structure from the outside, but he had not imagined what lay within. The front doors led into a chamber as wide and tall as many a castle in their own right. Its entry area dropped thirty steep steps to a wide floor which could be considered a pit, which then faced some yards distant a new high wall before it, covered in a confusing array of staircases and arrowslits; from which defenders, positioned behind that new interior wall, could rain fire on an unsuspecting enemy who might have made it inside. This meant they had the outer perimeter wall, then the main building's outer wall, and then this inside area at their disposal to hold back the King's Army. It was a miracle! But if it was, it was one that had been built for them centuries ago, by unaware architects and builders, but with perhaps the same desperation in mind for some future conflict: pitting a tiny defense against a sieging numberless horde.

The lieutenant had breathed a sigh of relief and clapped Rosczy on the back.

"I thought this might be of use," said Rosczy, "since no one was using it."

"You knew about all of this?" said Ivanti, pointing to the amazing structure.

Rosczy shook his head, "Hadn't a clue. But I had faith."

Ivanti noted this, too: Rosczy's words.

• • •

The King's army, perhaps with the taste of victory firing them forward, did not break off at sunset but pressed their attack. The siege of the outer walls did not take more than half an hour. Then a short, quarter of an hour later the defense of the outer part of the building collapsed. When the Prince strode into the great entrance, his men pouring through the door around him with cries of havoc, they either paused or immediately fell into the central well of this treacherous, unheard of bit of architecture, and the castle's defense was renewed with a hearty rebel shout from every window of the inner wall.

But that initial sense of tide-turning had diminished over the hours, as the Prince continued to send his men at the doors and windows and up the many staircases (some of which led to nowhere or to aptly named murderholes). And with a trained force of that size, pitted against a handful of untrained, untested men, it became obvious to the lieutenant there would be no miracles here.

The Black Castle was impregnable without siege engines, cannon, or a way to summit the main building's walls, which were as high as a cliff's. An invader had no other access points than through the front doors. So it should be impossible to take, as long as it was well manned. But the lieutenant's pitiable force was not enough. Unless the Prince called off his men for the night, the castle would be taken before dawn. Or unless there was another miracle.

"He gave me his word," muttered Ivanti, looking down from an upper window at the treetrunk being hauled inside to ram at the doors below. The soldiers carrying the load didn't seem the least tired, but only more energized and excited. "What happened?"

But what had happened didn't really matter, did it? There was no way of getting out of this. Ivanti Ion Vokent was staring directly at his end. He'd felt it before, on so many battlefields, and in nameless cities and fortresses, when the chances of war had blown back against the great General Volante. But there was always an exit at the backside of the army, another route to another day to take up the battle again. But this time, with Ivanti in charge, locked inside a surrounded castle, he'd run his luck out. A foolish place to die, and for a foolish cause, this venture with the mock 'silver army' was supposed to be just a diversionary tactic, not a last stand. He could have stayed on with Volante and, with some luck, enjoyed a long career and advanced in rank, with a sea of women underneath him. Putting that thought out of his head, because he knew it was wrong, knowing that he had no choice but to return to Ardeel, he realized it might have been better, after all, to have taken Amalina up on her odd, princely charade against the Count's Ladies of Title. He shouldn't be here, anyway. Not this, not this. *Anything but this …*

"You don't belong here," said Rosczy bluntly, staring at him, his hand firm on Vokent's arm. "Come."


• • •


Rosczy led them back up the way they'd descended, through the large room now become the casualty ward, and into a further off place that Basz had lit. It seemed like a bedroom of some kind, but it could have been a smaller audience chamber. There was a strange tarp crumpled in the middle of the floor.

"You don't belong here," he said again. "I can see it in your eyes. You are lost."

"What are you talking about?" snarled Vokent, feeling the eyes of a Volante death-sergeant on him; that he'd been accurately read by Rosczy and caught out.

"I'm saying this is not your fight. I don't know what is, but this one is not yours."

"I'll fight beside everyone else!"

"But not now," returned Rosczy, somberly. "Another day. I'll take over here."

"Because this is *your* fight?"

"Definitely."

"How?"

"We haven't the time, Lieutenant. We have to get you out of here now, before it's too late."

The lieutenant shuddered with relief, and anger, and pity, and finally confusion. "These are my men, my brothers."

"Lend them to me," said Rosczy. "And I will give you mine." He put his hands together and his sunken eyes narrowed. "For just a moment, I was afraid I would break. I'd find a way out of here and run, just run."

"We're surrounded," said Vokent with a bleak smile. "There's nowhere *to* run, man."

"But there's always a way out. Always. But then I thought, if I ran, I could go to my men, who are not too far away, and bring them back here. Surprise this army from the rear, at night, almost in equal number. And fresh."

"Could you do that?" said Vokent, feeling a positive stir, lifting his eyebrow.

"I could have. But I'm telling *you* to do it. Go. Tell them I sent you, and then bring them up."

Vokent swallowed, feeling unsure. "Why me?"

"Because if you stay, with that look in your eyes, I'm afraid by the time I return it will be too late. However, if I stay, and with the hope of a rescue, I can guide these courageous men. And fight harder than you ever could. And for you, knowing you're doing a good thing, helping save your friends, you will travel faster, and surer, and see that the rescue comes."

"But—"

"Listen," said Rosczy, "I can fight a man from behind a secure wall. You're a fighter who can use weapons and your own body to take someone down. There's a much better chance of you getting out of here than me. You see? Now, let's find some way to get you on your way."

To the lieutenant it suddenly felt like he was in a dream, that this was impossible. A fantasy. That he was still standing at the wall and waiting for the Prince to punch through and he'd gone insane. But Rosczy's hand was fixed on his arm, guiding him deeper into the castle, and upward.

"I don't understand," said the lieutenant.

"I made it very clear to you. While this isn't your fight, it's mine: I am here doing all I can to restore myself and the soul of this country. Better than you simply escaping, Ivanti Vokent, know that when you send my forces against the Prince we will beat them; beat them enough so that an escape for all can be made.

"And better still," said Rosczy with a light in his eye, "just as we did this morning and afternoon, I will command a rearguard action, as if in retreat, and lead these bastards further and further south. Away from Attila and Korr. Bronk wanted your men to make a name for themselves, and send up the false idea that they were the 'silver army' knocking down old castles, to throw off any scent to his own force, eh? what will soon be his real 'silver army.' Well, we'll carry out his plan and take that name for ourselves. But did you see those shiny ornaments and buttons all over the King's Army? They're silver too, eh? The Prince and his company are wearing it to shove in our faces that they are above the common law and the people. We will help the Prince spread that news. They will be known, this King's Army, as they follow us and hunt us down, as *another*, 'silver army'. There will be silver armies traipsing all around the Ardeel, and the Count won't ever know one from the other."

Vokent grinned roguishly. "Attila would like that."

Rosczy nodded, a serious look on his face. "It will happen. As long as you get out of this castle and reach my men."

He told the lieutenant where their camp was on the mountain, and just what to tell them.

"But why would they believe me?"

"They will know it is true by this." Rosczy took a small wooden cross out of his pocket, kissed it, crossed himself with it, and handed it to Ivanti. The lieutenant stared at it in his hand. "They know this is mine, they have seen it on me. They will believe you."

"*You* are religious, Rosczy?" asked Ivanti.

"No."

"How can you say—?"

"I am a *spiritual* man. I have my own religion. But I'm not *religious*; that is an outward thing. Nor do I work for a religious cause. Those people push their hidden agendas, using belief as a weapon to increase their power and against those innocents they wish to bend to their will. I am *not* religious. I am *nothing* like the Cardinal of Netz."

Ivanti nodded, not sure what to make of it. "But you're a holy man, all the same. You said you will fight. Killing won't be a problem for you?"

"Well," said Rosczy with an embarrassed shrug, "I am also a profound hypocrite. I will do what I have to. But keep that in mind when you meet with the Cardinal, and remember my warning to you. Keep safe, now. And believe I will do the same here. Whatever I have to."

"Good," said Ivanti, feeling an electric charge, "then I'll tell you what *you* have to do."

. . .

*I will do what I have to do,* **thought Rosczy.** *I will do and keep doing it until I have done what is needed to be done. And when that is over, I won't stop. That will be just the beginning. It won't end until I meet with the Cardinal, an audience of equals, and I pour him a drink. And he will only trust what I've offered him when he sees me swallow first. Even better: I will have him drink from my own cup, after I have had a good long taste from it. But when he is sputtering his last breath, staring at me uncomprehendingly how I could have poisoned him, I will show him my own secret method: how since the very first man I helped kill for the Cardinal, full of grief, I have taken small amounts of the slow-acting poison myself, so that now I could down a whole pitcher if I wanted to, without antidote. The Cardinal will curse himself. And though I might suffer greatly for it, I will live … and be triumphant.*

He would show the Cardinal. He *must* show the Cardinal!

Rosczy knew none of this would come to pass if he did not win the day. With the lieutenant gone away with Basz, he pulled himself upright and charged down to the doors to the entrance hall, where the king's soldiers were out there, ramming the tree trunks inward. On the inside, Ivanti's men were braced against the doors, forcing their shoulders into it, pinning their legs against the opposite wall. There was a whole procession waiting to relieve them, while others stood by with swords and iron picks and pitchforks and bills and the odd baldiche—field weapons or looted ones, the resources of a peasant army—readied for the first soldier to pop his Germanic head through. This defense would have to work. They would have to keep it up until Ivanti Vokent brought the thousand plus reinforcements screaming through the night and snow to save them.

He noticed some of the looks from the waiting men. Most were focused on the action but these others stared with eyes that pulled at him like so many abysses. Rosczy realized in an instant: It had been easy to arrange this moment, assembling Vogoneyevic's southern forces and leading them north, because it was easy to command on an empty battlefield. But in this moment of extreme danger, with other men counting on him, waiting on him for inspiration, or at least some kind of hope, Rosczy was not used to those starving eyes turned toward him, but looking past him to the Cardinal. Never at Rosczy directly!

How could he comfort them now? With his own private ambitions? *How,* went his plummeting thoughts, *can I prove anything of courage beyond the weakest of platitudes, when I've only ever been mediocre?*

Rosczy could feel the sinking of his spirit, which threatened to crash down his whole body before these famished eyes. How utterly foolish and empty were his boastful thoughts, mere seconds ago, of revenge against the

Cardinal? That in his arrogant pride he'd sent a more capable man running from this castle who could have seen them all through the crisis at hand! Hadn't this been what that vain, pompous villain, the Cardinal, had been trying to tell Rosczy all along? That he was worthless? and that Rosczy didn't rise even to his knees in ability? or was capable enough to carry through on anything alone, and without guidance? That Rosczy was, in the end, a disappointment; a failure?

In a shake of his spine, Rosczy knew he could not let these men down. And he would not. He refused to give in to the tyrant which had set up shop in his mind, and which now, with its infectious, poisonous corruption, sought to defeat him even in that most personal place. History was on the line here. He had only to keep the castle until the reinforcements arrived. Until then, he could only offer the command the lieutenant had left him with, the one that saves any defense on the brink.

"Hold!" shouted Rosczy, as he shoved past the lost men hovering at the edge and joined the blocking effort at the door, putting his own shoulder into it; offering a prayer that the lieutenant would make it through in time—and that the partisans would receive him without trouble.

"Hold, men!" cried Rosczy, firing them on, "Hold! Hold! Hold!"

# PART FIVE
# CASCADIA

## 42

## A Tall Dark Stranger

The Count sent word to his beloved Ladies of Title that he would be traveling to check on his eastern properties and so would be absent their company for at least several days. The morning following this announcement, and to Amalina's shock, *Prince Phillipe Castion of the Outer Meldines* was noticed by the obsessively bored Ladies of Title as he commenced parading about in the streets, outside their shops, restaurants, and the theatre; from the shadows, with out-sized gestures, ordering around his valet—a scruffy looking street urchin in an cheap, ill-fit livery—and flagrantly showering into his valet's cupped hand many gold crown coins; which were never really *spent* on anything. He was observed, again mostly in shadow, with his freshly shaved chin held high, his padded chest outthrust, and with either a large smile or a menacing scowl, sometimes alternating between the two within the same minute.

Amalina could not believe it. No matter how clownish it might have made him appear, Jakob's cheekbones (brought out majestically by careful touches of stage makeup), his lustrous chestnut hair (wig), and firmly toned body (more strategically placed padding), that bulged his suit at the seams, had the Ladies sitting forward in their chairs, their posture perfect, trying to observe him in all his glory to the minutest detail and yet at the same time not to look at him, but to discreetly laugh at him behind their hands and kerchiefs, hoping to encourage him further. The rumors of a Prince having entered Ardeel, sitting at the head of an army, helped sell the sham, in part, that this was he. Staying in shadow, which Jakob did almost to perfection, ensured most of the rest of the work that he likely was a lusty, besotted noble out for no good. The Ladies had seen plenty of examples at home, and had plenty of practice playing with their like. While Jakob did have nice looking legs in hose, which he extended from the shadows and flexed proudly, he seemed to have no idea what a fool he was making of himself.

Amalina had worried Cristine might notice this mysterious newcomer to the Ardeelian royal set and somehow recognize him as a native Netzian—a lowly curb crawler and common beggar at that—as she'd traveled to Netz before and who knew if their paths had crossed; he with his soiled shirt hung open to the waist, a crumpled hat out in his hand. If so, she might have him arrested on the spot as a nuisance and a scoundrel, and then, to buy his freedom, he could reveal to the authorities—and so the Ladies—that he was a player in an underhanded trick by the Countess Katarina. Which would have been a small disaster to be cleaned.

But Amalina's mischief with the little green bottle must have worked, Cristine had begged off playing with her friends, claiming she was too exhausted and needed rest. It was an added and unforeseen benefit, allowing her time to make this 'prince' disappear.

Amalina tried to shut him down with warning looks.

And yet, with great discretion and clock-work timing, the 'prince's valet' delivered private notes to the ladies who'd caught his eye. The Ladies took a while to giggle, before their own servants began returning oblique but favorable replies to him, composed on perfumed paper, just to see how he might respond. There was a wager who might be the first to pry some money out of him for a supper.

But still, there was a reluctance on their part to actually dine with the 'prince', at his invitation, or to meet with him personally for a chat. It was like they were admiring a beautiful bird at a distance, but feared to approach or he might fly away; or by doing so might anger the Count, on a claim of infidelity. This coquettishness on their part only encouraged the 'prince' further, feeling a strike was near.

Urgently but discreetly, as the days continued and the chance of the Count returning increased, Amalina sent notes to Jakob through his urchin. "Leave." "Stop." "I told you we weren't doing this." And finally: "I'm not paying you! *Go away!*"

But on receiving these dismissals, he'd read the card and seem to nod with satisfaction to his valet, nod to her, then lean into a candle's light for a brief second to wink.

"My god!" exclaimed Amalina, flustered beyond reason, tearing a cloth napkin in her hand, and realizing Jakob's bizarre persistence was diverting her from her own opportunity to drive the Ladies away. "Of all the …!"

• • •

"What is it, Katty?"

"We're all grown women," said Amalina, sounding reasonable despite her flushed cheeks and sweaty brow. "Everyone here knows that my uncle's idea is to have only a small permanent court … or was that not made clear?"

"What do you mean by a 'small permanent court'?" asked Greta La Nevers. "How small?"

"I believe I can tell you this: he's already confided to me that he can see no more than nine of my friends continuing on past this year."

"Nine?"

Amalina nodded. "And he's already chosen five. There can be only four more. That means you can't *all* expect to be considered."

Greta made a noise of upset, but then settled down at the other Ladies' looks around the wide table. *Everyone* knew what the score was at this point. They must.

"More than one is unnatural," said 'Maria' di Oscina, in a critical tone. "Nine? We aren't living among the heathen who permit harems."

"No," said Amalina, encouragingly. "You mustn't let uncle's peculiar beliefs and taste corrupt your fine sensibilities and moral principles, Princess di Oscina. He may be powerful and rich, but he is old and avaricious." Glancing over at the shadowed 'prince', she added, almost hopefully: "There's no need to let a younger, handsome prince, like this Castion, who is wealthy, available, and interested, pass us by without *anyone* joining him."

"Why don't *you* visit with this Prince Castion, Katty?" asked Elle VandeGarde. "You seem interested."

"No, that's not true," gulped Amalina. "And why should I? He hasn't written to me, as he has all of *you*."

"Maybe he's bashful and he hopes to get to you through us. He certainly can't keep his eyes off you, whatever the case."

"That isn't true at all," said Amalina, her cheeks glowing. They had noticed Jakob looking to her for instruction and mistaken it as genuine affection.

But somewhere in that moment Amalina realized that, much like the Count, she had something like a growing harem of her own—if she chose to look at it that way. Didn't she though? How many times in the past months had she heard the words of love aimed at her? Seen it spoken in so many eyes and felt it in tender touches. She held the overwhelming romantic interests of the Count, Ion Vokent, perhaps Pia, and almost certainly Aklan now. This thought made her blush even more out of embarrassment. It was something to think about, but she didn't want to consider!

Only then, pivoting on the shame of it, the heat within her turned, carrying her thoughts like the wind buffeting a windmill. *All this love*, she thought angrily now, and she could sneer at how the thought mocked her: *All this love; my harem.* The Count had assembled all of *his* loves, placed them before him in his palace of pleasures, picked and chose his menagerie. *He*'d had a choice at every step. Amalina hadn't had a choice in any of her so-called 'lovers'. They'd alternately snatched her, chased her, or come out of the woodwork, their adoration based on the lies she was tossing about just to survive. It wasn't real, none of it. Even if one tried to argue that she'd chosen Ivanti Vokent—which a part of her mind did argue, her heart's pace quickening—that she'd been in love with him since she was young and had pursued this relationship, she could easily flip it back using the same poor argument Ivanti had told her on breaking their engagement: they'd been thrown together as children in Korr, and then they were thrown together again, by circumstance, later in Paris. This wasn't a chosen love then. This wasn't—none of them were—part of the romantic notions Amalina had read or seen around her; what everyone else seemed to be able to have for themselves. Why couldn't *she* meet someone by chance; the tall dark stranger who she'd never seen before but would fall in love with at first sight? There would be the joy in the pursuit, the testing of each other's qualities, the pleasing discoveries, the mad plummet into possession and pitiful worship, or the rational and satisfying decision to carry on. Her embarrassment of riches then—all her lovers—now were a pile of false gold; cold, and a parody it was. *Where is the someone-out-of-the-blue who is destined for me and me for them?* wondered Amalina.

It was a discontent so upsetting that her body seemed to lurch in her chair, as if she were forcing something physical into the world and the world must respond to her grievance, this absolute injustice, in kind. Her friends observed her eyes, her color, her expression, her uncomfortable gyrations on her chair, and how tightly she gripped her shredded napkin.

Aria laughed at Amalina.

"What are you doing, Katja?" asked Claire Montraine, in a low voice at her side.

"You obviously like him," said VandeGarde, misreading the signals. "We've seen you sending notes, why pretend otherwise? We won't fault you for it. So why don't you give the Prince a try, then? But has anyone ever heard of the Castion line? or the Outer Meldines?" She whispered quickly as if Amalina was about to launch herself at him: "Do be careful, Katty."

"I believe I've heard of them," said Maibrigg Smeehaute. "The Meldines? Islands aren't they?"

"All the same," said VandeGarde, shaking her head to say Maibrigg's opinion meant little. "Do be careful of mysterious princes and adventurers, Katty. Are you listening to me?"

But Amalina's mind was locked around her missing stranger, which life was withholding from her, seeming just around the corner and out of sight, while foisting on her these many thin substitutes, collected in the hidden box of her heart like so many chewed and half-used pencils, all of them unworthy relationships by their circumstances, she undeserving of their affections, and at least a couple of them rightfully undeserving of hers.

• • •

Later, after the 'prince' had given up breakfast and left, and Amalina had had time to cool down, a stir in the dining room caught everyone's attention: A small, hunched figure entered shakily from the hotel's outer corridors, tottering as if the individual might fall over on the next step. Some of the noble Ladies gasped when they recognized who it was.

Cristine glowered at them, her face grey, with dark circles between cheeks and brows almost like a faded highwayman's mask. Staring out of that dark, fleshy ribbon, the crystal blue eyes of the mineral merchant's daughter were pale and misty and lacked the edge they used to hold. But they soon found Amalina and pointed at her in a fixed and malevolent way.

"Cristine," said Aria Ecci with a skewering lilt. "You've made it out of your room. But are you sure you should be? You look like you need more rest. A year of it, perhaps. Have you caught what the others have?"

"Ama—Amaaa—" muttered Cristine. "No, that is, Katarina. *Katarina!* Countess, if you would please? Can you help?"

She looked pathetic.

Amalina ran to Cristine's side and took her by the arm to steady her. "Oh, Cristine, let's get you back to bed. I can send for a doctor."

"What are you talking about?" whispered her friend weakly. "I'm fine. Feeling much better. I need some fresh air and new walls to look at."

Amalina peered down at Cristine and sensed a hidden strength that wasn't apparent from how she was crabbed over or carried herself. It was not the effect of the green bottle stimulant; that was gone. But maybe with the Count's absence she was regaining her blood? But still, that would mean there was a reason she was pretending she could hardly walk. For sympathy from Amalina, or the other Ladies?

Cristine looked back into the outer room and nodded. Then she whispered to Amalina, "Yes just help me, Katty. Don't let them see me weak. That's all they'd need, you know? But I can count on you, can't I? Thank you so much. I'm sorry for how I acted earlier. I'm so very sorry. Sometimes that bottle gets the better of me ..."

"It's okay, but are you sure? No one will mind if you get some more rest."

She smiled sharply. "They all want me to rest. I'm sure every one of them would be glad of it. To have me out of the way. But I can rely on you, can't I? Of course I can. My good friend. Always willing to help."

"Oh, of course," whispered Amalina, guiltily.

"You will always help me, won't you?" whispered Cristine in return, still smiling for the Ladies' benefit, though she was quickly fading. She hugged close to Amalina, as if she needed support. Then she glanced back toward the outer rooms again. "It's not like you would ever lie to me ... no ... you'd have to've trained yourself to become such a good liar ... or been the best from the start and I never suspected ... "

"What?" Amalina didn't know what she meant by that. And what was Cristine looking at behind her? Was the Count standing there? She helped

Cristine into a chair. "You really need to get some sleep. Are you sure you don't want to go back to your room?"

"Never mind me, Kat," sighed Cristine with a soft, deflated laugh. Her head turned once more, eyes flickering back to where she'd come. "Doesn't matter. And never mind what I said. I barely know what I'm saying. But I'm good enough to lay here like a dead fish on a rock ... can sit here all day and night and day and night ... better than anyone else ... who cares what I have to say? it's not like it will matter much at all, soon enough ..."

When Amalina stood, she glanced back through the doorway into the hotel's outer rooms and corridors. No one was there but a tall, roughly clad peasant, or servant of some kind, who walked in a heavy, limping fashion. Perhaps he'd helped bring Cristine down from her room. But now his back was to them and he was hobbling away. He turned down a corridor and out of sight.

"Looks like you could use a leech or two, Berzweckie," Maibrigg told Cristine, appearing suddenly at their side. "It's clear you still have a bad humour circulating inside your system. And—" There was a sudden positive flash in Maibrigg's eyes: "Oh! Cristine! There might be a prince in town who you'll find most interesting! Have you ever heard of the Outer Meldines?"

• • •

When Amalina went back upstairs to her room, she saw the peasant from earlier waiting at the end of the hallway in front of the window. He lifted his head and had a glimmer of recognition in his face. There was something familiar in him, too, but Amalina could not place it. A brief, unhappy smile spread on his thick lips, which settled into something grim. As Amalina walked to her door he stood from his crouching position and limped, slowly and unevenly, toward her. His large, dark, hairy hands flexed as if preparing for a strenuous bit of work.

Amalina hurried to open her door. She couldn't remember if there was some way to bar it from the inside, and she thought she might have to pile something to barricade it. But the man took a wide step forward, and in the cramped corridor he was already towering over her, one hand on the door, pushing it in as far as it could go.

"Um," said Amalina.

"Countess Katarina," whispered the man in a deep voice. Up close, his face was pincushioned with pockmarks, his eyes small and hateful divots on that field of undulating flesh. His breath, passing over parched lips, stank of fermented fish and cheap wine. "Get in."

As she tried to turn around and shove him back into the hall, he fell on her like a wave, sweeping her into the room. She stumbled and barely kept herself upright. He closed the door gently behind him, then blocked it bodily. The only way out was the window. And then two floors down.

"What do you want?" she asked.

But he was already smiling again. He took a piece of black metal from a pocket, did something with his hands, and then his right fist had a bar across the knuckles. He made sure to turn and flex his fingers to deepen his grip on it and to show off the piece, and let her see the two sharp points protruding from the front of it. He brandished the queer bar so she knew it was some kind of weapon. He brought the twin, twisted points up near his face. She was transfixed by this dangerous looking item; feeling its teeth already being driven into her, again and again, here and there.

"Don't want much," he muttered. "If you please."

His other hand shot out faster than she could react—on an arm that was longer than she had considered. His smelly palm clamped over her mouth, the thick, wild hairs on the back of his hand tickled her cheek, as he whispered, "No screaming."

She wanted to shake her head to assure him she wouldn't say a word, if he would only let her go. But he fired his other hand to her neck to join the first and began to squeeze hard. Her body convulsed as it tried to cough and choke in response, while her arms and legs lashed out at him. He was too ogrish and strong. He could hold this position all day with her battering him and wear herself out. When she tried to grab and pry at his hands her left palm landed painfully on the iron skewers and sprung away, the hard edge of the device scratched at the skin along her jaw.

As the room blackened around her, with bright sparks popping in the corners of her eyes, she realized that she was about to die and there was nothing she could do about it. He would use that weapon on her, tearing her flesh wherever he liked—however long he liked, perhaps poking out her eyeballs with it—when her breath was gone and there was nothing more she could do. She should have run when she'd seen him at the end of the hall. How stupid to die this way. How many times had she been at what she thought was the end, and any of *those* times would have been a preferable way to slip into eternity than to fall to this ugly man, a tall dark stranger with an unknown cause.

She remembered Korr turning out in force during the baker's strike to lynch her and her father; or she hanging off the high castle's tower, awaiting the plunge to the stones below; or the innumerable times the black wolf had been on the verge of ripping her to pieces; or the Strange Man slashing at her as a giant praying mantis. Even the Count had tried to crush her throat, with an undeniable strength; so much stronger than this man here. Her eyes were shut tight at the pain. But her mind carried on, seemingly undisturbed but maybe spurred on by the violence: and what about AXP's assassins? the one who'd tried to corner her in the high castle, and the tall one who'd come after her in the snow—?

The man's grip loosened as he fell off her, rolling to the side. Over the high whining sound in her ears, Amalina heard a couple rattling, metallic *clangs*. She tried to open her eyes, but even when she did her vision was obscured, with sparks firing within a dark mote underneath a flow of involuntary tears. She crawled quickly to the farthest edge of the room, one arm alternately swinging back to ward off a renewed attack, one hand massaging her throat, while gasping for breath. It didn't seem she could fill her body with enough air for how much she'd lost.

And still the clanging continued.

"Wha-Whah?" said the killer.

Clang! Wham! Clang!

Then there was the awkward crumpling sound of his large bulk settling onto the floor.

"Stay down," said Aklan, adding a string of curses.

"But I've orders ... " Spoken as if that were a logical, meaningful explanation; enraged and confused by this interruption.

Amalina blinked and suddenly saw the man on his knees. He lurched upward, searching for his attacker, throwing a hard punch with his iron-pronged fist, only to be met by the bed-warming pan again, swept around at the end of a long stick. Aklan swung it so fast and ruthlessly, and at an angle that allowed the hard iron disk to hit and deflect in a way to immediately be brought around again for another clean strike. The man now tried to hold up his other hand, a large, long knife in it; the bar with the points proven worthless. But the knife got knocked away, and Aklan managed to hit his head so that the pan opened and covered the man's face in coal ash. The man choked and gasped as Aklan—or it sounded like Aklan, there was nobody, *no body*, there—lifted the pan high, only to bring it straight down on his defenseless head, as if he were trying to drive a stake into the ground. Once, twice, three times, four. The man collapsed with a wheeze, his head striking hard the shards of the room's broken chamber pot.

The sheets on the bed suddenly wrapped up into the air like spaghetti on a fork. With a spitting sound, the bone bounced to the middle of the room, and Aklan was there in the sheets. Aklan bent at the waist and caught his breath. He squinted at Amalina to make sure she was safe, then directed his bedwarming pan at the man.

"There," said Aklan. "Not only have I killed someone, but I've done it to save you, you see? Eh?"

She looked.

"He isn't dead."

"Your eyes are as broken as his head. He's dead."

"You just knocked him out. He's still breathing."

"He's not."

"Check him. See if he isn't."

"If you aren't satisfied, you check him." Aklan began searching the room, probably for his clothes. "I'm calling for the law."

"Genadie will take care of this," muttered Amalina, grabbing Aklan by the sheet. "Nobody can know, or it'll get too complicated for the Count's liking."

"Well, as long as you don't forget what I did," panted Aklan, "and that I did it for *you*. More than Jakob or that lieutenant's ever done."

"Of course. Thank you," she said. Her throat ached and felt as if she were still being strangled. But she found the energy to snatch up the bone from the bed and tuck it into her hidden pocket. Aklan didn't notice, while circling for his clothes and staring at the body. Where had the boy come from, and just in time?

"Were you following me, Aklan? this whole time?"

"No, I—"

"Where were you staying this week? How did you eat?"

"I just saved you!"

"Yes, but how did you get in the room, what were you doing here?"

"I'd snuck in for some coins, but when I tried to sneak out, I saw this guy coming up the hall and ducked back in. And he didn't leave, and I began to wonder what he was up to. Saw him playing with those nasty knuckler knives, like he meant to use them." Aklan turned his blueberry eyes at her, questioning. "But who is he? Why did he attack you, Pretty Princess?"

Before starting to black out, Amalina had been thinking of AXP's first assassin preparing to kill her—only weeks ago—in the woods. That image hadn't left her yet. This tall dark stranger, now that she had time to consider, looked to be an almost exact copy, and so it wasn't too far a leap. And hadn't he said something about 'orders'?

Amalina said, thinking it truer by the moment: "Cristine. I think she sent him."

"Lady Berzweck? Your *friend*?"

"Well ... *you* didn't arrange for him to attack me just so you could play the hero, did you?"

"No! My gosh, what a suspicious mind you have, Pretty Princess."

She waved her hand at him, and rolled onto the bed into a more comfortable position to regain her breath, as her throat, both inside and out, throbbed. "You know, when I thought I was going to die just now, I saw my life. It was nothing more than a series of people trying to kill me."

"You need to change that around, Pretty Princess."

Amalina groaned.

But then, almost in reply, so did the tall dark stranger on the floor.

43

# Housekeeping

Amalina's life did seem to have devolved into one close escape after another. It wasn't a pleasant thought. And she resented this because that's not what life was supposed to be, was it? Constantly balanced on a knife's edge, prepared to be cut to ribbons or plunged into an abyss? The bible was filled with chosen people's suffering, but even for Job it never felt like such a continuous peril. There could be periods without misery and thriving was allowed. Poems and romances gave their subjects rest from their agonies, and lent them eternal friendships, and loves.

While it seemed what had just happened was unreal, and with every second that passed it fell further behind into the unreality of the past, and Amalina's body, as sore as it was, was still alive and fully in the world—as it always had been and she planned it to be—the mortal fear that had been throbbing inside Amalina during that short traumatic moment was now being replaced by feelings of triumph and elation, and a disturbing, gloating glee over this would-be killer; who was now captured, and rendered impotent. Because it disturbed her to feel so joyous over another's pain, no matter how well-deserved, and because her mind was agitated by the understanding that she was so continuously and unfairly put upon, Amalina took this energy and converted it to a deeper loop of rage: *I could have died!* At this very second, the sore second she was experiencing presently, she might have, instead, already ceased to be! Not breathing the cool air, not thinking these thoughts! The killer obscenely gloating over her lifeless form, her limp body, ravaged by his weapon, still caught in his filthy, stinking hands!

*There must be punishment! Someone needs to pay!*

Amalina remembered how with one stroke the Count had split in half the assassin that Margeta had sent after Pia. Well, she didn't need this stranger bisected, but where Margeta's cutthroat had paid the ultimate price and yet Margeta had continued to enjoy her standing in the high castle, with privileges unrestricted, Amalina would make sure the person responsible here would feel her wrath ... and Amalina would expect the same blameless grace that'd been afforded the Barnacle. As well, in this unforgivable act, though 'Prince Castion' had failed to lure away any of the Ladies, *she* would drive one of them from this court most certainly now, having provided

Amalina with the ammunition; Cristine would find herself ejected, on her way back home, and not so complacent anymore!

. . .

Amalina charged downstairs in a boiling rage, panting, with her mind roiling over—imagining all her friends had been in on the assassination and were laughing about it, right this very moment, alongside Cristine—only to discover the Ladies of Title weren't in the dining room, of course. But Cristine was: splayed out on a chair, mouth hanging open, as motionless as a dead fish, just where Amalina had left her. A couple young men of the hotel wait-staff, hovering behind her like liveried vultures, bowed their heads and backed away when Amalina arrived—one of their curious looks asking silently what should, or could, be done with her?

Finding Cristine in this unexpected condition—not the laughing, gloating mastermind of murder—took away some of Amalina's steam. But only some.

"What are you doing there?" snapped Amalina.

Cristine lifted her eyes drowsily to Amalina. "Eh? … Ama—Kat?"

"Yes! Surprised?"

"Can you help me …" muttered Cristine, slowly, with effort, "get out of this chair … and back to my room … ?"

Amalina waved the vultures away, who were circling the edge of the floor's carpet. They nodded and fell through the open doorway, scattering into the building. They could tell the young countess, or whatever she was, was seething, which—thinking it had to do with catching them up to no good—was less promising for their entertainment or continued engagement at the hotel.

"*Can* you help me …?" breathed Cristine.

"And why should I help you?" said Amalina, bitterly "Where are the others, eh?"

"They left …"

"Where?" Amalina gritted her teeth, not knowing where to aim her animosity. "You mean they abandoned you here? I told you they can be just a bunch of mean things, didn't I?"

"Well …" Cristine took a few breaths, trying to bring up her energy to defend them, or herself. " … what fun could I be? Eh? I told them … to leave me here… Anyway … we'll see who holds their hearts by the end of the month … you or me … we'll see … For the moment … I'm content to rest … Just need to get back … to my room … don't you think? Will you—?"

"Why not just lay around here?" said Amalina, frostily. "Your good friends might come back sometime later this week to eat, and find you waiting if you haven't expired already. And then you can join them."

"This is … *my* fault?' said Cristine. "Is that …what you mean? What's going … on? What's the matter … with you?"

"The matter with me? Maybe you should ask yourself why you're so surprised to see me standing here." Worked up again, Amalina leaned down close to Cristine and demanded: "What did you do, Cristine? Eh? Tell me. Admit it."

Cristine said nothing, only stared.

"You can't keep a secret from me, remember? We're sworn to tell the truth. Now—you confess to me, Cristine, just what you did."

"What am I to say?" said Cristine, thinly. Her lids lowering, bemused. "What could I have done?"

"Don't pretend. It'll only make things worse."

After clearing her throat, she said, still with a weak voice. "I've been here the whole time. What could I have done? Tell me, Kat."

"But you *haven't* been here the whole time. Not more than an hour ago you came walking downstairs and in through that door. And you called my name several times. And you hugged close to me. Why? To single me out. To signal to your man."

"*My man?*"

"He's still alive," said Amalina, "just so you know. And he'll admit everything, what orders you gave him, so you'd better be honest."

"Why bother if *he's* going to tell?" murmured Cristine with a smirk, closing her eyes. "I don't know what you're talking about, and I could have nothing to add. Please leave me alone." She turned on the chair as if to go to sleep, but then pointed feebly through the door. "You know … somehow my elixir spilled … though it was locked away. Very strange. You wouldn't know how it happened, would you? You didn't do it, did you?"

"So that's what you were talking about?" said Amalina, astonished, trying to play her own guilt into anger, a righteous anger. "You blamed me for doing something against you, and then you sent him to *kill me*, eh? '*It won't matter much at all, soon enough'*, that is what you said, because you thought I'd be dead. He'd be waiting for me at my room."

"Someone tried to kill you?" mumbled Cristine sarcastically. "Oh, that's terrible. Don't say it too loud, though, might give the hotel a nasty reputation …" She grinned, and adjusted her head on the chair's headrest to be more comfortable. "But you should run off to tell your uncle now, shouldn't you?"

"I will. The first chance I get. And he will hear your man's confession and that will be that for *you*."

"I doubt it very much. And I wouldn't go spreading your slander to the others, you'll look silly. Like you're jealous after they've shown such friendship and sympathy toward me and you're just trying to get their attention with a bit of made up drama. They won't believe you. Remember how that worked last time, Katty?" Cristine turned her cutting smile to face Amalina, to see if her words had had an effect.

"The next time you want to do me in for good, Cristine, you better come yourself."

. . .

When Amalina returned to her room, Genadie stood up from the stranger, now on the bed, and looked dismal. He wiped his knife clean. Under the stranger's body, blood was blooming into the bottom sheet and mixing with the ashes that had fallen off his head.

Aklan stood opposite Genadie, his face much paler than earlier.

"No," said Amalina, gulping and staring at the motionless, silent corpse. "Genadie, what have you done?"

Genadie shrugged. "Well, Ms. Dalca …"

"We needed him alive so he could tell us why he attacked me. Who sent him. Who gave him his orders."

"He was dead already, Ms. Dalca," said Genadie in a scratchy whisper. His skin was red, his face had dark patches where it looke like he might have suffered frost bite. But he was somber and delicate in the moment, despite his rough look. "I just helped him along. You weren't going to get him to do anything but make some noise and scare people."

"What difference does it make anyway?" said Aklan positioning himself between her and Genadie. "I killed him. You know it. He just wants credit."

"Shut your mouth, boy," snarled Genadie. "It's nothing to brag about. Now help me get this thing out of here … and take that contraption off his hand, so we don't tear up the sheets with it."

"And so I don't cut myself," muttered Aklan.

"And so you don't injure yourself. Yes, that's right. Though it might teach you a lesson."

"Like what?"

When Aklan tugged the weapon off the man's fingers, Amalina took it and turned it to see if she might find AXP stamped somewhere in the iron. The body shifted, Genadie had hold of an arm and was pulling it his way.

"Come on, you little bugger. Help."

"What are you going to do?" said Amalina, putting a hand on the man's chest before they could do anything more.

"Discard him," said Genadie. "Easy to lose a body. I could maybe talk to the Cardinal—"

"Hold off til tonight," said Amalina. "Let me think, first."

"Do you want me to kill your lady friend?" volunteered Aklan, looking at Amalina with a dead seriousness. "For what she did, you know? Then I'll have killed them *both*—two of them!—if that's what you'd like."

"You'll do no such thing," warned Genadie. He seized the back of the boy's jacket and shook him. "You hear me? There's enough death for one day. And it might not have been anyone's fault, either. Much less Miss Berzweck's. Looks like he comes from the mines. I suspect they use those knuckle pieces he wore to chip rock ..." He turned to Amalina. "He could be another of the killer's lot. I'm afraid the man, the man you've been afraid of for so long—that AXP—he might still be after you, after all."

"You told him about AXP?" said Aklan, surprised, pointing to Genadie.

"You told the boy about him?" echoed Genadie, before shrugging. "Well, what I said, Ms. Dalca, this about confirms it, eh? Look at him. Could be a brother to the one before. Don't you think?"

"But if this killer here works in the mines ... *then he works for Cristine's father*," said Amalina, hoping Genadie'd pick up the hint. When it looked like he wouldn't, but was lost in his own ruminations, she continued: "So *she* could have sent him. You know, she might have told her father about me, or sent for his help. And then he ordered this—"

"Leave Master to fix it ... when our Master returns," sniffled Genadie, then he added hopefully, leaning casually on the man's left leg—Amalina noticing the man's ears oddly bleeding on the bedding more than the slice at his neck—" ... should be any day now."

"But we don't have that kind of time."

44

## Time to Go

I

Lieutenant Ivanti Ion Vokent's escape from the Black Castle had been fraught from the very start. The main building was like a titanic stone capsule patterned with narrow windows—slits too thin for a man to fit through—starting at the third floor up; and with no entrances or exits beyond its front door. *A fire trap*, thought Ivanti. Maybe that was why the castle was as black as char, as if it had been burned; woe to the people trapped inside. *And that might also explain why it had been abandoned for so many years.*

The only signs of recent use led Basz and the lieutenant up near the roof, then out onto a long sprit which projected out toward the forest. This walkout, like the rest of the castle, was matte black, with barely a parapet around it. Without exact definition in the night, it could have been an icy, suicidal promenade, if the bright half-moon hadn't shone on some chipped stones and snow yet to sail off. Peering over an invisible ledge, the lieutenant could see the 1$^{st}$ Dragoons at work below, setting up fires and tents outside the castle walls, felling more trees, storing excess weapons and loading guns, before charging back inside. The chopping, cries, and shouts of their excited labor, blew upward on the wind to Ivanti and Basz.

Basz was already centered on the job at hand. He spooled out a long enough rope that, with the sizeable subcommander anchoring it above, Ivanti could lower himself on the lee side of the building, where only a few guards were posted. Most of the Prince's soldiers were eager for action, and the lieutenant supposed these few in the rear, or those relegated to the periphery, weren't the most watchful this late at night. They were probably dreaming of getting off their tired, frozen feet and lying down on a cot. He was counting on it.

Ivanti saluted Basz, said, "You're a good man, eh? Do whatever Roz tells you, he's in charge now," gripped the rope and went over the side.

On the way down, Ivanti felt Basz straining at the line, trying not to let go. He swore he could hear the man's exertions. Ivanti needed to get down fast before he found himself either discovered by the guards, their attention drawn by Basz's loud, protesting wheezes, or flying down to the courtyard with a loose rope in his hand.

But the promenade jutted out so far it tempted him to try to swing his body away from the building itself, with a shallow arc, over the outer wall's rampart. By doing so, and dropping onto the wall, he would avoid sentries in the courtyard, and then maybe find an easier, unseen exit to the grounds. Ivanti, with a kick at the wall, and using a toe-hold on one of the arrow slits, swung himself as far backward as he could, to build momentum, and then, sensing the unexpected move was too much for Basz, in the forward sweep he let himself go.

A second to plummet.

Ivanti landed on the icy bricks of the wall well enough. He wasn't injured; and Basz hadn't tumbled off the roof.

*Couldn't have gone better.*

The lieutenant crept as far forward as he could along the battlements, wanting to get a closer look at the activity in the forecourt. He'd already glimpsed some of the Prince's methods for laying seige and storming a castle, marked it well for if he had the chance to lead his own attack on the Count's high castle—so much different than the simple task of marauding already razed and defenseless ruins, which he'd been doing so far with his 'silver army'. He cast his eyes about and made more mental notes, before he was confident he'd seen all he could see and reminded himself that his men inside—and Rosczy—were counting on him.

He dropped over into darkness … hard onto snow-covered ground with a loud *oof!* His bones rattled together but nothing broke. He rolled into a crouch, turning his head in all directions.

Vokent assumed that since most of the action was inside, the walls would be patrolled by one or two soldiers; at most every quarter of an hour. That didn't mean there wouldn't be sentries posted at the far corners, staring down their length for suspicious activity. If the Prince knew of Rosczy's partisans camped nearby, they might be more alert.

But if that were so, goodness help the 'silver army'; goodness help them all.

There were no guards he could see, and the tree trunks were being harvested on the other side of the Black Castle, which meant he was free to roam.

Ivanti used the dense treeline to make his way to the front of the castle, hood over his head, as stealthy as he could. He didn't bother to keep a ready hold on the hilt of his dagger, better to have his hands free and not look suspicious.

The supply train had caught up to the action and were helping to prepare and properly compose the regiment's camp. At the rear of the action, out beyond the tents being raised and campfires started, the horses had been tied off to wait for their owners' return. Ivanti spotted the Prince's horse tied to a stanchion along with some others inside a small roped cordon, and he laughed to himself. A horse would be just the thing to get him away fast. The Prince's horse, a prize.

He checked all sides, and everyone's attention was focused on the black monolith under moonlight, and its lit-up courtyard. The courtyard was packed to capacity, maybe half the regiment, and it seemed they were waving as a body, as if their movements here on the outside might be being transmitted into the building and directed to those tree-trunks slamming against the barred doors inside. Or maybe it was the reverse. Whatever it was, it looked like a tide of royal-blue draped shoulders rolling toward the castle and breaking against its central bulk. Hundreds of bodies moved as one, truly a tidal force. With most of them in the same uniform, it reminded Ivanti of a tree he'd seen beset by a horde of insects, entirely covered; the tree inferred only as a shape under their chittering mass. There was also the sense that if they contracted at once, with a combined will, the trunk might be crushed, the tree brought down. Some of the soldiers grunted loudly, with the air of rutting, to drive their effort, or to exhort their comrades further along, and Ivanti took it as a rallying cry for him to leave.

But when Ivanti Vokent took the reins of the Prince's horse, a soldier stepped out from behind a tree, halberd in one hand, pistol drawn in the other.

"Who are you, and what do you think you're doing?" said the man, his eyes blinking stickily, his lids half-frozen together or gummed with sleep.

"I'm going to fetch the reinforcements," said the lieutenant in a low but commanding voice, annoyed to find the reins had also been laced with some others. No quick getaway.

"That ain't your horse," was the first thing he had to say.

"I was ordered to take the Prince's horse, so that they know the command comes directly from him."

"Reinforcements?" was the second thing he had to say. "What reinforcements? Why?"

"That's none of your business, is it?" snapped the lieutenant, returning to untangling the reins. "Now if you'll help me here, I'll be on my way. As soon as the reinforcements come, we can be relieved. Some of your comrades would like to get some rest tonight."

The sentry nodded, but still looked suspicious.

"What's the matter with you there? Who knotted these together? I said give me a hand."

"Why the Prince's horse?"

"I already told you, you idiot."

That might have been too much, Ivanti realized. The sentry came awake and stepped forward, eyes darting around the rear of the encampment. If he wasn't careful, the lummox might draw attention to them or even call to someone nearby for help.

"What else would I be doing with it?" he said.

The sentry looked to the castle, then back at Ivanti. "You have an accent."

"Of course I do."

"Why? You sound Ardeelian."

"Because I *am.*"

This surprised him and he advanced again, but still didn't call for help. Perhaps too afraid to step out of line with someone who might have been acting on direct orders from the Prince. The Prince was wild and unpredictable that way.

"What do you want to know?" said Ivanti, quickly but patiently, reasonably. "You think I might be some Ardeelian who escaped from that heap of black rock? How? How would I have gotten past everyone? And why would I run straight into the camp and for the Prince's horse?"

"If you thought you were being clever. Open your jacket, hunh?"

Ivanti shook his head in exasperation and threw open his great cloak, but kept the hood on, saying, "I *am* being clever."

"What the hell uniform is that? And let me see your face."

"Listen, fool," growled Ivanti stepping so close to the soldier—within the sweeping range of the halberd, and point blank range for the pistol—he could smell the contraband rations on his breath. "You aren't going to see my face. I am the king's master spy. If you laid eyes on me, I'd have to kill you. This uniform is the one I was wearing when I returned from the west, you've seen it if you've drilled with France. But I have no more time for this." He unbuttoned his inner jacket and pushed aside the cloth. He leaned forward into the light, to allow the sentry a good look. On his bare chest was the raised mark of the King's Army: the scarlike brand of the double-headed eagle. Created by fiery iron, not many men wore them, but they were fabled, and belonged to a brave and exclusive lot known as *Die Schwarzen Herzen*— the Black Hearts. "I've been at this game longer than you. Now, I am going to take this horse, and in an hour or two you will—maybe—be relieved of this post to curl up by a fire. Or maybe get your filthy hands on some loot inside. I hear they've got loads of gold. Sound good?"

"Sounds alright …"

"But I'm going to do you a favor. One greater. I'm going to let you in on some information even the king, even our prince, doesn't know."

The sentry seemed to rouse even more, though his eyes slitted slyly, as he cocked his head to hear this valuable intelligence.

Ivanti pointed to the sea of heaving backs pushing into the castle. "You're going to want to keep a close eye there. On our men and especially the castle. This Black Castle is the property of the Knight of Ardeel. Have you heard of him?"

"Knight?"

"He's no man, but a foul creature of incredible might, a powerful strigoi and wizard. And this is his home. His favorite home. It's why the rebels came here to hide. And if all this banging around should wake him, he will come screaming out and kill every last man who has disturbed his castle."

The sentry made a face. "What kind of fool do you think I am?"

"One who's never heard of the Knight of Ardeel: the knight who has lived in and protected this land—and his castles—for near five hundred years. He's slaughtered whole armies single-handed. Threw out the Ottomans by himself—"

"There ain't no such things as strigoi," sneered the sentry, perhaps coming too awake. He hiked his hand up on the halberd's pole.

"Not anywhere else, maybe," replied the lieutenant. "But you're in Ardeel now. This is a whole different place if you haven't noticed. They've got everything that crawls from the bowels of earth here, that's why I never wanted to return, but by the king's order." The lieutenant gritted his teeth in a show of grim certitude. "Now you're going to want to keep very close watch, like I told you. Don't look away, and don't bat an eye, because it happens very fast. You may hear a howl like a wolf, or a growl like a dragon, but then it will already be too late: those men over there will come flying up, one row after another, as if they were being blown to the sky by a cannon. That will be your signal to run as fast as you can off this mountain. If you don't, you'll be half-way to the moon, your arms and legs stuffed in your mouth or up your ass."

This gave the sentry a chill.

"It's the same for all the armies who've ever stepped foot in his castles, and it is why those Ottomans were driven off. That is true history."

"So then how come he's never made a peep yet over us?"

"Don't know," said the lieutenant. "Only a matter of time. Anyway, it's why I need to get those reinforcements, in case the prince needs saving. In the meantime, watch out for your own skin, and don't take your eyes off the doors of that black monstrosity!"

Ivanti was off before the sentry could say another word or get his wits together. Racing out of camp, nobody bothered to stop the Prince's horse, even with a cloaked rider aboard, it could always be their commander, anyway, anonymous and slipping away. But he didn't feel safe until he was out of sight of the torches and fires, and was the only figure moving through the lonely snowdrifts by moonlight. Ivanti turned in the luxuriously crafted saddle, admiring its polished smoothness—it felt as if the highly paid craftsman's genius was still at work, attentively pampering a royal bottom— and noted how dense and close round the forest was to the Black Castle. The woods, thick as they were even in winter, were a splendid blind for one army to come sneaking through—and out of—at night, charging and screaming at the last minute for effect.

And now at least one sentry would be looking in the wrong direction, his whole attention focused on preserving his life and not his regiment's vulnerable flanks. The lieutenant laughed to himself about that neat little parting trick.

From what Rosczy had told him, it wouldn't be far to the Vogoneyevic camp; around and over to a hidden valley. And though it began to worry the lieutenant that the secretly religious man might have been lying to him, to get him away in order to enact some sabotage for the Germans, very soon he found himself barreling into a new, large and deep encampment, with only a few fires and torches cautiously—or miserly—spaced apart. Rosczy hadn't been lying after all, and here were the reinforcements that would save everyone; pop out of the forest and stuff their weapons right up the backside of the Prince's exhausted troops.

The sudden elation he felt dropped to cold, numbed surprise, however, with the shock of three musket blasts on his flank, and the whir of lead balls zipping inches from his brow.

And why not? He'd made the mistake of charging into a camp of Ardeel partisans, wearing a foreign uniform and riding atop the Prince's horse.

More blasts came.

"Ion!"


## II


Amalina had tracked Ivanti down. He was still inside his carriage with the birds, and sleeping soundly; though, on closer inspection, he appeared to be moaning. For some reason, finding him this way enraged her. She had nearly been killed, and here he was stretched out comfortably, seemingly carefree, hadn't even bothered to shave from the looks of it. As if he'd been laying here the whole week! She woke him by calling his name and with a tap. He came up immediately, with a martial snappiness, almost a shout, and like he might strike her.

"Ama! Ama!" He was out of his mind, clutching at her now. "What are you doing here! But ... but ..." He looked around the small interior suddenly relieved, or his eyes made some adjustment in that direction. He settled down, shivered in the cold and rubbed his hands together. He mumbled irritably: "Thank goodness … But what are you doing here?"

"What are *you* doing here?" she returned automatically, as if accusing him of something.

"Trying to save this country," he muttered in exhaustion, rubbing his eyes. "Now your turn."

"Are you mad at me?"

He smiled at her, blearily, "Heavens no. But you startled me. Not wise to do with a warring soldier, eh? But here, go on, what is it, Ama?"

"Warring?"

"Don't ask. Go on."

Amalina nodded, composing herself, then said, as she'd first intended, round-about, almost casually: "When you're done here in Netz—whatever it is you're doing—were you heading back to Korr?"

When he tried to sit up, he grabbed at his side as if he'd been shot there.

"Are you all right, Ion?"

He grumbled and waved her off.

She suspected now he *had* been laying there the whole time and had locked up his body. But she said, "Looks like you need a good cleaning, anyway."

"When *am* I going to be done here, Ama?" he said, dropping back on the cushions, sounding frustrated. "Ardeel doesn't ever seem to let go!"

"You have to go back to Korr," she pressed on, ignoring his curious statement before it annoyed her. "For me. Right away."

"Do I? Right now?" he replied with a cool aloofness, as if bemused by her urgency. "Can't, though. With all I've been doing, there's still some more work to be done before I—"

"I get all that. You told me you came to protect me, didn't you?"

"To rescue you."

"Well, what's the difference?"

"Listen, you imperious little—" he cut himself off.

She stared at thim.

"Sorry … still waking up. Yes, well …" he scratched his head and looked up at her. "Will you have it now?"

"You'd be a little late," snarled Amalina, still unhappy with his sleepy distraction, and apparent unconcern. "I almost died!"

"Eh?"

Ion stared at Amalina in a groggy amazement, as she told her story of the assassin. It came in a torrent of words, but she felt a bit numb when doing so. Ivanti's jaw clenched by the end of it.

"My god, Ama …" he said, suddenly awake, glancing at her hands repeatedly as if he wanted to hold them. "I—I'm so sorry. You can't blame me for that, can you? I didn't know! And how can I protect you at all hours when I'm trying to conduct a serious mission of my own? I can't be everywhere. I-I only just got back!"

"No, of course it isn't your fault, Ion," she said, seeing how suddenly distraught he looked, touching his shoulder to reassure him that that was not what she meant. But she couldn't help wonder: *What mission? And, where has* he *been?* "But we need to put a stop to this. If Cristine's father is still trying to have me killed, still sending his men after me, that means that Attila doesn't know yet, and he hasn't figured it out—"

"*Ama!*" choked Ion. "Cristine's father is—he's *what?*"

Amalina saw his astonishment and realized she hadn't told the lieutenant *everything.* She did so now. All about AXP. And how Alexandru Berzweck fit it.

"My god! My god! I can't believe it!" cried Ivanti, looking shattered, sitting up now despite the pain in his side. "Old Boss Berzweck? No! It's too much, Ama!"

"You don't believe me?"

"It's just …"

"Why do I always have to prove to you that I'm telling the truth?" she grumbled hotly in frustration. "I don't have time to go round in circles with you, they'll notice I'm gone. What will it take for you to believe me once in a while?"

"It just doesn't seem possible, Ama!"

"Do you want me to drag the dead body out for you? The man just tried to kill me," she pointed to the red marks around her neck, "just like the others who tried before, sent by *him.*"

"But why would he …?" He looked lost. "Why would the Boss …?"

"It doesn't matter! I already told Mr. Bronk someone was working with the Count. Then I sent him a note who it was. I thought he'd got it. He didn't, I guess?"

"I suppose not." Ivanti seemed to recall something as he stared at the marks on her neck. "He never said anything to me if he knew who it was, or he'd figured it out. But that's Bronk. But the Boss is the *man-of-the-acronym?* Well …"

"And so that is even more reason you need to go back. I can't just send a bird from here to tell him. Even if I could, who knows what happened to the first? Do you see? You have to go. You have to let him know, to warn him."

"Yes, of course," said Ivanti, his teeth gritting. "They *have* to know. The Boss, I'll be. When I'm done here, I promise, I'll—"

"He's going to keep sending people after me until he's stopped. You have to go *now.*"

"Listen, I can leave tomorrow," he said, looking roused but exhausted again. "That's the soonest … and the lastest. I promise you. But … the Boss, Ama? … I can't believe it."

"You don't believe me?"

"I believe you. I want to believe you—"

"*Want* to?"

He clenched his fists. "I'd kill him right now for you. On your word, Ama. But do you have proof?"

"Proof?"

"Not for me. But how will anyone else believe it? The Boss supports half the town, he cut the rent on the farm when my father needed it, he's so nice—"

"Ion!"

"So how will the others ever believe me, much less believe Attila, that it could *ever* be him, the ol' Boss? I don't know, I don't know. Even if I ran back there screaming bloody murder before I cut him down for you, they'd have me hanging from a tree in two minutes."

"You wouldn't be doing this just for me."

Ivanti rubbed his chin, or shook his head against his hand, troubled and bewildered by it all. "My heavens, Ama, always with the surprises …"

"They'd listen to Sadra."

"Sure, Sadra," said Ivanti, hopelessly. "Without proof, though … even her …This is The Boss."

"I know it's 'The Boss'," snarled Amalina, touching her neck.

"Do you have any? *Any* proof?"

"We'll get a coffin," said Amalina. "You'll take the killer back to Korr. Right back to the man who sent him. See what he has to say."

"That won't be proof, though, will it? Even if it's all true, it's just a body."

"'*If* it's all true?" said Amalina, offended again, now pointing to her neck.

"Not me, I mean! Look, Ama, to everyone else, they'll just see the body of some stranger, an innocent. He doesn't have a sign hanging around his neck that says what he did to you, or who told him to do it. So it won't convince anyone that ol' Boss Berzweck did something wrong, and it'll only be a provocation; it'd just be a message to the Boss that you're still alive. He'll act before anyone else would dare counter him. I'm telling you, you need *definite* proof he's the one if you're going to get—"

"*I* need it?"

"*We* do."

Amalina nodded. "Okay. Good. Evidence. I have it, all right. And I have it in writing."

"Do you really?"

"Maybe Mr. Bronk wouldn't want me to tell you everything, but I have practically a whole book of evidence."

"Then let's have it. Why didn't you say that before?"

"It's not as easy as that," smirked Amalina. She pointed at the bench. "I have to get it. Wait here."

"That's what I was doing," he said, mustering a grin as if to humor her—though dimmed with fatigue—as she hurried out of the carriage.

With an annoyed turn of thought, as Amalina darted up the icy street, blowing out clouds of breath, she pictured Ion leaning down into the cushions and slipping back into sleep. She thought heatedly: *He wouldn't dare!*

## 45

# Soft Evidence

Aklan was nowhere to be found. Genadie was gone too, along with the body. On her bed was a fresh, clean sheet. A couple crusty red stains on the floor showed something leaky had been dragged out.

"Are you all right, milady?" gasped 'Prince Castion', as Amalina came right to his table in the shadows of a nearby lounge.

"What's the matter with you?"

"Milady?"

"I asked you time and again to leave!"

"Did you, milady?" Jakob's sandy eyebrows went up near his chestnut wig in surprise, rucking up a hundred wrinkles between them, while his face lengthened in dismay.

"I sent you note after note!"

"Oh, that ..." he smiled. "Can't read, though, can I?"

"Why didn't you have your boy read them to you, then?"

"That's generous for you, milady, to think my little nephew has the education."

"He can't, either?"

"We Gurvils survive by our wits, milady."

"So then who wrote your notes?"

"The theatre manager where I got my clothes fancies himself an excellent romancer by letters, and was glad to do it for a few extra coin. But I'm doubting his talents at this point."

"And where did you get all this money? I'm not paying you. Don't tell me Aklan—"

Jakob tossed his gold coins on the table. There were a couple of Aklan's pieces, the rest were wooden slugs painted gold. "Bought them with the suit, eh? Theatre has bags of 'em. Works like a charm. The little crab gave me three of his good bits to work with, but I've only needed quarters of the first—"

"But if I'm not paying you more, if I told you you weren't needed, why are you continuing this ridiculous charade?"

"Because it's a fine idea!" declared Jakob with a quarter of his teeth in view. "Never thought I'd be able to live like a prince. And to court some real Ladies? How could I resist? Haven't eaten like this in ages, and the proprietors are all my friends, you know, so they're helping me along, hoping for some more of my gold, which I show them often enough. They haven't yet caught on how large my tab has grown."

He was quite satisfied, he even kicked back in his chair, throwing his hands behind his head and beaming.

"Well, you need to stop," said Amalina.

"But as you say, this has nothing to do with you or the crab. I'm doing this for the livin' of it."

"*Would* you like to get paid? I'd pay you double for some quick work."

"Six pieces?"

"Real ones," said Amalina. "You just have to leave off this ridiculousness, you're only making youself a fool, and do something real for me. Straight away."

Jakob's chair came down on all fours, and he clapped his hands together and rubbed them as if he might be trying to start a fire. His eyebrows lowered in concentration. "What've you in mind, milady?"

"Get to a carpenter. Have a coffin—I mean, have a box—made up." She told him the dimensions, where to have it delivered, and what instructions should be given to the man who received it. "Tell him he must wait for us. But do it now … right now."

"And might I still continue my fun, if for a little while longer, when I've done so?"

"If you value your life, you'll knock it off with the princesses before the Count returns, which could be any time. This is on you."

"But I can continue my role, otherwise."

"To your heart's content, Jakob. But you'll get paid your six gold when you've done what I asked, and have it delivered before nightfall. No excuses."

Jakob nodded gravely, but still looked surprised. "You sound a bit croaky, milady. You coming down with something?"

"I'm getting better by the minute. Now get going."

· · ·

Clutching her throat and feeling as if she'd never catch her breath—as if the assassin's hands were wringing her neck still—Amalina knocked urgently on Pia's door. She was let into the dark and cold room, and Pia, who moved slowly with bowed head, kept the door open for a little light, strictly for her friend. Though Amalina was bursting to launch into a passionate pitch, she held back, feeling it would disturb the solemn air within; a thick gloom which seemed to emanate directly from the sullen, drifting column of red hair.

"I need to speak to you," said Amalina in a quiet hush, trying to fit the mood.

"Good, I do, too," replied Pia softly, as she led Amalina to a sofa.

When they sat, Pia enveloped her. She seemed to have a strange power in her arms even if she didn't exactly radiate physical warmth. Her expression seemed lost. Amalina reflected on the strange, melancholy atmosphere, and recalled the last time she'd been in the room: Pia and the Count's conversation. All about her dreadful changes. *How could I have forgotten?*

"Oh?" said Amalina. She crunched her own energy down, a breathless. fist-clenching charge, to fit it neatly underneath some politeness. But her hands quivered as if cold. "Well then, you begin ..."

"I'm so sorry," began Pia.

By her weary, pained look, Amalina suddenly knew this was to be Pia's confession: how she was feeling, that the transformation had really taken hold of her now; the deeper emptiness she'd described to the Count. It was to be a frank admission to the darker side of her change, the unhumanness. But she already knew all this. Amalina squeezed her hand to encourage her to the point, if only to get to her own.

But Pia said: "I really am sorry, Katty ... I just can't get out during the day anymore. I think the sunlight rather did me in more than I expected, and I've needed the rest ..."

*No*, thought Amalina, *she's apologizing.*

"No, please," said Amalina, apologetic, too. "That isn't why I'm here. *I've been neglecting you* these past few days. And I feel awful about it. But now—"

"It's all right," laughed Pia breathily, patting her hand. Trying to calm the anxiousness she sensed in Amalina. "It's all right. Really, it's all right." She sighed and said, in a sad but resolute tone, and with some finality: "You don't have to lie to me anymore, Katty."

"But I'm not lying—I didn't—"

"I've already deceived myself quite enough already. Don't you think? I'll be happier if I don't flatter myself anymore with delusions ..." Pia ran a finger through her own hair, reflectively. "I don't know what I was thinking really ... believing in phantoms ..."

*Phantoms?* Amalina was confused. "I haven't lied to you, Pia, I really *do* care for you. But I'm actually here to—"

"Yes, well, *you* do," sighed Pia, lost in her own concerns, absorbed by its drama, ignorant of Amalina's. "But the person I thought you were is only partly there, isn't she?" Then she rushed in: "*And that's all right.* Only now that I know the truth, and you've been kind enough to show me the truth, I've been thinking ... I'm happy to go." She nodded. "I'll be leaving. Which is what you've been asking of me all along, but I haven't listened."

"Leaving?"

"Why would I stay where I'm not wanted?" said Pia. "Not *really* wanted. So that's fine, that's good. I can go home—while I still can, as you say. And there I'll become myself. Whatever it is I'm becoming. And without having to worry about being thrown up on some wheel in a dungeon, whatever *that* is. I'll just enjoy myself, and my home, and my family, and maybe you'll come visit?"

"Oh, of course, absolutely—"

Then Amalina stopped and wondered if this wasn't some strange test.

"Right." Pia smiled cynically and shook her head, her pretty pink lips curled as if she'd scented a rotten lie. "That's fine. You'll help me on my way *out*, anyway, I suppose. Sorry I couldn't assist with your plans at the castle, after all. All the better I didn't try. I'll just see if I can't lend you a hand in moving some of these girls out of here while I can. That's good. That's fine. I mean, you *are* getting what you've always wanted, isn't it? Everyone out? Even me?"

"Thank you," was all Amalina could find to say, still feeling somewhat breathless. It didn't matter if it was a test. It would work. "But, you see, Pia, something's happened—just now, something important ..."

· · ·

Amalina rehashed her attack for a third time that morning, feeling ever more tired than before, though with throbs of distressed energy she summoned and relived vividly the smell and feel of the killer's fishy hands on her, throttling her. Pia hugged her tighter as the story went on.

When she was done explaining, Amalina sat back, clasped Pia's hands, and laid out her new proposal: "Pia ... what you were just saying ... you *can* leave Ardeel, and I can help. I have a man riding to Korr in the morning with some boxes. You'll stay in one—to avoid the sun, you see—and then that box will be posted to Rome. You'll be home before two weeks are out. Isn't that wonderful?"

Pia's chin slowly dropped to her chest, in a contemplative silence.

"I can't go with you right away," said Amalina, her voice low and reassuring, "not now. It's true. That's true. But I promise I'll follow soon after. I *do* need you to do this. You're the only one who can help me. There's a book back at the castle that must be brought to Korr. It will help them prove who's collaborating with the Count." She added: " ... having innocent girls killed—the man who wants *me* killed. If he isn't stopped, he'll always be after me. You understand?"

"You want me to deliver this book for you?"

"Just drop it off on your way out of the country. Give them the book and the codes, and they will understand everything. It will be a good thing. A very good thing. You trust me, don't you?"

"Of course. But I still don't understand why you want me to do this—"

"You can leap over the castle walls, can't you? You're that strong, didn't you tell me?"

"Yes, I do, I did. I can."

"You can get back to the castle faster than a horse, I think. And return here with what we need before the sun rises tomorrow, no? And you can do it without anyone seeing you?"

"Well, maybe ..."

"You want to see your family again, don't you? Your home country? Little Ge Ge?"

"My dog's name is Giussepina, actually." Pia said this so mournfully it was as if the pup was lost in time. "Ge Ge is what I called her."

"Giussepina, that's a pretty name," said Amalina, trying to cover her impatience. "But you do want to see her again, and you can. That's what you were saying. If the sun is beginning to burn you, and while Count Tepsji is away, this might be your only chance to escape; before it's too late. Do you understand? This is not *just* for me, but for you, too."

"I ... I suppose it is possible," said Pia, warily. "And didn't I already say yes?"

• • •

It was simple enough for Amalina to break away from her other companions. She told the Ladies she was going to meet with the apiary to secure some queen bees and some hives. Nobody was interested in finding out what such a natural experience was like, so they waved goodbye to their host and closed ranks into themselves. Amalina met Pia later on the darkening street.

"Let's hurry," encouraged Amalina.

• • •

"I've already put the queens snug in the skecs," the Master Apiar told Amalina a quarter hour later, intrigued by her attentiveness. "You shouldn't have any problem this spring, I should hope. Though one never knows. How did you get interested in honeymaking, may I ask, Countess?"

"Books," said Amalina. "Books on bees. There shouldn't be any problem if I don't keep them inside the castle but in a nearby woods?"

"Will you be tending to them? Is there a good stretch of flowers relatively close? They pretty much take care of themselves. But if they'll be unprotected up there in the mountains, I suggest you hang the skecs from the end of a tall branch so the bears can't get at them. Or at them easily, anyway."

Amalina didn't have to pay, the Count had settled everything for her. He'd kept his word, Pia helpfully noted for her. She and Pia left the bee keeper's small cabin, carrying between them five skecs, which looked like large, upside down wicker baskets.

"Good," said Amalina, "Now we only have to visit the carriage house, and put these in the castle sleigh for storage. If the timing is right …"

. . .

Ivanti Vokent was waiting for them beside his carriage, stamping his feet on the ground to warm his legs. He'd shaved and polished up in the hours between, and looked surprised at Amalina's tall, red-headed friend. It was as if seeing the two together—the common girl he knew from long ago and a highborn Lady lugging baskets together in Ardeel—was a sheer impossibility.

"Lieutenant Ivanti Ion Vokent," introduced Amalina, "this is Lady Pia Lampeda of Rome, Italy."

Ivanti clacked the heels of his boots together and bowed deep at the waist, which looked very soldierly even with the plain clothes he was now wearing. After a lingering pause, Pia held out her hand for a kiss, which Ivanti delivered with the expertise of an officer and a ladiesman.

"Lady Pia, this is Lieutenant Vokent … who will be doing me a great favor, though he doesn't know it yet."

"Oh?" Ivanti tipped back his long-brimmed hat and raised his handsome eyebrow to Amalina. "Something more? I assume it has to do with this long box Jakob dropped off? Thought it was a coffin. And these baskets …?"

"As it happens, Pia's people are in Korr waiting to receive her. Since you're returning there, and leaving in the early morning tomorrow—"

"At the latest, Katrina. I'd prefer to be on my way tonight."

"But you'll wait to leave, however long, *for her*." At this, he nodded his acceptance. "And she will ride with you in that box."

Ivanti gave Pia another long stare, sizing up the young woman who would be riding with him for the next day or so. But—

"In the box?" he asked curiously, unbelieving.

"She can't be seen," cautioned Amalina. "There's an intrigue and her life might be in danger anywhere along the route. As it is, someone made an attempt on her months ago, which she barely escaped. She will be traveling as a piece of stored luggage. You are not to open that box until you reach Korr, do you understand?"

Ion half smiled, regarding Amalina's no-nonsense delivery with affection, because it was a ridiculous request. "Whatever you like. But not until Korr? It's a long trip for a carriage in the winter time."

"I'll be fine," said Pia. "Just open it when we get there. Um, not in the daylight, um, where I can be seen. Only at night."

"Of course. You've only to holler and I will open the sarcophagus sooner. Well then, shall we shut you up now? or later, you said…?"

"'Or'," said Amalina. "She'll make her excuses to Tepsji's people and slip out tonight. Late tonight. You *will* wait for her?"

"Of course. I'm not ready to go yet, either. A few more hours, at least. But meet me at the St. Grigori church, then. Everything will be ready and we can leave when you arrive. The quicker the better. But don't be *too* long, I must return to Korr as soon as I can. I've stayed long enough myself and am sure to be in trouble if I make it any later. As it is, I'll be riding straight on, no stops for dining, or sleeping at inns, only to allow rest for the horses, or to switch them out if I can. Speed is most crucial here, you understand."

Amalina could tell he was worrying about Boss Berzweck running loose inside Attila's revolution. Along those lines, she said: "Lady Lampeda will also be bringing *something* with her for, um … for you all."

"That thing you were telling me about before?" He looked at her blandly with a nod. "The *proof*? I thought these baskets—"

"What she brings is very important to *the Cause*, yes," she allowed. "But you'll see. When you get to Korr, take Pia to the bakery, gather everyone important—not the Boss, of course. Pia will reveal at once, to everyone there, what we have, all the evidence, and then there will be no question of Boss Berzweck's guilt."

Ivanti gave Pia another surprised look. He sized her up once more, trying to gauge her importance, trying to understand how someone who looked like her—a young, regal Roman daughter with wild red hair and entrancing green eyes—would have crucial information to an Ardeelian revolution. And why had Amalina taken her into her confidence? Did Attila know about this one, too? He'd never mentioned.

"And these pretty baskets?" he asked.

"A hobby, nothing more. She and what she brings tonight is all you have to worry about, and to look after."

"Very well."

"You'll wait for her, Ion?"

"Of course, Amalina. I mean … Well, I mean … *Countess*." He clicked his heels again—which looked silly but charming to the two ladies—and bowed.

"Thank you for doing this favor for me," said Amalina to Pia as they walked back to the hotel.

"I'm also doing this for me," smiled Pia, her mood definitely lightening. "Am I not?"

46

## The Chrysalis

With one leap, Princess Pia Lampeda was thirty feet into the air, the wind whipping her hair like a long red flag, the ends snapping loudly. Though there was a fluffy layer of snow to cushion her impact when she came down, when she landed it hurt. But the pain didn't slow Pia or caution her to limit her effort. Instead, she kicked off from the ground ever fiercer, pushing hard into the twinkling sky.

The waxing gibbous moon lit the edge of the mountain before her. Where the snow remained, it glowed, making the mountain's ridges look like a weird set of grey fangs gnashing down onto some upthrust, lighter, patchy and scraggier, white ones. Underneath the canopy of the forest, even at her extreme height, where Pia felt she was elongating into a ribbon, she could sense all the life squirming below. From insects to birds to bats, to snakes to rodents to wildcats, to wolves to horses to deer and to other big game. Even beyond the thrumming of hearts and bodies pushing through the snow and underbrush, the straggling plants and lichen spoke to her with their scents. The mountain itself was alive with babbling waters, crackling ice, wailing winds, grinding stone, and tumbling snow and earth.

This land wasn't the city of Rome. Being so lonely and isolated, it was definitively not her birthplace, her home. And yet somehow, with every small, quiet thing presently flooding-to-overflowing her senses, she felt an attachment to the severe landscape like she'd never experienced before. Never mind Katarina, or her servants, or even down to her fellow citywoman, Margeta. The soul of the Ardeelian land itself was—somehow— becoming her dearest friend.

And she no longer questioned how impossible it was what she was now, very much, doing. It was completely natural to be speeding faster than any race horse, bounding higher than the mountaintops, barely perceiving the razor sharp winds of winter, or registering or submitting to the pain of doing so. If she could describe the experience it was exhilarating, intoxicating. There was, as always, the undeniable emptiness inside her, and fatigue, like a vacuum pulling in on itself, but this was also life. If only there were a way to explain to Katarina, or have her somehow experience the wondrous singularity with the natural world, so that she would not be so hesitant and frightened of the change!

Pia didn't leave this queer euphoria until she'd landed atop the castle and entered through the window into Katarina's room.

She found the book almost immediately. It was where Katarina had told her it might be, stuffed in the back of the boy's tall cabinet, but it stood out on its own. AXP in bright polished steel, the letters as large as her own hand, and carrying the trace herbal scent of Count Tepsji. She threw it open on the desk and studied the tiny rectangles of paper glued into it. Yes, and there were the odd little scribblings she couldn't read but strangely almost make sense of, a tickling in the back of her mind. And there were the pretty drawings of young women looking pleasing and innocent. *The dead.*

The thought of Count Tepsji ripping their throats out, the blood flowing everywhere, sent a shudder of pleasure throughout Pia's body. It was a surprising thrill, but a thrill nonetheless. Not displeasurable nor unwanted, really. And what he'd done to them was almost understandable, no? Just a natural act. Something Pia could do. And would do, depending on the circumstances. That these innocent girls should die—*oh, in such a glorious, showering fashion!*—was a cruel thing. But nature was cruel sometimes. And to stand the victor in a life or death struggle was a secret, shameful pleasure beyond all compare. Very nearly sexual. No wonder religion did its best to snuff out such thoughts.

Pia shut the feeling away on her own. She slammed Boss Berzweck's book and turned. She didn't want to touch it, but she knew the book itself wasn't the problem. It was the lust for blood, and the power within. Blood was the only way to fill the aching void inside her. It was unnatural to the Pia-that-once-had-been; the daughter to godly, pious parents. But she had broken out of that shell like a butterfly from its cocoon. She was something *greater-than* now.

*But*, she thought coolly, *that doesn't mean I can't retain the virtues of right and wrong. I'm not an animal. I can live, still, with the idea of love; and with solid moral principles, whatever I've become.*

She didn't know what she was. From what Katty had told her, even Count Tepsji hadn't known what he was until he'd read the diary of another such creature, one who'd been more introspective and daring than he.

*And so, like a fool, should I just take this new life as I find it? Or perhaps worse, take my instruction from one who is just as blind? Or should I proceed as an adult, being introspective and as daring as I can allow, to learn what my new life really means?*

She left Katarina's room and wound her way down, almost like dreaming, into the Count's counting house and further down to the message center. She almost laughed as she spun around the room, taking in all the shelves with their mounds of papers; so easy to see, though there wasn't a single source of light. How could this be? She should be blind there! But it felt like her eyes had expanded into two massive globes, with irises like an owl's and dilated so that only a strip of green color showed around them.

There was a flutter in her mind when she stopped twirling about. In another time and place, it would have been a thought; something like, "Jesus, what the hell am I doing?" and/or "Never mind *him*! Why am *I* doing this for *her*? Why so much effort for someone when I don't even know if she really loves me? And do I even care if she does? Do I even *really* care?" Pia had created an elaborate reasoning for why she loved the girl, and it sounded very nice. But getting right down to it, wasn't it only a good sounding reason to use because it rang that much better than something as common, artless, and vulgar as appreciating the size and shape of her breasts, marveling at her hips, enjoying the strange spark in her brown eyes, the odd sensation at her well-muscled forearms and hands, and her eagerness? It wasn't anger as such, this feeling within Pia, but something like frustration, when butted against the limitless power and freedom stirring inside her. *Why do anything for anyone else, anymore?*

The storm within Pia passed after a few minutes.

She exited the message center and went deeper: to find the other women who were turning.

. . .

Up, then down. Up, then down.

Up …oh, yes … then down.

It's never ending, this turning and turning. How long has it been? Why won't it stop? I want to scream, but I can't. But wait …

… a sound. Again it approaches. Someone … is someone there? Has that brat returned? She never comes. She just left … she never left … is she still here?

Amalina.

I will kill her.

Just let me loose, girl! Let me loose!

*"What is this?" said an unfamiliar voice. "What are you doing?"*

My—my mouth … it no longer burns …

*"Katarina showed me," said another.*

A voice who'd been here before, too. Arguing, wasn't it?

Hold on, I can breath. I can talk …

*"But that doesn't answer the question," said a third. "Who is she?"*

I can scream …

*"She is us."*

I SCREAM!

. . .

"Quiet!" hissed Pia. She slapped the head with the end of the silver chain. Now it was the dessicated head's turn to hiss. It sounded like a serpent. "Be quiet or I'll throw the chain right back in your mouth."

The head tried to open its eyes: the lids fluttered, the hanging eyes rolled on its withered cheeks. And it lolled drunkenly, unable to orient itself with the constant turn of the wheel.

"Whooo?" its voice scraped drily.

No one else appeared to want to speak up.

"We are three sisters," said Pia. "*Your* sisters."

"Have I sisters? I don't remember. It's been so long. No, I don't have any."

"Why are you here on this wheel? What did you do?"

"Get me off," it said greedily.

Anne Brignol stepped forward with two powerful strides. "Tell us what happened. Why does Count Tepsji keep you this way?"

"Count Tepsji?" it said in drunken wonder. "Is that his name? Oh, yes. Count Tepsji. Count Tepsji ... *Count Tepsji!*"

"Shut up," said Erin Epris. "Tell us what we want to know, woman."

The woman told them a story, in her dizzy delivery, of being ravaged by some monster at the edge of a moonlit falls. She had managed to survive, only to become a monster herself. And she vowed to find him, and punish him for doing this to her. He had no remorse. He wouldn't even kill her when he'd bested her, but put her up on this wheel, to examine her; to be condemned to a deathless torture.

"Unless ..." the head said. "There are *three* of you? *Sisters*? Are you *my* sisters? Or you're tainted then, having suffered the same indignity as I, so long ago; at the beginning of time itself?"

"We've heard enough." Epris motioned for Pia to replace the silver chain over the woman's mouth.

"Noooo," the head looked like it was trying to wriggle free of its body, its neck extending, but gravity and the wheel's ceaseless turning had it in an invisible cage. It tried to open its eyes, as it cried out blindly, "Sisters. *Sistersss*. Do not leave me! Listen! When I was alone, I was not strong enough. But together, we can stop him. Listen to your hearts. Your innocent hearts, dearest sisters! Reap this monster from the world, let us. Yes, let us do this good thing, so that no one else may be corrupted, and the men of god suffer."

"There's a thought." Epris motioned again, and this time Pia obeyed. As the woman on the wheel knew what was coming, she let out a tremendous wail. But, with a rapid speed even Pia could not believe, and the dexterity of a spider—and though hampered with thick leather gloves—she strung the silver chain around the woman's head, between her teeth, and fixed it in place so she could no longer move her head or use her mouth. The gut-wrenching wail choked and died away.

"Why did you show us this?" Anne Brignol questioned Pia.

"You both needed to see her," said Pia, removing the gloves. "To know what he's capable of."

"It's disgusting."

"I agree."

They left the room and shut the door. As they returned to their own lower cellar chambers, the squat, mildewy rooms, they engaged in a quiet conversation.

"But did you hear what she said?" said Epris. "The ugly little bitch isn't wrong."

"What do you mean?"

"*He* put her there, but he can't put us all there. Not if we don't let him. We are more than enough to set him right, if we want."

"I think he's much stronger than all of us together," said Pia.

"He might be stronger," sneered Epris, "but there are more of us. Did you ever hit a bee hive? One bee is nothing, but a swarm will kill you, no matter how strong you are."

Pia fell into musing at the mention of bees.

"Are you saying we should *kill* him?" asked Brignol after a moment, in disbelief. "After all he has done for us? How nice he's been? What power he has generously shared?"

"You've seen what he can do," hissed Epris now, pointing back toward the distant captive, bound and gagged. "He might have been nice to us, but he can be as cruel as a despot. And he will rule us if we aren't careful. Take away our dreams."

"What a scared little child you still are, Lady Epris," said Brignol. "I won't even consider what you're proposing. It is ungrateful."

"I didn't say kill him in his sleep. But if he were to go after one of us, as he did that one in there on the wheel, I say we should all stick together. Hm? What do you say?"

Pia heard in Epris' words something similar to her lovely Kat's words—well, in *Amalina's* words, wasn't it?

"I just wanted you both to know everything," said Pia, apologetically. "Not call for a council of war and treason. We should just be wary of what we're getting into."

"It's too late," scoffed Epris.

"No, I don't think so," said Pia. "We're changing, it's true. But we get to have a voice in our own destiny."

"Have we?" Erin Epris was livid and her face twisted angrily. "I think we made the one choice we were given. But now, here we are."

"What I'm saying is we don't have to do everything we're told. Not by our new nature, and certainly not by him. There are no rules. That hunger is there. Even that woman on the wheel has it. It's inside us now, driving us. But so are many *other* things driving us."

"What are you blathering about?" snarled Epris. "Get to the point."

"You *can* thrive by not killing, you know," said Pia, looking each woman in the eye. "Have you listened to Katty at all?"

The two ladies moaned.

"Do you see what he's doing to Cristine?" continued Pia, patiently, undeterred. "Just a little here and there. We can do that to anyone, too. Sip by sip. Quietly, quietly. *Secretly*. And anywhere we like. Nobody will have to know what we are. And nobody will have to die."

"Yes. Well. I suppose," said Brignol. "We don't really know, do we? What comes, I mean."

"But we can try. And *I* will try, of course. It's not a matter of being good or bad anymore. That time is past. But to be civil and joyous of life. To be civilized. Well, I *can* try. And why not?"

"Why are you telling us all this?" said Erin Epris. "You think just because you were the first that you're better than us?"

"Just like Noka?" added Brignol, suspiciously. "Trying to be better than us?"

"I already told you what this is about," said Pia. "If you'd listen. If we're going to stay here together—"

"*If?* Where are we going otherwise?"

"*If we're going to stay here*," repeated Pia, "we will have a great and wonderful future together. But only as long as we can pull together like a decent family. Set a good course for ourselves."

"No," said Epris, "not Noka, then. You're beginning to sound like Margeta. Have you been taking religious instruction?"

"I get what Pia's talking about," said Brignol. "And she's right. It's four against one now, five including the old hag on the wheel. Six if we count Cristine when he finally turns her. We can call the shots in this castle, and not have to be treated like a Vizier's concubines. Tepsji made us, but he doesn't own us."

"That's true," said Pia hopefully, "And with the six of us—"

"No, there are four of us," said Anne Brignol, tossing back her head, imperiously contradicting herself. "Forget the old hag, and forget that merchant's daughter. If it comes to it, it's us alone." Brignol curled he lip over a solid line of vicious teeth, "I mean, the merchant's daughter? She's a *merchant's* daughter, and our old boy's doing her as he is just to please Katty.

And the hag? She was a bit of a mistake, wasn't she? I mean, look at her. She's old and ugly. We're young and pretty. We still have our titles. I mean, he *chose* us for this new era. *We* are the chosen ones."

"That's true," murmured Epris. "Better tell Nok-Nok about this when she gets back. And whatever we do, we should probably find a way to get rid of that wheel so he can't do that to any of us."

"And throw out the old hag with it," said Brignol, with a harsh smirk. "She's a bit pointless."

As their cruel and calculating conversation carried on, they weren't aware someone was still listening to their every word, and marking it for later.

## 47

## Always an Answer to Everything

Lieutenant Ivanti Ion Vokent watched the stretch of moonlit street outside the St. Grigori church and played with the horse whip impatiently as he waited for Amalina's friend to come. He could still hear the low groans and steady, mechanical movements along the fence, the monotony of it—could still feel the effort in his arms, back, and his sticky, sweated-through clothes—though the work had ended hours ago. Strangely, the echo of their work seemed to have moved down the street, to the other side of the town, long after the bell.

"You're satisfied with what I've given you?" asked the Cardinal, beside him, wringing his hands to warm them. "Or will he be requiring more?"

"You've delivered what Mr. Bronk asked for—at this time, anyway," said Ivanti, feeling uncomfortable standing this close to a man of such high religious stature; even without Rosczy's warning against the Cardinal himself. For the lieutenant, generals were one thing, they were men. Men of god, however, they were something else altogether. He'd seen the violent results of holy fervor among his comrades. He'd heard tales of the extreme inhuman acts demanded by men who professed to be on speaking terms with God. General Volantes's description of what had happened at Magdeburg against the Protestants had put him off involvement with the devout of any kind; and put him off more so to those linked to the Roman Orthodoxy; as the Cardinal of Netz was. Adhering to Rosczy's advice, Ivanti had already turned down the Cardinal's offer for food or drink several times, and said he'd wait outside, where he could watch his long coach, anxious horses, and the loaded-down trailing wagon. "Thank you very much, your eminence."

"It feels strange to have the old iron back in place," murmured the Cardinal, looking across at the gate. "But I'm sure from your perspective, it was exhausting making the switch."

"I'm quite all right, your eminence. Thank you."

"Who exactly are you waiting for?"

"To be honest, I don't know," Ivanti said with a shy smile.

"I see ... following orders. Mr. Bronk is secretive in his way, isn't he?"

"I don't know him very well, to be honest."

"A good, honest lad," said the Cardinal. "But he's told you the secret, Lieutenant Vokent?"

"About?"

"About why silver is required?"

"I think I understand."

"Without this particular substance our church might not have withstood our common adversary." The Cardinal lifted his manicured eyebrow at Ivanti. "Mr. Bronk couldn't have told you *that* part of it, of course. He is unaware of our entire history. I've never told *him*."

"Oh."

"I trust you to keep my confidence, Lt. Vokent. I'm sharing it with you because you are a military man, and you're a strong youth of true Ardeelian blood, and so you might appreciate these facts."

"Yes, your eminence."

"You're a good, loyal boy, aren't you? Honest and true."

"Yes, your eminence."

"The Knight of Ardeel almost died on our grounds you know. In the lake. The silver in it, you see. There is silver in the surrounding mountains and it runs off into our lake. The bishop found him on the shore one night, screaming, crying out in pain. His body mostly shriveled, like a side of over-salted pork. The Knight was still strong enough—or the bishop too frightened, or too principled—for the bishop to take advantage and kill him in this vulnerable position. The Knight mended in time, unaware of the cause for his weakness against these waters. The bishop figured it out soon enough, however. Which is why he had our iron gates and fences replaced with silver and blacked it over. And to this day our acolytes spread water from the lake over our grounds, thinking it a holy rite; and once-upon-a time they did the same onto the church; and now it's onto this Cathedral being built over it. When the Knight would attempt to enter, he always found himself weakened and ailing. He stopped his arrogant presumption after awhile, without knowing why. The bishop had done a clever thing."

Ivanti didn't know what to say. He nodded and hoped the beautiful, ethereal Roman Lady would show before long. He needed to leave as soon as he could. But the Cardinal's presence made the time pass ever so much slower and uncomfortably. *Remember,* he thought to himself, *Mr. Bronk told you to tell nothing to the Cardinal he should not know. Well, what the hell* doesn't *he know?* He knew more than Bronk, anyway.

Attila's nebulous order for tight lips around the Cardinal of Netz, and Rosczy's dire warnings against the Cardinal, while idling next to the Cardinal himself, cracked the lieutenant's patience a little.

"Then how'd he sneak in?" asked Ivanti, sounding like a casual question.

"*He* sneak in where?"

"I thought he was tearing apart your yard. And the courageous hero, Neku Jonker, died in a stand against him."

"Neku Jonker!" the Cardinal exclaimed in surprise. Then he settled down in an artificial way, and patted his sleeves. "Ah, yes, Neku. A hero ... I suppose. From the way some folk tell it. Rumors don't always live up to the reality of course. Our opponent did gain access to these grounds, but only because Neku hadn't been the most diligent of our attendants. He drank, you see. If he hadn't been such a drunkard we would have been spared the inciting problem. So, a hero? Well, I can allow that Neku's actions, and his memory, have furnished the means to overcome this Count Tepsji. But let us not set his pedestal too high."

"Oh, no, your eminence. I'd only heard that Neku ..." but his words trailed off, unsure what exactly he understood of the situation. From the way he had been told the story, Ivanti'd pictured Neku a seven foot tall marvel holding back the monster with one hand. But that couldn't be true. And still, how had the Count entered if the grounds were poisoned to him?

The Cardinal filled in the silence: "You see, it is *my* church, the Roman Church, the true orthodoxy of Ardeel and its peoples, who have stood bravely against the forces arrayed against us. The natural and unnatural; all things alien."

"I suppose so," said Ivanti. By the way the old man kept blabbing on, the way he seemed to be looking at him expectantly, Ivanti now wondered if the Cardinal was waiting for something from him. *Do I need to kiss his hand to get him to leave?* "Yes, your eminence."

"Some even consider the Count as a bulwark against our enemies, of Ardeel." The Cardinal clucked his tongue. "The fables the older folk push around our land have him responsible for driving the Ottomans out of these, our mountains. You've heard the stories, I'm sure. But if he were the true patriot, why did he allow the Germanian invasion of our beloved country?"

After time passed, Ivanti realized he was supposed to offer an opinion. Or admit his ignorance. "I don't know, sir. I mean, your eminence."

"I've spoken to him, you know; this Count Tepsji, the Knight of Ardeel. As have the bishops of this church before me. *Did* you know that? Were you *aware?*"

"Really, sir?" he said, duly impressed. "Was he frightening?"

"That's not the point. The point is: the fathers of this church have never shrunk from our duties, even when confronting monsters."

"I had no doubt, your eminence." It never hurt to butter people up, or so Volante had told him. "You're on the side of heaven and the righteous."

"I am glad you see it that way, Lieutenant: Properly."

After another long pause, Ivanti asked: "So why did he allow the invasion? He could have thrown Germania back too, like the Ottomans, couldn't he?"

"He can do anything he wants. But you've spent time in foreign armies, fought their wars all over the continent. *You've* kept their company. Dare I say, also enjoyed it?"

"I guess I have. But I had little choice in it, your eminence. I was conscripted. And my Papa didn't have to feed me anymore if I left."

"Spoken like a faithful son of Ardeel," clucked the Cardinal, proudly, "whose loyalty still lays with his brethren, no matter how far he has traveled."

"Yes, your eminence."

The Cardinal nodded with satisfaction.

"But *was* there an answer to why? Why did he let the German invasion succeed instead of throwing them out?"

The Cardinal's face drooped. "Well, that is a private conversation between the Count and I."

"Oh! Yes, your eminence. I didn't mean—"

"Between you and I, Lieutenant?" interrupted the Cardinal, a look of intrigue on his face, "he had his reasons. Because the people of this country turned their backs on him, and in their intransigence they forgot their history. When the time came, he did not see why he should protect us. He thought we deserved to be conquered and to know what it felt like to be under foreign subjugation for a generation or two, so we knew what oppression really feels like."

"Oh, I see," said Ivanti.

"And after repelling the Ottomans he became more circumspect about patriotic sentiment. He would rather have a stronger western element controlling the land than an eastern exotic."

Ivanti nodded politely, but ground his teeth. He could take no more. He was already so inexcusably late in his delivery he would be dressed down by Attila when he reached Korr. And they had to be told the outstanding information he now held about the clashing silver armies in the south, and warned about Boss Berzweck. This added discomfort, the Cardinal's secret confessions, wasn't worth it. The lieutenant would give Amalina's Lady Lampeda another quarter hour to show. If she didn't, too bad. Beautiful or not, she could hire a coach like anyone else. He would leave without her.

. . .

*The impertinence*, thought the Cardinal as he marched slowly back to his room. *How easily he ignored you! It seems there's no hope. Even Rosczy, of all people, has abandoned me, scurried off to who knows where? No one is listening anymore. I am alone. So then Attila and his Protestant upstarts—and the foreigners—have won the day. And for all I'm giving up, handing over the silver, opening the grounds to trespass, stripping the Cathedral of its protection and exposing myself! For what? What's left for me in my vulnerable state?*

He grinned cleverly at a sudden thought: *Send a note to the governor! Redirect the King's Army from their wanderings in the south and instead throw them right against Attila and his army of fools in Korr. It shouldn't take much convincing. A little lie or two for that fat imbecile to get the Prince riled against Attila Bronk. The King's Army will not only smash them to pieces, but by doing so should gain me good favor with Count Tepsji, while also ridding me of an ungrateful rival. Yes, delicious: balance the scales and bring things back to normal.*

His inspiration ran on: *Then the Prince will learn—by innocent but incessant rumors whispered 'round his ears—how the information against the revolutionary had been supplied by* me, *the Cardinal of Netz; who is in touch with the soul of the people and knows all! And he will naturally ask himself, 'if that is true, then what's the purpose of having a governor here? The Cardinal can rule alone.'*

*And the Count, appreciating my gift of vanquishing the revolution without his needing lift a finger, will fall steadily, through the years, to my continued reminders of it, and he might then, at some point, become malleable, and bestow on me the most amazing gift, if I can bring myself to accept it. Certainly he would be willing to share the world with me, just as I would him. Didn't he call me a friend? Friends would do such a thing. Yes. Yes, very good.*

*You see,* thought the Cardinal, as he rubbed his manicured beard with intense satisfaction, *there is always an answer to everything.*

48

## The Innocents

### I

Somewhere in the night a strange hush fell on the hotel. The kind of silence that spoke of an odd pressure which made things seem outwardly calm but held inside it the hint of an invisible working. Amalina could picture a great snowstorm silently dumping yards of snow on the city, to be discovered in the morning. Or was it something else? Had this sensation just begun, or had it been there for a while and she'd just noticed?

Amalina felt wetness in the bed covers. She worried blood had seeped up from the mattress. When she opened her eyes, in the dim candlelight she saw Aklan's face, looking cherubic in his sleep. Wearing his jacket, he wasn't bothered by the damp. He was curled up on his side, facing her, just as he'd fallen asleep many hours before. She remembered now, how Aklan had sighed as he entered the bedroom and, without bothering to remove his snow-covered cloak, threw himself down on the bed.

. . .

"You're welcome," he'd sighed in exhaustion.

"Where have you been?"

"Doing your bidding, of course, Pretty Princess," he sighed again, forlorn. "As you wish."

"*My* bidding?" Amalina felt like she was the Count facing an unhappy subordinate. "I hope you don't feel I *force* you to do things."

"I was getting the water from the lake," explained Aklan. "About a dozen bottles's worth. Wasn't easy, had to get all the way around that church fence, which is pretty long you know. And there were men working on it off-and-on all evening, had to keep out of sight. And then had to break through the ice. Frozen over. Then I had to haul them back and hide them in our sleigh without being seen; especially by the rat, Genadie. He *lives* in that thing, I think." Aklan sighed for the third time, the longest yet. "But I did it even without that bone. Started the afternoon by dispatching a murderer for you, saving your life in the process, ended it by gathering all what you need in the freezing cold, dunking my hands in the lake until the bottles and my hands were icicles. That's right: killed for you, got silver water for you. What more *is* there to do?"

*Before you love me?* seemed to have been left off, but lingered in the air between them, anyway.

"I really do hope you don't feel I force you to do things," she said.

Aklan let a long time pass, he stared blankly at the ceiling. Amalina moved to speak again, to put her statement to him a third time, but he turned to her. He grinned.

"What?" asked Amalina, confused by his change in attitude.

"There's a problem with your plan, Pretty Princess," he continued to grin.

"What's that?"

"Your big plan with all the silver on the chandelier," he said. "Thought of it while I was filling them bottles. So we lower the hall's big chandelier to load all this silver and bottles of water onto it, right? and wrap the iron chains up with some new silver chains, right? But even if I wrap those silver chains with sleeves of black cloth—for them sleeves to slide off when the chandelier is dropped?—that cloth also has to be tied real tight to the pulley above. That way the sleeves are stripped away when everything comes down, because they're still holding to the pulley block … at the ceiling. We can't do that last little part with the chandelier on the ground. We can only tie the cloth to the block by going right up there, *all the way up there*, when the chandelier's already in place."

Amalina made a face. "I hadn't thought of that."

"No, you hadn't." He giggled. "That'll be pretty tricky. Not to mention not spilling what's sitting on the wheel by accidentally bumping into it, or swinging it."

"But I'm sure it can be done," said Amalina, trying to picture it being done. How? By crawling up the thick iron holding-chain at the release point on the wall, where it's pulled taught? Or some tall ladder? "It can be."

"Get *all* the way up there? when the chandelier is hanging loose in the air? And can swing free … so you can't put a ladder to it?"

"Yes."

"I don't see Pils or Anka trying."

"I wouldn't trust them to."

Aklan gulped. "So you mean *me*, Pretty Princess?"

"I didn't mean anything," she said.

"But you're going to need me to do it."

"I didn't say that. I could do it. I was just coming up with a solution right now."

Aklan scrunched his face disagreeably. "Almost fell to my death when I went out the privy drain, remember that? Can't swear I like heights much anymore. I'd be scared. Very"

"Well it's a good thing I'm not *making* you do it," hummed Amalina. But who *would* do it?

"You shouldn't, Princess. How're you going to explain if you're caught up there? Especially with all that silver? You *can't* do it, eh? I wouldn't have it."

"Well, if you can't, and Pils and Anka can't, and now you say I can't, who else is there? Not Genadie."

"No, Princess," murmured Aklan. "I didn't say I *can't* do it. I just said how tough it would be for me if I did."

"I'm telling you, very clearly, that I'm not forcing you to do anything, Aklan. I won't have anyone do anything I wouldn't do myself."

"*Would* you do it?" he asked, looking at her with his goofy smile, admiring her. "If you could?"

"If I have to, I'll do anything. Well, why not?"

"Of course you would. So you think I wouldn't?" Aklan questioned her hotly. "After all I've done for you already? Didn't I just recount all I did for you just today? Of course I'll do it!"

Amalina blew out a frustrated breath. "What exactly is this conversation about?"

But she knew it already. He was just underlining his heroics. Heroics done *for* her. And pulling off a dangerous stunt like tying socks around the silver chains and then attaching them to the pulley block all the way up on the great hall's ceiling would be nerve-wracking, even if someone held a ladder beneath you. But this would have to be done without help, silently, secretly, without a ladder. And if caught, especially by the house guard or the Count himself, it could mean death. Aklan wagged his bushy blond brows over his blueberry eyes at her. He was volunteering for the job. Did she get it? Was she impressed?

*Don't you love me yet?*

That's when she'd proposed they were both too tired to talk about it anymore and should take a quick nap.

• • •

In that moment, when Amalina came awake, and with Aklan still at her side and looking like a scruffy-haired angel from a venetian painting—one who'd grow a little, anyway—Amalina realized, and could categorize, the feeling she had for him. It was protective ... almost sisterly. And suddenly she was as surprised as when she'd discovered a familial tenderness toward that ugly old woman who her father had married last year, the Widow Lidsz, the one who must replace her long gone mother. How she'd hated and resented the Widow, unfairly so. But then by her sheer niceness and obliviousness to Amalina's hate, and her obvious affection for her father, the Widow had won Amalina to her side. So Amalina had a new mother. And now, with Aklan, Amalina had a little brother?

Was it possible to be gaining family this way?

The boy had tried to reach a hand out after they'd fallen asleep, perhaps to take hers. Who knows what he was dreaming, but Amalina knew he wanted her as a fairytale princess, whose hand, at the end of the story, he wins. But she saw him as a silly, starry-eyed little kid, and nothing more than that, which wouldn't make him too happy at all. If she were to tell him. Ah well, she didn't have to tell him right away and break his heart so soon.

Aklan's eyes came open, meeting hers.

"What?" he asked her.

"What?" she said in return.

"No, *you* what? You thinking something?"

"Um, about the love thing," said Amalina, clearing her throat. "You said—"

"I know," said Aklan.

"I just don't think of you in that way, Aklan. I think of you like—"

"I heard. I'm too young."

"Well, yes …"

"But I won't *always* be."

"I suppose that's true … "

"And I *am* a prince, a true prince. That's a far step above a simple lieutenant, a *subject*; a subject to courtmartials, stripping of rank, and cowardice on the battlefield. I will always be a prince, and if I marry you, you'll be a princess, a true princess. And when I'm king you'll be queen."

"You think you're still a prince after you've been gone from your home so long?"

"They'll have me back whenever I return, and gladly so. Especially if I have some battles with the barbarians under my belt. It's a splendid offer. What do you think?"

Amalina sighed, then: "Let's just get done what needs to get done. We can think about all that later."

"That's good enough for me," cheered Aklan, his face warming to an agreeable color.

That's when Amalina noticed, fully, the strange silence.

"What?" he said.

• • •

Amalina patted the air between them, quieting the boy. She pointed to her ear and then spun her hand to indicate the room around them. He propped himself up on his elbow and regarded the walls suspiciously.

It was still there. Or rather, was not there. Amalina and Aklan glanced at each other, noting the odd hush, then between them silently acknowledged the fact: The Count had returned to Netz.

He was in the hotel. There was no mistaking it.

"Did he hear us talking?" whispered Aklan, worried. "What we were … um … talking *about?*"

Amalina shook her head and put a finger to her lips.

The more important question: If he's here, where is he now? Amalina held up a finger and tiptoed for the door. She heard Aria Ecci's distant laugh.

Of course, *her.*

Aria's rooms were upstairs.

"Get the fire going again and light some candles," she said as she scrounged for a brush to fix her hair. "Something's going on and I'd better find out."

Amalina ran to the floor above and found the Count escorting some of the Ladies and their servants through the narrow passageway.

"Katarina!" yelled someone. Then Aria took over: "I'm sure we were just coming to get you, Kat-Kat. Your uncle has rescued us from our beds tonight! Now go and get something heavy on so you won't be cold."

They were wearing their winter coats.

Towering over them all, the Count looked as tired as ever, though had a game smile and a madcap gleam in his eye. He pulled lightly on one side of his long mustache. "Yes, my little mouse, I want you to come."

"Of course, uncle," said Amalina. To his surprise, she reached out and pulled on his hand. "But I need you privately for a moment."

"Eh?" he said as the Ladies protested.

"Another surprise to prepare," said Amalina with a confident tone. "Don't you remember?"

"Eh? What's this?" But he shook off the grasping hands of the Ladies and followed Amalina away. A couple of them moaned in disappointment.

"We'll meet you all downstairs," Amalina told them.

"What is it, Mouse?" said the Count when they were headed for her room. "We haven't that much time. I must oversee the evening happenings or, even so well planned by me, they will all fall apart. I can't have it, I need this to come off before it is too late. Or the season ends and it will have to be postponed yet another year."

Amalina was curious what the Count had in mind, but she quickly turned on him and launched into a speed rehashing of the would-be killer, her non-killing, and how she suspected Cristine had put him up to her murder. The

Count got the same look of admiration he wore when pondering Margeta's coldblooded ruthlessness. But now he was thinking of Cristine.

"Sir, you *can't* let her stay. Now she's trying to kill me."

He laughed and patted her on the shoulder. "Ah, my little mouse, see how she has you worked up?"

"You understand, sir, I really could have been killed. If Aklan and Genadie hadn't stopped him, I'd be dead, sir."

"But you're alive," he reminded her. "And may I say, much closer still to being able to not worry yourself over such little matters."

"You aren't listening to me."

He frowned at Amalina, most likely for delaying his more important engagement with the Ladies. "Look, you don't have to come if you don't want, this is for my other guests. Though I expect you to have fun, as well. Aria assures me you had the most wonderful time the other year, as did all the rest. But if you can't compose yourself …"

"*Cristine. Tried. To. Kill. Me.*"

"Of course. And what of it? What can you expect from someone so young and possessive? She must always feel inadequate to you and will seek to undermine you in the hopes of gaining my favor. No matter how I assure her, it will be this way. This is why it was a mistake not to perform the rite on her but extend this process needlessly—and, I will add, *cruelly*. She will never be assured or confident until she has lost her tether to this silly mortal world, and joined the plane of higher thought."

His delivery was convincing until Amalina remembered how the Count and the Strange Man had been as petty and territorial as the worst of men.

"Please, little mouse," said the Count. "Pay Miss Berzweck no mind. You will both be beyond these trivialities very soon, and we will all be able to laugh at them as what they are, the squabbles of rambunctious children. The innocents! Just get yourself dressed for this nippy evening and meet us outside. Uh, erm, that'll be, you will meet us on the lee side of the town."


## II


In addition to the permanent lampposts fixed on Netz's streets, torches were now set on both sides, and at so many paces apart, so that it looked like city was on fire. Amalina knew which way to go by the few citizens walking (or staring) in one direction. Accustomed to a lively city at night from her time in the west, it didn't strike her how unusual this was. She was swept up in the heightened festive atmosphere, until she noticed apprehension on some of the old faces, or a strain at trying to keep their smiles. Netz should have been shut up hours ago, like an armored animal folded into itself, never to peek its head out until the sun was up and the nightly cosmic threat was lifted.

But others, especially the young, were clamoring with excitement, and Amalina could hear a small roar at the edge of town. It was almost like daylight there, with squared away stalls bustling with life—a midnight market. And the torches extended well beyond that square of makeshift shops, which were hawking all kinds of wares and foods, the lights spread out in two intermittent lines that climbed up the side of the mountain in a wide path between the trees.

Joyous cries rang out in the valley from the people flying down the mountain's white slopes, just as if it had been in the daytime, riding all makes and manner of sleighs; overturned tables, strips of wood, animal hides. They careened, and fell, and ran into and over each other, hooting and having the time of their lives; while the rest picked themselves up from the snow, dodged the oncoming traffic, and hauled the debris back to the top for another run. These were the adventurers of Netz, willing to enjoy themselves alongside their noble guests from the other side of Europe. Only a couple men, this far out from the protection of the village, looked over their shoulders nervously, or up into the sky, fearful of the wrath of supernatural creatures; though ironically, as it was, one of those particular beings—the worst of them—was in their midst.

"Ho, beware," said a man, pointing into the distant tree line. "Look at that monster."

Amalina could barely see it without her glasses. But she could tell from its size and shape and movement that it had to be the black wolf. It had come down from the castle's mountain in search of her, it seemed.

"Someone get a musket. Bring out the dogs."

"Never mind him," called Amalina. They turned to her with surprised looks, and when they saw who it was, they stepped back a pace and half bowed.

"What are they going on about?" said Genevieve de Roye, arriving beside Amalina. "Just an ugly little wolf is it?"

*Little?* Amalina began fumbling for her glasses. But it seemed Genevieve was only putting on a brave face; and to add to her bravery, she took a step toward it.

"I wouldn't do that, Jenny," said Amalina, reaching to hold her back.

"Oh, really, it's very silly," said de Roye. "You mountain people are afraid of your own shadows. It's quite annoying sometimes: afraid of the night so that you can't open up. Wasting over half your lives away in fear. But look how marvelous and spirited the night has become if you shake off these superstitions. Wolves are nothing but cowards, scared of us humans and run away at our approach."

"I've seen otherwise," said Amalina, warningly, gripping her friend's arm tighter. When de Roye gave her a look as if she was a liar, she said, "Well, maybe your city wolves are used to civilization. You just haven't seen our mountain wolves. And they will tear apart a full grown man just as they would a moose."

"*You've* seen such a thing?" sniffed de Roye doubtfully. "Or were you told so?"

"*I've* seen it, if *she* hasn't," said Princess Noka Kunuru Sowa Iwebo, suddenly there and staring cautiously at the black wolf. Amalina and de Roye both took in a quick breath at the surprise and turned. As she spoke on, Noka's voice was calm and gentle, almost soothing, but with a reassuring undercurrent of bold confidence: "Jenny, living within your high gates, and paddling your feet in your fountains, you haven't seen the law of the wild at work as I have. Any animal in her kingdom has the ability and the mind to kill a human, and she only needs, on any given day, the inclination to do so."

"Well if *you* say so," said de Roye, looking more petrified by Noka's unexpected appearance than the wolf's. "Finally come out of your shell? Well, you look good tonight."

De Roye wandered off quickly, and without another look back.

Tall, lithe, and serene, this Noka Iwebo, wearing her favorite black, shawl-like mantilla, was the Noka whom Amalina had always admired, and nothing like the bloated, monstrous form of the last time she'd seen her. And for Amalina, unlike for de Roye, Noka's reentry was so casual and welcome, and her air so familiar and unchanged, it was almost like that horrible night had never happened, or it had been some unnatural imposter then, and this was an ordinary, comfortable chat between good friends.

"You know this one?" said Noka to Amalina. She pointed at the wolf. Amalina still hadn't found her glasses under the layers of clothing.

"I—what do you mean?"

"He knows you," said Noka. "He knows you very well."

"How can you tell?" But she already knew what the answer must be. She could speak to the animals. Maybe she could read their minds, or see messages in their eyes. She *was* the new Noka, after all. Whatever that meant.

"He's keeping an eye on you, protecting you. He's grown to care for you greatly."

"I can't imagine why. But it is nice to see you again, Noka. You do look well. You going to do some sledding with us?"

"I'm going to kill a bear," she said, pointing up into the treeline. "I will leave your wolf alone and find myself something stronger and more potent and dangerous. And I will prove my might and savor the power in its blood. *Ouaiii.*"

"I think it will be hard to find a bear. They sleep during the winter."

"Your dog, Genadie, tells me they're most dangerous when you wake them in their cave."

"Yes, that's probably true."

"I am counting on it," said Princess Noka.

"That's very brave," said Amalina. She wanted to say something else but had trouble finding the words. *What's it like? Do you feel you're still yourself?* All the usual prying questions, but she didn't have the confidence to ask. "You know, I've always admired you, Princess Kunuru Iwebo. I wish I could be just like you. But I'd never go fight a bear by choice."

"I pray that is never your burden. Goodbye, Katty."

Princess Noka gave the wolf a wide berth for Amalina's sake, and marched up into the forest. It seemed that Princess Noka removed her clothes with a simple swipe of her hand before entering; a lean dark figure stretched taught, and then leaping.

By this time, one of the local boys had returned with a musket.

"Oh, please leave him be," Amalina begged in a lower, embarrassed voice. "He's just checking out what all this excitement is about. I know him … from the castle. Almost domesticated. He won't hurt anyone." They looked at the wolf and then back at her, unconvinced. "With all this fire and all these people, he wouldn't dare."

Amalina made shooing motions to the wolf. It stood its ground, and, she assumed, stared raptly back at her. It had gone from being her tormenter to a worshipful protector in so many years, but still only obeyed its instincts. She patted around her clothes a little more and found her glasses inside her coat pocket. By the time she rubbed the grease off of the lenses and sat them on her face, the wolf was gone.

The men who'd first seen it were now turned back inward, watching something else.

The Count's laugh was low and like the booming of an avalanche. But what Amalina saw now did not match the merriness of it. Coming down the mountain at an incredible speed was the Count and the Ladies of Title. Somehow they had all piled onto one sleigh—packed themselves into it until some were barely inside but holding on—so that the contraption disappeared underneath them and they looked like a giant furry rodent, perhaps the size of a small elephant, with the Ladies' heads and hands sticking out, whooshing along at the speed of a comet while teetering and tottering on two thin runners; with the Count strapped perilously to the front of it all. He seemed to be pressed and held there by the twin actions of their mounting velocity and the tearing wind. And while Aria Ecci, 'Maria' di Oscina, Halma Inovala, Genevieve de Roye, Maibrigg Smeehaute, Elle VandeGarde, Claire Montraine, Elisavet Pattipo, Ivareta Bolso, Terza

Fleccevocarre, Marie Daume, Berrille de Jeane-Miesse, Cece Mineau, Stasia Auster, Jottes Chemirouge-Guillat, Eustine Keller, Candace Multiford and Greta La Nevers keened with total abandon and delight, their faces giant screaming, laughing holes, the Count's lips were drawn back in a rictus of forced pleasure; his large, wide eyes trying for joy, but only betraying a sublime condescension and confusion of why this should be so fun.

• • •

"Where is Princess Noka Kunuru Sowa Iwebo?" asked the Count later, having noticed her absence for some reason, despite the swarm of lively princesses around him, each trying to nab his attention for themselves.

It was odd how he'd recited her name so formally, as Margeta would have done, instead of the familiar 'Noka' or the silly but tender 'Nok-Nok'. Amalina took this to mean that he'd just come from Margeta's side, and his behavior and phrasing were shaped by her; little fragments and chunks of her stiff personality that were presently holding sway inside him. Like the warm smell of a mistress haunting the skin of your lover, thought Amalina with a sneer. He was a chameleon who had not yet realized the scenery had changed.

"I said, where is Noka?" repeated the Count.

"She told me she was going to hunt down a bear," answered Amalina. "Up on the mountain."

"And where is your friend, Pia Lampeda?"

"She's back at the hotel, no?" said Amalina, sounding her words with expert innocence.

## 49

## A Hunger in the Night

### I

"Come, it's night, no one's watching."

Pia pushed open the crate's lid, then ran a hand confidently through her hair as Ivanti Vokent stared at her swaddled in the box. *Well, that wasn't bad at all*, she thought, as she kicked away the heavy blanket. *Easy enough.*

"Let's get you something to eat," he said, and offered his hand to take her out. He was looking at her nervously, or in awe. "You *must* be starving."

Pia Lampeda took this young man's hand because she wanted to feel it. He was someone important to Katarina; or, that is, to Amalina. The girl loved him, perhaps. So how did he feel to the touch? He smelled like any other man, with hints of mountain food and acrid notes of oiled steel and gunpowder. *Well*, she thought, *his hand* is *strong, I suppose*. It felt no more substantial than a light layer of dough, which she could crush or tear apart. But compared to other hands she'd touched, like Amalina's, his was admittedly stronger. His heart, which was large and healthy, beat harder inside his chest. His blood pulsed through his flesh with a steady and powerful rhythm she could barely resist. She smiled at him politely. Though she was famished, she said: "No, I'm not hungry."

His brows went up. "We've been on the road for almost two days."

He'd tried to question her before, and to open the box more than a handful of times along the way, when he had to rest or trade out horses as he rushed them toward Korr, and was always answered with an admonishment, "Are we *there* already? No, I'm fine, Lieutenant. Leave me be."

Pia nodded presently at his surprise. If he was amazed by her lack of hunger, or that she hadn't wasted away in all that time, he only had to look into the box, or search the crumpled heavy blanket, to see that the bottles of water and wine, and the little tin of snacks he'd thoughtfully supplied her hadn't been touched. That would have really sent him reeling, or asking more questions.

Pia reached back into the box and pulled out a large square, long handled bag which she threw over her shoulder.

"If you will follow me, milady," said Ivanti. He smiled a sly, charming smile that was meant to challenge her. "Where we're going, you might reconsider having something to eat. You'll be very tempted, anyway, I'm sure."

Pia pushed down the call of her hunger; the emptiness that felt like a sucking void within her, causing her senses to lash out for anything living. She noted the six horses on the carriage, their hearts still pounding, but she knew the unpure taste of that particular species' blood, and besides, the lieutenant was guiding her away. She followed him with only a glance back. As they walked along a quaint, rustic old village street, she smelled the many garlic rounds, and the din of a thousand chimneys piping their burning wood. And cutting past the gentle perfume of snow, and the stench of open sewer, were the tiny packets of blood and meat scurrying in the alleys and tucked up under large roof overhangs: the furry mice and rats, and the feathery birds. If it weren't winter and the home fires burning, maybe she could identify the subtler mass of insects.

"Do you smell it?" said Ivanti with a smile, pointing to a small building.

Was he talking about the thin blanketing scent of leavening yeast, and smashed and fermented and burnt grains? *Oh*, she thought, *bread, of course.*

Ivanti rapped a distinct sequence on the door. She heard the bodies behind it, the breathing, the thumping chests. Bolts were thrown, then she was being led into the dark storefront, passing a large man with a voluminous beard who patted her gently on the shoulders.

"Ah, Ivanti, you've finally made it! But who is this? Who have you brought with you?"

"Yes," said a small man at the far side of the room in a wary tone, who watched her with a dull look, though his heart was beating quickly. "Who *have* you brought us?"

"Attila, Dragomir," said Ivanti, nodding his head to the two men and then Pia, "this is Lady Pia Lampeda."

"A noble lady," said the one named Attila.

Pia removed her hood fully and glanced at the two men. The larger one, Dragomir, who had welcomed them into the bakery, must be Amalina's father. She didn't see the resemblance except for maybe the sturdy frame, the dark hair, and brown eyes. Attila must be the revolutionary Amalina had spoken of. The two men, Attila and Dragomir, stared at her. Only the old wrinkled woman in the corner, who now exclaimed, "Oh, a princess!" curtsied low, as should be expected for a woman of Pia's rank. Pia wanted to laugh, because she had been taken aback by the men's lack of a proper bow; what would be considered an insolent reception to a Lady of Noble Birth. The outrage was a tickle of spirit from her former life.

So some part of her was still alive.

Another part, though—and she felt this entirely—demanded to be fed.

. . .

To Pia, the small one, Attila, appeared an unlikely leader. His delivery was without the barking and strutting energy of a commander in the field. She also didn't like the way his eyes always found hers, and seemed to try to crawl into her head through them, to rummage the secrets of her mind.

"Why have you come?" asked Attila.

"As Katar—ah, Amalina Dalca, that is—told the kind lieutenant here, I am leaving. And this was the most convenient—"

"Leaving the … ?" interrupted Attila.

"The country. I'm returning home."

"Your own carriage or a sleigh, with drivers and retainers, would seem more convenient than depending on our lieutenant, even if he's a friend of your friend."

"Under normal circumstances, I suppose it would be," she said with amusement. *Does he suspect something of me?*

"It is the height of winter. Not a likely time for such a long stretch of travel. Very treacherous."

"Spring is not too far off. And, anyway, I needed to leave now."

"Why?" he asked quickly, as if to cut off her escape.

"Is there something wrong?" Ivanti interrupted, with a puzzled look.

"Her timing is interesting. Coming from the castle, an associate of Count Tepsji, while his allies are putting us under pressure."

"What's happened?" said Ivanti, with concern. He squared his large shoulders. It looked impressive even to Pia, who'd seen many handsome officers in her life; and had recently killed a couple. His heart beat faster. "What are you talking about?"

"But that isn't for *mixed* company," said Attila, his eyes not leaving Pia.

*Does he know what I am?* she wondered. She started to bite her lip, then stopped before he took it as a sign of nervousness. She couldn't be nervous anymore, could she? Not really.

"Does the princess want something to eat?" said the old woman, curtsying again, "Cheese and cold meat? Or I could make some stew. I'm sure you must be so very hungry after a long trip. All the way from Netz! And so cold! Ivanti, boy, you should be ashamed of yourself. Let me heat some wine."

A warm red wine, a rare burgundy—so close to what she really had a taste for. Pia shook her head.

"Leave the princess be, my dear dumpling," said Dragomir gesturing to the door. "And stop spying. Go back to bed now."

"I just wanted to see who it was," said the dear dumpling, Pia noticing now that the old woman wore—what they all were wearing—were nightclothes. They'd been rousted out of bed. "And I didn't hear *her* opinion."

"I'm not hungry, Mrs. Dalca. Thank you for showing me your hospitality."

"Oh, *'Mrs. Dalca'*," said the old woman, as if surprised at being called that. "Well, have a good night, Princess—um, milady—um, princess." Then, as she shuffled away to some other room, genuflecting several times as she backed through the door, holding closed the top of her coarse, plain and patched nightgown, Pia smiled privately when she heard the woman behind the closing door mumble under her breath—none of the men heard her, no doubt—" … and thanks me for my hospitality, she does … She hasn't *seen* my hospitality … I would say she's *rejected* it. Oh, dear me, oh, well …"

"We're in danger?" said Ivanti when their harmless spy had gone away. His jaw was set and clenching. As if he could already predict some news.

"There have been some developments," said Attila, opaquely. "And setbacks. Which, again, makes the timing curious."

"Basz and the men?" asked Ivanti, eagerly.

"What about them?" said Attila.

"You've had word?"

"Nothing direct from those quarters. There have been many rumors floating around that they had traveled south hounded by a Germanian force, which the people came out against and have resoundingly beaten down."

"Oh?" The lieutenant looked entirely relieved, a smile breaking on his tense face. His heart leapt, which Pia heard. "Hurrah!"

"You know about this, Lieutenant?"

The lieutenant couldn't get his smile under control, though he tried for Attila. "I know about the King's Army, and the Prince, and that the dragoons were after us—"

"But then there have also been rumors that this force overran your men, swept up their remnants, and killed them all in Tsobl, at the Black Castle."

"What? No!" The smile was entirely blotted out, he grew pale, his heart pounded in a different way now.

"But since you are here, Lieutenant, I assume that is false, just like all rumors usually are. Maybe you will be able to clarify for us the facts in Tsobl." He eyed Pia for the lieutenant to catch on, "but at a more sensible time."

"Oh, of course, sir. Yes, sir."

"In any case, that is not what I was talking about," said Attila. "But perhaps this new mystery first. You brought Lady Lampeda here to the bakery for a reason, Lieutenant?"

"Oh, well, Amalina said she should ... well ... the lady carries a message or something for us." He seemed to become shy. "But I don't know where to begin. It has to do with Boss Berzweck. You'll never believe ... but ... *milady?*"

They all turned and stared at Pia. She stared back at them.

The three sweaty men were troubling Pia's senses. Or was it her growing hunger and the nearness of so much rich blood?

"So, do you want to explain yourself?" said Attila. "Now would be the time, no?"

"I've been sent to help you, sir," said Pia, aggressively, to push back and sideline her unwanted, intruding, ravening thoughts. "Amalina felt I could aid in your cause, and which I am doing despite what danger it might bring to me, or might even prevent my departure.

"My leaving was unexpected by the Count," she continued, her eyes level, assertive. "He'll be upset when he learns of my defection, if he doesn't know about it already. As it is, I rode here in a blind enclosure to hide my person in case any of his allies—as you say—might observe me and report to him. But here I am, as I promised Amalina—" she turned to Dragomir "—your daughter. Sir, she is well and safe and in little danger there." She turned back to Attila. "But I cannot say the same for the rest of the noble daughters. The atmosphere in that place is changing, and I *must* return home to my family, before it becomes impossible. Does that explain me well enough?"

"I see," said Attila, unconvinced. "And how will you get home from here without means?"

"About Berzweck," said Pia, not answering. She opened the bag slung over her shoulder and pulled out the large leather book with metal AXP on the cover. Attila's eyes goggled at it. As Pia opened the cover and paged through it, she took out the sticks. "I came to give you this; it's from Count Tepsji's office, and it is his secret correspondence with Alexandru Xerxes Przek, also known as Alexandru Berzweck, who I am told lives in this village. Here you will find him ordering the death of young women, at the Count's hands, for some awful purpose I don't know. As you can see, it's all written in code. But here are the ciphers, and you will see for yourself. Amalina has included on these sheets a kind of codex, so you can understand how the ciphers are used, with examples. I will leave you to mete out his justice."

Pia belched. The salt of their sweat she could taste on her tongue, and she felt the unrestrained joy of biting through a small layer of skin, and letting the gouts of blood slide down her throat. She had to leave. Now.

Attila was entranced by the book and was already playing with the sticks. Dragomir pointed to one of the rough, small rectangles of vellum, to a drawing on it, and said: "Isn't that poor little Natszja?"

"And Ezebeel," said the lieutenant, pointing at another one. "So it's true? Do you believe it, sir? Boss Berzweck?"

"Nothing's proven yet," said Attila, absorbed in the process of decoding. "Certainly not against Berzweck yet. But even if it proves to be iron clad, we must be prudent and stick to our roles … as ever before. Until we know how this information can be used against him."

"But why?" gasped Dragomir softly. "He had them killed, you say? Why would he?"

"If it were only one victim this might be simpler," muttered Attila. "But look how many … and did he know them all? It's almost industrial. It may point to a certain fascination with—"

"He was having affairs with them," guessed Pia, feeling another belch on the rise, but recognizing a different kind of intense carnal hunger in the pattern laid out on the notes and sketches of pretty young girls.

"Too early to say," said Attila, in a cautioning tone, simultaneously surveying the book and trying to work out a cryptified message on one slip using the codex sheets. "A good guess, but we must not leap with our assumptions; though it is a natural one, coming from a beautiful young woman such as yourself, who might be used to certain indecent, unwanted attentions. But these are merely points of data. And then they must come into line, to point to the truth; as all signs eventually do. The greater question is, if we establish these posts *do* define a system of murder between the two, as we're told they do, why he would have the Count—?"

"To cover him from blame," guessed Pia again, logically.

Attila lifted a finger of instruction, "Yes, of course, and that would be another assumption: notable men who wish to avoid scandal resorting to seconds to do their dirty work; devious scoundrels whom, as a beautiful young woman, you also must have encountered in your life. But you didn't let me finish, Princess. What I meant to say was, why he would have the Count—him specifically—do this, and even more important, how could Berzweck have the power to ask the services of that monstrous beast, time and time again?"

Pia was fascinated by Attila. How he was challenging her, reasoning to her at some higher order, when he was nothing more than a package of flesh and bone and blood; and blood; and blood; and blood; and blood. Her awareness of his precious blood pulsed with every squeeze of his heart.

Pia bowed and withdrew from the table, putting the hood over her head as he was saying, with his incessant condescending drone, "Though if we observe the similarity in the victims, and the almost regular spacings between each portrait, we can't ignore—but mustn't infer too much yet—a regularity and punctuality that would also suggest the inherent compulsions I've found in some amorous criminals …"

Attila pointed to her: "Where are you going?"

"I must leave." She belched once more. "Immediately."

"Are you sure you aren't hungry?" said Dragomir.

"You may leave, of course," said Attila. "But you still haven't answered my question. Where are you going? How can you get home when you have no means to return there? It is to Italy, is it? To Rome?"

Pia really hated how he was staring at her and plucking out her secrets like they were ripe apples on a tree. She thought: *I could bite through* his *apple!*

"And you haven't told us the exact danger that the Count poses to these innocent ladies; who, as I understand, are under his direct protection; and more, his *instruction*. Such a tutelage, with his age and insight, would seem to be an advantage to women wishing to understand the workings of the world. That *is* what he has to offer up there in his castle for you? other than his eligibility as a bachelor?"

"If Amalina didn't tell you everything there is to know about him," said Pia, agitated beyond annoyance now, but sounding her words politely, "let her explain it to you. She must have had a reason, and I haven't the time. He might already be looking for me. But I'm a daughter to a family with some means, of course, and I have my own people here awaiting my arrival. They would be unknown to you because they are discreet. And you will never know I have left, or what has become of me after tonight—unless any of you find yourselves in Rome, and calling at the pallazo di Lampeda. If so, announce yourself for an audience with me, Lady Pia Lampeda, and I will grant this to you gladly; ... and I will tell you all you want to know, if you still want for further explanation. Thank you, gentlemen, and I will leave you to your work. Good luck, and may heaven preserve you."

"At this hour?" asked Attila.

"Milady, at least take a bottle of wine and some of our bread," said Dragomir.

II

Less than an hour later, Attila and Lt. Vokent were treading through the soft snow, glancing nervously to make sure they were not seen, and noting the snowy street would make them easy to follow. As if to confirm this sentiment, Attila easily spotted the young lady's footprints running off in an uncertain direction, but he turned himself purposely away on his own route, trying to shuffle his feet to obscure the trail they were leaving, while not looking obvious about it. In the silent winter night with all the buildings sealed up, the town looked abandoned. It made Attila feel they were all the more conspicuous and vulnerable, should the Count suddenly appear. But why should he? He knew nothing of what was happening in Korr.

*However, he could come to track down his delinquent princess*, thought Attila. *But why suspect she came here? There are many routes out of Ardeel. Yet still … isn't this the most direct to Italy?*

To take his mind off his nerves he touched Ivanti's arm and spoke softly: "You came through for us splendidly, Lt. Vokent. Now we move to the next phase of our operation. Do you trust yourself to the training and command of these men?"

"Yes, sir," said Ivanti.

"Do you have confidence in them that they will be able to be molded into what we require?"

"They like me. And they trust me, sir. That's a good start."

"Trust is good. Being liked doesn't matter at all."

"I suppose not, sir."

"You will be taking their lives into your hands. This is not a personal game of puppy-dog love anymore, Lieutenant."

Ivanti cast his eyes down.

"You saw her in Netz," said Attila, with mild accusation. "She's the reason for the delay. The baker's daughter."

"That's not true. I saw her, but … My mission was hard going." Ivanti described to Attila a little of his mission's death defying adventures, the razing of the castles, the scrape with the Prince, and the turning of his men over to Rosczy who had Hak's partisans of the south, making sure to cut out anything but the facts—with the odd little man growing a wry, unheard-of smile when he learned of the now multiple decoy 'silver armies' grappling each other around the south (as long as one hadn't already slaughtered the other)—and gave no mention of Amalina trying to turn him into a false prince. No need for that. Better to lead him away from *that*. "There was some time finding all those birds and castles, on top of everything else with the Prince and his force on the hunt. It also took a while to get those bars switched out and not be noticed. Longer than expected." Ivanti cleared his throat. "But I understand what you're saying, Mr. Bronk. You've nothing to worry about. Maybe I returned for Amalina; to help her." He shrugged. "But I *know* what we're trying to do here and the importance of it all. Believe me."

"I like to think so." Attila cut a look to the lieutenant. "I knew a brave man in these same circumstances, but his heart wasn't in it. And he was a great disappointment. At least he only managed to kill himself, and not half the central and southern population of this country. You think your men and all these partisans, armed with pitchforks and what-you-will, led by a lackey priest, will be able to handle a trained, mounted, veteran army riding circles around them, armed with muskets?"

The Lieutenant swallowed hard.

"Can't say I'm not worried for them, sir. Of course. I'm honestly terrified for them. But you weren't there—"

"No I wasn't. And I was hoping I could trust you so that I don't have to be everywhere at once, to make *every* decision." At Vokent's second downcast look. "No, no, pay me no mind, Lieutenant. I've upbraided you enough—and I *have* chosen you to command. I trust you. So you've cast the die, and we will see how it lands. That's all we can do. But for now, while we have time, we must secure our safety. Put all these distractions which we can do nothing about out of our heads and think clearly. Which returns me to my original point, about the baker's daughter."

"Yeah, well, as to that: you may think you know all about me, sir, but I'm afraid you don't. Not as much as my old general."

"His knowledge of you bears something on this situation with the girl?" asked Attila, still sounding short and a little concerned.

"Exactly so. Bears it on *everything*, I should think."

"Well, don't let me stop you, Lieutenant. I'd like a good wake up."

"You know what General Volante told me before my mustering out to return to Ardeel?" asked Ivanti with a confident, if sudden, self-conscious grin, looking at Attila from the corner of his eye. "He told me I'd come waltzing back into his arms someday, if not by summer. He said I was a soldier if he ever met one. And maybe that's true. But he also let me in on a secret. He said there would always be a war to return to. He and the grand army are always in need to put out heresies, Catholic or anti-papal aggressions (whichever suits the crowns), and rebellions. There is always a king or a prince-of-the-blood needing him to swipe territories from an unsuspecting cousin, who would then show their bravery by rebuilding their army the following year to team up with another uncle—or some relation— looking for a fight and itching for glory. 'Yet *we* get the glory, boy,' he said to me. 'Do not worry that, we get the glory, too.'

"But that isn't glory, Mr. Bronk," continued Ivanti, with a serious tone. "It's a game of croquet with cannonballs, is all it is. And it's fun, and maybe a fancy I can never give up. He's right, I will return if given the chance. But I know I'll never be trusted there as a general. Not an eastern hick like me. Not for a long while anyway. But here I can prove myself in the field. And here, what we do, what we fight for, is something that's beyond glory, sir. This is a real fight. This has meaning that goes as deep as the roots of this country. How could I refuse it? How could I ignore it? How could I not be a part? That's what I'm here for."

*He's much more impressive than Hak Vogoneyevic*, thought Attila, startled by Vokent's passionate confession, feeling a little ashamed for doubting him a moment ago, and for scolding him like he'd often wished he had done to Sir

Hak. *What a stroke of luck our lieutenant came back to Ardeel, even if it was for the ridiculous Dalca girl.*

· · ·

When they arrived at the tall stone building, Attila nodded and Lt. Vokent knocked loudly on the door. The church was set far enough back that his thumps might not be heard by the surrounding residences. All the same, Attila scanned them for activity. It didn't take long before the lieutenant's efforts were answered by the sliding of a bolt.

The minister opened the door, Sadra stood behind him. Sadra did not react to seeing Attila in her doorway beyond an intensifying light in her eyes. The minister was obviously unsettled by the surprise appearance of the man he'd last seen curled up, savaged at the neck, and nearly bled white inside an earthy den outside of town—little did he know that, until recently, Attila had been hiding in his backrooms for weeks, supplied with meals by his own wife. Guilt jarred Attila's system.

Minister Smidt spoke directly and cordially to the man he knew: "Ivanti Vokent? Is that you?"

"Reverend," said Attila, inserting himself between them, "I am here to request sanctuary."

"Well, yes, certainly," said the minister without hesitation. "Sanctuary. It is a sacred duty of the church to shelter those in need and for any cause. The reason unspoken, nor requested."

However, it looked like the minister said all this because he'd really appreciate an explanation. He glanced inquisitively at the bandage on Attila's neck.

Attila motioned to Ivanti to hand him the long leather tarp, which looked to have a pole within it. He took that, and then the big bag which hung off his shoulder, and entered. "It will just be me, Reverend Smidt. Put me where you like."

As Ivanti said his goodbye and left, the minister became puzzled and then somewhat annoyed. Attila supposed it could also be that he was tired, having had his sleep interrupted and was short on patience.

"I won't be bothering you for very long, Reverend," Attila assured him. "But unfortunately this is most necessary. Less for myself than for this."

Attila took the large book with the flashing metal letters out of the bag.

"Oh," said the minister, looking at it unsurely. With its bold, aggressive, grandiose appearance, it might have looked like a strange, heretical work, or rival holy book.

"What have you brought into this house of God?" said Sadra. But she saw the letters clearly enough.

"This is the proof of certain unthinkable crimes. Murders written out in the criminal's own hand, and the account of his clandestine conspiracy with the Knight of Ardeel. Needless to say, it must remain safe until it can be revealed publicly."

"Oh," said the minister again, looking at it unsurely. Maybe it *was* a heretical work? In any case, it was more directly dangerous now.

"It wouldn't be safer in the deputy sheriff's custody?" asked Sadra. More questions waited behind her controlled voice.

"The man behind the book is powerful and his influence cannot be taken lightly. There are only two people within Korr who I can trust: the two who saved my life." He bowed briefly to Sadra and her husband. "And to add to that, your church grants me—and my valuable possessions here—the protection that a secular building cannot."

"Oh, yes, very well," mumbled the minister. It looked like he wanted to return to bed and to quickly forget what he'd just let in the front door. Or that he'd never risen to answer the door in the first place. "And what else do you have there?"

Attila looked down at the long, leather-wrapped pole in his hand. "That's best left for another time."

"I'll make up the visitor's room," said Sadra to her husband. "You go back to bed, minister. Early morning for you."

Sadra made up a small bedroom within the living quarters, but close to the back storage rooms where she'd first hid Attila. In any case, it was safely away from her and her husband's bedroom.

As she went about snapping the sheets onto the pallet bed, she said: "We know who it is now? AXP? And—?"

Attila quickly explained how he'd already used Amalina's codex to decipher some messages, and revealed just what the evidence from the two pages he'd sampled made clear: "Alexandru. The Boss. It can be no one else."

"So then you were right," said Sadra with a tight smile and a look of admiration. "If we'd told him of our suspicions—he an informer to the Count, and his collaborator—we would have ruined everything."

"As it is, my stunt with his silver bar was impetuous and might have tipped him," admitted Attila. "He's a very cautious and suspicious man. Look at the trouble he took with the codes. He may very well suspect my concerns regarding him without my having said anything."

"But at least he doesn't know we know for sure," said Sadra. After a pause, her tone changed and she whispered: "Why did you come here tonight, really? To let me in on everything, or ... ?"

"It's just as I said, Sadra. Boss Berzweck is a dangerous man. A little bakery is no place for me to hide, or for something so important as this book.

He can't just invade a church. Or send his men to do the dirty work to get what he wants."

"I see," she nodded curtly, her tight smile thinning into a straight line. "But you were right, after all, Attila. You should be happy, why do you seem irritated? What's the matter?"

"Do I seem anything to you?" he said behind his steady mask.

"Of course. Look to your telling hand."

Attila steadied his left hand with his right. Then with a heavy-lidded stare he said, "What I wanted most was to level justice on the Count. Now, without a doubt, I have to waste time dealing with one of his allies first. A powerful and dangerous one. It is greater distraction than I'd hoped."

"Well, either way, I'm glad you're back," she said, then stared at him hopefully.

There seemed to be a loud noise somewhere. A pop, or a sudden blast of thunder, or a heavy drift of snow breaking free in the mountains.

And in that moment, Sadra lunged at Attila.

She kissed him hard on the lips.

## 50

# The Midnight Meal

While Pia had been inside the box en route to the Dalca bakery, she had been unaware of time. Had she been asleep for all of it? Besides the young lieutenant's several concerned interruptions, insisting she needed to drink or get some air or to relieve herself, it didn't feel more than an hour had passed from when Pia closed her eyes in Netz to when he had called her out in Korr. But thinking back, so much had drifted by. Too much for it to have been just an hour; with the fleeting fragrances of flesh and blood passing like interesting clouds wrapped within the crisp scent of snowfall, pine needles, and ancient stone. She had been thinking a little, but could barely recall what. Two days locked away? And how long since she'd properly eaten? Now her hunger had woke to its full. She moved on instinct.

She reined it in—*just a little more*—as she leapt from street to street.

Two men stood warming their hands at a fire. One wore glasses, both had identical hats, long pole weapons and short swords on their belts. Some kind of Ardeelian night patrol. She landed around the corner and shuffled quickly through the snow to meet them.

"Ho, who is this?" said the first man with a startled look. It was as if he'd seen a ghost.

"Excuse me," said Pia, with an innocent voice and a heavy accent. "I need directions."

"Young woman, don't you know you shouldn't be outside at this hour? The bell rang long ago."

"*You're* out here."

"That's our job," said the second man, wiping his glasses, angry at being challenged, especially by a foreign woman, no matter how pretty. Pia imagined ripping his nasty little head off. She couldn't help it.

"She don't know," said the first to the other, nudging him with an elbow.

"But this is urgent and I need your help, if you could."

"You're not from around here."

"I'm from a kingdom far from here, yes. But I am returning home, and I have stopped in this village to deliver a message to Alexandru Przek."

"Berzweck, did you say?"

"A message from his daughter," nodded Pia. "She says he lives here."

"Are you from the … from the University in Netz?"

"Can you please help me find the Berzweck family residence?"

"The Boss' place?" began the first. "It's hard to miss."

"We'll take you there," said the second. "No need for a young woman like yourself to risk her life."

"Oh, of course," said the first. "We will show you the way."

Pia shook her head, staring at them levelly, "There's no need. If you could point me in the right direction."

"Too cold a night for stabbing around. He might not even open his door to a stranger at this hour. Not at all. We'll bring you. Keep you safe."

"If you feel you must. Thank you."

"Did you say you are from the University in Netz?" the man with the glasses tried again. "I heard his daughter is enrolled there."

"I hadn't really thought of it as a school. I was there visiting the Count's niece."

"The Count?" the first one gulped.

"I am at the school. Yes. Sorry, my language is not so good. I'm not sure what I am saying sometimes. Now, where is Mr. Perzweck?"

. . .

Pia was trembling but it felt artificial. Her body was betraying the need within. If she didn't act soon, her strength would fade or explode. Her body would collapse into itself. Become dormant.

She looked up. Did she feel this way because the moon was full? She'd never had so strong a desire to hunt that she could not resist it. But *now* …

*Well, if someone has to die tonight*, smirked Pia, *it will be the most deserving.*

She thought of those rancid heads stuck on spikes above the gate. The Count had put them there, and Amalina had said they'd belonged to AXP. He—the Count—shouldn't be too upset if *she* took out their boss—

Would he be upset? It wouldn't matter. She'd never see him again, unless he someday made it to Rome.

"Who's there?" came a heavy voice from behind the door.

"Boss? Hey, Boss, it's us. We found a visitor who wants to talk to you."

"What? A visitor?" The bolts on the the great red house's door were thrown, and the door opened. The man inside stared out at them. He was large but older, with a thinning pate and sodden look. He wore a thick house coat.

His eyes were Cristine's.

"Hey, Boss. You answer the door yourself?" said the first man. "Where's Polto?"

"This time of night?" answered the man with a hard grin of superiority. "Everyone's asleep. The servants most of all. Everyone, except *me*."

The great man seemed amused by himself. Pia kept her face hidden under the cowl, but her body shook again, wracked with hunger, knowing sustenance was close and demanding satisfaction. Fortunately, it would look to the three men like she was shivering from the cold.

"You are Alexandru? Cristine's father?" said Pia.

He looked her up and down. "Yes?"

"This is *Boss* Berzweck," said the first man to Pia, as if instructing her to understand his importance.

"Your daughter sent me here to give you a message. May I come in?"

"Eh? My daughter? What is it?"

"I am afraid it's complicated. And it is for you alone to hear. Please."

"And who are you exactly?"

The two men from the night patrol turned to her, looking as if they thought that was a fine question as well. Why hadn't they thought to ask her that before bringing her?

"Thank you for help," Pia told them, exaggerating her accent. "Please, if I may speak him alone?"

"She's from the University in Netz," the first one told Alexandru, helpfully.

"Yes," said Alexandru, looking her up and down again. "Yes, I understood that part. Well, come in out of the dark—I mean, out of the street and the cold and get near the fire. Can't have you freezing to death can I? I suppose I'll be putting you up for the night?"

Though she felt like walking in mysteriously and not answering, she thought that would leave a wrong parting note to the patrol. She said in a sweet voice, "That would be very kind of you, sir. So I won't have to go back out."

"Your daughter sent her, Boss," said the second one with the glasses, helpfully but belatedly.

"Goodnight boys," said Alexandru.

Pia entered into a room that stank of tobacco smoke. Alexandru shut the door and locked the bolt.

"Wait here," he told Pia. "By the fire. You're lucky I don't sleep much. Just set up the fire, should be nice and warm. Feel free to take off your coat. Mind you don't get any snow on the carpet."

Pia pulled off her hood. It would only get in the way.

"Hm. Very pretty. Coming into my home this late at night, it could give me a bad reputation," he winked. "I'll get you something to eat."

"No need," said Pia. Her insides began to agitate. Her blood rushed in her ears. Actually *rushed*. It felt right.

She had questioned herself in that long trip here, to Amalina's little town, inside the box. And she recalled some of it now: If she was to escape to Italy with the promise of Katarina to join her shortly, how could Katarina prove herself, really prove her words were true, if this man—who still had her under threat—succeeded in his designs against her? If Amalina Dalca died, so would Katarina Tepsji, and it would all have meant nothing. She would never be able to prove herself. *I want her to prove herself,* Pia had thought. *What am I going to do, leave it to others to solve the problem? Trust these weak and clueless, paper-thin fools to Amalina's protection against a violent, resourceful, persecuting shadow? Let* me *solve this for her, and then she must come to me. She would* owe *me that.*

The way to do it was easy enough.

For a second, Pia thought to pull that incriminating book from the bag and tear it apart before his eyes. But she didn't have it anymore, she'd left it in the bakery, and doing so would solve nothing. Tearing something *else* apart, she licked her lips, would solve two.

Pia sensed the hunger taking control and she stood back to let it have its way, full fury. "Are we alone here?"

He kept his hands jammed in his housecoat pockets but flapped them jovially. He was giving her a curious look, though. He encouraged her: "It's just us two."

"You are Cristine's father?"

"Yes. Cristine is my lovely daughter. She has something she wants me to know? You say you have come from the castle—?"

"Alexandru," said Pia, with a note of rising accusation. "Alexandru Przek. Alexandru Xerxes Przek. Who has innocent girls killed."

Alexandru winced. "What?"

"You ... Will ... Leave ... Amalina ... Alone ..."

Before she leapt, Pia reveled in the look of horror on his fat, ugly face.

His right pocket exploded.

Pia gasped and doubled over. It seemed as if her abdomen, her whole torso, was on fire. And all that winding fury inside of her was blowing out, escaping in all directions.

"Wha—?" she said, trying to stagger away from him.

With his jowls shaking furiously, and his eyes wide in terror, he pulled a pistol from his other pocket. At a glance, it was strangely shaped for a pistol, with a wide, horn-like mouth. He pointed it at her head.

# Entr'acte:
# Dawn of a Sunset

51

## A Talisman of Quality and Purpose

"Why must everything be done so indirectly with you?" asked Sadra with a squint, as she and Attila crunched through the snow, its whiteness near blinding under the bright morning sun.

"Straight lines offer clarity," said Attila, lugging the leather-wrapped pole, seeming unphased by the scenery, focused instead on the coming maneuver. "The last thing you want for an enemy to have is clarity. They must be rendered unsure, so that their movements are filled with hesitation, and their thoughts are stunted by doubt."

"At this point, who knows the whole truth of his identity?"

"Besides the Boss, you, and I? Only Dragomir and the young lieutenant. And the creature, of course. And whoever might be in league or under the influence of Berzweck, and who might have abetted him in his crimes. And because we don't know who that might be, or how wide his circle, we have our own cloud of doubt to work through."

"And so we carry on as if nothing has happened," hissed Sadra.

"He left us with a challenge for possession of the army that we must meet as if it were still real," said Attila calmly. "If we don't, he might suspect something; a false step. No, we have to counter him and press hard, see how he reacts." He adjusted his grip on the pole thoughtfully, so that the leather squeaked. "If you can't control yourself, Sadra, you shouldn't join us."

"I don't intend to join you," she returned sternly. "I'm just showing you the way and acting as your calling card through the village. Hopefully the Vokent boy will be there to act as your second. It's right up ahead here, you can't miss it."

"But what is this?" said Attila, stopping short after his eyes had followed where Sadra pointed. His expression did not change, but he stared intently at the large red house in the center of the next block. "Here, come around and act as if we are talking to each other."

Sadra glanced, trying to see what had interested him, but then did as he asked, circling and putting her back to the coming block and Alexandru's home. Attila looked over her shoulder as he spoke.

"Something's happened. It seems a window has been broken and repaired with new wood."

"That happens to every house in this town at some point. What—?"

"It's on the second floor, above the slope of the lower roof. And there appears to be a quantity of blood. And what appears to be several footprints, widely spaced, as if someone were running … or jumping. And a patch in the drift below where they hit the ground hard and fell flat. Dead."

Sadra's angular face twitched as it became harder for her not to turn around.

"I didn't see anything," she said.

"Lt. Vokent has arrived at the front door and he's spotted us," announced Attila, nodding forward, before returning to the matter at hand. "Now, the snow cover will be matted where the likely victim landed, or otherwise it's been worked into the cobblestones. Distinct footprints might be difficult to detect—as well as the path of a dragged corpse. You should examine underneath the repaired window, see if there's a trail of blood to follow. And if there is, where it ends. We will meet again in a quarter hour, for you to sneak me back into your church. Best we're not gone too long or your husband might think I've broken sanctuary."

When Sadra turned she blinked at the large, imposing, ostentatious house—the same as it had always been—and said angrily, in disappointment, "You made it sound like there was a massacre. I don't see any blood."

"Get closer and have a look," he said as he waved to the young lieutenant outside Alexandru's door, who half-waved in return.

• • •

"You two are lucky to have found me here," grumbled Boss Berzweck irritably. But he offered them something to drink and called for his wife to get it. He jammed his sizeable hands into his overcoat's pockets and led them deeper into his home.

"No servants?" said Attila, his eyes turning this way and that as they entered into a wide living space; walls cluttered with expensive decorations and oil paintings as if to fit in everything that could impress a visitor. The floor was bare, the furniture—well-turned benches, tables, and chairs—were pushed to the side. "Judging by the size of your home, I thought you would have as many servants as a lord in his castle."

"They're attending to other things just now. Our days start early." He turned his head and shouted: "Where are those drinks, eh?" and then to Attila and Vokent: "The lad might have had some coffee out west. But this should be your first taste, Bronk. You'll love it. And maybe it'll get a rise out of you. Finally."

Focused on Attila, the Boss didn't notice Ivanti's straight mouth and burning eyes.

"And I suppose you had a late night," muttered Attila. "Are you fond of dancing, sir?"

Boss Berzweck looked confused. "What are you talking about?"

"The furniture set aside. Your carpet has been rolled up and sits in the corner. I've seen that done when dancing instruction is given."

"Where do you think you are?" laughed the Boss. "This is Korr. No one takes dancing instruction. Too damned busy making livings."

"It's unusual to see a carpet rolled into a corner that way. It doesn't look new. There's a dark rosy cloud on it."

"Hm? What are you talking about?" His eyes darted between the rolled up rug and Attila. He grunted. "My wife likes wine, if you need to know. And sometimes she gets a little careless late at night. We've lost many rugs to it. Now why don't you tell me why you've come? Vokent lad, what are you holding there?"

Attila took the long package from Ivanti, who stood like a soldier at attention, mute, head level, and quite serious with his square jaw set. Attila nodded for him to keep calm, professional. He spun one end of the leather and unfurled it onto the polished piece of floor where the carpet used to be.

In the middle of the leather rectangle was a long silver spear.

Boss Berzweck's eyes saucered. He couldn't help himself but dropped to the floor and touched it. Tested it with his expert fingers. Attila watched this action and noted it.

"Where did you get this?"

"I've told you before," said Attila, coldly, "every part of this operation is held in secrecy. But since you demanded proof, it is here before you now, as promised: my silver."

"Very Late, Low Constable." He appealed to the lieutenant, "Vokent lad? Where did you get this?"

Lieutenant Vokent kept at attention, his eyes fixed on the spear, as rehearsed, and not the Boss.

"You know this metal is contraband," said the Boss, as if scolding him. "It's illegal to possess."

"As you keep reminding us," said Attila. "We have hundreds of such weapons. And armor. This army will be properly equipped to deal with our enemy. If you hoped your little trophy, a blob of silver, impressed our men of your seriousness in this business, believe that any of their lingering doubts about me and my entire operation are now quashed. I have produced a talisman of quality and purpose. And they know it has been accomplished by a source other than their Boss Berzweck."

"You could be arrested," he warned, still looking at Lt. Vokent. "Ivanti, I know you. I know your father. You won't speak to me?" He paused. His head began to turn as if to look at the rolled up rug, but snapped back at them before it did. The tiredness and indignation was gone from his face entirely now, replaced by a shrewd suspicion. "At least tell me how long this has been in Korr. Did you bring it back with you, lad? When did you arrive here?"

"Now let's get things straight between you and I," said Attila, without emotion. "I am in command here. You will follow my orders and respect my timetable, and receive information only when I deem it necessary and the time's right. For your part, from here on out, you won't reveal one aspect of our operation to anyone. Not a piece. To anyone. Not the slightest whisper. Do you hear me? Any violation by you and you'll find yourself under arrest. As it is, from this moment forward, to ensure these rules are followed, Lt. Vokent here will be your new personal assistant. Make some room for him in your home as he will be staying close at your side, awake, and available at every hour."

· · ·

"There's no real trail to speak of," Sadra told Attila as they returned up the empty street. He was holding the long leather-wrapped spear lengthwise with both hands again. "It ends at the back alley."

*It ends where the victim was loaded into some mode of transportation, a dead cart,* thought Attila. *For that must be the conclusion, mustn't it?* He quickly informed Sadra of the ruined carpet with the claimed wine stain. "Maybe he doesn't always dispose of these young women via the Count. Resorts to the monster only when he doesn't have direct access to the girl, or he needs an alibi to keep himself above suspicion. In any case, we must see if anyone in town has disappeared after last night. Or within the past two days, at least."

"You think he killed someone?" asked Sadra.

"That's where the evidence points. We must always trust to the signs."

"And there's something else," said Sadra, reading him somehow.

"Vokent will keep watch on him from now on, so there is little to worry there. But it was odd how Berzweck didn't seem as concerned as he should've been about me assigning him a handler or my curious questions. It seemed he was more interrogating me, just now, than I was him. Why did he want to know *when* this spear arrived?"

· · ·

And still later that day, at the very edge of town, after the revolution's new supplies were distributed and secreted throughout Korr to certain soldiers loyal to *the Cause*—"*A very special delivery from Lieutenant Vokent,*" it was whispered—a dramatic scene privately played out:

Lazru Skeldar surveyed the piles of precious metal before him. He felt the coming toil charge his heavy arms. His teeth clenched into something like a smile.

"What is this, Lazru?" asked Lazru's wife, shocked and concerned. "Where did you get silver? All of this silver!"

Lazru grunted humorlessly.

"Have you been drinking again?"

"Never again, wife," he muttered. "Now leave me alone. I've work."

"Tell me where this came from. And what're you doing with it, husband? And all this armor …?" his wife sucked in a breath, and she began fitting the different pieces together, especially the armor—and the rumors. "What's happening here, Lazru? Is Ardeel going to war again? That army that came off the highway people have been talking about …"

Finding himself unable to explain, the ability to communicate without hammers never learned, Lazru grabbed his wife's wrist and escorted her roughly out of his work room. If he had been drinking, it would have been worse. As she struggled with him, trying one last look at all that shining metal and relics of ancient warfare, she kept asking, "Why? Why? Why, Lazru?"

"The Knight will finally pay," he said grimly as he tossed her out.

"The knight? *Who*? What are you talking about?"

But he'd already closed the door on her.

"War is it?" she shrieked behind the thick wood, pounding on it with her fists, and then, later, scratching at it with her fingernails. "And where d'you fit into it, husband? The Knight you say? Do you mean it? Then I ask you, where are our sons? Where is Lucinda? Now I'm going to lose you, too? For *nothing*?"

Lazru fired up the ovens and ignored her. There was a lot of hard work ahead.

And in the days to come, as the late winter winds clapped everything down in Korr with a fresh, glistening snow, if one were close enough, and listened for it, one could hear the fiery gusts and the relentless clatter of iron-upon-iron: the sound of a smithy hard at work, hammering and folding metals into new shapes, ringing its notes out into the thickening air of a transitional season just off stage.

Part Six
Burn ... Burn the Flames

## 52

## The Left-Behind Ladies

Winter withdrew in the next week, as if minding the Count's boredom with it and his desire to move on to a more liberating season. The Ladies of Title showed little resistance to return to the high castle. They viewed any missed opportunities to carouse in Netz—that backward little city—as worthless compared what was on offer up in the mountains; though they tried hard to convince their friends to stay behind and indulge themselves for a few days more; and Amalina did her best to sell them on any array of new opportunities to make up for the sudden, and mysterious, disappearance of the best of the attractions: the buffoonish 'Prince Caspion of the Outer Meldines'.

"That's *Castion*," corrected de Roye.

But once back inside the castle, far from being refreshed, everyone took up the positions they held before; and the air of the place felt further degraded, as when the party-goers leave the hall to get some fresh air, to renew their spirits with outside drinks and food, and upon returning to that very same hall, there is only the leftover air of happiness-that-once-was grown stale. And now added to it is an inevitability which might be sad, but was also comforting: where everyone seeks a place to land, and where every hard bench and chair—even the cool and littered floor—appears as the most comfortable bed to lay down to rest and await the next day's sun. The festivities can no longer be repeated, the courtships are either completed or lost, the strivings failed or won, but the end has been reached, the conclusion clear.

The Count was mostly absent at this time, appearing in-the-round less frequently, and usually only to assure the Ladies that the continuing mountain shudders were not to be feared, to inquire if Noka or Pia had been seen yet, and to tell Amalina whom of their guests was to be turned next. Though he looked ever more tired each time, he announced his selection to Amalina with a cheerful tone and a twinkle in his eye, and to explain that he did not need her assistance anymore to perform the well-practiced rite of transformation.

. . .

"I just need to know what has become of our two lovely but misplaced Ladies," the Count said to Amalina, in one of their private consultations. "You've no idea?"

"I haven't seen them for weeks now," she assured him. "The last time for Pia was when we arrived at the hotel; Noka at the mountain during sledding."

When thinking of Pia, Amalina often wondered how far she'd gotten in her trek back to Rome. Had the fair skinned redhead faced any trouble trying to stay out of the sun? What would her parents say, how would they react, when their daughter arrived home with some new, peculiar habits? While Amalina sometimes worried for her friend, she was more given to a pleasant, warm, uplifting feeling that at least *someone* had escaped the Count and was safe—at least *one*, finally, had done it. That it had been accomplished by Amalina's help and insistence—with some little conniving, admittedly— added an extra ounce of enjoyment. It made her feel stronger and more effective than she normally considered herself.

"I'm reaching my perfect number, you understand," the Count carried on. "I need to know if those two are lost to us. I can't imagine what might have happened to Lady Lampeda."

Here Amalina almost broke into a guilty smile.

"But now, I must wonder, do I replace them? I cannot do so precipitously, should one or both suddenly reappear." His lips turned down at a thought: "Of course, I no longer expect our Silver Moon Goddess to return from her hunt. That one is quite out, I suspect, now that I think about it. Ah, well. The victim of her own bravery become the hubris of legend; an Icarus in her own right, our Noka." He shrugged and picked at his shirt, "But, anyway, for the first time in my existence I feel a lack of patience. And I have lived a long time, as you know. I wish to finish this process so we can get on with our lives."

"Who else would you consider?" said Amalina, then added, "sir."

"Haven't I told you between us there is no longer a need for formality, my dear little mouse?"

"No, you haven't. But, um … are you still counting Cristine in?"

"Miss Berzweck remains in our castle, does she not? Though, to admit, I *have* admonished her for her misbehavior. I'll just let her languish without my presence … or my remedies. I haven't continued our process. I suppose she's regaining her strength now—and her mortality—because of my neglect." He looked down on Amalina. "But I'm not sure which outcome would make you happiest?"

"To send her home and never allow her back in, sir." She reminded him how Cristine had just tried to have her killed, because he often needed reminding of things like that.

The Count scoffed softly and rubbed his face. "Let it go. She has as well, I'm sure. It will all be forgotten as a bad prank once you both have sloughed off these petty temporal concerns. However, I won't favor her with my renewed attentions until she can demonstrate to me a satisfactory ability to respect you."

"You really think she'll change that much?" asked Amalina. "She's very mad at me."

"She fears inadequacy; but for the moment. Once elevated, she can no longer feel such a thing. Not when one is linked with the universe. She needs reassurance, is all."

"I don't think that's it, sir."

"But I *know* so."

"But, sir," began Amalina, then hesitated. "… It doesn't have to do with jealousy, really, or inadequacy, sir. I know this because … She's mad at me because …" here Amalina hesitated again. It drew his large, dark eyes. *What was the point in keeping some secrets?* she thought. "I told Cristine her father was having you kill people, sir. That he's trying to kill me, too. I told her all of it. She didn't like it."

The Count thought for a moment with a dim glower, but then his head came up and he grinned curiously at her. "How could you know about her father, Ms. Dalca?"

"You showed me the book, sir. You gave me it. Don't you remember?"

"I never said who it belonged to. No. *Noooo.* I remember making a point *not* to tell you."

"But it wasn't too hard to figure out," said Amalina. "His initials are right across the cover."

"AXP?"

"I know his last name used to be Przek, and so … Alexandru …"

"Always very clever. Such a leap, mouse."

"Not clever enough to know why, though. Even Cristine doesn't know the answer, which I was trying to find out. I thought our friendship was strong enough for me to ask. But she wouldn't believe it when I told her. Rather, she thinks I'm trying to put her down in front of the Ladies or to ruin her family name."

"I will speak to Lady Berzweck if you cannot, Ms. Dalca," said the Count, patiently. "Make her understand there's nothing to fear and you mean her no harm. That your friendship is as strong as before and shall last forever."

"But it *is* true about AXP, isn't it?" asked Amalina. She leaned toward him. "Her father *is* the one. And he *is* trying to kill me … even now."

"However, not *now*; I put an end to that," he said, trying to derail her as fast as she was diverting him. "You've nothing to worry from this AXP anymore. And even if his daughter has been naughty and erred by following in his footsteps—"

"—by trying to have me killed, you mean."

"Let's move on," said the Count, testily. "Let us now consider our final candidates, as I said; should it prove to be that Pia, and we assume Noka, are among us no longer."

"But I wish you'd tell me, sir," persisted Amalina, hoping to get her answer and also to put off his own question, and final decisions, if a little longer. Any delay was a reprieve for her friends. "*Why* did her father have you attack all those girls? Eh, sir?"

The Count's shoulders seemed to drop, as if she'd set on him the final straw on an unbearable load. He knew she wasn't going to give in. And so *he* must. His face relaxed, he shook his head. He said casually, "I can't imagine, but I really don't know."

"You don't know?" she said in astonishment.

"I told you before, Ms. Dalca." Irritation at having his intellect questioned squeezed his words. "It was a trade. It was never my place to question him or his motives."

"But he was having you *murder* innocent young women, sir. Why would you just do something like that? whatever he wanted? It was evil!"

"You know, you're an angry little child sometimes," grumped the Count, looking sulky, knowing by having given in to her interrogation his selection of a Lady now had to be put off until another time. Or at least would happen out of her sight. Without her involvement. And he enjoyed her participation in these kinds of things. "Please grow up, my little mouse. Haven't I already told you the agreement between he and I is at an end? That should be enough for you, I should hope." He breathed heavily in and out. "And though it is highly unsatisfying for me, I have been making a point not to kill—not anyone—in my hunts. Which means I have to hunt more often to draw what's needed. And I have to be more careful so as to conceal my identity, and what I have done. Which means it takes longer than before. It is a hard and disagreeable practice but which I do to honor you and *your* wishes. Is that not *enough* for you?"

Amalina felt embarrassed and ashamed. Especially because he looked so drawn out when he was once so powerful, and it seemed his present condition was entirely her fault. "I know you've left off of Cristine," she said, contrite. "The ceremony doesn't replenish you? when you drink the Ladies' blood in the rite, even?"

"If it wasn't for this rite," explained the Count, matter-of-fact, chin resting on palm; two friends having a talk, his resolution entirely collapsed, "I might be worse off. But they only draw my spirit at the end of it, and so it is still *unsatisfying*."

"I'm sorry, sir." But then she flushed and grew mad for apologizing. How did she get to where she should feel sorry for *him*? or at fault for anything!

"It's nothing, my little mouse, but what I do for you," said the Count generously of himself. "Remember that. And try to forgive your friend Cristine. And do so—extend your magnanimity, I ask of you—even as far as including her father, now that it is over; there was no real crime in taking advantage of my abilities. There's no evil, as you say there is, in what I do. And to provide a service—even to him—why, it is only natural." He lifted a weary brow, and intensified his look at her until she felt the walls close in. "He is not the only one," he said in a low, confiding tone, "I could reveal things to you that would set your mind on fire."

. . .

Lady Princess Halma Inovala's sheer reluctance to commit herself—her body anyway—to the Count caused her to be his next choice for transformation. After Greta La Nevers intimated to the younger Lady (echoing Aria's oft-spoken fantasies) that the Count would be sexually intriguing mate as a husband, Halma (echoing di Oscina's prudish anxiety at such a thought) reacted privately to Amalina in horror: "Ew, that old man? But who would think of him *that* way? Really, he is too old and ugly. Why would I want to be with him like *that*?"

"Because, Lady Inovala," rumbled the Count, as he casually stepped out of a shadowy corner, as if he'd always been there, making them jump in their seats, "I am the old and ugly man who is also the richest and most powerful man on the face of the earth. I can bestow on you the same power. And, as well, the ability to live without fear of death ... or rather, give you *immortality*."

"Is that true?"

"With it, let's see how old *you* can get."

Lady Elisavet Pattipo, of the smooth cinnamon skin, came next: "because," reasoned the Count, "if Noka does not return to me I *will* need a dusky, dark complexion to round out the mix." Amalina noted how he was missing the point that Noka was greater than simply a unique hue, but more so a poignant personality: sweet, bold, and majestic.

Aria Ecci followed Pattipo, whom the Count welcomed into his arms without a word but a contented purr, which they both shared like tigers.

Margeta declared with a raised chin and in her pure unflappable confidence, as the seeming final slot was filled: "I said I was going to marry him. Isn't that what I said? I care not what he does with his seraglio's roster. I *will* be chosen. I refuse not to be. One way or another, he is mine and I am his. I have no other reason to be assured but this truth."

The Barnacle may have been hoping that something tragic might befall Cristine—who was in, as far as Amalina knew, a permanent stasis, as Amalina was kept away from Cristine's room, or far from Cristine herself when she left it; shielded by sympathetic Ladies who saw advantage in siding with her.

Despite the outstanding question of Cristine Berzweck, Margeta la Brichese saw her reward finally come, when it was generally felt that, after so long missing, Pia Lampeda *and* Princess Noka Kunuru Sowa Iwebo would, unquestionably, not be returning and a replacement for both their numbers would be required. "Because you've really stuck it out, and I suppose you deserve it, don't you, Lady la Brichese?" the Count muttered almost apologetically as he petted the visibly sour and flummoxed young woman on the head. That night, as Margeta headed for the marble tub and the rite, Bardina delivered a handwritten note to Amalina:

> *Didn't I tell you? And now it happens, cousin. Or does that make you my niece?*

Each Lady went through the rite in so many weeks. During that time, as the ranks grew, the movement below the castle increased, and the cellars crowded with new—if different—life. And Amalina felt a further isolation from her friends who'd gone through it—those reclining into inhumanity—as well as the ones who, as each spot filled, knew they had not been selected again, and began to grow resentful, or feel failure.

"Who do you like better?" asked Lady Daume, echoing a common quiet question from the left-behind-Ladies; another silly question that Amalina desperately wished to avoid, but never seemed to be able to dodge quick enough. "I don't mean to be cruel, but ... *VandeGarde?* ... who is it, do you think? Me or her? Her or me?"

"You're both rather nice in your own ways," Amalina answered diplomatically. *And tiresome in the same*, she added to herself.

Some showed their resentment towards Amalina when, as the Ladies had begun riding horses into the improving season, she brought out her well-muscled courser and they insulted it and its name to her face. "White Mist? And didn't you say it was White Snow before? But how can one keep up? And how silly and childish, isn't it? Snow and mist are *already* white. And this drafthorse of yours is barely so." Amalina's powerful warhorse—which is what a courser is—was discolored in patches where it had suffered mortal blows in its previous incarnations. They laughed cruelly at her, as if mocking her would slice the Count: "More like spoiled milk!" "No," said Amalina, coolly but bothered, wanting to spook them by suddenly naming it 'Ghost', or better, 'Wraith', but deciding that wasn't her style and so, summoning something bright and apropos instead, cut off the "White" and cheerfully re-christened it: "Spirit."

A couple Ladies, Terza Fleccevocarre and Maibrigg Smeehaute, shook off the Count's betrayal with a matching cheerfulness and self-possession. They began a daily service of rounding up newfound flowers from the forest and posting them at everyone's doors, tucked into a small leather loop, a fresh bouquet, in the hopes to boost the sinking mood. The charm of it delighted Amalina so much, she would speak to the Count in their favor. He ignored it.

Some of the quicker ones began to fear for their lives. What would happen to those Ladies who knew the castle's secrets, but had failed to meet with the Count's satisfaction?

And still others had their own peculiar reaction: "I ask you Lord, why do you tolerate your great emissary to make angels of the wicked?" Amalina heard Giordina 'Maria' di Oscina pray aloud, thinking herself alone in the chapel, her arms raised to the ceiling in supplication. "Or is it all wickedness, and my eyes were deceived, Lord? This I cannot believe. Am I truly to be forsaken? Reveal my faults to me! Save me, my lord, *save me*!"

With Amalina's fretting for her remaining guests, and the concern that Spring had come and the roads were opening, which meant if the revolutionary were to go forward with his plan a massacre would be arriving at the castle any day, she began to arrange all the elements to destroy the Count—but with even less vigor than before. At times it felt silly and pointless, and almost as half-hearted as when she'd first tried to do him in; when she didn't know—not even a little—how to do it but tried anyway. But she had grown used to him and here he was trying so hard to endear himself to her. And it seemed he *was* following the restrictions she'd given, so that he was not wantonly killing, but living a decent, if a still-parasitic existence. How could she think of trying to kill him now?

But she moved forward all the same. Automatically. Mechanically. Like the wheel in the cellar with the poor woman on it, continuing in its relentless cycle. Because she knew it had to be done. Countless lives needed to be avenged, much less Lucinda Skeldar's. His plan to spread the plague of his disease needed stopping. She had to save the men of her village, her father, and now Ivanti, from the coming folly. And she needed to end Count Tepsji before he turned Cristine, which despite his ambiguous words and hesitating, equivocal actions, she was now convinced he was going to do.

The dread of Cristine becoming a creature, with all that power and with all that hatred against her, left Amalina with a sick feeling in her stomach. She couldn't believe she could think so poorly about her friend, but those icy blue eyes, and that vicious smile, did not promise a pleasant experience if she should be placed above Amalina. The hateful girl would no longer need to rely on her father's assassins. Cristine could do in Amalina by herself; even without thinking.

The only other option to counter that, besides stopping the Count, was if Amalina allowed him to change her, too; before he did Cristine. So that being superior to her old friend—the first off the mark—she would have nothing to be afraid of. Amalina had seen enough of the Count and the Strange Man that she knew what was possible in a fight between creatures and what she could do to defend herself if her friend should attack while they both had equal strength.

Amalina was mulling this dilemma as she moved about in the forest just outside the high castle, checking the several bee nests she'd salted inside the treeline. So when she returned to the castle she was feeling nervous and guilty, like an unfaithful lover, as she put on a false smile and prepared to pretend that nothing was wrong. That nothing had changed. That she wasn't a threat to everyone there.

It was impossible to keep that smile in place, and it fell like a broken mask, when she noticed the fiery red hair in the darkness of her room, and found Princess Pia Lampeda was sitting on her bed.

## 53

# The Weapon

**P**ia was folded into herself at the waist. Amalina could see a thick cloth bound around her midsection underneath her loose-fitted blouse. Her right hand was apple red, scaly, puckered, and curled as if she had palsy. Her right leg was bent inward, too.

"What—?" cried Amalina. She wanted to wrap her arms around her friend, but held back for fear of hurting her. Instead, she brushed aside the drape of hair to better see Pia's face. Her skin was pale grey, her eyes a hazy jade. "What are you doing here? *How* are you here? *Why* are you here? ... What's happened?" Amalina's mind burned with what horrible possibilities, what turns of events, could have placed her *here* instead of on the road to— but it was all too obvious: "*He* caught you, *he* brought you back here, and *he* ... he-he-he—"

She meant the Count, of course.

"No," sighed Pia, "No ..."

"*He* did this to you!"

Pia squeezed Amalina's arm, lifted her uninjured hand and raised a finger: *keep quiet.*

"*He*—"

"Please," whispered Pia, weakly. "It wasn't him. Not at all."

"Are you sure?"

For a second Pia's face twitched so that she was either in agony or throbbing with a laugh, but there was no sound, and she fell limp again.

Amalina panted: "But—"

"My fault, Katty ..." Pia took in a slow, shallow breath and nodded. "All of it. Not him. Please ..."

Amalina watched her, still panting but willing to listen. "Okay ... but ..."

"Yes, 'But': I was in Korr, I could have left for home ... but ... " Pia managed a feeble smile, "I couldn't leave without trying to help you ..."

"What do you mean?" Again Amalina's thoughts began to race, to predict what Pia might say. She tried to slow herself, take things as they must have occurred, to make sense of it. "Ion took you there. You gave them the book, didn't you?"

Pia nodded. "And then I was stupid ..."

"No."

"… and … I mean, how could I trust …?" Pia tried to smile again, it was a thin line of teeth behind her lips. Like she was fighting off an all-consuming pain. "There was only one way to be sure."

"I don't understand."

Pia told her what she could remember. How she'd gone after Alexandru Berzweck. And how he had surprised her with a pistol. It's destructive force.

Amalina had seen the slight effect firearms had on the Count, and supposed now, regarding how Pia seemed broken by it, maybe she hadn't yet reached his level of invulnerability.

"It wasn't normal," said Pia, of the weapon. "It opened like a horn at the end. And it didn't have a single shot. There must have been hundreds of little pieces in there. That's what it felt like. Hundreds of tiny pebbles of *silver*. And they shot out in all directions. I couldn't get out of the way."

"But you got away."

"I escaped before he could shoot me again." She shuddered. The weak vibration passed through to Amalina's body. It only enervated her. "But I was lucky to've. It burned so much, I could barely move. I thought I was going to die. I didn't know what to do, or where to go. I found a place to hide … places. And I limped back here. Always at night … and I ate things along the way to give me what I needed. Anything …"

"You *walked* back? All the way?"

"I'm so lucky," murmured Pia. She gripped Amalina's hand and raised her eyes to meet her own, to press her meaning. "And I'm lucky your uncle has allowed me back in. I thought he would kill me. But he was so nice. He and Genadie removed the silver from my body. Oh, I can't tell you the torture it was."

"You could have died."

"Silver doesn't kill," said Pia. "It's like salt on a snail, as you said … but worse. You can only imagine … the skin doesn't evaporate, but the tissue dries; reduces and contracts to its smallest, inert state. Sapped of energy. It feels like a crushing weight, oh … where it touches it paralyzes." She heaved a sigh. "But *his* blood still stirs within me. It has power. Even if the skin needs to be renewed and revitalized … It will take time, that's all."

"You shouldn't have done that, Pia," whispered Amalina. "To go after him? What were you thinking?"

"To be honest," she said with a sad smile, "I was hungry. I thought it couldn't hurt. But I didn't know he'd be ready with something like that."

"You told … ?" Amalina pointed to the ground—to wherever the Count was lurking. "Everything?"

Pia shook her head. "He thinks I was running around at night carelessly and some hunter shot me. Someone who must know his special weaknesses. I said I couldn't remember where I was. Heaven help what hunter he might come across out there from now on. But I couldn't tell him the truth, not all of it."

"So Cristine's father is still alive, then?"

"And he thinks you sent me after him." She looked apologetic again and squeezed Amalina's hand. "I kind of said some mean things before I went after him. I didn't think he'd live—or that he'd have that kind of gun."

"What's he going to do, do you think?" said Amalina, fear rising within her.

"You're still safe. Your uncle won't take his side. Even if he comes to the castle with demands, he wouldn't."

"If the Boss *does* come, who knows what he'll say? He has *something* that makes the Count willing to do him favors. And if he believes what the Boss tells him—that I sent you after him—he might consider that too much to tolerate."

"I hope it doesn't come to that," said Pia. "If he tells your uncle anything I said, it will paint me a liar. And he'll know I was up to something ... He might not like it."

"I have to think about this," said Amalina as she began to contemplate the problem. Her thinking pushed the fear to the side at least; or sat on it, like a shovel full of damp earth thrown onto a fire. The anxiety cooled and eased. "Let's just hope Cristine doesn't somehow find out. That could only make her more—"

Pia quieted her with a gesture.

"There was another reason, though," said Pia, softly, "for what I did ... I *was* hungry, of course, but I'd decided to go after him long before I got there. When I was riding in the box. I thought if I could release you from him, from the fear of him, you'd be free. Just like you were freeing me, eh? A gift in return. Liberation for us both ..."

"Oh. Well ..."

"But maybe that's just not what we are supposed to be, you and I ..." said Pia, "... free."

Amalina gave her a look, not following.

"You see: here I am, and here you are, all over again." Pia batted her eyes slowly. "Maybe we really *are* meant to be together. We both tried the best we could to get away ... And yet ... we're right back here..."

Her words and the look in her eyes: it was all so earnest. But, after hearing what Pia had said to the Count that night in the hotel, about how she saw the world now, it was still hard to be certain she wasn't just acting; seeing Amalina as an object she needed to interact with and manipulate to keep it in its place, like a pet with a short attention span; or worse, a piece of furniture she needed to glue into its fitted slot and polish. Even staring deep into her eyes now, it was too hard to tell.

But the kiss was real. Their lips were pressed together and it felt warm enough. It wasn't until they realized their eyes were half-open and they were looking at each other, that they parted with a light laugh. But Pia's expression clouded in pain and weakness a moment later and she had to lay back.

Yawning loudly from the nest of pillows, Pia said, "Would you mind if I rest here with you for a few days? I'm sure I'll be better soon enough."

"No, of course."

"Listen Katty," she said, as if she were drifting off. Her body grew heavy against Amalina. "Whatever happened, they know everything now. Your friends, your father, the revolutionary. Everything. I made sure of it. Like you wanted."

"Yes, thank you."

"But the man is evil. Pure evil. He started that pact with your uncle because he wanted the girls he was sleeping with silenced; so they couldn't ruin his reputation and his business when he was done with them."

"Oh." It was still hard to think of Cristine's father in such a strange, rude light. It seemed impossible.

"I should have killed him, Kat. I should never have given him the chance to react. I should have torn him to pieces right when I saw him."

"But they'll be bringing him to justice now," said Amalina. "You think?"

"Soon ... if not already done. Yes. That must be so. So maybe he won't come then ..."

But this meant the timeline was advancing. Almost out of control, thought Amalina.

"You need to get her out of here," whispered Pia, her eyes closed, still drifting.

"Who?"

"Can't say what I'll do to her. That I can hold back. So evil, Katty. You didn't see him ..."

"What are you talking about?"

"Get her out of this castle. If not for my sake, or your sake, then for hers. She has his eyes."

"Cristine?"

"Those eyes ..." Pia nodded. "Those evil eyes ... And what she tried to do to you ... You know what I did to the men who I thought *might* harm you ... well she damn well *tried* ... I can't say I can stay my hand. When I recover. Or when I wake up ..."

"Are you serious? What are you saying?"

"I am a woman of Rome," mumbled Pia. "Her father tried to kill me, too. You should have seen his face. So ugly. I feel it in me now, Kat ... I will be driven by my own blood to punish ... to take my vengeance ... and I don't think I will be able to stop myself ...and ... she has his eyes ..."

• • •

At first Amalina couldn't believe that Pia, whom she thought she had gotten out of the castle and safely hundreds of miles away, moving in the other direction, was back —just like Amalina returned, without choice and with all speed! Was there really no escape? Then Amalina found herself frustrated and full of rage at her inability to send even *someone else* away. She looked at Pia now and wished she could sneak her back out, if only to prevent what her friend was afraid she might do to Cristine. But it was too late for Lady Lampeda, the Count knew she was here and there would be no getting her out again. Ever again.

But in her resentment and seeming impotence, Amalina knew she had to get one out—*at least one!*—or she would scream. With a turn of thought after Pia's warning, Amalina knew who it would be.

Her heart pounded as it had when she'd considered the approach of the revolutionary army. But this was worse: this was an immediate danger already inside the castle.

"I have to go," said Amalina. "I should be back soon."

"Good," mumbled the nearly unconscious Pia. "Don't open the window, please, whatever you do."

## 54

## Mean Things

Suddenly, Cristine was Amalina's dear friend once again, her recent abuses forgotten; the threats now arranged against the poor misguided girl—much worse than anything the Korr gang could have come up with—felt like they could melt the castle's walls. Whether Pia truly aimed to mete out justice on Cristine for her father's wrongs—*if only because they have the same eyes!*—if the villagers were coming with the notion of punishing the Count, and in their heads burned the heat of anger and revenge at the Berzweck name ... well, hadn't Amalina experienced the horrors of the lynch mob at the bakery door? Sat there in that terrifying moment, their shouting faces crushed into the windows, with the knowledge that they would not be satisfied when they were done with Dragomir? The whole bakery and the entire Dalca clan—or what was left of it—would have been removed from the earth before their lust was spent. A mob was mindless and awful and pitiless. Amalina doubted even now if Sadra at her fullest powers could've stopped it. And while the event had ended with her father facing them down, that mob had every reason to stop: he was their baker; he'd committed no real injustice. But with the Boss' crimes, as monstrous as they were, there would be no reason to quit. Cristine Berzweck would be punished with the Count, whether she was a creature like him or not. She would be the focus of their bitterness and rage—if they had lost their daughters, well wasn't *she* Berzweck's daughter? Wouldn't it be fair and some neat poetry, some equitable payback, if they were to savage her, as their daughters had been? This would be Cristine's bloody, unenviable fate.

*If* she were caught.

All Amalina had to do was get her away to someplace safe.

"I won't be too clever, I won't be too clever, I won't be too clever," she promised herself presently, as she wound her way downstairs, her mind scrambling after what would work.

But how she got Cristine away was just the follow-through. What mattered was that she tried.

. . .

Amalina found Genadie, in his grey cottage, cleaning the large iron emergency bell. Of course, this bell was part of Amalina's plan to bring down the Count and she was surprised to see the little rat hard at work on it, shining it with some unhappy but vigorous pride.

Amalina was just as dumbstruck by this unexpected scene as Genadie was amazed at her bursting through his door without warning, so that she had a moment to glance around the dull grey room for the forbidden weapons—which she had also requested be readied—and he hurried to cover the bell with a cloth carpet, as if she hadn't already gotten a good look at it. There was a pause in this process and they regarded each other. And then whatever encouragement Amalina had felt at finding him at work on the plan, or his guilt at being discovered—even if only by her—had to be left aside.

"Ehm ... uh ... Ms. Dalca?" he asked, sheepishly.

"You have the emergency bell," said Amalina excitedly.

"Of course. It's mine.

"But I thought we needed to find it. Captain Durok had it last. Isn't that what you told me before?"

"And I took it back from him. It's *my* bell. Don't tell him where it is."

"No, no, not at all."

"Was there something you wanted, Ms. Dalca?"

She was already returned to the panic that had brought her: "Genadie, prepare the fast sleigh. Put Spirit on it. We'll be leaving with Lady Berzweck for Korr immediately."

"Spirit?" he wondered.

Amalina had forgotten: she hadn't yet told him about the recent change to White Mist's name. She also woke to the fact that Korr, if it was riled against the Berzwecks, would not be the most suitable place for Cristine to hide.

No matter, they'd be leaving, Netz or Tsobl would do. Anywhere but here.

"Get going!"

She sent Genadie scrambling to the sleigh while she flew upstairs, three steps at a time in full dress, to steal Cristine away; even if she had to drag her friend by the hair.

. . .

Genevieve de Roye's smile wasn't a gentle one. "Of course you can't get in to see her, Kat. Cristine doesn't want you in her room, and her friends are more than willing to keep you away from her. She still hasn't forgiven you."

"Forgiven me!"

"But you'll be talking to her soon enough," de Roye assured Amalina. "Come with me and see if being my good friend doesn't have its benefits."

Before long, Lady de Roye had led Amalina to Margeta's chapel, which was silent and empty, with only a three-candle stand lighting the place, and a handful of squat, red-and-gold-glassed prayer candles burning in a neat votive box beside the confessional. It was to this confessional they were headed. De Roye unhooked a long cloak of a priest and threw it over Amalina's shoulders. Amalina noticed a false mustache stuck to one of the confessional box's posts. De Roye pulled it off the wood with a sticky sound, and then pressed it under Amalina's nose. Amalina almost sneezed at the smell of the glue.

"What's happening here?" said Amalina, touching the mustache on but wanting to pull it off, frustrated and impatient at de Roye's pleased look.

"An interesting game," answered de Roye. "Since Aria is 'unwell', Greta La Nevers has picked up the glove of the hostess for entertainments. She's hit on a good one: with Rosczy gone and we are without a proper father of the cloth, we will be taking each other's confessions, each one of us getting a turn to play confessor or the priest. Which is what the game is called: The Confessor and the Priest."

"Margeta has taken all our confessions before," said Amalina, not seeing the sport in it and still impatient, "when Rosczy isn't here."

"Different," said de Roye. "Because we know when the chapel is free from Margeta, or 'Maria', or any of those other old sticks—with their bead-wracking and carping—a pair of us come down at that given hour: one to play the priest, and the other to be the confessor. But just as the priest's part is being played, so is the role of the confessor. Whoever confesses is given *someone else's* name and declares *that person's* sins. Today Cristine is coming to confess, and you can't guess whose name she has drawn for it."

De Roye's smile was impish, her eyes were lit, her brows alternately lifted and swooping in anticipation, so it wasn't too hard to guess.

"Mine," said Amalina.

"Isn't that hilarious?"

"I can't believe she would do such a thing."

"She wouldn't," said de Roye confidently. "But she doesn't have a choice. Greta arranged the whole thing. Cristine is completely worn out and can barely get herself out of bed. As it happens, Greta also inherited—or rather hawked in to take—Halma Inovala's herbs, incenses, and medicines after she went down; that particular lot don't like strong smells anymore, you know. And Greta will only let Cristine have a batch of Halma's stuff—that she promises will restore her energy—if she plays our game. She also arranged for Cristine to pull your name to confess; figuring that would be the most fun, since she knows you the best, and probably has some good filthy secrets she'd like to share." De Roye bobbed her head before she moved on to the next delicious part: "Now, Elle drew Cristine's name for hearing confession, and Cristine had no objection to it. But I traded with Elle because Elle wanted to hear from Claire, who's drawn *her* name to confess as; and don't you know, I wanted to trade for Cristine's priest so I could find out what she had to say about you, good or bad, and intercept any gossip before it could spread; to protect you, Katarina."

De Roye stood there proudly, arms thrown wide, as if she'd just performed an impressive act. Amalina didn't know how to respond. This felt like some kind of delay, a putting off of what she wanted—needed—to do right now. And part of her wished she hadn't met Genevieve de Roye first when looking for Cristine, or hadn't asked after her friend. But how could she deny that if she hadn't done both she might not have reached Cristine at all, but only stood outside her locked door, speaking to angry silence.

"Well, now I gladly give you the floor, Katty—or the box, that is," said Genevieve, opening the half of the confessional that belongs to the priest. "You can have her all to yourself."

"Thank you, Jenny. I don't know how to thank you."

"You can thank yourself. Greta was inspired to her game when I recounted the little confession I made to you; remember, the one in the shitbox? Wasn't that fun? Well, now here we are. I'll go. Get yourself ready, she should be here any minute. It's up to you if you want to reveal yourself; or just sit back and hear first what nastiness she has to say … as Katarina Tepsji. Could be fun, Kat! Try to sound like VandeGarde trying to sound like Rosczy, if you want to keep up the game."

•  •  •

Amalina heard the chapel door open slowly with a dull creak on its hinges. It was already hot in the confessional, but now Amalina sweated harder underneath the priest's scratchy cloak and she felt like she was suffocating. Her face dripped and she took turns pushing the mustache into place and wringing her hands. Through the gauze of red cloth placed over the slatted view of the chapel, Amalina saw the low, bent silhouette make its way up the narrow side aisle. She recognized the movements of her old friend, even though the figure was nearly crawling. How often had Amalina found her friend struggling through an alley this way after having been jumped?

The shaky breaths of this dark lump were accentuated by bursts of air and grunts as she forced her body along. Eventually the door of the neighboring box scraped closed with three labored tugs. Then, after she'd knelt and let her body slump against the inside of the small cabinet, the girl released a loud sigh.

"I'm here," said Cristine, her voice scratchy and faint. "Let's get this over with, eh?"

Amalina tried to see past the latticework screen to assess her friend's appearance. She could only see Cristine's pale lips and grey skinned neck, which looked—amazingly—to have fresh scarlet holes raked into it: new bites. Amalina nearly gasped. Then realized the semi-screen worked both ways and righted her self and shrugged the cloak higher, to bring up the shoulders to shield her face. She also straightened the mustache.

"He's drawn blood from you again?" asked Amalina, reining in her breaths, sending her voice as deep and masculine as it would go, and attempted to affect Elle VandeGarde's accent to it. The resonance in the cramped box helped with the aural mask. "Recently?"

"What are you talking about?" rasped Cristine, overly annoyed. She lifted her arm weakly and shoved a small paper through the lattice.

Amalina took it and, lifting it close to her eyes in the the dim red light, read Greta's ladylike script: *I am Katarina Tepsji*. Oh, right. This was a game.

Amalina could not overcome her nerves, and felt shy to announce herself this soon, not knowing what Cristine's reaction would be. And there was a strange anticipation: what would Cristine say in the role of Katarina? Would she reveal Amalina's secret that there was no Katarina at all? expose what fraud had really been played on all of these western Ladies? Would she really do it?

*What nonsense*, thought Amalina to herself: *You have to get her out of this castle before Pia wakes! Go!*

"You don't have to pretend to be Katarina," said Amalina, her voice still concealed as Elle-as-Rosczy, easing into the coming revelation.

"Who would I be, then?"

"Yourself, Cristine. It's all right."

"And why would I do that? So you can report to Greta that I blew it right away?" She sounded so exhausted and angry that she might suddenly faint.

"I wouldn't—"

"Come on: *Deus, Pater misericordium, per mortem and resurrectionem Filii sui*—let's get to it, father ..."

"*Benedic mihi pater quia peccavi* ..." Amalina corrected Cristine, rather automatically.

"Yes, yes, yes, Bless me father," repeated Cristine quickly in the Ardeelian tongue, on a long, sighing exhale, "but you don't really need to bless me, father; I don't believe in Rome, in the pope, or any of your ridiculous rituals ..."

"I see," said Amalina; it was a synthesis of the Count's opinions delivered through Cristine's harsh voice. She was playing the exact part she'd been given as Katarina Tepsji. Or so it sounded.

"Good enough?" asked Cristine "Can I leave now, or do I really have to do the whole quarter hour? It's not like Greta's really God here, and who's to say how long we've been stuck in this airless crypt?"

Amalina agreed: "No, we really don't have to—"

"Alright, alright, blah-blah-blah," sighed Cristine, not waiting for the rejection, or listening. "Fine, but it's not like I have a conscience to examine, father. I mean, what's to examine when one has no soul, eh? As I, Katarina, do not."

"Oh … I …"

"'Oh', what?"

"Well, I don't know if Katarina would say *that*," said Amalina, feeling defensive suddenly. And Father Rosczy had always been a soft-spoken, mild creature. "No soul … ?"

"I'm telling you what I would say, father. What do *you* think I'd say?"

"I feel Katarina would be a bit more respectful—"

Despite her exhaustion, Cristine snorted.

Amalina lowered her imitation voice: "Look, I'm telling you, you don't have to do this, I'm not—"

"Okay, all right," snarled Cristine, "Bless me father for I have done whatever I felt like, and don't really care what you think, go tell your master as much. Eh? I am iniquity personified."

"Cristine …"

"Quit calling me that! Please, father! I am Katarina Tepsji, not that lovely, innocent, young woman, Lady Berzweck. Oh what a wonderful girl she is, isn't she? I suppose you would rather have her here in the box with you? Is that what you're saying? Are you having some thoughts, sir? I mean, really. Is there something you want to confess to *me*? What would my uncle say if I told him so? What do you think he would do to you, eh?"

"Cris—um—Katarina, my child," said Amalina, trying to soothe the heaving body next door. She put her hand to the cabinet, trying to feel the human weight of against the wood. If Cristine carried on any more she might begin sobbing; the victim of the gang again. Amalina guessed maybe her friend, in her own simple, crude way, was trying to protect Katarina by cutting the game, and any questions, short. Which was nice enough. *If only she'd let me help.* "I really don't like this game either, so let's not—"

"What game?"

"Please, calm yourself—"

"My god," moaned Cristine. "What more do you want? Bless me father, for I have sinned! I was raised in your opposing faith, and I am an unaccountable liar! I bear false-witness left-right-up-down and to everyone I meet, every way I can. I am so good at it, I do it even to myself as if for sport!"

"I don't think …"

"You heard me. I lied to all these women here, and told them I'm their friend. Then I told myself—convinced myself—they *are* my friends, which is the biggest lie of all."

"But that isn't true."

"And I've even fooled you—Wait … Can you say that, Father?"

"You *do* have friends, Katarina." Amalina had put back on the fake accent, though it seemed to have no sway on Cristine one way or the other. But she really did feel on the defensive now. What was Cristine trying to do here?

"Whose confession is this?"

"What of you and Cristine?" asked Amalina. "You two are good friends, the best of friends—"

"You're mistaken there, fool."

Amalina shifted. "How is that, Katarina? I was led to believe—"

"Led to believe," sneered Cristine. "Exactly. We are nothing to each other, her and me, Cristine and me. You see how good I am at it."

"But you grew up together."

"Let me tell you about Cristine Berzweck and I, Countess Katarina Tepsji …"

Peeking into the opposite box, Amalina watched Cristine blow out a hostile breath and close her eyes, though somehow her face was still screwed up with resentment and scorn. Curled up in the small dim space, it looked like she was having an unpleasant dream.

"Go on …" said Amalina, with a mounting dread, "uh, Katarina, my child."

"Bless me father, but I think there has been a mistaken impression here, and it is entirely my fault. I have spoken falsely about my friendship with that girl, of course."

"Have you?"

"Why, as I've said, I've lied to everyone about it. It was our conspiracy, her and I, to pull the wool over everyone's eyes. But there is no friendship to speak of between us, but cold agreements based on convenience, jealousy, and mutual interest. On my part, I would emphasize pure jealousy."

"No! But you were sisters—"

"Father Rosczy! You're not supposed to know about that little infamy of ours! Unless she's been talking … and good Cristine would never let a secret out. Well, however you heard, whatever you think, we were never sisters. Never sisters! And less so friends. I, Katarina Tepsji, was just, and have always been, a jealous little girl with a plain face, plain hair, stubby little arms, and drab clothes, because my father Dragomir—" here Cristine paused in a passionate outburst, and Amalina wondered if, at the precipice of revealing the truth about the charade of Katarina Tepsji, she was actually going to do it, to spill the story of Amalina Dalca, baker's daughter; Cristine was carefully considering her words "—my father, Dragomir ... who doesn't care for his older brother, the Count, and who has put all his time and invested all his moneys into trifles of the common people ... like bakeries—" she paused again, gathering her breath and assessing if she'd successfully avoided forbidden subjects "—and I have always wanted to be more like Lady Berzweck, who was pretty and, though without a true title, was richer than I, and smarter than I, and well dressed, and from a powerful family who have made their own way in the world. And what can I say for Cristine but she needed protection. She had nobody else to walk with her, or talk with her. Nobody else was at her level, and the commoners were just as jealous of her as I, but since I had a title to protect me, they took it out on her in their common ways; with their kicks and scratches. But here, Father, I am a schemer, and I can pretend friendship to get what I like. And so Cristine, the pretty rich girl, the innocent but practical girl of the world, who saw I could lend her aid and security, made do with what she could get; she made allies with the dull little girl that I am—who did not care for her any better than she did in return. She got what she wanted from me, and I got what I wanted from her."

Amalina felt slightly sick to her stomach. "Oh? But ..."

"And now I'd like to get Lady Berzweck out of this castle. There's no doubt about that. She's very close to receiving something I want. If you could help me, I'd do anything for you. Put in a good word with Uncle for Elle VandeGarde, if you'd prefer. Eh?" she pulled herself up closer to the screen. "That can be arranged. Will you help me? Will you get word to Elle for me, father? I know you have communication with her, eh? Well, I can convince uncle to choose her. I swear I can. But my enemy Cristine must be out of here before the Count gives her what belongs to *meee*."

"How could you think—!" started Amalina, furiously, "Have you *ever* heard me—Have *you* ever said—" she stumbled as she tried to regain her bearings "—Has Cristine ever heard *you* say such a thing like that?"

"Eh?" said Cristine. "Is that a question for the confessional, father? Or are you prying now?"

"You aren't jealous of anyone, Katarina. Especially for Cristine ... How could you be?"

"Am I not?" huffed Cristine. "How can you be so bold as to defend my honor, when I think I know myself best? How could I be jealous of Cristine, you ask? Father Rosczy, listen well: I lost my mother at a very young age, and I've been a jealous dog ever since. You could say I was born with that sin buried in my flesh like a poisonous thorn. I look about the world with my tainted eyes, glare with utter envy at what everyone else under heaven seems to have from birth, yet I did not. I was robbed!" Here Cristine seemed to laugh, using soft coughs. "My black heart cries at what was taken away from me so unfairly. And now, my father has married someone else ...some old woman who has stolen his affections away from me. How else should I feel! I tell you, sir, I am the most jealous sinner that—"

"Cristine!" cried Amalina, dropping the imitation voice and accentuating her own.

Cristine paused, stared levelly at the partition as if trying to see through it. Then, in a low voice: "What is this?"

"Cristine, it's me."

"What is this?" she repeated, displeasure in her tone.

"I can't believe you said that about me!"

"Amalina?" she guessed, an unhappy curl on her lip. "Where's Elle, eh? But I get it. And what were you expecting to hear, Ama?"

"Not that! That you would think of me like that!"

"And here you came to spy on me. What's to think about you? Was it to have some fun with me, eh? You deserved everything you just heard. Everything I just said."

"But it isn't true!"

Cristine sagged to the side and began to open the door. "I'm done with this."

"No wait," said Amalina, scrambling out of the booth to corner her before she could fly the cabinet, tugging off the mustache in one wild motion. She threw open the confessional door, and half of Cristine fell out at her feet. "I didn't come to spy on you! I'm here to save you!"

Cristine recoiled. "Don't touch me, idiot."

"Come, never mind," said Amalina, "I have to get you out of the castle."

"Of course. Why not? Get me as far away from here—"

"Not just you," said Amalina. "But—"

"You're leaving too, are you telling me?"

"Yes, I'm taking you with."

Cristine's eyes popped open and she glared. "Yes, while I'm weak and near death. Now you come to rescue me. Because you're afraid of what I am about to attain—"

"You don't want it though," insisted Amalina, trying to catch her friend's limp hands. "You haven't thought it through enough. You couldn't possibly want it."

"Why not? It's good enough for your other friends. It's good enough for *you*—"

"No! I'm telling you: I'm out. And have you spoken to any of *them*? Just listen to how they talk, what they say, how miserable it must really be—"

"Oh, I believe you," she grunted sarcastically. Her bleary eyes sharpened.

"It's not what it sounds like. But you must believe."

"Why should I?" said Cristine, flopping angrily within the box, trying to get to her feet while fending off Amalina. "I don't know what you've told *him*, but look at me. He's holding back. He keeps me lingering in this impossible state instead of just getting it over with." She sighed when she got her legs under her. "I tell him I'm ready, I tell him I want it. What can I do to convince him, eh? But he hesitates, and why would he do that? If it isn't because he favors you, if it isn't because *you* poison his mind against me, then why? Why?"

She sounded just like Margeta.

"Listen, Cristine—"

"You're trying to punish me still ... to ruin me. ..."

"No. I'm trying to save us—"

"... starting with my family ... "

"Oh, never mind all that," said Amalina, in a final gust. "Can't you? Can't you just listen? We're together. I'm taking us both out of here right now, before it's too late. Come out of there."

"Too late?" Cristine stumbled to the side while dodging Amalina's hands.

"You're in danger now."

"I'm so close to never being in danger again. You're the one standing in the way of it ... it must be. Admit it. Admit it!"

"I mean, you're going to die."

"You wish. It is more than death."

"I mean your life is in danger, real danger here. I'm not talking about Tepsji, there's something else."

"And you will still keep your hands off me! I'll face down anyone or anything. I'm scared of nothing you can come up with."

"You don't understand," Amalina scanned her mind and knew it was better not to bring Pia's name into this, so ... what else: "they've found your father out."

"Papa! The hell!" her teeth clenched. "*Who*?"

"Everyone knows now. And we don't want to be—"

Amalina paused as Cristine's impassioned expression suddenly fell, relaxing into a cool smirk and her lids lowered on her icy eyes. "Lies, as always. I'm sure I don't know what you're talking about."

"Wait, you have to listen. He was having them killed because he was forcing them to lay with him—"

She jerked. Wide awake again, the volcano's rage building. "Again with you, Ama! Always a fresh insult. And when did you figure this one out?"

"D'you understand? And he had to silence them before they talked and—"

"And that's why he wanted *you* killed too, eh? *You* were forced into his arms?"

"I knew who he was, that's all. And he knew it, and … And he thinks I made you come here and am keeping you here."

"What a laugh."

"Come on, Cristine, how can you not believe me … even now? You must! He sent that assassin to you, didn't he? He had you identify me to that man. You can't deny it!"

Cristine shook her head slowly, looking like she smelled something bad.

"I forgive you for it," said Amalina, in a poor choice of reasoning, "if you'd just listen. But you know—"

"The only thing I know," began Cristine, lifting her body again and straightening inside the box, looking like a corpse adjusting itself inside a narrow coffin to get a little more dignity, "is right when you thought you'd make yourself greater than me, what could be more frightening than my elevating myself before you? That's precisely what I know. And don't pretend. I've known you long enough I can see it in your eyes. Well, you can say whatever you like to these girls, what do I care? It's happening. And I'll be above you *before* you. He's promised me this much. However long it takes. However long … I won't have you trick me out of it now."

"Your father's bringing your family down," argued Amalina, continuing on her line of attack, imploring with a shake of her clasped hands, trying to appeal to her. "Why side with him? He cheated on your mother, Cristine. He brutalized girls; girls *we* knew. Had them killed."

"Lies, lies, and lies. Keep talking." But Cristine's staggered blinking showed Amalina was scoring hits.

"And if that doesn't upset you, you have to understand: he *will* be punished for his crimes. And then, when they are done with him, they are coming here. They will have their revenge on the man in this castle, who was a party to the conspiracy, and on anyone who stands with him. This is the truth! This is why we must leave, Cristine, dear Cristine, while there is still time." Amalina shoved her head forward, as if to try kissing their eyelashes. "Please, please, please, sister in blood!"

Cristine wrenched away, and shoved Amalina as hard as she could, which wasn't much; she ended up pushing herself and stumbled to the back of the box. "We've never been, Ama. We swore an oath, but what of it when one oathmaker is unfaithful? has never honored it unless it was convenient to her?"

"What's convenient for me here?" said Amalina. "I'm giving everything up! I'm risking my life! I came here to save you, to warn you!"

Cristine emitted a strange sound, pivoted at the hips, and sunk low on her legs, as if she were about to launch out of the box.

"Came to warn me?" snarled Cristine. "Let me warn you. Let me warn you. Let me warn you, Amalina, or Katarina, or whoever else you pretend to be: now all is at an end!" Cristine's eyes slitted. "We need nothing more from each other. We both see that, you monster of envy, you gossip, you outright liar. Convinced yourself you can destroy anyone in your way if you think you have to? When I'm brought forth into the new plane, I will defend myself harder where I should have done so before—and using what I have learned. I will fight and protect my family's honor. And you will see what I will do to you as just payment for everything; what I will do to your family."

"No, Cristine—"

"Yes, Cristine," she echoed cruelly, with a wan smile. "I promise you. That will be my *new* blood oath. Upon my word. I will demand Count Tepsji admit what a fake and a liar you really are and have always been. I will make him see through your cowardly front and know he can never trust you. And then where will you be, eh? A backbiter and a traitor, stripped of her protector? I can only hope he'll allow me the pleasure of taking you apart myself, because his wrath will be stirred against you till it boils over."

"You don't know what you're saying ..."

"I know enough to *convince* him I do." A tear trickled down from Cristine's eye and over her cheek. But the sharp grin was still blood-thirsty and vicious.

Amalina wiped her own tears away. Her knees were shaking, she felt like sobbing, but somewhere in the act of backing away from the confessional, a resolution formed inside her. Part of the heat of her sadness fell away into numbness.

As she reached the far door, Cristine called out: "Or does it have to be this way, eh? If you could only leave me alone. Let me win just this one time, Amalina ..."

• • •

The look in Cristine's eyes, and the deadly promise of some kind of dreadful, twisted revenge, hammered in Amalina's heart. The plea she'd given as Amalina left the room, soft, meek, and pitiable as it sounded, couldn't be trusted. Not anymore. It had been only a small, gentle, pleasing, foamy white cap on top of the giant wave of bitter hate roaring and swelling beneath it. Maybe it was the last shred of the truth of their friendship bursting in one final sad appearance. It *had* been real friendship, once upon a time. At least for Amalina. All there was left was the clearest intimation of violence against her. Count Tepsji's promise to wipe out Amalina's family if she did not obey him had always been slightly ambivalent, balanced by his apparent fondness for her and her father; and his need for her help, anyway. Cristine's threat, though, was adamantine.

When Amalina couldn't find Count Tepsji, she went to Genadie's room. The rat wasn't there, but the old, large, iron bell was, barely hidden under the worn cloth carpet. And that was what she was looking for. She hefted it up, remembering when it had last sounded out in the castle, calling the Count forward to meet some emergency.

Was this an emergency?

No.

How could she justify using it? She ran to an upstairs, unused room—neutral ground—stared at the bell for a minute, and then struck it anyway. She struck it twice.

Cristine had to go. Any which way Amalina looked at it, the girl had to go.

## 55

## The Emergency Bell

A loud hum sounded from the stone in the hall, then a rush of air swept through the open door. A black blur swirled before Amalina and suddenly he was there in full. Count Tepsji stared down at her, his large eyes tired, his thick brows lowered and heavy, his hair disheveled. He was in his white linen shirt which seemed to be stippled and striped with blood. He rubbed his hands together, their skin shimmered strangely yellow. A wave of unnatural heat blew in with him.

"Ms. Dalca? Are you waking the whole house?" He seemed almost to be seething. She couldn't tell if he was unhappy with her or just out of breath. "What's happened?"

"Sir, I'd asked you to leave Cristine be," whispered Amalina, as if her friend was in the other room. "But you're still changing her!"

"And you rang my bell …?" He sounded confused, and looked more so. "Why? I can only wonder at it, at a time of such importance, when your close friend, Lady Lampeda, is so dearly wounded—and by a weapon of unheard of power—you would bother me? Bother *meee*?"

Amalina cleared her throat at his strangely passionate, if wheezing, display. Perhaps this new weapon, having seen its effects, and knowing someone in these mountains had the courage to use it, had rattled his normal complacency. There was a tremble in his body. He looked bewildered, almost like a doddering ancient. Or had he been frightened by the sounding of the bell, thinking it had been the announcement of an attack on the castle? But his fear was irrelevant right now. Amalina cleared her throat again, as he stared questioningly down at her.

"She's threatening me, sir. She's done it again. Just a moment ago, sir. She threatened me and Papa with all kinds of awful … well …"

The Count appeared to recover. He took in a long breath, straightened his clothes, and nodded, then lifted the bell gently from her hands between his fingers as if it were nothing more than a dinner chime; he didn't see this as an emergency compared to his own considerable concerns.

"I think she's in no condition to endanger a mouse." He grinned patronizingly. "I mean, a real mouse, my little mouse."

"I'm not talking *now*. But when she—if she—becomes what you are, sir, she will have the power to do whatever she wants to me."

He waved a golden hand dismissively, his relief at this comparable nonsense now obvious. "Once she's on the other side, as I have already explained, Mouse, it won't even occur to her anymore."

Amalina, annoyed by his indifference, reminded him: "After you changed you went after all your enemies. That's what you told me. You drove off the Ottomans."

This reminiscence pleased him greatly. He petted one side of his mustache and smiled broadly at Amalina. "Yes. *Yesssss.* But I didn't know exactly *what* I was yet. I hadn't fully learned I was no longer one of the lesser species. Why, I didn't even know I had changed—changed beyond this world—at all. If I'd known, I might not have." He weighed that thought. "*Maybe* I might have. They were my enemies, after all. Enemies from my birth. But you two began very young, as the best of friends. There isn't a reason it shouldn't continue that way."

"She thinks I'm attacking her family."

"I can remedy all of this," said the Count. "No one need know of it. But you know that."

"I don't think you can solve anything about it, sir. Unless you mean you're going to kill her father or—"

"You want me to kill him?" he said, astonished, but roused by the surprise. "Or *her?*"

"No, no," gasped Amalina. "I don't want anyone to die! But ... her father is still, um ... still evil ... and still powerful ... and as long as he has so much power ..."

"What makes him powerful?" asked the Count, almost making it sound like a philosophical question.

"Well ... um ..." she hesitated.

"Yes?" his interest was piqued.

"Well, he convinced you to ..." she stared at him, unsure if he'd understand. "I mean, he got you to do what he wanted, didn't he? And you helped him ... for some reason. I mean, there was a reason, wasn't there? That means he has *some* kind of power. Even over you, you see?"

"You don't know what you are talking about," said the Count. "It doesn't quite work that way. No one has power over me at all, my little mouse. Rest assured. And they won't have it over you." He eyed her for a second. "But let me clear up a little mystery for you. Come."

• • •

Once upon a time, when the Count wanted someone to be somewhere else, he would pick them up and transport them, almost instantly, to that point. Regardless of their body's ability to handle such a sudden shock, with the neck snapping and the bones and flesh protesting, he would roll the person out right into whatever room was intended, where they would somersault to a stop, or crash painfully into furniture or a wall.

Amalina thought of this as he took her arm and walked with her out of the room, he still cradling the bell in his other arm, and escorted her through the castle. Step by step they went, making her feel the boredom of the slow commute. The halls and winding stairs seemed endless. She almost began to wish he would just scoop her up and do his old trick. Instead, the Count nodded at her with a polite smile, and hummed a tune to occupy their time, as servants and guards cleared their way.

"Master!" cried Genadie when they reached *l'entrée grande.*

"Your Eminence!" shouted Captain Durok, who stood at Genadie's side, sword drawn, a bewildered look on his jug-like, whiskered, helmeted head.

"Close that door!"

Genadie and Durok flew to the entrance and, while ramming into each other, closed the door and threw shut its locking bar.

"The alarm, Your Greatness?" said Durok, once they had protected their master and turned for a better look; though still glancing about for intruders, obviously frightened by their master's bloody and disarranged appearance. Some of the other guards now entered from side halls.

"However, my little mouse rang it," explained the Count with a broad smile for them. And by his expression, ringing tone, and body language he wished to push out of the entrance hall without any more drama.

"Eh, what were you doing with that, Ms. Dalca!" demanded Genadie pointing to the iron bell tucked in his master's arm. "That's *my* bell."

"*Whose* bell?" growled the Count, halted short by the insolent claim.

Genadie threw himself flat on the cold stones of the entryway, while Captain Durok kneeled and bowed his head.

"Yours, sir!" they both cried.

"Captain Radu!" rumbled the Count.

"Your Eminence?"

"Come before me, Captain Radu!"

Durok rose from his place, looking unsure, and hustled forward. "Yes, sir, yes, sir, yes, sir ... But, Your Lordship ... That is ... Durok? ... I'm Durok, sir."

"What's that?" the Count seemed startled to find Durok before him.

"Radu is my great-grandfather's name, sir. Then came Michael, then Came Boro. As you'll recall, sir. But I'm not Radu, he was my great-grandfather, as I said."

"Well, what's the difference?" said the Count, almost breezily now. As if ignoring an insult given to him by a child. "You're all the same aren't you? ... Radu, Michael, Boro, what's in a name? Just further down the line, you are. You certainly *look* like him … and look more like him than he did when he got old." Again the Count gained that struck look he'd had earlier, which Amalina had seen on the faces of the mind-shattered: confused eyes and vexed scowl. "How can I be expected to keep track? And why should I? For all I know you're playing a joke!"

"Oh, no, sir. Never, sir."

"But then you *are* him, eh?" he seemed to know the man standing before him once more. "Just as dependable? Have that grand loyal streak in your blood?"

"Oh, yes, Your Eminence. You can count on me."

"Well, that's what they all say," shrugged the Count. "We'll just have to see … Radu."

"Um, Durok, sir."

"What's that?"

"Um, never mind, sir."

"Captain Radu, Captain Durok, Captain *whatever*!"

"Yes, Your Eminence!"

Suddenly the bell shot so hard into Durok's stomach that he fell to the floor. "Oof! Sir!"

"You will retain the emergency bell from here on out and keep our little mouse away from it."

"Yes, Your Eminence!"

"And it's never to be rung unless there's a true emergency. Thus the name for it."

"Damned if it won't be so, Your Supreme Highness!"

"You'll be more than damned if it happens again."

"Oh, yes, sir!"

"Come," the Count told Amalina.

As the Count took Amalina's hand and tugged her toward their destination, Genadie cleared his throat and mumbled unhappily after her, "That *was* my bell, Ms. Dalca."


· · ·


The Count nabbed a torch off the wall, and eventually they were in the private study and then through the secret door into the treasury, and then down the side stairs into the Count's message center.

He lit more torches at the bottom. This moment hadn't been planned and he hadn't prepared the set properly. When he was done, he finally dropped the first torch into a ring holder on the wall. Then he opened his arms to gesture to it all: the long rectangular vault with a high ceiling, tall shelves, and the central island of shelving.

"Look at this, my dear little mouse."

"You've shown me before, sir."

"Oh, yes. Yes I did. That's when I showed you my correspondence with Cristine's father. Which might have been a mistake, now that I think of it. But here we are again, in my little world of Ardeel; and all the tasks, and missions, and favors and hopes of those who have reached out to me over these long years. Look at all of it. Would you say that every one of these people who I've done business with have power over me?"

In a dark thought, she imagined all the souls attached to these scraps of paper, scrolls, and bound volumes, coming forth at once. A massive army indeed. Perhaps Sadra's revolutionary was right: such a force could take him. They *must* be able to. Somehow. Despite the history that proved the opposite.

But the Count stood there proudly, arms still outstretched, like a statue in a city center, beaming with pride and satisfaction. And with little fear of such a thought that Amalina had, an army of vengeance.

"I told you before, I could reveal to you things that would set your head on fire. You don't believe me?"

"Of course I do, sir."

"I've never lied to you."

"Except when you pretended my father ordered me to serve you. You forged his note, sir."

The Count chuckled guiltily. "I meant lied on a higher order, of course. But let's go back to your accusation against poor Alexandru Przek, and my question. You said he is evil. Would you say every one of these people who have written to me are evil?"

"It would depend," said Amalina. She thought of the contract he had with the vast generations of the men of Ardeel which allowed him to persist in his taking of victims. She saw where he was going with this. "I'd say your *contract* with Ardeel is evil. But you know that already. And you forced it on them, so it's not like they—"

"I'm not talking about *that* nonsense," said the Count, irritated. "I am talking about the individual people who've sought me out. Personally. The ones who signed that contract and know who I am, and yet they came forward on their own to ask something further from me, they understanding I should ask a price in return, and knowing what I am capable of asking from them."

Amalina looked around at all the shelves. She remembered Kralov's men, and Kralov, and Piotr, running through this very room, sending bolts of sunlight at the Count, firing their pistols at him, slashing their swords, filling it up with gunpowder to blow the whole thing. And they had all died, of course. But this room was an enormous library of direct contact from people across the country and down through the centuries. They were people who had *sided* in some way with the Count. Perhaps their collective will, embodied in these innumerable letters, had worked against Kralov's siege in some way—the exact opposite of what Attila had predicted—and caused its failure.

"Shall we call them a power over me? Shall we call them all evil? All of Ardeel? From beginning to end? Because, Amalina, believe me, everyone comes to me eventually."

With that statement, the Count went to the small shelf for Korr, the smallest in the whole room devoted to one village. He reached into the space and poked his hand around, sifting and stirring through the piles of paper and scrolls and weird pieces of sticks. Without the bulky AXP book as his target, his task was not as easy. But it didn't take him long to find what he wanted.

He brought to his standing desk a small yellowed envelope, and wagged his finger to bring Amalina closer. He opened the envelope, and then straightened the long letter inside, and sounded a note of disgust as Amalina put on her glasses to examine it.

"Glasses," he muttered.

The type of parchment looked all too familiar. And so did the handwriting. It was Dragomir's.

> *Please, I beg you to help her. I love her so much, I can't lose her, not now. You have so much power, great old one, I will do anything for you. I will do anything you ask. Anything! I will pay any price, just save my Dasha while you still can.*

"She was already dying," said the Count. "There was nothing I could do to save her—your mother—even if I had wanted to. But if I had, Amalina, your father would be in my service, wouldn't he? They *all* come asking, Amalina."

"Another forgery," accused Amalina.

"This letter is what I used to make that one—my little joke to you—look convincing. I imitated the linework perfectly, don't you think? But this is very real."

Amalina stared at her father's pleas, written with desperate hatch strokes and blobs of ink and maybe even, the way the paper bubbled, the stains of his tears: *"I will do anything you ask. Anything!"*

"Everyone comes to me, Amalina." he repeated in a gentle rumble. "I'm not so bad. But, you see, when I saw you in the window that night, I remembered this," he said, taking the page from her and waving it. "And I did more than a favor to the poor man whom I pitied. Though I could not do right by his wife, as he had asked, I spared his daughter, who resembled her so. I have promised to myself, and to him, to give you something everlasting. A gift that will spare Dragomir from losing anything so precious in his life again. And haven't I told you time after time how I thank heaven every day that I found you that night in the window? It has been such a blessing for us both."

Though she felt like the room should be spinning—and maybe it would later—she experienced a weird clarity. As if the world had just become defined in a real way. Here was her poor father begging for her mother's life. Of course he would promise anything to anyone he thought could save her. *Of course he came to you, the all powerful and mysterious creature of death, you idiot!* Whatever the Count thought he was proving with this revelation—some equivalence he perceived between Dragomir and AXP's correspondence— this desperate, pathetic attempt to beg a personal favor wasn't even close to the same thing as Cristine's father's decades-long sordid dealings with the Count, even if he couldn't see it.

Only, her mind went on: maybe Boss Berzweck held a similar secret to Dragomir's tragic circumstance, and by pleading his case had inspired a like sympathy in the Count; one that had so moved him it had precipitated and leveled an identical protection for the Boss' daughter; the very same one Amalina enjoyed. Could that be? Could that be what he was getting at?

"If you are really worried by your friend's threats," said the Count, after a moment, in a condescending tone but then one of finality, "I will change you first. It is now decided."

Something clenched hard in Amalina's chest.

*No!*

"You can't just *not* change her?" growled Amalina, like a cornered animal. "You can't just send Cristine away?"

There was a flash deep in his eyes. Or … it was as if a veil lifted between them, and she saw the constant mischievous glimmer inside the darkness; and wondering at it, recognized it. A monstrous notion now visited Amalina: He would not be stopping with Cristine. The Count had always been a bit of a scientist of course, she'd seen him spend months at a time stooped over strange bulbs of boiling liquids, taking measurements with odd instruments, and meticulously logging results and scratching down notes or formulas or recipes or theories. He tested and prodded everything in the universe which he got hold of, even in his hobbies, to see if there was something interesting there, or what could be done or had with it, or if it would break or could be broken; and at what point. Wasn't the wailing woman just such an experiment? It could be the only explanation! And Amalina had made the mistake of putting into his head the idea of a languishing, half-drained victim, a transformation plotted out over so many days, or weeks, or months, and not done by a quick, simple—if violent—ritual; and now he had his clay, his toy, to have a go at it. Cristine Berzweck, locked in his castle, could be played with indefinitely to see just how long the process could be extended, the life within a thinning vessel preserved; and only when he was satisfied, or tired to boredom, or forced to do so by physical necessity, conclude at what point the deed had to be brought to completion. And, as a matter of course in this experiment, unless he erred somewhere—and his cold-blooded tinkering need be taken up again to determine where he'd gone wrong with Cristine, using some new model—he would see that the experiment ended successfully.

It didn't matter the threat Cristine posed to Amalina; he did not recognize it; nor would he believe it. It did not matter Amalina no longer wanted Lady Berzweck there, and that her presence at the castle—live or changed—would never please her. It didn't even matter that Pia was now aimed to kill her—if Amalina dare mention it. Amalina's and Pia's feelings about Cristine bore no weight at all. The only opinion that mattered in the equation here was the Count's.

But Cristine had to go.

However, in this thought, combined with the Count's earlier fear of the new weapon and the damage it had done to Pia, and the confusion brought on by the revelation of her father's letter, Amalina realized there might be another chord to be struck here to get what she needed from him—and without delay.

*Yes, without delay*, she thought. *Now!*

"You see," the Count was saying in some measure of triumph, as if to paper the moment over, or to divert from what she might have realized, "you're begging me for a favor, are you not? Knowing I could ask anything of you in return, as I have of all my correspondents ... but no, you would never do such a thing—"

"Did Pia tell you how she was injured ... sir?" asked Amalina, almost choking before she could talk. "Did she tell you it was some farmer who struck her on his property? Shot her with that odd weapon with the silver in it?" He stared at her, motionless. He didn't know what one had to do with the other. "She was covering the truth, sir. She went to kill him—to kill AXP—to protect me. Only he had that gun, and with it he almost killed her, instead."

The Count's right brow lifted, as the corner of his mouth turned down.

"Cristine sent that man to kill me in the hotel," said Amalina, with mounting confidence. "Or she contacted her father to have him do it. Or maybe *he* reached out to *her*, knowing I was there, and anyway had her identify me, so that I could be ambushed. And before you tell me I have nothing to worry about, I need you to think this through, sir. Those two,

Cristine and her father: they work together. And even if he has been your friendly correspondent all these years, and someone you might consider an ally, he has that weapon. He *made* that weapon, sir. And he certainly didn't make it for Pia, either. He made it because he doesn't trust you. He likely never has."

Oddly, the Count leaned against the side of the desk and began stroking his mustache with a grin of admiration. His eyes grew distant as these thoughts circled in his head.

But Amalina still had something else to add: "How much does he know about you? And still he sent his daughter to this castle? And from the very moment Cristine arrived, she has sought out your attention more than mine, hasn't she? She's supposed to be my friend, but … Listen to me, sir. She came here when I asked her to stay away. Why? Because she wanted to be here. Why? Not to be with me, but to *get* something from here."

Amalina leaned forward and touched the Count's hand, his eyes grew larger.

*Get her out of here*, though Amalina. *Now, now, now.*

She continued in a firm voice: "Somehow they must have known what you're up to, sir. Found it out or figured it out, eh? The changing. And their plan was for her to come here, then for you to transform her. Why? So she could help protect him from you, sir? Even if she doesn't have the strength to beat you, in time she might. Or maybe the plan was for her to go back to him, after learning how it's done from you, to *elevate* her father as well. So that it would be two against one; so that they should have nothing to fear from you ever again."

"Always thinking, my little mouse," said the Count at length. His body shuddered, and the skin on his face darkened as if black hair was about to spring forth. It was harder for him to talk from the way his teeth were elongating, but she understood what he said: "Always the sly, brilliant, little one. My dear Amalina. I can only thank you forever for being at that window … after I remove this deadly asp from my garden."

The air boomed in front of Amalina, knocking her, the tall desk, and the torchstand over. Amalina picked herself up and righted everything, stuffing her glasses and her father's tragic letter into her waistband.

Then she wondered what she had just unleashed on her old best friend— her once-upon-a-time sister-in-blood.

## 56

# The Silver War

When Attila Bronk finished swaddling the silver spear, he hefted the leather-wrapped pole and the bag that contained the AXP book. To Sadra, who stood next to him in this room within the church, his purposeful movement spoke to an auspicious day.

"Why can't I go?" asked Sadra in a casual tone as if wanting to be reminded the reason; but knowing already, was obviously disappointed.

"This affair is for Korr's men," answered Attila, also casually; minding custom, as could only be expected. "Men alone. Best not to involve you, or any other woman, in this town's sin."

"But I know what's to be covered—every part of it," she said, "as many other wives must. They aren't all innocent, you know. They went along with their husbands and their decisions. They married into that sin and accepted it. It's hard to pretend we aren't somehow involved."

"All the same," said Attila. "Leave it to the ones who started it."

Sadra nodded slowly, but still looked like she had something on her mind.

"My husband is a man, isn't he?" she challenged. "What about him?"

"Do you want Minister Smidt to have a part in this?"

"I don't want *anyone* to be involved." Sadra's voice thickened. "Most of all *you*."

Attila felt a spark in their shared look.

She began: "But—"

"Then you understand perfectly why I won't let you come." His expression didn't change, but he swayed toward her, even as he shook the leather wrap and the bag again, announcing his intention to leave. "*I* have no choice but to see this through. It's my job."

"And it has to happen *now*, Attila?"

"Berzweck's proven himself dangerous in more than several ways. Given time, and should he grow aware of our suspicions, or if innocent men still loyal to him feel him unfairly removed, it could prove dangerous to *the Cause*. It is, as I see it, too risky to let go any longer. The Boss will be rooted out today, along with any collaborators."

• • •

When Lieutenant Vokent led Alexandru Berzweck into the barn, the Boss saw, for the first time assembled together in their entirety, those hundred-some men who were in on Attila's plan; *the Cause*. Berzweck's eyes didn't widen in surprise, but thinned in recognition. He blew out a cloud into the cold air, rubbed his gloved hands together and moved for the central fire pit. Along the way he nodded and smiled at them.

"Gentlemen, gentlemen," he said. "What have we here today in Korr? Have we left our village protected by Daniel and our deputy by themselves? What will we tell our wives, children, and our servants?"

But he didn't expect many laughs. He saw the serious expressions in some. And the confused looks in others. There was the air of a public execution, which Alexandru was familiar enough with, as was anyone who'd lived for a decade or so in that time. Attila noted how little concerned Alexandru was, though he must understand what this was about and what it meant.

Finally Alexandru stepped back from the fire and ambled toward the table behind which Attila, Dragomir, and Ivanti now stood. On the table lay the silver spear.

"An open secret now," said Boss Berzweck, pointing to the spear. His grin was sharp and cold. He leaned forward and tapped the radiant weapon with his forefinger. "Only one single weapon for all of us to share, boys?"

"This spear is a symbol of our new Ardeelian Council of Korr," announced Attila, in the voice he had learned to address crowds with during his time with Sir Hak Vogoneyevic. It sounded commanding, even when he couldn't get his face to show too much excitement or a pumping wrath. He patted the spear with a steady hand. "It will attend all its official functions."

"Yes," said the Boss, sweeping his cutting look around to encourage the others. "You men of *Sobelburg* are fond of pageantry in your functions. Kind of you to import these foreign sensibilities here to our little town."

"I am an outsider to Korr," admitted Attila, predicting where the cagey man was headed and cut him off. "But I am as red-blooded a man of Ardeel as anyone in this room. I have fought for the ideals and the soul of this country in the face of all opposition. Even the opposition of people who would claim to be a true man of these great mountainlands."

"Alright, what's going on then?" demanded Berzweck. "By the looks on their faces, I think I speak for at least some here: why have you dragged us out? To humiliate me some more, *General*? To prove you have won our war of silver? Or maybe to place us all in the presence of an illegal amount of metal for which we, every one of us, can be arrested? the King's Army waiting outside to pounce? No?"

A smattering of nervous laughs accompanied turning heads.

"Everyone here saw the silver ingot you gave to Dragomir," said Attila. "He showed it to each and every one. Many even held it in their hand. But under questioning, none caused the marks placed on it, which were witnessed by Dragomir, Lt. Vokent, and myself." Dragomir nodded agreement for all to see. "Cut into the bar were the letters 'A and X.' and the beginning of another letter, which was left unfinished."

"Yes, I saw it, too," said the Boss. "If you remember. You showed it to me. I told you that someone was testing its purity, not trying to spell out a message. Letters? Happenstance."

"It wasn't an attempt to spell anything, no. They are initials. A;X;P. Alexandru Xerxes Przek."

There were some sounds of recognition among the men.

"My name is Alexandru Berzweck," he told them before any blood rose too high and began purpling faces, "of the Berzwecken Mining Concern. You all know that."

Attila nodded: "Only the older ones can still remember the distant time your family name was Przek. Before the invasions and your father's interest in having a more suitable Germanian name for Ardeel's conquerors—Germanians, who you so loudly pretend to eschew."

"And yet, my name is still Berzweck," the Boss grumped. "So what's the point of what my family name was once before? And what is your obsession with those pointless markings on my silver?"

"Did you test, or have caused to be tested, your ingot, to see if it had been shaved to cheat you of your wealth? as you accused Dragomir or myself of doing?"

"No," barked Berzweck, sourly. "What's the point?"

"Because had you really suspected someone of cheating you, you would have tested it—as you said you'd do—when you stormed out of Dragomir's bakery. In your anger, you would have gone straight home, or to your place of work, and determined what you swore you'd find out."

"Who are you to tell me what I'd do?"

"*Had someone shaved a fraction of your silver?*" said Attila, acting out Berzweck's frame of mind to the crowd. "*Had someone stolen from you?* You were so upset about this crime you slammed the door and stamped your feet through the snow. Do you recall?"

"I wasn't angry," smirked the Boss. Then, for the audience, he lifted his smirk's corners into a sharp grin which he then pointed at his interrogator. "I was annoyed by a petty nothing. And I have an easy-going nature, as everyone knows, and enough 'wealth', as you put it, that I couldn't care less if someone had shaved some off. If they'd stolen the whole thing, I would be as content as I am today. I was just talking in the moment, threatening nothing. A tempest that blew over once I was in the street."

"And so you did *not* have it tested, as you said you'd do?"

"No," he chortled. "Of course not."

"Then you can go get it for us. So that all of us can see what *is* on that bit of silver and determine for ourselves whether something is written on it or not."

Boss Berzweck lost his cutting grin. He stammered for a moment. "I ... I don't know."

"You don't know?"

"I'm not sure where it is."

"Are you telling us that you have carelessly misplaced an item of such considerable value as a block of silver? Are you sure you don't know where it is, Mr. Berzweck?"

"I-I really couldn't say at this moment," he continued to stammer. "No. I'm sorry if that is hard for you to believe, sir. I am a man of minerals; and one metal—no matter how valuable it might be to some—they are really all the same to me."

"And yet you just told us that we could all be arrested simply for being in the presence of this great silver spear sitting here on the table. Now, is it believable that you would not be careful in handling and hiding something that you know very well could put you into the dungeon of the high constable of Ardeel?"

The Boss' jowls shook and trembled as he scowled: "Will you have done with this already, sir? What is your obsession with that damnable ingot?"

"You will not produce it for us?"

"I cannot."

"Cannot or will not?"

"Cannot. I'm sorry, but that's the case."

"But you will admit to those in attendance today, that you saw the markings on it. Just as I and Dragomir have declared."

"And my wife saw it," said Dragomir. "I showed her too, Mr. Bronk. Sorry."

Some quiet laughs rippled in the crowd.

"We will not drag the womenfolk into it," said Attila.

"But we both *did* see it," said Dragomir to the men. "The Widow Lidsz and I."

"And you will concede the fact, Alexandru?" said Attila.

"I will concede whatever you like. There were markings on the silver. Very good. And if one wished, as you are determined to do, one could claim by the way the scratches met, there was an A and an X and maybe something else. What is your point?"

"My point is that those very letters match this." Attila took out of his bag the large book with AXP on the front of it and set it onto the table beside the spear. He pointed to the shining metal letters. "AXP. Quite a coincidence. A. X. Something, you said. You conceded. You admitted to us those letters were carved into your very own ingot of silver. But the coincidence continues: contained within this book," he opened the pages with their fluttering little notes, "Are the many communications between Alexandru Xerxes Przek and the Knight of Ardeel; a conspiracy of the murder of innocent women at Alexandru's behest."

The men tightened together to get a look at the book.

"I've never seen that book before," said Boss Berzweck, looking goggle-eyed at it. Just the expression Attila had been hoping to see. It was clear confirmation. As was the redness in the face, and the drops of sweat starting to come off him, wilting his eyebrows with dampness. Of course, he knew the book. He had furnished it as some kind of gift to the Count, perhaps to use as a ledger. He had no idea the Count had been using it to keep a collection of all their criminal correspondence. But he recognized the little strips glued onto its pages, and realized what had happened. "I don't know what this is."

"This is a record of your crimes, Alexandru Xerxes Przek," declared Attila. "In black and white, sir. In your own, quite distinctive block-style handwriting; where the X—for some significant reason no doubt—is slightly larger than its two flanking letters, marking it out; and this peculiarity is repeated—*without variation*—on every note, and even on that silver block; all the same. But I digress," said Attila humbly as if accidently stumbling onto a neat, incriminating point he wished he could move on from. "What is established here is your criminality! You are not only an ally of this land's greatest enemy, but a scoundrel in your own right: ordering the deaths of countless young women, and daughters of some of these men within the room."

"And so you see, Dragomir!" the Boss suddenly raged. "Now you see it!"

The tension suddenly broke as Boss Berzweck spun in place, and stabbed a finger high into the air in protest.

"He is here to humiliate me! But that's not good enough for him! He's here to assassinate my character!"

Attila stepped back with a look of supreme boredom. "This book is the clear evidence of your crimes, sir."

"Of course it is!" yelled the Boss, finger still held in the air. "And you see how he did it! How clever. First he tells you that there were several letters carved into my silver block. How many of you men saw those letters? How many, eh? And then he says the markings spell AXP, which match the letters on this book, even though it did not spell out AXP at all."

"It could have been AXP," said Attila. "It was an attempt—"

"Now it's an attempt!" crowed the Boss, the cutting grin back on his face, sharper and wider than before. "Just like this is an attempt to destroy me and my name! AXP, AXP, AXP! Here he says it is written in 'my' silver, then he links it to this book, which he says is mine. Only it wasn't those exact letters on the silver block, and who cares if it was? Who wrote them there? Me? Did anyone see me do it? And why would I do such a thing?"

All the heads turned to Attila for an answer.

"Because you are a man of extreme compulsions, Mr. Berzweck," said Attila. "And you are compelled to put your name on everything of value you own. Anything you think is yours. Everything that you possess must, in your mind, be touched by you, and carry your brand. That is why this book is emblazoned with your initials, with massive metal letters. And not only that, but each and every note within this book is signed off with those very initials."

"This seems to be a tribunal," sneered the Boss. "Or is this to be a mindless lynching?"

"This is the *New Ardeelian Council of Korr*," said Attila. "It is a body of law. You have rights."

"Though I'm without a lawyer," snapped the Boss. "No matter. I trust myself to your combined intelligence, my friends. My friends, who have known me my whole life, and who have known my family. I trust you will listen as I prove to you just what I've maintained from the outset. This is an attempt to destroy me, my standing in this community, and my family name. And nothing is more important than a man's reputation, his standing in the community, and his family name." He pointed to Dragomir. "Dragomir, you've received my post already, as have a handful of the men here I most trust. Did I sign the missive AXP?"

Attila saw Dragomir and a number of other men nod and then shake their heads.

"I am Alexandru Berzweck! I will always be him. And more, never has anyone in this room heard or even thought I have been called Xerxes. What are you playing at? I will tell you. Because I have told them. And I warned them. And see if my warnings were not true."

The Boss moved his arms and circled the floor as if getting ready to make a big presentation, or to give himself a greater room to work with. He was building up the tension again, but directing it like a wave at Attila.

"Dragomir, as you stand next to that outsider, you will tell the truth. I command you! You received my letter the previous day and you read it?"

"Yes." There were nods and shouts of agreement within the group.

The Boss nodded and smiled back, encouraging them.

"I don't know what to make of our lad," he continued, pointing at the lieutenant now, "young Ivanti Vokent. I can only hope that he is an innocent in this scheme to bring me down. Easily manipulated in his youth and naïvete to carry out unwittingly the orders of this Attila Bronk, and his ultimate master, our enemy, the Knight Ardeel!"

Lieutenant Vokent staggered backward, stunned by the words. Dragomir also made space between himself and Attila. Attila, now separated from the two, looked like he might fall asleep.

"You have some proof of what you're saying?" said Attila. "Some line of logic that would back this bold, yet false, accusation?"

"As Dragomir and my friends will attest: the past evening I was attacked in my own home by a woman possessing the same traits as the powerful Knight. She was shown, again unwittingly, by the patrol to my door, and when she entered, she proceeded to attack me. Fortunately, it was after the bell had sounded, and so my suspicion to any late caller was up. And I recognized the signs. I have a weapon that I hoped can kill this thing, should he ever accost my wife or my child, and which I had prepared for our mission against him. I tested it on her. And let me tell you: I am alive, she is not!"

The men shouted approvingly.

"We have seen the foreign ladies passing through our town. We have heard the rumors of a college of sorcery. I believe we now have certain proof that it exists. And the creature serves as its head, and awards his favorite pupils with a conversion into his own kind." He paused for gasps. "And that craven creature, knowing how I'm set against him, and have always been a champion of our people and our laws, has sent this man, Attila Bronk, in disguise as an x-factor guardian, to carry out a private war against me. He hoped to fool you all with displays of patriotism and promises of silver."

"These are accusations, not proof," muttered Attila.

"Who saw me write those letters in my ingot? Nobody! It was him! Who saw me write what he claims is written in this book? Nobody! It was him; he with the help of his dread lord and master. And see for yourself the greater coincidence: this book, this spear, and the female assassin entered this town on the very same day! Delivered by the Vokent boy, who came here from no less than Netz—where our forefathers first met with—in calamity—the Knight of Ardeel!"

"There is no coincidence in it," said Attila, breaking in before the men could be stirred too hard. "That's where—"

"That is where his orders came from, where his scheme was formulated, and where all this injustice stems."

"You said you killed the woman?" asked Attila, in a tone completely at odds with the heightened mood. He sounded like a curious child asking about the color of the sky. "With what?"

"I have a pistol."

"Can you show it to us?"

"You doubt me?"

"No, I hope it's true. It proves what I've said all along: these creatures can be killed. What did you do with her body?"

"These are the wrong questions, Bronk," spat the Boss. "If you're hoping to find her and to save her, she is no more."

"I just want proof. Proof that these new weapons will succeed where the others have failed. And proof that the creature can make more of his own kind, which is an even greater danger knowing how many innocent women are now living in his castle. Including your daughter and Dragomir's."

Now there was a great outburst and a swirl of unsure movement in the crowd. This was too much information and it was all too confusing.

"You see, he threatens Dragomir and I with the safety of our daughters," said the Boss. "You heard it."

"I pray for them," said Attila. "And I pray we can reach them before it's too late."

"Easy words," said the Boss. "But how do you answer to the charge against you? What proof do you have of your innocence?"

"In my defense? Only my actions since I came to town. My declarations against Count Tepsji, which some of you witnessed in the Rock Cup Inn before I introduced myself. It would seem a pointless and convoluted way of going about attacking you, when I could have simply entered Korr unannounced and shot you."

"What you've just said proves nothing of your innocence," growled the Boss. "Only that you're clever and conniving. Come everyone, we are done. It is time the whole town knew of this. Someone fetch Mayor Daniel and the deputy sheriff. Tomorrow we will have Korr law decide the truth; bring them out!"

Exclamations filled the air in the barn. But Attila's silence and unperturbed pose drew their attention back to him.

"And, as well, we will have the deputy sheriff bring *the Secret History of Korr*," added Attila, his voice a monotone but electrically charged. "And we will discover your name written out in the Knight's contract, and then know for a fact, finally, that your full name is indeed Alexandru Xerxes Przek."

The sharp look the Boss gave Attila could have cut a diamond.

## 57

# The End of the Silver War and the Day of Executions

The 'Silver War' between Attila Bronk and Boss Berzweck—that is, the first official meeting of the New Ardeelian Council of Korr—had ended unsatisfactorily for all: Boss Berzweck had not been found guilty of murder and a treasonous collaborator with Count Tepsji, as Attila had hoped; and, equally, Attila had not been proven a lying foreign scoundrel out to destroy Korr's leading man-of-business—and acting on the Count's behalf, no less— as Boss Berzweck had hoped. Without a clear winner to raise above their heads while the loser was ground to pulp below their snowy boots, and without a reliable judge to manage and direct the proceedings, the council broke apart with uncomfortable grumbles as everyone left on their own impulse, scattering in all directions, not wanting to be seen as part of one faction or another—in case the side they chose today might be the losing one tomorrow—with neither party demanding the other be put into custody, for fear the same demand might be leveled on them. So both contestants, Attila and the Boss, walked out of the barn free men; until the tribunal could be reconvened, presided over by a trusted and neutral arbiter.

But there were clear sides drawn. Dragomir Dalca and Lieutenant Vokent were Attila Bronk's allies. Boss Berzweck could count on more than a handful of men whom he employed in his various businesses, as well as the street sweeper and the tinkerer. Without consultation, yet with acceptance, Ivanti went to attend the Boss, while Gorga the Street Sweeper was detailed to keep an eye on Attila and his movements. In the meantime, two neutrals, Minister Smidt and Argus the Baker, who knew nothing certain of the matter but were roused from their homes and conscripted, would be used as dispassionate envoys to the mayor and the deputy sheriff. Dragomir and the Tinkerer, partisans for either camp, went along to make sure one side did not put an unfair spin on the details that might influence any later decisions at the trial.

"Must this be done at all?" Dragomir had asked Attila. "We've already divided Korr and lost our army. I don't think we can ever get it back."

"Once we prove our case it will be settled and we'll have our army again," said Attila.

"*If* we prove it."

"You don't believe we will prevail, Mr. Dalca?"

"What the ol' Boss said sounded pretty convincing," said Dragomir, unsettlingly unsure. "Even if I don't believe it. But he's been a lifelong friend, and he's been just that to most everyone here."

"When we find his name in the contract, and they understand his depravity, they will turn on him. Wouldn't you?"

"Of course," said Dragomir, still sounding … not so sure.

. . .

Briefing Mayor Daniel Hokz and the deputy sheriff of the tumult escalating within their town, of which they had been astoundingly unaware though they were Korr's highest ranked officers—and for them to be dismayed further at learning of a new *New Ardeelian Council of Korr*, of which they were not a part—took some tact by the reverend minister and Dragomir (Argus excusing himself from the duty for not being up to the task); and it resulted in so much delay and hurt feelings that the mediation of the silver war could not begin until the mayor and deputy were coaxed out of their resulting arm-crossed funk, which meant the middle of the next day.

But when the time came, after the bell tower rang out as if in celebration of a victory, or to warn of an invasion, Korr's Common House was stuffed to the rafters with most the whole city, both the men and the women. Mayor Daniel and the deputy sheriff were visibly upset by the turnout of the lady folk. Attila was shocked as well, though his face did not reflect it.

"The Boss' doing," said Ivanti, explaining the women to Attila. "He demanded the whole of Korr know the truth, the entire truth of what's revealed here today, and not have half the population be subject to rumors and gossip."

"No," said Attila. "He hopes to stifle whatever might be said here by means of the men's fear of upsetting traditions and superstitions. Well, he's in for a surprise. I welcome this. It will be an open window to let in fresh air; the presence of the good women of Korr won't divert me from the truth." The last part he muttered as if it might still be a challenge. Then he said, with the relish of combat: "I had wondered what maneuvers he might make during last night's ceasefire."

"More than one," said Ivanti. "The birdkeep reported all his pigeons were killed last night."

"That was mine," said Attila in a low voice. "I had arranged for it if our tribunal did not work yesterday."

"*You* did that?" gawped Ivanti. "That's a clever thing, taking out the messengers. I'll have to suggest it as a tactic for our spies to General Volante. But how did you slip past Gorga?"

"I said I arranged for it to happen, not that I did it myself, Lieutenant. I had predicted the potential consequences of yesterday's failure. And it's a good thing I did. But never mind who it was. Was there anything else Alexandru got up to in the night?"

"If he did, I didn't see it. I thought I'd missed him sending someone to kill the pigeons."

"Maybe nothing else then," said Attila, hopefully. "We'll have to wait to find out. The only thing I'm really concerned about now is that he was telling the truth about that young lady you brought here; that she actually did try to kill him and that she was a creature like Tepsji. I'm not bothered that he could prove it, or that we were responsible and sent her after him, but that the Count *can* make new creatures—and that we were in the presence of one and did not even suspect!"

"I knew there was something strange about her," said the lieutenant, gritting his teeth. "It was a very long trip and she did not eat or drink. She seemed to enjoy herself in that box, where any man would have been screaming to get out."

"Box?" Attila stared at the lieutenant with dull eyes, thinking any item of what he'd just said would have been a good thing to know earlier. Vokent, shamefaced, scrutinized the floor beneath his polished boots.

"Did you find his specialized weapons? Did you get him to show it to you?"

"No," mumbled the lieutenant, not looking up.

"And what of Amalina?" burst Dragomir. "The Boss isn't wrong about that, either! If he can turn women into strigoi, what of our daughters? There isn't time to be wasting, but we should act now!"

"If he had had such designs on your daughter, Mr. Dalca," said Attila, calmly, "she would already be one. Your concern should only be that we are properly outfitted and prepared for the precise moment to launch our attack, and not a minute sooner."

"You aren't worried about this?" said Dragomir, surprised.

"As it is, we have until these coming first weeks of spring."

"We have until the first weeks of spring?" asked Ivanti. "How is that?"

"Because Dragomir's daughter has a plan of her own and it is ridiculous and it will fail miserably and she will die if we don't strike first. But hers involves such absurd things as the use of bees—"

"Bees," said Dragomir in a haunted tone.

"Yes, bees."

"She loves bees," said Dragomir, with a wavering smile that made him look half-crazed. "But I gave her a book on insects, and she loved the chapter on bees so much she read it many times. The both of us."

"And they'll be the death of her if we don't get there before she tries to use them. But luckily for us, they don't emerge from hibernation until mid-spring at the earliest."

"Are you sure?" asked Lieutenant Vokent—for Dragomir and he both.

"I've probably read the same book," said Attila. "But before we focus on the next battle, we must now concentrate on the moment at hand and neutralize this Count's true minion. AXP."

To Attila's surprise, Sadra suddenly appeared at his elbow to announce she was praying for him.

• • •

At the front of Korr's Common House, from the center of a small, raised stage, Mayor Daniel Hokz, with a grave and sober voice, declared that he would be the fair judge of this court, and the trial he presided over, with complete impartiality, would weigh the two parties' guilt. The side found wanting would then be arrested and executed. At a desk behind the mayor, a secretary transcribed his opening remarks. Stage left, but closer to the audience, the deputy sheriff sat in a chair looking somberly out at them to convey the seriousness of the occasion, while playing absently with something heavy in his jacket's large sidepocket.

The two men of the controversy, Attila Bronk and Boss Berzweck, walked to the front of the stage's lip but were not allowed onto it. From this lower position they would be free to address those gathered, and respond to direct questions from the mayor or the opposing side. These rules were laid down by the mayor himself.

Boss Berzweck demanded that he speak immediately. He reminded everyone how long his family had lived in Korr; from the time of its birth, he declared, the Berzwecks had been there uplifting the common folk. And then he refreshed their memories on how much of a community pillar his family had always been, and how he himself has upheld that noble tradition: he was a religious man; a scrupulous man; an observer of all customs and superstitions; he gave liberally to those in need; his businesses were vital to the economic health of the town. And, he intimated, those important businesses would fall to ruin should he not be there to run them. Intimated, as well, the town would quickly follow suit.

"Please bear in mind," Attila called out, "Mr. Berzweck's family name is not Berzweck, but Przek."

When the crowd stirred and started to mumble, Boss Berzweck belted out a laugh. It was a long and uproarious laugh that caused many to start laughing too.

"This man has many lies to tell you," said the Boss. "But for once he is telling the truth. As many of you know, my family name was once Przek; now Berzweck or Berzwecken. But what falsity he will try to tempt you with is that my full given name is Alexandru Xerxes Przek. It is the only way he can lasso me into his scheme to debase me. Without this lie, he cannot tie me to his central prop: a meaningless book."

At this, Attila took the book from his bag and held it high in the air for everyone to see the letters AXP, turning it once towards the stage for the mayor and the deputy to get a good look. He spelled it out for those in the audience who might not be able to read. "A.X.P. Alexandru Xerxes Przek."

"And so the lies begin," said the Boss after another laugh. "How do we know what those individual letters mean at all?"

Attila opened the book while still holding it aloft and paged through it. A couple of the tiny notes broke free of their glue and fluttered out, dropped on his head and shoulders like large flakes of dried skin.

"It is a record of the most evil crimes. Here in this book are the messages, sent by carrier pigeon, to the criminal Count Tepsji—who at this very moment stands charged with the capital crime of marauding the graves at St. Grigori cemetery, and killing its most treasured attendant *Neku Jonker!*"

Gasps and excited murmuring in the Common House. Attila nodded to the mayor, acknowledging he had introduced an adequate crime for the 'gentler ladies': the deadly attack on the brave and valiant grave-attendant Neku Jonker of Netz; nothing spectacularly offensive, nor incriminating to his own community. However, the mayor and the deputy sheriff were both visibly peeved that the trial had commenced with Berzweck and Attila's immediate command of the floor, and so their expressions were like two riders who'd just dismounted for a drink only to see their horses run off without them.

"Yes, we are all aggrieved at what happened to Neku Jonker," the Boss pronounced with deep reverence to the rapt crowd. "But what has that crime in Netz to do with me?"

The people looked to Attila for the answer. He paused and stared dully back at them.

"Nothing," answered Attila. "Unless we can find in these many pages an order for the Count to kill Neku. Which is possible, I haven't the stomach to read it all the way through. But I do know, for a fact, that what will be found within this book are the orders, on so many occasions, for hundreds of young women to be killed by that Count."

Up went the roar again.

"And so the lies continue," said the Boss, flatly.

"Do you wish to lay out your statement against Attila Bronk, Boss?" said the mayor, hoping to reassert himself.

"No. Let him continue so that everyone can see how far he is willing to go with the attempt at my destruction. With that, you will better understand the character of this stranger who has wandered into our midst."

"Some of these women," continued Attila, undaunted, "listed for death are the daughters of families within this room. Families who have suffered the tragedy of their untimely death—or the mysterious disappearance—at the hands of this criminal Count, at the bidding of the man who pretends to be your friend."

"On these papers pasted into your book," said the Boss. "They have my name on them? Alexandru Berzweck, owner of the Berzwecken Mining Concern?"

"No, they—"

"I see. Let me correct myself. You insist on me keeping to my given birth name. Do they state, 'I, Alexandru Przek, demand that you, Count *whatever-name-I-have-never-heard-of-before-this-Attila-Bronk-came-to-my-town*, that you kill such-and-such and so-and-so?'"

Attila wasn't fazed by the Boss' sarcasm and the laughs it lifted from their audience. He just shook his head and said, "The name Alexandru Przek does not appear within these pages."

"Oh, I see. Let me correct myself again. I meant to say, does the name you wish to give me, Alexandru Xerxes Przek, appear in your book?"

"Over and over again," said Attila. "On every piece of paper in this book, there is one name written. One set of initials. And those are—" he held the book high again, and pointed to the giant metal letters, which could be read from the back of the room "—A.X.P."

"So *not* Alexandru Xerxes Przek."

"A.X.P."

"But not Alexandru Xerxes Przek."

"Those are the initials of your name."

"*If* my name is Alexandru Xerxes Przek."

"Alexandru Xerxes Przek," repeated Attila, helpfully. "A.X.P."

"And just to be sure," said the Boss, with a note of mocking, "does this AXP explicitly mention that he is talking to the count, Count Tepsji? Does he mention him by name, when he is asking for him to commit his crimes?"

"No," said Attila. "But the Count is kind enough to identify himself in the margins."

This caused a stir in the Boss. His eyes bugged at the book.

"The Count identifies himself in this book?"

"He makes notes in the margins. Comments on the messages he has received. His title and character is revealed in them. There would be no doubt to his identity."

The Boss swallowed hard. Then he chuckled to himself and shook his head. "So this liar wishes to present you with a book of lies, and tie it to me by saying that this AXP conspiring with another miscreant is me. But to do so, as I have said, he must make Alexandru Berzweck become Alexandru Xerxes Przek."

"Which is easily done."

"Not so easily," said the Boss. He strutted around the small semi-circle the crowd had given them. "Because not one person in this room has ever heard me referred to as Alexandru Xerxes Przek. Not one! Or *has* anyone?"

Heads shook as he looked challengingly at them.

"We only need to read it," said Attila. "In your own hand. When you wrote it into the contract with the Count—I mean, the Knight of Ardeel. Mayor Daniel, deputy sheriff, let us bring that *other* book forth so that we may all see what this man wrote as his *true* name, as he swore it to honor the agreement, as did you all, men of Korr."

There was an agitated shifting within the room. Some—primarily the women—didn't know what he was referring to. But the grim look of the men made it obvious there was something to what Attila was saying.

"Bring it forth," said Attila, raising his voice. "Bring it forth!"

His words were echoed by a few. Then the Boss joined in.

"Bring it forth! Bring it forth! Yes, bring it forth! Fetch it now so we can have done with this farce and rid ourselves of a liar." The Boss waved his arms at the mayor and the deputy sheriff, conducting them to do what the room was calling them to. When the deputy sheriff left the room, the Boss turned to Attila, but said loudly and confidently for those around to hear, "Won't you be embarrassed when you see the name Alexandru Berzweck? But it will be the last thing you see in your life, before the bonfire awaiting you."

Attila spoke confidentially to the Boss, holding up his hand to shield his mouth, "First, you were still a bit of Przek when you signed that contract. And I figure that when you signed, at the age of maturity, you were old enough to already possess the ego that has only grown stronger in time, and so you signed it with your full name to make your stamp, as you are wont to on everything else, including your dealings with the Count. And yet, being young still, you were absent the learned caution to withhold your middle name, as you do now with common correspondence."

The Boss smiled on and waved at the audience. Attila for a brief moment worried that he might have miscalculated. Why else would Berzweck be so confident and calling for the contract himself?

When the deputy sheriff returned he was holding the book: *the Secret History of the Sheriff of Korr*. A red leather-bound volume. Attila forgot his momentary apprehension and experienced a welling of greed. Here was the book he'd been trying to get his hands on from the beginning. To look into. To study its potential secrets and revelations. It was within a few yards. It had been a painfully longer road than he'd expected, but here it was.

"Now we shall see!" bellowed the Boss with great cheer. He jumped onto the stage. Attila and Dragomir followed him. They all went to the secretary's table as the crowd filled in the hole at the front of the stage.

The deputy sheriff moved with precise gestures, snapping open the book right to where the contract was pinned. He began paging quickly to the point where someone of Alexandru's age would have made his mark. Dragomir pointed to a page only to identify his own signature, and suggested the Boss's must be several before.

But after some searching, his name could not be found. The deputy looked annoyed. On one of the pages within the strata it should be found, there was a large burn mark. The kind that often removed personal names and cities within the book itself and the contract. For this burn, on one side was the letter A and then, at the end, a K. Attila dropped a finger down to touch the burnt edges. The ash clung to his skin.

"The name has been burnt out," said Attila. "Recently. This is it here. Alexandru Xerxes Przek. But it's—"

"Perfidy!" cried the Boss. He charged the front of the stage and swung his hands out toward their audience as if to levitate them with his outrage. "Utter perfidy! My name has been removed from the contract!"

The shouts started up again.

Attila's expression was blanked out. Here was a maneuver he had not anticipated. The Boss had the ability not only to access the book, but the permission to remove his name. He had done so in the intervening night. Did the deputy sheriff belong to him? Or had it been done secretly?

"Now it is clear for all to see!" shouted the Boss. "You are all witnesses. Mayor. Deputy Sheriff. Even you Dragomir, and Vokent, lad. This is outrage beyond compare. Beyond all thought! He has wiped my name from our most safeguarded, most inviolable document, just in order to continue his pursuit. He could not change the name I wrote, so he blots it out. Why, the ash is still on his fingers!"

The crowd went silent. Not for what he said, but for what he was going to say next. The deputy sheriff was plopping a large iron key in his hand with agitation as he stared severely toward Boss Berzweck.

"AXP! AXP! AXP!" the Boss shouted presently, stomping around the stage. "He can call me anything he likes without proof! And what good is the proof he has? Where is that damned AXP book he would have crush me? Where is it, but give it here!"

The book with the giant metal letters was suddenly in his hands. He tore through it, his eyes darting back and forth as if reading it at ten times the speed. Then he shoved it into the air as Attila had, the leaves wide open, revealing its contents.

"Look now!" he cried. "Look now upon what he would accuse me with! The writing is nonsense! Complete jibberish. Nonsense after nonsense after nonsense!"

"It's a code," shouted Attila, to answer the angry cries. "A secret code between he and the Count. I have the ciphers to reveal their true meaning!"

"Codes!" guffawed the Boss, leading the people into a new round of laughter. "Codes and ciphers! What is he talking about? *He* has them? Shouldn't *I* have them if it is *my* code?"

"It is your code. You might have them, or as a caution, you might have them memorized—"

"And where did you get this book, anyway? You said it is my correspondence with the Count. Is it *his* book, then? How could you have gotten it away from him, unless he gave it to you?"

Gasps were heard.

"That's the only possibility, other than you manufactured it yourself. Do you finally see this ugly plan for what it is, fellows? This stranger arrives in town and has a book nobody can understand except he. These could be spells of confusion. These could be recipes. These could be gobbledygook nonsense. There is no way to know. We can only trust him for what they say. And we are going to let him tell us what they mean?"

"If you just use the cryptographs to decipher the meanings—"

"But they can be changed to make these letters say anything he wants!"

"No," said Attila, nabbing the book away, throwing it into the crowd. "Look in the book. You will see the faces of young women drawn in there. Some of them images of your own fallen daughters of Korr. There can be no mistake!"

"The mistake was in our allowing you to tell your first lie!" declared the Boss. "And listen closely my friends, for here is the whole truth finally laid out for you, as I promised I would deliver to you. This Attila Bronk is in league with the Count himself. He created the book in order to mystify you and spread chaos so he might prevent the assault by myself and the men of my mines—able-bodied men who are ready to attack him even now! Now!"

Anger returned to the faces. They twisted into ugly shapes.

"Yes, you understand it! He is a spreader of falsities. He duped some of the best men in this town. Dragomir Dalca. Young and handsome Ivanti Vokent, Naram Vokent's son. Even me, your Boss Berzweck was taken in by his lies. I admit that! But worse than the fall he tried to work against me, he found a willing participant within this town who has bought in … *all* the way. Who has sold their soul to Count Tepsji, out of jealousy of my wealth, because I jilted her once long ago. Attila Bronk has seduced Sadra Smidt to his cause!" Gasps all around. "They writhe in each other's arms in the sin of adultery and carnality! She, who has pretended to be better than everyone here. Who has lorded her righteousness over every one of your littlest faults and frailties. Attila Bronk and Sadra are Korr's truest enemies, and now that they have been revealed, they must pay the price!"

Sadra was stunned, but her hesitation was enough to announce her guilt.

The Boss knew not to let up and just where to strike next. He pointed to Minister Smidt: "Reverend Minister? What have you to say for your wife? Do my accusations sound the truth? But speak, good man! You must tell us now, while we are at the precipice—or forever remain silent! Is Sadra innocent or guilty? The truth!"

Minister Smidt's eyes lowered as his eyebrows hoisted on his tilting head, his hands were pressed together, his lips sucked into his mouth. It was a look of pensiveness and unsureness. In its equivocal weakness it was as damning as a thunderclap.

"Good enough!" bellowed the Boss, following the admission from the heavens, opening the gates for the growing frenzy that was seeking its outlet. "So be it!"

Attila looked sleepily into the yelling crowd, who were lusting to tear their enemies to pieces. And he was now one of them.

"Guilty!" someone cried. "Guilty!"

With a wave of the Boss' hand the people were unleashed and rose as one.

Attila saw the book disappear into their hideous churn. As did Sadra seconds later. When Attila was shoved from the stage, he felt the hands pulling him off his feet.

The deputy sheriff put the large key back into his pocket and pointed the way to the bonfire.

• • •

Widow Lidsz was not one for crowds or mobs and had held back from the general crush of bodies as it had pressed closer, one step at a time, toward the stage as the proceedings heated up. She could barely hear what was being said there at the center, and was then startled as the assembly exploded outward in a charge of bodies. She hustled back to the wall to avoid them, and scanned the crowd for Dragomir to see if he was safe. She lightly regretted having chosen to stand—properly so—in the women's section instead of deeper in, by her husband's side.

In the darkness at the edge of the hall, the Widow nearly tripped over a body crouched on the ground. At first she thought it was someone who had been knocked down, and feared for a second she would fall too, to be trampled by the town now exiting the building with a roar of rage and excitement, and blind to innocents in their path.

"Oh, dear me."

But the Widow recovered herself and knelt to help the body up, only to find that the woman was deliberately there on the floor. She was crying and tearing at something in her hands. It was pieces of that book; several broken pages from it.

"Barbara? What are you doing there?" asked Widow Lidsz, as she took hold of the crying woman's shoulder and tried to shift her away from the ragged edge of beating legs and feet. "Barbara, is that you?"

The woman turned her head up, her eyes were squeezed in agony.

"It was all a lie," said Barbara, her head dropping back down. "There's nothing here ..."

"What are you talking about?"

"All these faces," she hissed hatefully, clutching the hard black pages as if to crumple them, pointing at the blond strips loosely held there. "She should have been here! She should be! But she isn't! These are the faces of strangers, absolute strangers. We were being fed lies, Lidsz! Infernal lies by the wicked! And I was so desperate to *believe*, I almost—"

"You only have a piece of the book," consoled Widow Lidsz, sympathetically but sensibly. "Look, there's poor little Lottie Groszja's face there on that note. That was from almost twenty years ago. Do you remember? How could your daughter be there when there were so many others? You haven't seen them all without having the rest of the book, so many are missing."

At this word, *missing*, Widow Lidsz paused, then straightened herself and looked at the eerily glowing, twisted or confused faces shifting away, spilling out the door and into the street.

"You know," said Widow Lidsz, "Today we got almost everyone here that's worth being here. But it's strange, someone's missing. Someone *is* missing. One person I did not see, but I should have ... "

"Lazru's locked himself away in his barn," moaned the woman, but whether to dismiss Lidsz's fervent scanning of the mob or out of angry frustration it was hard to tell. "He says he can't bother with anything like this. Too busy! Well, I'm glad he didn't come, only to find—"

"I didn't mean him," said the Widow. "There was someone else a little more important, I should think."

58

## The Man of Fire

As they carried Sadra to the upright pole in the center of the town square—and they shook her, and they tore at her—Attila understood now why Boss Berzweck had insisted the women of Korr attend the trial. From the start he had intended to bring the accusation of infidelity against Sadra. An excellent touch. Attila was an outsider and might easily have been burned for whatever crime was brought against him. But he wasn't very interesting. Sadra was personal to the town. She was one of its pillars, especially to the women. But she was also a nuisance. She was the town's strict enforcer of morals and its busybody, as Perdu had warned. Her corruption would be welcomed by her victims. It would demand her fall, and allow the release of their suppressed urges. The fire among the people would burn that much hotter now, and draw their attention away from any sins of their old friend, Boss Berzweck.

Sadra stared coldly and without emotion at those who had now turned on her. She did not react to the laughs and the taunts and the jeers; not even to the ambivalence of her husband, the minister, who walked at the back of the mob, his jaw clenched, his hands wrapped together in anxiety more than prayer. She did not once cry out to him, or beg his forgiveness, or look to him beyond confirming that he was there, watching.

Mayor Daniel and the deputy sheriff also brought up the rear, treading steadily along, trying to keep the appearance of solemn duty and self restraint. They were not part of the whirlwind.

But Boss Berzweck was leading it, yelling at the top of his lungs, throwing his arms about as if fanning them toward the event. He would not relinquish control now. He had to see it through to the end; until his enemies were turned to ash before his eyes.

In the light, late spring snow, Attila and Sadra were led onto a short platform and roped together to the tall stake. They were placed back to back, their shoulders and hands touching. Then the mounds of sticks were gathered into a knee-high pile around them.

Sadra said under her breath, "Don't hold my hand. They don't deserve the satisfaction."

"No," he agreed.

"But you know I hold your beautiful, strong, righteous soul within my heart, Attila. Always."

Attila scanned the crowd as the pyre was assembled. Dragomir and Lt. Vokent seemed to have been left behind, or had gone home, choosing not to witness what injustice was to come. Or maybe they, too, had been convinced by the Boss and were now disillusioned and consoling themselves somewhere else. *But that doesn't follow logically*, thought Attila; he, as always, removed from the excitement.

Attila spotted the Cardinal's man, Bishop Perdu, standing beside Mayor Daniel and the deputy sheriff. But he was sharing a look with Boss Berzweck, his face neutral. Then he turned his eyes on the condemned and sighed heavily. Attila assumed Perdu was shifting his soul inside his body to accommodate the new and coming guilt. He was not there to protect Attila, he was there to witness the execution—its gruesome particulars—perhaps in aid to a pleasing report to the Cardinal.

"No final words for those in league with our enemies!" crowed the Boss. "They can only be more vile, mendacious slurs, and we've heard enough today, haven't we, my dear friends—all my dear, dear friends? Let us rejoice as their last breaths are given over to the pain of their mortal punishment, before we send them over to damnation. Their Eternal damnation. To hell with them!"

The Boss was the first to throw a torch on the wood, aiming as deep as he could into the pile to send Attila and Sadra up fast. But Attila kicked out and the pile shifted and sent the torch tumbling back to the slushy outer edge.

"Burn!" He waved for another torch to be added, his piercing blue eyes wide and ecstatic. " … burn the flames!"

As several men came forward to touch their torches to the bottom of the stack, Attila yelled loud enough for them to hear, though looking as sleepy-eyed as ever, "I am Attila Bronk. Former Low Constable of Ardeel of Tsobl, under the aegis of—and on commision from—the governor of Ardeel to prosecute the murderer of Neku Jonker. Though I fail, whatever you do to me, I remain a man of Law and am righteous before Heaven's laws."

"Too late," mocked the Boss. "Much too late." He addressed the crowd. "Here, let us return their book of lies to them! Where is it? Send it to the pile! Send it off with them! Let it burn them that much hotter!"

The AXP book had been torn apart, but the cover was still intact with metal letters askew and its binding held a few of the pages. It was added to the fire. A grin ticked on Attila's face. *A master stroke to get rid of the evidence*, thought Attila, in deep admiration of the criminal who had outwitted him, even as the flames began to build and engulf the book. And he felt the first brush of intense heat.

"No!" came a shrill cry from behind the crowd. Some looked to see who it was: a woman, dressed all in black, charged up the street. "Stop it! Stop it now! Please, please, stop!"

The crowd parted as she ran to the pile. She was running awkwardly. From Attila's poor vantage, through the smoke, the shimmering, heated air, and his watering eyes, he noted that she seemed to carry something. But when she saw the book in the fire, she cried out and dropped her object to the ground.

"Don't let it be destroyed!" cried the woman, as she reached into the fire, careless of her own safety, and retrieved the book. She cast it into the trampled snow before the astonished crowd.

"What are you doing?" the Boss demanded of her. "Why are you here? You've no business!"

The Boss tried to grab her but she was fast and ducked him. Meanwhile she was thrashing at the pyre, throwing and kicking the sticks away.

"What is she doing there?" cried the deputy sheriff. "Alexandru, get control of your wife!"

"They're innocent! Both of them!" the woman shrieked at anyone who came near her. She pointed to her husband and then to Attila and Sadra. "*He*'s the one that lies! Listen to them! Free them! Save them!"

The crowd stirred again, but in an unsure way. They watched as the pyre was dispersed by the Boss' wife.

"The only one who should burn this day is the man of fire!" she shouted, pointing at him. "*Alexandru Xerxes Przek!*"

"What are you saying?" said the Boss, still trying to grab hold of her. He was snarling and barking at her, his face like a gargoyle's. "How dare you disobey your husband, you old, ugly woman!"

Down at the far end of the block, yet unseen by the villagers who were staring greedily into the fire or at the gossip-worthy fight between the Berzweck's, Dragomir, the Widow Lidsz, Ivanti, and a suit of silver armor turned the corner and strode quickly toward the crowded square.

"The truth!" shouted the silver knight, causing a new gasp from the mob as they finally noticed the amazing suit stomping at them. "Let us hear the truth!"

"Leave off her, Alexandru!" cried the Widow Lidsz.

"What is this?" said the Boss, a sharp smile suddenly on his face, though he was still half hunched over, ready to strike at his wife. The Boss tried to ignore the silver knight, looking past him to Dragomir. "What is this, Dragomir? Vokent lad?"

"Did you not look in the book?" the Boss' wife cried out to the crowd. "I did! And did you not find the faces of your daughters? Your granddaughters? And you shed no tears? And you said nothing? You did not even *think*?"

"It is a book of lies," chortled the Boss uncomfortably. "It was designed to manipulate and evoke emotion. What better way than with pictures of their cherished children?"

"Only they were victims!" cried his wife. "All of them! I did not know what evil Alexandru was capable of, or I would have stopped him myself. I swear to you! I beg your forgiveness, though I don't deserve it, I know. But I saw those faces in that book, and I knew them. Not just the ones from Korr, but faces from women all across the mountains." She stabbed her finger at Boss Berzweck. "Here is the face of adultery! Not Sadra! Not this stranger! But your good old *Boss*! He seduced these young women, and when he was done with them, he had them destroyed! Destroyed!"

Her shrieking voice drove the crowd backward a step as if she were a dangerous animal.

"When I saw the pictures I knew the whole truth! I could not believe it, but look! Look you all!" She opened the box she'd dropped, and from it she threw uneven and scorched bits of paper and full pages into the crowd. "The same portraits drawn by the same hand! My husband's! He tried to burn them, but I saved them. Every one I could. See if these pictures don't look the same. They do! And tell me you don't see the letters AXP written there!"

"Disobedient, perfidious woman, where did you get these drawings?" demanded the Boss, looking confused and incredulous. "Mary, tell me this instant! They're not mine, I swear to you! You've been given false information! They've put you up to this! But what is the reward?"

"Truth!"

"But what *is* the truth?" he appealed to the crowd. "Again we return to the question of these confounded initials. But they have no bearing on me! Hasn't it already been proven that I am not this man, because I do not have these initials?"

"But that isn't true either!" cried his wife. "All the men in his family have the name given to them. It is their pride, though they reveal it only to their sons, their family! They believe it is what gives them their great fortune and power. A fetish that has existed for centuries. From his great-grandfather, Alberus Xenu Przek, to his grandfather, Argus Xepheron Przek, to his father, Arron Xanther Przek. The mark of superiority to the inheritors of the royal blood line of Great King and conqueror, Emperor Xerxes, who once ruled the world. So secretly proud are they of it, their inherited superiority, and of themselves and of the X that marks them out! And for this generation, Alexandru was due to claim the eternal name Xerxes itself, which he was given with much celebration and ceremony among his male kin, and foretold of an auspicious life. Alexandru took this legacy to heart, he saw it a prophecy of his renown, and he sets his mark proudly on everything he owns!"

"That isn't so!" bellowed the Boss. "Look at all my papers and contracts! I haven't a name beyond Alexandru Berzweck! There isn't one X to be found!"

"This man before you, my husband, is AXP!" she declared defiantly. "And I can tell you that for a fact! Because I have told you that he is a man of fire, burning what he wishes to destroy, melting what he wants to mold. And as God as my witness, he is the one who branded me with this!"

She tore away her dress to reveal something that sent the crowd back another foot. They recoiled in shock as she threw away her dress and pointed to her naked body. When she turned, Attila could see the scars of a massive brand on her skin, on her breast over her heart, and on her inner thigh, put there by hot irons: AXP.

"My God, woman," said the Boss, his face in shock. "What have you done to yourself? This man, he has seduced you. Just as he did Sadra! You have sinned together at the foot of your criminal master and plotted this slander against me."

But his words were swallowed up by the light, petering northern wind and the silence of the crowd. They stared, unbelieving.

"Alexandru," said the mayor, his voice kind but firm.

"Well, it is obvious, isn't it?" growled the Boss. "She has betrayed me, her own husband. She's taken up their lies. Their hideous, awful lies. She has defiled her own flesh for them! You must believe me!"

The silver knight charged forward and grabbed the Boss by his coat. He shoved the heavy man backward and shook him. "You killed my daughter!"

Lazru brought his shiny fist down on Alexandru's head. When the large man collapsed the armor followed him down, raining new blows with his metal gauntlet. "Lucinda! Lucinda! Lucinda!"

There were cries of anguish within the assembly. Demands for justice. For revenge. For blood. The Boss wailed as the silver knight punished him.

"Put him on the pole!"

Dragomir had already been working the knots that bound Attila and Sadra. New hands joined in once the call went up. Someone had a knife and the straps were cut. Attila stepped lazily away from the square of rough-wood planks where he thought he would die.

"Thank you," said Attila.

"Thank my Lidsz," said Dragomir, who beamed suddenly with pride. "She's the one who noticed Alexandru's wife wasn't at the trial. She's the one who thought to get some pages of that book and bring it to her, to see if she knew anything of it, and to send for Lazru when the truth came out."

"I knew something was wrong with that man," said Widow Lidsz. "I always knew."

"The wife always knows!" declared Dragomir.

The Boss had been lifted to his feet, and he went to the pole, a dazed look on his face.

"No, wait," shouted the deputy sheriff. "We must have order! This cannot be the rule of the mob. We *will* have a proper hearing for this man!"

The crowd yelped as the silver knight, now tarnished with the Boss' blood, dropped the deputy sheriff with a punch.

"Wait!" shouted Attila, pointing to Berzweck, who'd now been tied to the pole and was staring out in disbelief. "Take him down!"

"Listen to him!" cried the Boss. "Let me be! Spare me! Spare me! Take me down!"

The silver knight stared at Attila, the black slits of the faceplate's eyes questioning him.

"He's no good to our cause if he's dead," said Attila, with an idle flap of his coat. "We need him."

The armor swung round and took a knife out of someone's hand. He cut away the ropes that secured the Boss. But then he pointed the knife at the Boss' chest, keeping him backed against the pole.

"Listen to this man," shouted Boss Berzweck for all to hear, his features jerking and twisting. "You *do* need me. You may not like me. You may hate me. But I am as necessary as the cleansing rain."

"Shut up," growled Lazru.

But Boss Berzweck, finding his confidence again, stepped forward and Lazru backed away.

"Just one thing more!" said the Boss, in appeal to the crowd. "You must consider this one thing, my dear friends of Korr! This stranger, who has come into our lives, say what you will about me, *he* aims to overthrow our town! He plans to dress us up in these suits of shiny armor and send us against the creature who has ruled these lands since our earliest ancestors settled here! The creature who killed so many of our people through the ages. The one who killed your daughters—not I—and would have done so even if I had never existed." The Boss gasped for breath now, a heavy sweat causing his cold eyes to blink rapidly. He cleared the sweat away with the back of his meaty hand, and then glared defiantly at the assembled mass of Korr. His face was a rubbery, hot pink in the frigid air. "You, men of this land, you signed the contract with the Knight of Ardeel, just as I did; just as our fathers' fathers did. It was for our own peace and security. Everything I have done in my life has been to keep the order of these mountains intact, to provide for you people, to maintain that peace which has lasted for centuries, and which you would have lived for the rest of your lives content with—*had this man not come.*

"You blame me for the deaths of your children," he continued. "Well, someone had to die. The Knight's promise was that he would do it. I stepped forward to do what no one else here could have ever done. I made the most difficult sacrifice. I sought out the weak and the unworthy among us, and revealed them for his foul purposes, so that everyone else, the good, righteous people, could live in peace. *Peace*, people, *peace*. Or are you telling me that that monster, who has sat observing us for so long, truly has a better understanding of our true nature? This is what he believes of us: that we think *'why have peace when we can have war? Hate? Death? Slaughter?'* That bad blood is what we relish, and what we crave ... Or is it? Will you let *him* be right? Or shall we finally choose peace again?"

The town was silent. This encouraged him.

"Now, my good people, we have worked ourselves up into an anger that is most unwise. It is best, in any business matter, to make a clear choice and with a cool mind, or you might regret your rash decision, which seemed to gratify you when the flames were burning. So now listen to me carefully, thoughtful minds: we do not have to do this. Just as you took me off the stake at the insight of this clever stranger in our company, let us be cleverer still: we can back away from further madness; from the turning away from our traditions and customs which have protected us from utter annihilation for our entire lives. Read the history again if you must. Understand its meaning, its warning. And then read the contract you signed once before, and think to yourselves which is the best choice to make? Our lives were once perfect."

There was a brief pause where only the heavy breathing of the masses could be heard; before the silver knight lifted the knife high in the air and shouted, "I will kill you!"

• • •

Before Lazru's knife could strike, before the crowd felt the rumble in the ground, they heard the heavy voice bellow: "Make way for the King's Army!"

# ENTR'ACTE:
# ONE LAST THING IN KORR

59

# The House of War

I

When the King's army arrived, everyone in the town square pulled back in awe as the street filled with an advancing wall of mounted soldiers. This army extended, from one side to the other, as far back as the street allowed, but the numbers seemed endless. Before it, two men on light horses declared the advance of the King's Army. In the front line were the royal blue banners and pendants studded with the silver sigils of the hunt held aloft at the tip of raised spears. Among the first rows was the Prince of Germania, sitting high in his saddle, his spine straight, his lips downturned into a ferocious scowl.

"Make way for the King's Army! Make way for the King's Army!"

But the people had already backed away, some of them dutifully scrambling to clear the execution stake, its logs and kindling, drifts of dirty snow, and clumps of mud. Even the debris of loose pages and AXP's private papers were scattered. Attila, looking back, saw that the silver armor and the Boss had disappeared. He saw, too, that lieutenant Vokent's mouth hung open as wide as his eyes, his face awash with surprise and guilt and terror.

"Lieutenant," said Attila.

"I should have stayed," muttered Vokent, in horror. "I let him down, I let them *all* down. I betrayed everyone by leaving them to die at the castle. I should have fought. And now we're undone."

"Lieutenant," said Attila, "step back and out of the Prince's way. Don't you see? They aren't here for us."

Vokent blinked as he allowed Attila to draw him back to the recess of a storefront.

"They've come to kill us all," said Vokent.

"Not so," he assured him. "Observe the Prince. He rides tall, full of pride, of course. But look at his hand: it is bandaged, as they do with battlefield injuries. And mark his eyes. They don't leave the ground."

True enough the front line passed them, stamping their hooves lazily into the slush and sludge, and then the rest continued by at a relaxed saunter, as the scouts continued to declare, even to the empty streets, way must be made for the King's Army. The lieutenant stared at the Prince, expecting him to look up, to recognize him, to sound the alarm and order a charge. But that didn't happen. Soon Vokent was looking at the back of the Prince's head, and then he'd disappeared behind the ranks following.

"What does it mean?" said Vokent as they continued by.

Attila put a steady hand on the lieutenant's. "They've lost. We've won."

"How do you—?"

"You said they entered Ardeel from the north. They leave now through Korr in the most direct route home. And count them. You said the regiment must have been over a thousand. I see and estimate only two hundred at best. They are a defeated army, racing back to Germania. Your partisans have done their work."

"I don't believe it."

"I'd hoped the fight might drag out a little longer, so that the word of the silver armies would spread far and wide and be a continuing rumor," said Attila, with dull lament. "But that's beside the point. Congratulations are in order, my dear lieutenant. You cast the die. This little war didn't take long. We now hold the entire field. Well, how do you feel about your first victory?"

"I don't know about a victory," muttered Ivanti. "And it certainly wasn't mine. I suppose I wish I'd still been there, to help."

"You were here with me, though. Seeing to *my* victory. Perhaps you bring good luck—you're the revolution's *good luck charm*."

"A bit corny for you, I think, Mr. Bronk," said the lieutenant, with a reluctant smile. "You'd never catch General Volante saying such a thing. But I really did nothing. It was Roz that took the Prince on. Here today, the credit goes to Widow Lidsz and the Skeldars … and Mrs. Berzweck."

"Mrs. *Przek*," corrected Attila, automatically.

"She married the Boss as a Berzweck, and I think she would have preferred it had stayed that way."

"However" said Attila, entering into an apology, "corny though it may be, my compliment to you sounded nice in the moment, Lieutenant, but let it pass. In any case, that means it *must* be your turn next for a win."

Lieutenant Vokent gulped.

Once the parade of grim-faced dragoons had passed and were gone, and the pitiful remnants of their supply train—three splintered wagons—creaked by even slower, and the people of Korr began to emerge from alleys and storefronts, with dazed or angry looks they still hadn't lost, Attila said to Vokent, "Good, very good, I was right. The Prince was just passing through."

"You mean you *didn't* know they weren't here for us—?"

"Nothing is guaranteed until it is proven, my dear lieutenant," said Attila, his eyes at half-mast. "Recover yourself. If I am not mistaken, when the

King's Army returns home, and the king lays eyes on his proud jewel and sees that it has been decimated by a bunch of hillside farmers, we will be visited again. As soon as the regular reserves can be reintegrated for spring, there will be a force twenty times their number combing these mountains for retribution and revenge. Two nations will be at war. This is what we've started. And if we don't succeed in our effort now, or fail to do so in time, we won't be able to prepare for them, and we will be much the worse off for when we meet. All that is to say: Now begins our real work. And we've *all* some serious work to do." Then he added, his right hand steadying the left: "And mind, lieutenant—or, that is, *Commander*, if you please—we've very little time left in which to do it."

. . .

Attila woke from this remembrance, recalling every detail perfectly as he'd lived it, and played it through his mind again, because it was a rare, pleasing moment. In a minute he'd have to roll out of bed and see how his *Cause* had progressed since then.

## II

After many weeks at his forge Lazru Skeldar the Armorer had outdone himself. He had converted so many oddments of antique armor, scrounged from all corners of Ardeel, into glorious, shining suits fit for the kings and emperors of old. He extended the plating where he could, bolted on sharp cones where their enemy might seek to lay a hand, built and reinforced the bevors, which protect the neck, articulating many with lames; creating what were essentially falling buffes, so the man inside could move his head freely. And he had even glazed or scalloped the under-leathers and chainmail with a sheen of silver, so that not one joint between the plating went unprotected.

But all this impressive, otherworldly armor would be set on the common men of Korr. And so it was time to see how Lieutenant Ivanti Ion Vokent was getting along in shaping these men into the formidable army of knights they needed to become.

. . .

"I'm afraid I can't do it," said Gorga the Street Sweeper, as he stumbled away from the immense barn at the outskirts of Korr where training was being held, his face, pointed at the ground, a display of guilt and shame.

"What do you mean?" asked Attila, who'd confronted Gorga instead of letting him pass.

"How can I?" He tried to dodge Attila. "Leave me alone."

"You'll come with me." Attila seized him by the collar and turned him around.

"I'm just a street sweeper. I wasn't meant for this."

"You were a member of the night watch. That was very brave of you, wasn't it? Come."

When they entered the barn, Attila surveyed the men of his army: some wore Lazru's armor and were running through the paces and drills with their glittering weapons, some men were falling while some were laughing, and some were strutting in front of each other to show off their fine looks. Ivanti stood in the middle of this sparkling bedlam, barking instruction and encouragement. Attila spotted Bishop Perdu in a dark corner, speaking to a man whose face was grave. The bishop glanced at who'd come through the door, and spotting both Attila and the sheepish Gorga in his grasp, shied away behind a short wall of stretched hides.

"You!" shouted Attila. The assembly came to a halt. "Yes, you there! What are you doing? Lieutenant, what is that man doing there?"

Ivanti turned once in a circle, confused. "Who? What?"

"The bishop." Attila shook Gorga's collar. "He spoke to you, didn't he? What did he tell you? Out with it!"

"Not all of us must go," said Gorga. "Someone should stay behind; just in case ..."

"And so it would be *you* to stay behind?" barked Ivanti. "I think not." He spun again quickly, and pointed a spearpoint at the bishop. "What *are* you doing here, eh? Haven't you come to join us? Who're you talking to over there? Come out into the open."

The bishop, with the grave man beside him, stepped toward the center of the clearing and into a bright blade of sunlight that shone down onto the scene from an open door in the loft. Gavril the Carter looked nervous and disgraced next to Perdu. The bishop wasn't smiling, his usual embellishment, but wore an expression of superiority now; of defiance. After staring everyone down, he took in a long breath and opened his mouth as if to begin a sermon.

"You forget yourself, Perdu," Ivanti cut him off. "This is not your holy house. This is a house of war. I took you in because I thought you were on our side and could do us some good by offering a harmless blessing or two. If you're here to sabotage us in any way, even if it's to spread word of discouragement, I will hang you from the rafters myself!"

There was a low gasp from a few of the men.

"Oh yes," said Ivanti, making a circuit of the room as he stared each man in the eye. "Make no mistake about it. This is a house of war. We are about to do battle, we men of Ardeel, we sons of Korr. And in war, we kill, do we not? We kill the enemy. And the enemy is anything that works against us. You think it's the Count alone? He is our target. But right *here* is the enemy, too. If the Bishop Perdu would seek to undermine our effort, he is the enemy. A traitor to us. And he must die, just the same as if he were the Count himself. Do you understand me?"

A couple men voiced agreement, as if they were ready to string up the bishop right that second, adding him gladly to the salted hams and hides hanging from the rafters. Others shifted on their feet and were uncomfortable.

"Oh yes," continued Ivanti, feeling an urgency he wished he'd had weeks ago at the Black Castle, when he could have spoken up but held back, but now the words were there for him. He felt the same urgency of when he'd seen the King's Army advancing on the town square. "And he's not the only enemy here. Just as we plucked out the Boss, we must pluck out every other collaborator and double dealer. And sad to say, traitors are amongst us even now. Even in our greatest friends, who we wouldn't suspect. Maybe the traitor hides even in yourself."

The men lifted themselves, thrust out their chests or massaged their arms, as if they'd just been challenged.

"Now listen to me," called Vokent. "I've campaigned up and down and straight across this continent, and I've seen it all. Here we are, training hard for a job that will be difficult, and we think it's nothing because today we're having a roll in the hay. Because we are serious and hardworking people who will do what must be done when it comes to it. But I see you, just as I have seen hundreds, thousands of men in training. In training you throw your punches, you get knocked on your ass, and you laugh at yourself and stand back up. The men I trained with, they were laughing at themselves, too. Before the day came. Before the fight. That's the moment when reality hits. When we find out who has the streak of cowardice; who remembers they have a family at home that they will miss; who has something of value or pleasure that they would not do without, not for the world, not even to protect the life of the man beside them; those pieces within us which can cause a man to question, and to hesitate when that moment is at hand and he must put his all into the effort, willing to sacrifice everything.

"Look to the men around you. God may be your judge, I don't know. But *we* will be your judge on that day; if you should fall to your fears and let us down. And know, if you don't give your last, if you run, or hold back at the crucial moment, you'll be your own judge, too. You'll hate your rotten guts when it's done, even if you've survived. Believe me.

"I know it's easy to talk. I've made my living at hard violence and you—all of you—are men of peace and good standing, who have lived lives of comfort. But *I* was once one of you, wasn't I? I come from Korr stock, and there is nothing different between us than experience. And while I might not be able to bake some bread, or make a clock out of a bunch of springs and cogs, there's nothing to war beyond learning a few tricks, learning to take a blow, and—most importantly—standing your ground no matter what. No matter what the enemy outside or inside tells you to do. Whatever the enemy says, they just want you to lie down and die. And if you listen to them, that is just what'll happen.

"If you think that it's easy for me to say, because you think I'm here out of my love for Amalina. You're wrong. If it helps you overcome your enemy, then by all means, think of someone you love and fight for them. Use that love to land the blow. But I have crossed this continent to restore the honor of my ancestors. In the west, they think of us as a lowly, subjugated people. Fools cowering with a foot on their neck. I had to prove them wrong, time and time again. But it is never enough. Oh yes. Gentlemen, there comes a time in everyone's life to take the test, and to show their mettle for all it is worth. And now, at this moment, it is the time for us—every one of us—to do the right thing and to rid this land of the beast which has made us less than animals. To declare ourselves to the world that we are indeed men, and kill anyone who would tell us no."

. . .

"That was a masterful little speech," Attila complimented Ivanti later, as they drank together at the Rock Cup Inn.

"Just flew into my head," said Ivanti into his mug. "I'll probably have to say it again when the time comes. Just to get their blood up and to focus. I've seen it done well before. Not by me."

"Too bad Perdu found time to sneak away during the oratory—even I was that caught up by your stirring words," said Attila.

The two shared a low laugh at having found when the speech was over their doomed man had escaped.

"Ah, we'll catch 'im," said Ivanti, still staring into his drink. "Can't get too far in this season without friends or a horse."

Attila then said, with a serious gesture toward the lieutenant, to return to matters at hand: "Still, quite a speech. If you aren't careful, Lieutenant, you're shaping up to become the people's true champion."

"It's your plan," shrugged Ivanti, his eyes still down. He took a swig of the drink and set the mug hard onto the table, his lower lip thrust out wetly, seemingly reflective or forlorn. "You can take all the credit. You deserve it. I'm just along for the ride."

"Is something wrong, Lieutenant?"

"Well, I lied," he said, taking another sour drink.

"How so?" Attila had a sudden vision of Sir Hak Vogoneyevic's downfall at the appearance and influence of alcohol, and glanced worriedly into the lieutenant's cup.

"People keep telling me why I am doing this. It is nothing noble."

"Love," murmured Attila. "Or honor, didn't you say?"

"I *do* love Amalina," said Ivanti, like it was the beginning of a confession. "And I *am* doing this to restore my people's honor, like I said at the barn. There *is* some truth there. I feel a certain responsibility. All true, I guess. But that's not why I came, really. It's just that … it seems that this place is a sucking whirlpool, and no matter how hard I paddle, or how far away I get in my little boat, all the way to France, even, I'm sucked back into it. Amalina was the bait this time. I'm never going to be free of these abysmal mountains—never—until I get rid of this constant, unending foe, who threatens everything, and will eventually reach out for me, wherever I am, if I don't stop him here and now. I just have to have it out. It's a selfish thing."

"That sounds reasonable," said Attila, relieved it wasn't a burgeoning alcohol problem, "I wouldn't be too hard on yourself, Lieutenant. Not something to go telling everyone, but it's led you on the right path. It works, whatever it is."

. . .

And it did work. For each and every one of them. For all causes are built on the foundations of a thousand different wants and needs, coalescing and aligning to a single fine edge. To a man, it was the case for Korr. Revenge, renewed status, inverted cowardice. Even for Dragomir, considered perhaps the finest among them, whose blinkered vision and sole desire was to see Amalina again, just to scramble her hair, to hold her tighter than he ever had before, and to kiss her on both cheeks—just the chance to do it—would power his legs forward in the coming march, and it felt worthy against the promise of bulk carnage.

. . .

That's what powered them forward. Admirably, so. But what assisted them—with the strength of a well placed fulcrum, or even a catapult—

would come later, somewhere along the way, once Bishop Perdu had his
chance to approach them again, in private, one-by-one, to whisper promises
to them all; skirting Attila.

# ACT THREE

## THE END OF IT ALL

PART SEVEN
THE END OF THE MYSTERIES

## 60

# The Happiness Business

Cristine's room was empty. Cristine, her clothes, and her luggage had been cleared out, making it appear she'd never been there. Nobody seemed to know or care where Miss Berzweck had gone. Anka and Pils were suspiciously tight-lipped, answering Amalina's queries with averted eyes, shakes of their head, and hurrying away before she could ask more. Pia Lampeda, who'd gone to sleep in Amalina's bed, had disappeared as well. So too the Count and the other Special Ladies. His private study was locked, and stone walls now barred previously opened passages, so the Special Ladies' cellar bedrooms were now off limits. It was as if the castle was closing up on itself, leaving those in the main building somehow outside of its embrace. Aklan had no information and even Genadie, whose lips were atremble over his god's absence, was at a loss.

Amalina could only assume this was her fault. She'd used Cristine's threats right back against her and stoked suspicion in the Count's overworked, overly active, and entirely unpredictable mind. What had she *actually* hoped to accomplish? To have Tepsji kick Cristine out? For him to zip off to Korr to punish, or somehow un-violently neuter her father? Whatever it was Amalina had been after, this unsure, mysterious quiet wasn't it.

Worrying for Cristine's safety and Pia's health, to occupy the tides of her mind, Amalina turned to her natural last resort: her preparations; completing a list or fulfilling some mindless task was always good, constructive, and distracting. So here she dared and challenged and pushed herself, clearing her thoughts by taking greater and greater risks.

And to her shock and delight, the most daring paid out. Having noticed the wailing woman's wheel room hadn't been blocked, she went diving in again, her breath held, her eyes wide, moving quickly, in the hopes to relieve the lady of more chains without setting her free. And as she prepared to disentangle another strand at the midsection, she discovered a heaping coiled pile of silver chain—mounds and mounds of the stuff—stuck in a corner behind the wheel, underneath a now conspicuous, ancient oiled leather tarp. It felt like a reward for her effort, her boldness.

But had it always been there? She couldn't remember it before. Or had it been recently brought in to prepare for additions to the wheel? Amalina didn't stop to think about that chilling possibility, but instead tried to figure out how to haul the windfall bounty upstairs unseen and undetected, to the great hall.


· · ·


"We have a question for you about our bouquets," said Maibrigg Smeehaute, catching Amalina in *l'entrée grande*.

This morning's bouquet, posted at every Lady of Title's door, was a thick bunch of orchids with vivid, purple tongues, and a few lillies with a spray of some red berry sprigs around it all.

"Very pretty," said Amalina, a light sweat sprouting like a dew between her skin and the chains wrapped around her waist, which were hidden underneath her thick, brocaded vest; probably looking pregnant for it all. "But I was just—"

"Mm, I'm not sure," said Terza Fleccevocarre, in a light, playful, but critical tone, her head bracketed by the giant, poofy white shoulder puffs of her dress, "we're really thinking of branching out, selecting a different type of arrangement for each person, not just all the same. Eh? Not so uniform." Maibrigg added: "Or monotonous. What do you think, Kat?"

"Sounds like a lot of work."

"Oh, but it could be fun! We'll be the ones doing it!"

"I guess that's true," admitted Amalina a little half-heartedly, confused but impressed at their buoyancy in the castle's brooding atmosphere. "But as I was saying—"

"Well," said Terza, not too concerned at Amalina's ambivalent response but sounding challenging anyway, as if Lady Katarina had any reason to be judgmental, "what are *you* up to?"


· · ·


Bringing down the chandelier, arranging the various loose lengths of silver chain on it—including Anka's necklaces—wrapping the black socks around the long silver strands which snaked around the real support chains, carefully placing bottles of lake water amidst it all, and then hoisting the great wheel back up was easy enough, though laborious. Shimmying up the main support chain afterwards, then across to the pulley at the ceiling, was terrifying and exhausting. Amalina was sweating heavily and nearly lost her grip several times, even as her invisible hands grew numb from grasping the thick metal links and hauling her weight around—while Aklan stood watch below, half keeping track of the door, and half bent backwards at the waist, anticipating where Amalina might be and trying to place himself underneath. He sweated and breathed heavily, between loud whispers: "You there yet, Pretty Princess?"

Such work was better for a monkey or two.

And suddenly it seemed all the Ladies had some reason to enter the great hall when it hadn't seen use during the day in ages. Amalina had to hang there above the floor for what felt like hours, holding her breath, the magic bone between her teeth, while they came and went, grudgingly harried along their way by Aklan. By the time she'd got to the center, and with only one hand tied the ends of the black socks to the blocky support pulley, so that they'd hold fast to it, she felt lucky she wasn't caught, but realized she was only halfway done. Now she had to get back down.

She looked at the drop to the floor, and wondered if it wouldn't be easier just to let go. Maybe Aklan could break her fall.

When Amalina did get down she was angry, and growled, "I just realized *on the way down*: how the hell can we ever light the candles on that thing? Now we *can't* bring it down!"

"We just won't light them," said Aklan, blowing out a breath.

Back in her dress, she and Aklan admired the work, none-the-less. Then Pils knocked at the door and informed them a visitor had arrived who wanted to speak directly to Countess Katarina Tepsji.

Walking through *l'entrée grande*, Amalina could hear his voice out in the courtyard before she saw him, and recognized his laugh.

"Hee, hee. Hm, hee."

. . .

Janusch Timorak, dressed in a long cloak with a deep hood that hid his face, had attracted Captain Durok's attention. Durok stood on the parapet, glowering down on the mysterious figure who'd entered the courtyard and refused to let himself be seen. But Janusch's caution wasn't evident in his loud voice and movements, as it looked as if he would skip to Amalina and hug her: "Countess! It is I! Janushti! Hee, hee!"

"I can see," she said in amazement. "But … what are you doing here?"

"Your Master's gone," declared Janusch with his babylike smile, though in a softer voice. "He's been gone for some days. Thought I: now would be the best time to visit the most splendid castle in the world! After he's eliminated, everyone will want to see it. But I want to be able to say I saw it while he was still alive—when it was in full bloom!"

"But how did you know he's gone?"

"Come let's go where we can talk freely," he said, ushering her into the main building. "You can tell that man up there giving me looks—and anyone who asks—I am a priest sent by the Cardinal to replace your former assigned shepherd, Rosczy. But then you will order me away, eh? You'll do that for Janushti?"

Amalina noticed Genadie on the wall staring down at them, as well as Captain Durok. "Yes, let's get inside."

The great hall was the perfect space for such a meeting, with Aklan posted outside the door to prevent entry.

"Ah!" chimed Janushti, throwing back his hood and admiring the room, "*the* chandelier, isn't it? And I see you've already prepared it! Was it difficult to get everything up?"

"You wouldn't believe," sighed Amalina, still sticky with sweat, "Wait, you can tell what's up there?"

Janushti grinned and shrugged, "Oh, I can't say I see it *all*, and it doesn't really matter. I knew to look—and what to look for! But nobody else will know, I'm sure … Unless you want me to take you away with me, eh? Now that I'm here, I can offer you the chance again."

"I don't think so."

"Very well."

"Now," said Amalina, "this is a most amazing surprise to see you at the castle. You're going to tell me why you came, Mr. Timorak?"

"But as I told you, he's gone and I wanted to take advantage of it. I love to live, good sister! And how could I say I have truly lived without seeing the inside of the high castle of Netz, the lair of the old Knight of Ardeel! But don't you worry, for you won't be disappointed, as I—*Janushti!*—have come bearing gifts. Of course I have!"

He smiled grandly and warmly, lifting his arms high in celebration. But there didn't seem to be anything attached to him, or that he was carrying. No reason for lifting his arms this way. There came from beneath his clothes an odd clanking sound.

"Really?" asked Amalina, wondering what he meant.

"Of course! I heard from the Master Apiar that you—or that is your Master and his niece—purchased some hives. Well, I have done more than tenfold better. I've brought some others for you." He pulled out a piece of paper from his cloak and handed it to her. It was a folded and roughly sketched map. "They've been placed within the forest, but close enough for you to find. And since I know what you're up to, I brought hives of the most dangerous bees that can be had. Extremely aggressive, with thorns in their bottoms that set fire to the skin and have been known to kill men and large animals, so watch out, my comrade. But they'll serve your purpose, should you wish to use them. As long as you plan to stay and don't want to make use of my previous proposition … now that I am here?" Again he gave her an entreating look as he repeated his offer.

"No," said Amalina. "I couldn't. But I don't know how to thank you."

"The map is accurate enough, I'd suggest you memorize it and then burn it when you can. You'll do that for your friend Janushti? Of course you will! But there's more than just bees."

"Oh?" said Amalina, still amazed that he was standing before her. She couldn't guess what else there might be.

"I've found your friend's son! Well, I know where he is, the area they roam."

"You have!" Amalina's heart beat hard.

"Yes, you've got your *incentive* now," said Janusch, giggling as if he'd been tickled. "Just look how happy you are!"

"And what about more of these bones?" She held out her hand, palm up, with the invisibility bone on it. His eyes went wide and he sucked in a breath.

"No," said Janusch, after a moment, crestfallen to the point he nearly lost his smile. By the way his eyes were fixed on it, Amalina was sorry she'd showed him the magic item, thoughtless as it was to do, but she'd been holding it in her hand and done so on impulse. She'd gotten a little greedy, too. "They said they didn't know any kind of magic like that. But why would they admit to it? I'm just an outsider. But, I see you still have it and you keep it at hand! You can never be too careful, eh? But of course, of course. And I *would* be willing to trade you for it."

Amalina closed her hand and didn't put it immediately back, not wanting him to learn where the secret pockets in her dress were. "I really still need it, though."

"Oh yes, of course, of course." He wiped his big brow. His eyes almost looked pleading. "But I *could* use it in my line of work. You could only imagine. And I *do* have the location of your friend's child. That information didn't come easy."

"Are you now trying to barter for it, Mr. Timorak?"

"Mr …? Oh! But it is Janushti! Of course, *always* Janushti!" He shrugged off whatever he was thinking, and the inner glow turned back on. "Please, don't mind, but it's an amazing thing you have. And now, shall we tell your friend? Or no … better you ready him by yourself and he doesn't know of Janushti. But you can prepare him first."

"Prepare him?"

"It might be a shock. I've been in the happiness business for a long while. People are unpredictable."

"It's been decades since he's seen his little boy, I can't see—"

"I know, and the boy is no longer just a boy, but he's a man, of course. But I should say no more, eh?"

"Where is he? Is he close by? Does he have children now?" asked Amalina, eagerly, trying to picture it for Genadie.

"No, best you don't know. The little the better. You will get him set to hear the news, and if he looks accepting—"

"I'm sure he will!"

"—let me know. I was told there's a chapel here. In the Roman Catholic fashion there will be a place for confession? Tell him to meet me there, where he can't look upon me but I can give him all the good news and nobody else might overhear. But let's not take too long, I should be out well before night."

"Yes, let me get him ready first!" said Amalina.

"And I've just the thing for that," said Janusch. He pulled from deep within the folds of his cloak the pretty ceramic teapot from the restaurant where they'd met. "Remember this, eh? It should make him nice and relaxed. Recall what it did for you? Well, it's a trick pot, you see," he said, demonstrating its mechanics in an off-hand way. "It can look like you're pouring the same drink to each person ... but really you deliver a soporific to someone else's cup." He touched the raised design of a blue iris. "Just press the pretty painted iris on the handle with your thumb when you need to. Eh? First the tea for you to drink, you see. Then push here, and the other gets the tea plus."

"Ah!" exclaimed Amalina. "That's how you did it."

"That's how it's done," encouraged Janusch. "But here, look again, and don't forget, just press the iris on the handle with your thumb when pouring for the other." Janusch demonstrated a second time. "Got it? Of course you do! And here are two doses you can use." He opened the lid and dropped in two little vials. "Very easy! Will make him very happy."

Amalina took the pot but looked at it unsurely. "Well, I suppose."

"Works every time. *Everyone* will be happy! You listen to me. Very happy."

"I don't know how to thank you, Mr. Janushti. But, thank you! Thank you!"

"It's nothing, my comrade, it's just your incentive." He winked at her and bobbled his head back and forth. "And I've done even *more* for you than that! Even better! You won't be able to say I've done nothing when they ask you and you remember the time before the Count fell, and what Janushti did for you! But you'll know soon enough. What else can I do for my pretty comrade but wish you all luck!"

*What else could he have done?* she wondered. But he seemed very pleased and she wasn't going to bug him yet. She didn't know how much time they had left. "Where will you be, again? The confessional? There should be a mustache for a disguise there if you like."

By the way he bobbled his big head again, he looked like he did like the sound of it.

"I *do* insist on a tour, though," he said with an angelic grin. "I *must* see the inside of this historic place while I'm here, or what would be the point of living?"

Amalina pulled Aklan into the room and instructed him to show the 'priest' around the castle's attractions, while she prepared Genadie for some very good news.

. . .

With the hot water poured into the separate holds of Janushti's trick pot, the scene was set: her room, a couple chairs by her desk, two cups, and an innocent helping of tea. Genadie entered her inner chamber, looking at her quizzically. She probably gave him the same back, wondering how you ready someone to learn their long lost son has been found without telling them their long lost son has been found. But she was so happy for him she could barely contain herself and covered her unsureness with an overly bright smile. She supposed she might have resembled Mr. Timorak.

"Genadie," said Amalina, in a sweet voice, trying not to project her nervous excitement into him. "We were speaking a few weeks ago, and on a certain subject you didn't seem to wish to talk about, but on which we are agreement. And now we must speak on it again."

"What would that be, Ms. Dalca?"

"Want some tea?" she grinned almost painfully. She could feel it in her cheeks. "I think it's some of the best I've ever tasted."

"Tea!" cried Genadie in surprise. He smiled and wiped his hands on his grimy pants as if to clean them. "What a luxury. From Asia by the smell of it? Can't imagine what's the occasion, Ms. Dalca."

"Like I said, something we're agreed on ... about a certain *eventuality*."

"Eventuality you say?"

"I know you must know what I mean," said Amalina, pressing the secret button on the teapot and pouring the steaming liquid into a fancy cup on the desk next to him. "I mean, you were polishing the bell. You were preparing it. You know what I mean, don't you?"

His eyes grew watery and he suddenly looked miserable, the way he had right after he'd patched up her 'good luck' bone, when he thought it might have been an offense against the Count. "I think I see, Ms. Dalca. I *see*. Em ... Is this because Master has gone away, that you want to talk about the ... uh? But the ... well, whatever you had in mind ... can't we just escape like you asked before, Ms. Dalca? And forget this whole business. I can ready the sleigh again, put your Spirit right on it, he'd love it."

"If I can figure a way to do it, Genadie, we will. Absolutely. I promise you. Of course, escape. Always escape." She looked steadily into his eyes. "But there's still my duty here to consider."

"Duty?"

"To my family," said Amalina. She blew on her own cup after pouring the tea in from the normal part of the trick pot, and then took a sip. She made some yummy sounds, and smacked her lips. "I'd forgotten it in Paris, you know. An easy thing to do when so far away, after so long gone. Even when it's family. But when it *is* family, after all … *family*, don't you think?"

He picked up his cup, his lips quivering, but he nodded. "Family. Yes."

"Yes. I owe my life to Papa, and that means leaving—escaping—isn't easy now as it once was. Do you understand? I'm here again and I remember what I owe him, my family, as his daughter. Very important, is family."

"Oh, I can only imagine." He glanced around uncomfortably. "You've made your room up very nice again, Ms. Dalca. Remember when we used to hold our language lessons here?"

She thanked him. Then, after a breath: "You don't have to imagine, though."

"Eh? What's that, Ms. Dalca?"

"Family."

"What?"

Maybe she was going too fast. He hadn't had any tea yet. And it was up to Janusch to tell him everything. She was just there to prepare him. And there was still the primary matter for which this *incentive* was to buy. Start with that. She leaned forward and whispered. "Listen. You still have those weapons you used on the Strange Man, don't you? Tell me now."

"Well, I …" Confused by the change in direction of the conversation again, his eyebrows went up. But then he looked suspicious, realizing they'd remained on the same track from the beginning.

"Don't pretend now you don't know what we're talking about."

"No, I believe I know … "

She stared into his tiny eyes. "We spoke about this, eh? We need them, just in case, to use against *him*, or against one of the Ladies here if they decide to come after me. Or worse, after you."

"*Who*?" said Genadie, wide eyed with shock as if she were saying she knew someone specific. "Oh! But why now? The Master would certainly protect us, Ms.—"

"But you understand, I'm only asking for you to help me if it comes to it. As I would you. We've been over this part, already. So where are they now, the weapons? I want to know."

"They're safe." Genadie nodded. His lips trembled again and his right eye produced a tear that trailed down the wrinkles on his face. He gulped as if trying to swallow a whole bag of millet at once. "If it comes to it. What were we talking about, family did you say… ?"

"I don't understand why this is so hard for you, Genadie. You killed the Strange Man, didn't you?"

"Zeus—uh, Master—helped me."

He'd just called the creature Zeus, she thought. In this private conversation? Not a good sign. She had to be careful. Calm, calm. Happy, happy.

"Just think of how relieved we all were when *that* one was dead," consoled Amalina, speaking of the malicious Strange Man. "And think how relieved—not happy, for it will be a sad day, of course, if it came to it—but how relieved we all will be without the Count's threat to our lives looming over us anymore and our families."

"Mm," he said with great trepidation. Nervously he brought the cup to his lips. Amalina watched in anticipation, the cup at his wriggling lower lip. She thought of Janushti. But then she had another thought.

She pushed Genadie's arm down and took the cup away. "No, sorry. The tea seems to have gone off. Not good at all."

"Oh."

*I could never drug him like that!* she frowned. It was easy for someone like Janushti to suggest. Everyone was at arm's length to him. An outsider. That wasn't how she saw or felt about the shivering little rat.

"Look, Genadie," began Amalina. "I need you to understand the proposal here, and appreciate what it is that I'm asking … for us both … Or …" Without him being stupefied by Janusch's tea, she would have to be delicate. "Or if you need to," she said, "just remember that *if it comes to it*, you are saving *my* life, Genadie. You are saving *me*." She paused and then said pointedly: "Think of when you couldn't save your wife, Mala, or your family, even as he killed them before your eyes. What you would have loved to've done to him that night to save them all, to save your dear wife, if you'd had the chance."

"You keep bringing that up, Ms. Dalca. You *are* very cruel."

"I just need to know that you will help me. That you would do such a thing to ol' Zeus for me the way you would have to save your family's life. Any of them."

"How could I say no?" His lips wriggled now for another reason, thinking on his family.

"Genadie, what if I told you now … just as a side thing … I could tell you where you son is? That he's still alive and—"

"My son, Ms. Dalca?" He looked at her in amazement, but also with a hopeful cast to his features.

A burble rose within Amalina and she looked to the teapot. Wondered if she might have done something wrong.

"Yes," she said.

"You know where my son is? Is it … *could that be true?*"

"But it is, Genadie," said Amalina with an encouraging smile. "I had someone search for him, to find him."

"And you just found out now, and you've come to tell me?" his body tensed strangely.

"Well, yes …"

"That man! That *stranger!*" Genadie bounded out of his chair in one leap, sending the chair into the wall, rusty dagger out of his belt. "I'll kill him! I'll kill him!"

"Genadie!"

## 61

# The Most Reluctant Recruit

Amalina couldn't catch Genadie as he threw himself down corridor after corridor declaring death to the visitor, demanding to know where he was. She decided it would be easier to find Janusch first, and get him out if they couldn't find a way to calm Genadie.

She found Janusch and Aklan wandering a hall, heads turned curiously in the direction of the sound of raving, as most everyone else was doing. She pushed the two into a side room and explained.

"He's going to kill Janushti!" exclaimed Janusch. "I told you I didn't trust that dog-man, did I not? What could you have told him, my sister?"

"Just that I knew where—"

"You didn't give him the tea!"

Amalina blushed.

"But didn't I tell you that would happen? What are we to do? With him like that, everyone will know I'm here when I should have been simply an anonymous priest."

"I'm very sorry, Mr. Timorak."

"Please, Janushti!"

"Mr. Janushti."

"I have an idea," he said, still not exactly having lost the last curl of his cherub smile. Now he sounded positive and excited. "Everyone will be looking about, but it is most important that Janushti, your dear friend, not be seen. Eh?"

"Why not?" asked Aklan.

"Aklan, shush," said Amalina. To Janusch: "What do you think we should do, then?"

"The answer is simple enough, we lend Janushti the special little item you have, my comrade, which will allow me to leave this castle unseen!" His hand seemed to crab toward the hidden pocket on Amalina's dress. Towards *her*, anyway.

"Unseen?" cried Aklan.

"I said, shush," said Amalina, touching his shoulder to pull him back from Janusch.

"It only makes sense," said Janusch. "Think of what I've done for you."

"What've you done?" demanded Aklan.

"But," said Amalina, "it's the only one I have. And I need it."

"I'll just use it to escape, comrade. Don't you trust Janushti, eh? Listen to him out there. It'll be the only way to make sure I'm safe and can make it out of here, eh?"

"But Mr. Janushti …"

Janusch began to pull off his robes. "There's no time, my dear comrade Amalina. Even if this lad of yours doesn't know, now's the time for him to learn. I'll borrow it until I get to the forest, and then I will wait for you to bring me these clothes and I will make my way back to the world from whence I came."

Aklan made another sound of disgust, either at the proposal or the sight of the huge man losing his clothes quickly, Janusch's taught white skin glistening.

"But … " said Amalina, protectively clutching the bone under her skirt's outer layers.

"I promise you I won't freeze," grinned Janusch proudly, "this spring day isn't so cold, and Janushti can withstand the bite of deepest winter for hours, without clothes. I swear!"

Amalina blinked at him, not having gotten to that part, hadn't even been worried over *that*, "But …"

"Let him do it," said Aklan with a serious look. He pulled his dagger. Then he started to gather up the outsized robes and the underclothes. "But I'll see him out."

"Yes," said Janusch, with a feverish look as Genadie's voice seemed to be closing in. "Whatever's best. As long as you don't actually see me—anyone sees me."

"No," said Aklan. "You'll get out all right. I'll make sure the gate is open. I'll stick these clothes in a bag and then meet you at the large, lone knotty oak twenty yards straight into the forest, through the opening between the two great spruces. You can't miss it."

Janusch was smiling, naturally, but there was a worried look in his eyes.

"I just showed you around the castle, didn't I?" said Aklan. "The pretty princess here trusts me. She trusts you. You'll get your clothes just as long as we get that bone back."

"Pretty princess?" said Janusch, at first confused. He glanced at Amalina. "Oh, I see. Yes. Everything you've just said sounds good. Large knotty oak, twenty yards straight in through the two great spruces, I will meet you there. But let's hurry!" Janusch paused, and had a look as if he'd swallowed something too large for his throat. He choked toward Amalina. "Uh … if your plan succeeds … well, I just had a horrible thought," he smiled sadly, "if your plan succeeds … and with *him* finally gone … might not the brightness of the light I bring and provide to the people be diminished, because his darkness has left?" He paused again as his fevered thoughts rattled around disagreeably in his head. Amalina and Aklan traded looks. Where had this come from? "But that's no matter no matter." His smile corrected itself, "But we *should* want that, of course, of course … and so if your plan succeeds, always remember Janushti's part in it, I helped so much!" Then, with another thought: "Oh, and don't forget: they sting ferociously!"

With incredible internal reluctance that Amalina could feel like invisible arms holding her limbs back, so that Janusch had to reach his big bear paw out to take the bone, she pulled the magic item out of her dress and presented it to him. No sooner was it in his hands than it was in his mouth and he disappeared, except for a loincloth and his fancy, furry boots. "O'k' I' s'y'eh t'r." said Janusch incomprehensibly, his body blinking into sight and then out as he spoke. The loincloth and boots came off.

"Right," said Amalina, trying to detect, besides a faint heat or odor, the giant man whom she could no longer see. "I'll find Genadie and calm him down. He'll have run his anger off soon enough. Especially if he can't find you."

The door slammed open, shoving Aklan aside with a yelp. He'd dropped the clothes but picked them back up.

"Make sure you get that bone back," said Amalina.

"Don't worry, Princess," he called, as he darted after Janusch.

• • •

"I just don't understand what came over you," soothed Amalina, when she'd finally settled Genadie—after he failed to find the visitor; though Janusch's horse was still idling in the courtyard. She brought him back to her room and considered giving him the tea now, if only to make sure he wouldn't have another outburst. People might start asking questions which could give away the game. "I thought it would've been the best news in the world, you can go see your son now."

"I wouldn't dare," said Genadie, suddenly nervous and looking over his shoulder, speaking in that strange French dialect. "No, Ms. Dalca. If I found him, it would connect us, wouldn't it? Him and I."

"Yes. But isn't that what you'd want?"

"Even if it were possible, if I were to track him down, Master would know. And he wouldn't be too happy. It would leave a trail that can be followed. I might only be leading Master to him, you see. So I won't dare. Best to avoid, you see. Best for me never to know. I told you that before, Ms. Dalca."

"You never told me that!"

"And if anyone else knows, that would connect him to me: and then it all leads back to him again, you see; and Master might follow through. My little boy must remain lost, Ms. Dalca. Nobody can know. Not now. Not ever!"

"But then you see my point in the first place," said Amalina, after giving him some time to loosen and sag. "Not that we *want* it to happen, Genadie, of course we *don't*. But if things come to pass. And we have to … you know … and then, naturally, if *he* isn't here anymore … he isn't here in Ardeel, or on earth … you understand … If he isn't, then he wouldn't be able to do anything like that; to track down your son or torture or slay him. And then you could find him and be with him, eh? Don't you see? I'm just trying to make you happy."

"Oh, no you're not. You're trying to compromise me, and force my hand to grab hold one of your crooked plots."

"A crooked plot *to free you*?"

"And now *that man* knows, Ms. Dalca! Who is he? How do you know him? How did you find him?" Genadie began to heat again. His tortured hands twitched, his legs shifted back and forth nervously.

"Forget about that. He's gone. You'll never find him. And I'll never tell anyone what he knows, not even to your Master, eh?"

Genadie nodded. But she suddenly wondered if he was thinking about her the way he just was about Janusch: murderously, to protect his son.

"Not that I know everything," said Amalina. "Only *he* knew it all. Are you okay, now? Are you? You're sure?"

He nodded.

And Amalina whispered, "Listen to me: We're alike, you and I, Genadie. We're separated from our families, with him threatening them if we don't do what he wants."

"Yes, that's true," mumbled Genadie. "Though you *can* still see your father."

"And you can see your son. We can all have our families back, if …" She eyed him suggestively. "I'm not saying anything else. But, if …"

"I see what you mean."

"Okay," said Amalina. "Good. And you'll get those weapons so they're handy if we need them, eh? To be quick. Just hide them in a safe spot."

He nodded nervously.

"And when the time is right, you'll know it.

"When?"

"*'If'* …but you know what I mean, I'm not pushing it," said Amalina, wishing him to just give in. *Just give in!* He finally had his son back, or the chance for it. That *must* mean something to him, after how many decades hoping. "You'll get those pieces out of hiding. You'll have some, and I'll have some. And we'll use them. When we do, then we'll be free, and we'll have our lives and our families back, and we can live anywhere we wish. Just think about that."

He heaved a long, trembling sigh as tears began to stream down his cheeks.

"How is that again, Ms. Dalca? What's to be done?"

She nodded as she felt the terrible weight give from him.

•  •  •

"The lower levels get smoked out, as you did before, eh?" said Amalina in the snappy delivery of a field commander. Genadie nodded. "Just like when the Strange Man was here. We'll seek him out if we have to. If he's in the lower chambers, he'll either be in his room, overcome and docile and unaware we are there to kill him, and that is what we do, eh?; or he'll notice the smoke and realize what's happening, and he'll run to the upper level where we can better strike him."

"How?"

"I'll do it myself, upstairs," said Amalina. "You just have the weapons ready for us both. You set the fires and spread the smoke throughout the cellars. You hunt him there. That's it."

"Uh, yes, Ms. Dalca."

Hard to tell if he was getting it.

"And I'll do my part ... upstairs, right?" She said, to remind him, or solidify it in his mind. "You downstairs, me upstairs. We're in it together."

"Of course, Ms. Dalca," he said with a blubbery nod.

"Thank you."

"If it comes to it," he said.

"If it comes to it. But we'll have our families back. Speak not a word of this to anyone."

He nodded. But he seemed to be quivering all over.

"Are you all right?" asked Amalina, worried.

"What life am I living?" he said taking his head in his hands.

"What do you mean?"

"What life is this? I don't understand. I thought it was one way, then it was nother, and now ..."

"It can be a good life, eh? It still *can* be."

"If it comes to it."

"If it comes to it."

•  •  •

Later in the evening there was a knock at her chamber door, Aklan entered with a big smile.

"You got the bone?" When Aklan held it up proudly, Amalina felt a wave of relief. "I thought it was lost as soon as I gave it to him."

"Oh, he tried to get away with it, Pretty Princess."

"Did he?"

"Sure. Why wouldn't he?"

"But how did you get it back, then? How did you find him?"

"Are you kidding?" said Aklan. "That's the first time he had the bone; and didn't I try to do the same thing in Paris? I had a whole city. This is just a castle. I knew right where he'd go. And when we met," here Aklan beamed proudly, "I was the only one there with a knife. Easy, Pretty Princess. Real easy."

## 62

## A Movement in the Treeline

On the day before Amalina's dark adventure with the Count came to an end, Amalina stood along the top of the castle's outer wall and stared deep into the treeline. It was difficult to imagine the happy bear that was Janusch Timorak so enraged at losing his coveted magic item—and losing it to Comrade Amalina's young servant no less, and under humiliating circumstances at that—that on finding himself returned to the forest without the invisibility bone, he had, in retaliation, taken back his gift. But, difficult though it was, she did imagine him doing just that; yanking down his score of hives and squashing them under foot, or packing them up in a box to be removed to a better situation. She pictured this retributive rampage every ten minutes, clear as if it had happened, as she waited impatiently for the general excitement of Genadie's mad, knife-wielding search of the castle to die down, before she felt it safe enough to go out to inventory and inspect Janushti's bee nests.

Over those couple days, she'd stood at windows and battlements, avoiding Genadie and Captain Durok, trying to spot the new skecs. Though she couldn't see them in the forest—which in the warm spring weather was thickening into a near-solid barrier of green and brown—at times she saw strange movement within the woods and up on the mountainside. She couldn't tell if it was Janusch's men, wild animals, perhaps Noka, or—with a quickening of her pulse—it might be scouts from Attila's revolutionary army.

Amalina committed to memory the skec positions marked down on Janusch's map so she wouldn't be found holding it later, but still didn't burn the map quite yet. Instead, before beginning her search, she folded the paper into the trick teapot's hidden chamber, now dry and emptied and sitting innocuously on her desk.

She took Aklan with her, who was, as usual, looking restless. She brought him and a long, hooked pole which she pretended was a shepherd's crook, or an unusually tall, eccentrically shaped walking stick.

. . .

"But why do we have to?" asked Aklan after they'd left the gate.

"We can't just sit around," answered Amalina in her commander's voice. She sent the bottom of the pole forward to test the ground's firmness, in case it was boggy, before setting her foot down.

"I get that. But why now?"

"Are you nervous or something, boy?"

Aklan scoffed.

"We're doing this because we need our bees up and working. The revolution could be coming any day," explained Amalina. "They could've already *been* here by now." Amalina guided him into the forest edge. "There's something coming … don't you feel it?"

"The ground shaking again?"

"No. The tension in the air; the change in the atmosphere."

"You're probably feeling a little rain coming," he said, dismissive, his eyes looking warily about. *He's scared*, thought Amalina. The boy still hadn't warmed to the idea of the bees no matter how she'd assured him it would be safe. In any case, he spoke in another direction, conversationally, as if to put the worrisome subject out of mind. "You know, I haven't felt one of those rumbles in a while. Maybe the mountain isn't going to collapse after all. Maybe things *are* really getting better."

"We have to be ready," she reminded him again. "Now watch out where you're walking. It should be safe, but his bees sound like they could be dangerous if we aren't careful."

That didn't improve Aklan's drifting morale, he looked angry and spit. His hand went to the knife's handle at his belt.

"*I* hope he took those blasted things away," said Aklan. "Why do you even care about 'em? Weren't *your* bees good enough?"

"The more the better."

"Well … don't know about that. Anyway, we know where ours are, and they're where we left them, I'm sure. And you heard him. He said our chandelier should do just nice. He didn't see *all* the stuff up there, so it's working, ain't it? Maybe we don't need anything else besides—"

"You're going to make me nervous if you keep talking."

"Are you nervous, Pretty Princess?"

"It's *you*, boy. You're scared."

"No, I'm not!" pouted Aklan with his pert little Spaarvierlet lips, which were comical under his cross, resentful eyes. "I'm not scared of nothin'!"

"Then what are you going on about—about these bees, eh?"

"All I'm saying, there's no need for *his* little beasts. You can't tell me I'm some coward just because I don't like 'em. I swear I'm going to be right at your side, Pretty Princess, when we go after *you-know-who*. I'm just saying, never mind them buzzing pests, we'll get him good with all our other stuff."

At Aklan saying this, Amalina realized that, despite all her token preparations, even this bee tour now, a reality she did not look forward to *was* creeping ever closer. A date she wished she could hold off forever. Along this line, in her own offhand way and echoing Genadie's refrain, she said to calm herself: "Yes. If we need to."

Aklan tilted his head, looking at her askance. "What's that? What do you mean 'if'? You mean 'when' we need to; *when* we use it. Right?"

*Oh, yes*, she thought, *with Genadie I have to be soft. With Aklan, definite.*

She was learning.

"I only mean," said Amalina, correcting herself, "if we *have* to use it, it means we're in trouble. And that means *the time has come*. But I hope we never have to. You see?"

"I see," said Aklan. Then he grumbled, "Went to a lot of trouble if we don't."

"First you want to, then you don't want to, then you *do* want to!"

"Of course I want to." He glanced at her and made a face. "You know, the same could be said for you."

"What I'm saying is," explained Amalina, making it sound very pat, "If we *don't* ever have to use the chandelier—or the bees—it would just mean something *better* has happened for us, eh? Let's hope for *that*. But then be prepared otherwise."

Aklan made a strange clucking sound.

• • •

Amalina was pleased to find her original skecs were in good shape and hadn't been tampered with. Each hive hooked, by a ring on its top, to a small metal half-loop driven into a short arm that sprouted off a tall, bare-wood scaffold—from a distance it looked a like a head, bound in a rough sack cloth, clung to a tall, thin gallows by the shortest of ropes. Anyway, the nests were there, and if the posts were too low or scalable, the waking bears and other greedy scavengers hadn't yet found enough interest to take them down.

Amalina and Aklan were impressed with the number of happy little drones crawling over the hung 'heads'. The dormant skecs from Netz's Master Apiar had finally bloomed to life.

"Why aren't they flying off?" said Aklan, one eye squinted critically under his bushy blond brows at them.

"Too soon. The bees still have plenty of comb to eat and the flowers aren't blooming so much yet—no matter how many Terza and Maibrigg are finding for their bouquets." Just a few lovely, colorful patches of early stock here and there were poking through the dense green underbrush. "The flowers all need to grow in more, I think, before they get active."

"I don't know about flowers," said Aklan, now batting his blueberry eyes, maybe warming to them, "but the bees look pretty, enough, I'll admit. Not exactly a swarm, though, are they?"

"A good thing. If we need them we'll have to move 'em. And if they're aggressive, we'd be getting stung along the way."

"But … didn't he say his *are* aggressive?"

"Well, that's true." Amalina nodded. "You understand how to move them, Aklan?"

"Me?"

"You never know. That's why I brought you along, it wasn't just for your company, boy. This is just in case *you* need to do it."

Amalina used the hooked pole she'd carried from the castle to lift the bubble-shaped hive off its supporting gibbet. After lowering it, swirling it gingerly about, and raising it again, she rehooked it above.

"There, that isn't too hard, is it?" said Amalina, feeling satisfied. "And the crook should be long enough for you."

"Doesn't look too hard." He squinted at it again, judging distances and the bees' mellow reaction to the movement.

"Good enough. Let's see if we can find one of Janusch's."

She closed her eyes for a second, recalling his map, then oriented herself and pointed to the northeast. "Shouldn't be too far."

They heard the buzzing before they reached it. Janusch had placed his skecs in the same manner she had, hung by a ring off a tall stand—though he'd had his 'gallows' decorated fancily, with false leaves and paint as camouflage.

The new skec here was about the same size and shape as the ones she'd gotten in Netz, but the bees were noticeably different. The drones were longer than the regular bees and reddish-orange in color. They appeared much more dangerous … and threatening. Their hive seemed to shake back and forth from the violent activity within it, or was that just the breeze? Amalina and Aklan gulped.

"*Those* are active," said Aklan.

"Looks like it."

"We really need them?"

"Bees are bees," said Amalina, straightening herself. She hefted the pole to prove she could unhook this hive just the same as any other. "Yeah, these look better. Who knows, maybe *you-know-who* had the Master Apiar give me a weak supply on purpose. Knowing how much he doesn't like them I wouldn't put it past him. But these …"

The skec came off the ring as easily as the first. The buzzing inside and around it increased, and some of the bees flew off and began to circle.

"Uh-oh," said Aklan.

"No," cooed Amalina, "we can definitely use these. I'll just throw a blanket over them before I pick one up. I'm just showing you now how to—"

"That's not why I said 'uh-oh'." Aklan pointed past the hive, to the left.

With a heavy pant, the black wolf came trotting into the small clearing. His one yellow eye was focused on Amalina—and it looked like his cracked dead eye, on the other side of its battle-damaged, ferocious head, was on her, too—as he came at her in a straight line.

"Oh, hello," said Amalina, feeling a nervous cold streak down her back and sweat grow on her forehead. Though she knew the wolf was friendly to her now, his hateful look and monstrous features—and that he was moving right at her—was still alarming. The skec suddenly felt ten times heavier and off balance.

The black wolf stopped to observe what she was doing.

"Just playing with our little friends," said Amalina with a soothing voice, as she swung the hive back toward its place.

But the black wolf lunged forward and snagged the hem of her dress with his teeth.

"Oh!"

Aklan fell back and pulled out his knife. But the wolf was only drawing steadily, and insistently on her dress, emitting little growls of effort. It looked like a game of tug-of-war.

"What are you doing?" said Amalina, annoyed. "Go on. Leave me alone. Let me just … put this back … before I drop it!"

As she resisted, he began a deeper low growl, and dug his body into it.

"What should I do?" asked Aklan.

"Nothing. He's just being stupid." She snarled at the wolf: "Leave me alone! I don't have time for games right now. What's the matter with you?"

The wolf suddenly let go and skittered backwards. Amalina dropped awkwardly and almost smashed the hive into the elevated post. The wolf kneeled and crawled backwards, good eye worried.

Pia stepped into the clearing.

. . .

She wore a long, heavy cloak and a hat with a wide brim. Her face was done up with a scarf. Her arms were sheathed in long, thick, patterned sleeves with matching gloves. She would have been unrecognizable if her flaming red hair wasn't falling over her shoulders down to her waist.

"He isn't playing with you," said Pia, from behind the scarf.

"Pia!"

"Milady," said Aklan, bowing his head.

"He sensed danger and he's trying to protect you."

"What danger?" asked Amalina. "You?"

"I think not," she smiled and winked a large, shaded green eye. "The bees."

"How do you know?" asked Aklan. He appeared a little peeved having to then add on, for proper servility: "Milady."

"It's obvious."

At their mystified looks, Pia added, "I can sense it from *him*, the wolf, just as he senses it. Isn't that right, you big beast?"

The wolf eyed her gently but kept its distance. She pulled her scarf down, making sure her face was well under the brim's protection, to send a friendly smile at him. Her green eyes flickered playfully.

"You're all right, then?" Amalina noted the bandages were gone. "You can walk and everything?"

"He helped me, your uncle. Helped me so much. I'll recover after all ..."

Pia moved back and forth in a carefree waltz, a little stiffly, to show them how well she was. Aklan seemed to be observing her closely, as if she might suddenly grow another head.

"Have to keep myself covered now, the direct sunlight is too much. Maybe the silver weakened my constitution. But otherwise—"

"The bees don't bother you, Princess?" asked Aklan.

"No," she said.

Aklan looked to Amalina for comment. *Shouldn't they bother her?*

Amalina explained to Pia, breezily, "The Count hates them. Bees, that is. More than anything else I've seen."

Aklan pressed, turning to Pia for the answer: "So if they don't bother *you*, Princess, why would *he* hate them?"

"I wouldn' know, but—" She thought about it for a second, then nodded. She looked to Amalina for confirmation that *she* was interested in knowing. "Or maybe I do. Yes. We—people of the Count's nature that is—are in touch with everything of ourselves and in the world. And it only becomes stronger over time." Her eyes went up and she had a wistful look: "You know, I don't know if he is playing with me, or it's true, but he says he can talk to insects in their own languages; spiders and flies and so many more. He says that while they don't understand our human languages, for a short time they do remember precisely what they hear. And so he can trick them, by speaking to them, to reproduce the vibrations they've heard in a room. And then he can translate these vibrations—and by doing so, listen to what was done and said by someone earlier in that same room. Isn't that a wonderful imagination?"

"What does that have to do with bees?" said Aklan. "Milady."

"Nothing. But these little creatures are different. They don't speak to us. Something else controls them. And there are too many of them, everywhere, zooming around for their own purposes, on their specified tasks. And so they're annoying. And they have the power to wound us over and over again. And if you think about it—"

"I was thinking it's because they make honey," said Amalina, cutting in. "Honey is lifegiving. It can be used for healing. For that, they are 'good' despite their stings. And *he*, being who he is, stands opposite anything that's 'good', and so—"

"Oh, no, Katty," chided Pia with a forgiving smile. "That's so simplistic and unfair. But I was going to say, maybe it's because bees are utterly selfless; which might be along the same lines you mean. 'Good', as you say. Bees are the only creature who will willingly kill themselves to protect their nest."

"There are plenty of animals and insects that are brave and selfless," said Amalina.

"But I'm not speaking of bravery," said Pia. "*Anyone* would be willing to fight for something they care about, even in the face of death."

"Yes," said Aklan. "Um, Princess."

"But what a bee does, it's completely different. When one attacks there is no chance it will survive. When it protects the hive ... when it stings you ... it dies. So in that one moment—that one shot of pain—they give their life. Even knowing that their single blow will likely not be enough to kill their enemy, they do it anyway. They make the sacrifice."

"My book didn't say that," said Amalina.

"Oh, but it's true," said Pia, seriously. She eyed the severe looking bees climbing over Janusch's hive. "It's amazing to think. They act as if each of them is nothing but a cell of skin to be shed when fighting an enemy. They are senseless of themselves and devoted to their cause. They can't be reasoned with. They are unfathomable and unreasonable in that way: to give away everything even when there is no hope to see their victory."

"That should make them noble and inspirational, I should think," marveled Amalina.

"I wouldn't go that far," said Pia. "But they're impressive, anyway, in their ability to intimidate beyond their small scope. Do you remember the elephants in the traveling show back in Rome, Katty? The most monstrous beasts on earth, they are. Twenty feet tall, I swear! Isn't it true? But Noka told me they're afraid of bees! And they'll run away from a nest if they find one, as fast as they can."

"Is that true?" Amalina wondered, more curious how and why such a subject between Noka and Pia had come up in conversation.

"She swears it. So, when bees get angry, they can shake the knees of any living thing, I suppose. So isn't it natural that your uncle might find an aversion to them?"

Aklan said, his teeth gritted: "Well, that makes more sense, anyway."

"More sense than what?" asked Pia, a little confused.

"Than what my mistress was speculatin' about her uncle, milady." Aklan, eyed Amalina, making it known he still wasn't impressed. "*Aversion*, did you say, milady? Or is it *fear*, like an elephant's?"

"Whose to say? I don't really know." Pia sounded suddenly disinterested, she turned away, to speak more directly to Amalina. She adjusted her scarf so that her face could be seen in the shadow of the hat's brim, and smiled at Amalina. "Anyway, they fly all around and are loaded with honey; one of the most life-giving of substances, as you've pointed out. And there are so many and they can't be controlled. Can't even be spoken to, and they resist any attempt. And they make such a tremendous racket and yet their language is impossible to understand. So, in time, never mind fear, I could see a mutual loathing turn into hate."

Amalina gave Aklan a look. *You see*, it said, *it* would *work if it had to.*

"But hate's different, isn't it?" Aklan said openly to Amalina. "If they don't *scare* her, I don't see how they'll scare him."

"You want your bees to scare your uncle?" asked Pia, with a confused look. Their following silence told her something. She carefully turned her head, her fingers paused at the edge of the scarf. "You want to scare him?"

Amalina blushed. She had meant to keep the different players in her plot against the Count separate, of course, but she needed to get control of Pia's sudden concern.

"The point isn't to scare him," Amalina tutted to Aklan as if there were nothing to this little secret. "It's to *distract* him. Nobody can just ignore thousands of little insects attacking you."

Pia made a face, then looked very grave. "Then you mean … even though I'm back, and you see that I am recovered, that he helped me …you're still planning to … ?"

"Nothing's changed, Pia. As far as I know, they're still coming. Especially if they've taken care of the Boss. If they do arrive, we have to have some way to neutralize *him*, don't we?"

"Neutralize?" said Aklan, disagreeably.

Pia smirked, and looked a little lost and sad for a moment. But this disappointment was replaced in a second thought, and a positive charge to her stance. "So then I'm glad I found you, Katty. There may be something else."

"Oh?"

"Yes, but you need to see for yourself, though."

"What is it?"

Pia waved to her and sounded more upbeat. She hiked the scarf back up. "I could never explain it. Come with me. Just see."

"Is it important?"

"I think so."

Amalina told Aklan to keep practicing moving the hives.

He shot a nervous glance between Pia and the black wolf. Then he shrugged and took the tall pole and went to work.

The black wolf followed Pia and Amalina to the edge of the forest, keeping a couple paces behind.

"What is it?" Amalina asked again, to Pia's back.

"Something *has* changed."

## 63

## The Eighth Wonder of the World

Pia escorted Amalina into the castle's busy kitchens, which drew the attention of the cooks and servants, and then led her down into the packed cellar area; past the hanging bodies of slaughtered pigs, which were hung almost as a screen. They moved through and kept heading down, and Amalina sucked in her breath, knowing whatever was coming along the route had to do with the wailing woman; and anything that had changed with her could not be promising. Maybe the stolen silver chains had been discovered.

In place of the wheel room door was a rough rock wall. The kind of reinforced support going up all over the castle as the Count had done in the Grand Gallery. Because this was a less conspicuous spot with no traffic the stone was even rougher and not selected for matching color.

"The door," said Amalina.

"Yes," said Pia, drawing her away. "That's gone. Or behind it, anyway. No matter, come; that isn't what we're here for."

Pia steered Amalina down a passage she did not recall being there before. She looked back to get her bearings, but then decided a wall had blocked this opening previously. Anything could be true. And now a new corridor was revealed, and it stretched a long way into the distance, until they came to a set of downward winding stairs. The faint grating of the turning wheel in the wheel room could still be heard, but now added to it, blowing up the stairway, was a heavy gust of wind. The torch in Amalina's hand sputtered. Pia led her down the rough-hewn stone steps.

"What's this way?"

"It won't be long," said Pia, removing her hat, loosening the scarf so that it fell and wrapped her shoulders lightly. "No sense spoiling it with my nonsense."

Pia had a look of confidence in her eyes. Here was something to counteract Amalina's plan, or her need to take down the Count. Pia was now on course to finish the race in her own favor, thought Amalina, *that's what this is about.*

But it was a long way, after all. A winding staircase that kept going down and down, so that Amalina began to suppose they would, from the outside of the high castle, be reaching the base of the mountain it sat on. On one turn the wind lightened, and a rush of water could be heard. Then on the next turn, there was a short hallway which led to a dark room.

But when they arrived at the hall's end, she found it was not a dark room after all. It opened out onto an outcropping; a ledge that overlooked the inside of a massive cave. A plunging cavernous space larger than what Amalina had once seen in the Black Castle in Tsobl. It looked like they were standing on the ledge of a cliff, but above them and to the sides—everywhere she looked—it was all-enclosed with mountain rock. Before them was a deep valley that had been carved out. Facing them, on the distant side, was another cliff wall. And within that immense chasm between and below was a courtyard of buildings and outbuildings, a small, intricate city, with a great castle backed—cut—hacked—deep into that far wall; all of it fashioned out of shimmering gold.

Pia led Amalina onward, following the ledge which then sloped gradually downward to the left, hugging the wall, to some point at the bottom. But Amalina now saw that, as they continued around this great hollow, the space opened up further, as if this cave were crescent shaped. And she saw, as they circled and more came into view, near the top of the cave there was a titanic golden balaur dragon's head spewing a tremendous waterfall out its mouth, which dropped to what looked to be a river running through some of the streets below, and which forked and tongued and led to a number of artificial ponds and fountains. The many streets of this densely packed golden city were lit by torches. The light reflected by the gold and the water was almost too bright to look at, so that she had to squint and shade it with her hand.

Pia pointed to the waterways. "See the pretty little bridges down there? Just like in Venice. Those are for Aria, I suppose. There's a little here in this place for everyone."

"But what is all this?" said Amalina, her heart hammering—half from the effort on the long descent, half from the incredible sight.

Just then, a clock gonged, and an immense curved golden mirror in the shape of the sun—with a titanic iron bowl suspended directly underneath it, by chains, which contained a raging bonfire—moved overhead, drawing their attention, reflecting and directing bright beams of flickering light from the ceiling down onto the wonder below, lighting it up from a different angle. Amalina released a moan of astonishment. Each house looked like a replica of some kind she'd seen in Venice, and in Rome, and over there was a bit of Parisian architecture. And there, further off, was some sensible Dutch.

"This has to be the eighth wonder of the world," said Pia. "Don't you think?"

"I can hardly ..." Amalina added nothing more.

They reached the streets at the bottom of the ramp. She saw that the gold wasn't entirely throughout, but it was the bulk of the city's streets, walkways, building walls, edges and roofs.

"Almost eerie how quiet it is, if not for the waterfall, and a few birds," said Pia. "But that will change. Once we move down here."

"Move down …?"

"You see, Katty, I had thought I'd come up with some idea to help you in your, um … your plans to deal with your uncle. Well, he'd mentioned some little trifling work he was up to, some inspiration from those caves under the Kyrgil castle. But I had no idea. I had encouraged him into whatever it was because I thought all the extra work would tire him out, make him easier for us to handle, or distract him or whatever, when the time came." Pia lifted her arms to wave at it all. "But he has outdone himself. He has recreated the world for us in here. So that we should never be bored, or miss the daylight world, eh? We will have it. With our own sun and everything. Anything we can ever want will be here for us. Oh, you won't believe …"

Pia brought Amalina through the central avenue and directly to the city's golden castle. Once inside, she saw that it was a combination of the high castle, with its *l'entrée grande* and familiar—if golden—design, and some of the better parts of his other castles. But Pia knew just where she was going and, slinking her arm through Amalina's, took her to the Grand Gallery, which was now stocked with most of the artwork that had been in the castle above.

"Isn't he clever?" chimed Pia. "He knew this was my favorite room. And he's moving it all down here for me."

She began leading Amalina around the gallery as she had before. As many of the princesses and Ladies had done with Amalina, in the original version, when they were smitten by the richness of it all.

"He's promised to bring in new works every season," said Pia.

"Every season. So you're planning to stay, then?"

"Why not?" Pia shrugged with a smile. "Look at this place. Who wouldn't want to be here? I imagine everyone in the world would want to come, if they knew of it. Isn't it amazing what he's put together?"

"Yes. It's unimaginable."

"No one has to stay *forever*," said Pia, squeezing Amalina's arm encouragingly. "That isn't the plan. This will tide us over until he can build a route of reinforced castles for us to reach the rest of the world. But, still, I can't imagine never wanting to return here, even if we did leave at some point. I'd come back again and again."

"So you *have* changed your mind," said Amalina, just to confirm what was already obvious.

"Some things have changed, yes, as I said. I … I tried to leave, but …" She touched her stomach unconsciously. There might've still been bandages there under the dress. "And now I feel there's an attachment deeper than I realized. His blood flows through me. I know who I am. I have my own thoughts. I am me. But I know I could never help you kill him, if that is what it came to. If that is what you're really up to, Katty. And that's really it, isn't it? I would help you every way I could. Distract him, whatever. But I can't harm him, just as I could never you."

"You said you wanted to return to Rome, to your family …"

"This isn't about me, Amalina. And this," she gestured to the castle around her, "this is all well and good for us. But I really think he made it for you. Do you understand? He's trying to show you what you've been asking him for, Kat. You were so worried. You had *me* worried. That woman on the wheel … what happened to her will never be our fate. I mean, look what he built for *us*—for *you*. This isn't a wheel of torture. He's fully committed to our happiness. That woman was an accident. Count Tepsji has *chosen* us; to create us into his own kind. And, to honor you, he is committed to becoming more civilized, yes? He's doing everything you ask of him."

"I can see that. But … "

"If you're worried about being trapped here … with him … well, *I'm* not. If I ever grow tired or bored of this, we don't ever have to wait for his pathway to the world. There's nothing stopping us from leaving the high castle. He's scared because he is still a fearful child at heart. But having traveled to Korr as I did, I can't see not posting myself in a box to any corner of the world if I feel like it. I'll be visiting my parents before long. But then I'll be back."

Amalina stared at this modern wonder with wide, uncomprehending eyes. But there was something inside her that called out a warning.

"I know," said Pia. "You're worried about the coming revolution."

"There's still that," muttered Amalina. "They might arrive at any hour. We'll be forced to take a side and I … I don't know how I could … even with this—"

"No," said Pia with a laugh. "You worry too much sometimes, dear Katty. Imagine how difficult it was for him to create this masterpiece. And in almost no time at all. Compared to such a magnificent feat, done out of love for us, it should be the simplest thing of all for you. If they come … some day … you just have to tell them that the ridiculous contract is no longer needed. That he has had a change of heart and will obey the laws of man and heaven. And all should be said and done. I'm telling you, Katty: This is ours for the taking and the living."

## 64

# Good Evening

Amalina and Pia played with a gold gondola through the city's narrow canals, with Amalina showing how to use the guidepole to push the slender boat along. The smell of the water was so fresh and clean compared to Venice, Amalina remarked, while Pia noted with a mischievous grin they should be having plenty of fun right now, because this diversion was created for Aria and yet they were at it first.

They lunched streetside, outside a restaurant in the French quarter. Amalina's meal—as she was the only one of the two to really eat—was prepared and brought down from the kitchens by a waitstaff tasked to this secret area, and were dressed in poorly realized costumes meant to simulate the outfits of a high class establishment. They looked more like dressed up performers from a city fair. So some aspects could be perfected. Otherwise, Amalina and Pia chatted and marveled at all that must have gone into the making of this spectacle; the bulk of it created during the time Amalina was away. Suddenly the reason for the esteemed engineers, for Wanger, Regio, and Balbo's presence in the high castle, was clear. The men had proved to be geniuses of their craft.

All the while that they admired the handiwork and the innovation, sometimes playfully sniffing at gold flowers in long gold planter beds, other times noting the variety of books and regular homey articles stocked meticulously inside the various buildings, the sun gonged its way across the sky until it disappeared behind some rocks that served as mountaintops. After the last of the sunset, there was a second of total darkness. Then, suddenly, the ceiling was alive with hundreds of bright dots; a simulated universe of stars made of glowing lichen.

"It's nighttime," said Pia, bringing her face closer to the candles on the table where they now ate supper, curbside again but at an Italian restaurant, so Amalina could see her above the many dishes of their fragrant and hearty feast. "That is, it's night outside, in the real world. The time when we are free to rise from this castle and run wild through the Ardeel mountains."

The night carried on.

They saw several other ladies, Brignol, Epris, and Inovala, wandering along lanes and over the fancifully shaped bridges, but the sight was jarring for all parties and they kept their distances.

"It seems Princess Epris is no longer unhappy about the prospect of not having children," said Amalina, as they turned to wander down a side street, away from her.

"I wouldn't say that," said Pia. "But she's getting over it in her own way. And the others are trying to help her along. Erin Epris was very proud of her wide hips, and how many children she could've had. She always wanted a large family, and I suppose she thought with eternity at her disposal she was going to have an infinite line of children with the Count. Anne Brignol has begun a campaign to convince her it isn't so much wide hips she has but incredibly narrow shoulders."

The two laughed.

"You haven't seen Margeta down here yet?" said Amalina, in a lightly worried tone, as she anticipated the appearance of yet another changed Lady of Title.

"Why her?"

"No real reason, but … to see *her* down here?"

"Hm." Pia agreed.

"What about Cristine? Do you know what happened to her? Is she still alive? He didn't kill her?"

Pia shrugged indifferently. "Can't say I really care anymore. But he said he's taken care of everything; and looking around, I can only believe him." This didn't settle Amalina, but that didn't bother Pia. She pointed to the golden display around them. "Well, never mind all that. What does it matter? He has such a wild mind, can you believe it?"

The wildness of the Count's mind became only more evident. They entered a lamplit square with a torch-ringed fountain. In the middle of the fountain, set atop a squat octagonal base, was a gold statue of a woman. The woman looked familiar to Amalina, but she could not place her at first. The dress soon reminded her exactly who this must be: the Count's first wife—whose body Amalina helped rescue from the clutches of Neku Jonker so many years ago. A gold plaque at the front of the fountain, which Pia was presently bent over, read: "The final resting place of my dear love. Never to have lived to see this beautiful castle and city. A dream I wish we could have shared together."

Pia straightened to admire the statue with a soft sigh. "I didn't know he was once so in love," she said. "Of course he told me of his first wife, but never with much passion. Not this much. But it's sweet."

"Yes."

"At first I thought that was you up there, Katty."

"Oh, no," said Amalina, disturbed at the thought.

"Kind of looks like you, though."

"No. Nothing alike." She cleared her throat. "I've seen her before, his first wife, in real life … And then, I've never been gold."

On the side of neighboring buildings there were two smaller burbling fountains. The rounded plaques attached to them read simply, one name to each: *Ragonde la Basca* and *Robine Beaujeulle.*

"A romantic," said Pia, curtly, almost like she disapproved. "Katty," she raised a green eye at her, "I wonder … are *you* a romantic?"

"Hm?"

"I wonder, after all this, have you decided who you are yet?" At Amalina's uncomfortable look, Pia laughed gently and slid her arm around her. "No, don't answer. I was just wondering. Because I've decided who I am. And to do so *I* have decided who you are. I know you own a rich and wonderful past, with a father and a trade profession and so many friends. That is all fine and I welcome it. But to me you are Katarina. That's the person I first met, that is who I've known and came to this castle for, who I fell in love with. And that's who you've been to me for so long. So that's *my* decision. What you decide is up to you. And I'll be fine."

Returning to the castle, each bedroom was bare but for a polished gold bedframe stuffed with thick, peashell mattresses covered by expensive ermine blankets; set pieces awaiting their players. Full of energy, Pia begged to return to the gallery; which she did, on her own. Left there by herself, Amalina was was so exhausted by the day that as soon as she lay her head on the virginal goose down pillows she was asleep.

Lucinda Skeldar did not show.

There were only a few hours left.

**65**

# What Terrible Sacrifice

An ice-cold hand stroked Amalina's cheek. The hand smelled of earthy herbs and rodent fur. Amalina kicked backward with a gasp, her eyes opened wide, seeing nothing.

"I didn't mean to startle you," rumbled the Count's voice in the cool, deep, inky darkness. "You've slept a long time. Why, you've nearly dreamt the whole night away."

"Sir, I—I can't see."

A candle leapt to life.

On the bed, the Count sat at her side, wearing his casual white linen shirt and purple velvet trousers. He looked cleaner than he had in some while, as if he'd recently bathed and shaved. He stared down at her for a time, completely still. This was one of those moments, she supposed, when he could stay there for hours until she activated him in some way.

"What do you want, sir?"

"It's almost dawn. I know how you don't like to waste a single hour." As he said this, his dead white fingers tickled the air as if playing a musical instrument.

Amalina nodded and yawned. The murkiness of the room, even with the golden reflections of the candle on the walls, made it seem it could be closer to midnight than dawn. She had a sudden thought and discreetly touched her neck. The Count chuckled knowingly. Her skin was smooth and unbroken, and she felt her pulse beating steadily underneath.

"Your room has no windows," he said matter-of-factly. "My sun clock can't shine in. And below the mountain the temperature is nearly the same year round, there's little need to use the fireplaces. Time is indeed difficult to place. But there's no reason for you to use the same room here as you have up there. You can pick any you like if you prefer something brighter."

Amalina was still in her clothes, she threw aside the blanket and began stretching.

"So like a cat you are," he observed.

"Sir, are you going to be staying in my room? I'm awake now."

"Of course, my little mouse, now that you know about this little creation of mine, we must have a talk."

"I can't tell anyone up in the high castle," she said, anticipating the conversation.

"There's that. But I think you can imagine there are a few *other* things as well …"

"Can I get some breakfast sent down, sir? Or do I have to go back up into the regular castle? I can go there, that's no problem."

"You can eat wherever you want, Ms. Dalca," he said with a note of annoyance. She had interrupted some monologue he'd wanted to start in on. "But I wonder, is that necessary for you *at this moment*?"

"Well, you don't need to know this, sir," she said shyly, "but maybe you already do, I *do* have a morning routine … and it doesn't include you. Why don't we just meet at the restaurant where Pia and I ate last night? The cooks and servants should know where. Is it easy to let them know?"

"Very. But you'll learn all the secrets soon enough. I will allow you …" from the roll of his eyes he picked a time from the back of his head "… one hour's indulgence."

As he left, he said before closing the gold door, "One hour."

• • •

When Amalina was alone, she didn't know what to do with herself. She thought of putting out the candle and going back to sleep. This room made the thought of hibernation seem real and tempting. But her body had come awake and so she took the candle stick and left the room.

The privy stall was placed just where it was in the main castle above. But of course here the closet was gold. And it was cool and filled with a soft, echoey whisper that seemed to be coming up from the hole in the bench. Amalina brought the candle forward and saw the chute wasn't empty: down below was a rushing stream of water, headed who knows where? *What an odd, but very practical idea*, thought Amalina. An innovation she might have expected in the more modern and advanced Italy or France. She also remarked to herself, that it felt strange to sit down on gold. It seemed the territory of a fairy tale. And here she was doing it!

After that, she spun through the hallways, comparing them to the high castle's. It seemed dimensions were exaggerated in places. Some things were a little bigger, some shrunk to nothing. She recalled the chalk map of the high castle she'd drawn on her old dress. Did she still have it hidden away somewhere? It might be interesting to compare the layouts.

The door to Cristine's room was open. Out of curiosity she wandered in, only to draw back quickly. After a second, she peeked back inside.

Cristine lay in bed; no longer grey but fish-belly white. Her eyes were closed and she didn't look like she was breathing. Amalina stepped carefully forward, not wanting to rouse her friend, but wondered what might have changed. The Count hadn't killed her after all. But why was she now down here?

On her neck there was a series of red dots. The blood had been cleaned away, leaving only the scars, which didn't seem as bad as they had once been. As if they were healing.

There were some items on a table next to the bed. A small cup, and a tall pitcher of water. There was also the angular green vial.

Amalina's stomach lurched.

"Amalina," came the Count's low rumble. "Amalina Dalca."

She ran from the room before his call woke Cristine. She assumed he was projecting his considerable voice throughout the castle the way he and the Strange Man could do. A trick these creatures had. But she noticed the sound grew and shrank at different points in the corridor. "*... Amalina, Amalina, my sleepy little mouse ...*" She slowed down.

In the nearby wall was a round hole. Looking into it, it was a polished metal tube, widening out at this end like the mouth of a horn. And here the Count was speaking to her.

"Sir?"

"An hour has passed. The sun will rise very, very soon. Please come down so that you don't miss it."

She wanted to say she'd already seen it, but was still marveling at the contraption in the wall. "I'll be right down."

"Don't be long."

But when the Count's voice withdrew, Amalina pressed her ear to the horn ... as it seemed there were other voices. No. A low whisper. A chant.

It was Margeta and the clacking of her beads. Somewhere in the castle she was close to one of these horns and muttering to herself in prayer. But it wasn't prayer, exactly. "What have I done?" went her mantra. "Sold myself. What have I done? Lost my soul. What have I done? Forsaken the Holy Spirit. What have I done?"

"P-p-p-p-p-p-p-p-please, my P-p-p-p-p-p-p-p-princess," said Bardina. "Y-y-you've done nothing wrong. F-f-forgive yourself, my P-p-princess. My P-p-p-p-princess ..."

"... Nothing to forgive. What have I done? Devoured the forbidden fruit. What have I done? Made a mistake. What have I done ...?"

"Margeta?" called Amalina into the opening. "Bardina?"

Neither answered.

. . .

When the Count met Amalina outside the gold castle, she said, "Margeta doesn't sound very happy."

"When has she ever been?" replied the Count, unconcerned. "The process seems to have intensified her. But she'll come round. Her regret is born from her innate sense of superiority and obstinacy. She thought she was being elevated. And she has been. But only to find herself now an equal at best within our clique of the higher set. It will naturally take a little longer for a headstrong maiden like our Lady la Brichese to adapt. But that isn't a subject for happy morning chatter, which is what I had planned for us."

"And Cristine's in there too, sir. I saw her."

"Yes," he said, his mustache twitching. "That *is* one of the things we're to discuss this morning."

"You didn't kill her, thank god," said Amalina, with genuine relief but an added concern. "But what is she doing …? Did you …? But you didn't … or did you?"

"She's mine now," he said, smiling. Beaming. "*Ours*, I should say."

"Ours?" Her face twisted. "You mean you went through with it then?"

He seemed mystified by Amalina's upset; he'd generously granted her a favor, done presumably to please her. But the thought of Cristine's change only worsened the misgivings inside Amalina.

"We can speak after you've had something to eat," he said, misreading her displeasure, and in his cluelessness apparently thinking it was hunger. "Any minute the sun will rise in its glory. You should see the colors."

"I don't want to eat here," growled Amalina, feeling she wanted to get as far away from Cristine and Margeta, this unhappy place of shining gold, a place suddenly of broken friendships and betrayal, before some trap mechanism crashed down on her; making it a gold prison for her and all the infinite captives. The dark rock around her, and over her head, was now as constricting as the innards of a giant gold snake that had swallowed her, keeping her from the air and daylight and freedom of movement which she enjoyed above. "I don't care to see your artificial sunrise. I've already seen the sorry thing, and now I want to go back up."

"What's the matter?" he asked, following along as she stormed away without a sure direction.

"You went and turned her! after all I warned you about Cristine and her papa!"

"My little mouse." He smiled condescendingly when she stopped and spun back around on him. "You don't understand. But you will."

*It's like* you *don't understand*, she thought hotly. But in another reasoning: "You just can't help yourself, can you? You just can't help yourself!"

"How many times must I convince you of the greater reality I grasp than you do, my little mouse?" said the Count charitably. "Cristine will forgo her past, as all must when they pass the immortality's threshold. She will forgive any trespasses against her. She will be your friend once more, better than ever. And she will be loyal only to me."

"And you believe it?"

"She has assured me as much."

"She'd tell you anything."

"It's not an empty promise," he said. "She will seal her assurance to me in blood."

Amalina thought of her and Cristine's old blood pact. Remembered cutting her skin, and rubbing their bloody palms against each other, and feeling that guilty thrill of doing something forbidden. But after all, what had that amounted to?

"I'm not sure what you are thinking," he said. "But it is not a little sacrifice she'll be making, little mouse."

"Sacrifice?"

"Her first kill will be her own father," he said with a bland smile, but large heated eyes. "Should she fail to do so, I will remove them both."

Amalina swallowed hard. "She … She said she would … kill him?"

"This doesn't please you? The dreaded AXP, as you say, brought to proper justice? by his own daughter, no less?"

Amalina shook her head. "But it's unthinkable. I could never—even if Papa were the worst—"

"Of course *you* wouldn't. And couldn't. Killing is not in your nature. And it never will be. But for Cristine it is but a little act. *That* is in her nature. And it preserves her life. And it proves her loyalty to *us*."

Amalina swallowed hard. She pictured Cristine promising to the Count that she'd kill *Papa Szeful*, ol' Boss Berzweck. It turned her stomach all over again. Those crystal blue eyes were the eyes of a ruthless animal who Amalina had always counted as a friend. She'd never known the true depth behind them. *Her own father!* Just to gain …

*Well, that isn't me*, she thought. *That will never be me.*

"Did she know about this place," asked Amalina, looking around, "before she made her promise?"

"Let's get you out of here, Mouse," he said gently, reading her thoughts from her expression. "If it offends you."

He pointed them to the opposite side of the cave, to the far left of where the ramp to the upper ledge began. There was an alcove with a large basket secured in it. He picked her up and set her in the basket. Then he said, "Up!"

The basket rose and Amalina's legs buckled under her.

"Hold there," he said, and pointed to the rope at her elbow. Amalina grabbed it to steady herself and then stood. He appeared to be rising alongside the rocky wall to keep pace with her, but just outside the basket, without anything underneath him.

Peering down at the city below, with its falls and waterways and fountains and its great golden castle, the view—the whole masterwork—amazed Amalina once more. She stared dumbfounded, even as she wanted to get a thousand miles from this mountain and never see it again. She couldn't help but stare in wonder, and feel a strange, downward pull toward it. How could she leave behind something so amazing, something some inquisitive part of her wanted to explore?

"Look what I have done," he said, looking on it, too. The amber light gave his skin an almost healthy glow. In his large brown eyes was a glistening gold reflection, like from a nearby fireplace. "Even you, with your contempt for me, you must admit how wonderful it is."

"Even I?" The way he was admiring his work, like a proud child, smiling openly, was a little endearing. "Well, it is *something* …"

"I was inspired … So many sights I've read about and seen the illustrations, you understand, but thought I should never see myself."

"So beautiful," admitted Amalina, with a quiet breath.

"Well, don't be too amazed," he smirked off-handedly, pulling on his mustache. "It's just gold pressed very thin. A patina over raw stone." He flexed his yellowed fingers on his opposite hand, studying them. "But it does the trick well enough, eh? Too bad we'll be missing the sunrise this morning. But here we are."

The basket stopped as its bottom came level with the ledge. He helped her out of the basket and they both looked back at the city one last time.

"I'm afraid our conversation didn't start as it should have," said the Count in a disconsolate tone, as he turned to guide her away.

"I'm all right now I think," said Amalina, apologetic and sorry she'd ruined his plan, whatever it had been. She kept them in place, not quite wanting to leave just yet. "The basket ride and the view took away some of the—well, never mind …"

"It *was* to be about you, and you alone: our little talk."

*Was it really?* thought Amalina, with an inward smirk, glancing up at him. *All about me? No 'I, me, I me, I, me'*'s?

But suddenly Amalina felt it was unfair to judge him, he was—apparently—being sincere right now. So very earnest. He was looking directly at her, but not in a weird or intimidating way, or with those expanding and depthless eyes that would send the room and her mind whirling. They were apologetic, and accommodating, it seemed. A rarity for him.

"So begin, sir. I'm sorry to have put you off. What was it you wanted to say?"

"Really? You will let me have my say, after all, Ms. Dalca?" The side of his mouth came up in a cautious grin.

"Of course, sir," she said, returning his smile, feeling oddly in command. "What is it?"

"Amalina Dalca," said the Count in a low rumble.

"Yes?"

He waved his arm out toward the gold city. "You know that I made all of this for you, don't you? You understand that?"

"I think you made it for every one of us."

"Without you," he began, "I would never have acted on my inspiration. You motivate me, little mouse. With your constant movement and fresh energy and wondrous curiosity and intellect. In some ways, I was seeking to best you here. I mean, look at it. How foolish and unrealistic and *fantastic*. Something out of a fairy tale. You know how much I loathe such inconsequential things. But you love them. And I sought to do you one better: I *made* it. With my own hands. And why would I want to best you, but to win you over?"

"Sir—"

"No longer call me that, my Amalina," his eyes seemed to grow larger. Depthless, once more.

"It just seems hard to believe …"

"You know, if you join us, you will forgive Cristine. You will forgive *any* wrongs against you. You will forgive even me. Time washes away all these feelings."

"Until you aren't human anymore," said Amalina. She cleared her throat. "I heard you talking to Pia, at the hotel. I heard what she said, what you both said. What it's like. What is the point of living if you have no more feelings?"

"It's not that dire, my dear," he smiled gently. "Of course you have them. But your perspective is placed at a much higher vantage. Like that of an eagle watching over the earth. You become more liberal and patient."

Amalina's face contorted in an effort not to burst into laughter.

"Oh, little mouse," said the Count, indulgently. "You wish to call me a hypocrite? That I am the most intolerant and impatient man you've ever met?"

"Well—"

"Very well," he interrupted her. "I can be accused quite cynically if you haven't a full understanding of what *my* reality is like. Perhaps I grow impatient sometimes, because I feel like time is rushing by, and I am grasping at water that cannot be held for a second. But how can one truly question—how can one presume—what one does not know unless one tries it for oneself?"

"I suppose …"

"I always thought you as a pragmatic sort. Now, I know a decision is a scary thing. But permanence is an illusion." He paused, observing her reaction. "Or else, since it is impossible to reason with you, or convince you of my authenticity, if arguments will only fail, if it will satisfy your heart, let me, instead, *prove* my love for you."

"Love?" Amalina took half a step back.

"A *feeling*, my Amalina. And the strongest of all. The greatest one, no? The *everlasting* one. But we have to be realistic, even when it comes to love. I would never claim to know a thing about eternity, but I know more about it than you. I have lived a very long time. And with it comes an understanding of what survives the longest, perhaps even into eternity: that love, true love, is an unselfish thing."

"*Welll ...*"

"Amalina, I know how much your family means to you. If you accept my terms, to allow me to perfect you, so that you might be with me forever, I will become one of your family, too. And from this day forward, I will remove my threat, so rashly and unkindly put upon your father. You are freed of that burden."

To Amalina, the lifting of a threat, even when framed as a gift, seemed more like the intensification of one. But before she could argue, he was already moving on.

"Before you say anything, I also know how much you cherish life," he said. "As if it is sanctified. As you know for these past months, I have refrained from taking one life to feed my own. And it was in honor of that belief you hold. I have followed your advice, and used only what I needed, and left my victims unwary in their sleep, and fully unharmed. Though I will draw the line at resorting to base animals, I will conduct myself in this way for the rest of my days upon this earth. And I vouch to you that, if you should join me, that your supposition was right: it *is* possible to survive in such a fashion. And so you know that you may live honorably, without ever killing; as is your innocent makeup."

He cleared his throat and nodded slowly, working himself up for this next part: "I see how much you enjoy your travels into the west. You love to read, and to explore, and to learn. I could never conquer such a thing, and I would never seek to. For that is what makes you you. Though I would prefer to have you at my side every day, from here and ever forward, because I cannot guarantee a freer movement into the world for some time if I were to change you, and out of my own caution: you will be free to pursue your passions as you like. Go see the world on your own terms, even with my own treasury— *our* own treasury—and even in such a vulnerable state, as is your current condition as a mortal. You will be untethered by any of my weaknesses, except for human frailty, and may venture in the sun and among all you choose to befriend. Do this with my blessings, only with the promise that when you have had your fill of it, as all do, you will then return to me, and allow me to bring you into this higher realm, to experience the world more vividly; as it truly is.

"And I will trust you to leave my court, innocent as you've always been, and do these things; and that you will return to me one day as my bride, and only then, at that time, accept my gift. As I wait for you patiently, as patient as time itself, I know I can look forward to your return, however long it might be, years, or decades, perhaps half a century if you like, because you *will* return; because you will have given me your word to do so You are a Lady of Honor and Truth. You do not forget your agreements. And I can do nothing else but believe you shall honor this one."

Count Tepsji stopped. His face seemed overcome with deep emotion, but he wasn't breathless as a lover might be after delivering such a speech. Amalina stared, not knowing how to respond.

"You can do whatever you want, Ms. Dalca," he said. "I made all of this for you. I've done all this. I have amended my ways. I make these bold promises to you that I've never vowed to any other mortal in my life. How much I care then, must be obvious. What more can I do to win you? What error or blemish do I possess that I will not gladly mend for you? Shall I fault this body? Yet it is but a plaything."

With these words, his body began to shimmer and move. And his features rearranged, his color changed, his thick mustache withdrew. His eyes altered shape and color. And, by reading her thoughts behind her eyes, what she might be looking for, for a brief moment it seemed as if he was about to become Ion.

"No!" shouted Amalina. "No, no, stop! Don't. It's too much. Don't ever."

He returned to his normal appearance, though a little more youthful, which gave him a handsome edge. But it was difficult for her to disregard how truly transient his body was.

"I just mean," she said, apologetically, "you can be yourself. You should be, and have to be, yourself."

"Okay," he said. But tears formed in his eyes now. "And you should be yourself. And you don't have to come back to me—to be with me forever— but visit me from time to time. But, Amalina, my dear Amalina, it must be obvious my love for you now. All I ask is that you agree to join with me in this, my loving compact; that you will take my hand and say yes."

Count Tepsji held out his hand, it almost looked like for a handshake, but it trembled with emotion.

Amalina stood there thinking. Is this just another game for him? Was he just using the same old trick he'd done with the other Ladies to get them to give in to his will? Contorting himself and his personality only to claim them as his next prize? Each one a game or an experiment? And *this*, this eighth wonder of the world, was what he thought it would take to buy her? But … what a length to go! Or was something like this, with unlimited power and time at his disposal, still nothing to him after all? Or, Amalina wondered, was it uncharitable for her to be so absolutely cynical about it? How could it really be one of his meaningless diversions if it was truly meant to last forever? And, when it came to his many other Ladies under his sway, what was the difference between him and Ivanti, with his own string of cheap women? Ivanti Vokent hid his affairs with lies. This one—her would-be lover—was coming to Amalina, again and again and again, despite his many other open loves. Doesn't that make him at least more honest, in a sense?

*But he is a criminal of the highest order! Evil.* Someone she had sought to kill from the very first. For the untold number of people who had suffered at his villainy, he deserved to pay a price. But really, the only people she'd seen the Count kill—men who'd she'd cared for, at that—had come with the purpose of doing the same to *him*. He'd been defending his own life. There was only one person she'd seen him kill who was innocent: Lucinda Skeldar. And that was an assassination that he'd carried out at the request of someone else. And for his part, he had simply been fulfilling his needs, acting out his natural impulses, unaware that he did not *need* to do it in order to sustain himself. And now that he did know, and had resolved to restrain his appetites and no longer destroy a living being for sustenance, and had turned against Cristine's father so he wouldn't be murdering anyone innocent anymore, didn't that make him a better man than he was? An improved man? A completely *new* man?

But … was he really a man at all?

Amalina needed to think about this. It felt like she needed an hour more, or a day, or a week. But what circumstance would change in that time? She was being given all the time in the world to make her decision, really. To live her life as she would have it, for as long as she wanted, wherever she desired, before she made up her mind. Maybe at some point she would come to a better understanding of what this all meant. But none of that would happen if she did not decide clearly now. And what decision was it considering the one—the absolute one—the men in Attila's revolution were making, the terrible sacrifice they were readily taking up? And so: what sacrifice was it for her? And all she had to do to gain this strange bargain for immortality was play the toadying accomplice for the many years past, and by his terms she would never have to do so again. Or maybe after all those years on, having lived as a foreign, moneyed noble in the world, she might have become someone else, and be in a different frame of mind, and beg for such an offer. There was only one way to know.

Amalina took his hand. "Yes, of course, sir. Why not?"

A gong sounded.

Light from the sun opened up on them, the heat of it warmed Amalina's face. They were looking into each other's eyes.

Only, the gong sounded again.

And again.

And again.

The Count hesitated, then shot away. A black blur. Amalina followed the long route after him.

When she reached the upper floors, out of breath, the cooks were looking at each other, confused. There seemed to be a stirring within the castle. Voices were raised. Doors were being banged here and there, with some Ladies' cries following. She caught the humming black blur slam through *l'entrée grande.*

As the gong continued, Amalina ran out into the courtyard and saw Captain Durok atop the wall, hammering away at Genadie's large iron emergency bell, as he stared over the outer wall to the clearing outside.

"What is it?" she yelled to him.

He ignored her, but she followed after another guard and one of Greta's male servants, as they charged up the stairs to see what was out front of the castle.

"Oh, no, no, no, no, no," said Amalina when she arrived at the top and leaned over the parapet.

There before the castle gates, stood the raggedly-arranged ranks of a small army, shining brightly even in the early morning light, with their armor and long spears and pikes made uniformly of silver.

# Part Eight
# The Silver Army

## 66

# The Peace

Amalina's legs wobbled and felt like they would collapse, pitching her over the side.

"Idiots, idiots, idiots," she grumbled. But she righted her shoulders and said to Captain Durok, "Where's Count Tepsji?"

"How would I know?"

"But he knows about this? It's too far into sunrise for him to come see for himself, you know, you should—"

"Sent a messenger inside already," he bristled at her. "The Master must know by now."

"Who's down there?"

"Can't tell," said Durok with a shrug. "A fancy sort. Look at 'em."

"Well, what are they doing?"

"Standing at attention. See for yourself, enh?"

"They haven't made their intentions known?"

"Haven't said a thing." Durok shook his head. "Just marched out of the forest like that and came to ranks. I can't imagine—"

There was a loud crack as a large-wheeled platform with a cannon mounted to it, riding the mountain decline, crashed out of the forest and into the clearing. Four silver-clad men charged from the treeline after it, and began to right it where it fell.

"Look over there!" said another guard.

A long cart loaded with straw was coming up the mountain road, pulled by four frothy, trotting horses. Amalina heard the ghostly echo of Commander Kralov's warning "never use horses"—or *any* creature, so the sentiment of warning went—that Count Tepsji might be able to influence. But in truth, how could the Count influence them when he couldn't expose himself to the light of day? Maybe there wasn't anything to worry about. They'd find out soon enough. The cart was making good time and didn't look like it would stop or be turned around.

But still, this looked and felt so similar to Commander Kralov's ill-fated siege. Amalina stared down on the silver army and could only feel pity for them, no fear at all. And she didn't want to pity the men she'd known from childhood. They were all there. Even her father. They were anonymous, hidden inside their all-encompassing silver suits. So she imagined her father's face behind any and all the helmets with black whiskers hanging out at the neckline. She could only identify Gulgas the Hunter by his great height, so that his armor hung like tin dinner plates strung onto his body, as well as his singularly long rifle strapped to his shoulder.

She caught herself before she cried out to him.

"Hey," shouted Captain Durok, more annoyed than concerned. "What're you doing down there?"

One of the suits of armor strutted forward, and bent backward at the knees to look directly up at the Captain. "We're here to announce the capital charge of murder against Count Miscael Ivanov Tepsji—known by many other names—and to place him under arrest. He is presently within this castle, is he not?"

Amalina's heart leapt. It was Ion. When he'd finished his declaration he waited with one hand gripping the shaft of a tall pike, its dull end planted next to his shining plated foot, its sharp end reaching close to the height of the wall. Captain Durok didn't answer the question. He leaned back from the ledge so he couldn't be seen and tapped the point of his sword thoughtfully against the stone walkway.

"Possession of this castle shall be turned over to the governor of Ardeel," Ivanti's voice sounded from below.

Durok cursed several times, looked over the ledge again, then yelled, "Take care with that cannon. The Master will see you pay for any damage."

Aklan, beside Amalina, laughed at this. Amalina grabbed him. "Aklan, ready the rope! String it out through the old route!"

Aklan scrunched his face and said, "The privy hole? But the privy's being *used* now!"

"Eh?" said Captain Durok, not understanding.

The other year the privy tunnels had been used to evacuate the castle, an unexpected and effective route because the larger out-chutes were hidden from the front gate and, from the landing point of the midden, gave safe access to the forest. But at the time, years ago, there weren't people using those particular holes. Now it wouldn't be so pleasant a journey to safety. However—

"Get the rope!" snarled Amalina, giving Aklan a directing shove. "Get it ready, now!"

As Aklan ran off, Amalina turned on Durok. "Have the gate opened."

"What?"

"I know them. I can call it off."

"Can you, Mouse?" he said, eyeing her doubtfully. "So do it from here."

"I have to speak to them face to face."

"Why?"

"Just do it. I'm commanding you."

"You aren't the Master."

"Shall I get him for you, Captain?" asked Amalina hotly. "To tell you to your face? He won't be very pleased. What are you afraid will happen if you open the gate? Now, as the Countess Katarina Tepsji, I order you, Captain Durok, to let me through. Lock it after me if you're worried, but I must parley with them immediately."

Durok seemed to enjoy that Amalina had called him Captain.

• • •

Amalina slid out the gate's narrow opening. As the giant wood door closed and the locking bolts clunked in place, a suit of armor ran forward while others cheered at the sight of her.

"Amalina," said Ivanti, seeming somehow alien with a perforated thick silver plate for a face. She couldn't even see his pretty eyes inside. He came off as a hulking, inhuman metal insect. He must have handed his pike off to someone else in the line. As he reached her, his silver glove seized her arm and pulled her back from the wall.

She dug in her heels. "Wait! No!"

"What's the matter? We have a valuable hostage now. Come away—"

"I said no. You have to stop. Stop this whole thing. There's no reason for it anymore."

Three more suits broke ranks and approached.

"Papa, you have to listen to me!" she called to one. The armor stopped short.

"I'm not your papa."

Amalina didn't recognize the voice. With a sudden fear, she said, "Wait, Boss—?"

"No!" the armor shuddered.

"Hey!" Ivanti shook her arm. "Don't speak to anyone. And don't say names. They can't know who we are, who is here. Now, what are you doing, eh? Get to safety; go to the back of the lines, take the cart before it leaves—there behind us, coming up, see. Only, we're taking over this castle. We're doing it right here and now, Ama."

"But you don't have to do it. Listen to me: he isn't the same. He's changed. He's agreed to rescind the contract. And he has committed himself to never harming anyone ever again in this land. Not one more death. Ardeel is free!"

"You mean to tell us," came one mocking voice from the front ranks, she couldn't tell who, "that we should spare a criminal who has been murdering for centuries just because he's suddenly become reasonable?"

"No, I—"

"Aye, and will he pay us back?" said a gruff voice, closer still, with a hollow metallic ring. "For all we've lost?"

"He has all the money in the world," said Amalina. "I'm sure he'd be willing—"

The gruff-voiced knight clanked forward aggressively, cutting her off. "*And will he pay us back?* Will he? For what he has taken from us? How could he possibly?"

Ivanti pushed this man back with a firm hand to his breastplate, then turned to Amalina again. "What matters if he's had a change of heart, Ama? Let heaven celebrate. This has nothing to do with him. Though we are here to give the monster hell on earth, *we*'re here to redeem our own souls, and the souls of our ancestors, by taking righteous action against the greatest evil to walk these lands. Do you hear me, Amalina? We do this not for your safety, nor anyone else's, nor against him, but to restore our *honor*."

"Yes, yes, of course," she said breathlessly, starting to sweat. "I understand what you're saying. But all of you are going to die if you try. And what use is that?"

"I thought you said he doesn't kill!" said the rough one. *Lazru Skeldar,* thought Amalina. *It must be.*

"Mr. Skeld—"

"Ama!" warned Ivanti. "No names!"

"Sir, I can't guarantee anything if you attack him. But he *has* pledged his life to peace from now on."

"That should make our work easier," said one of the other knights, maybe Jenz Timer, to a round of dark laughter.

"Don't you hear me? All of this—all of it—it won't work! You'll all be killed. Just let me take care of it, and—"

"Get away, girl!" shouted the rough-voiced Lazru. He charged forward again, his glove snapping at her. "Out! Leave the dirty work to us!"

"You need to get out of our way," said Ivanti, as he began to drag her again, leading her toward the long cart that had arrived at the far side and turned around, presenting its bed fluffed full of straw. Men were pulling from its back-end barrels and boxes and cannon balls. "It will be dangerous, but we will succeed. The plan is sound."

Lazru added on, enthused: "We've the advantage and the ability; and this is our hour! We shall never have it again!"

"General!" Amalina cried out at the rows of armor, digging in her heels, trying to spot the revolutionary, Mr. Bronk. It was difficult to picture him in such a manly suit. "Where are you? I need to speak to you!"

Ivanti caught Amalina and shook her hard. "I'm the general here."

"No, I mean—"

"I said *leave*, you stupid girl. And stop *speaking*!"

"Well, where is he? He needs to know he's about to get you all killed."

"He isn't here," whispered Ivanti coolly through the small round holes in the helmet. "Do you understand? This isn't stopping, Amalina. Because it's already begun."

"Where?" she worried. "Where is he?"

"Just get yourself—"

Amalina pulled her arm out of his grip and ran the several yards back to the gate. It was so easy to slip through Ivanti's slick glove, which was difficult for him to close fully, and she could distance him in that armor in any race. Yes, if they were to fight the Count, they would all be dead. She was sure of it.

"Ion," she said.

"Amalina, come back here."

She turned to address the army again. She saw the cannon being mounted into place, pointed right at the castle's main door.

"Papa! Papa! Go! Don't stay! I'm begging you!"

"Shut up, you harlot!" raged Lazru. He burst forward at her again, like a wild animal. "Lucinda will see you dead with my own hands if you speak one more word in his defense! One more word, and you die with him!"

Amalina dodged the slow moving armorer, circled to draw him off, and returned to the gate at a sprint. "Let me in! Let me in!" The door cracked open at her pounding, and she looked one last time at Ivanti, "Give me an hour before you present your demands again. I promise, you will see. One hour!"

One of the guards hauled her in and closed the door. Three massive bolts slid into place.

"Could have been killed, Countess. Do you really know them?" asked Captain Durok.

Amalina ran to the main building and slammed into Durok's messenger as he was running out. She demanded: "Where are you going?"

"He told me—"

She nabbed the little boy by the collar and brought him into *l'entrée grande*. The Count stood before the fireplace, dressed in his ceremonial robes, arm casually resting on the mantle. He hadn't been there earlier. Or had he and she hadn't noticed? He turned to them as they entered.

"Amalina," he said in his deep, rich, resonant voice. It looked like he'd been wakened from private thoughts "What are you doing there? Has he delivered my offer already? How long have I been standing here?"

"What are you doing, sir?"

"Awaiting the audience," said the Count, patting his mustache. "I will have my parley with these gentlemen and settle whatever grievance they have."

"They're here to execute you."

"But I haven't heard yet why they've come."

"And I've just told you, sir. To take the castle and execute you."

"You've spoken with them?"

"Leave," said Amalina. "If you aren't here, they can do nothing."

"They *can't* do anything," he said, amused. "Not to me. Though they never stop trying, do they? No matter the ample examples I have provided down through the centuries. Yet, I shall meet them with open arms, as ever."

"Didn't the messenger tell you? They're clad fully in armor; *silver* armor."

His eyebrows raised. "Silver armor, is it now? Very interesting. It's always something new."

"There's no need for anyone to get hurt," said Amalina, frustrated at his nonchalance. He didn't take his elbow off the mantle, refused to break his excellent, carefree pose.

"Nobody will be," he said. "Unless they won't listen to reason …"

"They're from Korr. My father is with them."

This news gave him pause. "Well, I can only promise so much. But I will spare him, even if they choose to carry on with this private war of theirs." He whispered slyly, "And is our Cristine's father with them, too?"

"I'm serious, sir. They have cannons. This looks dangerous."

"You remember what you did for our previous spring invasion? How many years ago was that now? But you remember, of course, Ms. Dalca." He nodded that she must. "Their quarrel is only with me. Take our guests who are still in the living quarters to a safer place outside and into the forest to wait this episode out. No sense them getting injured or in my way."

"It's already happening, but—"

"I knew I could trust you, little mouse," he smiled in delight.

"But why not move them down to your golden city?"

He shook his head, definitely. "As before, as before, Ms. Dalca. That first route should do as it did then. No sense giving them ideas they shouldn't have."

"But I meant, why don't *you* retreat down there, too? Go wait with the other Ladies in that golden castle. This army might search the palace and think you aren't here and leave."

"I'll do no such thing," said the Count, unruffled. "And what if they aren't satisfied, as their kind tend to be? Who knows what they might get up to unsupervised? With no one to stop them, what if they should search my high castle to its foundations? It's possible they will find my hidden city given time, and what then? I will not have mortals bumbling and stumbling through what belongs only to our genus. No, it stops here. I will invite them in and we will—"

"We still have our agreement, don't we?"

He looked baffled. "Agreement?"

"*Our* agreement, sir. Which we just made. Downstairs?"

"You mean my *proposal*? Our compact?"

"Oh, yes, whatever it is, yes, yes. It's still good isn't it?"

"I am a man of my word," he said, amused. "But I don't see how that—"

"Give me an hour," said Amalina. "You can help Aklan with the Ladies and their escape. That should calm them and I'm sure you can convince them it's their idea."

"Of course I can," said the Count, as if Amalina had voiced some doubt in his ability to do so.

"But don't engage the army before the hour is out," she cautioned him. "I've already gotten them to agree to hold that long before they resume their demands."

"Have you? And what will happen in an hour, little mouse? What can *you* do?" he looked genuinely intrigued at what she was about to say.

"Most know me. They trust me. I'll find something to change their minds. I just need time to think. But, if nothing else, standing in the morning sun with all that armor on, after a while they will be less likely to put up a good strong fight. They would be more willing to listen, and deal."

"Oh, ho, ho," said the Count, his face breaking into a wide grin. "My Amalina. Yes. Yes. *Yesssss*. Always so smart, always *so* clever. Boy," he turned to Durok's messenger, "belay my order to throw open the gates. Our little mouse will have her hour."

## 67

## A Plan into Motion

Amalina felt dragged out and guilty by the time she reached her room but she didn't see how this moment could be played any other way than how she'd so carefully constructed it over the preceding months. As she entered, Aklan tossed the long knotted rope behind her bed, then, seeing who it was, went to retrieve it.

"What are you doing here?" cried Amalina.

"Getting the rope."

"You haven't already?"

"The Ladies are readying themselves. Thought I'd put on an extra jacket and pants, too. Once we're down in the forest, I can change out. I mean, we have to go through those tubes, right? I'll be going first." He grimaced. "Even so, can't imagine how we'll get them Ladies down through 'em."

"Yes, you go first, and once you've secured the rope, get to the hives right away," commanded Amalina, breathlessly, snatching the skec pole from the corner and setting it next to him. "Their people will take care of them. But you'll have to see to the bees—bring them in for me."

"Why?" said Aklan, eyes rounding at the mention of the bees. "Didn't you talk to the—? What's happening now?"

"The idiots *are* attacking the castle," she whispered, shaking angrily. "Going to get themselves all killed. It's insane! I told them. I warned them. But they won't listen. Oh, Papa!"

"Silver armor," whispered Aklan, hopefully. "He won't be able to touch them. Their weapons will be extra deadly. They even got a cannon. They *might* be able to—"

"It'll be *worse* than last time," said Amalina, inspecting the coiled rope and its many hand-hold knots before offering it back to him. "It's up to us to stop them."

"How?"

"What do you mean how?" Amalina snarled at Aklan. "*The plan!* We're doing it! Right now! You go get the hives, while I put the rest in order."

"So I *am* getting your bees? You said you—"

"Now, Aklan!"

"Not arguing, Pretty Princess, just asking!" Aklan hopped in place and slung the coiled rope over his shoulder. Outsized compared to his slight body, it appeared like it didn't weigh a pound to him. He was suddenly radiant. "The plan! I can't wait! This castle will be *ours!*"

"Get going," she said. "I'll tell the others."

. . .

*How did the plan go again?* Amalina tried to recall as she ran up the hallway, her mind suddenly blank. Her nerves were working against her thoughts. She couldn't believe this was happening.

> Smoke: in the cellars, to confuse and distract the Count.
> Bees: also for distraction, upstairs, in the great hall.
> The Wailing Woman: for distraction and unpredictability, stalking the Count wherever he might be, and possibly a formidable counter-force to him, while directing him where he needed to go.
> The Chandelier and all its silver chains, water, etc.: for immobilizing the Count, and containment.
> Genadie's weapons: to land the finishing blow—*if need be.*
> Maybe she could still talk one side or the other down.

"Genadie, where are you going?" said Amalina, as she saw him limping slowly and sadly down an empty passageway.

"Captain Durok took my warning bell, remember?" he frowned. "First you took it. Now it's Durok. Durok!"

"Well, so what?" Amalina whispered quickly. "There's an army outside about to come in!"

"It's *my* bell, and *my* job to raise the emergency alarm, Ms. Dalca."

"Genadie!" she shook him by the shoulders as if trying to wake him. He seemed dazed. Maybe he already realized what was happening—and what that ultimately meant. He wanted to deny, or pretend this was something else. "The plan, Genadie! It's time! The bell's already been rung. We have to do this now or all of those poor men outside will be killed. Senselessly. " She snarled to herself ruefully, "Oh, they don't understand that he's changed!"

"Who's changed?" said Genadie, more confused; but almost hopeful and almost disturbed. "Master?"

"That's not the point!" hissed Amalina. "My *father* is out there with them. And they're all going to die if we don't strike first. This is our chance. He'll be even more distracted, no? We can save them and save ourselves. The plan, the plan! So let's go! Get your weapons!"

"But—"

"But what?"

"But wasn't our plan to prevent him from changing you? This isn't—"

"What are you talking about? Changing me is one thing. But killing the men of my village, my family, is worse! *Family!*"

"Oh, yes," said Genadie, a crooked, trembling finger on his lip. Amalina knew he must be remembering how he'd watched his wife and her people being tossed out of their wagons by the Count, like salt out of a shaker, and him killing them before his eyes. "I suppose that is true, Ms. Dalca."

"So get going, Genadie! We haven't any more time! For Mala!"

Genadie's eyes became watery. They also appeared lost. He turned his face up to her like a child asking for directions: "Um … *Where?*"

Amalina shook him, then slapped him in his gawping face. He fell back from her, looking like a wronged, ill-treated rat.

"I'm sorry, Genadie!" cried Amalina, flexing her hands, still feeling the stinging blow on her palm, thinking that it couldn't have been her that had done it. "Sorry! But we need to act! Now! Listen to me: Get the weapons! Gather the torches! Set the fires for the smoke! Come on! Build the confusion, set the trap."

"Me?" He was still hunched away from her, as if she were about to strike him again. She pulled on his wrist.

"What is this? I can't believe you, Genadie! Don't you want to see your son again?"

"My son … Yes, that would be nice. And what are *you* going to do while I'm—?"

"My gosh! I'm doing everything else, aren't I!" she hissed at him. *Or rather, Aklan's already getting our little buzzing friends out of the forest,* she thought. "We haven't any more time to waste. Please don't make me have to do this *all* by myself."

Genadie brushed his tears away and nodded gravely. "Oh, Olympus. What a terrible day. But what has started must be finished. Isn't that so, Ms. Dalca?"

"Just think of your son—what's his name?"

"I daren't say."

"Just think of him and let's get this done."

"What life is this?" he asked, gripping his head with both hands. "*What life is this?*"

• • •

"Where have you been?" said Pia as Amalina reached the kitchen's lower cellar. "I almost went looking for you."

Pia stood at the top of the entrance to the network of hallways that led to the wheel room, or, as it was now, led *up* from the golden cavern. She held a torch in her hand.

"So you know?" said Amalina. "And you're still with me? Good, let's go. We haven't time."

"Know what?" said Pia, looking confused.

"It's—it's time for *the plan*. Now."

"What? Why?" said Pia, now shocked. "What's happening? I—you weren't in your room downstairs and—"

"They're attacking the castle, Pia. The revolutionary. My father and Ion. All the men from my hometown are outside. They'll be killed if we don't— *he* will kill them if we don't—"

"But Katty," whispered Pia sadly.

"Genadie's already getting the weapons, and—" Amalina stopped herself short. Pia wasn't supposed to know about that part, was she?

"*Weapons?*" said Pia, looking distraught. "But I can't! I told you, his blood runs in my veins now. I could never strike at him. I mean, I *want* to help you so badly, but ..."

Amalina nodded quickly. "That's fine, Pia. I just need you to help me with *her*." she pointed down the corridor. "You don't have to maneuver him anymore. She'll be best for that. But I don't think I can do it alone. She did almost eat me last time I took her off the wheel."

"Yes, the woman, all right," she said, her lips pursed. "I think I can help you do that. I do so much want to help you, Katty. You know that ... it's just ..."

"Don't think of it as we're going to hurt him, Pia. We don't have to. We just need to get him under our control so that he doesn't kill *them*. Understand? But the only way we can do that is if we use *the plan*."

"Get him under control."

"Right. Get him where I need him do be. We just don't ... you know ... finish it all the way."

"So I wouldn't be hurting him, necessarily," said Pia, working herself up or convincing herself.

"Uh-huh. Let's go."

Amalina grabbed Pia's pale, cold hand and they hurried to the wheel room. Only to find the rough wall set up in front of it.

"Oh, right. Damn!"

"We're locked out," said Pia.

Amalina gave Pia an appraising look, from legs to shoulders. "How strong are you, do you think? As strong as *him*?"

"I can break down this wall if that's what you mean." She touched the heavy stones. "But these blocks seem pretty thick. It would take too long, maybe. And he'd hear us before that."

Amalina rubbed her chin and thought for a second. The strange thing was, Amalina suddenly saw herself pinning the Count down—and then not killing him. *Was* she telling Pia the truth then? Could they get away with sparing him? Capture him and just drag him away, out of sight of the army? Tell them he'd escaped? Or prove to their satisfaction that he is a changed man, and that he can make redress? It felt so possible!

But Ivanti's words were serious. They countered her easy fantasy. Someone was going to have to die if they got inside and the Count wasn't hidden yet. It was a race against time. That's what it had come to.

"Katty?" asked Pia.

"There's another way," said Amalina.

## 68

# The Wailing Woman Pt. 2

Amalina rushed Pia back up into the main castle. Ignoring the confused and unsettled servants in the kitchens, they moved to the castle's rear door which led to Genadie's shack and other outer barns and storages. Amalina cautiously peeked out into the narrow rear courtyard.

"The *light*, Katty," squealed Pia.

"Oh! Sorry, I forgot," said Amalina, patting her friend gingerly. Pia was bent over at the waist, her arm over her head for protection. "Is it getting that bad?"

Uncurling, Pia looked at the red streak on her hand. She touched her face, and felt at the edges of a similar streak on her cheek. The welt there had a blue tint, a notable contrast to her fiery hair.

"I'll be okay," she said.

"We have to go outside. Just for a moment."

"That's too long, maybe."

Amalina spotted a servant clearing a counter. She had him fetch a large, thick, heavy cloth, and he returned with something which might have been a rug or a tapestry. "This should work," she said hopefully.

"What if it doesn't?"

"That's trouble."

"You'll have to lead me like a blind woman," said Pia as she pulled the cloth over her head and wrapped herself tight from the inside as the servant stared on, confused.

"Fair enough."

Judging from the looks they were getting, Amalina knew they would be a spectacle in the courtyard—the lady of the house slowly ushering a teetering, human-sized, gift-wrapped bundle. Attention was not what Amalina wanted. But she opened the door and started out. At least they were taking an inconspicuous route from the rear of the main building.

With relief Amalina saw, as they rounded the main building, that all eyes and activity were focused on the army outside their walls; the impending siege. As she and Pia closed on the front of the courtyard, Amalina spotted Durok at the top of the battlement dividing his time yelling insults over the parapet and cursing at his men on the inside; including into his harangues the shivering handful of servants who'd been suddenly conscripted into his force, swords shaking or hanging loose in their hands.

"How much farther?" asked Pia from inside the cloth.

"Are you all right?"

"It's a little bright and a little hot. I think I can manage if it isn't for too much longer. Otherwise I might scream."

With Pia's steps constricted by her covering, the walk that should have taken less than a few minutes, was stretching into an agonizing length. But Amalina, guiding the bundle with two hands on either side, saw that their destination, a metal grate hugged-up against the side of the inner wall, was in shadow. If they were quick enough, they would soon be out of the light altogether. "Don't worry, we're almost there."

Amalina swung to the left and took an unspoken-for spear from a weapon stand. Then, after making sure nobody was watching, she centered Pia above the edge of the large metal grate. She had Pia kneel down to tent the cloth over it.

"You see this drain cover?" whispered Amalina. "Do you think you can open it? Just give it a pull and slide it away."

The last time Amalina had done this, it had taken the help of her horse— or what would become her horse, White Snow—to jar the heavy grate loose, and then all her strength to scootch it far enough aside to allow entry below. She had been much younger then, and Pia was older and stronger. But could she do it on her own?

The lump of cloth shifted. The iron clanged and scraped as it came up and slid open. Easy.

"There you go," said Pia. "Now what?"

"Down, of course."

But once Amalina joined Pia in the lower tunnel, coming down iron rungs in the wall, she realized that without a torch, she wouldn't be able to see the way.

"My turn," said Pia in the cramped, dim, stone corridor, now freed of the cloth. "Which way?"

Amalina pointed and Pia took her hand and led them.

"You can see?" asked Amalina once they reached the section of tunnel where there was no light at all, and the darkness seemed to press in on all sides.

"Well enough," she said casually. "Be careful how you step, Kat. It's very slick and there seems to be an angle to i—wheee!"

Pia's grip tightened reflexively, and painfully, on Amalina's hand as she tumbled forward and took them both down the long slimy chute. Amalina dropped the spear along the way, but it clattered into them when they ran into a wall at the bottom.

"Sorry," said Pia.

Amalina couldn't see, but she heard Pia pick herself up and then she was lifted to her feet. The spear was placed back in her hands and they were moving again down the tunnel.

At junction points and forks, Amalina tried desperately to remember the route. It had seemed so simple and straightforward before. Had things changed down here, too? Or was she misremembering? She had thought it would be easy, but so much time had passed, and she'd seen so many more halls and passages. Maybe if she could actually see the tunnel, she would be able to tell with confidence. Now she relied on flashes of pictures in her mind, which she wasn't sure were from this spot, or from earlier, or further on, or cobbled into her memory from some other country entirely. She guessed by impulse, hoping for the best, as the spear's length made angling through the turns difficult.

"See how much easier it would be if you were like me?" joked Pia, after hearing the unsure note in Amalina's voice, and her low cursing for the fifth time, following the clang and scrape of the spear's metal point on wet stone.

*But Pia isn't wrong*, thought Amalina, feeling frustrated and annoyed at being blind and helpless. How much more freeing it would be to be able to function in total darkness!

"We seem to be at the end," whispered Pia, after not too long.

"You're sure?"

"I don't see any other way. There are holes in the floor, to help drain out, but—"

"Are there holes in the wall?" Amalina pointed blindly to what she assumed was the terminating wall. She reached out with her fingers to probe it. "Vertical ones. Narrow. About at chest height, probably. And we should be able to hear the—"

"Yes!" said Pia. "I see them. And I hear it much better: the wheel. She's just on the other side?"

"I tried to dig through before. You'll see some place—"

"Yes, that, too," said Pia, sounding excited. "Some deep scratches. It's not easy, but I got it."

"Probably the best place to use this," said Amalina, holding up the spear, trying to be careful not to prod her hidden friend. "But I just thought of something. I'm going to need a light. Even if we get through, I need to be able to see her. She's too dangerous if I can't."

"Sounds right enough. How much time do we have?"

"I don't know. But I really need it. You're going to have to show me back up. You can come down on your own and start working on the wall. I'll be back with a torch and another spear or something."

"Very well," sighed Pia. With an unseen hint of impatience, Pia dragged Amalina back up the slippery tunnel.

"It really *would* have been easier if you were a little more like me," whispered Pia Lampeda in a flat tone, before they reached the top of the tunnels, and Amalina could see the drain access-hole ahead in the ceiling.

"I know," said Amalina with a shrug of helplessness. "I'll go now. You go get started, right?"

"Don't take too long."

Amalina glanced back. Even in the murky light, she could see the strained patience in Pia's smile. Pia didn't want to be doing this. Any unnecessary delay, and leaving her alone, wasn't making it easier for her.

"You can find your way?" asked Amalina.

"Simple enough. If I get lost, just give a shout when you come back down. I'll hear you and find you. But of course, so will *he* … So will all of *us*."

Amalina gulped. She hoped even with all the noise they will make in this sewer system, everyone else will be distracted by the greater threat at the gate.

"Thank you for being so brave for me," said Amalina before she left. "And for helping in the first place."

. . .

When Amalina poked her head up out of the tunnel and into the courtyard, it was like surfacing from a river, but only to find a greater silence than being submerged. Captain Durok had stopped his cursing, and it seemed as if the entire castle was bracing for a hit. Amalina was the only free element rattling around within the tensed body. In *l'entrée grande* she saw that the entrance hall was now laid out with two long tables, placed crosswise, with benches on one side to face inward. The Count's thronal chair was at the far end of the room pointed outward, to overwatch it all. But the Count wasn't in it. And he'd left the mantle. Who knew where he was at any given moment? but she prayed he was still distracted by trying to convince a dozen or so Ladies of Title why it would be a good idea to quit the castle and have a slide down a privy chute.

When Amalina dove back through the drain, she was met with a grinding noise—metal on stone—that was high and shrill and made her shiver. But it stopped almost immediately, and then the castle's hush dominated again. The way felt longer than before, and at the several turns in the tunnel, Amalina wondered if she hadn't gotten lost. In the torchlight, it all looked different than how she remembered it. Orange flickering stone instead of cool blue. Ceilings much lower, walls closer in. She was bigger now, but she had not grown *that* much since the last time she was here. It was so cramped it was hard to breathe.

When Amalina came to the end, she heard the scrape of the wheel first, and then she saw the large hole in the wall. Nine stones had been taken out with precision. Three above, three below. They'd been pushed *into* the wheelroom.

And there, inside the room, was Pia. She stood before the turning wheel, one hand on her hip, the other on the shaft of the worn and chipped spear. Amalina noted Pia was wearing thick leather gloves. *Helpful*, thought Amalina, *but where'd she get those?*

Pia turned when Amalina entered the room.

"Now what?" she asked Amalina.

"For a second, I thought you'd taken her down already."

"I wouldn't know what to do," said Pia. "Or what to say. We never discussed this part, did we? What *I* was going to do—what she's to do now." There was a strange look in Pia's eye. "What's to become of her?"

"It'll be her own free will, for the most part," said Amalina. "But I can only imagine. Here, we can't stop the wheel, I don't know how, but we can unwind the chains."

"Must we?"

"We have to," said Amalina. "She can't stay on another minute."

Pia looked hesitantly at the dried out body of the woman on the wheel. Like she was worried.

"She'll leave us alone," promised Amalina. "I'm sure of it, once she's free and she knows who freed her. We have a deal, her and I. And I could use as much of this chain as I can get. There aren't many left."

"You have a deal?"

"Please."

Pia nodded grimly. While Amalina tried to time her hands to the turning spokes, Pia expertly matched the rotation so that Amalina had to get out of the way as she unwound the chains. Even with the clumsiness of the leather gloves the links came off the nails, and the chain spun and piled onto the floor until there was nothing left holding the woman in place. The woman's body drooped in stages, and fell onto the loose, gleaming pile beneath her. She recoiled and hissed, defensively, her eyes sucking into their sockets, like snails back into their shells, and opened in confusion.

Pia moved to tie her up, like a spider binding its prey, but the chains were winding on the outside of the dress.

"No, it has to touch her skin to do any good."

In a whir, the old body was turned in all directions and her wrists and bare ankles were bound together. The large oil cloth from the corner of the room, which had hidden the extra chains, now went over the woman's head, forming a thick bag with wide tails, and a length of chain secured it around her neck.

"Wh-at?" said the woman from within the bag, her voice muffled, strangled, and dry.

"I'm Amalina, do you remember me?" whispered Amalina.

"A-ma-li-na," said the woman, testing out the word. "No... Yes ... *Yessss.*"

"You *do* remember me, then?"

"How could I forget? You bound me to the wheel."

"Count Tepsji put you there," corrected Amalina. "I've come to free you. Remember?"

"*You* tied me to the wheel, A-ma-li-na. Put the chain right over my mouth. You *silenced* me, when all I had for company was my own voice. My only release was to cry out for pity and against the injustice and you *shut me up.*"

Amalina glanced guiltily at Pia.

"He made me do it," said Amalina. The excuse was beginning to sound weak and tired to her. "You know how powerful he is. I had no choice. But now I do. *We all do.*"

The woman's hands couldn't move with the silver tying them together. She brought the paralyzed fingers up against the cloth bag over her head, as if wanting to tear it off.

"It burns, girl. I cannot move. Release me!"

The bag began to expand in different directions above her shoulders, all at once. As if her head were growing arms and punching against the fabric from the inside. It made Amalina feel sick.

Pia leapt forward and pressed the wailer's head down to the floor with her foot. Putting weight on it so that it was stuck there.

"I will release you," whispered Amalina quickly. "*We* will. But you must wait!"

"The *pain.*"

"I know. But you aren't on the wheel any more, are you? And just a little more, and you will be completely free."

"Why not *nowwww?*"

"Because we need you to listen, eh? You need to understand what's happening here. You need to know our plan."

"Get off my head."

Pia took her foot off the woman's head, but kept it poised above the bag. Just in case.

The woman's body began to slither snakelike on the ground, with slow, undulating movements. Her skin seemed to harden and grow scales. But this was only around the patches of her that were far away from the silver chain, and the scales quickly turned color and dropped off, like dried pieces of parchment.

"Are you listening to me?"

"Say what you will, girl."

"You must save your energy," said Amalina. "For the fight against the Count."

The woman remained silent.

"If we don't succeed now, then we could all die. And he'll put you back up on the wheel. You can't want that to happen."

The bag said nothing, but the writhing slowed.

"If you attack us, if you impair or spoil us, we will fail; and he *will* put you back up on the wheel. Do you understand? We need you, and you need us."

"I will kill him with my bare hands," she snarled. "Do you hear me?"

"You now have the chance," Amalina assured her. "But he's only grown stronger through the years. So you must accept our help and do what I say, or it will be ruin for us all. Please, forgive anything I might have done while under his influence. Appreciate that we have come to rescue you from an eternal torment."

"Forgive what you've done?" growled the wailing woman. "Eh? And ignore what you've said against me? *'Throw out the old hag'*? Is that what I am? Oh, yes, I heard *everything* you and your friends said about me, and what you've planned for me. Well, am I *'pointless'* now?"

Pia's head dropped. She'd been looking expectantly at the woman, and with some bit of fear. Amalina had assumed it was because Pia saw herself in the same predicament. But now she knew there was something else. But what could that be? Pia hadn't really spoken, or said anything disparaging like that about the wailing woman. Certainly Amalina never had.

"I've never spoken against you," said Amalina. "Did you, Pia?"

"Listen here," whispered Pia to the bag, harshly. "Whatever you think you might have heard, that was in your nightmares. We're here saving you now, and promise you complete freedom should we succeed. You can promise us the same, no? Or are you going back up on the mill right this instant, to spend life-with-no-end turning cartwheels?"

. . .

A short while later, after giving the wailing woman her instructions, Amalina asked Pia, "You'll be okay down here by yourself?"

Pia nodded.

Amalina looked back to the woman with her bagged head.

"Don't do anything to damage her. Just put her on the wheel if she gives you trouble."

"Of course, Katty."

"When it comes time, let her loose. Remind her of the plan, what she should do, where she's to go. I'm sure she'll be able to find him. Let her have the cloth if she's going to go out the way we came in. and then you can hide down here until—"

"No need. If it's as much of a carnival as you think it's going to be, we can push through the wall there blocking the door without anyone noticing. Or, even if they do hear us, what will they care?"

"Sounds about right," nodded Amalina. "Just wait for the signal then."

"But Katty," whispered Pia lower now, bringing her mouth closer to Amalina's ear. "If I can't raise my hand against your uncle, how can *she*? I mean, maybe that's why she failed the first time around. She couldn't do it when it came time. And she's still so weak."

A chill went up Amalina's back. But she ignored it. She'd heard the wail for so long, it had sounded so strong, even from below the castle. The woman had a reserve of power just waiting to be unleashed.

"All we can hope is that she'll try. It's the distraction that will count." Amalina hefted the extra coils of silver chain. "That should be enough. The rest is up to us."

## 69

# The Bees

Aklan tried for the third hive, though the bees from the second skec were still bombing him. Swooping at his thick, bushy blond head.

"Ach! Get away you nasty things!"

He surprised himself by shouting in Ardeelian. Normally a curse would have rolled out robustly in his native tongue. He guessed maybe something inside him thought the bees here only spoke the local mountain dialects. He remembered what the Roman Princess had said, that the Count claimed he could talk to any creature in their own specialized languages. Aklan thought, as he protected his face from the looping hail of hard-husked menaces—which was like fending off a sack of swooping, stinging, biting, probing, orange peanut shells: *That would be fun.*

He'd only received a couple stings so far. The small, red, painful lumps were on his wrist, getting agitated by the sleeve of his jacket. How the bees had wormed their way in through the length of glove, he didn't know. He'd been worried they would sting his face and eyes because he didn't have any protection there.

This part of the operation had become a larger pain than he'd thought it would be. At first it had been fun whooping down the privy hole as he'd done in years past, now trying to ignore the filth and the stench and concentrating on the coming drop outside the castle wall. Whee! Only, he—and his pretty princess—had forgotten that General Marosh, when he'd taken over the defense of the castle, and in his mania for security, had barred even the privy vents, no matter how high up they were. While the long skec pole, tied to the rope, had somehow slid right out between the bars, Aklan had slammed into the metal barrier, caked with layers of hardened unmentionables. Luckily the bars hadn't been too secure, and he only wasted a little more than a minute kicking them out. Then it was time to lower himself down the rope to the rocky, soiled midden below; and, of course, once on the ground, strip himself clean of the foul outer clothes in the warming spring air and then wipe off the pole. By that point, the first of the servants were shimmying down, their faces twisted with barely contained fury and outrage.

Moving on.

Aklan had given up on securing the first of Janusch's beehives because it was too high and he saw how unhappy the vicious-looking bees were getting with him trying to nab it with the end of his skec pole. He couldn't have known just how much more unhappy things were to become when he moved on to the second, and after missing the ring holder but unseating the skec it crashed to the ground. Suddenly there was a savage, humming cloud that followed him for nearly a meandering mile.

The third and forth hives were the closest to the castle, which was why he chose them last, so that he would not be spotted by anyone until near the end of his route. From his current vantage, through partings in the tree branches, he could see the upper reaches of the castle's main building and towers, and parts of its outer wall. His eyes kept flicking to them, despite himself, because he felt the silence in the forest was eerie, and he liked the feeling of civilization nearby. And he felt the excitement of what was about to come.

• • •

How long had they planned to escape from that overbearing *thing* parading in a human body? wondered Aklan, hotly. How long had they plotted to kill him? But Princess Amalina was always finding some reason to abandon one plan for another. He knew it was because she was afraid. And why shouldn't she be? For one, she was a girl. And all girls—except for the women in his own family, it seemed—were terrible cowards. Always crying into the man's chest. But for the pretty princess' part, she was also under the strict scrutiny of the Count. She couldn't assume he didn't already know what was about to happen.

Just like Amalina, Aklan had seen the battle of the giants in Kyrgil. With the Count and the Strange Man tearing down the castle and mountain as they sought to kill each other. It would seem an impossible thing to destroy such a creature of immense power. Even those two couldn't do it to each other!

But somehow Genadie had, and with just a knife and a little bit of smoke from the fireplace. That's what the Pretty Princess told him, anyway. And, in any case, it was done. The Strange Man was killed by someone, in order for the Count to return. It meant mortal hands had done it. It could be done!

And maybe the princess was a coward at times, and at others she was very brave. But at all times she was very, very clever. And so her plan seemed like it should work. And Aklan would be a part of it. He might even strike the deathblow. If he did, she would have to show him a little respect. That's true! And for helping her bring down the Count, she wouldn't be thanking that strutting oaf lieutenant, Ivanti Vokent.

*Not as long as I get there first, to save her!*

• • •

All these positive thoughts pushed Aklan forward as he tried to hook the pole through the metal loop above the hive. Any time the stick connected with the holding ring, he could feel the vibration of the population of insects inside that papery cocoon. And he could see how the bees from the second hive were bringing up the hackles of the bees of the third. If he weren't fast about it, or careful, he'd be caught between two stormclouds of stingers.

That's when he heard the low growl and his leg yanked backward. With a shout he looked around.

Behind him was a monster—no, the most hideous looking dog he had ever seen—no, the most hideous looking *wolf* he'd ever seen. All black fur, and a head so mangled that it looked as if it were really two or three wolf-heads stuck together. Princess Amalina's stupid black wolf. It had hold of his left trouser leg.

"What the hell are you doing?" he hissed, trying to sound fearless while he looked into the animal's raging, live-and-dead eyes.

Aklan glanced up and found that the tip of his pole had speared the hive and was stuck in it. The bees' volume—both their noise and their circling cloud—increased. "Damn it all!"

The wolf clamped down harder with its teeth and brought its shoulders low to the ground as it tried to tug him back.

"Leave me alone, I say!" snarled Aklan through his teeth. "I've got important things to do here! Don't let go and I'll add a knot to that ugly head of yours, just you see."

The wolf shook its head, pulling Aklan's body this way and that, causing him to lose his balance.

BAM!

It seemed the whole mountain shook. Birds trilled alarms, some shooting off from the branches; trees swayed, which sent down twigs, pieces of bark, needles, and some early leaves. The hive seemed to shake too, and the buzz of irritation grew that much louder; the cloud of bees waved as if hit by a current, separated unsurely then reformed angier than ever. The sound echoed around the forest a few times.

"What the hell was that!"

The wolf had fallen back a safe distance, maybe suspecting Aklan's rage had been the cause of the blast.

Through a parting of branches, a white/black cloud rose from the castle. Cannon fire.

Aklan ran. He passed Janusch's fourth hive, as well as the less interesting Netz hives, as he made his way to the forest edge, noting the fourth's location and the roving satellites of alarmed bees around it.

Before reaching the clearing, Aklan stopped. He positioned himself behind an elm and leaned out for a better view. He noticed the wolf's head at his hip, also having a look.

The cannon had been fired, that was for sure. The smoke belched from its mouth the way the artillery pieces had in Ivanti's old army camp. The silver knights around the cannon were calmly releasing the barrel from its mounts, while others poured water over it or secured ropes to it, in preparation to reposition it.

The castle's gate was open. From the smoke, he couldn't tell if the cannonball had cleared it, or someone had simply opened the door. The silver army, with their gleaming pikes and spears and muskets pointed into the castle, were marching. There was no fear in their movement. They looked like proud, true, courageous men.

And Ivanti Vokent was one of them!

Aklan couldn't tell which one, though. Probably the one pointing with his pike toward the open gate.

*Damn it all!* thought Aklan, as he headed back for the hives.

Janusch's fourth hive was the closest active one, and it was going to have to do. Aklan removed his gloves and then opened his jacket flat on the ground below the skec. Then the gloves went back on because he wasn't going to get his hands stung at this point.

He snatched up the pole again and speared the small ring as easily as if it were as wide as a fish barrel. Ha! But as he tried to remove the skec from the platform's hook, he was pulled backward again at the leg.

"What are you doing! What's wrong with you!" cried Aklan at the wolf, who now held his whole ankle in its mouth. "I need to go! This isn't a game, do you hear me? Don't make me have to tame you!"

But the wolf dug its claws into the ground and drew Aklan off his feet. Aklan glanced around nervously, expecting to see members of its pack readying to jump him. But it was on its own, and now that he was down on the ground, it let him go.

Aklan stared at the great beast, it stared back at him.

"That nest's gotta get in that castle or the princess will be in trouble," he told the wolf. "And boy, so will I! You going to let me, or do you want to play games?"

The wolf stretched its muscular jaws, showing its long, thick fangs. But its weird eyes were on him, anticipating his next move. Aklan's heart sank.

He plotted for a second. Then he sprang suddenly from the ground with a shout. The wolf leapt backward.

Hoping that move might have given him just enough time, Aklan had already turned in air. On landing, he darted for the castle. Could he slash or whack a wide enough hole at the top of this fourth hive, freeing it from its holding ring, so that it falls—falls right on his open jacket on the ground?—so that he could hug the jacket closed around it as he picked it up? Even if the jacket buzzed disagreeably, the skec's openings would still be wrapped—so no bee would be coming out, right?—and Aklan would run with it, sprinting and leaping though the underbrush toward the castle; with the wolf in close pursuit, Aklan yelling: "Let's go find the Count!"

Aklan thought, as he licked his lips eagerly, preparing to strike the nest and to continue his forward rush: *Now* that's *a great plan!*

## 70

## To Help My Katty

"What was that?" said the withered woman on the floor. The bag over her head, cinched at her neck, deadened her voice. Her skin was still at work building and shedding scales, so she now lay in a small flaky nest.

Pia stared with faint loathing at it all, and wondered what the sight might have looked like in torchlight. When in utter darkness, her nightvision—a gift from the birds she'd eaten? or perhaps the twitchy bat she'd tried in the loft?—made everything incredibly fuzzy and blue-grey. Maybe with real colors it would have been more sickening. Maybe the woman's shriveled hide was changing colors into something more snakelike.

"Hm?" said Pia, a little late to answer. "I believe that must be our signal."

"So you're going to free me now," said the woman.

"You haven't eaten in a very long time, have you?"

"No," she said hungrily. "*Noo-oooo.*"

"How long? Do you know?"

"Has it been an hour? Or has it been one hundred years?"

"You still have the strength to move," noted Pia calmly, trying to keep the curiosity out of her voice; but she needed to learn. "You're still alive, even after all this time?"

"Yes. But it hurts. It's so hard to move. I am so weak."

"You don't seem too weak to me."

"If only I were filled, *then* you would see … Let me go."

"You think you'll be able to take him? Really?"

"I almost killed him once. Release my hands. Remove this hood. Let me go now."

"Why didn't you do it? Or why couldn't you?"

"He was too fast. I'm no fighter. He tricked me somehow. It was so long ago, I don't remember."

"And yet you think you can handle him now? Starved as you are? Still untrained? While he has had time to grow and practice? Someone else much stronger than you tried their hand at him and it didn't work."

"Why are you bothering me? Are you going to set me free or not?"

"Perhaps I'll do more than that," whispered Pia closer to the wrapped head. "But first I want you to understand something. That young woman who spoke to you …"

"Ahhh-mahhh-lihhh-nahhh."

"Well, yes," said Pia, grudgingly. "Or Katarina. But no matter. She's the one who told me about you. She has been trying to rescue you for a very long time."

"Almost there," snarled the woman. "If you'd just unbind me it will be done."

"You must promise me, if you succeed in bringing him down, you will not touch her. Whatever her crimes against you you think she's committed."

There was an ominously long pause.

"Did you hear what I said?"

"I must not kill A-ma-li-na."

"And will you promise me?"

There was mumbling in the wrap, then: "I must promise you? … or what?"

"Well, I'll kill you," said Pia, matter-of-factly. "Right now. It would be easy to remove your head, with or without the silver." Pia set the spear's blade on the exposed part of the woman's back. By adding only a little pressure, the scales peeled away from it like parting water. The woman shivered and groaned.

"You wouldn't do that to me," said the woman, through the pain. "You haven't the guts. That's why you hesitate, or you would have done it already. But not if you want to save A-ma-li-na's skin."

"I can just leave you here," shot Pia, coldly. "How about that? You know nothing about me. So don't presume."

"Free me! Or put me back on that rack and have done with it!"

"You want to kill Count Tepsji." Just saying it made Pia shiver with revulsion. "So does Amalina, maybe. She needs to stop him. She needs to do so *right now*. But both of you can't do it alone. Do you understand me? She was telling the truth. If you just go right after him to have a fight, he'll do what he will with you, and you'll be back on that wheel. If you don't follow Amalina's plan, she'll fail, too. And she will die. You must both work together. And that is why you must promise me—"

"I promise, I promise," moaned the woman greedily. It sounded like her mouth was full of saliva. "You have my word, but let me go."

"You heard the instructions, all of them? You know what you must do? The sound you must listen for? Where you must go?"

"Must, must, must, yes, yes, yesss. You've told me everything. She's told me everything. I've had my instructions. What more, what more?"

"The door is blocked by a wall," said Pia as she sat down behind the woman's head. "When I get these bindings off of you, together we will break through it as fast as we can. And then you will find him and lead him, or drive him, where you both need him to be. But before that, because my flesh is weak, but my blood is strong ..."

Pia used the spear blade to cut her wrist. She dropped the weapon and with that freed hand flexed her fingers, her nails grew like talons. With one of these sharp hooks she tore a hole in the cloth and shoved her bleeding forearm into the opening. She felt the unseen lips and teeth as they surrounded her wound. The woman inside began suckling at it uncontrollably.

Pia knew even if her body was fully recovered she could not oppose Count Tepsji. Her transformation had been too complete. She didn't know if it was just in her mind, but he had power over her. Pia hoped her blood, however, was enough of her own making now that he would not gain any more influence over this wailing woman than he already had. That this woman could not only be energized by this transfusion, but would still have the will to strike him. And maybe ... *perhaps* ... there would be enough of Pia's spirit within her own blood—that her will in it would be fresh enough—to allow her some bit of control over what was to happen, so that this woman would not think to disobey. So that, after all, she would not go after Amalina.

"Not too much," cautioned Pia as the withdrawing of her lifeforce stung, and she listened to the horrible sucking noise and felt those scaly lips squirming at her wrist. And she wondered which guiding force might win out: anger, cool reason, or what's in the blood? "Just what you need ... to help my Katty."

## 71

# Forward

The cannon had blown a big enough hole through the gate that the castle guard simply fell back from their positions and allowed the silver army's first rank to push open the door's splintered remnants. The men of Korr entered the courtyard with audible huffs and wheezes inside their shiny suits. But they moved like soldiers passing for review before a king and queen: straight upright, with powerful, confident movements. This was their moment, their finest hour. Most likely they did not notice they were breathing heavily. They were still entranced by their fine armor, their solemn duty, and the novelty of the occasion.

"Well, sirs, you're in," called Captain Durok from a commanding spot on the wall. "Your Heaven preserve you!"

"Anyone who stands between us and the condemned," returned Ivanti with a hearty shout, "will be considered accomplices and struck down alongside him."

"You see us standing in your way, shit head?"

"You've been warned."

"And I'll leave *you* with a warning," laughed Captain Durok, pointing down at them, "In his body alone, wit' Count Tepsji, you will meet your match toda—"

With a crack and a puff of smoke, Durok's head snapped back as a mist of blood sprayed out its top, helmet flying free. The knight with the long hunting rifle immediately began to reload, his metal hand expertly working the ramrod, his loose armor clanking.

Ivanti, in the vanguard position, signaled directions with his hands as the remaining knights shuffled in through the gate. Two ranks trotted left and right to circle the main building. Their weapons prickled out on all sides like silvery quills. Nothing could strike or bite at them without getting stung back or properly skewered.

Meanwhile the shiny cannon was rolled forward and positioned before the main building's front doors. The cannoneer brought the burning wick to the modified wick feed, holding it just above the touch hole and the feed's tiny scoop of powder.

But the building's doors swung open before the cannon was lit. The army tensed with a clattering sound, and the glimmering needles of a hundred spearpoints and pike blades centered on the blackened hole of a doorway.

"What is your purpose here?" boomed the Count's voice. The deep baritone seemed to come from every direction, causing many helmets to turn here and there.

"Eyes forward!" commanded Ivanti. "Enemy forward."

"You come into my home and declare an enemy?" growled the Count. "You holler about someone condemned, before they are taken prisoner and tried before a court? Disperse, unlawful mob! Or parley as men on a battlefield, for this venture lacks all justice, and is nothing but a private war."

While the Count's voice was rattling their bodies, Ivanti wandered over and whispered to the cannoneer: "Can you see who's talking? Do you see him inside?"

"I reckon I mark a figure in there, yeah."

"Down the barrel?"

"So. More or less."

"Fire."

The burning wick touched the hole. The cannon burst. This time, instead of a spinning black mass barreling out of it, a whumping hot silver spray spewed at the entryway and into the castle. Silver blobs spattered all around the door; chipping off pieces of stone, plastering and fusing to the wall, or dropping off and bouncing as hot marbles.

"Did we get him?" said Ivanti.

"Can't rightly tell," said the cannoneer. "Can you?"

"Forward!" cried Ivanti, pointing now with a musket, with silver bayonet attached, into the castle. He trotted to the front of the army and climbed the small set of stairs, as the smoking cannon was unmounted and prepared for movement again.

## 72

## Let Go the World

First: the bell.

And now: the magic bone.

Amalina had been congratulating herself for swiping the emergency bell back from Captain Durok. She'd found it overturned on the deserted wall-walk, almost as if it had been left lying there by an unseen helper. Since she was on the upper level at the time, she'd decided to run with it wrapped in her arms full tilt all the way around to the main building's rear battlement accessway. It saved her minutes and having to deal with Durok or the silver army—to argue with Ivanti, Attila Bronk, or Lucinda's furious father; or her own—the whole lot now entering through the castle's ground floor.

But as she ran to fetch the invisibility bone from her room, she realized she should have gone to Genadie's shack first. There was no saying she wouldn't need his array of weapons—she swallowed a greasy lump in her throat—*to kill the Count.* It would be better to be fully armed, just in case, when roaming the building. Maybe when Genadie realized she wasn't coming to meet him, he'd bring them all on his own mission.

By now, Genadie should have clogged what fireplaces he could and lit the cellar fires with the specially oiled logs. It wouldn't be long before the lower part of the main castle filled with smoke. If the Count was loitering there in that original section—presuming he hadn't gone fully down into the golden city—the smoke would hinder him, and maybe even, if it was thick enough, push the silver plated fools back out of the castle and into the courtyard, out of the Count's reach. She seemed to sense the smoke presently, up here in the higher floors.

Amalina shoved past Stasia Auster who, along with Genevieve de Roye, Greta La Nevers, and Claire Montraine demanded an immediate explanation as to what was happening and what they should do; their confusion haunted by the fear of the castle's previous bloody outburst. And more, someone had set fire to all the gift bouquets. The bundles of flowers beside the Ladies' doors were either burnt to char stems or were still burning, like sad little torches, threatening to spread to the tapestries. This was the smoke Amalina had noticed. *What was happening?* But what *wasn't* happening was the Ladies hadn't been collected—by the Count, or Aklan—and hadn't been smuggled out through the privy tunnels. Or else they'd refused so objectionable a route; a frighteningly high, and certainly ignominious exit. And so: chaos in the upper chambers. Amalina pushed on. *Oh, well …*

One of Margeta's abandoned servants growled foully at Amalina in Italian: "I suppose there isn't some surprise cavern in *this* heap of stone we can hide?"

"As a matter of fact there is," replied Amalina, coolly. "Through the kitchens, down through the cellars, and keep going. Be quick and they'll never find you. And there you'll discover your recovering mistress, Lady Margeta, and Bardina!"

Amalina slammed through her suite door and ran to her bed to pull out the bone from under her mattress. She couldn't believe she had taken it out of her pocket. *Of all the times!* She felt for it. And felt for it again.

"What are you looking for, Kat-Kat?" asked Cristine. She closed the door behind her and stared coldly at Amalina. There was a manicness in her eyes. She had roused herself with the Count's green bottle stimulant. Maybe taken too much of it. A frenzied air existed outside of her, like an aura. Her skin was so pale.

"I thought you were sleeping downstairs with the others," said Amalina, calmly, still searching, pushing her hands deeper under the mattress, groping at air. At some point it occurred to her that she'd left the bone there because Aklan was to eventually use it, to position himself—invisible and at the ready—in the great hall, next to the chain release, so better to leave it in a neutral place. Though she'd sent him off to fetch the bees, when she'd interrupted him he might have already been preparing himself for his original task, just in case, or he then, dutifully, started preparing for his primary role. Or he'd simply found it when looking for the rope and decided to take it. Whichever the case, it meant the boy had the magic bone. Amalina gulped but carried on vainly for a few more seconds, wishing there was something she could pretend to find for Cristine's satisfaction. At least it kept her from facing her friend. "You should go back down where it's safe, I'm sending everyone else there right now, and I'll meet you soon. You need to rest, anyway, Cristine."

"Don't tell me what you think I want to hear: that you'll 'meet me soon'." Cristine took in a low, wavering breath. "Tell me what I need to know: like, what *are* you doing up here? You were already in the new castle with me last night. No need to come up again at all. Is it because Ivanti is here?"

Amalina's skin went cold but her cheeks flushed. She turned from the bed.

"Amalina, you can't possibly still care," sneered Cristine. "Not now. He's in the past. Or he soon will be. And *we* will go on forever."

"Papa's with him, too," said Amalina. "With them all."

"All? Who's all? Is *my* Papa here? Well, you know what I say? Who cares? Better if he is … *so I can prove myself.*"

Cristine's eyes flashed and then she had a little laugh at the thought, but it didn't look like the thought pleased her.

"You aren't really going to *kill* him … your own father …?" whispered Amalina.

"Of course, that's the choice I was given. Either him or me. So what's the choice? I mean, I had to face an awful clarity then, eh?" Cristine shook her head and sneered sharply again. "And aren't you the one who forced me to make this choice, Ama? So isn't it fair that you face *the same thing* with me?"

"What do you mean!" gasped Amalina. The horrible scenario presented itself suddenly in her mind: both Ivanti and Dragomir were in this very building. What was to prevent the Count from sparing them death only to force Amalina to kill them herself? to prove *her* loyalty to him, just as he was forcing Cristine? to have the two sisters-in-blood execute their fathers side by side for his entertainment?

*But he wouldn't do that*, thought Amalina. *Not now. Not to me.* Cristine's dilemma was born from her own crimes and the crimes of her father. Amalina and Dragomir had never shown themselves untrustworthy or treacherous. And out of love, hadn't the Count turned himself into something softer, and better, and favorable to her? This was Cristine's own problem, decided Amalina confidently.

Amalina then realized she was thinking all this while she was in the middle of a potentially fatal plot against the Count. She felt ill at the hypocracy of it and the contemplation of the deed. Better not to think of it.

"Why *are* you here?" she asked Cristine. "The Count sent you to fetch me back down, or—?"

"I'm not here for you, I didn't come all the way up here just for *you*. How typical to be so full of yourself … But to be honest, everyone *was* asking after you, Katja." Cristine's tone spoke envy. " *'Why isn't she down here with us?'* they asked me. They wanted me to find out, and it was good enough reason to leave them."

"But I'm—"

"If *we* can all let go the world," she continued, "what makes *you* better than us by refusing, eh? Nothing. So as your closest friend, and since you are here, maybe I can reason with you, to make you understand, to convince you."

"Convince?"

"Now, what's the matter?" asked Cristine, her eyes hardening. "You think you *can't* do it? To kill them: Ivanti? Your dear papa? Months ago I'd have done it to the Big Boss, I'm sure of it—long before my transformation— if given the chance. What is *that* look, eh? He was having all those girls murdered to keep them quiet, wasn't he? Isn't that what you told me? He was unfaithful in his vows and probably *forced* them to sleep with him, the greedy pig. He deserves it. If not for me, if not for them, then for betraying my mother, I could do it. But now, knowing the power I can reap … it'd be worth it for nothing else."

Amalina stood up, confused, not knowing what to do. The bone was gone. Who knew where Genadie was, or if the wailing woman had already been released and was on the hunt. And what if the silver army had already started the battle? And where was the revolutionary?

She needed to hurry downstairs. But here was Cristine, barring the way.

"You don't seem to have too much to say, Amalina. Don't you agree? Won't you join me, like I've joined you? Come, let us be sisters in blood again. All the way."

Amalina's lips moved up and down, but she didn't speak. She couldn't think. Cristine stared into Amalina with her icy blue eyes. Past Cristine's shoulder Amalina spotted the trick teapot and wondered if that could be of use. Something to counteract the nervous energy spilling out of her friend.

"You think you're father's too good to die?" smirked Cristine, as if dealing with a stubborn child. "He's pretty old, isn't he? He's going to anyway. Well, what does it matter if it's *you* who helps him along? Maybe we could trade services; I do him, you do mine? No?" Amalina must have made a face, Cristine scowled in return: "Haven't I told you you worry too much about everyone else? Why do you *always* bother about *everyone* else, Amalina? See to yourself. *See to yourself.* As it is, I'm leaving *everything* behind because I am growing away from it. It's time you think for yourself, too. It is *soooo* much easier."

Her blue eyes now had that same brutish cruelty Amalina remembered from so long ago, when she'd gloated over Korr's dead bad girls. Despite her transformation, something of Cristine's character *had* survived. The bad part.

Amalina gritted her teeth and said, almost past her control: "Yeah, you're awful."

"Ahhh," Cristine sighed back, her expression razor sharp. "How can we live with each other, come forever, if you're going to think like that? I really don't believe that can happen, do you? Living together under the same roof when we don't even *like* each other anymore?"

Cristine stepped forward in an animally fluid motion. Her movement made Amalina realize her old friend had been standing preternaturally still. The statue-stillness of the Count. Of the dead. *Have to remember*, thought Amalina, *Cristine is now one of these creatures. With their incredible power.*

And Amalina was without weapons. And no bone, at least, to make her disappear. She glanced at the teapot again.

Cristine was saying: "There's a part of me that, though I know you're my dearest friend—or you pretended to be, anyway—and that Count Tepsji cares for you ... just a little; I can feel it in me—in the end, it will have to come down to either one of us. But not both. You know? So there *would* be an advantage for me to act on this fear I have now, hm? If you're dead, Amalina ... well, he couldn't bring you back. He'd *have* to accept me. And I could always tell him you were planning to kill him. That you were a rotten traitor to us."

Cristine took another ominous step closer to Amalina. Her grin widened impossibly. The ends of her eye teeth seemed to angle and lengthen into spikes.

"With all that power you have now," said Amalina, feeling a bit desperate, "I can't believe that's what you'd think of doing to me, after all this time. To me, your friend. That doesn't sound very powerful at all."

"Oh, it's power. And why shouldn't I play with you? With everything that's within me, and all the time in the world ..." Cristine paused to consider her advantages, the savage thoughts toying the corners of her mouth. "I could do a lot of good with it, eh? I could return to Korr and save my father's reputation, couldn't I? I could prove to everyone your papa was the one killing all those girls all along. And they'd believe me. Who could argue otherwise? And with all the time in the world I could make sure the Dalca name is destroyed, while elevating my family to the greatest heights.

"Imagine what I can do, Amalina ... without you here."

Amalina shivered.

. . .

While keeping her eyes on Amalina, Cristine crossed to the desk, "Let's start with this, the real reason I came to your room."

Cristine slid open the desk's lower right drawer. Glancing inside, when she didn't see what she was after, she dug her hand further into it. Amalina shifted, moving closer to the door. Cristine pointed a warning finger at her.

"Where are they?" said Cristine. She threw the drawer out onto the ground. Then she ran to where Amalina had been rooting under the mattress. "Of course, here."

She shoved and kicked the mattress and bedding. But again found nothing.

"What have you done with them?"

"Done with what?" said Amalina, confused.

"Those little papers, and those sticks of yours, with which you tried to drag my father into infamy. I'll tear them and break them to pieces before your eyes. Where are they?" She was furiously opening drawers and cabinets, spilling Amalina's possessions everywhere. "Tell me, Amalina. If you don't give me something to break right now, I will have to start with you."

Amalina tried for the door, but Cristine leapt there first. So fast that even she seemed surprised at her speed. She panted like an animal, and looked at Amalina with an unsettling hunger. It was rising within her. Or she was willing it up to use. There was wonder—and willingness—in her smile as she hunched her back and centered her focus on Amalina's neck.

Amalina held out her hands, "I—"

"Say nothing more," growled Cristine. "You liar and cheat, I won't believe anything you say. And I won't give you breath to do it." She seemed to compress herself, all her muscles tensing under a sharp, taught, vicious smile. "I can't deny, Ama, I've always kind of wanted to do this."

Cristine leapt at Amalina. Her hands were outthrust and bared like claws.

Amalina shouted and tried to duck. Something within her wilted as she fell to the side—as she remembered the titanic battle between the creatures at Kyrgil and knew she'd already lost this fight and would die at her friend's hands. With no weapons, she had no way to stop a creature. How could she hope to?

Cristine clawed and punched at the back of Amalina's head, who was bent away from her, trying to avoid the blows. There was no pain, really, remarked Amalina, as Cristine pounded on her. She felt the hits, but they weren't much. The scratches slight stings.

This sent Cristine into a greater fury, her bloodlust rising. She was trying to get at Amalina's neck, but her strength wasn't enough to do it. It wasn't the violent victory as she had imagined.

Amalina cried in protest and tossed aside her friend's arms now, trying to find a safe route to the door. Cristine was faster and blocked every move. Her speed was beyond normal. Unnatural. But maybe it had more to do with the stimulant than having gone through the transformation. Because she lacked power. The inhuman strength they both had expected in her just wasn't there yet.

*Of course*, thought Amalina. *Cristine has only just changed*. These things take time. It was a miracle alone that she was out of bed, less leaping buildings and changing herself. Pia had had over a year to grow into whatever she was becoming. Cristine was still overcoming death, so this fight wasn't that impossible, thought Amalina, hopefully. Cristine might be intent on killing her, but they were relatively equal. Amalina might even have the advantage with her martial experience, compared to this pampered brat.

"No doubt you can beat me even now, Ama—I mean, *Katarina*," sneered Cristine, annoyed and out of breath. "You have those baker's arms."

"Baker's arms!" Amalina almost laughed.

"And I haven't given myself permission to really destroy you yet." When Cristine said this, she flexed her fingers as if cat claws might emerge from their tips. Again Amalina almost laughed at the theatricality of it.

But Amalina just couldn't find it in her to laugh.

Cristine shoved Amalina into the desk, knocking her breath out. But still, it wasn't as disastrous as she'd thought. She could still beat her friend … if she applied herself.

To test this theory, Amalina grabbed up Janusch's trick teapot, spun and slugged Cristine in the head with it. After a cracking *thunk-clank!* her friend fell backwards, stunned, tiny shards of chipped ceramic on her shirt and face. The solid pot had held together for the most part, with Amalina's finger still around its handle, as if the whole device was made of hard metal and the pottery just a decorative shell that had been glued on.

But suddenly Cristine was up again and she tossed Amalina onto the bed. Cristine leapt on her, wheeling her arms and kicking her legs. With one hand she grabbed Amalina's hair and began to tear it out painfully at the roots, bits of skin going with it. She began scratching.

"Ow! Ow! Ow!"

*Uh, oh,* thought Amalina within the storm of pain. *Doesn't mean I can't still die here.*

## 73

## Any Minute, Any Second

*L'entrée grande* lay riddled with shards and chunks of dull grey silver. Those bits didn't match the high polish of the revolutionary army's alloy armor, but they were obvious bright blemishes—hundreds upon hundreds of pock-marks—on the stone or embedded in the various overturned scraps of wood that were once tables and benches. In this fantastic wreckage, bodies flopped and groaned or lay still, wearing expensive looking servant's costumes now shredded and soaked in gore. None were Count Tepsji.

"You may upset the furniture," called the Count, as the knights entered the hall. "But you won't deny me my say! I am showing you my graciousness, my great generosity at your repeated unkindness. Venture no further, blood of Ardeel, but guarantee my right to address your grievances as men—as your honorable ancestors once did. Let us have *parley!*"

From a side hallway, a couple castle guards entered. They were struck down by two ringing shots.

One knight advanced and tossed light flakes of silver from a sidepouch, littering the floor. Another detached a capped set of bellows from his belt. Squeezing the bellows' arms, a wet hissing noise followed as the cap popped off and a clear fluid sprayed out over the floor, across the remaining pieces of benches, scraps of wood, and the intact long tables.

"I can't see," cursed Ivanti as he tried to turn his head in all directions. He plucked off the helmet.

"Son!"

Ivanti snapped his arm out as a signal for silence. *Immediate silence!* The Count must *never* know the identity of his opposition. It would be bad enough if he could recognize the lieutenant. But if he knew the commanding officer's father was among the men, he might understand these were not trained, professional, hardened combatants.

Ivanti shrugged in his armor and flexed his neck, trying to look more fierce and menacing than he already was. Centuries ago he would have shone as the most handsome and fearsome knight. A Lancelot.

"Accept my offer of peace," rumbled the Count from all corners.

"We've seen your peace," said Ivanti. "We've lived under its tyranny. And now—"

"And now you will make me wish I had never granted it? That I'd slaughtered your families all to a one, ages ago?"

"We will search this entire castle from top to bottom, and we will root you out of your hiding place. And justice will be meted today."

"If you ask justice, you will conduct yourselves with true honor by honoring my demands. We must have a parley, face-to-face. As men. Parley! Parley! Parley!"

Ivanti motioned for his men to search deeper into the hall, while he himself sought where the voice was coming from.

"You can have your parley, villain," shouted Ivanti in the meanwhile. "If you'll dare come out of hiding, and indeed face us as a man. Not as a specter. Come, you giant of fearlessness, show yourself and shake me by my hand." Ivanti held up his silver gauntleted hand, and smiled for his men. They laughed at his joke.

"Laugh at me?" The Count's voice shook. "Men of Korr, you think I can't recognize who has come this day, in violation of our covenant? Laugh at me, really, when you tear our binding document as if it weren't the labor of the long dead but the newly living? as if it were a simple garment, offensive to your modern taste? a folly out of your generational ignorance, in order to justify your mortal greed? Laugh at me? Instead of studying your history, and honoring your solemn vows, which you signed in your own blood? *Laugh at me, you children, you babies still fresh in this world? Laugh at meeeee?*"

"Ready," Ivanti whispered, as he waved in the last of his knights into the hall with his uplifted gauntlet. They were crowded in together, hunched, with their weapons—spears, pikes, pistols, muskets, bellows, cannon— primed to stab and slash and fire and splash and blast their enemy out of existence, if he would dare show himself. Ivanti felt a swelling of pride which the others shared, alongside their fear, with a great heaving sigh. They had reached their moment. "He will appear before us at any time, good men."

The army flinched as maids and cooks entered from the far doorway. They bore baskets full of parchment, sticks, papers, and envelopes. These servants were white faced and avoided looking at their sprawled comrades on the floor who'd been killed in the cannon blast, stepping around the blood and debris, as the Count's voice growled and rumbled, almost to itself: "What's this …? ah, I now see, worthless, worthless every one of you, to the very last man … Meaningless … So be it …" The servants spilled their baskets out before the army and then scurried away. There was a strange guttural noise among the army's ranks when this was done.

"Think I do not know who comes before me?" boomed the Count's voice again, addressing them fully once more. "Do you not remember all that you've privately asked of me, you deceitful beggars? Begged me for aid and comfort and help? Look what is now strewn across my floor, you worthless cowards. Do you not recognize your own work before your eyes? For your treachery to me now, should this not all be revealed—by me—to the world?"

Some of the knights leaned forward as others shifted half a step back. Silver armor rang together with the opposing moves.

"Hold," said Ivanti, not knowing what this was about, what the papers were. "Watch. Ready ..."

"Gorga, don't you remember how I helped you so?" When the Count said this, there was a gasp, and one of the knights trembled.

"Steady," commanded Ivanti. "Don't listen to him."

"Lygo, are you forgetting the services I rendered for your success? It is all right there, to be discovered by anyone curious enough to look and read. Harszu ... Harszu will you forsake your own oath to me? Who else is there, eh? Jenz Timer. Elto Pop. Simyon Tailor. Doctor Niszu. Homer Tolchok, weren't we on the closest of terms, I thought? Miden. Paulu. Gulgas. David. Reiku. Jeno. Bardoz. Hector. Dragomir, how much have I spared you, out of pity and affection? And Gyemes. Ilyanos. Midas. Kodyu the Smith. Tosjk. Etrensil. 'Dog'. Luto, you fool, even you? And Ngaszy. And James. Orson the Clerk, shame. And *Szocs*. Professor Lexio. Ivanszony, I would have thought better of you after our bargain, now laid bare upon the floor. And Efraim. Matteus. Konstantin Krumb. Dan Shoemaker. Jon Tomaszu. Doctor Taszu, what mysteries of the natural world did I pull back as a curtain for your understanding? And Lemn, don't think I don't see you there. Pacinto, could I not have expected a move so greedy? But Laszerball, have you no shame in coming here against me? Zakreba. Orgo. Yat Cooper. Kastar. Docra. Vladimy. Nashyu. Borszova. Han Watchmaker. Horvak. Juda. Desclu. Besel Bookbinder, what favors I showed and allowed, tsk, tsk. And Szimy. Grayol. Moshecai Weaver. Lenn. Castor Whitesmith. Balaszi Naeblin, did I not find and furnish you the most precious stones of these mountains? Ilya, the finest sands? John Boat Maker. Hans Klepp, it is you I have given service to the most. And Gralya, you would not be alive today if it wasn't for me. Karl, you know what you still owe. Boris, your very stink gives you away. Decebal ..."

As the names continued from the ceiling, from the floor, from the walls, in that confident drone, Ivanti saw it wearing down his men. Striking each one individually with a shudder. And as a whole, the tremor was communicated and amplified. A few held strong. Gulgas was a ramrod. But others succumbed and dropped to their knees, letting their weapons clatter to the ground.

"We should have listened to the Boss," one muttered in anguish and regret nearby.

"No," said Ivanti, still not comprehending what was at play here. "It's a trick. Don't listen! He doesn't know who all is here. He's bluffing. We shall be rid of him when the coward shows himself. You just need to hold strong. Eyes up! Eyes up! Ready! Ready …!"

Ivanti gestured with his raised hand and that picked a few up from their knees, renewed their strength, even as the list carried on. He held his weapon ready, his hand high, still waiting for the Count to come shake it.

"Any minute," said Ivanti. "Any second! Hold! Hold …!"

There was a black blur and a hum. Ivanti was the only one to see his arm come neatly off at the joint in the armor, though he didn't realize what it meant. Its shiny, scaled bulk just disappeared before his eyes. And before a splash of blood could erupt from where his forearm used to be, the blur took hold of one of the long tables still intact in the far end of the room and swung it in a fanning arc, reaching beyond the spear and pike points, and the muskets with their bayonets, and in its unearthly speed clapped the helmets unevenly arrayed behind them with a single, horrible crunch.

## 74

## The Stiletto

Attila might have smiled but he didn't. And he was relieved that both his hands were occupied, wrapped around a torch and a long spear respectively, or he would have had to steady the nervous tremor which normally overtook his left arm at moments like these. The excitement was getting to him: he'd heard the cannon's report which meant the army was at the castle, maybe already inside. Everything was going to plan.

The plan had been simple enough and the first part was accomplished easily. The miners returning after winter to the Berzwecken mines was an annual event. Blended into the workforce, unseen by even the Cardinal himself, was an added mix of outsiders: the men of Korr. Along with them came the convoy of new equipment, sealed in boxes and bound tightly in leather and rope. The explosives needn't be transported, they were already at the Berzwecken mine, in the mountains outside of Netz.

The resumption of mining activity gave Attila's army the cover it needed to press through the mountain woods undetected. It was a rugged and treacherous haul, but a route was scouted that held only a handful of pinchpoints. The army was slowed by steep precipices where just two men could cross at a time. But once they were on the final mountain and within sight of the castle, they could rest until the earliest morning light, don their armor and make their approach.

The only real treacherous moment had come before they left Korr, when he'd gone to supervise the lieutenant's training of the men and caught Bishop Perdu seeding doubt among them. But the lieutenant had acquitted himself well, the threat removed, and it was a smooth, level road from there.

. . .

Attila's route had diverged from the silver army well before the castle approach.

"Are you certain, Attila?" Lazru Skeldar had asked at the designated parting point. Dragomir and Lieutenant Vokent were standing behind him with their own looks of concern as Attila Bronk, the architect of the assault, prepared to leave them.

Feeling anticipation working on his body, Attila was willing to calmly explain it again, if only to tamp his own reservations: "Dragomir's daughter described a mill system within the castle. This would only be possible with a river's power. The rivers coming off these mountains were well mapped in Mr. Przek's engineering surveys. The one closest to the castle is too far away to realistically support the castle's millwork. But there are several river outlets below the castle, which implies an underground waterway. There will be a system of caves which the builders of the castle once accessed in order to install the wheels and gears, which will, of course, enter the castle structure itself, probably within a lower level or cellar.

"From anecdotes and confirmed by my own recent reconnaissance, there is now an unnatural buildup of rocks below the mountain within the riverbed. This rock has signs of being removed by explosives and tools, which means deliberate excavation. But there are no mines above, only the Netz castle. As I have observed personally last week: there is still a significant excess of silt within the stream, the waters turbid with it. Nothing natural within the mountains would be its cause. There is no longer a doubt, a cave system is up there somehow connected with the castle, from which this irregular accumulation emanates. I will find my entry there, and while you are working your way to the Count through his front door, and providing a deadly distraction, I will be cutting off any hopes of his escape, and putting a point into his back."

It sounded reasonable, and removed at least a little of the concern in their eyes. While the couple dozen miners he would bring with him were dressed in leather armor with silver plating here and there, Attila had only a plain leather jacket and a silver cap, which kept some of their concern circling. "I am not as strong as most, and I'll need my freedom of movement," explained Attila on his lack of plate armor. "You are the hammer. We are the stiletto."

The men, with their helmets under their arms, stared at him with a silent concern he found touching. They had been silent, most of them, since leaving the mines; but for the most basic communication, reticent to talk. Their nerves must be playing havoc with them, especially now with their armor on. But this expression of theirs was enough, the heavy-browed looks. How very Ardeelian of them.

"Good luck to you all," said Attila.

"Don't blow yourselves up," said Lt. Vokent. He smiled grimly and apologized: "It's what General Volante would tell the engineers on a mining mission before a siege. The way he says it sounds better. Anyway ..."

"You'll make a fine general someday," said Attila, charitably.

"He is one *today*," said Dragomir seriously, beaming proudly at the young man, clapping him on the armored back for encouragement.

• • •

Now the troop of miners behind Attila shifted uneasily as Attila stared ahead. He pointed with the spear but he didn't need to. The mouth of the cave was a large parting in the rock, reinforced at the sides and protected by an iron grating, a grillwork as high and wide as the opening itself. Echoing through the jail-like bars was the sound of rushing water, a distant river running deep inside the system. This is what they were looking for. And a black iron door in the grate promised that in less than a minute they would be lugging the barrels of black powder and silver powder down into the network of cellars below the castle.

"I don't wish to disappoint you," said Attila to the first man, after it seemed to everyone their leader had performed a little magic trick of unfurling a lengthy strip of jangling leather, extracted a couple slender metal tools from it, and then with less than a gesture and a couple clacks, had defeated the iron door's lock. The door now stood wide open. "You'll have the easiest, but the most crucial job. You will remain here with your petards. If you hear someone approach from within the tunnel but you don't hear our call and the return password, collapse this passage; blow it to bits. No hesitation."

• • •

The tunnel walls were uneven and rough. It was a natural fissure in the rocks of which the original architects of the castle must have taken advantage. This wasn't made clear for hundreds of yards in, as the cave began to slope precariously downward—and the men began to worry. With the amount of black powder and readied petards they hauled, torches were carried only by Attila and the engineer at the head of the small troupe, and then a couple of men at the rear. The paltry light, coupled with a steepening slope and the increasing roar of an internal river, made every step less sure than the last. But then Attila found a set of manmade stairs.

"This should make things easier," said Attila with encouragement over his shoulder. "Mind the dampness, the stones are still slippery."

The stairs were a long, sloping grade that ran on for what felt a mile. The roar of the hidden waterway grew so loud it became almost deafening. Attila could no longer communicate with the miners carrying the heavy kegs behind him.

"Will the humidity in this cave ruin the powder?" Attila shouted to the engineer. He had to repeat the question several times, while the engineer leaned close with one hand cupped behind his ear. The man was already half deaf as it was from his profession.

"As long as we don't take too long, should be all right," called the engineer.

"Two hours?" said Attila after some calculation.

"Should be more than enough time."

"Well, that's all we have. In two hours we will be either victorious or all of us dead." The engineer didn't seem to like that comment. Attila moved on before he began to question.

Further down, at a point where the cave's ceiling rose considerably above their heads, and broadened to the limits of their torchlight, they arrived at a landing that overlooked a wide, fast-moving river. Its current spun a large waterwheel at the far edge of the platform. Despite the water's powerful surge, the wheel turned slowly as the axle caught the energy and dispersed it elsewhere; the axle-pole ran through a smooth hole in the tunnel wall to the left. Close to that transition point there was a door. Attila nodded toward it, and pointed one of the pairs of men who carried a barrel between them to position themselves beside the doorway, with the instructions to blow it if there was trouble.

Through the door, they discovered a room composed of the same kind of smooth stone with which the castle was built. The waterwheel's pole entered through the caveside wall and ended with a massive wooden cage that served as a rotating cog. There were all sorts of these wooden cogs, and of every size, linked to it, and were spun in turn by its force. The meshes were worn but still solid. Each new cog fed a well-oiled pole that exited the room through its own hole in one wall or another. Some of these connecting gears had levers below them designed to brake the motion, or remove them from the rest of the machinery, so that they would be stilled.

Attila had an urge to pull some of the levers and stop whatever was being worked inside the castle. But then that would give away their presence. He decided to not even leave a detachment of miners within the room to blow it. The ones on the platform outside would be good enough to disrupt the whole apparatus.

Presently, the engineer pointed to a door in the room's opposite wall and whispered: "The castle?"

Attila put his finger to his lips. The roar of the river wasn't as strong here, and he wasn't confident their voices would be covered. He nodded but waved the engineer back out onto the platform. He closed the door.

"The castle is there," said Attila, in as low a voice as he could while shouting above the roaring water and laboring against the engineer's hairy, half-working ears. "But we still have a few minutes and we will scout this cave further on."

The engineer didn't quite get it all so Attila pointed.

There were rougher steps leading off the platform. Perhaps made by the original creators of the millwheel. But there was something about them that caused Attila to suspect differently. The stone should have been smoother after so much time, or rougher had they not been stairs at all. But these were hastily done, and seemed, by their variation of color from the surrounding stone, to be more recently cut. And the cave further on seemed to have been artificially widened. And, as well, he sensed a sharp, rotten-eggy smell in the air from discharged gun powder.

He waved the engineer to follow. They left one torch on the platform as he and the engineer followed the unsteady path ahead. Just a few minutes, thought Attila, wondering if it wasn't an internal fear that kept him exploring as long as he could, knowing that back through the door waited certain danger; a confrontation he'd so longed for and now shrank from.

But as they moved down these new steps, it was obvious there had been a more recent activity that had scratched out the inside of the cave system. The river was being channeled into a deep, narrower groove that seemed to make it flow harder and faster. And there came a groaning, humming sound above the water that suggested a snoring giant. Then they saw the waterwheel ahead.

It was a massive wheel made of iron, difficult to see against the black walls. It must have been almost three times the size of the wooden one upstream. It groaned and churned in the force of the river, its voice echoing in the tunnel. There were no doors on its landing, but the pole entered through another slick hole in the wall; what mechanisms this dynamo powered were out of sight and unreachable.

The engineer wanted to turn back. Attila held his arm and pointed forward. There were no obvious stairs or walkways, but the stone had been cut and widened again, further on. Maybe something more interesting lay ahead.

They passed under the mill axle and its greased fittings and made their way down. The roar of the river somehow lightened, though it was raging ever harder, almost flying over its banks. And the ceiling of the cave began to fill up with an odd, yellow light that did not come from their torch. It seemed they were about to discover a new mystery around the next turn in the cave system.

Suddenly a loud voice shook them to their knees.

"Count Tepsji!" came a high, shrill wail. "Vile creature! Our time together is at hand! I am *coming* for you! Ready yourself and despair! Yee-ah-haa-haaaa!"

"My God!" cried the engineer, picking himself up from the wet stone. "What was that?"

It had been a feminine shriek. Another of these daughter creatures? wondered Attila. Or was it the one he'd already met in Korr? From the sound of it, her words sprang out of the rock around him. He might have been terrified if he hadn't witnessed such enveloping cries at the battle of Kyrgil, where the two titans had gone at it.

Shaken and shaking still, the engineer began to stumble back toward the upper platform. Attila took his arm.

"We must leave!" cried the engineer. "It knows we're here! It's after us!"

"Nonsense! That voice called out against our adversary! It's a partisan for our side! Another distraction in the name of our cause! It's all part of the plan!"

"The boys'll blow the mouth of the cave," said the engineer, his pale, wrinkled face quivering. "We'll be sealed in!"

"Have you forgotten your niece?" snapped Attila, rocking the man by the lapel. "Have you forgotten the mayor of Netz' beautiful daughter, Ygardina? Both so cruelly slain, and at such a youthful age? You knew these women. And now you hold back at the moment of justice? You are not a coward, sir! Get hold of yourself!"

"Ygardina. Yes. She was beautiful. So innocent. She never deserved what happened to her."

"And now we will serve justice upon him. You and I!"

Before the engineer had another chance to reconsider, Attila spun him around and pushed him onward. By the strange glow ahead, he knew there would be more to see. Perhaps another way into the castle, or something that was of greater strategic importance.

It was just around the bend.

The mouth of the cave opened impossibly. And the light of the torch died in what seemed like a new kind of daylight. The water of the river gouted out beside them and fell an impossible distance to the bottom of a colossal cavern. Above them, on the ceiling of the cave, was what appeared to be a sun made of gold. It blazed down its rays onto a golden city below.

"My god," said the engineer.

· · ·

It wasn't a real sun at all, Attila saw, and it moved slowly, mechanically along a looping metal track fastened along the cave's ceiling. The track connected overhead, near to the falls' opening where they stood. At their feet, and hundred of yards down, stretched the fantastic city.

"You knew about this?" asked the engineer.

"Not in my wildest dreams," said Attila. "Have we enough to destroy it?"

"Destroy it!" The engineer was agog.

"This is the gate of hell."

"What are you thinking? Look at it, sir. Solid gold. So beautiful. This is the city of God!"

"Underground?" argued Attila. "Underneath the Knight of Ardeel's castle? This is an illusion from the master of lies. Pluck out your eyes before you believe them, in this Place of Perfidy. This is only a masterpiece of deceit and temptation. It must be taken out."

"If it is *unnatural*," said the engineer reluctantly, sheepishly, "I don't see how we could do anything to bring it down, even if we wanted."

"Let's assume this cave and these dwellings are still subject to the laws of earth, eh? Is there any way our supplies can destroy it?"

The engineer lifted his hand, squinted, and drew his calloused pointer finger along the ceiling, stopping here and there, as he made his survey. "It can be done, I suppose. But what of the castle above?"

"Can we afford to keep the kit still at the mouth of the cave? And at the entrance to the cellars back up the tunnel? Then that's enough for that. I imagine if we bring down this—and the Netz castle sits on top, let us not forget—we might just sink it, too."

The engineer nodded, but his mouth was curved down at the corners.

"Remember the mayor's daughter," reminded Attila. "The mayor's daughter."

"Yes, Ygardina ... We *have* to, don't we?"

"Tell me."

"I think it can be done," admitted the engineer. "We use the track of that beautiful sun to set the charges at the right spots in the ceiling. But to be sure we'll need to plant some barrels on the other side. You see that yonder upper landing?"

Attila saw a landing on the opposite side of the cave at the same height which, promisingly or threateningly, fed into a low, dark passageway that led away from this abomination of golden splendor. But he didn't see a direct path to the place from where they were. It could only be accessed from the city below them by an upward winding ramp.

"Is there a way to get down there from here?" asked Attila, indicating the foot of the ramp.

"I don't see one," said the engineer. He angled his head over the side. "How deep does that pool at the bottom of the falls look?"

"What are you suggesting?"

"It's the fastest way down," explained the engineer.

"There might be another way."

"But we don't have much time, do we? You're going to have to go if you want to make sure. Enough petards'll do the work. Blow the other side out, so even if the castle doesn't fall, the whole cavern will block up and be flooded. Could play havoc with the river below the mountain, but that's acceptable to you, isn't it?"

"Did you say *I* have to go?" said Attila, finding a sudden rise of fear within him. Maybe it was the sound of the rushing water at his side. The falls.

"I didn't say you, but I'm your engineer." *Can't risk me* was unspoken, but understood. "I'll see it gets done right on this side." The engineer looked over the falls again, gulped and pulled his head back quickly. He kept his face straight and took the torch from Attila. "I'm sure it is deep enough for a good dive and a swim. You'll make it fine."

"I've tumbled over enough falls in my life," said Attila, peering over the edge, trying to remember the Baibay Valley waterfall, his first time around, the one which had led him to Sir Hak Vogoneyevic's farm. He'd blacked out before going over, or didn't remember it anyway; how he had survived the descent. "I don't need to do it again—"

"For Ygardina!" Attila heard as he felt the calloused hand push him; and the river, hundreds of yards below, rushed up to meet him.

75

# The Chandelier

"Ms. Dalca," cried Genadie as he loped toward her. "Where have you been?"

Amalina could barely see him as she staggered down the hall. She was still catching her breath from the fight with Cristine, while holding all the items she needed. Everything she needed ... but the bone. What was she going to do in a fight if everyone could see her? She patted her hair to put it in place. Her head stung. The fingers on her right hand were still sore from holding the teapot's handle as she'd cracked it again and again over Cristine's head, until only the ring of the handle was left. But now she held the emergency bell and its hammer.

"Where were *you*, Genadie? You weren't in your room!"

"Don't you hear?" his voice rasped as he pointed to his ear. "The lady below has broken loose! Oh, Olympus, it's what I most feared from the very outset. Had I not warned him it would happen! Why didn't he kill her?"

"Genadie," said Amalina. "What are you talking about? This is the best news of all!"

He looked at her, shocked.

"Isn't this what we wanted?" she whispered positively. "We might not even have to fight him *ourselves* anymore ..."

"Oh, yes. I suppose that's true," he mumbled. "But ... what if we have to fight *her* then?"

"They might do each other in. Get them both outside somehow. Or into a room with a window."

"*You* didn't take her off the wheel, did you?"

"Why would I do that?" asked Amalina, sounding affronted. "*When* could I have?"

"How did you get hurt, Ms. Dalca?"

"Cristine," gasped Amalina, as if remembering. "She just tried to kill me. I've been wrestling with her for the past half hour, waiting for you to rescue me."

"Oh. I'm sorry. Where's that boy of yours?"

"Never mind that. While Cristine's out of the way, let's get where we're supposed to be."

"Where's that?"

"The great hall!"

Genadie shuffled in place nervously. "Well, now that you mention it. Why don't we wait here and see what's to happen; what's to become of Master and the Lady of the Midnight Wails?"

"Because that isn't our plan." Amalina continued down the corridor. "Come on then."

"But why the great hall?" He limped slowly after her, waving her back toward her room. His little eyes were blinking and twitching fast. "Doesn't have to be *there*. Could be anywhere. And they really *are* still at it. Could be for hours. You remember Kyrgil."

"Remember *the plan*, Genadie! Let's stick to it!"

"But, Ms. Dalca."

"'*Katarina*', Genadie; we're in the halls!"

"But Countess, if you will, there's no need to go downstairs. Really. I think you shouldn't—we shouldn't—"

"What's the matter with you?" said Amalina, sucking in breaths as she now circled down the stairs, trying to will more energy into her body. "Everything should be set. You did start the fires in the cellars, didn't you?"

There should at least be a little smoke coming up the stairs by now, shouldn't there? But there wasn't. Only what was left from the burning bouquets.

"You didn't?"

"I didn't have time. The lady on the ..." Suddenly a promising pair of orange-yellow bees zagged by, heading up from the floor below. As she watched them, Genadie lunged forward and tried to hook Amalina's arm. She dodged it and continued faster down the stairs. "But I don't think it's a good idea *anymore*, Ms. Dalca. I don't think you should go down there."

"On the first floor we have a whole army of knights on our side."

But as she said this, Amalina felt a terrible plunge in her stomach. She had arrived at the bottom of the staircase, and instead of the clamor of armor and grunting men, or some sort of fireworks, there was a hollow silence. Even the reverberating screeches of the lady-from-the-wheel tearing through the castle searching for the Count was hushed here.

Amalina had stepped in blood. The floor was washed with it. She'd seen this before. In silent courtyards. In vast castle rooms and cellars and corridors. Blood ... with bodies.

"He didn't mean to," said Genadie.

The entrance hall was a glittering, prickly carpet of silver armor. All stilled. Helmets were gathered in the corner, blood and pieces of beard hung raggedly out of them.

"Oh, no," cried Amalina.

"Ms. Dalca," rasped Genadie, as he tried to pull her back up the stairs. "Please, come back—"

She couldn't help but stare, her eyes roving over the bodies, looking for someone she might recognize by some detail. One that might be her father. One who might still be alive.

But all were without heads, and all were anonymous, like a hill of silver ants.

Except one.

"No, no, no, no, no," said Amalina. She sank to her knees, barely holding onto her instruments. But she crawled into the bloody mire. To see. To make sure. "No, no, no, no, no."

Ivanti Ion Vokent lay on the floor, heaped with the rest of them, but with his head still there, no helmet on, as beautiful and serene as if he were asleep. She didn't notice his severed arm, it was lost in the riot of metal. The twist of his neck proved his death.

It seemed so awful. So senseless. Hadn't she warned him? Hadn't she told him this very thing would happen? And still, here he was. *The fool.* For what? Some sense of useless obligation ... for her? For a stupid, senseless girl? Or, he'd said something else ... honor ... duty ... ?

Her village was laid out in death before her. It was all her fault.

"No no no no no no no."

"Ms. Dalca," said Genadie, sniffling. "It wasn't his fault. They pushed him ..."

There was a glint of something—something gold—at Ion's parted lips. Those once-perfect lips, now grey, loosened thoughtlessly. She reached out to his resting head and took it up: one of the Count's gold coins; with the Count, in profile on it, grimacing wryly. Strangely, there were was a line of markings cut into the metal. Block letters. They spelled out: IVANTI ION VOKENT. Some kind of sick joke or statement by the Count, no doubt. A little laugh he had prepared for the moment, which he would then explain to her later. And she would have to accept, and admit he thinks of everything. He always thinks of everything.

"No no no no no no no no!"

Amalina ran from the room, trying not to slip, leaping over arms and discarded spears, thinking hotly how, as much as he thinks of everything, he hadn't thought of the chandelier, had he? And had he anticipated what she would do next? She rammed herself against the doors to the great hall.

A swarm of bees hummed down toward her, only to swerve back at the last second. A few landed on her. Some thunked off the emergency bell in her arms. The swarm spread out and buzzed angrily, like a swirling orange-yellow storm. This only made her angrier, matching them in outrage. She saw the clump of hive smashed in the corner. Aklan was nowhere to be seen but his rumpled jacket was on the floor. At least *he* was following orders. He *must* have taken the bone for himself. He'd be at the release on the wall now. She didn't look, trusting him.

Amalina lifted the iron bell and began to hammer it. She screamed and cried as she did so.

The black blur pounded through the door. As she had expected. When he came to a stop, his hands flailed over his head, and he twisted in all directions, following the waves of bees.

"What is this?" he said, confused. "Is she here?"

"Why?" Amalina yelled at him. "Why did you do it?"

"Do what?"

"You didn't have to!"

"He didn't mean to," cried Genadie, in apology.

"I haven't the time," said the Count, looking ever more confused. "She—"

With a banshee wail, the lady from the wheel flew from the fireplace. He was too distracted by Amalina berating him and everything whirring around him to realize he was being attacked. He tried to alter himself as the wailer tackled him, her own head already changed to that of an enormous snake. Her jaw was unhinged and she aimed to swallow him from the head down.

He rammed them both into the wall, where the stone cracked. The Count howled his displeasure.

"Ms. Dalca," cried Genadie, knocking the bell from her hand and putting into her palm a pointed stake. "Get her! We must get her!"

He lifted a silver spear and tried to follow their bodies rolling around the room, looking to place a shot into the snake woman.

Amalina knew not to look up. She'd already memorized the chandelier's position by the markings on the floor, and she must not draw anyone's attention to what hung heavily above them all. She had only to get them centered underneath it. The wailing woman appeared to be trying her best. She kept glancing sidelong at Amalina, her forked tongue flickering a foot or so out of her slick green lips, looking expectantly with slitted, bright emerald eyes; searching for confirmation, between somersaults, when they would land on the center spot—where Amalina had finally stopped kicking and nudging the bell's hammer into place—with the weapon ready in Amalina's hands. The woman's fingers were ripping soaking red shreds of cloth off the Count's body. And Amalina was thinking, *if only I could trigger the—*

The ceiling seemed to fall. Amalina screamed and threw herself back. The chandelier missed her by inches. But with the wailing woman anchoring the Count to the spot, it crushed down on the two creatures like a grooved mallet. And the chains continued to pour down on them from the ceiling, as well as the many extra silver loops that'd been stuck up there with them.

The bottles of lake water hopped into the air on landing, then dropped into the center, either shattering or simply spilling their contents.

Amalina and Genadie started forward, but silver chains were already rearranging themselves on their own, crossing the exposed parts of the Count and the woman. The two creatures moaned, swore, and hissed.

Genadie did not hesitate for very long. He speared the woman's chest, then fell on her as she writhed. He took a knife from his belt and sawed through her neck, her thick tongue lashing at him.

While he did that, Amalina grabbed the length of chain from her blouse, the one that had once covered the woman's mouth, and wrapped it around the Count's head. She tried to fit it into his open mouth, but his whole body was twisting and turning as if anticipating her moves, splashing and vibrating in the painful water and chains. She got it around his eyes and his neck, and was trying to wrap the rest around one of the chandelier's thick spokes when she ran into something that knocked her over. She saw one end of the silver chain tying itself to the Count's grossly extending arm.

Amalina reached out and felt the hot skin and solid body she could not see.

"Go," she said to the invisible boy. "Get out of here! Go I said!"

She shoved Aklan, and one of the Count's fingers bent backward, with a claw extended and slashed. Blood spurted out into the air. Aklan cried out.

"No!" said Amalina, knocking Aklan away from the seeking claw. She pushed him and righted him and sent him toward the door. His body was trembling, and she could hear him whimpering, as too much blood erupted from random spots in the air and onto the floor. "Out!"

Amalina took up the dropped chain and whipped it at the slashing hand. Then she wrapped the silver around it, so that the limb shrank back to a normal size and appeared to age and flake away.

"Ms. Dalca!" rasped Genadie, his tone a warning. He held his dagger in his hand, covered in blood.

"Do it," said Amalina. "Do it."

His jaw trembled. His hand shook. His eye blinked. "Ms. Dalca … It is Master …"

Amalina tried to take the blade from him, but he backed away. "It is Master …"

"Genadie, he can't hurt you. But you have to—"

"I won't let you, Ms. Dalca. I warned him what you were up to, but he didn't believe me. Did you, Master? But look what she's done to you." His lower lip quivered and he scratched unsurely at his grizzled chin. He still held the knife in his gnarled hand. His body was in a profound argument with itself. Wanting to go forward to end the Count, but refusing to do it. Punishing himself for even thinking it.

"Genadie," whispered the Count, weakly. He looked like a crushed bug; what little of him stuck out from under the pile. His neck and brow were red and shriveled. "What's happened?"

"Master, it was Amalina," he cried, falling to his knees. "It was Ms. Dalca who has worked this treachery against you. I saw her … This was no accident. Forgive me."

"Get me out."

"Yes, Master. Right away, Master."

But Genadie hesitated. His eyes roamed the debris and the heap of silver chain. Then he gaped as the silver spear before him pulled out of the wailer's chest.

Sickening vibrations ran up the spear's shaft into Amalina's hands and up her arms. She almost dropped it from the stomach-turning sensation. She adjusted her grip.

"No, Ms. Dalca," whimpered Genadie. "You can't."

"He killed Papa. He killed your family, your Mala. He's killed everyone."

"But it's *impossible*, Ms. Dalca. He's Zeus!"

Amalina circled Genadie, finding the right spot to stab at the creature with so many chains in the way.

"Now you find it in you, little mouse?" growled the Count from below. "After all these years, you will end your innocence with *me*?"

"No, Master," said Genadie. "I'll protect you, as always. I'm your greatest servant, Master. Aren't I, Master?"

Amalina said: "Genadie, what about your so—"

She was about to say 'son', when Genadie cried out and grabbed the spear. Amalina tried to pull it away, but he countered. They tripped over each other, the chains, and the spokes of the giant fallen chandelier. Amalina was taller than Genadie, even when he straightened himself upright, and she was heavier. She swung him around in circles. But he held on, and he knew how to pivot and use her weight against her. Just when she gave a pull to take him off of his feet, he jumped forward and pressed out with his arms. Amalina stumbled and fell over backwards, tripping over one of the spokes. Her back, then head, clunked painfully on the chandelier. She saw comets and grasped at her skull protectively.

Genadie was already running from the room with the silver spear dragging behind him.

Amalina scrambled to her feet, scraping her knee on an iron stud in the wood. She danced in pain. Then, recovering herself, she charged after the surprisingly spry Genadie, rubbing at her knee against the pain, as she passed through the doorway into *l'entrée grande*.

She was right back on the floor again, face first. The bloody floor. Her head pulsed. She felt something strike her back: the shaft of the spear. Genadie was pummeling her with it.

"Genadie …!"

"You will learn, Ms. Dalca," he said, swatting her hard on the arm, so that it went numb. "You will never question his greatness or his power *ever* again." He whacked her on her lower back. "Have I taught you nothing? You've brought shame to us both." He struck her across her shoulder blades, so that she buckled and her nose and mouth smacked the floor, where her lips stuck to the stone. "And, should Zeus favor us with his mercy," whack to the head, "which as worms we do not deserve," smack to her hips; she was gasping, losing breath, "we must show our humility and reverence forever onward!"

She felt a blow to her back that sunk her deeper into the thickening pool, which was quickly followed by a stabbing pain. The weight on her wiggled back and forth violently, and she pictured Genadie above her, twisting the spear into her body in the most vindictive way. But she heard him make a sorrowful noise and there was a savage growl. The air around her was in motion, and the shiny spear clanged down in front of her face, splashing red droplets across it.

When she turned the stabbing pain eased from her back, as the beast above her adjusted to the change. It was the black wolf, and it was tearing at Genadie's chest and throat. He spun his arms like a frightened rabbit to keep the claws and fangs away from his body. But the giant mangled head spun from side to side, seeking a way into him. It tore open his jacket.

Genadie fell onto one of the headless knights. His coat was open and he fumbled for the pistols tucked in his belt. Amalina jumped to his side and took one, arcing it across the room. Then he was skidding out from under her.

He was screaming.

The black wolf had his teeth sunk into Genadie's ankle. It dragged him with intermittent shakes of his head to further claim his hold. Genadie held up his arms to Amalina, appealing to her for help. But the wolf looked at Amalina with his one good burning eye, to calculate where she was and how far he needed to drag his quarry to keep her safe. Growling hungrily, the wolf pulled Genadie, kicking and wailing, back from her and then out the front door; Genadie not finding a solid hold on all the slick silver armor along the way. At the last second, before he disappeared from sight, the little rat's hands scrambled at his waist and plucked out his other pistol.

## 76

# The Fall

Attila had always feared water; drowning in it, in particular. But as much as he had done his best to avoid it, he'd found himself one too many times floundering at the bottom of a river. This time, though, he felt he had finally reached that long hoped-against point. When he'd wheeled over the ledge to join the falls, he'd had little time to gather his breath. And, hitting the river below, what air he'd taken in was blown out. And worse, the artificial riverbed wasn't as deep as it appeared from above and he'd struck the bottom painfully after plowing through its unyielding surface. He hadn't had time to regain his senses and he was quickly pushed by the current so that he could not gain any footing, even while it seemed to press him down.

But it was his leather jacket, metal helmet, and the baggage of his many weapons that weighted him and kept him below. He shoved hard with his legs to launch his body upward, yet could barely break the surface long enough to grab a breath. He scrambled to shed his heavy clothes, but knew right away he couldn't fast enough. He calmed himself, let his body sink to the bottom. This was a manmade channel for the river. He need only walk to its edge and maybe he could grab hold of the side and crawl out. Or maybe there would be an upward grade or a set of stairs he would run into.

The flow kept him moving. Through his boots, as he scooted across the smooth riverbed, he felt the power against him, and realized he wasn't going to catch a grip. He was being shoved very quickly out of the cavern.

Until he struck something hard.

Just as there was an iron grillwork at the mouth of the cave, from which they'd passed into the tunnel leading here, there was one built at the end of this golden city's artificial river, allowing the water to pass through to a channel in the rocks and then out somewhere below the mountain. The grillwork was to prevent anything valuable—or *anyone*—being swept away and lost. Or was it to prevent an invasion from below?

Attila was pinned hard to the iron bars. He had just enough strength left to pull with his arms to bring himself up. His head popped above the water and he gasped for breath. He couldn't keep his eyes open for the rush and splash battering his face. But he only had to note where the side of this channel might be and then shimmy his shoulders, back, and legs, until his outstretched hand found the water's edge.

When he threw himself onto the cobblestones, he panted and sputtered, blinking wildly. Soon his eyes could open fully, and he saw the stones were the same gold as everything else. Smooth and bright yellow. He righted himself immediately. No one stood along the canal.

Looking up, he spotted the engineer's head staring down at him from inside what appeared to be the mouth of a spouting, gold balaur dragon. At this distance, Attila could not see the engineer's face clearly, but he had his hand up to his mouth, as if in fear for Attila's life, or apprehension that Attila had not died in the fall. Without emotion, Attila decided that had been the engineer's idea: let fate or heaven decide the matter. If he had simply wanted to murder Attila, he would have slunk off immediately like a coward and been halfway out of the tunnels already. Attila's fall was a flip of a coin. If Attila died, that was the end of the mission. If Attila survived, they would proceed.

Attila jogged in his stiffening, waterlogged clothes, just beginning to feel the full icy bite of the water in his limbs. He shivered once and then motioned with both of his hands to the man above. *The spear!*

The engineer waved, telling him to wait.

Attila opened his jacket to let the water run out, and danced to warm himself. Until he saw his spear being lowered. Fortunately they'd brought plenty of rope, and in ample lengths, in anticipation of steep mountain grades, cliff faces, and chasms that needed to be forded. The rope could have lent Attila a more graceful, and less frigid, ride to the city than the plunge over the falls. Being suddenly and conveniently remembered, the rope was another proof for Attila that the engineer's shove was more than innocent.

Attila unwound his spear, and after checking that he was still undetected, the large pack of petards was next. Now Attila took the opportunity to truly get his bearings. He held back a loud gasp.

Rising above this gold city, protruding from the wall far to the right of the waterfall, just around a bend, was a gold castle, much the same as the one they were under. Was it just an artificial castle, its features simulated against the rock? Or was there really a whole other building built into the walls behind it? If so, there wasn't going to be enough explosives to bring it down. The best they could hope for was that there wasn't a secret exit to that new golden castle somewhere in the back. They would just have to collapse the cavern and hope for the best.

Attila appeared entirely bored as he strapped the heavy pack of petards across his shoulders. A torch arced down and missed the water by a foot. It bounced with wild sparks along the river's edge and then came to rest on the gold street, guttering and hissing but still burning, its light reflected like a bright pool around it. This was his matchstick for the explosives. He picked it up and started walking.

He would find the bottom end of the ramp that wound back to the opposing ledge. He'd been about to say to the engineer that that far ledge most likely connected to the Count's high castle above, and so they might find their way to it through the door of the gear room back along the tunnel, when the old man had given him the heave-ho. Now that Attila was in the village though, he saw the engineer was right after all. He'd probably reach the upper ledge much faster from here than winding through a number of blind rooms; and who knew if they connected? or if doors were securely locked against them along the route?

As he marched inward, Attila noticed the streets had a slight curve to them in order to lend the place an organic feel, and to perhaps avoid a direct line of sight to the far cavern walls; which might ruin the city effect. As a side result, it was a maze. He'd get to the ledge in time as long as there weren't any deadends. But there had to be many, and in every direction.

Something clanged off the street beside him. He looked up and someone above was waving from the sun's support rail. The man there had pulled one of the rail's pins and accidently dropped it.

Overhead, a number of miners had already climbed the ropes leading to the rail system and were now running along it with their charges, inserting them into crevices cut into the ceiling. Two pairs were hauling heavy kegs over from the waterfall's jaw-ledge. These men were young, small and wiry, moving like trained monkeys high over the cavern floor, unquestioningly gleeful at the opportunity to destroy a wondrous creation they'd just set their eyes on, and filled with the confidence that they would do so and get out alive.

The small charges would be set along the ceiling, though far enough away from the waterfall to keep the river flowing. Some of the barrels would be installed above and behind the sun itself. When the sun reached the center of the cavern, it and all the other charges would be blown. Hopefully Attila will have placed his own charges at the facing entrance by then.

* * *

Attila crossed a bridge over a small canal and began to worry that the way to the ramp would not be as direct as he'd hoped. Then came a question from behind.

"Who are you?"

A woman's voice.

Turning, Attila saw it was one of the ladies to whom he had preached the day he'd visited the castle, weeks ago. Her name escaped him at the moment. Maybe it was because her face was so pale even in the golden light that he could not recall her exactly. Her skin looked too tight.

"Are you one of the house guard?" she asked pleasantly. "Did the Count send you down to protect us? Is the castle under attack?"

"I—uh," said Attila, his eyelids lowering further than normal. "That is to say—"

"Wait, I remember you. You're the priest. You performed the services in the chapel, didn't you? The Cardinal's man. Father Roszcy's replacement."

Attila agreed immediately and bowed in a solemn way a priest might. It looked ridiculous wearing a silver helmet, soggy leathers, holding a silver spear, a torch, and with a load of black powder charges strapped onto his back.

"Are we going to have services down *here*?" she asked, sounding surprised. She appeared a little dazed, unsure of what she was looking at.

"If the lady should want it …"

"What are you holding there?"

"Well, it's a—"

"Is that going to be a cross? How beautiful it is. Is that silver?"

She reached out. A cross? He wondered how she could see his spear as any thing but a weapon, considering it tapered to a needle-like point. That and his armor should have put her in another frame of mind. He watched in fascination as her hand moved to caress it. But she stopped short of touching.

"I'm not allowed to—I can't touch it, can I?" she asked, her eyes wide and fixed on the glimmering shaft.

Attila did not visibly react to the question, but inside, his guts knotted. She wasn't allowed to touch silver? So she is one of *them* too? Another? He thought to plunge the spear through her breast, right through her heart. For some reason he pulled it away.

"I'm not sure it should be touched," said Attila, agreeing. "The Cardinal has blessed it. Or is there another reason you shouldn't?"

"I'm not sure," she said, still looking confused, but wary of it now. "Looks more like a spear. Or a giant knitting needle."

"It's going to the chapel," said Attila, confidently. "Is there one down here?"

"There must be," she said. "There's everything else. He didn't tell you where to find it?"

"He's busy above."

Attila swore to himself. *Where is the Count?* This weapon and this whole operation was to end that creature. And now he was facing a new threat just when he didn't need it.

He glanced up but directed his eyes to the distant ramp ledge. He should have already been there, placing the charges. Risking detection, he sent his eyes in another direction. The men were now rolling the barrels on the rail to catch up to the sun. The waterfall's racket covered their movement.

Others were still setting the smaller bombs, and connecting them with a spider's web of thin, powder-infused cord.

"Well, let's find your place, shall we?" she said, starting off down the street. "If we can't find it we'll ask him. To be honest, I *am* surprised he'd permit you down here at all, much less have a church built. But he's interesting that way. You never can predict him and his surprises. Even now I don't think I'll have as much interest in what you have to offer anymore as I once did. But one must find distractions.

"I really like your outfit, by the way," the Lady chattered on. "More interesting than the traditional dress. I suppose it's eastern? Influenced by the Greek style or something from the Steppes? Or is it one of the Count's own designs? Oh, you know, if there isn't a church, I think I know a perfect spot for one. There's this pretty building ..."

As she went on, they were moving further from the foot of the ramp. Attila didn't know how to redirect her. Never mind about what she was saying, as if to further distract him. Again, he considered whether he should ram the spear through her—through her back now, because she was walking slightly ahead of him. She wouldn't even notice him tip the spear at her.

But was she really no longer what she was before? no longer human? She spoke like the lady he'd met in his sham services; had the same temperament, it seemed, from what little he'd known of her. She *had* been human *then*.

As they came up a street, there was a man in the upper window of a building. The window was open and he was hanging his head out of it. It looked to Attila like any common drunkard airing himself from his apartment. But the general yellow glow of the city gave him a sickly pallor. What didn't help was that someone had planted brightly colored spring flowers in the window planters, which added to the contrast. And as they got closer, it became obvious his over-all skin was unnaturally grey. His eyes were red inside darker circles, and stared without blinking and without focus. His tongue hung out of his mouth as if he'd been strangled. His white whiskered neck was a mottle of cuts and lesions.

The lady was passing the sight as if it were nothing to make note of, though looking at it directly.

"Is that the architect Balbo?" asked Attila, with a complete air of disinterest. As if discussing the the mildly unusual shape of a passing cloud.

"Yes. Not sure how much longer he'll last. Might need your services. Maybe that's why Tepsji sent you down here. But he is good for another day or two, I think."

Now Attila couldn't help but stop to look closer at Balbo, for signs of life.

"He agreed to this," said the lady, sounding apologetic. Maybe embarrassed by the unpleasantness of the sight, like a fouled chamber pot discovered in her bedroom. "I mean, the prisoners ran out, after all. Oh, but maybe you're here for the prisoners."

"Prisoners?"

"But no, it'd be a little late on that count, isn't that so?"

"Too late?"

"Of course, there will always be the next in line."

"The next in line?" Attila felt annoyed he was repeating everything she said, and was somehow behind on some terrible new aspect to this place.

"But you *do* know what we're up to here, of course," she said chirpily. "Don't you?"

There was a scream from above as something dropped from the ceiling.

A pretty dress was climbing at an incredible speed up the side of the cavern wall, above the top of the gold castle. It moved with the rapidity and sureness of a squirrel scampering up the trunk of a tree. But the lady inside that dress was screaming: "Look! Look …! Invaders!"

Attila was dumbfounded. *Still another one!* And while she didn't have the same superhuman quickness of the Count, she was more than human in dexterity and strength. She was an animal. A long, tall animal.

"Invaders?" said the woman in front of him, as she stared blankly at all the men now shouting and running along the sun's support rails. "Have the prisoners got out again …? But no, they're already gone. What—?"

*Here is the moment*, thought Attila. He needed to run her through. While she wasn't looking at him. But he couldn't imagine sending the spear into her. The feel of her death connected to him. It seemed unthinkable. Impossible. But the lady above had reached the support beam, and she was tearing into the men on her way to the sun, sending bodies to the ground with flat, smacking sounds. They were beginning to die.

"Do you know what's happening, priest?" the young lady asked Attila, above the screams.

"Blow it!" shouted Attila at the men. "Blow everything!"

"What?"

Attila turned and ran for where he figured the ramp must begin. If he was lucky, he'd be able to place the charges and seal the entrance there.

"Blow them! Blow everything!"

*Lady Inovala, that was her name*, said the part of his mind that was always thinking, always detached from the immediate proceedings. She was running behind him, faster than him, crying out, catching him at the shoulder, "What? What do you mean? What's happening?"

With a tremendous crash, the bonfire—which had been lurching and shifting within the sun's now tilted bowl—emptied some of its blazing contents onto the city below, sending fire and sparks bouncing across and crashing through the glittering golden roofs.

Lady Inovala spun and gasped at the sight.

When she turned back, fear in her eyes, Attila shoved the spear into her chest. She fell off her feet and dropped to the ground, looking confused at first, but then screamed. She tried to grab the shaft of the spear, but as she did, her hands flew away from it, as if it burned her. Not as dramatic an effect as Attila had thought, but she must be newly converted and perhaps not as sensitive. She was still dying, anyway, or seemed to be; screaming and thrashing on the gold cobbles as she did so.

If it came to it, Attila would need the spear for the Count. He had to take it. He scrambled his hand into his armor. Over the wide, automatic tunnel of her mouth, her eyes watched him: frantic crescent moons with little dots for pupils. He was holding the pistol now. What should he do with it? he wondered. *Oh, yes … but will it work after the dip into the river?*

He cocked the pistol's hammer, prayed the powder was just dry enough, pointed the barrel at her head, and pulled the trigger. A glittering flash of silver beads blasted her head into two pieces. Her screaming stopped. He gulped and felt as if he'd just lost something important.

The last of the bonfire fell, followed by the massive bowl itself. He wasn't sure who had loosed it, but it crashed with a great metallic whomp that vibrated the whole city.

The cavern's colossal light had gone out. But even with the smoke billowing up from the flames, the top of the cave erupted in a pale twinkling blue light. Attila knew it must be some thousand-fold smudges of phosphorescent lichens, but the effect was as if the dome above had turned into the night sky.

"My God," muttered Attila. What a magnificent place! His words were lost in the screams of the men above, who at this point had still failed to light their charges. They would never hear him in the racket, so he willed them: *Blow it! Blow it all!*

He quickly refilled his pistol with gun powder and silver shot. He made sure the silver knives were ready inside his pouch in case he needed them. Then he pulled the spear from Lady Inovala's body and turned for his final run to the ramp, nothing now to stop him.

Three Ladies, standing shoulder-to-shoulder in the street, stared at him.

Or rather, they stared at their dead friend on the ground at his feet, or at him. Their looks traded places between the points of interest as they tried to understand what was happening.

"You killed her?" asked one.

"Blow it all!" he shouted, darting forward. "Blow it all! … Vedya …!!!"

## 77

## Around in Circles

Amalina sat up. There seemed to be a rumbling in the floor. Like something deep below the castle was turning over. The way the Kyrgil mountain had felt before its collapse. She stood quickly. Or had it been a pistol shot? she wondered. Was that what had woke her, and not the rumbling? Amalina looked around.

Genadie was gone; at least for the moment. The Count was still in the great hall, he must be. The last she had seen of Aklan was blood spurting out of the air as he ran to *l'entrée grande*, where she was now.

"Aklan," she whispered. "Aklan? Are you here?"

How awful it would be, she thought, if he was dying and he still had that bone clamped between his teeth. She'd never find him. There was blood everywhere, and his had joined—disappeared—into the rest. She grasped in circles for the boy.

"Aklan?"

"Ms. Dalca," came the deep basso voice. It wasn't so strong that it shook her bones. But it was enough to make her spin and expect to see him standing behind her. He wasn't there. His voice was projecting from the other room.

Amalina looked at the open doorway to the courtyard. How bright it was outside. She picked up a silver spear and walked quietly to the great hall.

"Come to me, Ms. Dalca." His voice was weakening, she could barely hear it. Was he dying under all that metal? Could it be? "Come closer to me, so that I might speak to you, and you might hear me better."

*I, me, I, me, I, me,* she thought. He was still himself even in his closing hour.

When she arrived at the chandelier, she could barely see him. It looked as if a massive wagonwheel lay atop a squashed mound of iron and silver spaghetti, with dampened bits of broken bottles, cloth, and skin showing through. As she closed in on it, she would see his shoulders, or the top of his head, and maybe the wailer's headless body—or bodiless head. Amalina stopped, lifted the spear with both hands, and pointed it aimlessly at the heap.

*You only have to find his heart, and stab it.*

"How many times have I told you, little mouse, how proud I was the night I first saw you at your window? How I knew you would be so good for me, that you would improve me and my life? That I fell in love with you that very second?" Something in the pile shifted. Silver links rose slightly, glinted, clinked, and then subsided, as if they were sighing. "This I have confessed to you."

*Don't listen to him*, thought Amalina. Or was it Lucinda's voice? Or the voices of her father? Of Ivanti? Of the men of Korr? *Kill him! Kill him now!*

Several bees landed on the spear's shaft and started crawling around, one toward her hand. Their anger was spent. Hers wasn't. She only had to find the right spot to sink the spear in and she wouldn't have to listen to him any more. Find the head. Or the heart. Her eyes roamed.

"And this is how you betray me?" he continued. "You stand there with a spear in your hand like a conqueror over his humbled enemy, instead of freeing me from my agony under this wreckage?"

"You *need* my help?" mumbled Amalina, her heart filled with rage but trying, as ever, to sound polite. "You can't free yourself, sir?"

She stepped onto the mound, listening for where his voice might come next. But also trying to avoid looking past its margins, where she might catch sight of the severed wailer's trunk.

"Shall I listen to your lying mouth anymore?" said the Count acidly. "You conspired to put me in this position! To render me into a helpless victim was your goal from the beginning. And how could that be? When I was willing to do so much for you. To live with you. To live *for* you. For my very love for you, I am rejected?"

As he spoke, she saw the top of his head. But before she slammed the spear into it, she realized that it seemed too flat. Almost like a pancake. That it didn't have the chains wrapped around the eyes the way it should. Because his skin wouldn't be able to pull away from the silver, would it? But then she saw the hairy bulb of the top of his head just a foot to the right. Then she saw another. And then, in another geometrical opening between the chains near her feet, his mustache and the side of his mouth appeared, moving to match his words. But was it real? Was he just trying to draw her into striking at a phantom piece of himself, an unimportant part of him that he had altered to look like his head? Did he know what she was going to do and was he trying to distract her?

A dead white hand emerged from the silver. Riddled in spots with welts, it looked like a scabbed albino spider. It paused. A thin, grotesquely elongated arm extended behind it, leading from—or to—its puppet. The hand sat there, with a weak, ticking, throbbing movement. As if it was deciding something. Eyes like little black bubbles opened along the knuckles. Its forefinger lifted and pointed at her.

"You!" growled the Count from all around. "*Yessssss.* How I curse the night I saw you in that window! Even then I knew I should have killed you! I loathed you! I hated you as the nasty little beast you are, and have proven to be! I should have torn you to pieces then, instead of giving into my weakness for your father's pathetic, pitiable cries for help against his fate! A fate he most deserved. As do you!"

The hand leapt.

Amalina screamed in surprise. Reflexively she swung the spear up to whack the gruesome hand aside. As it sizzled away, she stabbed into the heap of chain, feeling it strike something soft and sink until it hit stone. The Count groaned. She pulled the spear out and stabbed again. Only, in the meantime, the hand had snuck outward and began to circle the floor; extending and looping the arm around the mound. So that it might constrict suddenly and catch her in the coil of a newly formed tentacle!

She moaned as she lanced the silver mass repeatedly, throwing all her strength into it. But all she was doing was wearing herself out. That, and shifting the chains; loosening the pile. The Count's hand was secretly conducting her movements, herding her around by her fear of when or where it might strike. But, she saw, if she wasn't careful, she was going to move one chain too many, and clear enough off him so that he could escape.

But if he could escape now and kill her outright, he would have already. Which meant, he *was* trapped. His center was immobilized except for that thin little part—

The livid hand with razorlike claws slashed out at her. She screamed again and stabbed it right through. The spear flew out of her grip as the hand retracted. And as the Count howled in pain, Amalina was already springing over the many obstacles on her way out of the great hall. Behind her, she heard the chandelier creak and the chains shift ominously.

"You will pay, Amalina Dalca, *yesssss,*" he hissed in agony behind her. "All of you will suffer! I renounce you, you lying, conniving, unreasonable creatures!"

She entered *l'entrée grande* but kept running.

"And you, my mouse …! I wish I'd never met you! I will destroy you! I will destroy everything you have ever loved!"

A rustling of chains came from the inner chamber.

Amalina gathered up spears and pikes along her way, and was still running as she headed for the open front doors and the daylight. But her route seemed to billow and expand, the uneven field of silver and blood stretching in front of her so she could only trip, or slip, and never leave.

"I will bury these accursed mountains into the ground, my little mouse! Oh, yes! Should you ever look back over your ungrateful shoulder, you will know I have survived this betrayal, and you will recognize my hand at work, when you see this land shrouded over by an immense, expanding, tenebrous and terrible black cloud! Yes! Oh, yes! And within its impenetrable folds I will be rewriting Ardeel's history, so that no one in the world will ever believe this wretched, undeserving place had ever existed! Ha! Do you hear me? You shall see! You shall see, Amalina Dalca! Korr erased! Tsobl vanished! Netz unheard of! Ardeel entirely blotted from the world! And your family's name, as a consequence, removed from all good men's memory! Yes! *Yes, yes*! And then, when that good work is done, Amalina ... when it is complete, and the storm parts, leaving nothing the same, it shall have only been my first step ... for, when I am done here, Amalina, I will then rise to finish the job I began ... I will come for *you*!"

It sounded as if the chandelier collapsed to the ground.

Amalina charged out the castle doors, and blinked against the brightness. It seemed the courtyard was empty. She didn't stay to make sure, but kept on running, dumping the weapons to lighten her load. If the Count had just freed himself, he wasn't coming out into the light. But she didn't feel safe. She needed to keep running.

It was still morning, wasn't it? She had hours before sunset.

Outside the castle walls, along the treeline were a couple of the Ladies of Title and their frightened servants. One called to her, trying to flag her over. Pils and Anka waved at her too.

But she wasn't stopping. No matter how exhausted she already was, her body kept moving. Just as her life had seemed to become after meeting the Count, it seemed she was now just a passenger within a carriage, a helpless observer as the world passed by outside. She wasn't stopping for anyone, or turning back. She wanted to yell to them: "It's over! Run! Escape! Follow me!" But she had no control over her mouth either, and while she had invited them to the castle, hadn't she tried, again and again, to warn them against the dangers there? tried and failed to get them to leave *his* side and this land? What more could she do for them, what more could she say? They were their own women in the end, and anyway, they passed outside of her vision as her body turned and continued on its way. But what about Genadie? *Oh, to hell with him, the traitor*, she thought. But what about Aklan? And Pia; what had happened to her? She should turn around and find them, search for them, help them. Only she couldn't. Her body was running on its own. Running without her control. Running, running, running, as if she would never stop.

A large shape joined Amalina at her side. It was the black wolf, bounding along at a fast trot. It looked at her. Its muzzle and fangs were covered in blood. It seemed to nod to Amalina, and then it broke towards the far edge of the forest, sprinting away to safety; far from any more humans.

Epilogue

## Always Remember

### I

When Amalina reached the top of the long sloping descent to the valley below, she felt like she was going to collapse. It was too far to run. To escape.

*He's buried under all those chains. And he's bound to the wheel, just like the wailing woman had been, once upon a time. Even if he isn't spinning, he's too weak; he'll never get out. You have all the time in the world.*

Or maybe only a day ... before he works himself free.

Or two days.

Maybe.

On foot she'd be lucky to reach Netz in that time.

*As if Netz can save me*, she thought. She'd heard his vow: he was going to overturn everything. *Everyone* was going to die.

As she slowed, and her breath relaxed, her tunnel vision lightened and she saw the long cart halfway down the mountain slope, facing away. There was a horse attached to it, but the horse was fixed in place, head bowed, chewing the grass. Its three companions had been loosed and were grazing freely further along the decline.

On the rider's bench, hunched forward, sat a silver figure. One of the knights. She wondered why he was there and what he was waiting for. The way the rider and cart were positioned with their back to her, they seemed like a ghostly apparition. Something to haunt the mountainside as a future warning for anyone on their way up. A silver-armored scarecrow.

It would be appropriate.

She felt like she should cry, but the tears weren't coming. She was too tired, too worn out. Too driven to put a distance between her and the castle. Because she *was* escaping now, wasn't she? What she had meant to do all along. For so many years.

She didn't even care who exactly was on the cart, she would grab the reins and work that horse into a gallop. Never mind the steep downward grade, either.

Amalina crawled onto the riding bench and said: "Go! Let's go!"

The armor turned on the seat and the helmet angled toward her.

She reached for the reins as she said quickly: "He's behind us, sir. They're all dead."

"Amalina?" said Dragomir.

. . .

After all the crying and Amalina's assurances that the blood on her was not her own, came the explanations. The first was when they turned the dog leg round the mountain and Amalina realized Dragomir had gotten uncomfortably quiet. Had been so for some time.

"Are you all right, Papa?" When he didn't answer: " ... *Are* you?"

She tried to take off his helmet but he held it on.

"Leave it be," he said.

"For what, Papa? Take it off."

"It is a shameful thing," he breathed heavily inside the metal can. "They treated me like a child. Like an outsider."

"Who did?"

"All of them. I told them if it was my daughter in the castle, then I'm the one who should risk his neck. The only one who should fight. But all along they had planned I wouldn't. When the time came and we donned our armor and readied for it, they sent me away. Told me to watch the cart, that I wasn't welcome. That I should wait like the village idiot for them to come once they were done and everything was over. Or, if they had not signaled me by noon, I should ride home to Korr. Leave the valley before nightfall, before the Count found me. Well, as you can see, I would have waited there until midnight for them. I would never abandon them."

"Yes, Papa. I'm sure they didn't mean anything by it."

"Of course they did. They thought I was too old. They thought I was too foolish. They couldn't trust me."

"That isn't true."

"Ivanti told me I wouldn't think clearly in the fight. That the Count would use you against me if he found I was with them. Like I was a plain fool. I said 'It's my daughter in there!' And Ivanti said, 'I'm fighting for her, too. It's my fault she's in there. I drove her to it.' Of all the nonsense. As if it wasn't my fault from the beginning. I should have never given you a room with a window. Or a book on the night sky."

"Papa."

Dragomir remembered grimly Ivanti looking straight at him—just hours ago it was—and saying: "Old man, if we're going to the trouble to get her out of there, there's no sense losing you in the effort. She won't think it was worth it."

It had made sense at the time.

"He called me an old man," said Dragomir, more fondly than offended. "And you know what Lazru said? He said, 'If we're all wiped out, who will bake the bread in Korr? Argus? You're staying behind, Dragomir.' Well, that's what he said. And now he's dead and they all are. And I'm riding along in a cart on a sunny day."

"With me," added Amalina.

"That's true. But it doesn't feel right, somehow. It doesn't feel fair."

"I'm glad you're alive, Papa."

• • •

The second explanation came early the next day, after Dragomir's shame had passed and they were back on the road from Netz to Korr, and Amalina felt some talking was needed to pass the time.

"What of Mr. Berzweck, Papa? He wasn't with you?"

"The Boss?" said Dragomir, as if roused into surprise after a moment of contemplation. "No. But you sent us word he was the traitor, didn't you? He was removed before we ever left."

Dragomir recounted what had happened in Korr after the trial and then the executions.

"That Attila was a smart one," said Dragomir admiringly, becoming chatty after she'd drawn him out of his silence. "He figured out the whole scheme between those two. Old Alexandru was mining silver out of the mountains as a favor to the Count. Been at it forever, I suppose. That's why the Count felt indebted enough to let him ask for one girl or another to be killed."

*Or Tepsji was pretending that exchange was the reason*, thought Amalina. *Just enjoying the Boss' scheme as another novelty entertainment by the humans. Meanwhile, and only as a side benefit, the silver he was so scared of was getting hauled out of his beloved mountains. Making him all the safer in his high castle. It was a win on top of a win.*

"Who would ever have thought the Boss was as bad as he was?" growled her father, at the end. "Pure evil, what he had going. It's strange, and hard to understand him. Alexandru seemed to think he'd been doing us a favor all along. Or that's what he tried to tell us."

"A favor to us? But he was working with the Count! That's confused."

"I'm so glad he didn't get you mixed up in that business, anyway, dear child."

But, of course, she *had* been 'mixed up' in the Count's affairs. Her father must've realized he'd said something that wasn't quite right because he went quiet and thoughtful for several miles.

"Anyway, that Attila was a clever one, Amalina, my little dumpling. He said you'd come up with a plan to kill the Count on your own."

"I did."

"That's what he said. And he said that if he had calculated properly, based on what you told him about your experience with Tepsji, even if our assault were to fail, your plan would then be able to work. Because he would be distracted by us, too. Isn't that a clever thing to do?"

"But he's still alive," said Amalina in a low voice. She explained how she'd left the creature underneath all those chains in the castle. Dragomir was quiet for another mile. "I couldn't kill him, Papa. I'm sorry."

"No, I'm glad you didn't," said Dragomir, patting her knee with his heavy silver gauntlet. "It isn't a job for a young girl like you."

"No," she said, quickly trying to correct him. "I just *couldn't*."

"Of course not. Such a thing like killing isn't in your nature, dearest. I remember how frightened you were of the wolves when they would threaten us on the way to the mill. Remember that? And you'd shame me for firing at them. So cute. No, that kind of thing isn't in you. You are meant for life; and for making life better."

"Papa," she groaned in frustration, "I'm saying that after all this, after everyone dying, I don't think he *can* be killed. He may be trapped for a good long while but he's lived too long, and become too strong, to allow himself to be killed so easily. If ever. He's still up in that castle, Papa."

The silver bucket-helmet stared into the distance and said nothing.

But Amalina was struck by a sudden thought: what if she was wrong about what had happened in the great hall? Had the Count really threatened her only to anger her and drive her to attack him because he *is* utterly indestructible and immune to death? and her repeated stabs into the mound of chains would help loosen something in it, or shift the unbearable load, which might then allow him to set himself free, later, once she was gone? Or … Or maybe … maybe he isn't invulnerable and *can* be killed … and perhaps, even if he possessed the strength and speed that he could've broken free of the trap the moment it was sprung on him … instead he'd allowed it to happen, the trap to catch him, and he'd squirmed just enough under the pile to let her *think* he was ready to bust loose, just to scare her off; to drive her away before she might actually keep up the attack and kill him.

That was a thought. But there was more to it:

Maybe he had driven her away not to save himself from death, but because he'd wanted to preserve the ultimate purity and innocence he seemed to cherish in her—even in the moment of her betraying him. If Amalina had killed him, she'd no longer be pure; the *blood innocent* as he'd called her.

What a strange thing to think. But by how perfectly it fit his nature to do such an odd thing, she couldn't discount it.


## II


The cart slowed and Amalina began to wonder if her father wasn't delaying their return to Korr for some reason. The helmet would turn from time to time, and she didn't know what he was looking at, or if he was trying to get his bearings. Amalina, an expert now on traveling the highways of Ardeel, would tell him which way they should go and he would nod, with a hollow clank, and keep to the highway. But still, at some point when Amalina wasn't paying attention, they'd veered off onto a road that led into an unfamiliar wood in an untraveled valley. Before she could say anything to get him to turn around, the light dimmed, and the thick tendrils of a fog had surrounded and captured them. The landscape was now an unsettling tableau of the blackest silhouettes of gnarled, twisted, skeletal trees submerged within a grey-white mist, the outer daylight lending it a dreamlike luminescence.

But by Dragomir's movements, and his forward stoop, he appeared to be satisfied that they had arrived somewhere. He stopped the cart.

"Papa?"

He lifted his hand to silence her. She could hear nothing but a light wind between the trees and over the surrounding mountains, and the mournful cry of a loon and some chatterings of a jackdaw.

"This is it," said Dragomir, wrestling himself off the bench, his armor scratching heavily on the wood. "You wait here, Amalina. Wait right here until I come back. I won't be gone long."

He pointed his silver glove at the ground right where she should stay put, but then turned and walked up the road.

"Where are you going?"

"Mind me, daughter. Have to get rid of this suit and back into my proper clothes."

A few minutes later, once her father had disappeared into the mist without another word or sound, with her heart beating loudly in her chest, Amalina threw aside the reins and followed after him, patting the side of the worn-out horses as she passed by. At a hundred yards in—she could only suppose that was how far she'd gone—a parked wagon appeared to her left, just off the trail inside the tree line, then came another, and soon she was walking beside an encampment of wagons. They looked like vardos—gypsy wagons—though the bright, motley colors of those peculiar transports, covered in various patterns and decorations, had been leeched out by the fog into haunted, muted hues or necral grays. And there were bodies within the fog now, standing between the wagons as if they'd been planted there; flat, like wooden cut-outs, black and anonymous. Amalina began to wonder, because this looked like it was a gypsy caravan, that this might have something to do with Janusch Timorak, and she might be about to meet Genadie's son.

"Hello? Papa?"

"Amalina?"

It wasn't Dragomir's voice, but a familiar one that caused her to suck in a breath and feel confused, frightened, and elated all at once.

Ivanti Ion Vokent stepped toward her through the fog, the silhouette of a man gaining value and detail until it was him.

"Ion!"

Amalina wanted to run to him, and she took a few quick faltering steps forward, until she recognized that particular troubled look on his face. That apologetic smile she'd seen a disappointing number of times before. She stopped a couple paces from him. He was as grey and colorless as the wagons, even his beautiful hazel eyes. But the fog could not rob him of his smile and other charms.

"Ion, what's going on? What's happening here? You're alive?"

She looked past him and saw the giant shadow of Gulgas the Hunter standing not too far away. And Lazru. And Jenz Timer. And wasn't that the Inn Keeper? But it must be!

"Everyone? You're all here? But at the castle … "

Ion shook his head with a wider, but pale, smile. "We're all here."

"But I saw you, everyone … !" she said, unable to understand. Her chest heaved a couple times, almost reliving the upset. But they *were* all here. She could see them. They were moving, staring at her. It was confusion.

"It wasn't us," said Ion.

"I saw your face!"

"Well, I suppose it *was* us," he said. "But not exactly so."

"I don't understand, what … ?" she couldn't tell if she wanted to cry from happiness or fear, she began to feel angry at the puzzlement.

What had her father told her …?

Seeing her brow cross down, Ion laughed and patted the air. "Those were our *substitutes*. Father Perdu came to us and told us of a deal that'd been worked out. A deal to save ourselves, Amalina. It *seemed* we could win against the Count, but you know … there's no ever telling." He laughed again, mirthlessly. "Well, you see how that worked out, eh?"

"What was this deal?"

"On our behalf, and through some strange merchant whose name escapes me, we were given the opportunity to have others fight in our place.

They would be us, you see—but us placed *inside* other bodies. It's an old magic, I'm told. Very old. Something to do with faeries, or something like that, I think ..."

"I don't understand, how could ..."

"The deal, as it was, we needed to pay our way. Five gold coins each. Three per head paid to the one who would perform the rite, and two to be used per man in the rite. The only conditions were that it would be done only if all agreed to it—all or none—and no one could tell anyone else outside our circle, especially not Attila Bronk, who would be sure to put a stop to it. But now, since it's done and over we can tell anyone we'd like. But for what use I couldn't guess. But *you* should know it, anyway."

They seemed to be gathering a crowd. Amalina recognized more faces. They looked downcast and ashamed.

"And so you are all safe and alive," said Amalina. "But that's wonderful!"

"There was another exchange within the agreement, Amalina," said Ion Vokent, with a shrug. "On our way to the castle, from the Netz mine, Perdu delivered us to a woods such as this, maybe this is it, I can't tell ... Where are we, Ama, do you know? ... But in those strange woods, with the spring rains the ground was soft and boggy. And the man performing the rite led us to a nearby shallow fen that had swollen in the season to the needed size. There he performed the rite and wrapped us up in silk tethers with gold designs on them, and we were made to dig through the mud and expose the roots of ancient trees. We used specialized tools, engraved with strange markings, to open the roots. Roots longer and wider than the size of a man, and inside held a body that resembled the man who opened it. We were to embrace the body, speak certain words into its ears—words we didn't understand—and bring it out of the fen.

"Their eyes were open, but they seemed as simple as babies and lacked power. Each of us scratched out our name on the face of a gold coin. And then did so again, writing our name in reverse on the tail side of the second coin. After kissing the coins, and giving the second a drop of our blood, and touching the two pieces together so the blood met and they had a bloody kiss of their own, the coin with our reversed names were placed in our mouths. And when the coin with our real names were placed in the mouth of our double, they became us. Our consciences went into them, and though we were still in our own bodies, it was like the world had been reversed. We, in the unearthed bodies, stood above ourselves, now laid out on the ground and helpless. But we controlled the new bodies; we saw, felt, and heard what they saw, felt, and heard. We could move any way we liked and we could speak through them. And they spoke and they did what we thought to do, and after an hour or two we couldn't tell the difference anymore, it was like we were in a dream and those bodies were now us, we believed we were them. But those bodies had a power and quickness we had never felt before, the strength of ancient trees and sunlight's speed. We could not have hoped to do better. The older among us were like young men, the young of us were unstoppable, invincible. It then seemed to us our victory, through this little trick, was guaranteed, and we were cheered, Amalina. That's how we felt, and how we went forward, controlling these new bodies and feeling like they were our own, convinced we were them, forgetting everything about the exchange but that we'd commited to some pact and we needed to keep the coins in our mouths. Nobody could tell the difference, not even Attila Bronk. Especially when we put on the armor."

"That must have been scary but amazing," said Amalina, in a hopeful tone. "It was a good thing you did, though, considering ..."

"The bargain we struck had one caveat to it, the most crucial one," said Ion. "After we were done with the bodies, we would return them to the roots they came from, and remove the coins from their mouths, restoring us to our own bodies properly. But if any man should die while in the new body, that is where their soul will stay, you see. The conscience, which was in the old body, would be there, still alive, but the soul would be forever lost to them. We could never return to Korr, or pretend to be whom we no longer were, but carry on as wanderers of the earth. Lost to our old selves.

"With our confidence in Attila's plan," continued Ion, "*even with that*, we still weren't sure who would make it out alive. It seemed a great bargain to all of us. We didn't need much persuasion from Perdu. We all took the deal and were glad for it."

"But ... then ..." said Amalina. "You *are* still alive ...?"

He shrugged his manly shoulders with a lost grin, "We're alive. But who are we now? We've lost our souls. We can't return to our old lives. We aren't 'we' anymore."

Amalina felt tears welling up in her eyes. "Why would you do such a thing—?"

"Now don't get like that, Ama," said Ion, just as he might have before he'd lost everything. Which was further confusing. "Please don't get mad. Anyone would have taken that deal. I mean, why not?"

"Attila wouldn't have."

"Mr. Bronk, no," agreed Ion. "But you ...? Oh now, don't look like that, that's a fancy thing to pretend on your part, Ama. You think *you* wouldn't have?"

He seemed to be amused she'd believe otherwise, he wasn't so mad about it. The others looked on without expression now, just a wall of adult men she used to know. Slack, gray, familiar faces.

"I'd never ..." she said. "You think I would?"

"I tried to cheat … to hell with it, we *all* tried to cheat death," grinned Ion guiltily. "And hasn't that been what you've been up to all along? and to get everything you want, eh, Princess Ama?"

"Should've heeded the Boss," one of the closer shadows grumbled.

"You need to stop that," warned Ion, half turning to address the ghost in the darkness.

"He was right," joined another.

"Look you, all of you," he admonished the gathered army, "Amalina's alive; so's Drag. If they are here and they are alive, then we did it. Whatever the cost, we are victorious, we won." He turned back to Amalina. "Didn't we?"

"Amalina!" shouted her father. He ran at her from the far side of the encampment, chugging along as a shadow, and then, as he neared, clearly himself, now wearing his regular clothes. He even wore the old crusty baker's bib. "I told you to wait at the cart! I told you to stay there! You aren't supposed to see *any* of this! Go!"

He grabbed Amalina by the arm and shoved her back toward the road.

"But Ion …"

"That isn't him," growled Dragomir.

"Good bye, Amalina!" called Ion.

"When are you going to start minding me!" her father growled again as Amalina tried to turn and wave, to see Ion one last time at least. It *must* still be him.

"Here!" Ion expertly tossed something from his spot. "Something to remember me by. Remember me. Remember us all!"

There was a murmur and groan of agreement from the shadows in the fog. Dragomir twirled her around and forced her back to the cart. She'd caught what Ion had thrown, and without resisting her father, as she stumbled away from the lost men of Korr, she looked down in her hand and saw a gold piece with TNEKOV NOI ITNAVI—'IVANTI ION VOKENT' in reverse, it took a moment for her to see it—scratched into its tail side as if by point of a dagger.

She'd wondered where they'd gotten the gold, but it had the Count's face embossed on it, just like the one that had fallen out of Ion's mouth in the entrance hall. These were the pieces Amalina had given her father, when she'd tried to bribe him to leave the country. He'd spent it all on this misguided stunt.

She couldn't bring herself to ask Dragomir if it were true, but stared at the side of his unhelmeted face as they left the fog and the sun grew brighter and hot, and the wind whipped the sides of his beard. Had he just been changing out of the armor and back into his clothes at the camp, she wondered, just saying good bye to his old friends? Or had she been sitting beside his armored, unnatural double the whole time, talking to him, confessing to him? he lying to her about his own story and his own grief? or he, as a double, believing it was true? He'd been in on the deal with everyone else after all, hadn't he? And then he'd put himself back in the root of a marsh tree.

In the spring sunlight, out of the grey mist, she didn't care to ask. What did it matter? And before her father could ask what Ion had thrown to her, she tucked the coin and the memories of handsome Lieutenant Ivanti Ion Vokent away.

. . .

After the rumors spread through Ardeel about a strange occurrence outside of Netz, and the collapse of the mines there, and about the sudden disappearance of all the strong men in Korr—which shamefully spoke of a strain of succubi working the country's border towns—things got quiet. And a family that silently shuttered their business and moved away went unnoticed.

Whether getting away from something or going to, Amalina felt a great thrill of happiness as she held her father and new mother's hands and they boarded the boat destined to the far, far away island of manly men, the legendary audacious queen, and a certain brilliant, ancient poet—England. With her, she brought some glimmering plans for the future and the quick mind of an entreprenuer. And while she tried to remember all the men of her town, and those many souls she'd met in her dark adventures in Ardeel, she never could dream of them.

But as the years passed—and to her continued shock and surprise—one perplexing dream rose again and again: the one about a blue sky, a sunny summer day with a field full of barley, and a certain angry young girl skipping through it; coming straight for her, whispering dark words …

Which seemed unfair somehow.

**Acknowledgements:**

Any book has a number of unspoken helpers to get it to print. This series owes a great deal of debt to a core skeleton crew of editors and advisors; namely Rob Errera, my friend, eagle-eyed editor and publisher, who guided the extended narrative along its winding way, and especially wrestled this final episode through my own writerly trials to its conclusion; also Meghan Allen, friend and writer, who was there for the bulk of the series, helping immensely with sage observations and advice. And then there is my wife, who backstopped and bore with me throughout the writing of it, and beyond a doubt if it wasn't for her this story, as it is, would not exist.